DICK FRA

Omnibus 7

Dick Francis has written over forty international best-
sellers and is widely acclaimed as one of the world's finest thriller
writers. His awards include the Crime Writers' Association's
Cartier Diamond Dagger for his outstanding contribution to the
crime genre, and an honorary Doctorate of Humane Letters
from Tufts University of Boston. In 1996 Dick Francis was made
a Mystery Writers of America Grand Master for a lifetime's
achievement and in 2000 he received a CBE in the Queen's
Birthday Honours list.

DICK FRANCIS

Omnibus 7

NERVE
BLOOD SPORT
IN THE FRAME

PAN BOOKS

Nerve first published 1964 by Michael Joseph Ltd
And by Pan Books in 1976
Bloodsport first published 1967 by Michael Joseph Ltd
And by Pan Books in 1969
In the Frame first published 1976 by Michael Joseph Ltd
And by Pan Books in 1978

This omnibus edition published 2004 by Pan Books
an imprint of Pan Macmillan Ltd
Pan Macmillan, 20 New Wharf Road, London N1 9RR
Basingstoke and Oxford
Associated companies throughout the world
www.panmacmillan.com

ISBN 1 4050 4930 8

1 3 5 7 9 8 6 4 2

A CIP catalogue record for this book is available from
the British Library.

Printed and bound in Great Britain by
Mackays of Chatham plc, Chatham, Kent

NERVE

One

ART MATHEWS shot himself, loudly and messily, in the centre of the parade ring at Dunstable races.

I was standing only six feet away from him, but he did it so quickly that had it been only six inches I would not have had time to stop him.

He had walked out of the changing-room ahead of me, his narrow shoulders hunched inside the khaki jerkin he had put on over his racing colours, and his head down on his chest as if he were deep in thought. I noticed him stumble slightly down the two steps from the weighing-room to the path; and when someone spoke to him on the short walk to the parade ring, he gave absolutely no sign of having heard. But it was just another walk from the weighing-room to the parade ring, just another race like a hundred others. There was nothing to suggest that when he had stood talking for two or three minutes with the owner and trainer of the horse he was due to ride, he would take off his jerkin, produce from under it as he dropped it to the ground a large automatic pistol, place the barrel against his temple and squeeze the trigger.

Unhesitating. No pause for a final weighing-up. No good-byes. The casualness of his movement was as shocking as its effect.

He hadn't even shut his eyes, and they were still open as he fell forwards to the ground, his face hitting the grass with an audible thud and his helmet rolling off. The bullet had passed

3

straight through his skull, and the exit wound lay open to the sky, a tangled, bloody mess of skin and hair and brain, with splinters of bone sticking out.

The crack of the gunshot echoed round the paddock, amplified by the high back wall of the stands. Heads turned searchingly and the busy buzz and hum of conversation from the three-deep railside racegoers grew hushed and finally silent as they took in the appalling, unbelievable, indisputable fact that what remained of Art Mathews lay face downwards on the bright green turf.

Mr John Brewar, the owner of Art's prospective mount, stood with his middle-aged mouth stretched open in a sound-less oval, his eyes glazed with surprise. His plump, well-preserved wife toppled to the ground in the graceless sprawl of a genuine faint, and Corin Kellar, the trainer for whom both Art and I had been about to ride, went down on one knee and shook Art by the shoulder, as if he could still awaken one whose head was half blown away.

The sun shone brightly. The blue and orange silk on Art's back gleamed: his white breeches were spotless, and his racing boots had been polished into a clean, soft shine. I thought inconsequentially that he would have been glad that – from the neck down at least – he looked as immaculate as ever.

The two stewards hurried over and stood stock-still, staring at Art's head. Horror dragged down their jaws and narrowed their eyes. It was part of their responsibility at a meeting to stand in the parade ring while the horses were led round before each race, so that they should be both witnesses and adjudicators if anything irregular should occur. Nothing as irregular as a pub-lic suicide of a top-notch steeplechase jockey had ever, I im-agined, required their attention before.

The elder of them, Lord Tirrold, a tall, thin man with an executive mind, bent over Art for a closer inspection. I saw the muscles bunch along his jaw, and he looked up at me across Art's body and said quietly, 'Finn . . . fetch a rug.'

I walked twenty steps down the parade ring to where one of the horses due to run in the race stood in a little group with his owner, trainer and jockey. Without a word the trainer took the rug off the horse and held it out to me.

'Mathews?' he said incredulously.

I nodded unhappily and thanked him for the rug, and went back with it.

The other steward, a sour-tempered hulk named Ballerton, was, I was meanly pleased to see, losing his cherished dignity by vomiting up his lunch.

Mr Brewar pulled down his unconscious wife's rucked-up skirt and began anxiously to feel her pulse. Corin Kellar kept passing his hand over his face from forehead to chin, still down on one knee beside his jockey. His face was colourless, his hand shaking. He was taking it badly.

I handed one end of the rug to Lord Tirrold and we opened it out and spread it gently over the dead man. Lord Tirrold stood for a moment looking down at the motionless brown shape, then glanced round at the little silent groups of the people who had runners in the race. He went over and spoke to one or two, and presently the stable lads led all the horses out from the parade ring and back to the saddling boxes.

I stood looking down at Corin Kellar and his distress, which I thought he thoroughly deserved. I wondered how it felt to know one had driven a man to kill himself.

There was a click, and a voice announced over the loud-speaker system that owing to a serious accident in the parade ring the last two races would be abandoned. Tomorrow's meeting would be held as planned, it said, and would everyone please go home. As far as the growing crowd of racegoers round the ring were concerned, this might never have been said, for they remained glued to the rails with all eyes on the concealing rug.

Nothing rivets human attention as hungrily as a bloody disaster, I thought tolerantly, picking up Art's helmet and whip from the grass.

Poor Art. Poor badgered, beleaguered Art, rubbing out his misery with a scrap of lead.

I turned away from his body and walked thoughtfully back to the weighing-room.

While we changed back from riding kit into our normal clothes the atmosphere down our end of the changing-room was one of irreverence covering shock. Art, occupying by general consent the position of elder statesman among jockeys, though he was not actually at thirty-five by any means the eldest, had been much deferred to and respected. Distant in manner sometimes, withdrawn even, but an honest man and a good jockey. His one noticeable weakness, at which we usually smiled indulgently, was his conviction that a lost race was always due to some deficiency in his horse or its training, and never to a mistake on his own part. We all knew perfectly well that Art was no exception to the rule that every jockey misjudges things once in a while, but he would never admit a fault, and could put up a persuasive defence every time if called to account.

'Thank the Lord,' said Tick-Tock Ingersoll, stripping off his blue and black checked jersey, 'that Art was considerate enough to let us all weigh out for the race before bumping himself off.' Tick-Tock's face emerged from the woolly folds with a wide grin which faded comically when no one laughed.

'Well,' he said, dropping his jersey absentmindedly in a heap on the floor. 'If he'd done it an hour ago we'd all have been ten quid out of pocket.'

He was right. Our fees for each race were technically earned once we had sat on the scales and been checked out as carrying the correct weight, and they would be automatically paid whether we ran the race or not.

'In that case,' said Peter Cloony, 'we should put half of it into a fund for his widow.' He was a small, quiet young man prone to over-emotional, quickly roused and quickly spent bouts of pity both for others and for himself.

'Not ruddy likely,' said Tick-Tock, who disliked him openly. 'Ten quid's ten quid to me, and Mrs Art's rolling in it. And snooty with it. Catch me giving her the time of day, you'll be lucky.'

'It's a mark of respect,' said Peter obstinately, looking round at us with rather damp large eyes and carefully refraining from returning young Tick-Tock's belligerent glare.

I sympathized with Tick-Tock. I needed the money, too. Besides, Mrs Art had treated me, along with all the other rank-and-file jockeys, with her own particularly arctic brand of coolness. Giving her a fiver in Art's memory wouldn't thaw her. Pale, straw-haired, light-eyed, she was the original ice maiden, I thought.

'Mrs Art doesn't need our money,' I said. 'Remember how she bought herself a mink coat last winter and used it as a hedge against all of us who didn't measure up to her standards? She hardly knows two of us by name. Let's just buy Art a wreath, and perhaps a useful memorial, something he would have appreciated, like some hot showers in the washroom here.'

Tick-Tock's angular young face registered delight. Peter Cloony bent on me a look of sorrowful reproof. But from the others came nods of agreement.

Grant Oldfield said violently, 'He probably shot himself because that whey-faced bitch short-changed him in bed.'

There was a curious little silence. A year ago, I reflected, a year ago we might have laughed. But a year ago Grant Oldfield would have said the same thing amusingly and perhaps vulgarly, but not with this ugly unsmiling venom.

I was aware, we all were, that he didn't know or care a jot about the private practices of Art's marriage; but in the past months Grant had seemed more and more to be consumed by some inner rage, and lately he could scarcely make the most commonplace remark without in some way giving vent to it. It was caused, we thought, by the fact that he was going down the ladder again without ever having got to the top. He had always been ambitious and ruthless in character, and had developed a riding style to match. But at the vital point when he had attracted public attention with a string of successes and had begun to ride regularly for James Axminster, one of the very top trainers, something had happened to spoil it. He had lost the Axminster job, and other trainers booked him less and less. The race we had not run was his only engagement that day.

Grant was a dark, hairy, thick-set man of thirty, with high cheek-bones and a wide-nostrilled nose bent permanently out of shape. I endured a great deal more of his company than I would have liked because my peg in the changing-room at nearly all racecourses was next to his, since both our kit was looked after by the same racecourse valet. He borrowed my things freely without asking first or thanking afterwards, and if he had broken something, denied he had used it. When I first met him I had been amused by his pawky humour, but two years later, by the day Art died, I was heartily sick of his thunderous moods, his roughness and his vile temper.

Once or twice in the six weeks since the new season had begun I had found him standing with his head thrust forward looking round him in bewilderment, like a bull played out by a matador. A bull exhausted by fighting a piece of cloth, a bull baffled and broken, all his magnificent strength wasted on something he could not pin down with his horns. At such times I could pity Grant all right, but at all others I kept out of his way as much as I could.

Peter Cloony, paying him no attention as usual, indicated the peg on which Art's everyday clothes hung, and said, 'What do you think we had better do with these?'

We all looked at them, the well-cut tweed suit neatly

arranged on a hanger, with the small grip which contained his folded shirt and underclothes standing on the bench beneath. His almost obsessive tidiness was so familiar to us that it aroused no comment, but now that he was dead I was struck afresh by it. Everyone else hung up their jackets by the loop at the back of the neck, hooked their braces on to the pegs, and piled their other clothes into the tops of their trousers. Only Art had insisted on a hanger, and had provided his valet with one to bring for him.

Before we had got any further than an obscene suggestion from Grant, a racecourse official threaded his way down the changing-room, spotted me, and shouted, 'Finn, the stewards want you.'

'Now?' I said, standing in shirt and underpants.

'At once.' He grinned.

'All right.' I finished dressing quickly, brushed my hair, walked through the weighing-room, and knocked on the stewards' door. They said to come in, and in I went.

All three stewards were there, also the clerk of the course, and Corin Kellar. They were sitting in uncomfortable-looking, straight-backed chairs around a large, oblong table.

Lord Tirrold said, 'Come along in and close the door.'

I did as he said.

He went on, 'I know you were near Mathews when he . . . er . . . shot himself. Did you actually see him do it? I mean, did you see him take the pistol out and aim it, or did you look at him when you heard the shot?'

'I saw him take out the pistol and aim it, sir,' I said.

'Very well. In that case the police may wish to take a statement from you; please do not leave the weighing-room building until they have seen you. We are waiting now for the inspector to come back from the first-aid room.'

He nodded to dismiss me, but when I had my hand on the

door-knob he said, 'Finn . . . do you know of any reason why Mathews should have wished to end his life?'

I hesitated a fraction too long before I turned round, so that a plain 'No' would have been unconvincing. I looked at Corin Kellar, who was busy studying his fingernails.

'Mr Kellar might know,' I said, non-committally.

The stewards exchanged glances. Mr Ballerton, still pallid from his bout of sickness by Art's body, made a pushing away gesture with his hand, and said, 'You're not asking us to believe that Mathews killed himself merely because Kellar was dissatisfied with his riding?' He turned to the other stewards. 'Really,' he added forcefully, 'if these jockeys get so big for their boots that they can't take a little well-earned criticism, it is time they looked about for other employment. But to suggest that Mathews killed himself because of a few hard words is irresponsible mischief.'

At that point I remembered that Ballerton himself owned a horse which Corin Kellar trained. 'Dissatisfied with his riding,' the colourless phrase he had used to describe the recent series of acrimonious post-race arguments between Art and the trainer suddenly seemed to me a deliberate attempt at oiling troubled waters. You know why Art killed himself, I thought; you helped to cause it, and you won't admit it.

I shifted my gaze back to Lord Tirrold and found him regarding me with speculation.

'That will be all, Finn,' he said.

'Yes, sir,' I said.

I went out and this time they did not call me back, but before I had crossed the weighing-room the door opened again and shut and I heard Corin's voice behind me.

'Rob.'

I turned round and waited for him.

'Thanks very much,' he said sarcastically, 'for tossing that little bomb into my lap.'

'You had told them already,' I said.

'Yes, and just as well.'

He still looked shocked, his thin face deeply lined with worry. He was an exceptionally clever trainer but a nervous, undependable man who offered you life-long friendship one day and cut you dead the next. Just then, it appeared, he needed reassurance.

He said, 'Surely you and the other jockeys don't believe Art killed himself because . . . er . . . I had decided to employ him less? He must have had another reason.'

'Today was supposed to be his last as your jockey in any case, wasn't it?' I said.

He hesitated and then nodded, surprised at my knowing what had not been published. I didn't tell him that I had bumped into Art in the car park the evening before, and that Art, bitterly despairing and smarting from a corroding sense of injustice, had lowered the customary guard on his tongue enough to tell me that his job with Kellar was finished.

I said only, 'He killed himself because you gave him the sack, and he did it in front of you to cause you the maximum amount of remorse. And that, if you want my opinion, is that.'

'But people don't kill themselves because they've lost their jobs,' he said, with a tinge of exasperation.

'Not if they're normal, no,' I agreed.

'Every jockey knows he'll have to retire sometime. And Art was getting too old . . . he must have been mad.'

'Yes, I suppose so,' I said.

I left him standing there, trying to convince himself that he was in no way responsible for Art's death.

Back in the changing-room the discussion on what to do with Art's clothes had been ended by his valet taking charge of them, and Grant Oldfield, I was glad to find, had finished dressing and gone home. Most of the other jockeys had gone also, and the valets were busy tidying up the chaos they had left behind, sorting dirty white breeches into kit bags, and piling helmets, boots, whips and other gear into large wicker hampers. It had been a dry sunny day, and for once there was no mud to wash off.

I reflected as I watched the quick, neat way they flipped the things into the baskets, ready to take the dirty ones home, clean them and return them laundered and polished on the following day, that possibly they did deserve the very large fees we had to pay them for the service. I knew I would loathe, after a day of travelling and of dressing jockeys, to have to face those hampers and bags when I reached home; take out the grubby piles and set to work. Ugh.

I had often seen Art paying his valet, counting through a wad of notes. At the height of the season it always amounted to over twenty pounds each week. My own valet, Young Mike (in his middle forties), twitched my helmet up from the bench and smiled at me as he went by. He earned more than most of the dozen or so jockeys he regularly looked after, and decidedly more than I did. But all the same . . . ugh!

Tick-Tock, whistling the latest hit tune between his teeth, sat on the bench and pulled on a pair of very fancy yellow socks. On top of those went smooth, slim-toed shoes reaching up to the ankle bone. He shook down the slender legs of his dark tweed trousers (no turn-ups), and feeling my gaze upon him looked up and grinned at me across the room.

He said, 'Look your fill on the "Tailor and Cutter's" dream boy.'

'My father in his time,' I said blandly, 'was a Twelve Best Dressed man.'

'My grandfather had vicuna linings in his raincoats.'

'My mother,' I said, dredging for it, 'has a Pucci shirt.'

'Mine,' he said carefully, 'cooks in hers.'

At this infantile exchange we regarded each other with high good humour. Five minutes of Tick-Tock's company were as cheering as rum punch in a snowstorm, and some of his happy-go-lucky enjoyment of living always rubbed off on to the next man. Let Art die of shame, let the murk spread in Grant Oldfield's soul; surely nothing could be really wrong in the racing world, I thought, while young Ingersoll ticked so gaily.

He waved his hand at me, adjusted his Tyrolean trilby, said 'See you tomorrow,' and was gone.

But all the same there *was* something wrong in the racing world. Very wrong. I didn't know what; I could see only the symptoms, and see them all the more clearly perhaps, since I had been only two years in the game. Between trainers and jockeys there seemed to be an all-round edginess, sudden outbursts of rancour, and an ebbing and flowing undercurrent of resentment and distrust. There was more to it, I thought, than the usual jungle beneath the surface of any fiercely competitive business, more to it than the equivalent of grey-flannel-suit manoeuvring in the world of jodhpurs and hacking jackets; but Tick-Tock, to whom alone I had in any way suggested my misgivings, had brushed the whole thing aside.

'You must be on the wrong wavelength, pal,' he said. 'Look around you. Those are smiles you can see, boy. Smiles. It's an O.K. life by me.'

The last few pieces of kit were disappearing into the hampers and some of the lids were already down. I drank a second cup of sugarless tea, lukewarm, and eyed the moist-looking pieces of fruit cake. As usual it took a good deal of resolution not to eat one. Being constantly hungry was the one thing I did not enjoy about race riding, and September was always a bad time of the year, with the remains of the summer's fat still having to be starved off. I sighed, averted my eyes from the cake, and tried to console myself that in another month my appetite would have shrunk back to its winter level.

Young Mike shouted down the room from the doorway

through which he had been staggering with a hamper, 'Rob, there's a copper here to see you.'

I put down the cup and went out into the weighing-room. A middle-aged, undistinguished-looking policeman in a peaked cap was waiting for me with a notebook in his hand.

'Robert Finn?' he asked.

'Yes,' I said.

'I understand from Lord Tirrold that you saw Arthur Mathews put the pistol against his temple and pull the trigger?'

'Yes,' I agreed.

He made a note: then he said, 'It's a very straightforward case of suicide. There won't be any need for more than one witness at the inquest, apart from the doctor, and that will probably be Mr Kellar. I don't think we will need to trouble you any further.' He smiled briefly, shut the notebook and put it in his pocket.

'That's all?' I asked rather blankly.

'Yes, that's all. When a man kills himself as publicly as this there's no question of accident or homicide. The only thing for the coroner to decide is the wording of his verdict.'

'Unsound mind and so on?' I said.

'Yes,' he said. 'Thank you for waiting, though it was your stewards' idea, not mine. Good afternoon, then.' He nodded at me, turned, and walked across towards the stewards' room.

I collected my hat and binoculars and walked down to the racecourse station. The train was already waiting and full, and the only seat I could find was in a compartment packed with bookmakers' clerks playing cards on a suitcase balanced across their knees. They invited me to join them, and between Luton and St Pancras I fear I repaid their kindness by winning from them the cost of the journey.

Two

THE FLAT in Kensington was empty. There were a few letters from the day's second post in the wire basket on the inner side of the door, and I fished them out and walked through into the sitting-room, sorting out the two which were addressed to me. As usual, the place looked as if it had lately received the attentions of a minor tornado. My mother's grand piano lay inches deep in piano scores, several of which had cascaded to the floor. Two music-stands leant at a drunken angle against the wall with a violin bow hooked on to one of them. The violin itself was propped up in an armchair, with its case open on the floor beside it. A 'cello and another music-stand rested side by side like lovers along the length of the sofa. An oboe and two clarinets lay on a table beside another untidy pile of music, and round the room and on all the bedroom chairs which filled most of the floor space lay a profusion of white silk handkerchiefs, rosin, coffee cups and batons.

Running a practised eye over the chaos I diagnosed the recent presence of my parents, two uncles and a cousin. As they never travelled far without their instruments, it was safe to predict that the whole circus was within walking distance and would return in a very short while. I had, I was thankful to realize, struck the interval.

I threaded a path to the window and looked out. No sign of returning Finns. The flat was at the top of a house two or three streets back from Hyde Park, and across the rooftops I could see the evening sunlight striking on the green dome of the Albert Hall. The Royal Institute of Music, where one of my uncles taught, rose in a solid dark mass beside it. The large airy apartment which was the headquarters of the Finn family was held by my father to be an economy, as it was within walking distance of where so many of them from time to time worked.

I was the odd one out. The talents with which both my parents' families had been lavishly endowed had not descended to me. This had become painfully clear to them when at the age of four I had failed to distinguish between the notes of an oboe and a *cor anglais*. To the uninitiated there may not seem to be much difference between them, but my father happened to be an oboist of international reputation, against whom other oboists were measured. Also, high musical talent, if it exists, is apparent in a child from an extremely early age, earlier than any other form of inborn ability, and at three years (when Mozart began composing), concertos and symphonies made less impression on me than the noise of the men emptying the dustbins.

By the time I was five my shattered parents had reluctantly faced the fact that the child they had bred by mistake (I had caused an important American tour to be cancelled) was unmusical. Unmusical, that is, in their pure sense. I was not tone deaf and soaring flights of melody had drawn from me childish tears, but I never had, and still have not, their complete understanding, intellectual, emotional, technical and spiritual, of the effect of putting certain sounds in certain orders.

My mother never being one to do things by halves, I had henceforth been shuffled off from London between school terms to a succession of long holidays on farms, ostensibly for my health, but in reality, I knew later, to free my parents for the complicated and lengthy concert tours in which they were engaged. I grew up into a sort of truce with them, in which it was tacitly agreed that as they had not intended to have a child in the first place, and as he had proved to be less than a (musical) credit to them in the second, the less we saw of each other the better.

They disapproved of my venture into jockeyship for no other reason than that racing had nothing to do with music. It was no use my pointing out that the one thing I had learned on the various holiday farms was how to ride (for I was enough my father's son for farming itself to bore me stiff), and that my present occupation was directly due to their actions in the past. To what they did not want to hear my acute-eared parents were sublimely deaf.

There was still no sign of them down in the street, nor of the uncle who lived with us who played the 'cello, nor the visiting uncle and cousin, violin and clarinet.

I opened my two letters. The first informed me that my income tax returns were overdue. I slit the second envelope with a smiling and complacent anticipation of enjoyment, which just shows how often life can get up and slap you when you least expect it. In a familiar childish hand the letter said:

Dearest Rob,
I am afraid this may come as a surprise to you, but I am getting married. He is Sir Morton Henge, who you may have heard of, and he is very sweet and kind and no cracks from you about him being old enough to be my father etc. I don't think I had better ask you to the reception, do you? Morton doesn't know about you and you will be a great dear not to let on to anybody about us, if you don't mind. I shall never forget you, dearest Rob, and all the sweet times we had together. Thank you for everything, and goodbye.
Your loving Paulina.

Sir Morton Henge, middle-aged widower and canning tycoon. Well, well. I wondered sardonically how his serious-minded son, whom I knew slightly, would enjoy the prospect of a cuddly twenty-year-old model for a stepmother. But being in a lopsided way able to laugh at Paulina's catch made it no less of a blow.

In the eighteen months since I had first met her she had progressed from mousy-haired obscurity to blonde blossoming on the cover of at least one glossy magazine a week. In the last month her radiant eyes had smiled at me (and eight million other men) from a cigarette advertisement in every underground station in London. I had known that it was inevitable that one day she would forsake me if she struck gold in her profession, and our whole relationship had from the start been based on that assumption; but a future without her happy inanity and her generous love-making seemed all of a sudden more bleak than I had expected.

I went through to my bedroom and putting down Paulina's letter on the chest of drawers, caught sight of myself in the oval mirror on the wall above it. That is the face, I thought, that she has been pleased to see beside her on her pillow, but which was no match for a title and a canning fortune. Looking objectively at my reflection I noted the black hair, black eyebrows and lashes, brown eyes . . . not a distinguished face, nor handsome; too thin perhaps. Not bad, not good. Just a face.

I turned away and looked around the little sloping-ceilinged room which had been converted for me from a lumber room when I came home from my travels. There was very little in it; a bed, the chest of drawers, an armchair and a bedside table with a lamp on it. One picture, an impressionistic sketch of racing horses, hung on the wall facing my bed. There were no other ornaments, few books, no clutter. In six years of wandering round the world I had become so used to living with a minimum of possessions that although I had now occupied this little room on and off for two years, I had amassed nothing to put in it.

A clothes cupboard had been built for me across one end of the room. I opened the door and tried to look at its contents as

Paulina must have looked, the twice she had been there. One good dark grey suit, one evening jacket with black trousers, one hacking jacket, two pairs of grey slacks, and a pair of jodhpurs. I took off the suit I was wearing and hung it at the end of the meagre row, a tweed mixture of browns. They were enough for me, those clothes. They covered every situation. Sir Morton Henge probably counted his suits in dozens and had a man-servant to look after them. I shrugged my shoulders. There was no profit in this melancholy stocktaking. Paulina was gone, and that was that.

Picking up a pair of black sneakers, I shut the cupboard door and changed into jeans and an old checked shirt. That done, I contemplated the desert of time between then and the next day's racing. The trouble with me was that steeplechasing had got into my blood like a drug addiction, so that all the normal pleasures of life, and even Paulina herself, had become merely ways of passing as quickly as possible the hours away from it.

My stomach gave an extra twist, which I would like to have believed was due to romantic desolation at my blasted love life, but which I knew very well was only the effect of not having eaten for twenty-three hours. Admitting wryly that being jetti-soned had not spoiled my appetite, I made for the kitchen. Before I reached it, however, the front door of the flat banged open and in trooped my parents, uncles and cousin.

'Hello, darling,' said my mother, presenting a smooth sweet-smelling cheek for a kiss. It was her usual greeting to everyone from impresarios to back row chorus singers, and when applied to me still utterly lacked any maternal quality. She was not a motherly person in any way. Tall, slender and immensely chic in a style that looked casual but was the result of much thought and expenditure, she was becoming more and more a 'presence' as she approached fifty. As a woman I knew her to be passionate and temperamental; as an artist to be a first-class interpretative vehicle for the genius of Haydn, whose piano concertos she

19

poured out with magical, meticulous, ecstatic precision. I had seen hardened music critics leave her performances with tears in their eyes. So I had never expected a broad motherly bosom to comfort my childish woes, nor a sock-darning, cake-making mum to come home to.

My father, who treated me always with polite friendliness, said as a form of greeting, 'Did you have a good day?' He always asked. I usually answered briefly yes or no, knowing that he was not really interested.

I said, 'I saw a man kill himself. No, it wasn't a good day.'

Five heads swivelled towards me.

My mother said, 'Darling, what do you mean?'

'A jockey shot himself at the races. He was only six feet away from me. It was a mess.' All five of them stood there looking at me with their mouths open. I wished I hadn't told them, for it seemed even more horrible in memory than it had done at the time.

But they were unaffected. The 'cello uncle shut his mouth with a snap, shrugged, and went on into the sitting-room, saying over his shoulder, 'Well, if you will go in for these peculiar pursuits . . .'

My mother followed him with her eyes. There was a bass twang as he picked up his instrument from the sofa, and as if drawn by an irresistible magnet the others drifted after him. Only my cousin stayed long enough to spare Art a thought, then he too went back to his clarinet.

I listened to them re-tuning and setting up the music stands. They began to play a jigging piece for strings and woodwind that I particularly disliked. The flat was suddenly intolerable. I went out and down into the street and began to walk.

There was only one place to go if I wanted a certain kind of peace, and I didn't care to go there too often for fear of wearing out my welcome. But it was a full month since I had seen my cousin Joanna, and I needed some more of her company. Need. That was the only word for it.

She opened the door with her usual air of good-humoured invitation.

'Well, hello,' she said, smiling. I followed her into the big converted mews garage which served her as sitting-room, bed-room and rehearsal room all in one. Half of the roof was a slop-ing skylight, through which the remains of the evening sun still shone. The size and comparative bareness of the room gave it unusual acoustic qualities; if one spoke ordinarily it was like any other room; if one sang, as Joanna did, there was a satisfying illusion of distance and some good amplification from concrete walls.

Joanna's voice was deep and clear and resonant. When she liked, in singing dramatic passages, she could colour it with the suggestion of graininess, a very effective hint of a crack in the bell. She could have made a fortune as a blues singer; but hav-ing been born a true classical Finn, so commercial a use of her talent was out of the question. Instead she preferred songs which were to me unmelodic and unrewarding, though she seemed to be amassing a fair-sized reputation with them among people who enjoyed that sort of thing.

She had greeted me in a pair of jeans as old as my own and a black sweater streaked here and there with paint. On an easel stood a half-finished portrait of a man, with some brushes and paints on a table beside it.

'I'm trying my hand at oils,' she said, picking up a brush and making a tentative dab at the picture, 'but it's not going very well, damn it.'

'Stick to charcoal, then,' I said. She had drawn with flowing lines the racing horses which hung in my bedroom, short on anatomy, but full of life and movement.

'I'll finish this, at least,' she said.

I stood and watched her. She squeezed out some carmine.

Without looking at me she said, 'What's the matter?'

I didn't answer. She paused with her brushes in the air and turned and regarded me calmly for some seconds.

'There's some steak in the kitchen,' she said.

A mind reader, my cousin Joanna. I grinned at her and went out into the long narrow lean-to where she both took her bath and did her cooking. It was rump steak, thick and dark. I grilled it with a couple of tomatoes and made some french dressing for a lettuce I found already prepared in a wooden bowl. When the steak was done I divided it on to two plates and took the whole lot back to Joanna. It smelt wonderful.

She put down her brush and came to eat, wiping her hands on the seat of her pants.

'I'll say one thing for you, Rob. You cook a mean steak,' she said, after her first mouthful.

'Thanks for nothing,' I said, with my mouth full.

We ate every scrap. I finished first, and sat back and watched her. She had a fascinating face, full of strength and character, with straight dark eyebrows and, that night, no lipstick. She had tucked her short wavy hair in a no-nonsense style behind her ears, but on top it still curled forward on to her forehead in an untidy fringe.

My cousin Joanna was the reason I was still a bachelor, if one can be said to need a reason at twenty-six years of age. She was three months older than I, which had given her an advantage over me all our lives, and this was a pity, since I had been in love with her from the cradle. I had several times asked her to marry me, but she always said no. First cousins, she explained firmly, were too closely related. Besides which, she added, I didn't stir her blood.

Two other men, however, had done that for her. Both were musicians. And each of them in their turn in a most friendly way had told me how greatly having Joanna for a lover had deepened their appreciation of living, given new impetus to their musical inspiration, opened new vistas, and so on and so on. They were both rather intense brooding men with undeniably handsome faces, and I didn't like hearing what they had to say. On the first occasion, when I was eighteen, I departed in speed and grief to foreign lands, and somehow had not returned for six years. On the second occasion I went straight to a wild party, got thoroughly drunk for the first and only time in my life, and woke up in Paulina's bed. Both adventures had turned out to be satisfying and educational. But they had not cured me of Joanna.

She pushed away her empty plate and said, 'Now, what's the matter?'

I told her about Art. She listened seriously and when I had finished she said, 'The poor man. And his poor wife . . . Why did he do it, do you know?'

'I think it was because he lost his job,' I said. 'Art was such a perfectionist in everything. He was too proud . . . He would never admit he had done anything wrong in a race . . . And I think he simply couldn't face everyone knowing he'd been given the sack. But the odd thing is, Joanna, that he looked as good as ever to me. I know he was thirty-five, but that's not really old for a jockey, and although it was obvious that he and Corin Kellar, the trainer who retained him, were always having rows when their horses didn't win, he hadn't lost any of his style. Someone else would have employed him, even if not one of the top stables like Corin's.'

'And there you have it, I should think,' she said. 'Death was preferable to decline.'

'Yes, it looks like it.'

'I hope that when your time comes to retire you will do it less drastically,' she said. I smiled, and she added, 'And just what will you do when you retire?'

'Retire? I have only just started,' I said.

'And in fourteen years' time you'll be a second-rate, battered, bitter forty, too old to make anything of your life and with nothing to live on but horsy memories that no one wants to listen to.' She sounded quite annoyed at the prospect.

'You, on the other hand,' I said, 'will be a fat, middle-aged, contralto's understudy, scared stiff of losing your looks and aware that those precious vocal cords are growing less flexible every year.'

She laughed. 'How gloomy. But I see your point. From now on I'll try not to disapprove of your job because it lacks a future.'

'But you'll go on disapproving for other reasons?'

'Certainly. It's basically frivolous, unproductive, escapist, and it encourages people to waste time and money on inessentials.'

'Like music,' I said.

She glared at me. 'For that you shall do the washing-up,' she said, getting to her feet and putting the plates together.

While I did my penance for the worst heresy possibly in the Finn family she went back to her portrait, but it was nearly dusk, and when I brought in a peace offering of some freshly-made coffee she gave it up for the day.

'Is your television set working?' I asked, handing her a cup.

'Yes, I think so.'

'Do you mind if we have it on for a quarter of an hour?'

'Who's playing?' she asked automatically.

I sighed. 'No one. It's a racing programme.'

'Oh, very well. If you must.' But she smiled.

I switched on, and we saw the end of the variety show. I enjoyed the songs of the last performer, a vivacious blonde, but Joanna, technique-minded, said her breath control creaked. A batch of advertisements followed, and then the fluttering urgent opening bars of 'The Galloping Major', accompanied by speeded-up superimposed views of horses racing, announced the weekly fifteen minutes of *Turf Talk*.

The well-known good-looking face of Maurice Kemp-Lore came on the screen, smiling and casual. He began in his easy

24

charming way to introduce his guest of the evening, a prominent bookmaker, and his topic of the evening, the mathematics involved in making a book.

'But first,' he said, 'I would like to pay a tribute to the steeplechase jockey, Art Mathews, who died today by his own hand at Dunstable races. Many of you have watched him ride . . . I expect nearly all of you have seen televised races in which he has appeared . . . and you will feel with me a great sense of shock that such a long and successful career should end in a tragedy of this sort. Although never actually champion jockey, Art was acknowledged to be one of the six best steeple-chase riders in the country, and his upright incorruptible char-acter has been a splendid example to young jockeys just starting in the game . . .'

Joanna lifted an eyebrow at me, and Maurice Kemp-Lore, neatly finishing off Art's glowing obituary, reintroduced the bookmaker, who gave a clear and fascinating demonstration of how to come out on the winning side. His talk, illustrated with films and animated charts, described the minute by minute deci-sions made daily in a big London starting price office, and was well up to the high standard of all the Kemp-Lore programmes.

Kemp-Lore thanked him and rounded off the quarter of an hour with a review of the following week's racing, not tipping particular animals to win but giving snippets of information about people and horses on the basis that there would be more interest in the outcome of a race if the public already knew something of the background of the contestants. His anecdotes were always interesting or amusing, and I had heard him called the despair of racing journalists since he so often beat them to a good story.

He said finally, 'See you all next week at the same time,' and 'The Galloping Major' faded him out.

I switched off the set. Joanna said, 'Do you watch that every week?'

'Yes, if I can,' I said. 'It's a racing must. It's so full of things one ought not to miss, and quite often his guest is someone I've met.'

'Mr Kemp-Lore knows his onions, then?' she said.

'He does indeed. He was brought up to it. His father rode a Grand National winner back in the thirties and is now a big noise on the National Hunt Committee; which,' I went on, seeing her blank look, 'is the ruling body of steeplechasing.'

'Oh. And has Mr Kemp-Lore ridden any Grand National winners himself?' she asked.

'No,' I said. 'I don't think he rides much at all. Horses give him asthma, or something like that. I'm not sure . . . I only know him by sight. He is often at the races but I have never spoken to him.'

Joanna's interest in racing, never very strong, subsided entirely at this point, and for an hour or so we gossiped amicably and aimlessly about how the world wagged.

The door bell rang. She went to answer it and came back followed by the man whose portrait she was attempting, the second of her two blood stirrers, still stirring away. He put his arm possessively round her waist and kissed her. He nodded to me.

'How did the concert go?' she asked. He played a first violin in the London Symphony Orchestra.

'So so,' he said; 'the Mozart B flat went all right except that some fool in the audience started clapping after the slow movement and ruined the transition to the allegro.'

My cousin made sympathetic noises. I stood up. I did not enjoy seeing them so cosily together.

'Going?' asked Joanna, detaching herself.

'Yes.'

'Good night, Rob,' he said, yawning. He took off his black tie and loosened the neck of his shirt.

I said politely, 'Good night, Brian.' And may you rot, I thought.

Joanna came with me to the door and opened it, and I stepped out into the dark cobbled mews and turned to say good-bye. She was silhouetted against the warm light in the studio room where Brian, I could see, was sitting down and taking off his shoes.

I said flatly, 'Thank you for the steak . . . and the television.'

'Come again,' she said.

'Yes. Well, good night.'

'Good night,' she said, and then in an afterthought added, 'How is Paulina?'

'She is going to marry,' I said, 'Sir Morton Henge.'

I am not sure what I expected in the way of sympathy, but I should have known. Joanna laughed.

Three

TWO WEEKS after Art died I stayed a night in Peter Cloony's house.

It was the first Cheltenham meeting of the season, and having no car I went down as usual on the race train, carrying some overnight things in a small suitcase. I had been engaged for two races at the meeting, one on each day, and intended to find a back street pub whose charges would make the smallest possible dent in my pocket. But Peter, seeing the case, asked me if I were fixed up for the night, and offered me a bed. It was kind of him, for we were not particularly close friends, and I thanked him and accepted.

From my point of view it was an unexciting day. My one ride, a novice hurdler revoltingly called Neddikins, had no chance of winning. His past form was a sorry record of falls and unfinished races. Tailed-off and pulled-up figured largely. I wondered why on earth the owner bothered with the wretched animal, but at the same time rehearsed in advance some complimentary things to say about it. I had long ago discovered that owners hated to be told their horses were useless and often would not employ again a jockey who spoke too much unpalatable truth. It was wiser not to answer the typical question, 'What do you think we should do with beautiful Neddikins next?' with an unequivocal 'Shoot it.'

By working hard from start to finish I managed to wake Neddikins up slightly, so that although we finished plainly last, we were not exactly tailed off. A triumph, I considered it, to have got round at all, and to my surprise this was also the opinion of his trainer, who clapped me on the shoulder and offered me another novice hurdler on the following day.

Neddikins was the first horse I rode for James Axminster, and I knew I had been asked because he had not wanted to risk injury to his usual jockey. A good many of that sort of ride came my way, but I was glad to have them. I reckoned if I could gain enough experience on bad horses when nothing much was expected of me, it would stand me in good stead if ever I found myself on better ones.

At the end of the afternoon I joined Peter and we drove off in his sedate family saloon. He lived in a small village, scarcely more than a hamlet, in a hollow in the Cotswold Hills about twenty miles from Cheltenham. We turned off the main road into a narrow secondary road bordered on each side by thick hedges. It seemed to stretch interminably across bare farm land, but eventually, turning a corner, it came to the edge of the plateau and one could see a whole village spread out in the small valley below.

Peter pointed. 'That bungalow down there is where I live. The one with the white windows.'

I followed his finger. I had time to see a neatly fenced little garden round a new-looking house before a curve in the road hid it from view. We slid down the hill, rounded several blind corners with a good deal of necessary horn blowing, and at the beginning of the village curled into an even smaller lane and drew up outside Peter's house. It was modern, brick-built, and freshly attractive, with neatly edged flower beds and shaven squares of lawn.

Peter's wife opened the white front door and came down the path to meet us. She was, I saw, very soon to have a child. She herself looked hardly old enough to have left school. She spoke shyly.

'Do come in,' she said, shaking my hand. 'Peter telephoned to say you were coming, and everything is ready.'

I followed her into the bungalow. It was extremely neat and clean and smelled of furniture polish. All the floors were covered with mottled soft blue linoleum with a few terracotta rugs scattered about. Peter's wife, she told me during the evening, had made the rugs herself.

In the sitting-room there was only a sofa, a television set, and a dining-table with four chairs. The bareness of the room was to some extent disguised by one wall being almost completely covered in photographs. They had been framed by Peter himself and were edged in passe-partout in several different bright colours, so that the effect was gay and cheerful. Peter showed them to me while his wife cooked the dinner.

They were clearly devoted to each other. It showed in every glance, every word, every touch. They seemed very well matched; good natured, quickly moved to sympathy, sensitive, and with not a vestige of a sense of humour between them.

'How long have you two been married?' I asked, biting into a wedge of cheese.

Peter said, 'Nine months,' and his wife blushed beguilingly.

We cleared away the dishes and washed them, and spent the evening watching television and talking about racing. When we went to bed they apologized for the state of my bedroom.

'We haven't furnished it properly yet,' said Peter's wife, looking at me with anxious eyes.

'I'll be very comfortable indeed,' I said. 'You are so kind to have had me at all.' She smiled happily.

The bedroom contained a bed and a chair only. There was the blue linoleum on the floor, with a terracotta rug. A small mirror on the wall, some thin rust-coloured curtains at the window, and a hook and two hangers on the back of the door to serve as a wardrobe. I slept well.

In the morning, after breakfast, Peter did a lot of household jobs while his wife showed me round the small garden. She seemed to know every flower and growing vegetable individually. The plants were cherished as thoroughly as the house.

'Peter does most of my housework just now,' she said, looking fondly back to the house. 'The baby is due in six days. He says I mustn't strain myself.'

'He is a most considerate husband,' I said.

'The best in the world,' she said fervently.

It was because Peter insisted at the last minute on driving down to the village shop to fetch a loaf of bread to save his wife the walk that we started out for Cheltenham later than we had intended.

We wound up the twisty hill too fast for prudence, but nothing luckily was on its way down. At least, it seemed to be lucky until we had streaked across the farm land and were slowing down to approach the turn into the main road. That was when we first saw the tank carrier. It was slewed across the road diagonally, completely blocking the way.

Peter's urgent tooting on the horn produced one soldier, who ambled over to the car and spoke soothingly.

'I'm very sorry, sir, but we were looking for the road to Timberley.'

'You turned too soon. It's the next road on the right,' said Peter impatiently.

'Yes, I know,' said the soldier. 'We realized we had turned too soon, and my mate tried to back out again, but he made a right mess of it, and we've hit the hedge on the other side. As a matter of fact,' he said casually, 'we're ruddy well stuck. My mate's just hitched a lorry to go and ring up our H.Q. about it.'

We both got out of the car to have a look, but it was true. The great unwieldy articulated tank carrier was solidly jammed across the mouth of the narrow lane, and the driver had gone.

Pale and grim, Peter climbed back into his seat with me beside him. He had to reverse for a quarter of a mile before we came to a gateway he could turn the car in: then we backtracked down the long bend-ridden hill, raced through the village and out on to the road on the far side. It led south, away from Cheltenham, and we had to make a long detour to get back to the right direction. Altogether the tank carrier put at least twelve miles on to our journey.

Several times Peter said, 'I'll be late,' in a despairing tone of voice. He was, I knew, due to ride in the first race, and the trainer for whom he rode liked him to report to him in the weighing-room an hour earlier. Trainers had to state the name of the jockey who would be riding their horse at least three-quarters of an hour before the event: if they took a chance and declared a jockey who had not arrived and then he did not arrive at all, however good the reason, the trainer was in trouble with the stewards. Peter rode for a man who never took this risk. If his jockey was not there an hour before the race, he found a substitute; and since Peter was his jockey, the rule was a good one, because he was by nature a last-minute rusher who left no time margin for things to go wrong.

We reached the racecourse just forty-three minutes before the first race. Peter sprinted from the car park, but he had some way to go and we both knew that he wouldn't do it. As I followed him more slowly and walked across the big expanse of tarmac towards the weighing-room I heard the click of the loud-speakers being turned on, and the announcer began to recite the runners and riders of the first race. P. Cloony was not among them.

I found him in the changing-room, sitting on the bench with his head in his hands.

'He didn't wait,' he said miserably. 'He didn't wait. I knew he wouldn't. I knew it. He's put Ingersoll up instead.'

I looked across the room to where Tick-Tock was pulling his boots up over his nylon stockings. He already wore the scarlet jersey which should have been Peter's. He caught my eye and grimaced and shook his head in sympathy: but it was not his fault he had been given the ride, and he had no need to be too apologetic.

The worst of it was that Tick-Tock won. I was standing beside Peter on the jockeys' stand when the scarlet colours skated by the winning post, and he made a choking sound as if he were about to burst into tears. He managed not to, but there was a certain dampness about his eyes and his face had changed to a bloodless, greyish white.

'Never mind,' I said awkwardly, embarrassed for him. 'It's not the end of the world.'

It had been unfortunate that we had arrived so late, but the trainer he rode for was a reasonable man, if impatient, and there was no question of his not engaging him in future. Peter did in fact ride for him again that same afternoon, but the horse ran less well than was expected, and pulled up lame. My last glimpse of him showed a face still dragged down in lines of disappointment and he was boring everyone in the weighing-room by harping on the tank carrier over and over again.

For myself, things went slightly better. The novice chaser fell at the water jump, but went down slowly and I suffered nothing but grass stains on my breeches.

The young hurdler I was to ride for James Axminster in the last race on the card had as vile a reputation as his stablemate the previous day and I had made completing the race my sole target. But for some reason the wayward animal and I got on very well together from the start, and to my surprise, an emotion shared by every single person present, we came over the last hurdle in second place and passed the leading horse on the uphill stretch to the winning post. The odds-on favourite finished fourth. It was my second win of the season, and my first ever at Cheltenham: and it was greeted with dead silence.

I found myself trying to explain it away to James Axminster in the winner's unsaddling enclosure.

'I'm very sorry, sir,' I said. 'I couldn't help it.'

I knew he hadn't had a penny on it, and the owner had not even bothered to come to see the horse run.

He looked at me broodingly without answering, and I thought that there was one trainer who would not employ me again in a hurry. Sometimes it is as bad to win unexpectedly as to lose on a certainty.

I unbuckled the girths, pulled the saddle off over my arm and stood waiting for the storm to break.

'Well, go along and weigh in,' he said abruptly. 'And when you're dressed I want to talk to you.'

When I came out of the changing-room he was standing just inside the weighing-room door talking to Lord Tirrold, whose horse he trained. They stopped talking and turned towards me as I went over to them, but I could not see their expressions clearly as they had their backs to the light.

James Axminster said, 'What stable do you ride for most?'

I said, 'I ride mainly for farmers who train their own horses. I haven't a steady job with a public trainer, but I have ridden for several when they have asked me. Mr Kellar has put me up a few times.' And that, I thought a little wryly, is the true picture of the smallness of the impression I had made in the racing world.

'I have heard one or two trainers say,' said Lord Tirrold, speaking directly to Axminster, 'that for their really bad horses they can always get Finn.'

Axminster grinned back at him. 'Just what I did today, and look at the result! How am I going to convince the owner it was as much a surprise to me as it will be to him when he hears about it? I've told him often that the horse is pretty useless.' He turned to me. 'You have made me look a proper fool, you know.'

'I'm sorry, sir,' I said again: and I meant it.

'Don't look so glum about it. I'll give you another chance; several in fact. There's a slow old plug you can ride for me on

Saturday, if you're not booked already for that race, and two or three others next week. After that . . . we'll see.'

'Thank you,' I said dazedly. 'Thank you very much.' It was as if he had thrust a gold brick into my hands when I had expected a scorpion: if I acquitted myself at all well on his horses he might use me regularly as a second-string jockey. That would be, for me, a giant step up.

He smiled a warm, almost mischievous smile which crinkled the skin round his eyes and said, 'Geranium in the handicap chase at Hereford on Saturday, then. Are you free?'

'Yes,' I said.

'And you can do the weight? Ten stone?'

'Yes,' I said. I'd need to lose another three pounds in the two days, but starvation had never seemed so attractive.

'Very well. I'll see you there.'

'Yes, sir,' I said.

He and Lord Tirrold turned away and went out of the weighing-room together, and I heard them laugh. I watched them go, the thin angular Lord Tirrold and the even taller trainer, a pair who had between them won almost every important event in the National Hunt calendar.

James Axminster was a big man in every sense. Six foot four and solidly bulky, he moved and spoke and made decisions with easy assurance. He had a big face with a prominent nose and a square-looking heavy lower jaw. When he smiled his lower teeth showed in front of the upper ones, and they were good strong teeth, evenly set and unusually white.

His stable was one of the six largest in the country: his jockey, Pip Pankhurst, had been champion for the past two seasons; and his horses, about sixty of them, included some of the best alive. To have been offered a toe-hold in this set-up was almost as frightening as it was miraculous. If I messed up this chance, I thought, I might as well follow Art into oblivion.

I spent most of the next day running round Hyde Park in

three sweaters and a wind-cheater and resisting the temptation to drink pints of water to replace what I had sweated off. Some of the other jockeys used dehydrating pills to rid their bodies of fluid (which weighs more than fat and is easier to shift) but I had found, the only time I took some, that they left me feeling almost too weak to ride.

At about six o'clock I boiled three eggs and ate them without salt or bread, and then removed myself hurriedly, for my mother was entertaining some friends to dinner, and the girl who came to cook for us on these occasions was beginning to fill the kitchen with demoralizing savoury smells. I decided to go to the pictures to take my mind off my stomach; but it wasn't a great success as I chose the film somewhat carelessly, and found myself watching three men staggering on their parched way through a blazing desert sharing their rations into ever dwindling morsels.

After that I went to the Turkish baths in Jermyn Street and spent the whole night there, sweating gently all evening and again when I woke in the morning. Then I went back to the flat and ate three more boiled eggs, which I no longer cared for very much, and at last made my way to Hereford.

The needle quivered when I sat on the scales with the lightest possible saddle and thin boots. It swung up over the ten stone mark and pendulumed down and finally settled a hair's breadth on the right side.

'Ten stone,' said the clerk of the scales in a surprised voice. 'What have you been doing? Sandpapering it off?'

'More or less,' I grinned.

In the parade ring James Axminster looked at the number boards where the weights the horses carried were recorded, if they differed from those printed in the race cards. He turned back to me.

'No overweight?' he asked.

'No, sir,' I said matter-of-factly, as if it were the easiest thing in the world.

'Hm.' He beckoned the lad who was leading round the slow old plug I was to ride and said, 'You'll have to kick this old mare along a bit. She's lazy. A good jumper, but that's about all.'

I was used to kicking lazy horses. I kicked, and the mare jumped: and we finished third.

'Hm,' said Axminster again as I unbuckled the girths. I took my saddle and weighed in – half a pound lighter – and changed into the colours of the other horse I had been engaged to ride that afternoon, and when I walked out into the weighing-room, Axminster was waiting for me. He had a paper in his hand. He gave it to me without a word.

It was a list of five horses running in various races during the following week. Against each horse's name he had put the weight it had to carry and the race it was to run in. I read through them.

'Well?' he said. 'Can you ride them?'

'I can ride four of them,' I said. 'But I'm already booked for that novice chase on Wednesday.'

'Is it important? Can you get off?' he asked.

I would dearly have liked to say yes. The paper I held was an invitation to my personal paradise, and there was always the chance that if I refused one of his mounts, the man who got it might corner all the future ones.

'I . . . no,' I said, 'I ought not to. It's for the farmer who gave me my first few rides . . .'

Axminster smiled faintly, the lower teeth showing in front. 'Very well. Ride the other four.'

I said, 'Thank you, sir. I'd be glad to.' He turned away, and I folded up the precious list and put it in my pocket.

My other ride later that afternoon was for Corin Kellar. Since Art's death he had employed several different jockeys and moaned to them about the inconvenience of not having a first-class man always on call. As it was his treatment of Art which had driven a first-class man to leave him in the most drastic possible way, Tick-Tock and I considered him a case for psychiatry; but both of us were glad enough to ride his horses, and Tick-Tock had ridden more of them than anyone else.

'If Corin asks you,' I said as we collected our saddles and helmets ready to weigh out for the race, 'will you accept Art's job?'

'If he asks me, yes,' said Tick-Tock. 'He won't harass *me* into the hereafter.' He looked up slantwise from under his rakishly tilted eyebrows, the thin-lipped, wide mouth stretched in a care-free grin. A vivid, almost aggressive sanity moulded the angular planes of his face, and for a moment he seemed to me more than ever to have been born too soon. He was what I pictured twenty-first century man should be – intensely alive, curiously innocent, with no taint of apathy or anger or greed. He made me feel old. He was nineteen.

We went out together to the parade ring.

'Paste on a toothy leer,' he said. 'The eye of the world has swivelled our way.'

I glanced up. From its draughty platform a television camera swung its square snout towards us as it followed the progress of a grey horse round the ring. It tracked briefly over us and moved on.

'I'd forgotten we were on the air,' I said indifferently.

'Oh, yes,' said Tick-Tock, 'and the great man himself is here somewhere too, the one and only M. Kemp-Lore, no less. Puff pastry, that man is.'

'How do you mean?' I asked.

'A quick riser. And full of hot air. But rich, man, and tasty. A good crisp flavour, nice and crunchy.'

I laughed. We joined Corin and he began to give us both our instructions for the race. Tick-Tock's mount was a good one, but I was as usual riding a horse of whom little was expected, and quite rightly, as it turned out. We trailed in a long way behind, and I saw from the numbers going up in the frame that Corin's other horse had won.

Corin and Tick-Tock and the horse's owner were conducting a mutual admiration session in the winner's enclosure when I walked back to the weighing-room with my saddle, but Corin caught me by the arm as I went past and asked me to come straight out again, when I had dumped my saddle and helmet, to tell him how the horse had run.

When I rejoined him he was talking to a man who had his back towards me. I hovered, not wanting to interrupt, but Corin saw me and beckoned, and I walked across to them. The man turned round. He was in his early thirties, I judged. Of average height and slim build, with good features and light hair. It never ceases to be disconcerting, meeting for the first time in the flesh a man whose face is as familiar to you as a brother's. It was Maurice Kemp-Lore.

Television is unflattering to everybody. It fattens the body and flattens the personality, so that to sparkle from the small screen an entertainer must be positively incandescent in real life, and Kemp-Lore was no exception. The charm which came over gradually in his programme was instantly compelling when one met him. Intensely blue eyes looked at me from a firm, sun-tanned face; his hand shake was quick and strong, his smile, infectious and warm, indicated his delight in meeting me. But it was a professional delight, and even as I responded to him I recognized that the effect he had on me was calculated. His stock in trade. All good interviewers know how to give people confidence so that they expand and flower, and Kemp-Lore was a master of his art. Dull men had shone as wits in his programme, taciturn men chattered, bigoted men thought again.

'I see you were last in the race,' he said. 'Bad luck.'

'Bad horse,' said Corin, put into smiling good humour by his presence.

'I've been wanting for some time to do a programme on – if you'll forgive me – an unsuccessful jockey.' His smile took the sting out of his words. 'Or at least, a jockey who is not yet successful. Perhaps that would be a fairer way of putting it?' His blue eyes twinkled. 'Would you consider coming on my programme and telling viewers what sort of life you lead? I have in mind your financial position, your reliance on chance rides, insecurity . . . that sort of thing. Just to give the public the reverse side of the coin. They know all about big retainers and fat presents and jockeys who win important races. I want to show them how a jockey who seldom wins even unimportant races manages to live. A jockey on the fringe.' He smiled his warm smile. 'Will you do it?'

'Yes,' I said, 'certainly. But I'm not really typical. I . . .'

He interrupted me. 'Don't tell me anything now,' he said, 'I know enough about your career to find you suitable for what I have in mind, but I always prefer not to know the answers to my specific questions until we are actually on the air. It makes the whole thing more spontaneous. I have found that if I rehearse with my subject what we are going to say the programme comes over stiffly and unconvincingly. Instead, I will send you a list of the sort of questions I will be asking, and you can think out your replies. O.K.?'

'Yes,' I said. 'All right.'

'Good. Next Friday then. The programme goes out at nine o'clock. Get to the studios by seven-thirty, will you? That gives time for seeing to lighting, make-up, and so on, and perhaps for a drink beforehand. Here is a card which will tell you how to get there.' He produced a card which had 'Universal Telecast' printed in large capitals on one side and a simplified map of Willesden on the other.

'Oh, and by the way, there will be a fee, of course, and your expenses.' He smiled sympathetically, letting me know that he knew that that was good news.

'Thank you,' I smiled back. 'I'll be there.'

He spoke a word to Corin and strolled away. I turned to Corin and caught on his face as he watched the retreating figure of Kemp-Lore, the same expression that I saw so often on hangers-on round my parents. The smug, fawning smirk which meant 'I am on speaking terms with a famous person, clever me.' It would have been more impressive, I thought, if like most other trainers he had taken knowing the illustrious Kemp-Lore entirely for granted.

'I know Maurice quite well,' said Corin aloud, in a self-satisfied voice. 'He asked my advice about whether you'd be any good as his – er – unsuccessful jockey, and I told him to go ahead.'

'Thanks,' I said, as he waited for it.

'Yes, a grand fellow, Maurice. Good family, you know. His father won the National – an amateur of course – and his sister is the best lady point-to-point rider there has been for years. Poor old Maurice, though, he hardly rises at all. Doesn't even hunt. Horses give him the most ghastly asthma, you know. He's very cut-up about it. Still, he'd never have taken to broadcasting if he'd been able to race, so perhaps it's all for the best.'

'I dare say,' I said. I was still in lightweight silk colours and breeches and the afternoon was growing cool. I dragged the conversation back to the horse I had just come last on, got the post-mortem over, and eventually went back to the weighing-room to change.

The jockeys had already gone out for the last race, but several others were standing about in various stages of undress, gossiping and putting on their street clothes. As I went down the room I saw Grant Oldfield standing by my peg, holding a paper in his hand, and I was annoyed to find, drawing nearer, that it was the list of horses James Axminster had given me. Grant had been going through my pockets.

My protest was never uttered. Without a word, without any warning, Grant swung his fist and punched me heavily in the nose.

Four

THE AMOUNT of blood which resulted would have done credit to a clinic full of donors. It splashed in a scarlet stain down the front of my pale green silk shirt and made big uneven blotches on the white breeches. There were large spots of it on the bench and on the floor and it was all over my hands where I had tried to wipe it out of my mouth.

'For God's sake, lay him down on his back,' said one of the valets, hurrying over. His advice was almost unnecessary, since I was already lying down, mostly on the floor but half propped up by the leg of the bench. It was where that one blow, catching me off balance, had felled me.

Grant stood at my feet, looking down as if surprised to have caused so much mess. I could have laughed if I had not been so busy swallowing what seemed like cupfuls of my own blood.

Young Mike thrust a saddle under my shoulders and pushed my head backwards over it. A second later he was piling a cold, wet towel across the bridge of my nose; and gradually the breath-clogging bleeding lessened and stopped.

'You'd better stay there for a bit,' said Mike. 'I'll go and get one of the first-aid men to see to you.'

'Don't bother,' I said. 'Please don't bother, it's all right now.'

He came back irresolutely from the door and stood by my head. He looked upside down to me, as my eyes were level with his ankles.

'What the hell did you do that for?' he said to Grant.

I wanted to hear his answer too, but Grant did not reply. He scowled down at me, then turned on his heel and pushed his way out of the changing-room against the incoming tide of the jockeys returning from the last race. The list of Axminster horses fluttered to the floor in his wake. Mike picked it up and put it into my outstretched hand.

Tick-Tock dumped his saddle on the bench, tipped back his helmet, and put his hands on his hips.

'What have we here? A blood bath?' he said.

'Nose bleed,' I said.

'You don't say.'

The others began crowding round and I decided I'd been lying down long enough. I lifted the towel off my face and stood up gingerly. All was well. The fountains had dried up.

'Grant socked him one,' said one of the jockeys who had been there all the time.

'Why?'

'Ask me another,' I said. 'Or ask Grant.'

'You ought to report it to the stewards.'

'It's not worth it,' I said.

I cleaned myself up and changed, and walked down to the station with Tick-Tock.

'You must know why he hit you,' he said. 'Or was it merely target practice?'

I handed him Axminster's list. He read it and gave it back.

'Yes, I see. Hatred, envy and jealousy. You're stepping into the shoes he couldn't fill himself. He had his chance there, and he muffed it.'

'What happened?' I asked. 'Why did Axminster drop him?'

'I don't honestly know,' Tick-Tock said, 'you'd better ask Grant and find out what mistakes not to make.' He grinned. 'Your nose looks like a vulgar seaside postcard.'

'It's good enough for the goggle box,' I said. I told him about Maurice Kemp-Lore's invitation.

'My dear sir,' he said, sweeping off his Tyrolean hat, and making me a mocking bow. 'I am impressed.'

'You're a fool,' I said, grinning.

'Thank God.'

We went our ways, Tick-Tock to his digs in Berkshire and I to Kensington. The flat was empty, the usual state of affairs on Saturday evenings, a busy night for concerts. I took half the ice cubes from the refrigerator, wrapped them in a plastic bag and a tea towel and lay down on the bed with the ice bag balanced on my forehead. My nose felt like a jelly. Grant's fist had had the power of severe mental disturbance behind it.

I shut my eyes and thought about them, Grant and Art; two disintegrated people. One had been driven to violence against himself, and the other had turned violent against the world. Poor things, I thought rather too complacently, they were not stable enough to deal with whatever had undermined them: and I remembered that easy pity, later on.

On the following Wednesday Peter Cloony came to the races bubbling over with happiness. The baby was a boy, his wife was fine, everything was rosy. He slapped us all on the back and told us we didn't know what we were missing. The horse he rode that afternoon started favourite and ran badly, but it didn't damp his spirits.

The next day he was due to ride in the first race, and he was late. We knew before he arrived that he had missed his chance, because five minutes before the deadline for declaring jockeys his trainer had sent an official into the changing-room to find out if he was there, and he wasn't.

I was standing outside the weighing-room when Peter finally came, forty minutes before the first race. He was running over the grass, anxiety clear on his face even from a distance. His trainer detached himself from the group of people he had been talking to and intercepted him. Fragments of angry remarks floated across to me.

'Is this your idea of an hour before the first? . . . I've had to get another jockey . . . very stupid of you . . . second time in a week . . . irresponsible . . . not the way to go on if you want to keep your job with me . . .' He stalked away.

Peter brushed past me, white, trembling and looking sick, and when I went back into the changing-room a short time later he was sitting on a bench with his head in his hands.

'What happened this time?' I asked. 'Is your wife all right? And the baby?' I thought he must have been so busy attending to them that he had forgotten to watch the clock.

'They're fine,' he said miserably. 'My mother-in-law is staying with us to look after them. I wasn't late setting out . . . only five minutes or so . . . but . . .' he stood up and gazed at me with his large, moist-looking eyes, '. . . you'll never believe it but there was something else stuck across the lane, and I had to go miles round again, even further than last time . . .' His voice trailed off as I looked at him in disbelief.

'Not another tank carrier?' I asked incredulously.

'No, a car. An old car, one of those heavy old Jaguars. It had its nose in the hedge and one front wheel in the ditch, and it was jammed tight, right across the lane.'

'You couldn't have helped its driver push it straight again?' I asked.

'There wasn't any driver. No one at all. And the car doors were locked, and the hand-brake was full on, and he'd left the thing in gear. The stinking bastard.' Peter seldom used such strong language. 'Another man had driven up the hill behind me and we both tried to shift the Jag, but it was absolutely hopeless. We had to reverse again for miles, and he had to go first, and he wouldn't hurry a yard . . . he had a new car and he was afraid of scratching it.'

'It's very bad luck,' I said inadequately.

'Bad luck!' he repeated explosively, apparently near to tears. 'It's more than bad luck it's – it's awful. I can't afford . . . I need the money . . .' He stopped talking and swallowed several times, and sniffed, 'We've got a mortgage to pay off,' he said, 'and I didn't know babies could cost so much. And my wife had to stop working, which we hadn't reckoned on . . . we didn't mean to have a baby so soon.'

I remembered vividly the new little bungalow with its cheap, blue linoleum, its home-made terra cotta rugs, its bare, bare furnishings. And he had a car to run and now a child to keep. I saw that the loss of a ten-guinea riding fee was a calamity.

He had not been booked for any other ride that afternoon, and he spent the whole day mooching about the weighing-room so as to be under the eye of any trainers looking hurriedly for a jockey. He wore a desperate, hunted look all the time, and I knew that that alone would have discouraged me, had I been a trainer. He left, unemployed and disconsolate, just before the fifth race, having done himself no good at all in the eyes of every trainer at the meeting.

I watched him trailing off to the car park as I walked down from the weighing-room to the parade ring for my own one-and-only ride of the day, and I felt a surge of irritation against him. Why couldn't he pretend a little, make light of his misfortune, shrug it off? And why above all didn't he leave himself a margin for error on his journeys, when unprompt arrivals cost him so much? A punctured tyre, a windscreen shattered by a flying stone, anything might make him late. It didn't have to be as unforeseeable as a tank carrier or a locked Jaguar wedged immovably across his path. And what a dismal coincidence, I reflected, that it should have happened twice in a week.

James Axminster smiled his disconcerting, heavy-jawed smile in the parade ring and introduced me to the owner of the horse I was to ride. He shook hands and we made the usual desultory

pre-race conversation. The middle-aged handicap hurdler plod-
ding sleepily round the ring was the third Axminster horse I had
ridden during the week, and I had already grown to appreciate
the sleekness and slickness of his organization. His horses were
well schooled and beautifully turned out, and there was nothing
makeshift or second-best in any of his equipment. Success and
prosperity spoke from every brightly initialled horse rug, every
top quality bridle, every brush, bandage and bucket that came
to the meetings.

In the two earlier races that week I had been riding the
stable's second string while Pip Pankhurst took his usual place
on the better horses. Thursday's handicap hurdle, however, was
all my own because Pip could not do the weight.

'Anything under ten stone six, and it's yours,' he told me,
cheerfully, when he found I was riding some of his stable's
horses. 'Anything under ten six is hardly worth riding, anyway.'

By eating and drinking very little I had managed to keep my
riding weight down to ten stone for a whole week. This meant
a body weight of nine stone eight, which was a strain at my
height, but with Pip in that ungrudging frame of mind it was
well worth it.

James Axminster said, 'At the fourth hurdle, you want to be
somewhere in the middle. About three from home, providing
they're not too strung out, you want to lie about fourth. He
takes some time to get into top gear, so start him moving going
into the second last. Keep him going, try to come up to the
leader at the last and see how much you can gain in the air there.
This horse is a great jumper, but has no finishing speed. Very
one-paced. See what you can do, anyway.'

He had not given me such detailed instructions before, and
it was the first time he had mentioned anything about what to
do at the last obstacle. I felt a deep quiver of excitement in my
stomach. At last I was about to ride a horse whose trainer would
not be thoroughly surprised if he won.

I followed my instructions to the letter, and coming into the last hurdle level with two other horses I kicked my old mount with all the determination I could muster. He responded with a zipping leap which sped him clean past the other horses in mid-air and landed us a good two lengths clear of them. I heard the clatter of the hurdles as the others rapped them, and basely hoped they had made stumbling, time-wasting landings. It was true that the old hurdler could not quicken. I got him balanced and ran him straight to the winning post, using my whip hardly at all and concentrating mainly on sitting still and not disturbing him. He held on gamely, and still had half a length in hand when we passed the post. It was a gorgeous moment.

'Well done,' said Axminster matter-of-factly. Winners were nothing out of the ordinary to him. I unbuckled the girths and slid the saddle off over my arm, and patted the hurdler's sweating neck.

The owner was delighted. 'Well done, well done,' he said to the horse, Axminster and me indiscriminately. 'I never thought he'd pull it off, James, even though I took your advice and backed him.'

I looked quickly at Axminster. His piercingly blue eyes regarded me quizzically.

'Do you want the job?' he asked. 'Second to Pip, regular?'

I nodded and dragged in a deep breath, and said, 'Yes.' It sounded like a croak.

The hurdler's owner laughed. 'It's Finn's lucky week. John Ballerton tells me Maurice is interviewing him on his television programme tomorrow evening.'

'Really?' Axminster said. 'I'll try and watch it.'

I went to weigh in and change, and when I came out Axminster gave me another list of horses, four of them, which he wanted me to ride the following week.

'From now on,' he said, 'I don't want you to accept any rides without finding out first if I need you. All right?'

'Yes, sir,' I said, trying not to show too much of the idiotic delight I was feeling. But he knew. He was too old a hand not to. His eyes glimmered with understanding and friendliness and promise.

I telephoned Joanna. 'How about dinner? I want to celebrate.'

'What?' she asked economically.

'A winner. A new job. All's right with the world,' I said.

'You sound as if you've been celebrating already.'

'No,' I said. 'Any drunkenness you can hear in my voice is due to being hit on the head by good luck.'

She laughed. 'All right then. Where?'

'Hennibert's,' I said. It was a small restaurant in St James's Street with a standard of cooking to match its address, and prices to match both.

'Oh yes,' said Joanna. 'Shall I come in my golden coach?'

'I mean it,' I said. 'I've earned forty pounds this week. I want to spend some of it. And besides, I'm hungry.'

'You won't get a table,' she said.

'It's booked.'

'I'm sold,' she said. 'I'll be there at eight.'

She came in a taxi, a compliment to me as she was a girl who liked walking. She wore a dress I had not seen before, a slender straight affair made of a firm, deep-blue material which moved with a faint shimmer when the light fell on it. Her springy dark hair curved neatly down on to the nape of her neck, and the slanting outward tapering lines she had drawn on her eyelids made her black eyes look bigger and deep set and mysterious. Every male head turned to look at her as we walked down the room: yet she was not pretty, not eye-catchingly glamorous, not even notably well dressed. She looked . . . I surprised myself with the word . . . intelligent.

We ate avocados with french dressing and *boeuf stroganoff* with spinach, and late crop strawberries and cream, and a mushroom and bacon and prune savoury. For me, after so many bird-sized meals, it was a feast. We took a long time eating and drank a bottle of wine, and sat over our coffee talking with the ease of a friendship which stretched back to childhood. Most of the time, after so much practice, I could keep my more uncousinly feelings for Joanna well concealed from her; and it was necessary to conceal them because I knew from past experience that if I even approached the subject of love she would begin to fidget and avoid my eyes, and would very soon find a good reason for leaving. If I wanted to enjoy her company, it had to be on her terms.

She seemed genuinely pleased about the James Axminster job. Even though racing didn't interest her, she saw clearly what it meant to me.

'It's like the day the musical director at the Handel Society picked me out of the choir to sing my first recitative. I felt like a pouter pigeon and so full of air that I thought I would need guy-ropes to keep my feet on the ground.'

'Heady stuff,' I agreed. My first elation had settled down to a warm cosy glow of satisfaction. I did not remember ever having felt so content.

I told her about the television programme.

'Tomorrow?' she said. 'Good, I think I'll be free to watch you. You don't do things by halves, do you?'

I grinned. 'This is just the start,' I said. I almost believed it.

We walked all the way back to Joanna's studio. It was a clear crisp night with the stars blazing coldly in the black sky. Depth upon depth of infinity. We stopped in the dark mews outside Joanna's door and looked up.

'They put things into proportion, don't they?' she said.

'Yes.' I wondered what it was that she needed to see in proportion. I looked at her. It was a mistake. The up-tilted face with starlight reflected in the shadowy eyes, the dark hair tousled again by our walk, the strong line of throat, the jut of breasts close to my arm, they swept me ruthlessly into the turmoil I had been suppressing all evening.

'Thank you for coming,' I said abruptly. 'Good night, Joanna.'

She said, surprised, 'Wouldn't you like some more coffee . . . or something?'

Or something. Yes.

I said, 'I couldn't eat or drink another thing. Anyway . . . there's Brian . . .'

'Brian's in Manchester, on tour,' she said. But it was a statement of fact, not an invitation.

'Oh. Well, all the same, I think I'd better get some sleep,' I said.

'All right, then.' She was undisturbed. 'A lovely dinner, Rob. Thank you.' She put her hand for a moment on my shoulder in a friendly fashion and smiled good night. She put the key in her door and opened it and waved briefly to me as I turned and started back down the mews. She shut her door. I swore violently, aloud. It wasn't much relief. I looked up at the sky. The stars went on whizzing round in their courses, uncaring and cold.

Five

THEY GAVE me what in the Finn family was known as F.I.P. treatment at the Universal Telecast Studios. Fairly Important Person. It meant being met by someone well enough up in the hierarchy of the organization for it to be clear that trouble was being taken, but not so high that he needed to be supported by lieutenants.

My mother was a connoisseur of all the shades between V.I.P. and F.I.P. and invariably noticed every detail of the pains or lack of them taken to make her feel comfortable. Her awareness had rubbed off on to me at a very early age and the whole gambit caused me a lot of quiet amusement when I grew up. Years of being a U.I.P. (Unimportant Person) had only sharpened my appreciation.

I went through the swinging glass doors into the large echoing entrance hall and asked the girl at the reception desk where I should go. She smiled kindly. Would I sit down, she said, gesturing to a nearby sofa. I sat. She spoke down the telephone, 'Mr Finn is here, Gordon.'

Within ten seconds a burly young man with freckles and a rising-young-executive, navy-blue, pin-striped suit advanced briskly from one of the corridors.

'Mr Finn?' he said expansively, holding out a hand protruding from a snowy, gold-linked shirt cuff.

'Yes,' I said, standing up and shaking hands.

'Glad to have you here. I am Gordon Kildare, Associate

53

Producer. Maurice is up in the studio running over the last-minute details, so I suggest we go along and have a drink and a sandwich first.' He led the way down the corridor he had come from and we turned in through an open door into a small impersonal reception room. On the table stood bottles and glasses and four plates of fat freshly cut and appetizing-looking sandwiches.

'What will you have?' he asked hospitably, his hands hovering over the bottles.

'Nothing, thank you,' I said.

He was not put out. 'Perhaps afterwards, then?' He poured some whisky into a glass, added soda and raised it to me, smiling. 'Good luck,' he said. 'Is this your first time on television?'

I nodded.

'The great thing is to be natural.' He picked up a sandwich with a pink filling and took a squelchy bite.

The door opened and two more men came in. Introduced to me as Dan something and Paul something, they were a shade less carefully dressed than Gordon Kildare, to whom they deferred. They too dug into the sandwiches and filled their glasses, and wished me luck and told me to be natural.

Maurice Kemp-Lore strode briskly in with a couple of sports-jacketed assistants in tow.

'My dear chap,' he greeted me, shaking me warmly by the hand. 'Glad to see you're here in good time. Has Gordon been looking after you? That's right. Now, what are you drinking?'

'Nothing just now,' I said.

'Oh? Oh well, never mind. Perhaps afterwards? You got the list of questions all right?'

I nodded.

'Have you thought out some answers?'

'Yes,' I said.

'Good, good. That's fine,' he said.

Gordon handed him a well-filled glass and offered him the sandwiches. The assistants helped themselves. It dawned on me that the refreshments provided for the entertainment of visitors probably served all of them as their main evening meal.

Kemp-Lore looked at his watch. 'Our other guest is cutting it rather fine.' As he spoke, the telephone rang. Gordon answered it, listened briefly, said 'He's here, Maurice,' and opened the door.

Kemp-Lore went out first, followed by Gordon and either Dan or Paul, who looked very much alike. It was a more impressive welcoming committee than had been accorded me: I smiled to think of what my mother would have said.

A sports-jacketed assistant offered me sandwiches.

'No?' he said. 'Oh, well, a lot of people feel like that beforehand. You'll be very hungry afterwards.' He put two sandwiches carefully together and stretched open his mouth to bite them.

The voice of Kemp-Lore could be heard coming back along the corridor talking with someone who spoke in a harsh voice with a nasal twang. I wondered idly who the other guest would be and whether I knew him. At the doorway Kemp-Lore stood respectfully back to let his guest precede him into the room. My spirits sank. Paunch and horn-rims well to the fore, Mr John Ballerton allowed himself to be ushered in.

Kemp-Lore introduced all the television men to him. 'And Rob Finn, of course, you know?' he said.

Ballerton nodded coldly in my direction without meeting my eyes. Evidently it still rankled with him that I had seen him sicking up beside Art's body. Perhaps he knew that I had not kept it a secret from the other jockeys.

'It's time we went up to the studio, I think,' Kemp-Lore said, looking enquiringly at Gordon, who nodded.

We all filed out into the corridor, and as I passed the table I noticed the sandwich plates now held nothing but crumbs and a few straggly pieces of cress.

The smallish studio held a chaotic-looking tangle of cameras trailing their thick cables over the floor. To one side there was a shallow carpet-covered platform on which stood three low-slung chairs and a coffee table. A tray with three cups, cream jug and sugar basin shared the table with three empty balloon brandy glasses, a silver cigarette box and two large glass ash-trays.

Kemp-Lore took Ballerton and me towards this arrangement.

'We want to look as informal as possible,' he said pleasantly. 'As if we had just had dinner and were talking over coffee and brandy and cigars.'

He asked Ballerton to sit in the left-hand chair and me in the right, and then took his place between us. Set in front and slightly to one side stood a monitor set with a blank screen; and in a semicircle a battery of cameras converged their menacing black lenses in our direction.

Gordon and his assistants spent some time checking their lights, which dazed us with a dazzling intensity for a few moments, and then tested for sound while the three of us made stilted conversation over the empty cups. When he was satisfied, Gordon came over to us. 'You all need make-up,' he said. 'Maurice, you'll see to yours as usual? Then Mr Ballerton and Mr Finn, I'll show you where to go, if you will follow me?'

He led us to a small room off one corner of the studio. There were two girls in pink overalls and bright smiles.

'It won't take long,' they said, smoothing coloured cream into our skins. 'Just a little darkener under the eyes . . . that's right. Now powder . . .' They patted the powder on with pads of cotton wool, carefully flicking off the excess. 'That's all.'

I looked in the mirror. The make-up softened and blurred both the outlines of the face and texture of the skin. I didn't much care for it.

'You'd look ill on television without it,' the girls assured us. 'You need make-up to look natural and healthy.'

Ballerton frowned and complained as one of them powdered the bald patch on his head. The girl insisted politely. 'It'll shine too much otherwise, you see,' she said, and went on patting his head with the cotton wool.

He caught me grinning at him and it clearly made him furious, raising a dark flush under the sun-tone make-up. There was no question of his ever sharing a rueful joke at his own expense, and I should have known it. I sighed to myself. This made twice that I had seen him at what he considered a disadvantage, and though I had not meant at all to antagonize him, it seemed that I had made a thorough job of it.

We went back into the studio and Kemp-Lore beckoned to us to take our places in the chairs on the platform.

'I'll just run through the order of the programme,' he said, 'so that you will know what to expect. After the introductory music I am going to talk to you first, John, along the lines we discussed. After that, Rob will tell us what his sort of life entails. We have some film of a race you rode in, Rob, which we are using as an illustration, and I plan to fit that in fairly near the beginning of our talk. It will be thrown on to that screen over there.' He pointed.

'For the last few minutes, John will have a chance to comment on what you have said and we might have a final word or two from you. We'll see how it goes. Now, the great thing is to talk naturally. I've explained that too much rehearsal spoils the spontaneity of a programme like this, but it means that a lot of the success of the next quarter of an hour depends on you. I'm sure you will both do splendidly.' He finished his pep talk with a cheerful grin, and I did in fact feel confidence flowing into me from him.

One of the sports-jacketed assistants stepped on to the shallow platform with a coffee pot in one hand and a brandy bottle in the other. He poured hot black coffee into the three cups, and put the pot down on the tray. Then he uncorked the brandy and wet the bottom of the balloon glasses.

'No expense spared,' he said cheerfully. He produced three

cigars from the breast pocket of the sports jacket and offered them to us. Ballerton accepted one and sniffed it and rolled it between his fingers, curving his bad-tempered mouth into what passed with him for a smile.

'Two minutes,' shouted a voice.

The spotlights flashed on, dazzling as before, blacking out everything in the studio. For a moment the monitor set showed a close-up of the coffee cups: then it went dark and the next picture on it was an animated cartoon advertising petrol. It was tuned now to what was actually being transmitted.

'Thirty seconds. Quiet please. Quiet please,' Gordon said.

A hush fell over the whole area. I glanced at the monitor set in front of us. It was busy with a silent advertisement for soap flakes. Dimly seen beyond the lights, Gordon stood with his hand raised. There was dead silence. Steam rose gently from the three coffee cups. Everyone waited. Kemp-Lore beside me arranged his features in the well-known smile, looking straight ahead at the round black lens of the camera. The smile stayed in position for ten seconds without wavering.

On the monitor set the superimposed horses galloped and faded. Gordon's hand swept down briskly. The camera in front of Kemp-Lore developed a shining red eye and he began to speak, pleasantly, intimately, straight into a million sitting-rooms.

'Good evening . . . tonight I am going to introduce you to two people who are both deeply involved with National Hunt racing, but who look at it, so to speak, from opposite poles. First, here is Mr John Ballerton . . .' He gave him a good build-up but overdid the importance. There were about forty-nine other members of the National Hunt Committee, including Kemp-Lore's own father, all at least as active and devoted as the fat man now basking in praise.

Skilfully guided by Kemp-Lore, he talked about his duties as one of the three stewards at a race meeting. It involved, he said,

NERVE

hearing both sides if there was an objection to a winner and awarding the race justly to the more deserving, and yes, summoning jockeys and trainers for minor infringements of the rules and fining them a fiver or a tenner a time.

I watched him on the monitor set. I had to admit he looked a solid, sober, responsible citizen with right on his side. The aggressive horn rims gave him, on the screen, a definite air of authority; also for the occasion his habitually sour expression had given way to a rather persuasive geniality. No one watching the performance Kemp-Lore coaxed out of him would have suspected him to be the bigoted, pompous bully we knew on the racecourse. I understood at last how he had come to be voted on to the National Hunt Committee.

Before I expected it, Kemp-Lore was turning round to me. I swallowed convulsively. He smiled at the camera.

'And now,' he said with the air of one producing a treat, 'here is Rob Finn. This is a young steeplechase jockey just scratching the surface of his career. Few of you will have heard of him. He has won no big races, nor ridden any well-known horses, and that is why I have invited him here tonight to meet you, to give us all a glimpse of what it is like to break into a highly competitive sport . . .'

The red light was burning on the camera pointing at me. I smiled at it faintly. My tongue stuck to the roof of my mouth.

'First,' he went on, 'here is a piece of film which shows Finn in action. He is the rider with the white cap, fourth from last.'

We watched on the monitor set. I was all too easy to pick out. It was one of the first races I ever rode in, and my inexperience showed sorely. During the few seconds the film lasted the white cap lost two places, and as an illustration of an unsuccessful jockey it could not have been bettered.

The film faded out and Kemp-Lore said, smiling, 'How did you set about starting to be a jockey, once you had decided on it?'

I said, 'I knew three farmers who owned and trained their own horses, and I asked them to let me try my hand in a race.'

'And they did?'

'Yes, in the end,' I agreed. I could have added, 'After I had promised to return the riding fees and not even ask for expenses'; but the method I had used to persuade a string of farmers to give me rides was strictly against the rules.

'Usually,' Kemp-Lore said, turning towards the camera which immediately glowed with its red eye, 'jumping jockeys either start as amateur steeplechase riders or as apprentices on the flat, but I understand that you did neither of these things, Rob?'

'No,' I said. 'I started too old to be an apprentice and couldn't be an amateur because I had earned my living riding horses.'

'As a stable lad?' He put it in the form of a question but from his intonation he clearly expected me to say yes. It was, after all by far the commonest background of jockeys riding as few races as I had been doing.

'No,' I said.

He was waiting for me to go on, his eyebrows a fraction raised in a tinge of surprise mingled with what looked like the beginning of apprehension. Well, I thought in amusement, you wouldn't listen when I said I was hardly typical, so if my answers are not what you expect, it's entirely your own fault.

I said, 'I was away from England for some years, wandering round the world, you know? Mainly in Australia and South America. Most of the time I got jobs as a stockman, but I spent a year in New South Wales working as a hand in a travelling rodeo. Ten seconds on the bucking bronc: that sort of thing.' I grinned.

'Oh.' The eyebrows rose another fraction, and there was a perceptible pause before he said, 'How very interesting.' He sounded as if he meant it. He went on, 'I wish we had more time to hear about your experiences, but I want to give viewers a picture of the economics of a jockey in your position . . . trying to make a living on a race or two a week. Now, your fee is ten guineas a time, that's right? . . .'

He took me at some length through my finances, which didn't sound too good when dissected into travelling expenses, valets' fees, replacement of kit, and so on. It emerged quite clearly that my net income over the last two years was less than I could have earned driving a delivery van, and that my future prospects were not demonstrably much better. I could almost feel the thought clicking into the viewers' heads that I was a fool.

Kemp-Lore turned deferentially to Ballerton. 'John, have you any comment to make on what we have been hearing from Rob?'

A trace of purely malicious pleasure crept into Ballerton's man-of-authority smile.

'All these young jockeys complain too much,' he stated in his harsh voice, ignoring the fact that I had not complained at all. 'If they aren't very good at their job they shouldn't expect to be highly paid. Racehorse owners don't want to waste their money and their horses' chances by putting up jockeys in whom they have no confidence. I speak as an owner myself, of course.'

'Eh . . . of course,' said Kemp-Lore. 'But surely every jockey has to make a start? And there must always be large numbers of jockeys who never quite reach the top grade, but who have a living to make, and families to support.'

'They'd be better off in a factory, earning a fair wage on a production line,' said Ballerton, with heavy, reasonable-sounding humour. 'If they can't endure the fact that they are unsuccessful without snivelling about how poor they are, they ought to get out of racing altogether. Not many of them do,' he added with an unkind chuckle, 'because they like wearing those bright silks.

People turn to look at them as they go by, and it flatters their little egos.'

There was a gasp somewhere out in the dark studio at this ungentlemanly blow below the belt, and I saw out of the corner of my eye that the red spot on the camera pointing at me was glowing. What expression it had initially caught on my face I did not know, but I raised a smile for Mr Ballerton then, as sweet and cheerful and forgiving a smile as ever turned the other cheek. It was made easier by the certain knowledge that wearing bright shirts was if anything an embarrassment to me, not a gratification.

Kemp-Lore's head switched to me. 'And what do you say to that, Rob?'

I spoke truthfully, vehemently, and straight from the heart. 'Give me a horse and a race to ride it in, and I don't care if I wear silks or . . . or . . . pyjamas. I don't care if there's anyone watching or not. I don't care if I don't earn much money, or if I break my bones, or if I have to starve to keep my weight down. All I care about is racing . . . racing . . . and winning, if I can.'

There was a small silence.

'I can't explain it,' I said.

Both of them were staring at me. John Ballerton looked as if a squashed wasp had revived and stung him, and his earlier animosity settled and deepened into a scowl. And Kemp-Lore? There was an expression on his face that I could not read at all. There were only a few empty seconds before he turned smoothly back to his camera and slid the familiar smile into place, but I felt irrationally that something important had taken place in them. I found it oddly disturbing not to have the slightest clue to what it was.

Kemp-Lore launched into his usual review of the following week's racing, and was very soon closing the programme with the customary words, 'See you all next week at the same time . . .'

The image on the monitor faded on Kemp-Lore's smile and changed to another soap advertisement. The hot spotlight flicked off and my eyes began to get used to not being dazzled.

Gordon strode up beaming. 'A very good programme. It came over well. Just what they like, an argument with an edge to it. Well done, well done, Mr Ballerton, Mr Finn. Splendid.' He shook us both by the hand.

Kemp-Lore stood up and stretched and grinned around at us all. 'Well, John. Well, Rob. Thank you both very much.' He bent down, picked up my brandy glass and handed it to me. 'Drink it,' he said, 'you deserve it.' He smiled warmly. He crackled with released tension.

I smiled back and drank the brandy, and reflected again how superlative he was at his job. By encouraging Ballerton to needle me he had drawn from me, for the ears of a few million strangers, a more soul-baring statement than I would ever have made privately to a close friend.

A good deal of back-slapping followed, and more plates of sandwiches were dealt with downstairs in the reception room before I left the television building and went back to Kensington. In view of the approval which had been generously, if undeservedly, heaped upon Ballerton and me after the show, I wondered why it was that I felt more apprehensive than I had before I started.

Six

THREE WEEKS and a day after the broadcast, Pip Pankhurst broke his leg. His horse, falling with him and on him at the last hurdle of the second race on a dreary, drizzly mid-November Saturday afternoon, made a thorough job of putting the champion jockey out of action for the bulk of the 'chasing season.

The first-aid men beside the hurdle were slow to move him into the ambulance for the good reason that a sharp arrow of shin bone was sticking out at a crazy angle through a tear in the thin leather racing boot; and they finally managed to lift him on to a stretcher, one of them told me later, only because Pip slid off into a dead faint.

From the stands I saw only the white flag waving, the ambulance creeping down over the bumpy ground, and the flat, ominously unmoving figure of Pip on the grass. It would be untrue to say that I went down the stairs to the weighing-room with a calm heart. However sincere my pity for his plight might be, the faint chance that I might take his place in the following race was playing hop, skip and jump with my pulse.

It was the big race of the day, the big race of the week, a three-mile chase with a substantial prize put up by a firm of brewers. It had attracted a good number of top horses and had been well discussed on the sports pages of all the day's papers. Pip's mount, which belonged to Lord Tirrold, was the rising star of the Axminster stable; a stringy six-year-old brown gelding with nothing much to recommend him at first sight, but intelligent, fast, and a battler. He had all the qualities of a world beater, and his best years lay ahead. At present he was still reckoned 'promising'. He was called Template.

Stifling hope is a hopeless business. As I went into the weighing-room I saw James Axminster talking to Pip's close friend, another leading jockey. The jockey shook his head, and across the room I watched his lips say, 'No, I can't.'

Axminster turned slowly round looking at faces. I stood still and waited. Gradually his head came round and he saw me. He looked at me steadily, pondering, unsmiling. Then his eyes were past me and focused on someone to my left. He came to a decision and walked briskly past me.

Well, what did I expect? I had ridden for him for only four weeks. Three winners. A dozen also-rans. During the past fortnight I had taken digs in the village near his stable and ridden out at exercise on his horses every morning; but I was still the new boy, the unknown, unsuccessful jockey of the television programme. I began to walk disconsolately over to the changing-room door.

'Rob,' he said in my ear. 'Lord Tirrold says you can ride his horse. You'd better tell Pip's valet; he has the colours.'

I half-turned towards them. They stood together, the two tall men, looking at me appraisingly, knowing they were giving me the chance of a lifetime, but not sure that I was up to it.

'Yes, sir,' I said; and I went on into the changing-room, queerly steadied by having believed that I had been passed over.

I rode better than I had ever done before, but that was probably because Template was the best horse I had ever ridden. He was smooth and steely, and his rocketing spring over the first fence had me gasping; but I was ready for it at the second, and exulted in it at the third; and by the fourth I knew I had entered a new dimension of racing.

Neither Axminster nor Lord Tirrold had given me any orders in the paddock on how to shape the race. They had been too concerned about Pip, whom they had just briefly visited. The sight of his shattered leg had left them upset and preoccupied.

Axminster said only, 'Do the best you can, Rob,' and Lord Tirrold, unusually tactless for so diplomatic a man, said gloomily, 'I put a hundred on Template this morning. Oh, well, it's too late to cancel it, I suppose.' Then seeing my rueful amusement, added, 'I beg your pardon, Rob. I'm sure you'll do splendidly.' But he did not sound convinced.

As the pattern of the race shifted and changed, I concentrated solely on keeping Template lying in about fourth position in the field of twelve runners. To be farther back meant leaving him a lot to do at the end, and to be farther forward meant that one could not see how well or how badly everyone else was going. Template jumped himself into third place at the second last fence, and was still not under pressure. Coming towards the last I brought him to the outside, to give him a clear view, and urged him on. His stride immediately quickened. He took off so far in front of the fence that for a heart-breaking second I was sure he would land squarely on top of it, but I had underestimated his power. He landed yards out on the far side, collecting himself without faltering and surged ahead towards the winning post.

One of the two horses close in front had been passed in mid-air over the fence. There remained only a chestnut to be beaten. Only. Only the favourite, the choice of the critics, the public and the press. No disgrace, I fleetingly thought, to be beaten only by him.

I dug my knees into Template's sides and gave him two taps with the whip down his shoulder. He needed only this signal, I found, to put every ounce into getting to the front. He stretched his neck out and flattened his stride, and I knelt on his withers and squeezed him and moved with his rhythm, and kept my whip still for fear of disturbing him. He put his head in front of the chestnut's five strides from the winning post, and kept it there.

I was almost too exhausted to unbuckle the saddle. There was a cheer as we went into the unsaddling enclosure, and a lot of smiling faces, and some complimentary things were said, but I felt too weak and breathless to enjoy them. No race had ever before taken so much out of me. Nor given me so much, either.

Surprisingly Lord Tirrold and Axminster were almost subdued.

'That was all right, then,' said Axminster, the lower teeth glimmering in a smile.

'He's a wonderful horse,' I said fervently.

'Yes,' said Lord Tirrold, 'he is.' He patted the dark sweating neck.

Axminster said, 'Don't hang about then, Rob. Go and weigh in. You haven't any time to waste. You're riding in the next race. And the one after.'

I stared at him.

'Well, what did you expect?' he said. 'Pip's obviously going to be unfit for months. I took you on to ride second to him, and you will stand in for him until he comes back.'

Tick-Tock said, 'Some people would climb out of a septic tank smelling of lavender.'

He was waiting for me to change at the end of the afternoon.

'Six weeks ago you were scrounging rides. Then you get yourself on television as a failure and make it obvious you aren't one. Sunday newspapers write columns about you and your version of the creed gets a splash in *The Times* as well. Now you do the understudy-into-star routine, and all that jazz. And properly too. Three winners in one afternoon. What a nerve.'

I grinned at him. 'What goes up must come down. You can pick up the pieces later on.'

I tied my tie and brushed my hair, and looked in the mirror

at the fatuous smile I could not remove from my face. Days like this don't happen very often, I thought.

'Let's go and see Pip,' I said abruptly, turning round.

'Okay,' he agreed.

We asked the first-aid men where Pip had been taken, and as they were leaving in any case they gave us a lift to the hospital in the ambulance. It was not until they told us that we realized how seriously the leg was broken.

We saw Pip only for a few moments. He lay in a cubicle in the casualty department, a cradle over his leg and blankets up to his chin. A brisk nurse told us he was going to the operating theatre within minutes and not to disturb the patient, as he had been given his pre-med. 'But you can say hello,' she said, 'as you've come.'

Hello was just about all we did say. Pip looked terribly pale and his eyes were fuzzy, but he said weakly, 'Who won the big race?'

'Template,' I said, almost apologetically.

'You?'

I nodded. He smiled faintly. 'You'll ride the lot now, then.'

'I'll keep them warm for you,' I said. 'You won't be long.'

'Three bloody months.' He shut his eyes. 'Three bloody months.'

The nurse came back with a stretcher trolley and two khaki-overalled porters, and asked us to leave. We waited outside in the hall, and saw them trundle Pip off towards the open lift.

'He'll be four months at least with a leg like that,' said Tick-Tock. 'He might just be ready for Cheltenham in March. Just in time to take back all the horses and do you out of a chance in the Champion Hurdle and the Gold Cup.'

'It can't be helped,' I said. 'It's only fair. And anything can happen before then.'

*

I think Axminster had trouble persuading some of his owners that I was capable of taking Pip's place, because I didn't ride all of the stable's horses, not at first. But gradually as the weeks went by and I seemed to make no unforgivable bloomers, fewer and fewer other jockeys were engaged. I became used to seeing my name continually in the number boards, to riding three or four races a day, to going back to my digs contentedly tired in body and mind and waking the next morning with energy and eagerness. In some ways, I even became used to winning. It was no longer a rarity for me to be led into the first's enclosure, or to talk to delighted owners, or to see my picture in the sporting papers.

I began earning a good deal of money, but I spent very little of it. There was always the knowledge, hovering in the background, that my prosperity was temporary. Pip's leg was mending. Tick-Tock and I decided, however, to share the cost of buying a car. It was a second-hand cream-coloured Mini-Cooper which did forty miles to the gallon on a long run and could shift along at a steady seventy on the flat, and a friend of Tick-Tock's who kept a garage had recommended it to him as a bargain.

'All we want now are some leopard-skin seat covers and a couple of blondes in the back,' said Tick-Tock, as we dusted the small vehicle parked outside my digs, 'and we'll look like one of those gracious-living advertisements in the *Tatler*.' He lifted up the bonnet and took at least his tenth look at the engine. 'A beautiful job of design,' he said fondly.

Gracious living, good design or not, the little car smoothed our paths considerably, and within a fortnight I could not imagine how we had ever managed without it. Tick-Tock kept it where he lived, seven miles away, near the stable he rode for, and came to collect me whenever Axminster himself was not taking me to meetings in his own car. Race trains came and went without any further support from either of us as we whizzed homewards through the black December afternoons in our cosy box on wheels.

While the Gods heaped good fortune on my head, others fared badly.

Grant had offered neither explanation nor apology for hitting me on the nose. He had not, in fact, spoken one word to me since that day, but, as at the same time he had also stopped borrowing my kit, I was not sure that I minded. He withdrew more and more into himself. The inner volcano of violence showed itself only in the stiffness of his body and the tightness of his lips, which seemed always to be compressed in fury. He loathed to be touched, even accidentally, and would swing round threateningly if anyone bumped into him in the changing-room. With my peg at most meetings still next to his I had knocked into him several times, for however hard I tried it was impossible in those cramped quarters not to, and the glare he gave me each time was frankly murderous.

It was not only to me that he had stopped speaking. He no longer said much at all. The trainers and owners who still employed him could get him neither to discuss a race beforehand nor explain what had happened afterwards. He listened to his orders in silence and left the trainer to draw his own conclusions through his race-glasses about how the horse had run. When he did speak, his remarks were laden with such a burden of obscenity that even the hardened inmates of the changing-room shifted uncomfortably.

Oddly enough Grant's riding skill had not degenerated with his character. He rode the same rough, tough race as always; but he had, we knew, begun to let out his anger on his mounts, and twice during November he was called before the stewards for 'excessive use of the whip'. The horses in question had each come in from their races with raw red weals on their flanks.

The Oldfield volcano erupted, as far as I was concerned, one cold afternoon in the jockeys' and trainers' car park at Warwick.

I was late leaving the meeting as I had won the last race and had been taken off to the bar afterwards by the elated owner, one of my farmer friends. Tick-Tock had gone to a different meeting, and I had the car. By the time I got there the park was empty except for the Mini-Cooper and another car which was standing almost next to it, and two or three cars further on down the row.

I went towards the Mini still smiling to myself with the pleasure of this latest win, and I did not see Grant until I was quite close to him. I was approaching the cars from behind, with Grant's on the right of mine. His near hind wheel lay on the grass, surrounded by a collection of implements spilling out of a holdall tool bag. A jack held up the bare axle of his black saloon and he was kneeling beside it with the spare wheel in his hand.

He saw me coming, and he saw me smiling, and he thought I was laughing at him for having a puncture. I could actually see the uncontrollable fury rise in his face. He got to his feet and stood rigidly, his thickset body hunched with belligerence, the strong shoulders bunching under his coat, his arms hanging down. Then he bent forward and from among the mess of tools picked up a tyre lever. He swished it through the air, his eyes on me.

'I'll help you with your puncture, if you like,' I said mildly.

For answer he took a step sideways, swung his arm in a sort of backwards chop, and smashed the tyre lever through the back window of the Mini-Cooper. The glass crashed and tinkled into the car, leaving only a fringe of jagged peaks round the frame.

Tick-Tock and I had had the car barely three weeks. My own anger rose quick and hot and I took a step towards Grant to save my most precious possession from further damage. He turned to face me squarely and lifted the tyre lever again.

'Put it down,' I said, reasonably, standing still. We were now about four feet apart. He told me to do something which was biologically impossible.

'Don't be an ass, Grant,' I said. 'Put that thing down and let's get on with changing your tyre.'

'You—' he said, 'you took my job.'

'No,' I said. It was pointless to add more, not least because if he was going to try to hit me I wanted to have all my concentration focused on what he was doing, not on what I was saying.

His eyes were red-rimmed above the high cheek bones. The big nostrils flared open like black pits. With his wild face, his bursting anger, and the upheld quivering tyre lever, he was a pretty frightening sight.

He slashed forward and downward at my head.

I think that at that moment he must have been truly insane, for had the blow connected he would surely have killed me, and he couldn't have hoped to get away with it with his car standing there with the wheel off. He was beyond thought.

I saw his arm go up a fraction before it came down and it gave me time to duck sideways. The lever whistled past my right ear. His arm returned in a backhand, again aiming at my head. I ducked again underneath it, and this time, as his arm swung wide and his body lay open to me, I stepped close and hit him hard with my fist just below his breast bone. He grunted as the wind rushed out of his lungs, and the arm with the tyre lever dropped and his head came forward. I took a half pace to the right and hit him on the side of the neck with the edge of my hand.

He went down on his hands and knees, and then weakly sprawled on the grass. I took the tyre lever from his slack fingers and put it with all the other tools into the holdall, and shut the whole thing into the boot of his car.

It was getting very cold and the early dusk was turning colours to black and grey. I squatted beside Grant. He was hovering on the edge of consciousness, breathing heavily and moaning slightly.

I said conversationally, close to his ear, 'Grant, why did you get the sack from Axminster?'

He mumbled something I could not hear. I repeated my question. He said nothing. I sighed and stood up. It had been only a faint chance, after all.

Then he said distinctly, 'He said I passed on the message.'

'What message?'

'Passed on the message,' he said, less clearly. I bent down and asked him again, 'What message?' But although his lips moved he said nothing more.

I decided that in spite of everything I could not just drive off and leave him lying there in the cold. I took out the tools again, and sorting out the brace, put the spare wheel on and tightened up the nuts. Then I pumped up the tyre, let the jack down and slung it with the punctured wheel into the boot on top of the tools.

Grant was still not properly conscious. I knew I hadn't hit him hard enough to account for such a long semi-waking state, and it occurred to me that perhaps his disturbed brain was finding this a helpful way to dodge reality. I bent down and shook his shoulder and called his name. He opened his eyes. For a split second it seemed as though the old Grant smiled out of them, and then the resentment and bitterness flooded back as he remembered what had happened. I helped him sit up, and propped him against his car. He looked desperately tired, utterly worn out.

'O God,' he said, 'O God.' It sounded like a true prayer, and it came from lips which usually blasphemed without thought.

'If you went to see a psychiatrist,' I said gently, 'you could get some help.'

He didn't answer; but neither did he resist when I helped him into the passenger seat of the Mini-Cooper. He was in no state to drive his own car, and there was no one else about to look after him. I asked him where he lived, and he told me. His car was safe enough where it was, and I remarked that he could fetch it on the following day. He made no reply.

Luckily he lived only thirty miles away, and I drew up where he told me outside a semi-detached featureless house on the outskirts of a small country town. There were no lights in the windows.

'Isn't your wife in?' I asked.

'She left me,' he said absently. Then his jaw tensed and he said, 'Mind your own—business.' He jerked the door open and climbed out and slammed it noisily. He shouted, 'Take your bloody do-gooding off and—it. I don't want your help, you—'. He appeared to be back to his usual frame of mind, which was a pity, but there didn't seem to be any point in staying to hear more so I let in the clutch and drove off: but I had gone only half a mile down the road when I reluctantly came to the conclusion that he shouldn't be left alone in an empty house.

I was at that point in the centre of the little town whose brightly lit shops were closing their doors for the day, and I stopped and asked an elderly woman with a shopping basket where I could find a doctor. She directed me to a large house in a quiet side street, and I parked outside and rang the door bell.

A pretty girl appeared and said, 'Surgery at six,' and began to close the door again.

'If the doctor is in, please let me speak to him,' I said quickly, 'it's not a case for the surgery.'

'Well, all right,' she said and went away. Children's voices sounded noisily somewhere in the house. Presently, a youngish, chubby, capable-looking man appeared, munching at a piece of cream-filled chocolate cake and wearing the resigned, enquiring expression of a doctor called to duty during his free time.

'Are you by any chance Grant Oldfield's doctor?' I asked. If he weren't, I thought, he could tell me where else to go.

But he said at once, 'Yes, I am. Has he had another fall?'

'Not exactly,' I said, 'but could you please come and take a look at him?'

'Now?'

'Yes, please,' I said. 'He . . . er . . . he was knocked out at the races.'

'Half a mo,' he said and went back to the house, reappearing with his medical bag and another piece of cake. 'Can you run me down there? Save me getting my car out again for those few yards.'

We went out to the Mini-Cooper and as soon as he sat in it he made a remark about the broken window, not unreasonably, since gusts of December wind blowing through it were freezing our necks. I told him that Grant had smashed it and explained how I had come to bring him home.

He listened in silence, licking the cream as it oozed out of the side of the cake. Then he said, 'Why did he attack you?'

'He seems to believe I took his job.'

'And did you?'

'No,' I said. 'He lost it months before it was offered to me.'

'Are you a jockey too, then?' he asked, looking at me curiously, and I nodded and told him my name. He said his was Parnell. I started the car and drove the few hundred yards back to Grant's house. It was still in complete darkness.

'I left him here not ten minutes ago,' I said as we went up the path to the front door. The small front garden was ragged and uncared for, with rotting dead leaves and mournful grass-grown flower beds dimly visible in the light from the street lamp. We rang the bell. It sounded shrilly in the house, but produced no other results. We rang again. The doctor finished his cake and licked his fingers.

There was a faint rustle in the darkness of the patch of garden. The doctor unclipped from his breast pocket the pen-shaped torch he normally used for peering into eyes and down throats, and directed its tiny beam round the bordering privet hedge. It revealed first some pathetic rose bushes choked with last summer's unmown grass; but in the corner where the hedge dividing the garden from the next door one met the hedge bordering the road, the pin point of light steadied on the hunched shape of a man.

We went over to him. He was sitting on the ground, huddling back into the hedge, with his knees drawn up to his chin and his head resting on his folded arms.

'Come along old chap,' said the doctor encouragingly, and half-helped, half-pulled him to his feet. He felt in Grant's pockets, found a bunch of keys, and handed them to me. I went over and unlocked the front door and turned on the lights in the hall. The doctor guided Grant through the hall and into the first room we came to, which happened to be a dining-room. Everything in it was covered with a thick layer of dust.

Grant collapsed in a heap on a dining chair and laid his head down on the dirty table. The doctor examined him, feeling his pulse, lifting up his eyelid and running both hands round the thick neck and the base of the skull. Grant moved irritably when Parnell's fingers touched the place where I had hit him and he said crossly, 'Go away, go away.'

Parnell stepped back a pace and sucked his teeth. 'There's nothing physically wrong with him as far as I can see, except for what is going to be a stiff neck. We'd better get him into bed and I'll give him something to keep him quiet, and in the morning I'll arrange for him to see someone who can sort out his troubles for him. You'd better give me a ring during the evening if there's any change in his condition.'

'I?' I said. 'I'm not staying here all evening . . .'

'Oh yes, I think so, don't you?' he said cheerfully, his eyes shining sardonically in his round face. 'Who else? All night too, if you don't mind. After all, you hit him.'

'Yes, but,' I protested, 'that's not what's the matter with him.'

'Never mind. You cared enough to bring him home and fetch me. Be a good chap and finish the job. I do really think someone ought to stay here all night . . . someone strong enough to deal with him in a crisis. It's not a job for elderly female relatives, even if we could rake one up so late in the day.'

Put like that, it was difficult to refuse. We took Grant upstairs, balancing his thick-set body between us as he stumbled up the treads. His bedroom was filthy. Dirty tangled sheets and blankets were piled in heaps on the unmade bed, dust lay thick on every surface, and soiled clothes were scattered over the floor and hung sordidly over chairs. The whole room smelled of sour sweat.

'We'd better put him somewhere else,' I said, switching on lights and opening all the other doors on the small landing. One door led into a bathroom whose squalor defied description. Another opened on to a linen cupboard which still contained a few sheets in a neat pile, and the last revealed an empty bedroom with bright pink rosebuds on the walls. Grant stood blinking on the landing while I fetched some sheets and made up the bed for him. There were no clean pyjamas. Doctor Parnell undressed Grant as far as his underpants and socks and made him get into the fresh bed. Then he went downstairs and returned with a glass of water, wearing so disgusted an expression that I knew without being told what state the kitchen must be in.

Opening his case, he shook two capsules on to his hand and told Grant to swallow them, which he docilely did. Grant at this time seemed as if he were sleep-walking; he was only a shell, his personality a blank. It was disturbing, but on the other hand it made the business of putting him to bed much easier than it might have been.

Parnell looked at his watch. 'I'm late for surgery,' he said as Grant lay back on his pillow and shut his eyes. 'Those pills ought to keep him quiet for a bit. Give him two more when he wakes up.' He handed me a small bottle. 'You know where to find me if you want me,' he added with a callous grin. 'Have a good night.'

I spent a miserable evening and dined off a pint of milk I found on the back doorstep. Nothing else in the stinking kitchen was any longer edible. There were no books and no radio to be found, and to pass the hours I made an effort to clean up some of the mess, but what that dreadful house really needed was a breezy spring day, lashings of disinfectant, and an army of strong-minded charwomen.

Several times I went softly in to see how Grant was doing, but he slept peacefully, flat on his back, until midnight. I found him then with his eyes open, but when I went close to him there was no recognition in them. He was still in a withdrawn blank state and he obediently, without a word, swallowed the capsules when I offered them to him. I waited until his eyes had closed again, then I locked his door and went downstairs and eventually fell uneasily asleep myself, wrapped in a travelling rug on a too short sofa. There was no sound from Grant all night, and when I went up to him at six in the morning he was still sleeping quietly.

Dr Parnell at least had the decency to release me at an early hour, arriving with a middle-aged male nurse at 7.30 in the freezing dawn. He had also brought a basket packed by his wife, containing eggs, bacon, bread, milk, and coffee, and from his medical bag he produced a powerful battery razor.

'All mod cons,' he said cheerfully, his round face beaming.

So I went back to the races washed, shaved and fed. But thinking of the husk of a man I left behind me, not in a happy frame of mind.

Seven

'THE TROUBLE is, there's such a shortage of jockeys just now,' said James Axminster.

We were on our way to Sandown, discussing whom he should engage to ride for him the following week when he would be sending horses to two different places on the same day.

'You'd almost think there was a hoodoo on the whole tribe,' he said, expertly swinging his large car between a wobbly girl cyclist and an oncoming pantechnicon. 'Art shot himself, Pip's broken his leg, Grant's had a breakdown. Two or three others are out with more ordinary things like busted collar bones, and at least four quite useful chaps took that wretched Ballerton's misguided advice and are now churning out car bodies on assembly lines. There's Peter Cloony . . . but I've heard he's very unreliable and might not turn up in time; and Danny Higgs bets too much, they say, and Ingersoll doesn't always try, so I've been told . . .'

He slowed down while a mother pushed a perambulator and three small children untidily across the road in front of us, and went on talking. 'Every time I think I've found a good up-and-coming jockey I seem to hear something to his disadvantage. With you, it was that film, the one they showed on that television programme. It was shocking, wasn't it? I watched it and thought, my God, what have I done, asking this clod to ride for me, however will I explain it away to the owners.' He grinned.

'I was on the point of ringing them all up and assuring them you'd not be on their horses after all. Luckily for you I remembered the way you had already ridden for me and I watched the rest of the programme first, and when it had finished I had changed my mind. I had even begun to think I had perhaps struck oil in annexing you. Nothing that has happened since,' he glanced at me sideways, smiling, 'has led me to alter that opinion.'

I smiled back. In the weeks since Pip broke his leg I had come to know him well, and liked him better with every day that passed. Not only was he a superb craftsman at his job and a tireless worker, but he was reliable in other ways. He was never moody: one did not have to approach him circumspectly every time to see if he were in a good or bad humour because he was always the same, neither boisterous nor irritable, just reasonable and receptive. He said directly what he thought, so that one never had to search for innuendoes or suspect hidden sarcasm and it made any relationship with him stable and free from worry. He was, on the other hand, in many ways thoroughly selfish. Unless it were a strictly business matter, his own comfort and convenience came first, second and third, and he would do a favour for someone else only if it caused him absolutely no personal sacrifice of time or effort. Even this was often a blessing to his stable lads since it was typical of him, if the occasion arose, to give them a generous travelling allowance out of his own pocket to visit their homes, rather than go five miles out of his way to drop them on their doorsteps.

He had seemed from the first to be as satisfied with my company as I was with his, and had quite soon told me to drop the 'sir' and stick to 'James'. Later the same week as he drove us back from Birmingham races, we passed some brightly lit posters advertising a concert which was to be held there that evening.

'Conductor, Sir Trelawny Finn,' he read aloud, the enormous lettering catching his eye. 'No relation, I suppose,' he said jokingly.

'Well, yes, as a matter of fact, he's my uncle,' I said.

There was a dead silence. Then he said, 'And Caspar Finn?'

'My father.' A pause.

'Anyone else?'

'Dame Olivia Cottin is my mother,' I said, matter-of-factly.

'Good God,' he said explosively.

I grinned.

'You keep it very quiet,' he said.

'It's really the other way round,' I said cheerfully. 'They like to keep me quiet. A jockey in the family is a disgrace to them, you see. It embarrasses them. They don't like the connexion to be noticed.'

'All the same,' he said thoughtfully, 'it explains quite a lot about you that I had begun to wonder about. Where you got that air of confidence from . . . and why you've said so little about yourself.'

I said, smiling, 'I'd be very glad . . . James . . . if you'd not let my parentage loose in the weighing-room, as a favour to them.'

He had said he would not, and he had kept his word, but he had accepted me more firmly as a friend from then on. So when he ran through the reported shortcomings of Peter Cloony, Danny Higgs and Tick-Tock, it was with some confidence that I said, 'You seem to have heard a great many rumours. Do you know all these things for a fact?'

'For a fact?' he repeated, surprised. 'Well, Peter Cloony definitely missed two races a few weeks back because he was late. That's a fact.'

I told him about Peter's atrocious luck in twice finding a vehicle stuck across the mouth of the narrow lane from his village to the main road. 'As far as I know,' I said, 'he hasn't been late since then. His reputation for lateness seems to be built mainly on those two days.'

'I've heard several times that he can't be trusted to turn up,' said James obstinately.

'Who from?' I asked curiously.

'Oh, I don't know. Corin Kellar for one. And of course Johnson who employs him. Ballerton too, though it's against my better judgement to pay too much attention to what he says. It's common knowledge though.'

'How about Danny Higgs, then?' I said. Danny was an irrepressible cockney, tiny in size, but ferociously brave.

'He bets too heavily,' James said positively.

'Who says so?' I asked. I knew Danny broke the regulations by backing horses, but from what he said in the changing-room, it was only in amounts of five or ten pounds, which would cause few trainers to look askance at him.

'Who says? I . . . er . . . Corin,' he finished lamely. 'Corin, come to think of it, has told me so several times. He says he never puts him up because of it.'

'And Tick-Tock?' I said. 'Who says Ingersoll doesn't always try?'

He didn't answer at once. Then he said, 'Why shouldn't I believe what Corin says? He has no axe to grind. He's an excellent trainer, but he depends as we all do on securing good jockeys. He certainly wouldn't deny himself the use of people like Cloony or Higgs if he didn't have a good reason.'

I thought for a few moments, and then said, 'I know it's really none of my business, but would you mind very much telling me why you dropped Grant Oldfield? He told me himself that it was something to do with a message, but he wouldn't explain what.' I refrained from mentioning that he had been semiconscious at the time.

'A message? Oh yes, he passed on the message, I couldn't have that.'

I still looked mystified. Axminster squeezed through the traffic lights on the amber and glanced sideways at me.

'The message,' he said impatiently, 'you know, the news. He was passing on the news. If we had a fancied runner he would tip off a professional backer. The owner of the horse didn't get good odds to his money because the professional was there before him and spoiled the market. Three of my owners were very angry about it – no fun for them having to take two or three to one when they expected sixes or sevens. So Grant had to go. It was a pity; he was a strong jockey, just what I needed.'

'How did you discover it was Grant passing on the information?'

'Maurice Kemp-Lore found out while he was working on one of those programmes of his. Something to do with how professional backers work, I think it was, and he found out about Grant more or less by accident. He told me very apologetically, and just said it would be wiser not to let Grant know too much. But you can't work properly with a jockey and keep secrets from him, it's a hopeless set-up.'

'What did Grant say when you sacked him?' I asked.

'He denied the whole thing very indignantly. But of course he would. No jockey would ever confess to selling information if he wanted another trainer to take him on.'

'Did you talk to the professional backer in question?' I asked.

'Yes I did, as a matter of fact,' he said. 'I didn't want to believe it, you see. But it was open and shut. I had to press him a bit, because it didn't reflect well on him, but Lubbock, the professional, did admit that Grant had been tipping him off over the telephone, and that he had been paying him ever since he had started to ride for me.'

It seemed conclusive enough, but I had an elusive feeling that I had missed something, somewhere.

I changed the subject. 'Going back to Art,' I said, 'why was he always having rows with Corin?'

'I don't really know,' James said reflectively. 'I heard Corin say once or twice that Art didn't ride to orders. Perhaps it was that.' He neatly passed two slow lorries on a round-about, and glanced at me again. 'What are you getting at?'

'It seems to me sometimes that there is too much of a pattern,' I said. 'Too many jockeys are affected by rumours. You said yourself that there seems to be a hoodoo on the whole tribe.'

'I didn't mean it seriously,' he protested. 'You're imagining things. And as for rumours, what rumour made Art kill himself or broke Pip's leg, or made Grant sell information? Rumour didn't make Cloony late either.'

'Danny Higgs doesn't bet heavily,' I said, feeling I was fighting a rearguard action, 'and Ingersoll rides as honestly as anyone.'

'You can't know about Higgs,' he pointed out, 'and Ingersoll, let me remind you, was called in before the stewards last week for easing his mount out of third place. John Ballerton owned the horse and he was very annoyed about it, he told me so himself.'

I sighed. Tick-Tock's version was that since Corin had told him not to overwork the horse, which was not fully fit, he had decided that he ought not to drive the horse too hard just for the sake of finishing third. Better to save the horse's energy for winning next time, he had thought, adopting a view commonly held and acted on by at least half the jockeys and trainers engaged in the sport: but owners and members of the public who had backed the horse for a place were liable to disagree. After the enquiry, changing with the wind as usual, Corin had been heard condemning Tick-Tock for his action.

'I may be quite wrong about it all,' I said slowly, 'I hope so. Only . . .'

'Only?' he prompted as I paused.

'Only,' I finished lightly, 'if you ever hear any rumours about me, will you remember what I think . . . and make utterly sure they're true before you believe them?'

'All right,' he said, humouring me. 'I think it's nonsense, but all right, I'll agree to that.' He drove in silence for a while, and then said with an impatient shake of his big head, 'No one stands to gain anything by trying to ruin jockeys. It's nonsense. Pointless.'

'I know,' I said. 'Pointless.'

We changed the subject.

Christmas came, and during the week before it, when there was no racing, I spent several days in Kensington. My parents greeted me with their usual friendly detachment and left me to my own devices. They were both preoccupied with crowded Christmas schedules, and my mother also spent each morning working at her piano on a new concerto which was to have its first performance in the New Year. She started daily at seven punctually, and played with short interruptions for coffee and thought until twelve-thirty. I awoke as so often during my life to the sound of warming-up chromatics and wrist-loosening arpeggios, and lay lazily in bed listening to her pick her way phrase by phrase through a dissonant modern score, repeating and repeating each section until she was satisfied she knew it, until the notes flowed easily in their intended order.

I could picture her exactly, dressed for work in a cashmere sweater and ski pants, sitting upright on her special stool, with her head thrust forward as if to hear more from the piano than the notes themselves. She was digging the bones out of the piece, and I knew better than to interrupt her. Digging the bones, the essence, the composer's ultimate intention: and when she had these things firmly in her mind, she would begin the process of clothing them with her own interpretations, sharpening the contrasts of mood and tone, until the finished conception emerged clear and shining and memorable.

My mother might not have been a comforting refuge in my childhood nor take much loving interest in me now I was a man, but she had by her example shown me many qualities to admire and value. Professionalism, for instance; a tough-minded single-ness of purpose; a refusal to be content with a low standard when a higher one could be achieved merely by working. I had become self-reliant young and thoroughly as a result of her rejection of motherhood, and because I saw the grind behind the gloss of her public performances, I grew up not expecting life's plums to be tossed into my lap without any effort from me. What mother could teach her son more?

Joanna's time was tangled inextricably with several perform-ances in different places of the Christmas Oratorio. I managed to hook her only for one chilly morning's walk in the Park, which was not a success from my point of view since Bach easily shoved me into second place for her attention. She hummed bits of the Oratorio continuously from the Albert Gate to the Ser-pentine, and from the Serpentine to Bayswater Road. There I put her into a taxi and gave her a Christmassy lunch at the Savoy, where she appeared to restrain herself with difficulty from burst-ing into full song, as the acoustics in the entrance hall appealed to her. I couldn't decide whether or not she was being irritating on purpose, and if she was, why?

She was definitely a great deal less serene than usual, and there was a sort of brittleness in her manner which I didn't like and couldn't understand, until when we were half-way through some excellent mince pies it belatedly occurred to me that she might be unhappy. Unhappiness was not a state I had seen her in before, so I couldn't be sure. I waited until the coffee came, and then said, casually, 'What's up, Joanna?'

She looked at me, then she looked round the room, then at me again, then at her coffee.

Finally she said, 'Brian wants me to marry him.'

It wasn't what I expected, and it hurt. I found myself looking down at my own coffee: black and bitter, very appropriate, I thought.

'I don't know what to do,' she said. 'I was content as we were. Now I'm unsettled. Brian keeps talking about "living in sin" and "regularizing the position". He goes to church a lot now, and he can't reconcile our relationship with his religion. I never thought of it as sinful, just as enjoyable and fruitful and . . . and comfortable. He is talking about buying a house and settling down, and sees me as the complete housewife, cleaning, mending, cooking, and so on. I'm not that sort of person. The thought appals me. If I marry him, I know I'll be miserable . . .' Her voice trailed off.

'And if you don't marry him?' I asked.

'I'll be miserable then, too, because he refuses to go on as we are. We're not easy together any more. We nearly have rows. He says it's irresponsible and childish not to want to marry at my age, and I say I'll gladly marry him if we live as we do now, with him coming and going from the studio when he likes, and me free to work and come and go as I please too. But he doesn't want that. He wants to be respectable and conventional and . . . and stuffy.' The last word came out explosively, steeped in contempt. There was a pause while she stirred her coffee vigorously. There was no sugar in it. I watched the nervous gesture, the long strong fingers with the pink varnished nails gripping the spoon too hard.

'How much do you love him?' I asked painfully.

'I don't know,' she said unhappily. 'I don't know any more what love is.' She looked straight across the little table. 'If it means that I want to spend my life attending to his creature comforts, then I don't love him. If it means being happy in bed, then I do.'

She saw the movement in my face, and said abruptly, 'Oh hell . . . Rob, I'm sorry. It's so long since you said anything . . . I thought you didn't still . . .'

'Never mind,' I said. 'It can't be helped.'

'What . . . what do you think I should do?' she said after a pause, still fiddling with the coffee spoon.

'It's quite clear,' I said positively, 'that you should not marry Brian if you can't bear the prospect of the life he intends to lead. It wouldn't work for either of you.'

'So?' she said, in a small voice.

But I shook my head. The rest she would have to resolve for herself. No advice I could give her would be unbiased, and she must have known it.

She left presently to go to a rehearsal, and I paid the bill and wandered out into the festive streets. I bought some presents for my family on the way, walking slowly back to the flat. The sort of marriage which Joanna had offered Brian, and which he had spurned, was what I most wanted in the world. Why, I wondered disconsolately, was life so ruddy unfair.

On Boxing Day Template won the King 'Chase, one of the ten top races of the year. It put him conclusively into the star class and it didn't do me any harm either.

The race had been televised, and afterwards, as was his custom, Maurice Kemp-Lore interviewed me as the winning jockey before the cameras. Towards the end of the brief talk he invited me to say hullo directly to Pip, who, he explained to viewers, was watching at home. I had seen Pip only a week or two earlier and had discussed big-race tactics with him, but I obligingly greeted him and said I hoped his leg was mending well. Kemp-Lore smilingly added, 'We all wish you a speedy recovery, Pip,' and the interview was over.

On the following day the sporting press was complimentary about the race, and a number of trainers I had not yet ridden for offered me mounts. I began to feel at last as though I were being accepted as a jockey in my own right, and not principally as a substitute for Pip. It even seemed likely that when Pip returned to his job I would not fade back into the wilderness, for two of the new trainers said they would put me up on their horses as often as I was free.

I had, of course, my share of falls during this period, for however fortunate I was I couldn't beat the law of averages: but no damage was done except for a few bruises here and there, and none of them was bad enough to stop me riding.

The worst fall from the spectators' point of view happened one Saturday afternoon in January, when the hurdler I was riding tripped over the flight of hurdles nearest to the grandstand and flung me off on to my head. I woke up dizzily as the first-aid men lifted me into the ambulance on a stretcher, and for a moment or two could not remember where I was.

James's face, looming over me, as they carried me into the first-aid room, brought me back to earth with a click, and I asked him if his horse was all right.

'Yes,' he said, 'how about you?'

'Nothing broken,' I assured him, having explored my limbs rather drunkenly during the short trip back in the ambulance.

'He rolled on you,' he said.

'I'm not surprised.' I grinned up at him. 'I feel a bit squashed, come to think of it.'

I lay for a while on a bed in the first-aid room, but there was nothing wrong with me that a good sleep wouldn't cure, and at the end of the afternoon I went back to Berkshire with James as expected.

'Are you all right?' he asked once, on the way.

'Yes,' I said cheerfully. 'Fine.' Actually I felt dizzy now and then, and also shivery and unsettled, but concealing one's true state of health from trainers was an occupational habit, and I knew I would be fit again to ride on Monday.

The only person who was openly annoyed at the run of good luck I had had was John Ballerton, and I had caught him several times in the parade ring staring tight-lipped at me with a patent and most unstewardly animosity.

Since the day of our joint broadcast we had exchanged the fewest possible words, but I had heard from Corin, who repeated it to me with sly relish, that Ballerton had said loudly to him and Maurice Kemp-Lore in the members' bar at Kempton, 'Finn isn't worth all the fuss that's being made of him. He'll come down just as quickly as he's gone up, you'll see. And I for one won't weep about it.'

In view of this it was astonishing that on the day after my fall I should be offered a ride on one of his horses. At first I refused to take Corin seriously. His telephone call woke me on the Sunday morning, and I was inclined to think the concussion had returned.

'If it were a choice between me and a sack of potatoes,' I said sleepily, 'he'd choose the potatoes.'

'No, seriously Rob, he wants you to ride Shantytown at Dunstable tomorrow.' Corin's voice held no trace of humour. 'I must say, I don't really understand why, as he's been so set against you before. But he was quite definite on the telephone, not five minutes ago. Perhaps it's an olive branch.'

And perhaps not, I thought. My first instinct was to refuse to ride the horse, but I couldn't think of a reasonable excuse, as Corin had found out I was free for the race before he told me whose the horse was. A point-blank excuseless refusal was, while possible, a senseless course. It would give Ballerton a genuine grievance against me, and if he sincerely wanted to smooth over his hostility, which I doubted, I should only deepen it by spurning his offer.

Shantytown was no Template. Far, far from it. His uncertain temper and unreliable jumping were described to me in unreassuring terms by Tick-Tock on the way to Dunstable the following morning.

'A right one,' he said, putting his foot down on the Mini-

Cooper's accelerator. 'A knacker's delight. Dog-meat on the hoof.'

'His form's not bad,' I protested mildly, having looked it up the previous day.

'Hmph. Any time he's won or been placed it's because he's dragged his jockey's arms out of the sockets by a blast-off start and kept right on going. Hang on and hope, that's how to ride him when he's in that mood. His mouth is as hard as Gibraltar. In fact I cannot,' finished Tick-Tock with satiric formality, 'I cannot instantly recall any horse who is less receptive of his jockey's ideas.'

There was no bitterness in his voice, but we were both aware that a few weeks ago riding Shantytown would have been his doubtful pleasure, not mine. Since his parade before the stewards for not pushing his horse all out into third place, he been ignored by Corin Kellar. It was the sort of injustice typical of Corin, to sack a man who ran into trouble looking after his interests, and it had done nothing to lay the unfair rumour that Tick-Tock was a habitual non-trier.

Apart from abruptly lessening the number of races he rode in, the rumour had had little effect on Tick-Tock himself. He shrugged his shoulders, and with a determined look on his angular young face stated, 'They'll change their minds again in time. I'll mash every horse I ride into a pulp. I'll do my nut on every hopeless hack. No one henceforth will see me finish eighth when by bashing the beast I could be sixth.'

I had smiled to hear these fighting words from one whose chief asset was his lightness of touch, but was relieved, too, that he was intact in spirits. No suicides, no mental breakdowns for him.

Shantytown, when it came to the race, was not what I had been led to expect. The damp raw January afternoon had drawn only a small crowd of stalwarts to watch a second-class pro-gramme at a minor meeting, and as I watched the big chestnut plod round the parade ring I thought how well he matched the circumstances. Uninspiring.

But far from pulling my arms out of their sockets, Shantytown seemed to me to be in danger of falling asleep. The start caught him flat-footed, so little interest was he taking in it, and I had to boot him into the first fence. He rose to it fairly well, but was slow in his recovery, and it was the same at every jump. It was puzzling, after what Tick-Tock had said, but horses do have their off-days for no discernible reason, and I could only suppose that this was one of them.

We trailed round the entire three miles in the rear of the field, and finished ingloriously last. All my efforts to get him to quicken up the straight met with no response. Shantytown hadn't taken hold of his bit from the beginning and at the end he seemed to be dead beat.

A hostile reception met us on our return. John Ballerton, with whom I had exchanged coldly polite 'Good afternoons' in the parade ring before the race, now glowered like a July thunderstorm. Corin, standing on one leg and wearing an anxious, placatory expression, was obviously going to use me as the scapegoat for the horse's failure, to save his face as its trainer. That was always one of the hazards to be run in riding Corin's horses.

'What the hell do you think you were doing?' Ballerton said aggressively, as I slid off on to the ground and began to unbuckle the saddle girths.

'I'm sorry, sir,' I said. 'He wouldn't go any faster.'

'Don't talk such bloody rubbish,' he said, 'he always goes faster than that. I've never seen a more disgusting display of incompetence . . . you couldn't ride in a cart with a pig net over it. If you ask me, the horse wasn't given a chance. You missed the start and couldn't be bothered to make it up.'

'I did say,' said Corin to me reproachfully, 'not to let him run away with you, and to keep tucked in behind for the first two miles. But I do think you carried my orders a bit too far . . .'

'A bit too far!' interrupted Ballerton furiously. 'Were you afraid to let him go, or something? If you can't manage to ride a decent race on a horse which pulls, why the hell do you try to. Why not say straight out that you can't? Save us all a lot of time and money.'

I said, 'The horse didn't pull. There was no life in him.'

'Kellar,' Ballerton was nearly shouting. 'Is my horse a puller or is he not?'

'He is,' said Corin, not meeting my eyes.

'And you told me he was fit. On his toes.'

'Yes,' said Corin. 'I thought he'd win.'

They looked at me accusingly. Corin must have known that the horse had run listlessly because he had seen the race with experienced eyes, but he was not going to admit it. If I had to ride often for Corin, I thought wryly, I would soon have as many rows with him as Art had had.

Ballerton narrowed his eyes and said to me, 'I asked you to ride Shantytown against my better judgement and only because Maurice Kemp-Lore insisted I had been misjudging you and that you were really a reliable man who would ride a genuine race. Well, I'm going to tell him he is wrong. Very wrong. You'll never ride another horse of mine, I promise you that.'

He turned on his heel and stalked off, followed by Corin. My chief feeling, as I went back to the weighing-room, was of irritation that I hadn't relied on instinct and refused to ride for him in the first place.

By the end of the afternoon the puzzlement I had felt over Shantytown's dead running had changed to a vague uneasiness, for neither of the other two horses I rode afterwards did anything like as well as had been expected. Both were well backed, and both finished nearly last, and although their owners were a great deal nicer about it than Ballerton had been, their disappointment was obvious.

On the following day, still at Dunstable, the run of flops continued. I had been booked for three horses, and they all ran badly. I spent the whole depressing afternoon apologetically explaining to owner after owner that I had not been able to make their horse go faster. The third horse, in fact, went so badly that I had to pull him up half-way round. He was a slow jumper on the best of days, but on that particular one he took so long putting himself right and so long starting off again when he landed, that the rest of the field were a whole fence ahead by the time we had gone a mile. It was hopeless. When I reined him in he slowed from a reluctant gallop to a walk in a couple of strides, sure sign of a very tired horse. I thought as he was trained by a farmer-owner who might not know better, that he must have been given too stiff a training gallop on the previous day, but the farmer said he was sure he had not.

Runs of bad luck are commoner in racing than good ones, and the fact that six of my mounts in a row had made a showing far below their usual capabilities would not have attracted much notice had it not been for John Ballerton.

I changed into street clothes after the fifth race and strolled out of the weighing-room to find him standing close by with a small circle of cronies. All the heads turned towards me with that sideways, assessing look which meant they had been talking about me, and Ballerton said something forceful to them, of which the word 'disgrace' floated across clearly.

Jockeys being as accustomed as politicians to abuse I gave no sign of having heard what had obviously been intended for my ears, and walked casually off to the stands to watch the last race; but I did wonder how long and how maliciously Ballerton would hold Shantytown's failure against me, and what effect his complaints would have on the number of horses I was asked to ride. He was not a man to keep his grudges to himself, and as a

National Hunt Committee member he was not without influence either.

Up on the stands Maurice Kemp-Lore came across to talk to me. We had met briefly on racecourses several times now, and were on superficially friendly terms, but in spite of his charm, or perhaps because it sometimes seemed too polished, I felt his friendship came strictly into the professional, 'might be useful' category. I did not believe that he liked me for my own sake.

He smiled vividly, the charm turned on to full wattage, his slim figure radiating health and confidence and his blue eyes achieving the near impossible of twinkling on a grey January afternoon. I smiled back automatically: one couldn't help it. All his impressive success stemmed from the instantaneous, irresistible feeling of well-being he inspired in whomever he talked to, and there was no one from the Senior Steward downwards who did not enjoy his company, even if, like me, one suspected his unfailing motive was the gathering of material for his programme.

'What bad luck, Rob,' he said cheerfully. 'I hear the good word I put in for you with John Ballerton has gone awry.'

'You can say that again,' I agreed. 'But thanks for trying anyway.'

The blue eyes glimmered. 'Anything to help,' he said.

I could hear distinctly a faint high-pitched wheeze as he drew breath into his lungs, and I realized it was the first time I had encountered him in an asthmatic attack. I was vaguely sorry for him.

The horses for the sixth race cantered past, going down to the start.

'Are James's plans fixed for the Midwinter Cup?' he asked casually, his eyes on the horses. I smiled. But he had his job to do, I supposed, and there was no harm in telling him.

'Template runs, all being well,' I said.

'And you ride him?'

'Yes,' I agreed.

'How is Pip getting along?' he asked, wheezing quietly.

'They think his leg is mending well, but he is still in plaster,' I said. 'It comes off next week, I believe, and he might be ready for Cheltenham, but of course he won't be fit for the Midwinter.'

The race in question was a richly endowed new event at Ascot, introduced to provide a high spot in mid-February, and nicely timed to give three full weeks for recovery and retuning before the Cheltenham Gold Cup. It lay almost a month ahead, on that day at Dunstable, and I was looking forward to it particularly as it seemed possible that it would be my last chance on Template. Pip would do his very best to be fit to ride him in the Gold Cup, and so would I have done in his place.

'What chance do you give Template in the Midwinter?' Maurice asked, watching the start through his race glasses.

'Oh, I hope he'll win,' I said, grinning. 'You can quote me.'

'I probably will,' he agreed, grinning back. We watched the race together, and such was the effect of his personality that I left Dunstable quite cheerfully, the dismal two days' results temporarily forgotten.

Eight

IT WAS a false security. My charmed run of good luck had ended with a vengeance, and Dunstable proved to be only the fringe of the whirlpool. During the next two weeks I rode seventeen horses. Fifteen of them finished in the rear of the field, and in only two cases was this a fair result.

I couldn't understand it. As far as I knew there was no difference in my riding, and it was unbelievable that my mounts should all lose their form simultaneously. I began to worry about it, and that didn't help, as I could feel my confidence oozing away as each disturbing and embarrassing day passed.

There was one grey mare I particularly liked riding because of the speed of her reactions: she often seemed to know what I intended to do a split second before I gave her signals, rather as if she had sized up the situation as quickly as I had and was already taking independent action. She was sweet-tempered and silken-mouthed, and jumped magnificently. I liked her owner too, a short jolly farmer with a thick Norfolk accent, and while we watched her walk round the parade ring before her race he commiserated with me on my bad luck and said, 'Never mind, lad. The mare will put you right. She'll not fail you. You'll do all right on her, never fear.'

I went out smiling to the race because I too believed I would do all right on her. But that week she might have been another horse. Same colour, same size, same pretty head. But no zip. It was like driving a car with four flat tyres.

The jolly farmer looked less jolly and more pensive when I brought her back.

'She's not been last ever before, lad,' he said reproachfully.

We looked her over, but there was nothing wrong with her that we could see, and she wasn't even blowing very hard.

'I could get her heart tested I suppose,' the farmer said doubtfully. 'Are you sure you gave her her head, lad?'

'Yes,' I said. 'But she had no enthusiasm at all today.'

The farmer shook his head, doleful and puzzled.

One of the horses I rode belonged to a tall sharp-faced woman who knew a great deal about racing and had no sympathy with bunglers. She laid straight into me with her tongue after I had eased her ultra-expensive new gelding from last into second last place only feet from the winning post.

'I suppose you realize,' she said in a loud, hard voice, unashamedly listened to by a large group of racegoers, 'that in the last five minutes you have succeeded both in halving the value of my horse and making me look a fool for having paid a fortune for him.'

I apologized. I suggested possibly that her animal needed a little time.

'Time?' she repeated angrily. 'For what? For you to wake up? You speak as if it were my judgement that is at fault, not yours. You lay far too far out of your ground. You should have taken closer order from the beginning . . .' Her acid lecture went on and on and on, and I looked at the fine head of her glossy black high-bred gelding and admitted to myself that he was probably a great deal better than he had appeared.

One Wednesday was the big day for a ten-year-old schoolboy with sparkly brown eyes and a conspiratorial grin. His wealthy eccentric grandmother, having discovered that there was no minimum age laid down for racehorse owners, had given Hugo a colossal chestnut 'chaser twice his height, and was considerate enough to foot the training bills as well.

I had become firm friends with Hugo. Knowing that I saw his horse most mornings at James's, he used to send me tiny parcels containing lumps of sugar filched from the dining table at his prep school, which I conscientiously passed on to their intended destination: and I used to write back to Hugo, giving him quite detailed accounts of how his giant pet was progressing.

On that Wednesday Hugo had not only begged a day off from school to see his horse run, but had brought three friends with him. The four of them stood with me and James in the parade ring, Hugo's mother being the rare sort who liked her son to enjoy his limelight alone. As I had walked down from the weighing-room she had smiled broadly to me from her station on the rails.

The four little boys were earnest and excited, and James and I had great fun with them before the race, treating them with seriousness and as man-to-man, which they obviously appreciated. This time, I promised myself, this time, for Hugo, I will win. I must.

But the big chestnut jumped very clumsily that day. On the far side of nearly every fence he ducked his head, and once, to prevent myself being hauled over in a somersault, I had to stretch forward down his neck with one hand only, leaving go of the reins entirely with the other. The free arm, swinging up sideways, helped to bring my weight far enough back to keep me in the saddle, but the gesture known as 'calling a cab' was not going to earn me any bonus points with James, who had denounced it often as the style of 'bad, tired, scared or unfit amateurs'.

Hugo's little face was pink when I dismounted, and the three friends glumly shuffled their feet behind him. With them as witnesses there would be no chance of Hugo smoothing over the disaster with the rest of his schoolmates.

'I'm very sorry, Hugo,' I said sincerely, apologizing for

everything – myself, the horse, the race, and the miserliness of fate.

He answered with a stoicism which would have been a lesson to many of his seniors. 'I expect it was an off day,' he said kindly. 'And anyway, someone always has to be last. That's what Daddy said when I came bottom in History.' He looked at the chestnut forgivingly, and said to me, 'I expect he's keen really, don't you?'

'Yes,' I agreed. 'Keen, very.'

'Well,' said Hugo, turning bravely to his friends. 'That's that, then. We might as well have tea.'

Failures like these were too numerous to escape anyone's attention, but as the days passed I noticed a change in the way people spoke to me. One or two, and Corin in particular, showed something like contempt. Others looked uncomfortable, others sympathetic, others pitying. Heads turned towards me wherever I went, and I could almost feel the wave of gossip I left in my wake. I didn't know exactly what they were saying, so I asked Tick-Tock.

'Pay no attention,' he said. 'Ride a couple of winners and they'll be throwing the laurel wreaths again, and back-pedalling on everything they're saying now. It's badpatchville, chum, that's all.'

And that was all I could get out of him.

One Thursday evening James telephoned to my digs and asked me to go up to his house. I walked up in the dark, rather miserably wondering whether he, like two other trainers that day, was going to find an excuse for putting someone else up on his horses. I couldn't blame him. Owners could make it impossible for him to continue with a jockey so thoroughly in the doldrums.

James called me into his office, a square room joining his house to the stable yard. Its walls were covered with racing photographs, bookshelves, a long row of racing colours on clothes hangers, and filing cabinets. A huge roll-top desk stood in front of the window, which looked out on to the yard. There were three broken-springed armchairs with faded chintz covers, a decrepit Turkish carpet on the floor, and a red-hot coal fire in the grate. I had spent a good many hours there in the past three months, discussing past performances and future plans.

James waited for me and stood aside to let me go in first. He followed me in and shut the door, and faced me almost aggressively across the familiar room.

'I hear,' he said without preamble, 'that you have lost your nerve.'

The room was very still. The fire crackled slightly. A horse in a near-by loose box banged the floor with his hoof. I stared at James, and he stared straight back, gravely.

I didn't answer. The silence lengthened. It was not a surprise. I had guessed what was being said about me when Tick-Tock had refused to tell me what it was.

'No one is to blame for losing his nerve,' James said noncommittally. 'But a trainer cannot continue to employ someone to whom it has happened.'

I still said nothing.

He waited a few seconds, and went on, 'You have been showing the classic symptoms . . . trailing round nearly last, pulling up for no clear reason, never going fast enough to keep warm, and calling a cab. Keeping at the back out of trouble, that's what you've been doing.'

I thought about it, rather numbly.

'A few weeks ago,' he said, 'I promised you that if I heard any rumours about you I would make sure they were true before I believed them. Do you remember?'

I nodded.

'I heard this rumour last Saturday,' he said. 'Several people sympathized with me because my jockey had lost his nerve. I didn't believe it. I have watched you closely ever since.'

I waited dumbly for the axe. During the week I had been last five times out of seven.

He walked abruptly over to an armchair by the fire and sat down heavily.

Irritably he said, 'Oh sit down, Rob. Don't just stand there like a stricken ox, saying nothing.'

I sat down and looked at the fire.

'I expected you to deny it,' he said in a tired voice. 'Is it true, then?'

'No,' I said.

'Is that all you've got to say? It isn't enough. What has happened to you? You owe me an explanation.'

I owed him much more than an explanation.

'I can't explain,' I said despairingly. 'Every horse I've ridden in the last three weeks seems to have had its feet dipped in treacle. The difference is in the horses . . . I am the same.' It sounded futile and incredible, even to me.

'You have certainly lost your touch,' he said slowly. 'Perhaps Ballerton is right . . .'

'Ballerton?' I said sharply.

'He's always said you were not as good as you were made out to be, and that I'd pushed you too fast . . . given you a top job when you weren't ready for it. Today he has been going round smugly saying "I told you so." He can't leave the subject alone, he's so pleased.'

'I'm sorry, James,' I said.

'Are you ill, or something?' he asked exasperatedly.

'No,' I said.

'They say the fall you had three weeks ago was what frightened you – the day you got knocked out and your horse rolled on you. But you were all right going home, weren't you? I remember you being a bit sore, but you didn't seem in the least scared of falling again.'

'I didn't give that fall another thought,' I said.

'Then why, Rob, why?'

But I shook my head. I didn't know why.

He stood up and opened a cupboard which contained bottles and glasses, poured out two whiskies, and handed one to me.

'I can't convince myself yet that you've lost your nerve,' he said. 'Remembering the way you rode Template on Boxing Day, only a month ago, it seems impossible. No one could change so fundamentally in so short a time. Before I took you on, wasn't it your stock in trade to ride all the rough and dangerous horses that trainers didn't want to risk their best jockeys on? That's why I first engaged you, I remember it clearly. And all those years you spent in wherever it was as a stockman, and that spell in a rodeo . . . you aren't the sort of man to lose his nerve suddenly and for nothing, and especially not when you're in the middle of a most spectacularly successful season.'

I smiled for almost the first time that day, realizing how deeply I wanted him not to lose faith in me.

I said, 'I feel as if I'm fighting a fog. I tried everything I knew today to get those horses to go faster, but they were all half-dead. Or I was. I don't know . . . it's a pretty ghastly mess.'

'I'm afraid it is,' he said gloomily. 'And I'm having owner trouble about it, as you can imagine. All the original doubters are doubting again. I can't reassure them . . . it's like a Stock Exchange crash; catching. And you're the bad stock that's being jettisoned.'

'What rides can I still expect?' I said.

He sighed. 'I don't exactly know. You can have all the Broome runners because he's on a cruise in the Mediterranean and won't hear the rumours for a while. And my two as well; they both run next week. For the rest, we'll have to wait and see.'

I could hardly bring myself to say it, but I had to know.

'How about Template?' I asked.

He looked at me steadily. 'I haven't heard from George

Tirrold,' he said. 'I think he will agree that he can't chuck you out after you've won so many races for him. He is not easily stampeded, there's that to hope for, and it was he who drew my attention to you in the first place. Unless something worse happens,' he finished judiciously, 'I think you can still count on riding Template in the Midwinter a week on Saturday. But if you bring him in last in that . . . it will be the end.'

I stood up and drained the whisky.

'I'll win that race,' I said, 'whatever the cost, I'll win it.'

We went silently together to the races the following day, but when we arrived I discovered that two of my three prospective mounts were mine no longer. I had been, in the expressive phrase, jocked off. The owners, the trainer in question brusquely explained, thought they would have no chance of winning if they put me up as planned. Very sorry and all that, he said, but no dice.

I stood on the stands and watched both the horses run well: one of them won, and the other finished a close third. I ignored as best I could the speculative, sideways glances from all the other jockeys, trainers and pressmen standing near me. If they wanted to see how I was taking it, that was their affair; just as it was mine if I wanted to conceal from them the inescapable bitterness of these two results.

I went out to ride James's runner in the fourth race absolutely determined to win. The horse was capable of it on his day, and I knew him to be a competent jumper and a willing battler in a close finish.

We came last.

All the way round I could barely keep him in touch with the rest of the field. In the end he cantered slowly past the winning post with his head down in tiredness, and mine down too, in defeat and humiliation. I felt ill.

It was an effort to go back and face the music. I felt more like driving the Mini-Cooper at top speed into a nice solid tree.

The freckle-faced lad who looked after the horse deliberately did not glance at me when he took hold of the reins in the paddock. He usually greeted me with a beaming smile. I slid off the horse. The owner and James stood there, their faces blank. No one said anything. There was nothing to say. Finally, without a word, the owner shrugged his shoulders and turned on his heel, and walked off.

I took my saddle off the horse and the lad led him away.

James said, 'It can't go on, Rob.'

I knew it.

He said, 'I'm sorry. I'm very sorry. I'll have to get someone else to ride my horses tomorrow.'

I nodded.

He gave me a searching look in which puzzlement and doubt were tinged for the first time with pity. I found it unbearable.

'I think I'll go to Kensington tonight after the races,' I said, trying to speak evenly. 'Instead of coming back with you.'

'Very well,' he said, obviously relieved at not having to face an embarrassing return journey. 'I really am sorry, Rob.'

'Yes,' I said. 'I know.'

I took my saddle back to the weighing-room, acutely aware of the glances which followed me. The conversation in the changing-room died into an embarrassed silence when I walked in. I went over to my peg and put the saddle on the bench, and began to take off my colours. I looked at the circle of faces turned towards me, reading on some curiosity, on some hostility, on some sympathy, and on one or two, pleasure. No contempt: they would leave that to people who didn't ride, to the people who didn't know at first hand how formidable a big fence can look to a jockey on a bad horse. In the changing-room there was too much consciousness in their minds of 'there but for the grace of God go I,' for them to feel contempt.

They began to talk again, but not much to me. I guessed they didn't know what to say. Nor did I.

I felt neither more nor less courageous than I had done all my life. It was surely impossible, I thought confusedly, to be subconsciously afraid, to keep out of trouble and yet think one was as willing as ever to accept risks. Three weeks earlier, I would have laughed at the idea. But the shattering fact remained that none of the twenty-eight horses I had ridden since I had been knocked out in that fall had made any show at all. They were trained by several different trainers and owned by different owners: all they had had in common was me. There were too many of them for it to be a coincidence, especially as those I had been removed from had done well.

Round and round in a jumble went the profitless thoughts, the hopeless statistics, the feeling that the sky had fallen. I put on my street clothes and brushed my hair, and was surprised to see in the mirror that I looked the same as usual.

I went outside on to the steps outside the weighing-room and heard the normal chatter which my presence had muffled in the changing-room break out cheerfully again as soon as I was gone. No one outside either seemed very anxious to talk to me: no one, that is, except a weedy little ferret of a man, who worked, I knew, for one of the minor sporting papers.

He was standing with John Ballerton, but when he caught sight of me he came directly over.

'Oh, Finn,' he said, taking a notebook and pencil out of his pocket and looking at me with a sly, malicious smile. 'May I have a list of the horses you are riding tomorrow? And next week?'

I looked across at Ballerton. There was a smirk of triumph on his heavy face. I took a great grip on my rising temper and spoke mildly to the pressman.

'Ask Mr Axminster,' I said. He looked disappointed, but he didn't know how close he had come to feeling my fist in his face.

I had just enough sense to know that letting fly at him would be the worst thing I could do.

I strode away from him, seething with rage; but the day had not done with me, even yet. Corin, crossing my path purposefully, stopped me and said, 'I suppose you've seen this?' He held out a copy of the paper for which the ferrety little man wrote.

'No,' I said. 'And I don't want to.'

Corin smiled thinly, enjoying himself. 'I think you ought to sue them. Everyone thinks so. You'll have to sue them when you've read it. You can't ignore it, or everyone will think . . .'

'Everyone can think what they damn well please,' I said roughly, trying to walk on.

'Read it,' insisted Corin, thrusting the paper in front of my eyes. 'Everyone else has.'

It needed only a half glance to see the headline. There was no missing it. In bold type it said, 'Nerve Lost.'

Against my will I began to read.

'Nerve, depending on how it takes you, is either fear overcome by an effort of will, or a total lack of imagination. If you ride steeplechasing it doesn't matter which sort you have, as long as you have one of them.

'Does anyone understand why one man is brave and another is not? Or why a person can be brave at one time and cowardly at another?

'Maybe it is all a matter of hormones! Maybe a bang on the head can destroy the chemical make-up which produces courage. Who knows? Who knows?

'The crumbling of a jumping jockey's nerve is a pathetic sight, as every recent racegoer will realize. But while one may extend sympathy to a man for a state which he cannot help, one must at the same time ask whether he is doing the right thing if he continues to seek and accept rides in races.

'The public deserves a fair run for its money. If a jockey can't give it to them because he is afraid of hurting himself, he is taking fees under false pretences.

'But it is only a matter of time, of course, before owners and trainers withdraw their custom from such a man and, by forcing him into retirement, protect the betting public from wasting any more of its money.

'And a good thing too!'

I gave the paper back to Corin and tried to loosen the clamped tension of my jaw muscles.

'I can't sue them,' I said. 'They don't mention my name.'

He didn't look surprised, and I realized sharply that he had known it all along. He had wanted only the pleasure of watching me read, and there was still about his eyes a remnant of a very nasty smile.

'What did I ever do to you, Corin,' I asked, 'to make you feel the way you do?'

He looked taken aback, and said weakly, 'Er . . . nothing . . .'

'Then I'm sorry for you,' I said stonily. 'I'm sorry for your spiteful, mean, cowardly little soul . . .'

'Cowardly!' he exclaimed, stung and flushing. 'Who are you to call anyone else cowardly? That's a laugh, that really is. Just wait till they hear this. Just wait till I tell . . .'

But I didn't wait. I had had far, far more than enough. I went back to Kensington in as deep and terrible a mood of despair as I ever hope to have to live through.

There was no one in the flat, and for once it was spotlessly tidy. The family, I concluded, were away. The kitchen confirmed it. There was no food or milk in the refrigerator, no bread in the bin, no fruit in the basket.

Back in the silent sitting-room I took a nearly full whisky bottle out of the cupboard and lay down full length on the sofa. I uncorked the bottle and took two large gulps. The neat spirit bit into my gums and scorched down to my empty stomach.

I put the cork in the bottle and the bottle on the floor beside me. What is the point of getting drunk, I thought: I'd only feel worse in the morning. I could stay drunk for several days perhaps, but it wouldn't do any good in the end. Nothing would do any good. Everything was finished. Everything was busted and gone.

I spent a long time looking at my hands. Hands. The touch they had for horses had earned me my living all my adult life. They looked the same as always. They were the same, I thought desperately. Nerves and muscles, strength and sensitivity, nothing was changed. But the memory of the last twenty-eight horses I had ridden denied it: heavy, cumbersome and unresponsive.

I knew no other skill but riding, nor had ever wanted any. I felt more than whole on horseback: I felt extended. Four extra limbs and a second brain. More speed, more strength, more courage . . . I winced at the word . . . and quicker reactions. A saddle was to me as the sea to a fish, natural and easy. Home. And a racing saddle? I drew in a breath, shivering. For a racing saddle, I thought bleakly, I am not sufficient.

It wasn't enough after all to *want* to race as well as anybody, one had to have the talent and the staying power as well; and I was face to face with the conviction that I was not good enough, that I was never going to be good enough, to take firm hold of the position which had been so nearly in my grasp. I had thought myself capable of seizing the incredible opportunity I had been given. The mess I had made of it, the weak, degrading retreat from the brink of success, was tearing to shreds all I had known or believed about myself.

I picked up the whisky bottle and held it on my chest. It was all the company I had, and it offered sleep, at least. But I suppose old habits cling hard: I held the bottle to my chest like a life-jacket to a drowning man and knew I wouldn't pull the cork out again. Not for a while. Not that night, anyway.

And what of the future? I could return during the next week and race on one or two of James's horses, if he would still let me, and perhaps even on Template in the Midwinter. But I no longer either expected or hoped to do well, and I could feel myself shrink at the prospect of going back to a racecourse to face all those stares and insults again. Better to start a new life at once, perhaps. But a new life doing what?

It couldn't be the old life. Being a stockman might have suited me at twenty, but it was not what I would want at thirty, nor at forty, nor fifty. And whatever I did, wherever I went now, I would drag around with me the knowledge that I had totally failed at what I had tried hardest to do.

After a long time I stood up and put the bottle back into the cupboard.

It was then a good twenty-six hours since I had eaten, and despite everything my stomach was beginning its squeezing routine. On a second inspection the kitchen revealed only some assorted tins of *escargots*, cheese straws and *marrons glacés*, so I went out and along the streets until I came to a decent-looking pub where I was sure I was not known by sight. I didn't want to have to talk.

I ordered ham sandwiches and a glass of beer, but when it came the thick new white bread stuck tastelessly in my mouth and my throat kept closing convulsively against all attempts to swallow. This can't go on, I thought. I've got to eat. If I can't get drunk and I can't have Joanna and I can't . . . I can't be a jockey any more . . . at least I can eat now as much as I like, without worrying about gaining a pound or two . . . but after ten minutes trying I had swallowed only two mouthfuls, and I couldn't manage another bite.

The fact that it was Friday had meant nothing to me all evening, and the approach of 9 o'clock went unnoticed. But just when I pushed away the sandwiches and was eyeing the beer with the beginnings of nausea, someone turned up the volume of the television set which stood at one end of the bar, and the opening bars of the 'Galloping Major' suddenly blared out across the tinkling glasses and the buzzing voices. A large bunch of devotees who had settled themselves with full pint pots in front of the set made shooshing noises to those nearest to them, and by the time Maurice Kemp-Lore's tidy features materialized there was a more or less attentive audience to receive him. My little glass-topped table was as far as it could be from the door, so that it was more because leaving meant weaving my way through the sprawling silent crowd, than from a positive desire to watch, that I stayed where I was.

'Good evening,' Maurice said, the spellbinding smile in place. 'This evening we are going to talk about handicapping, and I have here to meet you two well-informed men who look at weights and measures from opposing angles. The first is Mr Charles Jenkinson, who has been an official handicapper for several years.' Mr Jenkinson's self-conscious face appeared briefly on the screen. 'And the other is the well-known trainer Corin Kellar.'

Corin's thin face glowed with satisfaction. We'll never hear the last of this, I thought; and then with a stab remembered that I wouldn't be there to hear any of it anyway.

'Mr Jenkinson,' said Maurice, 'will explain how he builds a handicap. And Mr Kellar will tell you how he tries to avoid having his horses defeated by their weights. The battle between handicappers and trainers is none the less fierce for being conducted in gentlemanly and largely uncomplaining reticence, and perhaps tonight you will capture a whiff of that unrelenting struggle.' He smiled engagingly. 'A handicapper's pinnacle of success is for every single runner in a race to pass the winning post in a straight line abreast – a multiple dead-heat – since it is his aim to give each horse an exactly equal chance. It never actually happens, but handicappers dream about it in their softer moments.' He grinned sideways in a friendly fashion towards his guest, and when Mr Jenkinson appeared on the screen one could almost see the self-confidence begin to flow in him as he started to talk about his job.

I listened with only half my mind, the rest being submerged in persistent misery, and Corin had been speaking for some moments before I paid much attention to him. He was being of necessity less than frank, since the bald truth would have lost him his licence very smartly. In practice he felt no qualms at all when giving his jockey orders to start at the back and stay there, but in theory, I was sardonically amused to see, he was right-eously on the side of the angels.

'Horses from my stable are always doing their best to win,' he said, lying without a tremor.

'But surely you don't insist on them being ridden hard at the end when they've no chance at all?' said Maurice, reasonably.

'As hard as necessary, yes,' Corin asserted. 'I hate to see jockeys easing up too soon, even if they are beaten. I dismissed a jockey a short while ago for not riding hard enough at the end. He could have come third if he had ridden the horse out . . .' his voice droned on, pious and petulant, and I thought of Tick-Tock, thrown to the stewards for obeying his orders too conscien-tiously and now having trouble getting other trainers to trust him. I thought of Art, nagged and contradicted and driven to death; and the active dislike I already felt for Corin Kellar sharp-ened in that dim pub corner into hatred.

Maurice dragged him back to handicapping and finally wrung from him a grudging admission that from the point of view of the weight he would be allotted in future, it was better for a horse to win by one length than by ten. Maurice would have done better, I thought, to have chosen almost anyone else to show how to dodge the handicapper; or perhaps he did not know Corin well enough to expect him hypocritically to deny in public what he had said in private. Every jockey who had ridden the Kellar horses had learned it the hard way.

'One is always in the hands of one's jockey,' Corin was saying.

'Go on,' said Maurice encouragingly, leaning forward. A light somewhere in the studio lent his eyes a momentary shimmer as he moved. Corin said, 'You can slave away for weeks preparing a horse for a race and then a jockey can undo it all with one stupid mistake.'

'It does the handicap good though,' Maurice interrupted, laughing. The pub audience laughed too.

'Well . . .' agreed Corin, nonplussed.

'If you look at it that way,' Maurice continued, 'there is always some compensation for a jockey not getting the most out of a horse. Whatever the reason, trivial, like a mistake, or more serious, like a failure of resolution at a crucial point . . .'

'No guts, you mean?' said Corin flatly. 'I'd say that that would be as obvious to a handicapper as to everyone else, and that he'd take it into account. There's a case in point now . . .' he hesitated, but Maurice did not try to stop him, so he went on more boldly, 'a case now where everything a certain jockey rides goes round at the back of the field. He is afraid of falling, you see. Well, you can't tell me any handicapper thinks those particular horses are not as good as they were. Of course they are. It's just the rider who's going downhill.'

I could feel the blood rush to my head and begin to pulse there. I leaned my elbows on the table and bit my knuckle. Hard.

The voices went on inexorably.

Maurice said, 'What are your views on that, Mr Jenkinson?'

And the handicapper, looking embarrassed, murmured that 'Of course . . . er . . . in certain circumstances, one would . . . er . . . overlook the occasional result.'

'Occasional!' said Corin. 'I wouldn't call nearly thirty races in a row occasional. Are you going to overlook them all?'

'I can't answer that,' protested Jenkinson.

'What do you usually do in these cases?' Maurice asked.

'I . . . that is . . . they aren't usually as blatant as this. I may have to consult . . . er, others, before coming to a decision. But it really isn't a thing I can discuss here.'

'Where better?' said Maurice persuasively. 'We all know that this poor chap took a toss three weeks ago and has ridden . . . er . . . ineffectively . . . ever since. Surely you'd have to take that into account when you are handicapping those horses?'

While the cameras focused on Jenkinson hesitating over his answer Corin's voice said, 'I'll be interested to know what you decide. One of those horses was mine, you know. It was a shocking exhibition. Finn won't be riding for me again, or for anyone else either, I shouldn't wonder.'

Jenkinson said uneasily, 'I don't think we should mention names,' and Maurice cut in quickly, saying, 'No, no. I agree. Better not.' But the damage was done.

'Well, thank you both very much for giving us your time this evening. I am sorry to say we have come nearly to the end once again . . .' He slid expertly into his minute of chit-chat and his closing sentences, but I was no longer listening. Between them he and Corin had hammered in the nails on the ruins of my brief career, and watching them at it on the glaring little screen had given me a blinding headache.

I stood up stiffly as the chatter broke out again in the crowded pub and threaded my way a little unsteadily to the door. The bunch of racing enthusiasts were downing their pints and I caught a scrap of their conversation as I squeezed around them.

'Laid it on a bit thick, I thought,' one of them said.

'Not thick enough,' contradicted another. 'I lost a quid on Finn on Tuesday. He deserves all he gets, if you ask me, the windy b—.'

I stumbled out into the street, breathing in great gulps of cold air and making a conscious effort to stand up straight. It was no use sitting down and weeping in the gutter, which would have been easy enough to do. I walked slowly back to the dark, empty flat, and without switching on any lights lay down fully dressed on my bed.

The glow from the street below dimly lit the small room, the window frame throwing an angular distorted shadow on the ceiling. My head throbbed. I remembered lying there like that before, the day Grant's fist pulped my nose. I remembered pitying him, and pitying Art. It had been so easy. I groaned aloud, and the sound shocked me.

It was a long way down from my window to the street. Five storeys. A long, quick way down. I thought about it.

There was a chiming clock in the flat below ours, counting away the quarter-hours, and in the quiet house I could hear it clearly. It struck ten, eleven, twelve, one, two.

The window threw its shadow steadily on the ceiling. I stared up at it. Five storeys down. But however bad things were I couldn't take that way, either. It wasn't for me. I shut my eyes and lay still, and finally after the long despairing hours drifted into an exhausted, uneasy, dream-filled sleep.

I woke less than two hours later, and heard the clock strike four. My headache had gone, and my mind felt as clear and sharp as the starry sky outside: washed and shining. It was like coming out of a thick fog into sunshine. Like coolness after fever. Like being re-born.

Somewhere between sleeping and waking I found I had regained myself, come back to the life-saving certainty that I was the person I thought I was, and not the cracked-up mess that everyone else believed.

And that being so, I thought in puzzlement, there must be some other explanation of my troubles. All – *all* I had to do was find it. Looking back unsympathetically on the appalling desolation in which I had so recently allowed myself to flounder, I began at last, at long last, to use my brain.

Half an hour later it was clear that my stomach was awake too, and it was so insistent to be filled that I couldn't concentrate. I got up and fetched the tins of cheese straws and *marrons glacés* from the kitchen, but not the snails. How hungry would one have to be, I wondered idly, to face those molluscs cold and butterless at five o'clock in the morning?

I opened the tins and lay down again, and crunched up all the cheese straws while I thought, and peeled and chewed half of the syrupy weight-producing chestnuts. My stomach quietened like a dragon fed its daily maiden, and outside the stars faded into the wan London dawn.

In the morning I took the advice I had given to Grant, and went to see a psychiatrist.

Nine

I HAD known the psychiatrist all my life as he was a friend of my father, and, I hoped, I knew him well enough to ring him up for help on a morning which he always reserved for golf. At eight o'clock I telephoned his house in Wimpole Street where he lived in a flat above his consulting rooms.

He asked after my father. He sounded in a hurry.

'Can I come and see you, sir?' I said.

'Now? No. Saturday. Golf,' he said economically.

'Please . . . it won't take long.'

There was a brief pause.

'Urgent?' A professional note to his question.

'Yes,' I said.

'Come at once, then. I'm due at Wentworth at ten.'

'I haven't shaved . . .' I said, catching sight of myself in the looking-glass and realizing what a wreck I looked.

'Do you want to shave, or do you want to talk?' he said, exasperated.

'Talk,' I said.

'Then arrive,' he said, and put down his receiver.

I took a taxi, and he opened the door to me with a corner of toast and marmalade in his hand. The eminent Mr Claudius Mellit, whose patients usually saw him in striped trousers and black jacket, was sensibly attired for winter golf in waterproof trousers and a comfortably sloppy Norwegian sweater. He gave me a piercing preliminary glance and gestured, 'Upstairs.'

117

I followed him up. He finished his breakfast on the way. We went into his dining-room, where he gave me a seat at the oval mahogany table and some lukewarm coffee in a gold-rimmed cup.

'Now,' he said, sitting down opposite me.

'Suppose . . .' I began, and stopped. It didn't seem so easy, now that I was there. What had seemed obvious and manifest at five in the morning was now tinged with doubt. The dawn hours had shown me a pattern I believed in, but in the full light of day I felt sure it was going to sound preposterous.

'Look,' he said, 'if you really need help my golf can go hang. When I said on the telephone that I was in a hurry I hadn't seen the state you are in . . . and if you will excuse my saying so, your suit looks as if you had slept in it?'

'Well, yes, I did,' I said, surprised.

'Relax then, and tell me all.' He grinned, a big bear of a man, fifty years old and formidably wise.

'I'm sorry I look so untidy and unshaven,' I began.

'And sunken-eyed and hollow-cheeked,' he murmured, smiling.

'But I don't feel as bad as I suppose I look. Not any more. I won't keep you away from your golf if you'll just tell me . . .'

'Yes?' he waited for me calmly.

'Suppose I had a sister,' I said, 'who was as good a musician as Mother and Father, and I was the only one in the entire family to lack their talent – as you know I am – and I felt they despised me for lacking it, how would you expect me to act?'

'They don't despise you,' he protested.

'No . . . but if they did, would there be any way in which I could persuade them – and myself – that I had a very good excuse for not being a musician?'

'Oh, yes,' he said instantly, 'I'd expect you to do exactly what you have done. Find something you can do, and pursue it fanatically until in your own sphere you reach the standard of your family in theirs.'

I felt as if I'd been hit in the solar plexus. So simple an explanation of my compulsion to race had never occurred to me.

'That . . . that isn't what I meant,' I said helplessly. 'But when I come to think of it, I see it is true.' I paused. 'What I really meant to ask was, could I, when I was growing up, have developed a physical infirmity to explain away my failure? Paralysis, for instance, so that I simply couldn't play a violin or a piano or any musical instrument? An apparently honourable way out?'

He looked at me for a few moments, unsmiling and intent.

'If you were a certain type of person, yes, it's possible. But not in your case. You had better stop waltzing round it and ask me your question straight out. The real question. I am very well accustomed to hypothetical questions . . . I meet them every day . . . but if you want a trustable answer you'll have to ask the real question.'

'There are two,' I said. I still hesitated. So very much, my whole life, depended on his answers. He waited patiently.

I said at last, 'Could a boy whose family were all terrific cross-country riders develop asthma to hide the fact that he was afraid of horses?' My mouth was dry.

He didn't answer at once. He said, 'What is the other question?'

'Could that boy, as a man, develop such a loathing for steeplechase jockeys that he would try to smash their careers? Even if, as you said, he had found something else which he could do extremely well?'

'I suppose this man has that sister you mentioned?'

'Yes,' I said. 'She is getting to be the best girl point-to-point rider for a generation.'

He slouched back in his chair.

'It obviously matters so desperately to you, Robert, that I can't give you an answer without knowing more about it. I'm not giving you a couple of casual yeses and find afterwards I've let you stir up disastrous trouble for all sorts of people. You must tell me why you ask these questions.'

'But your golf,' I said.

'I'll go later,' he said calmly. 'Talk.'

So I talked. I told him what had happened to Art, and to Grant, and to Peter Cloony, and Tick-Tock, and myself.

I told him about Maurice Kemp-Lore. 'He comes from a family who ride as soon as walk, and he's the right build for steeplechasing. But horses give him asthma, and that, everyone knows, is why he doesn't race himself. Well . . . it's a good reason, isn't it? Of course there are asthmatics who do ride – asthma doesn't stop people who think that racing is worth the wheezing – but no one would dream of blaming a man who didn't.'

I paused, but as he made no comment, I went on, 'You can't help being drawn to him. You can't imagine the spell of his personality unless you've felt it. You can see people wake up and sparkle when he speaks to them. He has the ear of everyone from the stewards down . . . and I think he uses his influence to sow seeds of doubt about jockeys' characters.'

'Go on,' Claudius said, his face showing nothing.

'The men who seem to be especially under his spell are Corin Kellar, a trainer, and John Ballerton, a member of the ruling body. Neither of them ever has a good word to say for jockeys. I think Kemp-Lore picked them out as friends solely because they had the right sort of mean-mindedness for broadcasting every damaging opinion he insinuated into their heads. I think all the ruinous rumours start with Kemp-Lore, and that even the substance behind the rumours is mostly his work. Why isn't he content with having so much? The jockeys he is hurting like him and are pleased when he talks to them. Why does he need to destroy them?'

He said, 'If this were a hypothetical case I would tell you that

120

such a man could both hate and envy his father – and his sister – and have felt both these emotions from early childhood. But because he knows these feelings are wrong he represses them, and the aggression is unfortunately transferred on to people who show the same qualities and abilities that he hates in his father. Such individuals can be helped. They can be understood, and treated, and forgiven.'

'I can't forgive him,' I said. 'And I'm going to stop him.'

He considered me. 'You must make sure of your facts,' he said, stroking his thumbnail down his upper lip. 'At present you are just guessing. And as I've had no opportunity to talk to him you'll get no more from me than an admission that your suspicions of Kemp-Lore are *possibly* correct. Not even probably correct. He is a public figure of some standing. You are making a very serious accusation. You need cast-iron facts. Until you have them, there is always the chance that you have interpreted what has happened to you as malice from outside in order to explain away your own inner failure. Asthma of the mind, in fact.'

'Don't psychologists ever take a simple view?' I said, sighing.

He shook his head. 'Few things are simple.'

'I'll get the facts. Starting today,' I said. I stood up. 'Thank you for seeing me, and being so patient, and I'm sincerely sorry about your golf.'

'I won't be very late,' he reassured me, ambling down the stairs and opening his front door. On the doorstep shaking hands, he said as if making up his mind, 'Be careful, Robert. Go gently. If you are right about Kemp-Lore, and it is just possible that you are, you must deal with him thoughtfully. Persuade him to ask for treatment. Don't drive him too hard. His sanity may be in your hands.'

I said flatly, 'I can't look at it from your point of view. I don't think of Kemp-Lore as ill, but as wicked.'

'Where illness ends and crime begins . . .' he shrugged. 'It has been debated for centuries, and no two people agree. But take care, take care.' He turned to go in. 'Remember me to your parents.' He smiled, and shut the door.

Round a couple of corners, first during a luxurious shave in a fresh-smelling barber's and second over a triple order of eggs and bacon in the café next door, I bent my mind to the problem of how the cast-iron facts were to be dug up. On reflection, there seemed to be precious few of them to work on, and in the digging, to start with at least, I was going to come up against the barrier of pity and contempt which my recent performances had raised. Nasty medicine; but if I wanted a cure, I'd have to take it.

Using the café's telephone, I rang up Tick-Tock.

'Are you riding this afternoon?' I asked.

He said, 'Do me a favour, pal. No unkind questions so early in the day. In a word – negative.' A pause. 'And you?' Innocently, too innocently.

'You're a bastard,' I said.

'So my best friends tell me.'

'I want the car,' I said.

'Not if you're thinking of driving it over Beachy Head.'

'I'm not,' I said.

'Well, I'm relieved to hear it. But if you change your mind, let me know and I'll join you.' His voice was light and mocking; the desperate truth underneath needed no stating.

'I want to call at some stables,' I began.

'Whose?' he interrupted.

'Several people's . . . about six altogether, I think, apart from Axminster's. And Kellar's. I'll have to go there as well.'

'You've got a nerve,' said Tick-Tock.

'Thank you,' I said. 'You're about the only person in the country who thinks so.'

'Damn it . . . I didn't mean . . .'

I grinned into the telephone. 'Save it. Where's the car now?'

'Outside the window.'

'I'll come down to Newbury by train and pick it up, if you'll meet me at the station,' I said.

'It's no use going to any stables today,' he said. 'The trainers will all be at the races.'

'Yes, I sincerely hope so,' I agreed.

'What are you up to?' he asked suspiciously.

'Retrieving the fallen fortunes of the House of Finn,' I said. 'I'll catch the 10.10. You meet it. O.K.?' And I put the receiver down, hearing and ignoring a protesting 'Hey' before I cut him off.

But when I stepped off the train at Newbury he was waiting, dressed in a dandyish waisted riding jacket of almost eighteenth-century length on top of some unbelievably narrow cavalry cord trousers. He enjoyed his moment ironically while I looked him up and down.

'Where's the cravat, the ruffles and the sword?' I asked.

He said, 'You don't get the message. I'm tomorrow's man. My sword will be a do-it-yourself instant anti-radiation kit. You must fit your defence to the danger you meet . . .' He grinned.

Young Tick-Tock, I reflected, not for the first time, took an uncompromisingly realistic view of the world.

He opened the car door and settled himself behind the wheel.

'Where to?' he said.

'You're not coming,' I said.

'I certainly am. This car is half mine. Where it goes, I go.' He was clearly determined. 'Where to?'

'Well . . .' I got in beside him, fished out of my pocket a list I had made on the train, and showed it to him. 'These are the stables I want to go to. I've tried to arrange them in order so that there isn't too much back-tracking, but even so it means a lot of driving.'

'Phew,' he said. 'There's a lot of them. Hampshire, Sussex, Kent, Oxford, Leicester, and Yorkshire . . . how long will you be staying in each place? We'll never cover this lot in one day. Especially as you look tired already.'

I glanced at him, but he was looking down at the paper. It was true that I felt tired, but disconcerting that it should be so obvious. I had thought that the shave and breakfast and the return of self-confidence would have wiped away the ravages of the previous day and night.

'You needn't come,' I began.

'We've been through all that,' he interrupted. 'We'll start by going to your digs and mine for overnight things, and then make for Kent. And on the way you can tell me why we're going.' He calmly let in the clutch and drove off; and truth to tell I was very glad of his company.

We collected our things, and Tick-Tock pointed the Mini-Cooper's blunt nose towards the first stable on the list, Corin Kellar's, in Hampshire.

'Now,' he said. 'The works.'

'No,' I said. 'I'm not going to tell you why we're going. Listen and watch, and then you tell me.'

'You're a cagey blighter,' he said, without arguing. He added, 'I suppose you've taken into account all that about saps rushing in where angels wouldn't plonk their holy feet? I mean, to put it mildly, we are neither of us in the red carpet bracket just now. Strictly doomsville, us.'

'You are so right,' I said, smiling.

Tick-Tock turned his head and gave me a surprised stare.

'Keep your eyes on the road,' I said mildly.

'I'll never know you,' he said. 'I'd have thought you'd take it very hard . . . what has happened . . . but since I picked you up at the station I've felt more cheerful than I have for weeks.' His foot went down on the accelerator and he began to whistle.

We arrived at Corin's extensive, well-groomed stable while the lads were doing up the horses after the second morning exercise. Arthur, the head lad, was crossing the yard with a bucket of oats when we climbed out of the little car, and the crinkling smile with which he usually greeted me got half-way to his eyes before he remembered. I saw the embarrassment take over and the welcome fade away.

'The guvnor isn't here,' he said awkwardly. 'He's gone to the races.'

'I know,' I said. 'Can I speak to Davey?'

Davey was the lad who looked after Shantytown.

'I suppose so,' said Arthur doubtfully, 'but you won't make no trouble?'

'No,' I said. 'No trouble. Where is he?'

'Fourth box from the end over that side,' he said, pointing. Tick-Tock and I walked over, and found Davey tossing and tidying the straw bed round a big chestnut, Shantytown. We leaned over the bottom half of the door, and watched Davey's expression too change from warmth to disgust. He was a short, tough, sixteen-year-old boy with flaming red hair and an intolerant mouth. He turned his back on us and ran his hand down the horse's neck. Then he spat into the straw. Tick-Tock took a sharp breath and his hands clenched into fists.

I said quickly, 'Davey, there's a quid for you if you feel like talking a bit.'

'What about?' he said, without turning round.

'About the day I rode Shantytown at Dunstable,' I said. 'Three weeks ago. Do you remember?'

'I'll say I remember,' he said offensively.

I ignored his tone. 'Well, tell me what happened from the moment you arrived on the course until I got up on Shantytown in the parade ring.'

'What the hell do you mean?' he said, wheeling round and coming over to the door. 'Nothing happened. What should happen?'

I took a pound note out of my wallet and gave it to him. He

looked at it for a second or two, then shrugged, and thrust it into his pocket.

'Start when you set off from here. Don't leave anything out,' I said.

'Are you off your nut?' he said.

'No,' I said, 'and I want my quid's worth.'

He shrugged again, but said, 'We went in the horse box from here to Dunstable, and . . .'

'Did you stop on the way?' I asked.

'Yes, Joe's Caff, same as always when we go to Dunstable.'

'Did you see anyone there you knew?'

'Well . . . Joe, and the girl who pours out the char.'

'No one you wouldn't expect?' I pressed.

'No, of course not. Like I said, we got to the course and unloaded the horses, two of them, in the stables there, and went and got another cuppa and a wad in the canteen, and then I went round the bookies, like, and put ten bob on Bloggs in the first, and went up on the stands and watched it get stuffed . . . sodding animal didn't try a yard . . . and then I went back to the stables and got Shantytown and put on his paddock clothing and led him out into the paddock . . .' His voice was bored as he recited the everyday racing routine of his job.

'Could anyone have given Shantytown anything to eat or drink in the stables, say a bucket of water just before the race?' I asked.

'Don't be so ruddy stupid. Of course not. Who ever heard of giving a horse anything to eat or drink before a race? A mouthful of water, I dare say, a couple of hours beforehand, but a bucketful . . .' The scorn in his voice suddenly changed to anger. 'Here, you're not suggesting I gave him a drink, are you? Oh no, mate, you're not putting the blame on me for the balls you made of it.'

'No,' I said, 'no, Davey. Calm down. How tight is the security on the Dunstable stables? Would anyone but a lad or a trainer get in there?'

'No,' he said, more moderately, 'it's as tight as a drum. The last gateman got sacked for letting an owner in alone without a trainer, and the new man's as pernickety as they come.'

'Go on, then,' I said. 'We've got you as far as the paddock.'

'Well, I walked the horse round the assembly ring for a bit, waiting for the guvnor to bring the saddle up from the weighing-room . . .' He smiled suddenly, as at some pleasant memory '. . . and then when he came I took Shanty into one of the saddling boxes and the guvnor saddled up, and then I took Shanty down into the parade ring and walked him round until they called me over and you got up on him.' He stopped. 'I can't see what you wanted to hear all that for.'

'What happened while you were walking round the assembly ring?' I asked. 'Something you enjoyed? Something you smile about when you remember it?'

He sniffed. 'It's nothing you'd want to know.'

I said, 'The quid was for telling everything.'

'Oh, very well then, but it's nothing to do with racing. It was that chap on the telly, Maurice Kemp-Lore, he came over and spoke to me and admired the horse. He said he was a friend of the owner, old man Ballerton. He patted Shanty and gave him a couple of sugar knobs, which I wasn't too keen on, mind, but you can't be narky with a chap like him, somehow, and he asked me what his chances were, and I said pretty good . . . more fool me . . . and then he went away again. That's all. I told you it wasn't anything to do with racing.'

'No,' I said. 'Well, never mind. Thanks for trying.'

I straightened up and turned away from the door, and Tick-Tock had taken a step or two towards the car when Davey said under his breath behind me, 'Trying . . . you two could both do a bit more of that yourselves, if you ask me.' But Tick-Tock fortunately didn't hear, and we folded ourselves back into the Mini-Cooper and drove unmourned out of the yard.

Tick-Tock exploded. 'Anyone would think you'd killed your mother and robbed your grandmother, the way they look at you. Losing your nerve isn't a crime.'

'Unless you can put up with a few harmless sneers you'd better get out at the next railway station,' I said cheerfully, having blessedly discovered in the last half-hour that they no longer hurt. 'And I haven't lost my nerve. Not yet, anyway.'

He opened his mouth and shut it again and nicked a glance at me, and drove another twenty miles without speaking.

We reached the next yard on my list shortly before one o'clock, and disturbed the well-to-do farmer, who trained his own horses, just as he was about to sit down to his lunch. When he opened the door to us a warm smell of stew and cabbage edged past him, and we could hear a clatter of saucepans in the kitchen. I had ridden several winners for him in the past two years before disgracing his best horse the previous week, and after he had got over the unpleasant shock of finding me on his doorstep, he asked us, in a friendly enough fashion, to go in for a drink. But I thanked him and refused, and asked where I could find the lad who looked after the horse in question. He came out to the gate with us and pointed to a house down the road.

We winkled the lad out of his digs and into the car, where I gave him a pound and invited him to describe in detail what had happened on the day I had ridden his horse. He was older, less intelligent and less truculent than Davey, but not much more willing. He didn't see no sense in it, he didn't. He said so, several times. Eventually I got him started, and then there was no stopping him. Detail I had asked for, and detail I got, solidly, for close on half an hour.

Sandwiched between stripping off the paddock clothing and buckling up the saddle came the news that Maurice Kemp-Lore had lounged into the saddling box, said some complimentary things to the farmer-owner about his horse, meanwhile feeding the animal some lumps of sugar, and had drifted away again leaving behind him the usual feeling of friendliness and pleasure.

'A proper corker, ain't he?' was how the lad put it.

I waited until he had reached the point when the farmer had given me a leg up on the horse, and then stopped him and thanked him for his efforts. We left him muttering that we were welcome, but he still didn't see the point.

'How odd,' said Tick-Tock pensively as we sped along the road to the next stable, eighty miles away. 'How odd that Maurice Kemp-Lore . . .' but he didn't finish the sentence; and nor did I.

Two hours later, in Kent, we listened, for another pound, to a gaunt boy of twenty telling us what a smashing fellow that Maurice Kemp-Lore was, how interested he'd been in the horse, how kind to give him some sugar, though it wasn't really allowed in his stables, but how could you tell a man like that not to, when he was being so friendly? The lad also treated us with a rather offensive superiority, but even Tick-Tock by now had become too interested to care.

'He drugged them,' he said flatly, after a long silence, turning on to the Maidstone by-pass. 'He drugged them to make it look as if you couldn't ride them . . . to make everyone believe you'd lost your nerve.'

'Yes,' I agreed.

'But it's impossible,' he protested vehemently. 'Why on earth should he? It can't be right. It must be a coincidence that he gave sugar to three horses you rode.'

'Maybe. We'll see,' I said.

And we did see. We went to the stables of every horse (other than James's) that I had ridden since Shantytown, talking to every lad concerned. And in every single case we heard that Maurice Kemp-Lore had made the lad's afternoon memorable (before I had blighted it) by admiring the way the lad had looked after his horse, and by offering those tempting lumps of sugar. It took us the whole of Saturday, and all Sunday morning, and we finished the last stable on my list on the edge of the Yorkshire moors at two o'clock in the afternoon. Only because I wanted my facts to be as cast-iron as possible had we gone so far north. Tick-Tock had become convinced in Northamptonshire.

I drove us back to our respective digs in Berkshire, and the following morning, Monday, I walked up to the Axminster stables to see James.

He had just come in from supervising the morning exercise, and the cold downland air had numbed his toes and fingers.

'Come into the office,' he said when he saw me waiting. His tone was neutral, but his protruding lower jaw was unrelenting. I followed him in, and he turned on an electric heater to warm his hands.

'I can't give you much to ride,' he said, with his back to me. 'All the owners have cried off, except one. You'd better look at this; it came this morning.' He stretched out his hand, picked up a paper from his desk, and held it out to me.

I took it. It was a letter from Lord Tirrold. It said,

Dear James,

Since our telephone conversation I have been thinking over our decision to replace Finn on Template next Saturday, and I now consider that we should reverse this and allow him to ride as originally planned. It is, I confess, at least as much for our sake as for his, since I do not want it said that I hurried to throw him out at the first possible moment, showing heartless ingratitude after his many wins on my horses. I am prepared for the disappointment of not winning the Midwinter and I apologize to you for robbing you of the chance of adding this prize to your total, but I would rather lose the race than the respect of the racing fraternity.

Yours ever, George.

I put the letter back on the desk.

'He doesn't need to worry,' I said thickly. 'Template will win.'

'Do you mean you aren't going to ride it?' said James, turning round quickly. There was a damaging note of eagerness in his voice, and he saw that I had heard it. 'I . . . I mean . . .' he tailed off.

'James,' I said, sitting down unasked in one of the battered armchairs. 'There are a few things I'd like you to know. First, however bad it looks, and whatever you believe, I have not lost my nerve. Second, every single horse I have ridden since that fall three weeks ago has been doped. Not enough to be very noticeable, just enough to make it run like a slug. Third, the dope has been given to all the horses on sugar lumps. I should think it was some form of sleeping draught, but I've no way of knowing for sure.' I stopped abruptly.

James stood looking at me with his mouth open, the prominent lower teeth bared to the gums as his lip dropped in shocked disbelief.

I said, 'Before you conclude that I am out of my mind, do me the favour of calling in one of the lads, and listening to what he has to say.'

James shut his mouth with a snap. 'Which lad?'

'It doesn't really matter. Any of them whose horse I have ridden in the last three weeks.'

He paused dubiously, but finally went to the door and shouted for someone to find Eddie, the lad who looked after Hugo's big chestnut. In less than a minute the boy arrived, out of breath, and with his curly hair sticking up in an uncombed halo.

James gave me no chance to do the questioning. He said brusquely to Eddie, 'When did you last talk to Rob?'

The boy looked scared and began to stutter, 'N-not since l-l-last week.'

'Since last Friday?' That was the day James himself had last seen me.

'No sir.'

'Very well, then. You remember the big chestnut running badly last Wednesday week?'

'Yes sir.' Eddie treated me to a scornful glance.

'Did anyone give the chestnut a lump of sugar before the race?' There was now only interest to be heard in James's voice: the severity was masked.

'Yes sir,' said Eddie eagerly. The familiar remembering smile appeared on his grubby face, and I breathed an inward sigh of bottomless relief.

'Who was it?'

'Maurice Kemp-Lore, sir. He said how splendidly I looked after my horses, sir. He was leaning over the rails of the assembly ring and he spoke to me as I was going past. So I stopped, and he was ever so nice. He gave the chestnut some sugar, sir, but I didn't think it would matter as Mr Hugo is always sending sugar for him anyway.'

'Thank you, Eddie,' said James, rather faintly. 'No matter about the sugar . . . run along, now.'

Eddie went. James looked at me blankly. The loud clock ticked.

Presently I said, 'I've spent the last two days talking to the lads of all the horses I've ridden for other stables since I had that fall. Every one of them told me that Maurice Kemp-Lore gave the horse some lumps of sugar before I rode it. Ingersoll came with me. He heard them too. You've only to ask him if you can't believe it from me.'

'Maurice never goes near horses at the races,' James protested, 'or anywhere else for that matter.'

'That's precisely what helped me to understand what was happening,' I said. 'I talked to Kemp-Lore on the stands at Dunstable just after Shantytown and two other horses had run hopelessly for me, and he was wheezing quite audibly. He had asthma. Which meant that he had recently been very close to horses. I didn't give it a thought at the time, but it means a packet to me now.'

'But Maurice . . .' he repeated, unbelievingly. 'It's just not possible.'

'It is, however, possible,' I said, more coldly than I had any right to, having believed it myself for twelve awful hours, 'for me to fall apart from a small spot of concussion?'

'I don't know what to think,' he said uncomfortably. There was a pause. There were two things I wanted James to do to help me: but in view of his ingrained disinclination to do favours for anyone, I did not think my requests would be very enthusiastically received. However, if I didn't ask, I wouldn't get.

I said slowly, persuasively, as if the thought had just occurred to me, 'Let me ride a horse for you . . . one of your own, if the owners won't have me . . . and see for yourself if Kemp-Lore tries to give it sugar. Perhaps you could stick with the horse yourself, all the time? And if he comes up with his sugar lumps, maybe you could manage to knock them out of his hand before the horse eats them. Perhaps you could pick them up yourself and put them in your pocket, and give the horse some sugar lumps of your own instead? Then we would see how the horse runs.'

It was too much trouble; his face showed it. He said, 'That's too fantastic. I can't do things like that.'

'It's simple,' I said mildly, 'you've only to bump his arm.'

'No,' he said, but not obstinately. A hopeful no, to my ears. I didn't press him, knowing from experience that he would irrevocably stick in his toes if urged too vehemently to do anything he did not want to.

I said instead, 'Aren't you friendly with that man who arranges the regular dope tests at the races?' One or two spot checks were taken at every meeting, mainly to deter trainers of doubtful reputation from pepping up or slowing down their horses with drugs. At the beginning of each afternoon the stewards decided which horses to test – for example, the winner of the second race, and the favourite in the fourth race (especially if he was beaten). No one, not even the stewards, always knew in advance exactly which horses would have their saliva taken, and the value of the whole system lay in this uncertainty.

James followed my thoughts. 'You mean, will I ask him if any of the horses you have ridden since your fall have been tested for dope in the normal course of events?'

'Yes,' I agreed. 'Could you possibly do that?'

'Yes, I'll do that,' he said. 'I will ring him up. But if any of them have been tested and proved negative, you do realize that it will dispose of your wild accusations absolutely?'

'I do,' I agreed. 'Actually, I've ridden so many beaten favourites that I can't think why such systematic doping has not already been discovered.'

'You really do believe it, don't you?' said James, wonderingly.

'Yes,' I said, getting up and going to the door. 'Yes, I believe it. And so will you, James.'

But he shook his head, and I left him staring frozen-faced out of the window, the incredible nature of what I had said to him still losing the battle against his own personal knowledge of Kemp-Lore. James liked the man.

Ten

LATE THAT Monday evening James rang me up at my digs and told me that I could ride his own horse, Turniptop, which was due to run in the novice 'chase at Stratford-on-Avon on the following Thursday. I began to thank him, but he interrupted, 'I'm doing you no favour. You know it won't win. He's never been over fences, only hurdles, and all I want is for you to give him an easy race round, getting used to the bigger obstacles. All right?'

'Yes,' I said. 'All right.' And he rang off. There was no mention of whether he would or would not contemplate juggling with sugar knobs.

I was tired. I had spent the whole day driving to Devon and back to visit Art Mathews's beautiful widow, the ice maiden. A fruitless journey. She had been as chilly as ever. Widowhood had warmed her no more than wifehood had done. Blonde, well-bred and cold, she had answered my questions calmly and incuriously and with a complete lack of interest. Art had been dead four months. She spoke of him as though she could hardly remember what he had looked like. No, she did not know exactly why Art had quarrelled so continuously with Corin. No, she did not know why Art had thought fit to shoot himself. No, Art had not got on well with Mr John Ballerton, but she did not know why. Yes, Art had once appeared on television on *Turf Talk*. It had not been a success, she said, the shadow of an old grievance sharpening her voice. Art had been made to look a

135

fool. Art, whose meticulous sense of honour and order had earned him only respect on the racecourse, had been made to look a cantankerous, mean-minded fool. No, she could not remember exactly how it had been done, but she did remember, only too well, the effect it had had on her own family and friends. They had, it appeared, loudly pitied her on her choice of husband.

But I, listening to her, inwardly pitied poor dead Art on his choice of wife.

On the following day, Tuesday, I again appropriated the Mini-Cooper, much to Tick-Tock's disgust. This time I went towards Cheltenham, and called at Peter Cloony's neat, new bungalow, turning down the narrow, winding lane from the high main road to the village in the hollow.

Peter's wife opened the door to me and asked me in with a strained smile. She no longer looked happy and rosily content. She was too thin, and her hair hung straight and wispy round her neck. It was very nearly as cold inside the house as it was outside, and she wore some tattered fur boots, thick stockings, bulky clothes, and gloves. With no lipstick and no life in her eyes, she was almost unrecognizable as the loving girl who had put me up for the night four months ago.

'Come in,' she said, 'but I'm afraid Peter isn't here. He was given a lift to Birmingham races . . . perhaps he'll get a spare ride . . .' She spoke without hope.

'Of course he will,' I said. 'He's a good jockey.'

'The trainers don't seem to think so,' she said despairingly. 'Ever since he lost his regular job, he's barely had one ride a week. We can't live on it, how could we? If things don't change very soon, he's going to give up racing and try something else. But he only cares for horses and racing . . . it will break his heart if he has to leave it.'

She had taken me into the sitting-room. It was as bare as before. Barer. The rented television set had gone. In its place stood a baby's cot, a wickerwork basket affair on a metal stand. I went over and looked down at the tiny baby, only a small bump under the mound of blankets. He was asleep. I made admiring remarks about what I could see of him, and his mother's face momentarily livened up with pleasure.

She insisted on making us a cup of tea, and I had to wait until the question of no milk, no sugar, no biscuits had all been settled before asking her what I really wanted to know.

I said, 'That Jaguar – the one which blocked the lane and made Peter late – who did it belong to?'

'We don't know,' she said. 'It was very odd. No one came to move it away and it stayed across the lane all that morning. In the end the police arranged for it to be towed away. I know Peter asked the police who owned it, because he wanted to tell the man just what his filthy Jaguar had cost him, but they said they hadn't yet traced him.'

'You don't happen to know where the Jaguar is now?' I asked.

'I don't know if it is still there,' she said, 'but it used to be outside the big garage beside Timberley Station. They're the only garage round here with a breakdown truck, and they were the ones who towed it away.'

I thanked her and stood up, and she came out to the car with me to say goodbye. I had spent some time going through the form book adding up the number of races Peter had ridden during the past few weeks, and I knew how little he had earned. I had brought with me a big box of groceries, butter, eggs, cheese and so on, and a stack of tins, and also a string of plastic ducks for the baby. This collection I carried back into the bungalow and dumped on the kitchen table, ignoring her surprised protest as she followed me in.

I grinned. 'They are too heavy to take back. You'll have to make the best of it.'

She began to cry.

'Cheer up,' I said, 'things will get better soon. But meanwhile, don't you think the bungalow is too cold for a baby? I read somewhere that some babies die every winter from breathing freezing air, even though they may be as warmly wrapped up as yours is.'

She looked at me aghast, tears trickling down her cheeks.

'You ought to heat that room a little, and especially keep it warm all night too, if he sleeps in there,' I said.

'But I can't,' she said jerkily, 'the payments on the bungalow take nearly all we have . . . we can't afford a fire, except just in the evenings. Is it really true about babies dying?'

She was frightened.

'Yes, quite true,' I said. I took a sealed envelope out of my pocket and gave it to her. 'This is a present for the baby. Warmth. It's not a fortune, but it will pay your electricity bills for a while, and buy some coal if you want it. There's likely to be a lot of cold weather coming, so you must promise to spend most of it on keeping warm.'

'I promise,' she said faintly.

'Good.' I smiled at her as she wiped her eyes, and I went back to the car and drove away up the lane.

The garage at Timberley Station was a modernized affair with the front all snowy plaster and the back, when I walked round there, of badly pointed cheap brickwork. The elderly abandoned Jaguar stood there, tucked away between the burnt-out remains of a Standard 8 and a pile of old tyres. I went back to the front of the garage to talk to the man in charge, and I asked him if I could buy the car.

'Sorry, sir, no can do,' he said breezily. He was a dapper thirtyish man with no oil on his hands.

'Why not?' I said. 'It doesn't look good for anything but the scrap heap.'

'I can't sell it to you because I don't know who it belongs to,' he said regretfully, 'but,' he brightened, 'it's been here so long now that it might be mine after all . . . like unclaimed lost property. I'll ask the police.'

With a bit of prompting he told me all about the Jaguar being stuck across the lane and how his firm had fetched it.

I said, 'But someone must have seen the driver after he left the car?'

'The police think he must have got a lift, and then decided the car wasn't worth coming back for. But it's in good enough order. And it wasn't hot . . . stolen, I mean.'

'What's it worth?' I asked.

'To you, sir,' he smiled glossily, 'I'd have let it go for a hundred pounds.'

A hundred. I parted from him and strolled out on to the forecourt. Was it worth a hundred to Kemp-Lore I wondered, to ruin Peter Cloony? Was his obsessive hatred of jockeys so fierce? But then a hundred to Kemp-Lore, I reflected, was probably a lot less than a hundred to me.

Timberley railway station (six stopping trains a day and twenty-two expresses) lay on my left. I stood and considered it. The station was nearly four miles from the top of the lane leading to Peter's village; say an hour's quick walk. Peter had found the Jaguar across the lane at eleven o'clock, and it had to have been jammed in position only seconds before he came up the hill, as his had been the first car to be obstructed. I had a vivid mental picture of Kemp-Lore parked in the gateway where the lane began to curve downwards, watching Peter's house through binoculars, seeing him go out and get into his car and start on his way to the races. There wouldn't have been much time to force the Jaguar into position, lock its door and disappear before Peter got there. Not much time: but enough.

And then? The one tremendous disadvantage Kemp-Lore had to overcome, I thought, was his own fame. His face was so well known to almost the entire British population that he could not hope to move about the country inconspicuously, and wherever he went he would be noticed and remembered. Surely, I thought, in this sparsely populated area, it should be possible to find someone who had seen him.

As I was there anyway, I started with the station. Outside, I looked up the times of the stopping trains. There was, I found, a down train at twelve-thirty but no up train until five o'clock. The only other trains ran early in the morning and later in the evening. The booking office was shut. I found the clerk-ticket-collector-porter nodding over a hot stove and a racing paper in the parcels office. A large basket of hens squawked noisily in a corner as I walked in, and he woke with a jerk and told me the next train was due in one hour and ten minutes.

I got him talking via the racing news, but there was nothing to learn. Maurice Kemp-Lore had never (more's the pity he said) caught a train at Timberley. If it had happened when he was off-duty, he'd have heard about it all right. And yes, he said, he'd been on duty the day they'd fetched the Jaguar down to the garage. Disgusting that. Shouldn't be allowed, people being rich enough to chuck their old cars in the ditch like cigarette ends.

I asked him if the station had been busy that day: if there had been a lot of passengers catching the midday train.

'A lot of passengers?' he repeated scornfully. 'Never more than three or four, excepting Cheltenham race days . . .'

'I was just wondering,' I said idly, 'whether the chap who left his Jaguar behind could have caught a train from here that morning?'

'Not from here, he didn't,' the railway man said positively. 'Because, same as usual, all the people who caught the train were ladies.'

'Ladies?'

'Yeh, women. Shopping in Cheltenham. We haven't had a man catch the midday – excepting race days of course – since young Simpkins from the garage got sent home with chicken-pox last summer. Bit of a joke it is round here, see, the midday.'

I gave him a hot tip for Birmingham that afternoon (which won, I was glad to see later) and left him busily putting a call through to his bookmaker on the government's telephone bill.

Timberley village pub, nearly empty, had never been stirred, they told me regretfully, by the flashing presence of Maurice Kemp-Lore.

The two transport cafés along the main road hadn't heard of any of their chaps giving him a lift.

None of the garages within ten miles had seen him ever.

The local taxi service had never driven him. He had never caught a bus on the country route.

It wasn't hard at each place to work conversation round to Kemp-Lore, but it was never quick. By the time a friendly bus conductor had told me, over a cigarette at the Cheltenham ter-minus, that none of his mates had ever had such a famous man on board because they'd never have kept quiet about it (look how Bill went on for days and days when Dennis Compton took a tenpenny single), it was seven o'clock in the evening.

If I hadn't been so utterly, unreasonably sure that it was Kemp-Lore who had abandoned the Jaguar, I would have admitted that if no one had seen him, then he hadn't been there. As it was, I was depressed by the failure of my search, but not convinced that there was nothing to search for.

The army tank carrier that had blocked Peter's and my way to Cheltenham was there accidentally: that much was clear. But Peter had got into such trouble for being late that a weapon was put straight into the hand of his enemy. He had only to make Peter late again, and to spread his little rumours, and the deed was done. No confidence, no rides, no career for Cloony.

I found I still hoped by perseverance to dig something up, so I booked a room in a hotel in Cheltenham, and spent the evening in a cinema to take my mind off food. On the telephone

Tick-Tock sounded more resigned than angry to hear that he would be car-less yet again. He asked how I was getting on, and when I reported no progress, he said, 'If you're right about our friend, he's as sly and cunning as all get out. You won't find his tracks too easily.'

Without much hope I went down in the morning to the Cheltenham railway station and sorted out, after a little difficulty with old time-sheets and the passing of a pound note, the man who had collected the tickets from the passengers on the stopping train from Timberley on the day the Jaguar was abandoned.

He was willing enough, but he too had never seen Kemp-Lore, except on television; though he hesitated while he said so.

'What is it?' I asked.

'Well, sir, I've never seen him, but I think I've seen his sister.'

'What was she like?' I asked.

'Very like him, of course, sir, or I wouldn't have known who she was. And she had riding clothes on. You know – jodhpurs, I think they're called. And a scarf over her head. Pretty she looked, very pretty. I couldn't think who she was for a bit, and then it came to me, afterwards like. I didn't talk to her, see? I just took her ticket when she went through the barrier, that's all. I remember taking her ticket.'

'When was it that you saw her?' I asked.

'Oh, I couldn't say. I don't rightly know when it was. Before Christmas though, some time before Christmas, I'm certain of that.'

He flipped the pound I gave him expertly into an inner pocket. 'Thank you, sir, thank you indeed,' he said.

I dressed and shaved with particular care on the Thursday morning as, I supposed, a sort of barrier against the reception I knew I was going to meet. It was six days since I had been racing, six days in which my shortcomings and the shreds of my riding reputation would have been brought up, pawed over and discarded. Life moved fast in the changing-room; today was important, tomorrow more so; but yesterday was dead. I belonged to yesterday. I was ancient news.

Even my valet was surprised to see me, although I had written to say I was coming.

'You are riding today then?' he said. 'I was wondering if you wanted to sell your saddle . . . there's a boy just starting who needs one.'

'I'll keep it a bit longer,' I said. 'I'm riding Turniptop in the fourth. Mr Axminster's colours.'

It was a strange day. As I no longer felt that I deserved the pitying glances to which I was treated, I found that they had, to a great extent, ceased to trouble me, and I even watched with fair equanimity the success of two of my ex-mounts in the first two races. The only thing I worried about was whether or not James would have both sugar lumps in his pocket and willingness in his heart.

He was so busy with his other runners that I did not exchange more than a few words with him during the first part of the afternoon, and when I went out into the parade ring to join him for Turniptop's race, he was standing alone, thoughtfully gazing into the distance.

'Maurice Kemp-Lore's here,' he said abruptly.

'Yes, I know,' I said. 'I saw him.'

'He has given sugar to several horses already.'

'What?' I exclaimed.

'I have asked quite a few people . . . Maurice has been feeding sugar to any number of horses during the past few weeks, not only to the ones you have ridden.'

'Oh,' I said weakly. Cunning as all get out, Tick-Tock had said.

'None of the horses you rode were picked for the regulation

dope test,' said James, 'but some of the other horses Maurice gave sugar to were tested. All negative.'

'He only gave doped sugar to my mounts. The rest were camouflage, and he was damn lucky that the horses I rode weren't tested,' I said. It sounded improbable, but I was sure of it.

James shook his head.

'Did you . . ?' I began without much hope. 'Did he . . . Kemp-Lore . . . try to give Turniptop any sugar?'

James compressed his lips and stared into the middle distance. I positively held my breath.

'He did come into the saddling box,' he said grudgingly. 'He admired the horse's coat.'

Turniptop ambled past glowing with good health, but before James could say any more one of the stewards came over to talk to him, and I had no chance to find out about the sugar before it was time to mount and go out for the race.

I knew by the second fence that whether Kemp-Lore had fed him sugar or not, Turniptop was not doped. The leaden sluggishness which had afflicted my last twenty-eight mounts and which I had been forced to believe was due to my own deficiency had lifted like a spent thundercloud.

Turniptop leapt and sprang and surged, pulling like a train and doing his damnedest to run away with me. I could have shouted aloud with relief. He was an untidy jumper with more enthusiasm than judgement, a style which had brought him no especial grief over hurdles; but now, in his first steeplechase, he showed signs of treating fences with the same disrespect. It wouldn't really do; there's a world of difference between a single-thickness, easily knocked-down hurdle and a three-foot-wide fence, solidly built of birch twigs, particularly when an open ditch lies in front of it. But Turniptop did not want to be steadied. He was eager. He was rash.

With things as they were, and with James to be convinced,

I must admit that my mood matched Turniptop's exactly. We infected each other with recklessness. We took some indefensible risks, and we got away with them.

I kept him continually on the rails, squeezing forward into tiny openings and letting him take all the bumps that came his way. When he met a fence dead right he gained lengths over it, and when he met one wrong he scrambled through and found a foot to land on somehow. It was more like a roller-coaster ride than the sensible, well-judged race James had indicated, but it taught the tough-minded Turniptop just as much about getting himself out of trouble as going round quietly on the outside would have done.

Coming into the second-to-last fence, I was afraid we would win. Afraid, because I knew James wanted to sell the horse and if he had already won a novice 'chase he would not be as valuable as if he had not. An apparent paradox: but Turniptop, young and still green, showed great promise. Too early a win would disqualify him from entering a string of good novice 'chases in the following season.

It would be far, far better, I knew, to come second. To have shown what he could do but not actually to have won would have put hundreds on his value. But we had run too fierce a race, and at the second-last the disaster of winning seemed unavoidable. There was only one other tiring horse alongside, and I could hear no others on my tail.

Turniptop rose, or rather fell to the occasion. In spite of my urging him to put in another stride, he took off far too soon and landed with his hind feet tangled hopelessly in the birch. His forelegs buckled under the strain and he went down on to his knees, with my chin resting on his right ear and my hands touching each other round his throat. Even then his indomitable sense of balance rescued him, and he staggered back on to his feet with a terrific upthrust of his shoulders, tipping me back into the saddle, and, tossing his head as if in disgust, he set off again towards the winning-post. The horse which had been alongside was now safely ahead, and two that had been behind me had jumped past, so that we came into the last fence in fourth position.

I had lost my irons in the débâcle and couldn't get my feet into them again in time to jump, so we went over the last with them dangling and clanking in the air. I collected him together and squeezed with my legs, and Turniptop, game to the end, accelerated past two of the horses ahead and flashed into second place four strides from the post.

James waited for me to dismount in the unsaddling enclosure with a face from which all expression had studiously been wiped. Poker-faced to match, I slid from the saddle.

'Don't ever ride a race like that for me again,' he said.

'No,' I agreed. I undid the girth buckles and took my saddle over my arm, and at last looked into his eyes.

They gleamed, narrowed and inscrutable. He said, 'You proved your point. But you could have killed my horse doing it.'

I said nothing.

'And yourself,' he added, implying that that was less important.

I shook my head, smiling faintly. 'Not a chance,' I said.

'H'm.' He gave me a hard stare. 'You'd better come up to the stable this evening,' he said. 'We can't talk about . . . what we have to talk about . . . here. There are too many people about.'

As if to punctuate this remark the owner of the winner leant over the dividing rails to admire Turniptop and I had to loop up the girths and go and weigh in, still without knowing exactly what had happened in the saddling box before the race.

Tick-Tock was standing by my peg in the changing-room, one smoothly shod foot up on the bench and the Tyrolean hat pushed back on his head.

'Before you ride like that again, you might make a will leaving me your half of the car,' he said. 'It would solve so many legal complications.'

'Oh, shut up,' I said, peeling off first the crimson and white sweater, James's colours, and then the thin brown jersey underneath. I took a towel from the valet and went along to the washbasin.

'A lot of people,' said Tick-Tock in a loud voice across the room, 'are going to have a fine old time eating their words, and I hope it gives them indigestion.' He followed me along and watched me wash, leaning languidly against the wall. 'I suppose you realize that your exploits this afternoon were clearly visible to several million assorted housewives, invalids, babes in arms, and people hanging about on the pavement outside electric shops?'

'What?' I exclaimed.

'It's a fact. Didn't you really know? The last three races are filling up the spare time between *Sex for Sixth Forms* and *Goggle with Granny*. Universal T. C. Maurice's lot. I wonder,' he finished more soberly, 'what he'll do when he knows you've rumbled the sugar bit?'

'He may not know,' I said, towelling my chest and shoulders. 'He may think it was accidental . . . I haven't heard yet from James what happened before the race.'

'Anyway,' said Tick-Tock confidently, 'his campaign against you is over. He won't risk going on with it after today.'

I agreed with him. It just shows how little either of us understood about obsession.

James was waiting for me in the office, busy with papers at his big desk. The fire blazed hotly and the light winked on the glasses standing ready beside the whisky bottle.

He stopped writing when I went in, and got up and poured our drinks, and stood towering above me as I sat in the battered armchair by the fire. His strong heavy face looked worried.

'I apologize,' he said abruptly.

'Don't,' I said. 'No need.'

'I very nearly let Maurice give Turniptop that damned sugar,' he said. 'I couldn't believe him capable of a scheme as fantastic as doping every horse you ride. I mean, it's . . . it's ridiculous.'

'What happened in the saddling box?' I asked.

He took a sip from his glass. 'I gave Sid instructions that no one, absolutely no one, however important they were, was to give Turniptop anything to eat or drink before the race. When I reached the box with your saddle, Maurice was in the box next door and I watched him giving the horse there some sugar. Sid said no one had given Turniptop anything.' He paused and drank again. 'I put on your number cloth, weight pad and saddle, and began to do up the girths. Maurice came round the partition from the next box and said hello. That infectious smile of his . . . I found myself smiling back and thinking you were mad. He was wheezing a bit with asthma . . . and he put his hand in his pocket and brought out three lumps of sugar. He did it naturally, casually, and held them out to Turniptop. I had my hands full of girths and I thought you were wrong . . . but . . . I don't know . . . there was something in the way he was stand-ing, with his arm stretched out rather stiffly and the sugar flat on the palm of his hand, that didn't look right. People who are fond of horses stroke their muzzles when they give them sugar, they don't stand as far away as possible. And if Maurice wasn't fond of horses, why was he giving them sugar? Anyway, I did decide suddenly that there would be no harm done if Turniptop didn't eat that sugar, so I dropped the girths and pretended to trip, and grabbed Maurice's arm to steady myself. The sugar fell off his hand on to the straw on the ground and I stepped on it as if by accident while I was recovering my balance.'

'What did he say?' I asked, fascinated.

'Nothing,' said James. 'I apologized for bumping into him, but he didn't answer. Just for a second he looked absolutely furious. Then he smiled again, and . . .' James's eyes glinted, '. . . he said how much he admired me for giving poor Finn this one last chance.'

'Dear of him,' I murmured.

'I told him it wasn't exactly your last chance. I said you would be riding Template on Saturday as well. He just said "Oh really?", and wished me luck and walked away.'

'So the sugar was crunched up and swept out with the dirty straw,' I said.

'Yes,' he agreed.

'Nothing to analyse. No evidence.' A nuisance.

'If I hadn't stepped on it, Maurice could have picked it up and offered it to Turniptop again. I hadn't taken any sugar with me . . . I hadn't any lumps to substitute . . . I didn't believe I would need them.'

He hadn't intended to bother, I knew. But he had bothered. I would never stop feeling grateful.

We drank our whisky. James said suddenly, 'Why? I don't understand why he should have gone to such lengths to discredit you. What has he got against you?'

'I am a jockey, and he is not,' I said flatly. 'That's all.' I told about my visit to Claudius Mellit and the answers he had given me. I said, 'It's no coincidence that you and most other trainers have had trouble finding and keeping a jockey. You've all been swayed by Kemp-Lore, either by him directly, or through those two shadows of his, Ballerton and Corin Kellar, who soak up his poison like sponges and drip it out into every receptive ear. They've said it all to you. You repeated it to me yourself, not so long ago. Peter Cloony is always late, Tick-Tock doesn't try, Danny Higgs bets too heavily, Grant sold information, Finn has lost his nerve . . .'

He stared at me, appalled. I said, 'You believed it all, James, didn't you? Even you? And so did everyone else. Why shouldn't they, with so much evident foundation for the rumours? It doesn't take much for an owner or a trainer to lose confidence in a jockey. The thought has only to be insinuated, however fleetingly, that a jockey is habitually late, or dishonest, or afraid, and very soon, very soon indeed, he is on his way out . . . Art. Art killed himself because Corin sacked him. Grant had a mental breakdown. Peter Cloony is so broke his wife was starving herself in a freezing cold house. Tick-Tock makes jokes like Pagliacci . . .'

'And you?' asked James.

'I? Well . . . I haven't exactly enjoyed the last three weeks.'

'No,' he said, as if thinking about it from my point of view for the first time. 'No, I don't suppose you have.'

'It's been so calculated, this destruction of jockeys,' I said. 'Every week in *Turf Talk*, looking back on it, there has been some damaging reference to one jockey or another. When he had me on the programme he introduced me as an unsuccessful rider, and he meant me to stay that way. Do you remember that ghastly bit of film he showed of me? You'd never have taken me on if you'd seen that before I'd ridden for you, would you?'

He shook his head, very troubled.

I went on, 'On every possible occasion – when Template won the King 'Chase for instance – he has reminded everyone watching on television that I am only substituting for Pip, and that I'll be out on my ear as soon as that broken leg is strong again. Fair enough, it's Pip's job and he should have it back, but that patronizing note in Kemp-Lore's voice was calculated to make everyone take it for granted that my brief spell in the limelight was thoroughly undeserved. I dare say it was, too. But I think a lot of your owners would have been readier to trust your judgement in engaging me, and less quick to chuck me overboard at the first sign of trouble, if it hadn't been for the continual deflating pin-pricks Kemp-Lore had dealt out all round. And last Friday . . .' I tried, not too successfully, to keep my voice evenly conversational. 'Last Friday he led Corin and that handicapper on until they said straight out that I was finished. Were you watching?'

James nodded, and poured us another drink.

'It's a matter for the National Hunt Committee,' he said firmly.

'No,' I said. 'His father is a member of it.'

James gasped sharply. 'I had forgotten . . .'

I said, 'The whole Committee's a stronghold of pro-Kemp-Lore feeling. They're all sold on Maurice. Most of them wear the same old school tie,' I grinned. James wore it too. 'I would be very glad if you would say nothing to any of them, just yet. They would take even more convincing than you did, and there aren't any facts that Kemp-Lore couldn't explain away. But I'm digging.' I drank. 'The day will come.'

'You sound unexpectedly cheerful,' he said.

'O God, James.' I stood up abruptly. 'I wanted to kill myself last week. I'm glad I didn't. It makes me cheerful.'

He looked so startled that I relaxed and laughed, and put down my glass. 'Never mind,' I said, 'but you must understand I don't think the National Hunt Committee meets the case at the moment. Too gentlemanly. I favour something more in the biter-bit line for dear Maurice.'

But I had as yet no useful plan, and dear Maurice still had his teeth, and they were sharp.

Eleven

ALTHOUGH NEITHER Tick-Tock nor I had any rides the next day I pinched the car from him to go to the meeting at Ascot, and walked round the course to get the feel of the turf. There was a bitterly cold north-east wind blowing across the heath and the ground was hard with a touch of frost in the more exposed patches. It had been a surprisingly mild winter so far, but the high clear sky spoke ominously of ice to come. One more day, that was all I asked; only one more day. But prodding the earth on the landing side of the water jump with my heel I felt it jar instead of give.

I finished the circuit, planning the race in my mind as I went. If the ground remained firm it would be a fast-run affair, but that suited Template well, especially with top weight to carry. Lugging packets of lead around in the mud was not what his lean streamlined frame was best fitted for.

Outside the weighing-room Peter Cloony stopped me. His face was white and thin and mournful, and lines were developing on his forehead.

'I'll pay you back,' he said, almost belligerently. He seemed prepared to argue about it.

'All right. One day. No hurry,' I said mildly.

'You shouldn't have gone behind my back and given my wife that money and the food. I wanted to send it back at once but she won't let me. We don't need charity. I don't approve of it.'

'You're a fool, Peter,' I said. 'Your wife was right to accept what I gave her, and I'd have thought her a stubborn ass if she hadn't. And you'd better get used to the idea: a box of groceries will be delivered to your house every week until you're earning a decent screw again.'

'No,' he almost shouted, 'I won't have it.'

'I don't see why your wife and baby should suffer because of your misplaced pride,' I said. 'But if it will ease your conscience, I'll tell you why I'm doing it. You'll never get much work as long as you go around with that hang-dog expression. Looking weak and miserable isn't going to persuade anybody to employ you. You need to cheer up, get fit again, and prove you're worth having. Well – all I'm doing is removing one of your worries so that you can think a bit more about racing and a bit less about your cold house and empty larder. So now you can get on with it . . . it's all up to you. And don't ever even risk being late.'

I walked off and left Peter standing with his mouth open and his eyebrows half-way to his hair.

What Kemp-Lore had pulled down, I could try to rebuild, I thought. When I had arrived I had seen him in the distance, talking animatedly to one of the stewards, who was laughing. Slim, vital and wholesome-looking, he seemed to attract the light of the day on to his fair head.

In the weighing-room after the fourth race I was handed a telegram. It said, 'Pick me up White Bear, Uxbridge, 6.30 p.m. Important, Ingersoll.' I felt like cursing Tick-Tock soundly because Uxbridge was in the opposite direction from home. But the car was half his, after all, and I'd had more than my fair share of it during the past week.

The afternoon dragged. I hated having to watch, hated it even more after my reassuring ride on Turniptop, but I tried to take my own advice to Peter and look cheerful: and I was rewarded, as time went on, with a definite thawing of the cold shoulder. It made life much easier not finding everyone still too embarrassed to speak to me; but I was also in no doubt that most final judgements were being reserved until after Template's race. I didn't mind that. I was confident that he was the fastest 'chaser in training and I had James's promise that he would be guarded every second against being doped.

I dawdled after racing ended, with two hours to kill before turning up at Uxbridge to collect Tick-Tock. I watched the men from Universal Telecast erecting their scaffolding towers, ready to televise the Midwinter the next day, and recognized a man directing them as Gordon Kildare, still in navy-blue pinstripe suiting and still looking like a rising young executive who knew the score. He passed by me with the practised half smile which from a man of his sort always means that he doesn't know who he's smiling at, but smiles all the same in case he should later find out it was someone important. However, he had only gone two steps past me when he turned and came back.

'We've had you on the programme,' he said pleasantly. 'No don't tell me . . .' His brow furrowed; then he snapped his fingers. 'Finn, that's it, Finn.' But his smile at the triumph of his memory began ludicrously to slip and I knew he was also remembering what had been said about me on his programme a week ago.

'Yes, Finn,' I said, taking no notice. 'All set for tomorrow?'

'Eh, oh, yes. Busy day. Well now, I'm sorry to have to rush off but you know how it is . . . we've got the programme to put out tonight and I'm due back in the studios. Maurice went ages ago.'

He looked at his watch, gave me a noncommittal smile, and gracefully retreated.

I watched him drive off in the latest streamlined Ford, picturing the studio he was going to; the ranks of cameras, the dazzling lights, the plates of sandwiches; they would all be the same. And who, I wondered, who was to be Kemp-Lore's victim this evening? For whom was the chopper poised, the false charm ready?

There was so little I could do against him. Pick up some of the pieces, start some counter rumours? Try to undermine his influence? All that, yes. But I didn't have his sparkle, nor his prestige, nor yet his ruthlessness. I thrust my hands into my pockets, went out to the Mini-Cooper, and drove off to fetch Tick-Tock.

Mine was only the second car in the dark park beside the White Bear. It was one of those disappointing pubs built of tidy pinkish bricks with cold lighting inside and no atmosphere. The saloon bar was empty. The public bar held only a droopy-moustached old man pursing his lips to the evening's first half-pint. I went back to the saloon bar and ordered a whisky. No Tick-Tock. I looked at my watch. Twenty to seven.

The green plastic seats round the walls were so inhospitable that I didn't wonder the pub was empty. The dark-green curtains didn't help. Nor the fluorescent strip-lights on the ceiling.

I looked at my watch again.

'Are you by any chance waiting for someone, sir?' asked the characterless barman.

'Yes, I am,' I said.

'You wouldn't be a Mr Finn?'

'Yes.'

'Then I've a message for you, sir. A Mr Ingersoll telephoned just now and said he couldn't get here to meet you, sir, and he was very sorry but could you go and pick him up from the station at six fifty-five. The station is just down the road, first turning left and straight on for half a mile.'

Finishing my drink, I thanked the barman and went out to the car. I climbed into the driving seat and stretched my hand out to turn on the lights and the ignition. I stretched out my hand . . . but I didn't reach the lights.

My neck was gripped violently from behind.

There was movement then in the back of the car as the arms

shifted to get a better leverage, a rustling of clothes and the scrape of shoe across the thin carpet.

I flung up my hands and clawed but I couldn't reach the face of whoever was behind me, and my nails were useless against his gloves. Thick leather gloves. The fingers inside them were strong, and what was worse, they knew exactly where to dig in and press, each side of the neck, just above the collarbone, where the carotid arteries branched upwards. Pressure on one carotid, I remembered wildly from some distant first-aid course, stops arterial bleeding from the head . . . but pressure on both at once blocked all blood supplies to the brain.

I hadn't a chance. My struggles were hampered by the steering wheel and gained me nothing. In the few seconds before a roaring blackness took me off, I had time for only two more thoughts. First that I should have known that Tick-Tock would never meet me in a dreary pub like that. Secondly, angrily, that I was dead.

I couldn't have been out very long, but it was long enough. When consciousness slowly and fuzzily returned, I found I could open neither my eyes nor my mouth. Both were covered with sticking plaster. My wrists were tied together, and my ankles, when I tried to move them, would only part a foot or two: they were hobbled together, like a gipsy's pony.

I was lying on my side, awkwardly doubled up, on the floor in the back of a car which, from the size and smell and feel, I knew to be the Mini-Cooper. It was very cold, and after a while I realized that this was because I was no longer wearing a jacket or an overcoat. My shirt-sleeved arms were dragged forward between the two front seats so that I couldn't reach the sticking plaster to rip it off, and I was extremely, horribly uncomfortable. I tried once with all my strength to free my arms, lifting and jerking at the same time, but they were securely fastened, and a fist – I supposed – crashed down on them so brutally that I didn't attempt it again. I couldn't see who was driving, and driving fast, but I didn't need to. There was only one person in the world who could have set such a trap; complicated but effective, like the Jaguar in the lane. Only one person who had any reason to abduct me, however mad that reason might be. I had no illusions. Maurice Kemp-Lore did not intend that I should win the Midwinter Cup, and was taking steps to prevent it.

Did he know, I wondered helplessly, that it was no accident that Turniptop had not eaten the doped sugar? Did he guess that I knew all about his anti-jockey activities? Had he heard about my trek round the stables or my enquiries about the Jaguar? If he did know these things, what was he going to do with me? To this last rather bleak question I was in no hurry to discover the answer.

When the journey had been going for some time, the car swung suddenly to the left and bumped on to an unevenly surfaced side road, increasing my discomfort. After a while it slowed, turned again, and rolled to a stop.

Kemp-Lore got out of the car, tipped forward the driver's seat, and tugged me out after him by the wrists. I couldn't get my feet under me because of the hobble, and I fell out on to the back of my shoulders. The ground was hard and gravelly. My shirt tore, and the sharp stones scraped into my skin.

He pulled me to my feet, and I stood there swaying, blinded by the plaster on my eyes and unable to run even if I could have wrenched myself from his grasp. He had some sort of lead fixed to my tied wrists, and he began to pull me forward by it. The ground was uneven and the rope joining my ankles was very short. I kept stumbling, and twice fell down.

It was very unpleasant, falling when I couldn't see, but I managed somehow to twist before hitting the ground, landing on my shoulders instead of my face. Always he pulled my hands so far in front of me that I couldn't reach the sticking plaster: the second time I fell I made a great effort to get it off, but he wrenched my arms roughly over my head and dragged me along the ground on my back for a long way, I very painfully lost a good deal more skin.

At length he paused and let me stand up again. He still didn't speak. Not a word. And I couldn't. There was only the sound of our footsteps on the stony ground and the faint sigh of the sharp north-easter in some near-by trees. My tattered shirt was no shield against that wind, and I began to shiver.

He stopped, and there was the sound of a door being opened, and I was tugged in. This time there was a step up, as I realized a fraction too late to prevent myself falling again. I hadn't time to twist, either. I fell flat on my stomach, elbows and chest. It knocked the wind out of me and made me dizzy.

It was a wooden floor, I thought, with my cheek on it. It smelled strongly of dust, and faintly of horses. He pulled me to my feet again and I felt my wrists being hauled upwards and fastened to something just above my head. When he had finished and stepped away I explored with my fingers to find out what it was; and as soon as I felt the smooth metal hooks, I knew exactly the sort of place I was in.

It was a tack-room. Every stable has one. It is the place where the saddles and bridles are kept, along with all the brushes and straps and bandages and rugs that horses need. From the ceiling of every tack-room hangs a harness hook, a gadget something like a three-pronged anchor, which is used for hanging bridles on while they are being cleaned. There were no bridles hanging from these particular hooks. Only me. I was securely fastened at the point where they branched off their stem.

Most tack-rooms are warm, heated by a stove which dries damp rugs and prevents leather getting mildewed. This tack-room was very cold indeed, and in the air the ingrained smells of leather and saddle soap were overlaid by a dead sort of mustiness. It was an unused room: an empty room. The silence took on a new meaning. There were no horses moving in the boxes.

It was an empty stable. I shivered from something more than cold.

I heard him step out into the gritty yard, and presently there was a familiar rattle of bolts and the clang of a stable door being opened. After a few seconds it was shut again, and another one was opened. This again was shut, and another opened. He went on down the row, opening six doors. I thought he must be looking for something, and numbly wondered what it was, and began to hope very much that he wouldn't find it.

After the sixth stable door shut he was gone for some time, and I couldn't hear what he was doing. But the car had not been started, so I knew he must still be there. I could make no impression at all on the strands of rope twined round my wrists. They were narrow and slippery to touch, and felt like nylon, and I couldn't even find a knot, much less undo one.

Eventually he came back, and dumped down outside the door something that clattered. A bucket.

He stepped into the room and walked softly on the wooden floor. He stopped in front of me. It was very quiet everywhere. I could hear a new sound, the high, faint asthmatic wheeze of the air going into his lungs. Even an empty stable, it seemed, could start him off.

Nothing happened for a while. He walked all round me, slowly, and stopped again. Walked and stopped. Making up his mind, I thought. But to do what?

He touched me once, dragging his gloved hand across my raw shoulders. I flinched, and his breath hissed sharply. He began to cough, the dry difficult asthmatic's cough. And may you choke, I thought.

He went outside, still coughing, and picked up the bucket and walked away across the yard. I heard the bucket clatter down and a tap being turned on. The water splashed into the bucket, echoing in the stillness.

Jack and Jill went up the hill, said my brain ridiculously, to fetch a pail of water. Jack fell down and broke his crown and Jill threw the water all over him.

Oh no, I thought, oh no, I'm so cold already. Part of my mind said I wouldn't mind what he did to me if only he'd let me go in time to ride Template, and the rest said don't be a fool, that's the whole point, he won't let you go, and anyway if you do get away you'll be so cold and stiff after this you won't be able to ride a donkey.

He turned off the tap and came back across the yard, the water splashing slightly as he walked. He brought the bucket with him into the tack-room and stopped behind me. The handle of the bucket clanked. I ground my teeth and took a deep breath, and waited.

He threw the water. It hit me squarely between the shoulder blades and soaked me from head to foot. It was bitterly, icy cold, and it stung like murder on the skinned patches.

After a short pause he went across the yard again and refilled the bucket. I thought I was almost past caring about that. You can't be wetter than wet and you can't be colder than freezing. And my arms, with being hauled up higher than my head, were already beginning to feel heavy and to ache. I began to worry less about the immediate future, and more about how long he intended to leave me where I was.

He came back with the bucket, and this time he threw the water in my face. I had been wrong about not caring. It was at least as bad as the first time, mostly because too much of it went up my nose. Couldn't he see, I thought desperately, that he was drowning me. My chest hurt. I couldn't get my breath. Surely he'd pull the plaster off my mouth, surely . . . surely . . .

He didn't.

By the time a reasonable amount of air was finding its way into my heaving lungs he was across the yard again, with more water splashing into the bucket. In due course he turned the tap off, and his feet began once more to crunch methodically in my direction. Up the step and across the wooden floor. There wasn't anything I could do to stop him. My thoughts were unprintable.

He came round in front of me again. I twisted my face sideways and buried my nose against my upper arm. He poured the whole arctic bucketful over my head. After this, I thought, I am going to have more sympathy for those clowns in circuses. I hoped the poor blighters used warm water, anyway.

It seemed that he now thought that I was wet enough. In any case he dumped the bucket down outside the door instead of going to fill it again, and came back and stood close beside me. His asthma was worse.

He put his hand in my hair and pulled my head back, and spoke for the first time.

He said in a low voice, with obvious satisfaction, 'That should fix *you*.'

He let go of my hair and went out of the room, and I heard him walk away across the yard. His footsteps faded into the distance and after a while there was the distant slam of the Mini-Cooper's door. The engine started, the car drove off, and soon I could hear it no more.

It wasn't very funny being abandoned in a trussed condition soaking wet on a cold night. I knew he wouldn't be back for hours, because it was Friday. From eight o'clock until at least nine-thirty he would be occupied with his programme; and I wondered in passing what effect his recent capers would have on his performance.

One thing was clear, I could not meekly stand still and wait to be released. The first necessity was obviously to get some of the sticking plaster off. I thought that as it was wet it would come away fairly easily, but it was very adhesive, and after a good deal of rubbing my mouth against my arm, I only succeeded in peeling back one corner of it. It was enough to let in a precious extra trickle of air, but no good for shouting for help.

The cold was a serious problem. My wet trousers clung clammily to my legs, my shoes were full of water, and my shirt, what was left of it, was plastered against my arms and chest. Already my fingers were completely numb, and my feet were going through the stage that precedes loss of feeling. He had left the door open on purpose, I knew, and although the biting wind was not blowing straight in there were enough eddies swirling off the walls outside for me to be in a considerable draught. I shivered from head to foot.

Harness hooks. I considered their anatomy. A stem with three upward-curving branches at the bottom. At the top, a ring, and attached to the ring, a chain. The length of chain depended on the height of the ceiling. At the top of the chain, a staple driven into a beam. As the whole thing was solidly constructed to resist years of vigorous stablemen putting their weight on bridles while they cleaned them, it was absolutely hopeless to try and tug it straight out of the ceiling.

I had seen harness hooks which were only hitched on to their chains and would detach easily if lifted instead of being pulled down, but after some fruitless and tiring manoeuvring I knew the one I was fixed to was not so obliging.

But somewhere, I thought, there must be a weak link. Literally a weak link. When they were bought, harness hooks didn't have chains on. Chain was cut to the length needed and added when the hook was installed in the tack-room. Therefore, somewhere there was a join.

The bottom curve of the hooks brushed my hair, and my wrists were tied some three inches above that. It gave me very little leverage, but it was the only hope I had. I started pivoting, leaning my forearms on the hooks and twisting the chain, putting a strain on it and hearing the links rub hollowly together. In two and a half full turns, as near as I could judge, it locked solid. If I could turn it further, the weak link would snap.

The theory was simple. Putting it into operation was different. For one thing, twisting the chain had shortened it, so that my arms were stretched higher above my head and gave me less leverage than ever. And for another, they had begun to ache in earnest.

I pressed round as hard as I could. Nothing happened. I unwound the chain a fraction, and forcefully jerked it tight again. The jolt ran right down my body and threw me off my feet.

I stumbled miserably upright again, and with my legs braced, repeated the process. This time the jolt shook only the top part of my body. I did it again. The chain didn't break.

After that, as a respite from rattling my arms in their sockets, I got back to work on the sticking plaster and a while later dislodged it entirely. It meant that at last I could open my mouth and yell.

I yelled.

No one came. My voice echoed round the tack-room and sounded loud in my ears, but I feared that outside the wind would sweep it away. I shouted, on and off, for a long while. No results.

It was at this point, perhaps an hour after Kemp-Lore had gone, that I became both very frightened and very angry.

I was frightened for my hands, which I could no longer feel. I was now not only shivering but shuddering with cold, and the blood supply to my hands was having, to put it literally, an uphill job; and with the weight of my aching arms to support, the rope tying my wrists was viciously tight.

The dismal fact had to be faced that if I had to stay where I was all night my hands might be dead in the morning. My imagination trotted on unasked with scarifying pictures. Dead. Gangrenous. Amputated.

He can't have meant that, I thought suddenly. Surely he hadn't meant that all along. No one could be so savagely cruel. I remembered the satisfaction in his voice. 'That should fix *you*,' he said. But I'd thought he meant for the next day only. Not for life.

Being angry gave me both strength and resolution. I would not, I absolutely would not let him get away with it. The chain had got to be broken.

I wound it up tight again and jerked. It took my breath away. I told myself not to be a baby. I loosened and jerked, loosened and jerked, pushing against the hooks, trying to twist them round with all my strength. The chain rattled, and held.

I started doing it rhythmically. Six jerks and a rest. Six jerks and a rest. On and on, six jerks and a rest, until I was sobbing.

At least, I thought, with a last flicker of humour, the exercise is making me warmer. But it was little consolation for the cracking pain in my arms and shoulders, or the red-hot pincers which seemed to have attached themselves to the back of my neck, or the bite of the rope into my wrists as the friction rubbed away the skin.

Six jerks and a rest. Six jerks and a rest. The rests got longer. Anyone who has tried crying with sticking plaster over his eyes will know that the tears run down inside the nose. When I sniffed, they came into my mouth. Salty. I got tired of the taste.

Six jerks and a rest. I wouldn't stop. I refused to stop. Six jerks. Rest. Six. Rest.

After a while I unwound the chain by turning round and round where I stood and wound it up again in the opposite direction. I thought that jolting it the other way might both snap it more quickly and be easier on my protesting muscles; but I was wrong on both counts. Eventually, I wound back again.

Time passed. Because I couldn't see I became giddy as I grew tired. I began to sway and buckle at the knees if I didn't concentrate, and neither of these things did my arms any good.

Why – jerk – wouldn't – jerk – the ruddy chain – jerk – jerk – break. I wasn't going to admit it was too much for me without struggling to the end, though the disgusting temptation gradually grew to give up the excruciating wrenching and just hang and faint away and get some peace. A temporary, deceptive, useless, dangerous peace.

I went on jerking for what seemed like hours, sometimes sobbing, sometimes cursing, sometimes maybe praying as well.

I was quite unprepared for it when it happened. One minute I was screwing up the dregs of willpower for another series of jerks, and the next, after a convulsive, despairing heave, I was collapsing in a tumbled heap on the floor with the harness hook clattering down on top of me, still tied to my wrists.

For a moment or two I could hardly believe it. My head was whirling, all sense of direction gone. But the floor was hard beneath my body, dusty smelling and real, damp and reassuring.

After a while, when my head cleared, I rolled into a kneeling position so that the blood was flowing down my arms at last, and put my hands between my thighs to try to warm them. They felt like lumps of frozen meat, with no sensation and no movement. The rope round my wrists didn't cut so much now that it had no weight to support, and there was room for the blood to get back into my hands, I thought, if only it would.

The unimaginable relief of having my arms down made me forget for some time how cold I was, and how wet, and how far still from getting warm and dry. I felt almost cheerful, as if I had won a major battle; and indeed, looking back on it, I know I had.

Twelve

KNEELING VERY soon became uncomfortable, so I shuffled across the floor until I came to a wall, and sat with the bottom of my spine propped against it and my knees bent up.

The plaster on my eyes was still stuck tight. I tried to scrape it off by rubbing it against the rope on my wrists, but made no headway. The hooks hindered me and bumped into my face, and in the end I gave it up and concentrated again on warming my hands, alternately cradling them between my thighs and thumping them against my knees to restore the circulation.

After a time I found I could move my fingers. I still couldn't feel them at all, but movement was a tremendous step forward, and I remember smiling about it for at least ten minutes.

I put my hands up to my face and tried to scrape the plaster off with my thumbnail. My thumb slid across my cheek, checked on the edge of the plaster and, when I pushed from the elbow, bent uselessly and slithered away. I tried again. It had to be done, because until I could see where I was going I couldn't leave the tack-room. It was colder outside, and my ankles were still hobbled, and wandering about blind in those conditions did not appeal to me a bit.

I bent my head down and put my right thumb in my mouth, to warm it. Every few minutes I tested the results on the edge of the plaster and at least got to the stage where the thumb would push without bending. I only needed to prise a corner up, but even that took a long time. Eventually, however, my nail had pushed a flap unstuck which was big enough for me to grip between my wrists, and with several false starts and a fair selection of oaths, I managed in the end to pull the obstinate thing off.

Dazzling moonlight poured through the open door and through a window beside it. I was sitting against the end wall with the door away on my left. Above my head and all round the room there were empty wooden supports for saddles and bridles, and bare shelves and a cupboard on the wall facing me. An efficient-looking stove occupied the corner on my right, with a few dead cinders still scattered on the ground beside it.

From the centre of the ceiling, pale in the moonlight, hung twenty inches of sturdy galvanized chain.

I looked down at my hands. The harness hook glinted with reflected light. No wonder it had been so difficult to break, I thought. The chain and the hook were almost new. Not the dark, old, rusty things I had been imagining all along. I swallowed, really shattered. It was just as well I hadn't known.

My hands themselves, including the thumb I had tried to warm, were white. Almost as white as my shirt-sleeves. Almost as white as the nylon rope which wound round the hooks. Only my wrists were dark.

I stretched my feet out. More white nylon rope ran from one ankle to the other, about fifteen inches of it.

My fingers wouldn't undo the knots. My pockets had been emptied; no knife, no matches. There was nothing in the tackroom to cut with. I stood up stiffly, leaning against the wall, and slowly, carefully, shuffled over to the door. My foot kicked against something, and I looked down. On the edge of a patch of moonlight lay the broken link. It was a grotesquely buckled piece of silvery metal. It had given me a lot of trouble.

I went on to the door and negotiated the step. The bucket stood there, dully grey. I looked round the moonlit L-shaped yard. Four boxes stretched away to my right, and at right angles to them there were two more, on the short arm of the L. Over there too, was the tap; and beside the tap, on the ground, an object I was very glad to see. A boot-scraper made of a thin metal plate bedded in concrete.

With small careful steps I made my way to it across the hard-packed gravel, the cutting wind ripping the last remnants of warmth from my body.

Leaning against the wall, and with one foot on the ground, I stretched the rope tautly over the boot-scraper and began to rub it to and fro, using the other foot as a pendulum. The blade of the scraper was far from sharp and the rope was new, and it took a long time to fray it through, but it parted in the end. I knelt down and tried to do the same with the strands round my wrists, but the harness hook kept getting in the way again and I couldn't get anything like the same purchase. I stood up wearily. It looked as though I'd have to lug that tiresome piece of iron-mongery around with me a while longer.

Being able to move my legs, however, gave me a marvellous sense of freedom. Stiffly, shaking with cold, I walked out of the yard round to the house looming darkly behind it. There were no lights, and looking closer I found the downstairs windows were all shuttered. It was as empty as the stable; an unwelcome but not unexpected discovery.

I walked a bit unsteadily on past the house and down the drive. It was a long drive with no lodge at the gate, only an estate agent's board announcing that this desirable country gentleman's residence was for sale, together with some excellent modern stabling, forty acres of arable land and an apple orchard.

A country lane ran past the end of the drive giving no indication as to which way lay civilization. I tried to remember from which direction the Mini-Cooper had come, but I couldn't. It seemed a very long time ago. I glanced automatically at my left wrist but there was only rope there, no watch. Since it had to be one thing or the other, I turned right. It was a deserted road with open fields on the far sides of its low hedges. No cars passed, and nowhere could I see a light. Cursing the wind and aching all over, I stumbled on, hanging on to the fact that if I went far enough I was bound to come to a house in the end.

What I came to first was not a house but something much better. A telephone box. It stood alone, brightly lit inside, square and beckoning, on the corner where the lane turned into a more main road, and it solved the embarrassing problem of presenting myself at some stranger's door looking like a scarecrow and having to explain how I had got into such a state.

There were a lot of people I could have called. Police, Ambulance or the Fire Brigade for a start; but by the time I had forced my still nearly useless hands to pull the door open far enough for me to get my foot in, I had had time to think. Once I called in authority in any form there would be unending questions to answer and statements to make and like as not I'd end up for the night in the local cottage hospital. I hated being in hospitals.

Also, although I felt so bone cold, it was not, I thought, actually freezing. The puddles at the side of the road had no ice on them. They would be racing at Ascot the next day. Template would turn up for the Midwinter, and James didn't know his jockey was wandering around unfit to ride.

Unfit . . . Between seeing the telephone box and clumsily picking up the receiver I came to the conclusion that the only satisfactory way to cheat Kemp-Lore of his victory was to go and ride the race, and win it if I could, and pretend that tonight's misfortunes had not happened. He had had things his own way for far too long. He was not, he was positively not, I vowed, going to get the better of me any more.

I dialled O with an effort, gave the operator my credit card number, and asked to be connected to the one person in the world who would give me the help I needed, and keep quiet about it afterwards, and not try to argue me out of what I intended to do.

Her voice sounded sleepy. She said, 'Hello?'

'Joanna . . . are you busy?' I asked.

'Busy? At this hour?' she said. 'Is that you, Rob?'

'Yes,' I said.

'Well, go back to bed and ring me in the morning,' she said. 'I was asleep. Don't you know what time it is?' I heard her yawn.

'No,' I said.

'Well, it's . . . er . . . twenty to one. Good night.'

'Joanna, don't go,' I said urgently. 'I need your help. I really do. Please, don't ring off.'

'What's the matter?' She yawned again.

'I . . . I . . . Joanna, come and help me. Please.'

There was a little silence and she said in a more awake voice, 'You've never said "please" like that to me before. Not for anything.'

'Will you come?'

'Where to?'

'I don't really know,' I said despairingly. 'I'm in a telephone box on a country road miles from anywhere. The telephone exchange is Hampden Row.' I spelled it out for her. 'I don't think it's very far from London, and somewhere on the West, probably.'

'You can't come back on your own?' she asked.

'No,' I said. 'I've no money and my clothes are wet.'

'Oh.' A pause. 'All right, then. I'll find out where you are and come in a taxi. Anything else?'

'Bring a sweater,' I said. 'I'm cold. And some dry socks, if you have any. And some gloves. Don't forget the gloves. And a pair of scissors.'

'Sweater, socks, gloves, scissors. O.K. You'll have to wait while I get dressed again, but I'll come as soon as I can. Stay by the telephone box.'

'Yes,' I said.

'I'll hurry, don't worry,' she said. 'Good-bye.'

'Good-bye . . .' I fumbled the receiver back on to its rest. However quick she was, she wouldn't arrive for an hour. Well, what was one more hour after so many? I had had no idea it was so late: the evening had certainly seemed to me to be going on for an eternity, but I had lost all sense of actual time. And Kemp-Lore hadn't come back. His show had been over for hours, and he hadn't come back. The bloody, murdering bastard, I thought.

I sat down on the floor of the box and leaned gingerly against the wall beside the telephone, with my head resting on the coin box. Exercise and the bitter wind outside, inactivity and shelter inside; one looked as cold a prospect as the other. But I was too tired to walk any more if I didn't have to, so the choice was easy.

I put my hands up to my face and one by one bit my fingers. They were icy cold and yellowish white, and none of them had any feeling. They would curl and uncurl, but slowly and weakly, and that was all. I got to work on them seriously then, rubbing them up and down against my legs, bumping them on my knees, forcing them open and shut, but it seemed to make little difference. I persevered from fear that they should get worse if I didn't, and paid for it in various creaks from my sore and sorely misused shoulders.

There was a good deal to think about to take my mind off my woes. That sticking-plaster for instance. Why had he used it? The strip over my mouth, I had assumed, had been to stop me shouting for help; but when I got it off at last and shouted, there was no one to hear. No one could have heard however loud I yelled, because the stable was so far from the lane.

The strip over my eyes should have been to prevent my seeing where I was going, but why did it matter if I saw an empty yard and a deserted tack-room? What would have happened differently, I wondered, if I had been able to see and talk.

To see . . . I would have seen Kemp-Lore's expression while he went about putting me out of action. I would have seen

Kemp-Lore . . . that was it! It was himself he had not wanted me to see, not the place.

If that were so it was conceivable that he had prevented me from talking simply so that he should not be trapped into answering. He had spoken only once, and that in a low, unrecognizable tone. I became convinced that he had not wanted me to hear and recognize his voice.

In that case he must have believed I did not know who had abducted me, that I didn't know who he was. He must still believe it. Which meant that he thought James had knocked Turniptop's doped sugar out of his hand by accident, that he hadn't heard about Tick-Tock and me going round all the stables, and that he didn't know that I had been asking about the Jaguar. It gave me, I thought, a fractional advantage for the future. If he had left any tracks anywhere, he would not see any vital, immediate need to obliterate them. If he didn't know he was due for destruction himself, he would not be excessively on his guard.

Looking at my bloodless hands and knowing that on top of everything else I still had to face the pain of their return to life, I was aware that all the civilized brakes were off in my conscience. Helping to build up what he had broken was not enough. He himself had hammered into me the inner implacability I had lacked to avenge myself and all the others thoroughly, and to do it physically and finally and without compunction.

She came, in the end.

I heard a car draw up and a door slam, and her quick tread on the road. The door of the telephone box opened, letting in an icy blast, and there she was, dressed in trousers and woolly boots and a warm blue padded jacket, with the light falling on her dark hair and making hollows of her eyes.

I was infinitely glad to see her. I looked up at her and did my

best at a big smile of welcome, but it didn't come off very well.
I was shivering too much.

She knelt down and took a closer look at me. Her face went
stiff with shock.

'Your hands,' she said.

'Yes. Did you bring the scissors?'

Without a word she opened her handbag, took out a sensible-
sized pair, and cut me free. She did it gently. She took the harness hook from between my knees and laid it on the floor, and
carefully peeled from my wrists the cut pieces of rope. They were
all more brown than white, stained with blood, and where they
had been there were big corrugated raw patches, dark and deep.
She stared at them.

'More bits of rope down there,' I said, nodding towards my
feet.

She cut the pieces round my ankles, and I saw her rubbing
my trouser leg between her fingers. The air had been too cold
to dry them and my body had not generated enough heat, so
they were still very damp.

'Been swimming?' she said flippantly. Her voice cracked.

There was a step on the road outside and a man's shape
loomed up behind Joanna.

'Are you all right, miss?' he said in a reliable-sounding cockney voice.

'Yes, thank you,' she said. 'Do you think you could help me
get my cousin into the taxi?'

He stepped into the doorway and looked down at me, his
eyes on my wrists and my hands.

'Christ,' he said.

'Very aptly put,' I said.

He looked at my face. He was a big sturdy man of about fifty,
weather-beaten like a sailor, with eyes that looked as if they had
seen everything and found most of it disappointing.

'You've been done proper, haven't you?' he said.

'Proper,' I agreed.

He smiled faintly. 'Come on then. No sense in hanging about here.'

I stood up clumsily and lurched against Joanna, and put my arms round her neck to save myself from falling; and as I was there it seemed a shame to miss the opportunity, so I kissed her. On the eyebrow, as it happened.

'Did you say "cousin"?' said the taxi driver.

'Cousin,' said Joanna firmly. Much too firmly.

The driver held the door open. 'We'd better take him to a doctor,' he said.

'No,' I said. 'No doctor.'

Joanna said, 'You need one.'

'No.'

'That's frostbite,' said the driver pointing to my hands.

'No,' I said. 'It isn't freezing. No ice on the puddles. Just cold. Not frostbite.' My teeth were chattering and I could only speak in short sentences.

'What happened to your back?' asked the driver, looking at the tattered bits of shirt sticking to me.

'I . . . fell over,' I said. 'On some gravel.'

He looked sceptical.

'It's a terrible mess, and there's a lot of dirt in it,' said Joanna, peering round me and sounding worried.

'You wash it,' I said. 'At home.'

'You need a doctor,' said the driver again.

I shook my head. 'I need Dettol, aspirins and sleep.'

'I hope you know what you're doing,' said Joanna. 'What else?'

'Sweater,' I said.

'It's in the taxi,' she said. 'And some other clothes. You can change as we go along. The sooner you get into a hot bath the better.'

'I'd be careful about that, miss,' said the driver. 'Don't go warming those hands up too fast or the fingers will drop off.' A comforting chap. Inaccurate too, I trusted. Joanna looked more worried than ever.

We walked from the telephone box to the taxi. It was an ordinary black London taxi. I wondered what charm Joanna had used to get it so far out into the country in the middle of the night; and also, more practically, whether the meter was still ticking away. It was.

'Get in, out of the wind,' she said, opening the taxi door.

I did as I was told. She had brought a suitcase, from which she now produced a thin, pale blue cardigan of her own, and a padded man-size olive-coloured anorak which zipped up the front. She looked at me judiciously, and out came the scissors. Some quick snips and the ruins of my shirt lay on the seat beside me. She cut two long strips of it and wound them carefully round my wrists. The taxi driver watched.

'This is a police job,' he suggested.

I shook my head. 'Private fight,' I said.

He held up the harness hook, which he had brought across from the telephone box.

'What sort of thing is this?' he asked.

'Throw it in the ditch,' I said, averting my eyes.

'You'll be needing it for the police,' he insisted.

'I told you,' I said wearily, 'no police.'

His disillusioned face showed that he knew all about people who got themselves beaten up but wouldn't report it. He shrugged and went off into the darkness, and came back without the hook.

'It's in the ditch behind the telephone box, if you change your mind,' he said.

'Thanks,' I said.

Joanna finished the bandages and helped my arms into both the garments she had brought, and fastened the fronts. The next thing the suitcase produced was a pair of fur-lined mittens which went on without too much trouble, and after that a thermos flask full of hot soup, and some cups.

I looked into Joanna's black eyes as she held the cup to my mouth. I loved her. Who wouldn't love a girl who thought of hot soup at a time like that?

The driver accepted some soup too, and stamped his feet on the ground and remarked that it was getting chilly. Joanna gave him a pained look, and I laughed.

He glanced at me appraisingly and said, 'Maybe you can do without a doctor, at that.' He thanked Joanna for the soup, gave her back the cup, settled himself in the driving seat and, switching off the light inside the taxi, started to drive us back to London.

'Who did it?' said Joanna.

'Tell you later.'

'All right.' She didn't press. She bent down to the case and brought out some fleecy slippers, thick socks and a pair of her own stretchy trews. 'Take your trousers off.'

I said ironically, 'I can't undo the zip.'

'I forgot . . .'

'Anyway,' I said, 'I'll settle for the socks; can't manage the trousers.' Even I could hear the exhaustion in my voice, and Joanna without arguing got down on her knees in the swaying cab and changed my wet socks and shoes for dry ones.

'Your feet are freezing,' she said.

'I can't feel them,' I said. The moon shone clearly through the window and I looked at the slippers. They were too large for me, much too large for Joanna.

'Have I stepped into Brian's shoes?' I asked.

After a pause she said neutrally, 'They are Brian's, yes.'

'And the jacket?'

'I bought it for him for Christmas.'

So that was that. It wasn't the best moment to find out.

'I didn't give it to him,' she said after a moment, as if she had made up her mind about something.

'Why not?'

'It didn't seem to suit a respectable life in the outer suburbs. I gave him a gold tie-pin instead.'

'Very suitable,' I said dryly.

'A farewell present,' she said quietly.

I said sincerely, 'I'm sorry.' I knew it hadn't been easy for her.

She drew in a breath sharply. 'Are you made of iron, Rob?'

'Iron filings,' I said.

The taxi sped on.

'We had a job finding you,' she said. 'I'm sorry we were so long. It was such a big area, you see.'

'You came, though.'

'Yes.'

I found sitting in the swaying taxi very uncomfortable. My arms and shoulders ached unceasingly and if I leaned back too heavily the raw bits didn't like it. After a while I gave it up, and finished the journey sitting on the floor with my head and my hands in Joanna's lap.

I was of course quite used to being knocked about. I followed, after all, an occupation in which physical damage was a fairly frequent though unimportant factor; and, especially during my first season, when I was a less efficient jockey and most of the horses I rode were the worst to be had, there was rarely a time when some area of my body was not black and blue. I had broken several of the smaller bones, been kicked in tender places, and dislocated one or two joints. On my general sense of well-being, and on my optimism that I wouldn't crash unmendably, none of these things had made the slightest dent. It seemed that in common with most other jockeys I had been born with the sort of resilient constitution which could take a bang and be ready for business, if not the following day, at least a good deal quicker than the medical profession considered normal.

Practice had given me a certain routine for dealing with discomfort, which was mainly to ignore it and concentrate on something else: but this system was not operating very well that evening. It didn't work, for instance, when I sat for a while in a light armchair in Joanna's warm room with my elbows on my knees, watching my fingers gradually change colour from yellowy white to smudgy charcoal, to patchy purple, and finally to red.

It began as a tingle, faint and welcome, soon after we had got back and Joanna had turned both her powerful heaters on. She had insisted at once on removing my clammy trousers and also my pants, and on my donning her black trews, which were warm but not long enough by several inches. It was odd, in a way, letting her undress me, which she did matter-of-factly and without remark; but in another way it seemed completely natural, a throwback to our childhood, when we had been bathed together on our visits to each other's houses.

She dug out some rather powdery-looking aspirins in a bottle. There were only three of them left, which I swallowed. Then she made some black coffee and held it for me to drink. It was stiff with brandy.

'Warming,' she said laconically. 'Anyway, you've stopped shivering at last.'

It was then that my fingers tingled and I told her.

'Will it be bad?' she said prosaically, putting down the empty coffee mug.

'Possibly.'

'You won't want me to sit and watch you then,' she said.

I shook my head. She took the empty mug into the kitchen and was several minutes coming back with a full one for herself.

The tingle increased first to a burning sensation and then to a feeling of being squeezed in a vice, tighter and tighter, getting more and more agonizing until it felt that at any minute my fingers would disintegrate under the pressure. But there they were, harmlessly hanging in the warm air, with nothing to show for it except that they were turning slowly puce.

Joanna came back from the kitchen and wiped the sweat off my forehead.

'Are you all right?' she asked.

'Yes,' I said.

She nodded, and gave me a faint edition of the intimate smile that had had my heart doing flip-flaps from boyhood, and drank her coffee.

When the pulse got going, it felt as though my hands had been taken out of the vice, laid on a bench, and were being rhythmically hammered. It was terrible. And it went on too long. My head drooped.

When I looked up she was standing in front of me, watching me with an expression which I couldn't read. There were tears in her eyes.

'Is it over?' she said, blinking to disguise them.

'More or less.'

We both looked at my hands, which were now a fierce red all over.

'And your feet?' she asked.

'They're fine,' I said. Their awakening had been nothing.

'I'd better wash those grazes on your back,' she said.

'No,' I said. 'In the morning.'

'There's a lot of dirt in them,' she protested.

'It's been there so long already that a few more hours won't hurt,' I said. 'I've had four anti-tetanus injections in the last two years, and there's always penicillin . . . and I'm too tired.'

She didn't argue. She unzipped and helped me take off the anorak, and made me get into her bed, still incongruously dressed in her black trews and blue cardigan and looking like a second-rate ballet dancer with a hangover. The sheets were rumpled from her lying in them before I had woken her up, and there was still a dent in her pillow where her head had been. I put mine there too, with an odd feeling of delight. She saw me grin, and correctly read my mind.

'It's the first time you've got into my bed,' she said. 'And it'll be the last.'

'Have a heart, Joanna,' I said.

She perched herself on the edge of the mattress and looked down at me.

'It's no good for cousins,' she said.

'And if we weren't cousins?'

'I don't know . . .' she sighed. 'But we are.'

She bent down to kiss me good night on the forehead.

I couldn't help it; I put my arms up round her shoulders and pulled her down on to my chest and kissed her properly, mouth to mouth. It was the first time I had ever done it, and into it went all the pent-up and suppressed desire I had ever felt for her. It was too hungry, too passionate, much too desperate. I knew it, but I couldn't stop it. For a moment she seemed to relax and melt and kiss me back, but it was so brief and passing that I thought I had imagined it, and afterwards her body grew rigid.

I let her go. She stood up abruptly and stared at me, her face scrubbed of any emotion. No anger, no disgust; and no love. She turned away without speaking and went across the room to the sofa, where she twisted a blanket around herself and lay down. She stretched out her hand to the table light and switched it off.

Her voice reached me across the dark room, calm, self-controlled. 'Good night, Rob.'

'Good night, Joanna,' I said politely.

There was dead silence.

I rolled over on to my stomach and put my face in her pillow.

Thirteen

I DON'T know whether she slept or not during the next four hours. The room was quiet. The time passed slowly.

The pulse in my hands went on throbbing violently for a while, but who cared? It was comforting, even if it hurt. I thought about all the fat red corpuscles forcing their way through the shrunken capillaries like water gushing along dry irrigation ditches after a drought. Very nice. Very life-giving. By tomorrow afternoon, I thought – correction, this afternoon – they might be fit for work. They'd got to be, that was all there was about it.

Some time after it was light I heard Joanna go into her narrow bathroom-kitchen where she brushed her teeth and made some fresh coffee. The warm roasted smell floated across to me. Saturday morning, I thought. Midwinter Cup day. I didn't leap out of bed eagerly to greet it; I turned over slowly from my stomach on to one side, shutting my eyes against the stiffness which afflicted every muscle from neck to waist, and the sharp soreness of my back and wrists. I really didn't feel very well.

She came across the room with a mug of steaming coffee and put it on the bedside table. Her face was pale and expressionless.

'Coffee,' she said unnecessarily.

'Thank you.'

'How do you feel?' she asked, a little too clinically.

'Alive,' I said.

There was a pause.

'Oh, go on,' I said. 'Either slosh me one or smile . . . one or the other. But don't stand there looking tragic, as if the Albert Hall had burned down on the first night of the Proms.'

'Damn it, Rob,' she said, her face crinkling into a laugh.

'Truce?' I asked.

'Truce,' she agreed, still smiling. She even sat down again on the edge of the bed. I shoved myself up into a sitting position, wincing somewhat from various aches, and brought a hand out from under the bedclothes to reach for the coffee.

As a hand it closely resembled a bunch of beef sausages. I produced the other one. It also was swollen. The skin on both felt very tender, and they were still unnaturally red.

'Blast,' I said. 'What's the time?'

'About eight o'clock,' she said. 'Why?'

Eight o'clock. The race was at two-thirty. I began counting backwards. I would have to be at Ascot by at the latest one-thirty, preferably earlier, and the journey down, going by taxi, would take about fifty minutes. Allow an hour for hold-ups. That left me precisely four and a half hours in which to get fit enough to ride, and the way I felt, it was a tall order.

I began to consider ways and means. There were the Turkish baths, with heat and massage; but I had lost too much skin for that to be an attractive idea. There was a work-out in a gym; a possibility, but rough. There was a canter in the park – a good solution on any day except Saturday, when the Row would be packed with little girls on leading-reins – or better still a gallop on a racehorse at Epsom, but there was neither time to arrange it nor a good excuse to be found for needing it.

'What's the matter?' asked Joanna.

I told her.

'You don't mean it?' she said. 'You aren't seriously thinking of racing today?'

'I seriously am.'

'You're not fit to,' she said.

'That's the point. That's what we are discussing, how best to get fit,' I said.

'That isn't what I mean,' she protested. 'You look ill. You need a long, quiet day in bed.'

'I'll have it tomorrow,' I said, 'today I am riding Template in the Midwinter Cup.' She began more forcibly to try to dissuade me, so I told her why I was going to ride. I told her everything, all about Kemp-Lore's anti-jockey obsession and all that had happened on the previous evening before she found me in the telephone box. It took quite a time. I didn't look at her while I told her about the tack-room episode, because for some reason it embarrassed me to describe it, even to her, and I knew then quite certainly that I was not going to repeat it to anyone else.

When I had finished she looked at me without speaking for half a minute – thirty solid seconds – and then she cleared her throat and said, 'Yes, I see. We'd better get you fit, then.'

I smiled at her.

'What first?' she said.

'Hot bath and breakfast,' I said. 'And can we have the weather forecast on?' I listened to it every morning, as a matter of routine.

She switched on the radio, which was busy with some sickening matinee music, and started tidying up the room, folding the blanket she had slept in and shaking the sofa cushions. Before she had finished the music stopped, and we heard the eight-thirty news headlines, followed by the forecast.

'There was a slight frost in many parts of the country last night,' said the announcer smoothly, 'and more is expected tonight, especially in exposed areas. Temperatures today will reach five degrees centigrade, forty-one Fahrenheit, in most places, and the north-easterly wind will moderate slightly. It will be bright and sunny in the south. Further outlook: colder weather is expected in the next few days. And here is an announcement. The stewards at Ascot inspected the course at

eight o'clock this morning and have issued the following statement. "Two or three degrees of frost were recorded on the racecourse last night, but the ground on both sides of the fences was
protected by straw, and unless there is a sudden severe frost during the morning, racing is certain." '

Joanna switched off. She said, 'Are you absolutely determined to go?'

'Absolutely,' I said.

'Well . . . I'd better tell you . . . I watched that programme
last night on television. *Turf Talk.*'

'Did you now!' I said, surprised.

'I sometimes do, since you were on it. If I'm in. Anyway I
watched last night.'

'And?' I prompted.

'He,' she said, neither of us needing help to know who she
meant, 'he talked about the Midwinter Cup nearly all the time;
potted biographies of the horses and trainers, and so on. I was
waiting to hear him mention you, but he didn't. He just went
on and on about how superb Template is; not a word about you.
But what I thought you'd like to know is that he said that as it
was such an important race he personally would be commentat-
ing the finish today, and that he personally would also interview
the winning jockey afterwards. If only you can win, he'll have to
describe you doing it, which would be a bitter enough pill, and
then congratulate you publicly in full view of several million
people.'

I gazed at her, awestruck.

'That's a great thought,' I said.

'Like he interviewed you after that race on Boxing Day,' she
added.

'That was the race that sealed my fate with him, I imagine,'
I said. 'And you seem to have done some fairly extensive view-
ing, if I may say so.'

She looked taken aback. 'Well . . . didn't I see you sitting unobtrusively at the back of a concert I gave in Birmingham one night last summer?'

'I thought those lights were supposed to dazzle you,' I said.

'You'd be surprised,' she said.

I pushed back the bedclothes. The black trews looked even more incongruous in the daylight.

'I'd better get going,' I said. 'What do you have in the way of disinfectant and bandages, and a razor?'

'Only a few minute bits of Elastoplast,' she said apologetically, 'and the razor I de-fuzz my legs with. There's a chemist two roads away though, who will be open by now. I'll make a list.' She wrote it on an old envelope.

'And A.P.C. tablets,' I said. 'They are better than just aspirins.'

'Right,' she said. 'I won't be long.'

When she had gone I got out of bed and went into the bathroom. It's easy enough to say, but it wasn't all that easy to do, since I felt as if some over-zealous laundress had fed me several times through a mangle. It was exasperating, I thought bitterly, how much havoc Kemp-Lore had worked on my body by such simple means. I turned on the taps, took off the trews and socks, and stepped into the bath. The blue cardigan had stuck to my back and the shirt bandages to my wrists, so I lay down in the hot water without tugging at them and waited for them to soak off.

Gradually the heat did its customary work of unlocking the worst of the cramps, until I could rotate my shoulders and turn my head from side to side without feeling that I was tearing something adrift. Every few minutes I added more hot water, so that by the time Joanna came back I was up to my throat in it and steaming nicely, warm to the backbone and beyond.

She had dried my trousers and pants overnight, and she pressed them for me while I eased myself out of the blue cardigan and reluctantly got out of the bath. I put on the trousers and watched her setting out her purchases on the kitchen table, a dark lock of hair falling forward into her eyes and a look of concentration firming her mouth. Quite a girl.

I sat down at the table and she bathed the grazes with disinfectant, dried them, and covered them with large pieces of lint spread with zinc-and-castor-oil ointment which she stuck on with adhesive tape. She was neat and quick, and her touch was light.

'Most of the dirt came out in the bath luckily,' she observed, busy with the scissors. 'You've got quite an impressive set of muscles, haven't you? You must be strong . . . I didn't realize.'

'At the moment I've got an impressive set of jellies,' I sighed. 'Very wobbly, very weak.' And aching steadily, though there wasn't any point in saying so.

She went into the other room, rummaged in a drawer, and came back with another cardigan. Pale green, this time; the colour suited my state of health rather well, I thought.

'I'll buy you some new ones,' I said, stretching it across my chest to do up the fancy buttons.

'Don't bother,' she said, 'I loathe both of them.'

'Thanks,' I said, and she laughed.

I put the anorak on again on top of the jersey and pushed the knitted cuffs up my forearms. Joanna slowly unwound the blood-stained bandages on my wrists. They still stuck a bit in spite of the soaking, and what lay underneath was a pretty disturbing sight, even to me, now that we could see it in daylight.

'I can't deal with this,' she said positively. 'You must go to a doctor.'

'This evening,' I said. 'Put some more bandages on, for now.'

'It's too deep,' she said. 'It's too easy to get it infected. You can't ride like this, Rob, really you can't.'

'I can,' I said. 'I'll dunk them in a bowl of Dettol for a while, and then you wrap them up again. Nice and flat, so they won't show.'

'Don't they hurt?' she said.

I didn't answer.

'Yes,' she said. 'Silly question.' She sighed, and fetched a bowl full of warm water, pouring in Dettol so that it turned a milky white, and I soaked my wrists in it for ten minutes.

'That's fixed the infection,' I said. 'Now . . . nice and flat.'

She did as I asked, fastening the ends of the bandages down with little gold safety pins. When she had finished the white cuffs looked tidy and narrow, and I knew they would be unnoticeable under racing colours.

'Perfect,' I said appreciatively, pulling down the anorak sleeves to cover them. 'Thank you, Florence.'

'And Nightingale to you, too,' she said, making a face at me. 'When are you going to the police?'

'I'm not. I told you,' I said. 'I'm not going at all. I meant what I said last night.'

'But why not; why not?' She didn't understand. 'You could get him prosecuted for assault or for causing grievous bodily harm, or whatever the technical term is.'

I said, 'I'd rather fight my own battles . . . and anyway, I can't face the thought of telling the police what happened last night, or being examined by their doctors, and photographed; or standing up in court, if it came to that, and answering questions about it in public, and having the whole rotten lot printed in gory detail in the papers. I just can't face it, that's all.'

'Oh,' she said slowly. 'I suppose it would be a bit of an ordeal, if you look at it like that. Perhaps you feel humiliated . . . is that it?'

'You may be rather bruisingly right,' I admitted grudgingly, thinking about it. 'And I'll keep my humiliation to myself, if you don't mind.'

She laughed. 'You don't need to feel any,' she said. 'Men are funny creatures.'

The pity about hot baths is that although they loosen one up beautifully for the time being, the effect does not last; one has to consolidate the position by exercise. And exercise, my battered muscles protested, was just what they would least enjoy; all the same I did a few rather half-hearted bend-stretch arm movements while Joanna scrambled us some eggs, and after we had eaten and I had shaved I went back to it with more resolution, knowing that if I didn't get on to Template's back in a reasonably supple condition he had no chance of winning. It wouldn't help anyone if I fell off at the first fence.

After an hour's work, though I couldn't screw myself up to swinging my arms round in complete circles, I did get to the stage where I could lift them above shoulder height without wanting to cry out.

Joanna washed up and tidied the flat, and soon after ten o'clock, while I was taking a breather, she said, 'Are you going on with this health and beauty kick until you leave for Ascot?'

'Yes.'

'Well,' she said, 'it's only a suggestion, but why don't we go skating instead?'

'All that ice,' I said, shuddering.

She smiled. 'I thought you had to remount at once, after a fall?'

I saw the point.

'Anyway,' she said, 'it's good, warming exercise, and far more interesting than what you've been doing.'

'You're a blooming genius, my darling Joanna,' I said fervently.

'Er . . . maybe,' she said. 'I still think you ought to be in bed.'

When she was ready we went along to my family's flat where I borrowed one of my father's shirts and a tie and also his skates, which represented his only interest outside music. Then we called at the bank, since the taxi ride the night before had taken nearly all Joanna's cash, and apart from needing money myself I wanted to repay her. Lastly, we stopped at a shop to buy me a pair of brown, silk-lined leather gloves, which I put on, and finally we reached the ice rink in Queensway where we had both been members from the days when we were taken there as toddlers on afternoons too rainy for playing in the Park.

We had not skated together since we were sixteen, and it was fascinating to see how quickly we fell back into the same dancing techniques that we had practised as children.

She was right about the exercise. After an hour of it I had loosened up from head to foot, with hardly a muscle that wasn't moving reasonably freely. She herself, sliding over the ice beside me, had colour in her cheeks and a dazzling sparkle in her eyes. She looked young and vivid.

At twelve o'clock, Cinderella-like, we slid off the rink.

'All right?' she asked, smiling.

'Gorgeous,' I said, admiring the clear, intelligent face turned up to mine.

She didn't know whether I meant her or the skating, which was perhaps just as well.

'I mean . . . how are the aches and pains?'

'Gone,' I said.

'You're a liar,' she said, 'but at least you don't look as grey as you did.'

We went to change, which for me simply meant substituting my father's shirt and tie for the pale green cardigan, and putting back the anorak on top, and the gloves. Necessary, the gloves. Although my fingers were less swollen, less red, and no longer throbbed, the skin in places was beginning to split in short thread-thin cracks.

In the foyer Joanna put the cardigan and my father's skates into her bag and zipped it up, and we went out into the street.

She had already told me that she would not come to Ascot with me, but would watch on television. 'And mind you win,' she said, 'after all this.'

'Can I come back to your place, afterwards?' I said.

'Why, yes . . . yes,' she said, as if surprised that I had asked.

'Fine,' I said. 'Well . . . good-bye.'

'Good luck, Rob,' she said seriously.

Fourteen

THE THIRD cruising taxi driver that I stopped just round the corner in Bayswater Road agreed to take me all the way to Ascot. During the journey, which was quick and skilfully driven, I kept the warmth and flexibility going in my arms by some minor exercises and imaginary piano playing; and if the driver saw me at it in his mirror he probably imagined I was suffering from a sad sort of St Vitus dance.

He announced, when I paid him at the gate, that he thought as it was his own cab that he might as well stay and have a flutter on the races himself, so I arranged for him to drive me back to London again at the end of the afternoon.

'Got any tips?' he said, counting my change.

'How about Template, in the big race?' I said.

'I dunno,' he pursed his lips. 'I dunno as I fancy that Finn. They say as he's all washed up.'

'Don't believe all you hear,' I said, smiling. 'See you later.'

'Right.'

I went through the gate and along to the weighing-room. The hands of the clock on the tower pointed to five past one. Sid, James's head travelling lad, was standing outside the weighing-room door when I got there, and as soon as he saw me he came to meet me, and said, 'You're here then.'

'Yes,' I said. 'Why not?'

'The governor posted me here to wait for you. I had to go and tell him at once if you came. He's having lunch . . . there's a rumour going round that you weren't going to turn up, see?' He bustled off.

I went through the weighing-room into the changing-room.

'Hello,' said my valet. 'I thought you'd cried off.'

'So you came after all,' said Peter Cloony.

Tick-Tock said, 'Where in hell have you been?'

'Why did everyone believe I wouldn't get here?' I asked.

'I don't know. Some rumour or other. Everyone's been saying you frightened yourself again on Thursday and you'd chucked up the idea of riding any more.'

'How very interesting,' I said, grimly.

'Never mind that now,' said Tick-Tock. 'You're here, and that's that. I rang your pad this morning, but your landlady said you hadn't been back all night. I wanted to see if it was O.K. for me to have the car after racing today and for you to get a lift back with Mr Axminster. I have met,' he finished gaily, 'a smashing girl. She's here at the races and she's coming out with me afterwards.'

'The car?' I said. 'Oh . . . yes. Certainly. Meet me outside the weighing-room after the last, and I'll show you where it is.'

'Super,' he said. 'I say, are you all right?'

'Yes, of course.'

'You look a bit night-afterish, to my hawk eyes,' he said. 'Anyway the best of luck on Template, and all that rot.'

An official peered into the changing-room and called me out. James was waiting in the weighing-room outside.

'Where have you been?' he said.

'In London,' I said. 'What's this rumour about me not turning up?'

'God knows,' he shrugged. 'I was sure you wouldn't have stayed away without at least letting me know, but . . .'

'No,' I said. 'Of course not.' Not unless, I thought, I had still been hanging in a deserted tack-room in the process of being crippled for life.

He dismissed the subject and began to talk about the race. 'There's a touch of frost in the ground still,' he said, 'but that's really to our advantage.' I told him I had walked round the course the day before, and knew which parts were best avoided.

'Good,' he said.

I could see that for once he was excited. There was a sort of uncharacteristic shyness about his eyes, and the lower teeth gleamed in an almost perpetual half smile. Anticipation of victory, that's what it is, I thought. And if I hadn't spent such a taxing night and morning I would have been feeling the same. As it was, I looked forward to the race without much joy, knowing from past experience that riding with injuries never made them better. Even so, I wouldn't have given up my place on Template for anything I could think of.

When I went back into the changing-room to put on breeches and colours, the jockeys riding in the first race had gone out, leaving a lot of space and quiet behind them. I went along to my peg, where all my kit was set out ready, and sat down for a while on the bench. My conscience ought to have been troubling me. James and Lord Tirrold had a right to expect their jockey to be in tip-top physical condition for so important a race, and, to put it mildly, he wasn't. However, I reflected wryly, looking down at my gloved hands, if we all owned up to every spot of damage, we'd spend far too much time on the stands watching others win on our mounts. It wasn't the first time I had deceived an owner and trainer in this way and yet won a race, and I fervently hoped it wouldn't be the last.

I thought about the Midwinter. Much depended on how it developed, but basically I intended to start on the rails, sit tight in about fourth place all the way round, and sprint the last three furlongs. There was a new Irish mare, Emerald, who had come over with a terrific reputation and might take a lot of beating, especially as her jockey was a wily character, very clever at riding near the front and slipping the field by a hard-to-peg-back ten lengths round the last bend. If Emerald led into the last bend, I decided, Template would have to be close to her by then, not still waiting in fourth place. Fast though he was, it would be senseless to leave him too much to do up the straight.

It is not customary for jockeys to stay in the changing-room while a race is on, and I saw the valets looking surprised that I had not gone out to watch it. I stood up, picked up the under-jersey and Lord Tirrold's colours and went to change into them in the washroom. Let the valets think what they like, I thought. I wanted to change out of sight, partly because I had to do it more slowly than usual but mostly so that they shouldn't see the bandages. I pulled down the sleeves of the finely knitted green and black jersey until they hid those on my wrists.

The first race was over and the jockeys were beginning to stream into the changing-room when I went back to my peg. I finished changing into breeches, nylons and boots and took my saddle and weight cloth along to the trial scales for Mike to adjust the amount of lead needed to bring me to twelve stone.

'You've got gloves on,' he pointed out.

'Yes,' I said mildly, 'it's a cold day. I'd better have some silk ones for riding in, though.'

'O.K.' he said. He produced from a hamper a bundle of whitish gloves and pulled out a pair for me.

I went along to the main scales to weigh out, and gave my saddle to Sid, who was standing there waiting for it.

He said, 'The governor says I'm to saddle Template in the stable, and bring him straight down into the parade ring when it's time, and not go into the saddling boxes at all.'

'Good,' I said emphatically.

'We've had two private dicks and a bloody great dog patrolling the yard all night,' he went on. 'And another dick came with us in the horse-box, and he's sitting in Template's box at this very minute. You never saw such a circus.'

'How's the horse?' I asked, smiling. Evidently James was splendidly keeping his word that Template would not be doped.

'He'll eat 'em,' Sid said simply. 'The Irish won't know what hit them. All the lads have got their wages on him. Yeah, I know they've been a bit fed up that you were going to ride him, but I saw you turn that Turniptop inside out on Thursday and I told 'em they've nothing to worry about.'

'Thanks,' I said, sincerely enough; but it was just one more ounce on a load of responsibility.

The time dragged. My shoulders ached. To take my mind off that I spent some time imagining the expression on Kemp-Lore's face when he saw my name up in the number frame. He would think at first it was a mistake. He would wait for it to be changed. And at any moment now, I thought maliciously, he will begin to realize that I am indeed here.

The second race was run with me still sitting in the changing-room, the object of now frankly curious looks from the valets. I took the brown gloves off and put on the greyish white ones. They had originally been really white, but nothing could entirely wash out a season's accumulated stains of mud and leather. I flexed my fingers. Most of the swelling had gone, and they seemed to be getting fairly strong again in spite of the cracked and tender skin.

Back came the other jockeys again, talking, laughing, swearing, dealing out friendly and not so friendly abuse, yelling to the valets, dumping down their kit – the ordinary, comradely, noisy changing-room mixture – and I felt apart from it, as if I were living in a different dimension. Another slow quarter of an hour crawled by. Then an official put his head in and shouted, 'Jockeys out, hurry up there, please.'

I stood up, put on the anorak, fastened my helmet, picked up my whip, and followed the general drift to the door. The feeling of unreality persisted.

Down in the paddock where in June the chiffons and ribbons

fluttered in the heat stood cold little bunches of owners and trainers, most of them muffled to the eyes against the wind. It seared through the bare branches of the trees beside the parade ring, leaving a uniformity of pinched faces among the people lining the rails. The bright winter sunshine gave an illusion of warmth which blue noses and runny eyes belied. But the anorak, as I had been pleased to discover, was windproof.

Lord Tirrold wore on his fine-boned face the same look of excited anticipation that I could still see on James's. They are both so sure, I thought uneasily, that Template will win. Their very confidence weakened mine.

'Well, Rob,' said Lord Tirrold, shaking me too firmly by the hand, 'this is it.'

'Yes, sir,' I agreed, 'this is it.'

'What do you think of Emerald?' he asked.

We watched her shamble round the parade ring with the sloppy walk and the low-carried head that so often denotes a champion.

'They say she's another Kerstin,' said James, referring to the best steeplechasing mare of the century.

'It's too soon to say that,' said Lord Tirrold: and I wondered if the same thought sprang into his mind as into mine, that after the Midwinter, it might not be too soon, after all. But he added as if to bury the possibility, 'Template will beat her.'

'I think so,' James agreed.

I swallowed. They were too sure. If he won, they would expect it. If he lost, they would blame me; and probably with good cause.

Template himself stalked round the parade ring in his navy-blue rug, playing up each time as he came face on to the wind, trying to turn round so that it blew on his quarters, with his lad hanging on to his leading-rein like a small child on a large kite.

A bell rang, indicating it was time for the jockeys to mount.

James beckoned to the boy, who brought Template across to us and took off his rug.

'Everything all right?' James asked.

'Yes, sir.'

Template's eyes were liquid clear, his ears were pricked, his muscles quivering to be off: the picture of a taut, tuned racing-machine eager to get on with the job he was born for. He was not a kind horse: there was no sweetness in his make-up and he inspired admiration rather than affection: but I liked him for his fire and his aggressiveness and his unswerving will to win.

'You've admired him long enough, Rob,' said James teasingly. 'Get up on him.'

I took off the anorak and dropped it on the rug. James gave me a leg up into the saddle and I gathered the reins and put my feet into the irons.

What he read in my face I don't know, but he said suddenly, anxiously, 'Is anything wrong?'

'No,' I said. 'Everything's fine.' I smiled down at him, reassuring myself as much as him.

Lord Tirrold said, 'Good luck,' as if he didn't think I needed it, and I touched my cap to him and turned Template away to take his place in the parade down the course.

There was a television camera on a tower not far down the course from the starting gate, and I found the thought of Kemp-Lore raging at the sight of me on his monitor set a most effective antidote to the freezing wind. We circled round for five minutes, eleven of us, while the assistant starter tightened girths and complained that anyone would think we were in perishing Siberia.

I remembered that Tick-Tock, the last time we had ridden together on the course on a cold day, had murmured 'Ascot's blasted Heath. Where are the witches?' And I thought of him now, putting a brave face on his inactivity on the stands. I thought briefly of Grant, probably hating my guts while he watched the race on television, and of Peter Cloony's wife, with no set to watch on at all, and of the jockeys who had given up and gone into factories, and of Art, under the sod.

'Line up,' called the starter, and we straightened into a ragged row across the course, with Template firmly on the inside, hugging the rails.

I thought of myself, driven to distraction by having it drummed into me that I had lost my nerve, and I thought of myself dragged over flinty ground and tied to a piece of galvanized chain; and I didn't need any more good reasons for having to win the Midwinter Cup.

I watched the starter's hand. He had a habit of stretching his fingers just before he pulled the lever to let the tapes up, and I had no intention of letting anyone get away before me and cut me out of the position I had acquired on the rails.

The starter stretched his fingers. I kicked Template's flanks. He was moving quite fast when we went under the rising tapes, with me lying flat along his withers to avoid being swept off, like other riders who had jumped the start too effectively in the past. The tapes whistled over my head and we were away, securely on the rails and on the inside curve for at least the next two miles.

The first three fences were the worst, as far as my comfort was concerned. By the time we had jumped the fourth – the water – I had felt the thinly healed crusts on my back tear open, had thought my arms and shoulder would split apart with the strain of controlling Template's eagerness, had found just how much my wrists and hands had to stand from the tug of the reins.

My chief feeling, as we landed over the water, was one of relief. It was all bearable; I could contain it and ignore it, and get on with the job.

The pattern of the race was simple from my point of view, because from start to finish I saw only three other horses, Emerald and the two lightly-weighted animals whom I had allowed to go on and set the pace. The jockeys of this pair, racing ahead of me nose for nose, consistently left a two-foot gap between themselves and the rails, and I reckoned that if they were still there by the time we reached the second last fence in the straight, they would veer very slightly towards the stands, as horses usually do at Ascot, and widen the gap enough for me to get through.

My main task until then was keeping Emerald from cutting across to the rails in front of me and being able to take the opening instead of Template. I left just too little room between me and the front pair for Emerald to get in, forcing the mare to race all the way on my outside. It didn't matter that she was two or three feet in front: I could see her better there, and Template was too clever a jumper to be brought down by the half-length trick – riding into a fence half a length in front of an opponent, causing him to take off at the same moment as oneself and land on top of the fence instead of safely on the ground the other side.

With the order unchanged we completed the whole of the first circuit and swept out to the country again. Template jumped the four fences down to Swinley Bottom so brilliantly that I kept finding myself crowding the tails of the pacemakers as we landed, and had to ease him back on the flat each time to avoid taking the lead too soon, and yet not ease him so much that Emerald could squeeze into the space between us.

From time to time I caught a glimpse of the grimness on Emerald's jockey's face. He knew perfectly well what I was doing to him, and if I hadn't beaten him to the rails and made a flying start, he would have done the same to me. Perhaps I had Kemp-Lore to thank that he hadn't even tried, I thought fleetingly; if the bonfire Kemp-Lore had made of my reputation had led the Irishman to misjudge what I would do, so much the better.

For another half-mile the two horses in front kept going

splendidly, but one of the jockeys picked up his whip at the third last fence, and the other was already busy with his hands. They were dead ducks, and because of that they swung a little wide going round the last bend into the straight. The Irishman must have had his usual bend tactics too fixed in his mind, for he chose that exact moment to go to the front. It was not a good occasion for that manoeuvre. I saw him spurt forward from beside me and accelerate, but he had to go round on the outside of the two front horses who were themselves swinging wide, and he was wasting lengths in the process. The mare carried seven pounds less weight than Template, and on that bend she lost the advantage they should have given her.

After the bend, tackling the straight for the last time, with the second last fence just ahead, Emerald was in the lead on the outside, then the two tiring horses, then me.

There was a three-foot gap then between the innermost pacemaker and the rails. I squeezed Template. He pricked his ears and bunched his colossal muscles and thrust himself forward into the narrow opening. He took off at the second last fence half a length behind and landed a length in front of the tiring horse, jumping so close to him on one side and to the wings on the other that I heard the other jockey cry out in surprise as I passed.

One of Template's great advantages was his speed away from a fence. With no check in his stride he sped smoothly on, still hugging the rails, with Emerald only a length in front on our left. I urged him a fraction forward to prevent the mare from swinging over to the rails and blocking me at the last fence. She needed two lengths' lead to do it safely, and I had no intention of letting her have it.

The utter joy of riding Template lay in the feeling of immense power which he generated. There was no need to make the best of things, on his back; to fiddle and scramble, and hope for others to blunder, and find nothing to spare for a finish. He had enough reserve strength for his jockey to be able to carve up the race as he wished, and there was nothing in racing, I thought, more ecstatic than that.

I knew, as we galloped towards the last fence, that Template would beat Emerald if he jumped it in anything like his usual style. She was a length ahead and showing no sign of flagging, but I was still holding Template on a tight rein. Ten yards from the fence, I let him go. I kicked his flanks and squeezed with the calves of my legs and he went over the birch like an angel, smooth, surging, the nearest to flying one can get.

He gained nearly half a length on the mare, but she didn't give up easily. I sat down and rode Template for my life, and he stretched himself into his flat-looking stride. He came level with Emerald half-way along the run in. She hung on grimly for a short distance, but Template would have none of it. He floated past her with an incredible increase of speed, and he won, in the end, by two clear lengths.

There are times beyond words, and that was one of them. I patted Template's sweating neck over and over. I could have kissed him. I would have given him anything. How does one thank a horse? How could one ever repay him, in terms he would understand, for giving one such a victory?

The two tall men were pleased all right. They stood side by side, waiting for us in the unsaddling enclosure, the same elated expression on both their faces. I smiled at them, and shook my feet out of the irons and slid off on to the ground. On to the ground: down to earth. The end of an unforgettable experience.

'Rob,' said James, shaking his big head. 'Rob.' He slapped Template's steaming shoulder and watched me struggle to undo the girth buckles with fingers shaking from both weakness and excitement.

'I knew he'd do it,' Lord Tirrold said. 'What a horse! What a race!'

I had got the buckles undone at last and had pulled the

saddle off over my arm when an official came over and asked Lord Tirrold not to go away, as the Cup was to be presented to him in a few minutes. To me, he said, 'Will you come straight out again after you have weighed in? There's a trophy for the winning jockey as well.'

I nodded, and went in to sit on the scales. Now that the concentration of the race was over, I began to be aware of the extra damage it had done. Across the back of my shoulders and down my arms to the fingertips every muscle felt like lead, draggingly heavy, shot with stabbing and burning sensations. I was appallingly weak and tired, and the pain in my wrists had increased to the point where I was finding it very difficult to keep it all out of my face. A quick look revealed that the bandages were red again, and so were the cuffs of the silk gloves and parts of the fawn under-jersey. But if the blood had soaked through the black jersey as well, at least it didn't show.

With a broad smile Mike took my saddle from me in the changing-room and unbuckled my helmet and pulled it off my head.

'They are wanting you outside, did you know?' he said.

I nodded. He held out a comb. 'Better smarten your hair a bit. You can't let the side down.'

I obediently took the comb and tidied my hair, and went back outside.

The horses had been led away and in their place stood a table bearing the Midwinter Cup and other trophies, with a bunch of racecourse directors and stewards beside it.

And Maurice Kemp-Lore as well.

It was lucky I saw him before he saw me. I felt my scalp contract at the sight of him and an unexpectedly strong shock of revulsion ran right down my body. He couldn't have failed to understand it, if he had seen it.

I found James at my elbow. He followed my gaze.

'Why are you looking so grim?' he said. 'He didn't even try to dope Template.'

'No,' I agreed. 'I expect he was too tied up with his television work to be sure of having time to do it.'

'He has given up the whole idea,' said James confidently. 'He must have seen there was no chance any more of persuading anyone you had lost your nerve. Not after the way you rode on Thursday.'

It was the reckless way I had ridden on Thursday that had infuriated Kemp-Lore into delivering the packet I had taken on Friday. I understood that very well.

'Have you told anyone about the sugar?' I asked James.

'No, since you asked me not to. But I think something must be done. Slander or no slander, evidence or not . . .'

'Will you wait,' I asked, 'until next Saturday? A week today? Then you can tell whoever you like.'

'Very well,' he said slowly. 'But I still think . . .'

He was interrupted by the arrival at the trophy table of the day's V.I.P., a pretty Duchess, who with a few well-chosen words and a genuinely friendly smile presented the Midwinter Cup to Lord Tirrold, a silver tray to James, and a cigarette box to me. An enterprising press photographer let off a flash bulb as the three of us stood together admiring our prizes, and after that we gave them back again to the clerk of the course, for him to have them engraved with Template's name and our own.

I heard Kemp-Lore's voice behind me as I handed over the cigarette box, and it gave me time to arrange my face into a mildly smiling blankness before turning round. Even so, I was afraid that I wouldn't be able to look at him without showing my feelings.

I pivoted slowly on my heels and met his eyes. They were piercingly blue and very cold, and they didn't blink or alter in any way as I looked back at them. I relaxed a little, inwardly, thankful that the first difficult hurdle was crossed. He had searched, but had not read in my face that I knew it was he who had abducted me the evening before.

'Rob Finn,' he said in his charming television voice, 'is the jockey you just watched being carried to victory by this wonder horse, Template.' He was speaking into a hand microphone from which trailed yards of black flex, and looking alternately at me and at a camera on a scaffolding tower near by. The camera's red eye glowed. I mentally girded up my loins and prepared to forestall every disparaging opinion he might utter.

He said, 'I expect you enjoyed being his passenger?'

'It was marvellous,' I said emphatically, smiling a smile to outdazzle his. 'It is a great thrill for any jockey to ride a horse as superb as Template. Of course,' I went on amiably, before he had time to speak, 'I am lucky to have had the opportunity. As you know, I have been taking Pip Pankhurst's place all these months, while his leg has been mending, and today's win should have been his. He is much better now, I'm glad to say, and we are all delighted that it won't be long before he is riding again.' I spoke truthfully: whatever it meant to me in fewer rides, it would benefit the sport as a whole to have its champion back in action.

A slight chill crept into the corner of Kemp-Lore's mouth.

'You haven't been doing as well, lately . . .' he began.

'No,' I interrupted warmly. 'Aren't they extraordinary, those runs of atrocious luck in racing? Did you know that Doug Smith once rode ninety-nine losers in succession? How terrible he must have felt. It makes my twenty or so seem quite paltry.'

'You weren't worried, then, by . . . er . . . by such a bad patch as you've been going through?' His smile was slipping.

'Worried?' I repeated lightheartedly. 'Well, naturally I wasn't exactly delighted, but these runs of bad luck happen to everyone in racing, once in a while, and one just has to live through them until another winner comes along. Like today's,' I finished with a grin at the camera.

'Most people understood it was more than bad luck,' he said sharply. There was a definite crack in his jolly-chums manner, and for an instant I saw in his eyes a flash of the fury he was controlling. It gave me great satisfaction, and because of it I smiled at him more vividly.

I said, 'People will believe anything when their pockets are touched. I'm afraid a lot of people lost their money backing my mounts . . . it's only natural to blame the jockey . . . nearly everyone does, when they lose.'

He listened to me mending the holes he had torn in my life and he couldn't stop me without giving an impression of being a bad sport; and nothing kills the popularity of a television commentator quicker than obvious bad-sportsmanship.

He had been standing at right angles to me with his profile to the camera, but now he took a step towards me and turned so that he stood beside me on my left side. As he moved there was a fleeting set to his mouth that looked like cruelty to me, and it prepared me in some measure for what he did next.

With a large gesture which must have appeared as genuine friendship on the television screen, he dropped his right arm heavily across my shoulders, with his right thumb lying forward on my collar bone and his fingers spread out on my back.

I stood still, and turned my head slowly towards him, and smiled sweetly. Few things have ever cost me more effort.

'Tell us a bit about the race, then, Rob,' he said, advancing the microphone in his left hand. 'When did you begin to think you might win?'

His arm felt like a ton weight, an almost unsupportable burden on my aching muscles. I gathered my straying wits.

'Oh . . . I thought, coming into the last fence,' I said, 'that Template might have the speed to beat Emerald on the flat. He can produce such a sprint at the end, you know.'

'Yes, of course.' He pressed his fingers more firmly into the back of my shoulder and gave me what passed for a friendly shake. My head began to spin. Everything on the edge of my vision became blurred. I went on smiling, concentrating desperately on the fair, good-looking face so close to mine, and was rewarded by the expression of puzzlement and disappointment in his eyes. He knew that under his fingers, beneath two thin jerseys, were patches which must be sore if touched, but he didn't know how much or how little trouble I had had in freeing myself in the tack-room. I wanted him to believe it had been none at all, that the ropes had slipped undone or the hook fallen easily out of the ceiling. I wanted to deny him even the consolation of knowing how nearly he had succeeded in preventing me from riding Template.

'And what are Template's plans for the future?' He strove to be conversational, normal. The television interview was progressing along well-trodden ways.

'There's the Gold Cup at Cheltenham,' I said. I was past telling whether I sounded equally unruffled, but there was still no leap of triumph in his face, so I went on, 'I expect he will run there, in three weeks' time. All being well, of course.'

'And do you hope to ride him again in that?' he asked. There was an edge to his voice which just stopped short of offensiveness. He was finding it as nearly impossible to put on an appearance of affection for me as I for him.

'It depends,' I said, 'on whether or not Pip is fit in time . . . and on whether Lord Tirrold and Mr Axminster want me to, if he isn't. But of course I'd like to, if I get the chance.'

'You've never yet managed to ride in the Gold Cup, I believe?' He made it sound as if I had been trying unsuccessfully for years to beg a mount.

'No,' I agreed. 'But it has only been run twice since I came into racing, so if I get a ride in it so soon in my career I'll count myself very lucky.'

His nostrils flared and I thought in satisfaction, 'That got you squarely in the guts, my friend. You'd forgotten how short a time I've been a jockey.'

He turned his head away from me towards the camera and I saw the rigidity in his neck and jaw and the pulse which beat visibly in his temple. I imagined he would willingly have seen me dead: yet he was enough in command of himself to realize that if he pressed my shoulder any harder I would be likely to guess it was not accidental.

Perhaps if he had been less controlled at that moment I would have been more merciful to him later. If his professionally pleasant expression had exploded into the rage he was feeling, or if he had openly dug his nails with ungovernable vindictiveness into my back, I could perhaps have believed him more mad than wicked, after all. But he knew too well where to stop; and since I could not equate madness with such self-discipline, by my standards he was sane; sane and controlled, and therefore unlikely to destroy himself from within. I threw Claudius Mellit's plea for kid gloves finally overboard.

Kemp-Lore was speaking calmly towards the camera, finishing off his broadcast. He gave me a last, natural-looking little squeezing shake, and let his arm drop away from my shoulders. Slowly and methodically I silently repeated to myself the ten most obscene words I knew, and after that Ascot racecourse stopped attempting to whirl round and settled down again into brick and mortar and grass and people, all sharp and perpendicular.

The man behind the camera on the tower held up his thumb and the red eye blinked out.

Kemp-Lore turned directly to me again and said, 'Well, that's it. We're off the air now.'

'Thank you, Maurice,' I said, carefully constructing one last warm smile. 'That was just what I needed to set me back on top of the world. A big race win and a television interview with you to clinch it. Thank you very much.' I could rub my fingers in his wounds, too.

He gave me a look in which the cultivated habit of charm struggled for supremacy over spite, and still won. Then he turned on his heel and walked away, pulling his black microphone lead along the ground after him.

It is impossible to say which of us loathed the other more.

Fifteen

I SPENT most of the next day in Joanna's bed. Alone, unfortunately.

She gave me a cup of coffee for breakfast, a cosy grin, and instructions to sleep. So I lazily went on snoozing in the pyjamas she had bought me, dreaming about her on her own pillow, doing nothing more energetic than occasionally raise my blood pressure by thinking about Kemp-Lore.

I had arrived in a shaky condition on her doorstep the evening before, having first taken Tick-Tock and his space-age girlfriend by taxi to the boring White Bear at Uxbridge where, as I had imagined, the Mini-Cooper stood abandoned in the car park. It had seemed to me certain that Kemp-Lore had driven to the White Bear in his own car, had used the Mini-Cooper for his excursion to the abandoned stables, and had changed back again to his own car on the return journey. His route, checked on the map, was simple: direct almost. All the same I was relieved to find the little Mini safe and sound.

Tick-Tock's remarks about my carelessness with communal property trickled to a stop when he found my wrist-watch and wallet and the other things out of my pockets on the glove shelf, and my jacket and overcoat and a length of white nylon rope on the back seat.

'Why the blazes,' he said slowly, 'did you leave your watch and your money and your coats here? It's a wonder they weren't pinched. And the car.'

'It's the north-east wind,' I said solemnly. 'Like the moon, you know. I always do mad things when there's a north-east wind.'

'North-east my aunt fanny.' He grinned, picked up the coats, and transferred them to the waiting taxi. Then he surprisingly shovelled all my small belongings back into my trousers pockets, and put my watch into my gloved hand.

'You may have fooled everyone else, mate,' he said lightly, 'but to me you have looked like death inefficiently warmed up all day, and it's something to do with your maulers . . . the gloves are new . . . you don't usually wear any. What happened?'

'You work on it,' I said amiably, getting back into the taxi. 'If you haven't anything better to do.' I glanced across at his little hep-cat, and he laughed and flipped his hand, and went to help her into the Mini-Cooper.

The taxi driver, in a good mood because he had backed three winners, drove me back to Joanna's mews without a single complaint about the roundabout journey. When I paid him and added a fat tip on top he said, 'Were you on a winner, too, then?'

'Yes,' I said. 'Template.'

'Funny thing that,' he said. 'I backed him myself, after what you said about not believing all you hear. You were quite right, weren't you? That fellow Finn's not washed up at all, not by a long chalk. He rode a hell of a race. I reckon he can carry my money again, any day.' He shifted his gears gently, and drove off.

Watching his tail-light bump away down the cobbled mews, I felt ridiculously happy and very much at peace. Winning the race had already been infinitely worth the cost, and the taxi driver, not knowing who he was speaking to, had presented me with the bonus of learning that as far as the British racing public was concerned, I was back in business.

Dead beat but contented, I leaned against Joanna's doorpost and rang her bell.

That wasn't quite the end of the most exhausting twenty-four hours of my life, however. My thoughtful cousin, anticipating correctly that I would refuse to turn out again to see a doctor, had imported one of her own. He was waiting there when I arrived, a blunt no-bedside manner Scot with bushy eyebrows and three warts on his chin.

To my urgent protests that I was in no state to withstand his ministrations, both he and Joanna turned deaf ears. They sat me in a chair, and off came my clothes again, the leather gloves and the silk racing ones I had not removed after riding, then the anorak, my father's shirt and the racing under-jersey, also not returned to Mike, then the bits of lint Joanna had stuck on in the morning, and finally the blood-soaked bandages round my wrists. Towards the end of all this rather ruthless undressing, the room began spinning as Ascot had done, and I regrettably rolled off the chair on to the floor, closer to fainting than I had been the whole time.

The Scotsman picked me up and put me back in the chair and told me to pull myself together and be a man.

'You've only lost a wee bit of skin,' he said sternly.

I began to laugh weakly, which didn't go down well, either. He was a joyless fellow. He compressed his mouth until the warts quivered when I shook my head to his enquiries and would not tell him what had happened to me. But he bound me up again comfortably enough and gave me some pain-killing pills which turned out to be very effective; and when he had gone I got into Joanna's bed and sank thankfully into oblivion.

Joanna worked at her painting most of the next day and when I surfaced finally at about four o'clock in the afternoon, she was singing quietly at her easel. Not the angular, spiky songs she specialized in, but a Gaelic ballad in a minor key, soft and sad. I lay and listened with my eyes shut because I knew she would stop if she found me awake. Her voice was true, even at a level not much above a whisper, the result of well-exercised vocal cords and terrific breath control. A proper Finn, she is, I thought wryly. Nothing done by halves.

She came to the end of the ballad, and afterwards began another. 'I know where I'm going, and I know who's going with me. I know who I love, but the dear knows who I'll marry. Some say he's black, but I say he's bonny . . .' She stopped abruptly and said quietly but forcefully, 'Damn, damn and blast.' I heard her throw down her palette and brushes and go into the kitchen.

After a minute I sat up in bed and called to her, 'Joanna.'

'Yes?' she shouted, without reappearing.

'I'm starving,' I said.

'Oh.' She gave a laugh which ended in a choke, and called, 'All right. I'll cook.'

And cook she did; fried chicken with sweetcorn and pine-apple and bacon. While the preliminary smells wafted tantaliz-ingly out of the kitchen I got up and put my clothes on, and stripped her bed. There were clean sheets in the drawer beneath, and I made it up again fresh and neat for her to get into.

She carried a tray of plates and cutlery in from the kitchen and saw the bundle of dirty sheets and the smooth bed.

'What are you doing?'

'The sofa isn't good for you,' I said. 'You obviously haven't slept well . . . and your eyes are red.'

'That isn't . . .' she began, and thought better of it.

'It isn't lack of sleep?' I finished.

She shook her head. 'Let's eat.'

'Then what's the matter?' I said.

'Nothing. Nothing. Shut up and eat.'

I did as I was told. I was hungry.

She watched me finish every morsel. 'You're feeling better,' she stated.

'Oh, yes. Much. Thanks to you.'

'And you are not sleeping here tonight?'

'No.'

'You can try the sofa,' she said mildly. 'You might as well find out what I have endured for your sake.' I didn't answer at once, and she added compulsively, 'I'd like you to stay, Rob. Stay.'

I looked at her carefully. Was there the slightest chance, I wondered, that her gentle songs and her tears in the kitchen and now her reluctance to have me leave meant that she was at last finding the fact of our cousinship more troublesome than she was prepared for? I had always known that if she ever did come to love me as I wanted and also was not able to abandon her rigid prejudice against our blood relationship, it would very likely break her up. If that was what was happening to her, it was definitely not the time to walk out.

'All right,' I said smiling. 'Thank you. I'll stay. On the sofa.'

She became suddenly animated and talkative, and told me in great detail how the race and the interview afterwards had appeared on television. Her voice was quick and light. 'At the beginning of the programme he said he thought your name was a mistake on the number boards, because he had heard you weren't there, and I began to worry that you had broken down on the way and hadn't got there after all. But of course you had . . . and afterwards you looked like life-long buddies standing there with his arm round your shoulders and you smiling at him as if the sun shone out of his eyes. How did you manage it? But he was trying to needle you, wasn't he? It seemed like it to me, but then that was perhaps because I knew . . .' She stopped in mid-flow, and in an entirely different, sober tone of voice she said, 'What are you going to do about him?'

I told her. It took some time.

She was shaken. 'You can't,' she said.

I smiled at her, but didn't answer.

She shivered. 'He didn't know what he was up against, when he picked on you.'

'Will you help?' I asked. Her help was essential.

'Won't you change your mind and go to the police?' she said seriously.

'No.'

'But what you are planning . . . it's cruel.'

'Yes,' I agreed.

'And complicated, and a lot of work, and expensive.'

'Yes. Will you make that one telephone call for me?'

She sighed and said, 'You don't think you'll relent, once everything has stopped hurting?'

'I'm quite certain,' I said.

'I'll think about it,' she said, standing up and collecting the dirty dishes. She wouldn't let me help her wash up, so I went over to the easel to see what she had been working at all day: and I was vaguely disturbed to find it was a portrait of my mother sitting at her piano.

I was still looking at the picture when she came back.

'It's not very good, I'm afraid,' she said, standing beside me. 'Something seems to have gone wrong with the perspective.'

'Does Mother know you're doing it?' I asked.

'Oh no,' she said.

'When did you start it?'

'Yesterday afternoon,' she said.

There was a pause. Then I said, 'It won't do you any good to try to convince yourself your feelings for me are maternal.'

She jerked in surprise.

'I don't want mothering,' I said. 'I want a wife.'

'I can't . . .' she said, with a tight throat.

I turned away from the picture, feeling that I had pressed her too far, too soon. Joanna abruptly picked up a turpentine-soaked rag and scrubbed at the still wet oils, wiping out all her work.

'You see too much,' she said. 'More than I understood myself.'

I grinned at her and after a moment, with an effort, she smiled back. She wiped her fingers on the rag, and hung it on the easel.

'I'll make that telephone call,' she said. 'You can go ahead with . . . with what you plan to do.'

On the following morning, Monday, I hired a drive-yourself car and went to see Grant Oldfield.

The hard overnight frost, which had caused the day's racing to be cancelled, had covered the hedges and trees with sparkling rime, and I enjoyed the journey even though I expected a reception at the end of it as cold as the day.

I stopped outside the gate, walked up the short path through the desolate garden, and rang the bell.

It had only just struck me that the brass bell push was brightly polished when the door opened and a neat dark-haired young woman in a green wool dress looked at me enquiringly.

'I came . . .' I said. 'I wanted to see . . . er . . . I wonder if you could tell me where I can find Grant Oldfield?'

'Indoors,' she said. 'He lives here; I'm his wife. Just a minute, and I'll get him. What name shall I say?'

'Rob Finn,' I said.

'Oh,' she said in surprise; and she smiled warmly. 'Do come in. Grant will be so pleased to see you.'

I doubted it, but I stepped into the narrow hall and she shut the door behind me. Everything was spotless and shining; it looked a different house from the one I remembered. She led the way to the kitchen and opened the door on to another area of dazzling cleanliness.

Grant was sitting at a table, reading a newspaper. He glanced up as his wife went in, and when he saw me his face too creased into a smile of surprised welcome. He stood up. He was much thinner and older-looking, and shrunken in some indefinable inner way; but he was, or he was going to be soon, a whole man again.

'How are you, Grant?' I said inadequately, not understanding their friendliness.

'I'm much better, thanks,' he said. 'I've been home a fortnight now.'

'He was in hospital,' his wife explained. 'They took him there the day after you brought him home. Dr Parnell wrote to me and told me Grant was ill and couldn't help being how he was. So I came back.' She smiled at Grant. 'And everything's going to be all right now. Grant's got a job lined up too. He starts in two weeks, selling toys.'

'Toys?' I exclaimed. Of all incongruous things, I thought.

'Yes,' she said, 'they thought it would be better for him to do something which had nothing to do with horses, so that he wouldn't start brooding again.'

'We've a lot to thank you for, Rob,' Grant said.

'Dr Parnell told me,' his wife said, seeing my surprise, 'that you would have been well within your rights if you'd handed him over to the police instead of bringing him here.'

'I tried to kill you,' Grant said in a wondering voice, as if he could no longer understand how he had felt. 'I really tried to kill you, you know.'

'Dr Parnell said if you'd been a different sort of person Grant could have ended up in a criminal lunatic asylum.'

I said uncomfortably, 'Dr Parnell appears to have been doing too much talking altogether.'

'He wanted me to understand,' she said, smiling, 'that you had given Grant another chance, so I ought to give him another chance too.'

'Would it bother you,' I said to Grant, 'if I asked you a question about how you lost your job with Axminster?'

Mrs Oldfield moved protectively to his side. 'Don't bring it all back,' she said anxiously, 'all the resentment.'

'It's all right, love,' Grant said, putting his arm around her waist. 'Go ahead.'

'I believe you were telling the truth when you told Axminster you had not sold information to that professional punter, Lubbock,' I said. 'But Lubbock did get information, and did pay for it. The question is, who was he actually handing over the money to, if he thought he was paying it to you?'

'You've got it wrong, Rob,' Grant said. 'I went over and over it at the time, and I went to see Lubbock and got pretty angry with him . . .' He smiled ruefully, 'and Lubbock said that until James Axminster tackled him about it he hadn't known for sure who he was buying information from. He had guessed it was me, he said. But he said I had given him the information over the telephone, and he had sent the payments to me in the name of Robinson, care of a Post Office in London. He didn't believe I knew nothing about it, of course. He just thought I hadn't covered myself well enough and was trying to wriggle out of trouble.' There was a remarkable lack of bitterness in his voice; his spell in a mental hospital, or his illness itself, seemed to have changed his personality to the roots.

'Can you give me Lubbock's address?' I asked.

'He lives in Solihull,' he said slowly. 'I might know the house again, but I can't remember the name of it, or the road.'

'I'll find it,' I said.

'Why do you want to?' he asked.

'Would it mean anything to you, if I happened to prove that you were telling the truth all along?'

His face came suddenly alive from within. 'I'll say it would,' he said. 'You can't imagine what it was like, losing that job for something I didn't do, and having no one believe in me any more.'

I didn't tell him that I knew exactly what it was like, only too well. I said, 'I'll do my best, then.'

'But you won't go back to racing?' his wife said to him anxiously. 'You won't start all over again?'

'No love. Don't worry,' he said calmly. 'I'm going to enjoy selling toys. You never know, we might start a toy shop of our own, next year, when I've learned the business.'

I drove the thirty miles to Solihull, looked up Lubbock in the telephone directory, and rang his number. A woman answered. She told me that he was not in, but if I wanted him urgently I would probably get hold of him at the Queen's Hotel in Birmingham, as he was lunching there.

Having lost my way twice in the one-way streets, I miraculously found a place to park outside the Queen's, and went in. I wrote a note on the hotel writing-paper, asking Mr Lubbock, whom I did not know even by sight, if he would be so very kind as to give me a few minutes of his time. Sealing the note in an envelope, I asked the head porter if he would have one of the page-boys find Mr Lubbock and give it to him.

'He went into the dining-room with another gentleman a few minutes ago,' he said. 'Here, Dickie, take this note in to Mr Lubbock.'

Dickie returned with an answer on the back of the note: Mr Lubbock would meet me in the lounge at two-fifteen.

Mr Lubbock proved to be a plumpish, middle-aged man with a gingery moustache and a thin section of lank hair brushed across a balding skull. He accepted from me a large brandy and a fat cigar with such an air of surprised irony that I was in no doubt that he was used to buying these things for jockeys, and not the other way about.

'I want to know about Grant Oldfield,' I said, coming straight to the point.

'Oldfield?' he murmured, sucking flame down the cigar. 'Oh

yes, I remember, Oldfield.' He gave me a sharp upward glance. 'You . . . er . . . you still work for the same firm, don't you? Do you want a deal, is that it? Well, I don't see why not. I'll give you the odds to a pony for every winner you put me on to. No one could say fairer than that.'

'Is that what you paid Oldfield?' I said.

'Yes,' he said.

'Did you give it to him personally?' I asked.

'No,' he said. 'But then he didn't ask me personally. He fixed it up on the telephone. He was very secretive: he said his name was Robinson, and asked me to pay him in uncrossed money orders, and to send them to a Post Office for him to collect.'

'Which one?' I asked.

He took a swig at the brandy and gave me an assessing look. 'Why do you want to know?'

'It sounds a good idea,' I said casually.

He shrugged. 'I can't remember,' he said. 'Surely it's unimportant which Post Office it was? Somewhere in a London suburb, I know, but I can't remember where after all this time. NE7? N12? Something like that.'

'You wouldn't have a record of it?'

'No,' he said decisively. 'Why don't you ask Oldfield himself, if you need to know?'

I sighed. 'How many times did he give you information?' I asked.

'He told me the names of about five horses altogether, I should think. Three of them won, and I sent him the money on those occasions.'

'You didn't know it was Oldfield selling you tips, did you?' I asked.

'It depends what you mean by "know",' he said. 'I had a pretty good idea. Who else could it have been? But I suppose I didn't actually "know" until Axminster said "I hear you've been buying information from my jockey," and I agreed that I had.'

'So you wouldn't have told anyone before that that it was Oldfield who was selling you tips?'

'Of course not.'

'No one at all?' I pressed.

'No, certainly not.' He gave me a hard stare. 'You don't broadcast things like that, not in my business, and especially if you aren't dead sure of your facts. Just what is all this about?'

'Well . . .' I said. 'I'm very sorry to have misled you, Mr Lubbock, but I am not really in the market for information. I'm just trying to unstick a bit of the mud that was thrown at Grant Oldfield.'

To my surprise he gave a fat chuckle and knocked half an inch of ash off the cigar.

'Do you know,' he said, 'if you'd agreed to tip me off I'd have been looking for the catch? There's some jockeys you can square, and some you can't, and in my line you get an instinct for which are which. Now you . . .' he jabbed the cigar in my direction . . . 'you aren't the type.'

'Thanks,' I murmured.

'And more fool you,' he said nodding. 'It's not illegal.'

I grinned.

'Mr Lubbock,' I said, 'Oldfield was not Robinson, but his career and his health were broken up because you and Mr Axminster were led to believe that he was.'

He stroked his moustache with his thumb and forefinger of his left hand, wondering.

I went on, 'Oldfield has now given up all thought of riding again, but it would still mean a great deal to him to have his name cleared. Will you help to do it?'

'How?' he said.

'Wouldn't you just write a statement to the effect that you saw no evidence at any time to support your guess that in paying Robinson, you were really paying Oldfield, and that at no time before James Axminster approached you did you speak of your suspicions as to Robinson's identity.'

'Is that all?' he said.

'Yes.'

'All right,' he said. 'It can't do any harm. But I think you're barking up the wrong tree. No one but a jockey would go to all that trouble to hide his identity. No one would bother, if his job didn't depend on not being found out. Still, I'll write what you ask.'

He unscrewed a pen, took a sheet of hotel writing-paper and in a decisive hand wrote the statement I had suggested. He signed it, and added the date and read it through.

'There you are,' he said. 'Though I can't see what good it will do.'

I read what he had written and folded the paper, and put it in my wallet.

'Someone told Mr Axminster that Oldfield was selling you information,' I said. 'If you hadn't told anyone at all – who knew?'

'Oh.' His eyes opened. 'I see, yes, I see. Robinson knew. But Oldfield would never have let on . . . so Oldfield was not Robinson.'

'That's about it,' I agreed, standing up. 'Thank you very much, Mr Lubbock, for your help.'

'Any time.' He waved the diminishing cigar, smiling broadly. 'See you at the races.'

Sixteen

ON TUESDAY morning I bought a copy of the *Horse and Hound* and spent a good while telephoning a few of the people who had advertised their hunters for sale. With three of them I made appointments to view the animal in question in two days' time.

Next I rang up one of the farmers I rode for and persuaded him to lend me his Land-Rover and trailer on Thursday afternoon.

Then, having borrowed a tape measure out of Joanna's work-box – she was out at a rehearsal – I drove the hired car down to James's stables. I found him sitting in his office dealing with his paper work. The fire, newly lit in the grate, was making little headway against the raw chill in the air, and outside in the yard the lads looked frozen as they scurried about doing up their horses after the second morning exercise.

'No racing again today,' James remarked. 'Still, we've been extraordinarily lucky this winter up to now.'

He stood up and rubbed his hands, and held them out to the inadequate fire. 'Some of the owners have telephoned,' he said. 'They're willing to have you back. I told them . . .' and his lower teeth gleamed as he looked at me from under his eyebrows, '. . . that I was satisfied with your riding, and that you would be on Template in the Gold Cup.'

'What!' I exclaimed. 'Do you mean it?'

'Yes.' The glimmer deepened in his eyes.

'But . . . Pip . . .' I said.

'I've explained to Pip,' he said, 'that I can't take you off the horse when you've won both the King' Chase and the Midwinter on him. And Pip agrees. I have arranged with him that he starts again the week after Cheltenham, which will give him time to get a few races in before the Grand National. He'll be riding my runner in that – the horse he rode last year.'

'It finished sixth,' I said, remembering.

'Yes, that's right. Now, I've enough horses to keep both Pip and you fairly busy, and no doubt you'll get outside rides as well. It should work out all right for both of you.'

'I don't know how to thank you,' I said.

'Thank yourself,' he said sardonically. 'You earned it.' He bent down and put another lump of coal on the fire.

'James,' I said, 'will you write something down for me?'

'Write? Oh, you'll get a contract for next season, the same as Pip.'

'I didn't mean that,' I said awkwardly. 'It's quite different . . . would you just write down that it was Maurice Kemp-Lore who told you that Oldfield was selling information about your horses, and that he said he had learned it from Lubbock?'

'Write it down?'

'Yes. Please,' I said.

'I don't see . . .' He gave me an intent look and shrugged. 'Oh, very well then.' He sat down at his desk, took a sheet of paper headed with his name and address, and wrote what I had asked.

'Signature and date?' he said.

'Yes, please.'

He blotted the page. 'What good will that do?' he said, handing it to me.

I took Mr Lubbock's paper out of my wallet and showed it to him. He read it through three times.

'My God,' he said. 'It's incredible. Suppose I had checked carefully with Lubbock? What a risk Maurice took.'

'It wasn't so big a risk,' I said. 'You wouldn't have thought of questioning what he put forward as a friendly warning. Anyway, it worked. Grant got the sack.'

'I'm sorry for that,' James said slowly. 'I wish there was something I could do about it.'

'Write to Grant and explain,' I suggested. 'He would appreciate it more than anything in the world.'

'I'll do that,' he agreed, making a note.

'On Saturday morning,' I said, taking back Lubbock's statement and putting it with his in my wallet, 'these little documents will arrive with a plop on the Senior Steward's doormat. Of course they aren't conclusive enough to base any legal proceedings on, but they should be enough to kick friend Kemp-Lore off his pedestal.'

'I should say you were right.' He looked at me gravely, and then said, 'Why wait until Saturday?'

'I . . . er . . . I won't be ready until then,' I said evasively.

He didn't pursue it. We walked out into the yard together and looked in on some of the horses, James giving instructions, criticism and praise – in that order – to the hurrying lads. I realized how used I had grown to the efficiency and prosperity of his organization, and how much it meant to me to be a part of it.

We walked slowly along one row of boxes, and James went into the tack-room at the end to talk to Sid about the cancellation of the following day's racing. Unexpectedly I stopped dead on the threshold. I didn't want to go in. I knew it was stupid, but it made no difference. Parts of me were still too sore.

The harness hook hung quietly from the centre of the ceiling, with a couple of dirty bridles swinging harmlessly on two of its curving arms. I turned my back on it and looked out across the tidy yard, and wondered if I would ever again see one without remembering.

Up in the rolling, grassy hills a mile or so away from his stable, James owned an old deserted keeper's cottage. In the past it had been the home allotted to the man who looked after the gallops, James had told me once on a journey to the races, but as it had no electricity, no piped water and no sanitation, the new groundsman preferred, not unnaturally, to live in comfort in the village below and go up the hill to work on a motor-bike.

The old cottage lay down an overgrown lane leading off a public but little used secondary road which led nowhere except up and along the side of the hill and down again to join the main road four miles further on. It served only two farms and one private house, and because of its quietness it was a regular route for the Axminster horses on roadwork days.

After leaving James I drove up to the cottage. I had not seen it at close quarters before, only a glimpse of its blank end wall from the end of the lane as I rode by. I now found it was a four-roomed bungalow, set in a small fenced garden with a narrow path leading from the gate to the front door. The neglected grass had been cropped short by sheep. There was one window to each room, two facing the front and two the back.

Getting in without a key presented no difficulty as most of the glass in the windows was broken; and opening one, I climbed in. The whole place smelt of fungus and rot, though faintly, as if the decay were only warming up for future onslaught. The walls and floorboards were still in good condition, and only one of the rooms was damp. I found that all four rooms opened on to a small central hall inside the front entrance; and as I made my tour I reflected that it could not have been more convenient if I had designed it myself.

I let myself out of the front door, and walking round to the back I took out Joanna's inch tape and measured the window frame; three feet high, four feet wide. Then I returned to the front, counted the number of broken panes of glass, and measured one of them. That done, I returned to James and asked him to lend me the cottage for a few days to store some things in for which there was no room at my digs.

'As long as you like,' he agreed absently, busy with paper work.

'May I mend some of the windows, and put on a new lock, to make it more secure?' I asked.

'Help yourself,' he said. 'Do what you like.'

I thanked him, and drove into Newbury, and at a builder's merchants waited while they made me up an order of ten panes of glass, enough putty to put them in with, several pieces of water pipe cut to a specified length, a bucket, some screws, a stout padlock, a bag of cement, a pot of green paint, a putty knife, a screwdriver, a cement trowel and a paint brush. Loaded to the axles with that lot I returned to the cottage.

I painted the weather-beaten front door and left it open to dry, reflecting that no one could blame a keeper, or his wife for that matter, for not wanting to live in that lonely, inconvenient cul-de-sac.

I went into one of the back rooms and knocked out all the panes of glass which still remained in their little oblong frames. Then, outside in the garden, I mixed a good quantity of cement, using water from the rain butt, and fixed six three-foot lengths of water pipe upright in a row across the window. That done, I went round into the hall, and on the doorpost and door of the same room screwed firmly home the fittings for the padlock. On the inside of the door I unscrewed the handle and removed it.

The final job was replacing the glass in the front windows, and it took me longest to do, chipping out all the old putty and squeezing on the new; but at last it was done, and with its whole windows and fresh green door the cottage already looked more cheerful and welcoming.

I smiled to myself. I retrieved the car from where I had parked it inconspicuously behind some bushes, and drove back to London.

The Scots doctor was drinking gin with Joanna when I let myself in.

'Oh no,' I said unceremoniously.

'Oh yes, laddie,' he said. 'You were supposed to come and see me yesterday, remember.'

'I was busy,' I said.

'I'll just take a look at those wrists, if you don't mind,' he said, putting down the gin and standing up purposefully.

I sighed and sat down at the table, and he unwrapped the bandages. There was blood on them again.

'I thought I told you to take it easy,' he said sternly. 'How do you expect them to heal? What have you been doing?'

I could have said 'Screwing in screws, chipping out putty and mixing cement,' but instead I rather uncooperatively muttered, 'Nothing.'

Irritated, he slapped a new dressing on with unnecessary force and I winced. He snorted, but he was gentler with the second one.

'All right,' he said, finishing them off. 'Now, rest them a bit this time. And come and see me on Friday.'

'Saturday,' I said. 'I won't be in London on Friday.'

'Saturday morning then. And mind you come.' He picked up his glass, tossed off the gin, and said a friendly good night exclusively to Joanna.

She came back laughing from seeing him out. 'He isn't usually so unsympathetic,' she said. 'But I think he suspects you were engaged in some sort of sadistic, disgusting orgy last week, as you wouldn't tell him how you got like that.'

'And he's dead right,' I said morosely. He had stirred up my wrists properly, and they hadn't been too good to start with, after my labours at the cottage.

For the third night I went to bed on the sofa and lay awake in the darkness, listening to Joanna's soft sleeping breath. Every day she hesitantly asked me if I would like to stay another night in her flat, and as I had no intention of leaving while there was any chance of thawing her resistance, I accepted promptly each time, even though I was progressively finding that no bread would have been more restful. Half a loaf, in the shape of Joanna padding familiarly in and out of the bathroom in a pretty dressing-gown and going to bed five yards away, was decidedly unsatisfying. But I could easily have escaped and gone to a non-tantalizing sleep in my own bed in my family's flat half a mile away; if I didn't, it was my own fault, and I pointed this out to her when every morning she remorsefully apologized for being unfair.

On Wednesday morning I went to a large photographic agency and asked to see a picture of Maurice Kemp-Lore's sister Alice. I was given a bundle of photographs to choose from, varying from Alice front-view in spotted organza at a Hunt Ball to Alice back-view winning over the last fence in a point to point. Alice was a striking girl, with dark hair, high cheek-bones, small fierce eyes, and a tight aggressive mouth. A girl to avoid, as far as I was concerned. I bought a copy of a waist-length photograph which showed her watching some hunter trials, dressed in a hacking jacket and headscarf.

Leaving the agency, I went to the city offices of my parents' accountants, and talked 'our Mr Stuart' in the records department into letting me use first a typewriter and then his photo-copying machine.

On plain typing paper I wrote a bald account of Kemp-Lore's actions against Grant Oldfield, remarking that as a result of Axminster's relying on the apparent disinterestedness of Kemp-Lore's accusation, Oldfield had lost his job, had subsequently suffered great distress of mind, and had undergone three months' treatment in a mental hospital.

I made ten copies of this statement and then on the photocopier printed ten copies each of the statements from Lubbock and James. I thanked 'our Mr Stuart' profusely and returned to Joanna's mews.

When I got back I showed her the photograph of Alice Kemp-Lore, and explained who she was.

'But,' said Joanna, 'she isn't a bit like her brother. It can't have been her that the ticket-collector saw at Cheltenham.'

'No,' I said. 'It was Kemp-Lore himself. Could you draw me a picture of him wearing a head-scarf?'

She found a piece of cartridge paper and with concentration made a recognizable likeness in charcoal of the face I now unwillingly saw in dreams.

'I've only seen him on television,' she said. 'It isn't very good.' She began to sketch in a head-scarf, adding with a few strokes an impression of a curl of hair over the forehead. Then, putting her head on one side and considering her work, she emphasized the lips so that they looked dark and full.

'Lipstick,' she murmured, explaining. 'How about clothes?' Her charcoal hovered over the neck.

'Jodhpurs and hacking jacket,' I said. 'The only clothes which look equally right on men and women.'

'Crumbs,' she said, staring at me. 'It was easy, wasn't it? On with head-scarf and lipstick, and exit the immediately recognizable Kemp-Lore.'

I nodded. 'Except that he still reminded people of himself.'

She drew a collar and tie and the shoulders of a jacket with revers. The portrait grew into a likeness of a pretty girl dressed for riding. It made my skin crawl.

I found Joanna's eyes regarding me sympathetically.

'You can hardly bear to look at him, can you?' she said. 'And you talk in your sleep.'

I rolled up the picture, bounced it on the top of her head, and said lightly, 'Then I'll buy you some ear plugs.'

'He was taking a big risk, all the same, pretending to be a girl,' she said, smiling.

'I don't suppose he did it a minute longer than he had to,' I agreed. 'Just long enough to get from Timberley to Cheltenham without being recognized.'

I filled ten long envelopes with the various statements, and stuck them down. I addressed one to the Senior Steward and four others to influential people on the National Hunt Committee. One to the Chairman of Universal Telecast, one to John Ballerton, and one to Corin Kellar, to show them their idol's clay feet. One to James. And one to Maurice Kemp-Lore.

'Can't he get you for libel?' asked Joanna looking over my shoulder.

'Not a chance,' I said. 'There's a defence in libel actions called justification, which roughly means that if a man has done something dishonest you are justified in disclosing it. You have to prove it is true, that's all.'

'I hope you are right,' she said dubiously, sticking on some stamps.

'Don't worry. He won't sue me,' I said positively.

I stacked nine of the envelopes into a neat pile on the book-shelf and propped the tenth, the unstamped one for Kemp-Lore, up on end behind them.

'We'll post that lot on Friday,' I said. 'And I'll deliver the other one myself.'

At eight-thirty on Thursday morning Joanna made the telephone call upon which so much depended.

I dialled the number of Kemp-Lore's London flat.

There was a click as soon as the bell started ringing, and an automatic answering device invited us to leave a recorded message. Joanna raised her eyebrows; I shook my head, and she put down the receiver without saying anything.

'Out,' I said unnecessarily. 'Damn.'

I gave her the number of Kemp-Lore's father's house in Essex and she was soon connected and talking to someone there. She nodded to me and put her hand over the mouthpiece, and said, 'He's there. They've gone to fetch him. I . . . I hope I don't mess it up.'

I shook my head encouragingly. We had rehearsed pretty thoroughly what she was going to say. She licked her lips, and looked at me with anxious eyes.

'Oh? Mr Kemp-Lore?' She could do a beautiful cockney-suburban accent, not exaggerated and very convincing. 'You don't know me, but I wondered if I could tell you something that you could use on your programme in the newsy bits at the end? I do admire your programme, I do really. It's ever so good, I always think . . .'

His voice clacked, interrupting the flow.

'What information?' repeated Joanna. 'Oh, well, you know all the talk there's been about athletes using them pep pills and injections and things, well I wondered if you wanted to know about jockeys doing it too . . . one jockey, actually that I know of, but I expect they all do it if the truth were known . . . Which jockey? Oh . . . er . . . Robbie Finn, you know, the one you talked to on the telly on Saturday after he won that race. Pepped to the eyebrows as usual he was, didn't you guess? You was that close to him I thought you must have . . . How do I know? Well I do know . . . you want to know how I know . . . well . . . it's a bit dodgy, like, but it was me got some stuff for him once. I work in a doctor's surgery . . . cleaning you see . . . and he told me what to take and I got it for him. But now look here, I don't want to get into no trouble, I didn't mean to let on about that . . . I think I'd better ring off . . . Don't ring off? You won't say nothing about it then, you know, me pinching the stuff?

'Why am I telling you? . . . Well, he don't come to see me no more, that's why.' Her voice was superbly loaded with jealous spite. 'After all I've done for him . . . I did think of telling one of the newspapers, but I thought I'd see if you were interested first. I can tell them if you'd rather . . . Check, what do you mean check? . . . You can't take my word for it on the telephone? Well, yes, you can come and see me if you want to . . . no, not today, I'm at work all day . . . yes, all right, tomorrow morning then.

'How do you get there? . . . Well, you go to Newbury and then out towards Hungerford . . .' She went on with the directions slowly while he wrote them down. 'And it's the only cottage along there, you can't miss it. Yes, I'll wait in for you, about eleven o'clock, all right then. What's my name? . . . Doris Jones. Yes, that's right. Mrs Doris Jones . . . Well ta-ta then.' The telephone clicked and buzzed as he disconnected.

She put the receiver down slowly, looking at me with a serious face.

'Hook, line and sinker,' she said.

When the banks opened I went along and drew out one hundred and fifty pounds. As Joanna had said, what I was doing was complicated and expensive; but complication and expense had achieved top-grade results for Kemp-Lore, and at least I was paying him the compliment of copying his methods. I grudged the money not at all: what is money for, if not to get what you want? What I wanted, admirable or not, was to pay him in his own coin.

I drove off to the Bedfordshire farmer who promised to lend me his Land-Rover and trailer. It was standing ready in the yard when I arrived at noon, and before I left I bought from the farmer two bales of straw and one of hay, which we stowed in the back of the Land-Rover. Then, promising to return that evening, I started away to the first of my appointments with the *Horse and Hound* advertisers.

The first hunter, an old grey gelding in Northamptonshire, was so lame that he could hardly walk out of his box and he was no bargain even at the sixty pounds they were asking for him. I shook my head, and pressed on into Leicestershire.

The second appointment proved to be with a brown mare, sound in limb but noisy in wind, as I discovered when I cantered her across a field. She was big, about twelve years old and gawky, but quiet to handle and not too bad to look at, and she was for sale only because she could not go as fast as her ambitious owner liked. I haggled, bringing him from the hundred he had advertised her for down to eighty-five pounds, and clinched the deal. Then I loaded the mare, whose name, her ex-owner said, was Buttonhook, into the trailer and turned my face south again to Berkshire.

Three hours later, at half past five in the afternoon, I turned the Land-Rover into the lane at the cottage, and bumped Buttonhook to a standstill on the rough ground behind the bushes beyond the building. She had to wait in the trailer while I got the straw and spread it thickly over the floorboards in the room with the water pipes cemented over the window, and again while I filled her a bucket of water out of the rain butt and carried an armful of hay into the room and put it in the corner behind the door.

She was an affectionate old thing, I found. She came docilely out of the trailer and made no fuss when I led her up the little garden path and in through the front door of the cottage and across the little hall into the room prepared for her. I gave her some sugar and rubbed her ears, and she butted her head playfully against my chest. After a while, as she seemed quite content in her unusual and not very spacious loose box, I went out into the hall, shut the door, and padlocked her in. Then I walked round the outside of the cottage and shook the water-pipe bars to see if they were secure, as the frosty air might have prevented the cement from setting properly. But they were all immovably fixed.

The mare came to the window and tried to poke her muzzle through the glassless squares of the window frame and through the bars outside them, but the maze defeated her. I put my hand through and fondled her muzzle, and she blew contentedly down her nostrils. Then she turned and went over to the corner where her hay was, and quietly and trustfully put her head down to eat.

I dumped the rest of the hay and straw in one of the front rooms of the cottage, shut the front door, manoeuvred the trailer round with some difficulty into the lane again, and set off back to Bedfordshire. In due course I delivered the Land-Rover and trailer to their owner, thanked him, and drove the hired car back to Joanna's mews.

When I went in, she kissed me. She sprang up from the sofa where she had been sitting reading, and kissed me lightly on the mouth. It was utterly spontaneous; without thought: and it was a great surprise to both of us. I put my hands on her arms and smiled incredulously down into her black eyes, and watched the surprise there turn to confusion and the confusion to panic. I took my hands away and turned my back on her to give her time, taking off the anorak and saying casually over my shoulder, 'The lodger is installed in the cottage. A big brown mare with a nice nature.'

I hung up the anorak in the cupboard.

'I was just . . . glad to see you back,' she said in a high voice.

'That's fine,' I said lightly. 'Can I rustle up an egg, do you think?'

'There are some mushrooms for an omelette,' she said, more normally.

'Terrific,' I said, going into the kitchen. 'Not peeled, by any chance?'

'Damn it, no,' she said, following me and beginning to smile. She made the omelette for me and I told her about Buttonhook, and the difficult moment passed.

Later on she announced that she was coming down to the cottage with me when I went in the morning.

'No,' I said.

'Yes,' she nodded. 'He is expecting Mrs Doris Jones to open the door to him. It will be much better if she does.'

I couldn't budge her.

'And,' she said, 'I don't suppose you've thought of putting curtains in the windows? If you want him to walk into your parlour, you'll have to make it look normal. He probably has a keen nose for smelling rats.' She fished some printed cotton material out of the drawer and held it up. 'I've never used this . . . we can pin it up to look like curtains.' She busily collected some drawing pins and scissors, and then rolled up the big rag rug which the easel stood on and took a flower picture off the wall.

'What are those for?' I said.

'To furnish the hall, of course. It's got to look right.'

'Okay, genius,' I said, giving in. 'You can come.'

We put all the things she had gathered into a tidy pile by the door, and I added two boxes of cubed sugar from her store cupboard, the big electric torch she kept in case of power cuts, and a broom.

After that springing kiss, the sofa was more of a wasteland than ever.

Seventeen

WE SET off early and got down to the cottage before nine, because there was a good deal to be done before Kemp-Lore arrived.

I hid the car behind the bushes again, and we carried the rug and the other things indoors. Buttonhook was safe and sound in her room, and was delighted to see us, neighing purringly in her throat when we opened her door. While I tossed her straw and fetched her some more hay and water, Joanna said she would clean the windows at the front of the cottage, and presently I heard her humming softly as she wiped away the grime of years.

The putty round the new panes had hardened well, and after I had finished Buttonhook, and Joanna was stepping back admiring the sparkle of the glass, I fetched the paint and began the tedious job of covering the patchwork of old decayed black paint and pale new putty with a bright green skin. Joanna watched me for a while and then went indoors. She put down the rug in the little hall, and I heard her banging a nail into the wall to hang up the picture just inside the front door where no visitor could fail to see it. After that she worked on the inside of the windows while I painted their outsides. She cut the flowery material into lengths and pinned it so that it hung like curtains.

When we had both finished we stood at the gate in front of the cottage admiring our handiwork. With its fresh paint, pretty curtains, and the rug and picture showing through the half-open door, it looked well cared for and homely.

'Has it got a name?' Joanna asked.

'I don't think so. It's always called "The Keeper's Cottage," as far as I know,' I said.

'We should name it Sundew,' she said.

'After the Grand National winner?' I said, puzzled.

'No,' she said soberly, 'the carnivorous plant.'

I put my arm round her waist. She didn't stir.

'You will be careful, won't you?' she said.

'Yes, I will,' I assured her. I looked at my watch. It was twenty minutes to eleven. 'We'd better go indoors in case he comes early.'

We went in and shut the front door and sat on the remains of the hay bale in the front room, giving ourselves a clear view of the front gate.

A minute or two ticked by in silence. Joanna shivered.

'Are you too cold?' I said with concern. There had been another frost during the night and there was, of course, no heating in the cottage. 'We should have brought a stove.'

'It's nerves as much as cold,' she said, shivering again.

I put my arm round her shoulders. She leaned comfortably against me, and I kissed her cheek. Her black eyes looked gravely, warily into mine.

'It isn't incest,' I said.

Her eyelids flickered in shock, but she didn't move.

'Our fathers may be brothers,' I said, 'but our mothers are not related to them or to each other.'

She said nothing. I had a sudden feeling that if I lost this time I had lost for ever, and a leaden chill of despair settled in my stomach.

'No one forbids marriage between cousins,' I said slowly. 'The Law allows it and the Church allows it, and you can be sure they wouldn't if there were anything immoral in it. And in a case like ours, the medical profession raises no objection either. If there were a good genetic reason why we shouldn't marry, it would be different. But you know there isn't.' I paused, but she still looked at me gravely and said nothing. Without much hope I said, 'I don't really understand why you feel the way you do.'

'It's instinct,' she said. 'I don't understand it myself. It's just that I've always thought of it as wrong . . . and impossible.'

There was a little silence.

I said, 'I think I'll sleep in my digs down here in the village tonight, and ride out at exercise with the horses tomorrow morning. I've been neglecting my job this week . . .'

She sat up straight, pulling free of my arm.

'No,' she said abruptly. 'Come back to the flat.'

'I can't. I can't any more,' I said.

She stood up and went over to the window and looked out. Minutes passed. Then she turned round and perched on the window-sill with her back to the light, and I couldn't see her expression.

'It's an ultimatum, isn't it?' she said shakily. 'Either I marry you or you clear out altogether? No more having it both ways like you've given me this past week . . .'

'It isn't a deliberate ultimatum,' I protested. 'But we can't go on like this for ever. At least, I can't. Not if you know beyond any doubt that you'll never change your mind.'

'Before last week-end there wasn't any problem as far as I was concerned,' she said. 'You were just something I couldn't have . . . like oysters, which give me indigestion . . . something nice, but out of bounds. And now' – she tried to laugh – 'now it's as if I've developed a craving for oysters. And I'm in a thorough muddle.'

'Come here,' I said persuasively. She walked across and sat down again beside me on the hay bale. I took her hand.

'If we weren't cousins, would you marry me?' I held my breath.

'Yes,' she said simply. No reservations, no hesitation any more.

I turned towards her and put my hands on the sides of her head and tilted her face up. There wasn't any panic this time. I kissed her; gently, and with love.

Her lips trembled, but there was no rigidity in her body, no blind instinctive retreat as there had been a week ago. I thought, if seven days can work such a change, what could happen in seven weeks?

I hadn't lost after all. The chill in my stomach melted away. I sat back on the hay bale, holding Joanna's hand again and smiling at her.

'It will be all right,' I said. 'Our being cousins won't worry you in a little while.'

She looked at me wonderingly for a moment and then unexpectedly her lips twitched at the corners. 'I believe you,' she said, 'because I've never known anyone more determined in all my life. You've always been like it. You don't care what trouble you put yourself to to get what you want . . . like riding in the race last Saturday, and fixing up this fly-trap of a cottage, and living with me how you have this week . . . so my instinct against blood relatives marrying, wherever it is seated, will have to start getting used to the idea that it is wrong, I suppose, otherwise I'll find myself being dragged by you along to Claudius Mellit to be psychoanalysed or brain-washed, or something. I will try,' she finished more seriously, 'not to keep you waiting very long.'

'In that case,' I said, matching her lightheartedness, 'I'll go on sleeping on your sofa as often as possible, so as to be handy when the breakthrough occurs.'

She laughed without strain. 'Starting tonight?' she asked.

'I guess so,' I said smiling. 'I never did like my digs much.'

'Ouch,' she said.

'But I'll have to come back here on Sunday evening in any case. As James has given me my job back, the least I can do is show some interest in his horses.'

We went on sitting on the hay bale, talking calmly as if

nothing had happened; and nothing had, I thought, except a miracle that one could reliably build a future on, the miracle that Joanna's hand now lay intimately curled in mine without her wanting to remove it.

The minutes ticked away towards eleven o'clock.

'Suppose he doesn't come?' she said.

'He will.'

'I almost hope he doesn't,' she said. 'Those letters would be enough by themselves.'

'You won't forget to post them when you get back, will you?' I said.

'Of course not,' she said, 'but I wish you'd let me stay.'

I shook my head. We sat on, watching the gate. The minute hand crept round to twelve on my watch, and passed it.

'He's late,' she said.

Five past eleven. Ten past eleven.

'He isn't coming,' Joanna murmured.

'He'll come,' I said.

'Perhaps he got suspicious and checked up and found there wasn't any Mrs Doris Jones living in the Keeper's Cottage,' she said.

'There shouldn't be any reason for him to be suspicious,' I pointed out. 'He clearly didn't know at the end of that television interview with me last Saturday that I was on to him, and nothing I've done since should have got back to him, and James and Tick-Tock promised to say nothing to anyone about the doped sugar. As far as Kemp-Lore should know, he is unsuspected and undiscovered. If he feels as secure as I am sure he does, he'll never pass up an opportunity to learn about something as damaging as pep pills . . . so he'll come.'

A quarter past eleven.

He had to come. I found that all my muscles were tense, as if I were listening for him with my whole body, not only my ears. I flexed my toes inside my shoes and tried to relax. There were traffic jams, breakdowns, detours, any number of things to delay him. It was a long way, and he could easily have misjudged the time it would take.

Twenty past eleven.

Joanna sighed and stirred. Neither of us spoke for ten minutes. At eleven-thirty, she said again, 'He isn't coming.'

I didn't answer.

At eleven-thirty-three, the sleek cream nose of an Aston Martin slid to a stop at the gate and Maurice Kemp-Lore stepped out. He stretched himself, stiff from driving, and glanced over the front of the cottage. He wore a beautifully cut hacking jacket and cavalry twill trousers, and there was poise and grace in his every movement.

'Glory, he's handsome,' breathed Joanna in my ear. 'What features! What colouring! Television doesn't do him justice. It's difficult to think of anyone who looks so young and noble doing any harm.'

'He's thirty-three,' I said, 'and Nero died at twenty-nine.'

'You know the oddest things,' she murmured.

Kemp-Lore unlatched the garden gate, walked up the short path and banged the knocker on the front door.

We stood up. Joanna picked a piece of hay off her skirt, swallowed, gave me a half-smile, and walked unhurriedly into the hall. I followed her and stood against the wall where I would be hidden when the front door opened.

Joanna licked her lips.

'Go on,' I whispered.

She put her hand on the latch, and opened the door.

'Mrs Jones?' the honey voice said. 'I'm so sorry I'm a little late.'

'Won't you come in, Mr Kemp-Lore?' said Joanna in her cockney-suburban accent. 'It's ever so nice to see you.'

'Thank you,' he said stepping over the threshold. Joanna

took two paces backwards and Kemp-Lore followed her into the hall.

Slamming the front door with my foot, I seized Kemp-Lore from behind by both elbows, pulling them backwards and forcing him forwards at the same time. Joanna opened the door of Buttonhook's room and I brought my foot up into the small of Kemp-Lore's back and gave him an almighty push. He staggered forwards through the door and I had a glimpse of him sprawling face downwards in the straw before I had the door shut again and the padlock firmly clicking into place.

'That was easy enough,' I said with satisfaction. 'Thanks to your help.'

Kemp-Lore began kicking the door.

'Let me out,' he shouted. 'What do you think you're doing?'

'He didn't see you,' said Joanna softly.

'No,' I agreed, 'I think we'll leave him in ignorance while I take you into Newbury to catch the train.'

'Is it safe?' she said, looking worried.

'I won't be away long,' I promised. 'Come on.'

Before driving her down to Newbury I moved Kemp-Lore's car along and off the lane until it was hidden in the bushes. The last thing I wanted was some stray inquisitive local inhabitant going along to the cottage to investigate. Then I took Joanna to the station and drove straight back again, a matter of twenty minutes each way, and parked in the bushes as usual.

Walking quietly I went along the side of the cottage and round to the back.

Kemp-Lore's hands stuck out through the glassless window frames, gripping the water-pipe bars and shaking them vigorously. They had not budged in their cement.

He stopped abruptly when he saw me and I watched the anger in his face change to blank surprise.

'Who did you expect?' I said.

'I don't know what's going on,' he said. 'Some damn fool of

a woman locked me in here nearly an hour ago and went away and left me. You can let me out. Quickly.' His breath wheezed sharply in his throat. 'There's a horse in here,' he said looking over his shoulder, 'and they give me asthma.'

'Yes,' I said steadily, without moving. 'Yes. I know.'

It hit him then. His eyes widened.

'It was you . . . who pushed me . . .'

'Yes,' I said.

He stood staring at me through the criss-cross of window frame and bars.

'You did it on purpose? You put me in here with a horse on purpose?' His voice rose.

'Yes,' I agreed.

'Why?' he cried. He must have known the answer already, but when I didn't reply he said again, almost in a whisper, 'Why?'

'I'll give you half an hour to think about it,' I said, turning to walk away.

'No,' he exclaimed. 'My asthma's bad. Let me out at once.' I turned back and stood close to the window. His breath whistled fiercely, but he had not even loosened his collar and tie. He was in no danger.

'Don't you have some pills?' I said.

'Of course. I've taken them. But they won't work with a horse so close. Let me out.'

'Stand by the window,' I said, 'and breathe the fresh air.'

'It's cold,' he objected. 'This place is like an ice house.'

I smiled. 'Maybe it is,' I said. 'But then you are fortunate . . . you can move about to keep warm, and you have your jacket on . . . and I have not poured three bucketfuls of cold water over your head.'

He gasped sharply, and it was then, I think, that he began to realize that he was not going to escape lightly or easily from his prison.

Certainly, when I returned to him after sitting on the hay bale for half an hour listening to him alternately kicking the door and yelling for help out of the window, he was no longer assuming that I had lured him all the way from London and gone to the trouble of converting a cottage room into a loose box merely to set him free again at his first squawk.

When I walked round to the window I found him fending off Buttonhook, who was putting her muzzle affectionately over his shoulder. I laughed callously, and he nearly choked with rage.

'Get her away from me,' he screamed. 'She won't leave me alone. I can't breathe.'

He clung on to a bar with one hand, and chopped at Buttonhook with the other.

'If you don't make so much noise she'll go back to her hay.'

He glared at me through the bars, his face distorted with rage and hate and fright. His asthma was much worse. He had unbuttoned the neck of his shirt and pulled down his tie and I could see his throat heaving.

I put the box of sugar cubes I was carrying on the inner window-sill, withdrawing my hand quickly as he made a grab at it.

'Put some sugar on her hay,' I said. 'Go on,' I added, as he hesitated. 'This lot isn't doped.'

His head jerked up. I looked bitterly into his staring eyes.

'Twenty-eight horses,' I said, 'starting with Shantytown. Twenty-eight sleepy horses who all ate some sugar from your hand before they raced.'

Savagely he picked up the box of sugar, tore it open, and sprinkled the cubes on the pile of hay at the other end of the room. Buttonhook, following him, put her head down and began to crunch. He came back to the window, wheezing laboriously.

'You won't get away with this,' he said. 'You'll go to jail for this. I'll see you're pilloried for this.'

'Save your breath,' I said brusquely. 'I've a good deal to say to you. After that, if you want to complain to the police about the way I've treated you, you're welcome.'

'You'll be in jail so quick you won't know what hit you,' he said, the breath hissing through his teeth. 'Now, hurry up and say whatever it is you want to say.'

'Hurry?' I said slowly. 'Well now, it's going to take some time.'

'You'll have to let me out by two-thirty at the latest,' he said unguardedly. 'I've got rehearsals today at five.'

I smiled at him. I could feel it wasn't a pleasant smile.

I said, 'It isn't an accident that you are here on Friday.'

His jaw literally dropped. 'The programme . . .' he said.

'Will have to go on without you,' I agreed.

'But you can't,' he shouted, gasping for enough breath, 'you can't do that.'

'Why not?' I said mildly.

'It's . . . it's television,' he shouted, as if I didn't know. 'Millions of people are expecting to see the programme.'

'Then millions of people are going to be disappointed,' I said.

He stopped shouting and took three gulping, wheezing breaths.

'I know,' he said, with a visible effort at moderation and at getting back to normal, 'that you don't really mean to keep me here so long that I can't get to the studio in time for the programme. All right then,' he paused for a couple of wheezes, 'if you let me go in good time for the rehearsals, I won't report you to the police as I threatened. I'll overlook all this.'

'I think you had better keep quiet and listen,' I said. 'I suppose you find it hard to realize that I don't give a damn for your influence or the pinnacle the British public have seen fit to put you on, or your dazzling, synthetic personality. They are a fraud. Underneath there is only a sick mess of envy and frustration and spite. But I wouldn't have found you out if you hadn't doped twenty-eight horses I rode and told everyone I had lost my nerve. And you can spend this afternoon reflecting that you wouldn't be missing your programme tonight if you hadn't tried to stop me riding Template.'

He stood stock still, his face pallid and suddenly sweating.

'You mean it,' he whispered.

'Indeed I do,' I said.

'No,' he said. A muscle in his cheek started twitching. 'No. You can't. You did ride Template . . . you must let me do the programme.'

'You won't be doing any more programmes,' I said. 'Not tonight or any night. I didn't bring you here just for a personal revenge, though I don't deny I felt like killing you last Friday night. I brought you here on behalf of Art Mathews and Peter Cloony and Grant Oldfield. I brought you because of Danny Higgs, and Ingersoll, and every other jockey you have hit where it hurts. In various ways you saw to it that they lost their jobs; so now you are going to lose yours.'

For the first time, he was speechless. His lips moved but no sound came out except the high, asthmatic whine of his breathing. His eyes seemed to fall back in their sockets and his lower jaw hung slack, making hollows of his cheeks. He looked like a death's-head caricature of the handsome charmer he had been.

I took the long envelope addressed to him out of my pocket and held it to him through the bars. He took it mechanically, with black fingers.

'Open it,' I said.

He pulled out the sheets of paper and read them. He read them through twice, though his face showed from the first that he understood the extent of the disaster. The haggard hollows deepened.

'As you will see,' I said, 'those are photostat copies. More like them are in the post to the Senior Steward and to your boss at

Universal Telecast, and to several other people as well. They will get them tomorrow morning. And they will no longer wonder why you failed to turn up for your programme tonight.'

He still seemed unable to speak, and his hands shook convulsively. I passed to him through the bars the rolled-up portrait Joanna had drawn of him. He opened it, and it was clearly another blow.

'I brought it to show you,' I said, 'so that you would realize beyond any doubt that I know exactly what you have been doing. All along you have found that having an instantly recognizable face was a big handicap when it came to doing things you couldn't explain away, like ramming an old Jaguar across Peter Cloony's lane.'

His head jerked back, as if it still surprised him that I knew so much.

I said calmly, 'A ticket collector at Cheltenham said you were pretty.'

I smiled faintly. He looked very far from pretty at that moment.

'As for that Jaguar,' I said, 'I haven't had time yet to find out where it came from, but it can be done. It's only a question of asking. Advertising its number in the trade papers . . . tracing its former owner . . . that sort of thing. Tedious, I dare say, but definitely possible, and if necessary I will do it. No one would forget having you for a customer.

'You must have bought it in the week after the tank carrier blocked Cloony's lane, because that is what gave you the idea. Do you think you can explain away the time sequence of acquiring the Jaguar and abandoning it exactly where and when and how you did? And disappearing from the scene immediately afterwards?'

His mouth hung open and the muscle twitched in his cheek.

'Most of your vicious rumours,' I said, changing tack, 'were spread for you by Corin Kellar and John Ballerton, who you found would foolishly repeat every thought that you put into their heads. I hope you know Corin well enough to realize that he never stands by his friends. When the contents of the letter he will receive in the morning sink into that rat-brain of his, and he finds that other people have had letters like it, there won't be anyone spewing out more damaging truth about you than him. He will start telling everyone, for instance, that it was you who set him at loggerheads with Art Mathews. There won't be any stopping him.

'You see,' I finished after a pause, 'I think it is only justice that as far as possible you should suffer exactly what you inflicted on other people.'

He spoke at last. The words came out in a wheezing croak, and he was past caring what admissions he made. 'How did you find it out?' he said disbelievingly. 'You didn't know last Friday, you couldn't see . . .'

'I did know last Friday,' I said, 'I knew just how far you had gone to smash Peter Cloony, and I knew you hated me enough to give yourself asthma doping my mounts. I knew the dope business had gone sour on you when it came to Turniptop at Stratford. And you may care to learn that it was no accident that James Axminster jogged your arm and stepped on the sugar lumps; I asked him to, and told him what you were doing. I knew all about your curdled, obsessive jealousy of jockeys. I didn't need to see you last Friday to know you . . . there wasn't anyone else with any reason to want me out of action.'

'You can't have known all that,' he said obstinately, clinging to it as if it mattered. 'You didn't know the next day when I interviewed you after the race . . .' His voice tailed off in a wheeze and he stared at me hopelessly through the bars.

'You aren't the only one who can smile and hate at the same time,' I said neutrally. 'I learned it from you.'

He made a sound like a high-pitched moan, and turned his back towards me with his arms bent upwards and folded over his head in an attitude of the utmost misery and despair. It may be regrettable, but I felt no pity for him at all.

I walked away from his window, round the cottage and in at the front door, and sat down again on the hay in the front room. I looked at my watch. It was a quarter to two. The afternoon stretched lengthily ahead.

Kemp-Lore had another spell of screaming for help through the window, but no one came; then he tried the door again, but there was no handle on his side of it for him to pull, and it was too solidly constructed for him to kick his way through. But-tonhook grew restive again from the noise and started pawing the ground, and Kemp-Lore shouted to me furiously to let him out, let him out, let him out.

Joanna's great fear had been that his asthma would make him seriously ill, and she had repeatedly warned me to be careful; but I judged that while he had enough breath for so much yelling he was in no real danger, and I sat and listened to him without relenting. The slow hours passed, punctuated only by the bursts of fury from the back room, while I stretched myself comfort-ably across the hay and day-dreamed about marriage to my cousin.

At about five o'clock he was quiet for a long time. I got up and walked round the outside of the cottage and looked in through the window. He was lying face down in the straw near the door, not moving at all.

I watched him for a few minutes and called his name, but as he still did not stir I began to be alarmed, and decided I would have to make sure he was all right. I returned to the hall, and having shut the front door firmly behind me, I unlocked the padlock on the back room. The door swung inwards, and But-tonhook, lifting her head, greeted me with a soft whinny.

Kemp-Lore was alive, that at least was plain. The sound of his high, squeezed breath rose unmistakably from his still form. I bent down beside him to see into just how bad a spasm he had been driven, but I never did get around to turning him over or feeling his pulse. As soon as I was down on one knee beside him he heaved himself up and into me, knocking me sprawling off balance, and sprang like lightning for the door.

I caught his shoe as it zipped across three inches from my face and yanked him back. He fell heavily on top of me and we rolled towards Buttonhook, with me trying to pin him down on the floor and he fighting like a tiger to get free. The mare was frightened. She cowered back against the wall to get out of our way, but it was a small room and our struggles took us among Buttonhook's feet and under her belly. She stepped gingerly over us and made cautiously for the open door.

Kemp-Lore's left hand was clamped round my right wrist, a circumstance which hindered me considerably. If he'd been clairvoyant he couldn't have struck on anything better calculated to cause me inconvenience. I hit him in the face and neck with my left hand, but I was too close to get any weight behind it and was also fairly occupied dodging the blows he aimed at me in return.

After he had lost the advantage of surprise, he seemed to decide he could only get free of me by lacing his fingers in my hair and banging my head against the wall, for this he tried repeatedly to do. He was staggeringly strong, more than I would have believed possible in view of his asthma, and the fury and desperation which fired him blazed in his blue eyes like a furnace.

If my hair hadn't been so short he would probably have succeeded in knocking me out, but his fingers kept slipping when I twisted my head violently in his grasp, and the third time my ear grazed the plaster I managed at last to wrench my right hand free as well.

After that, hauling off a fraction, I landed a socking right jab in his short ribs, and the air whistled out of his lungs screeching like an express train. He went a sick grey-green colour and fell slackly off me, gasping and retching and clawing his throat for air.

I got to my feet and hauled him up, and staggered with him over to the window, holding him where the fresh cold air blew into his face. After three or four minutes his colour improved and the terrifying heaving lessened, and some strength flowed back into his sagging legs.

I clamped his fingers round the window frames and let go of him. He swayed a bit, but his hands held, and after a moment I walked dizzily out of the room and padlocked the door shut behind me.

Buttonhook had found her way into the front room and was placidly eating the hay. I leaned weakly against the wall and watched her for a while, cursing myself for the foolish way I had nearly got myself locked into my own prison. I was badly shaken, not only by the fight itself but by the strength with which Kemp-Lore had fought and by the shocking effect my last blow had had on him. I ought to have had more sense, I knew, than to hit an asthmatic with that particular punch.

There was no sound from the back room. I straightened up and walked round to the window. He was standing there, holding on to the frames where I had put him, and there were tears running down his cheeks.

He was breathing safely enough, the asthma reduced to a more manageable wheeze, and I imagined it would not get any worse from then on, as Buttonhook was no longer in the room with him.

'Damn you,' he said. Another tear spilt over. 'Damn you. Damn you.'

There wasn't anything to say.

I went back to Buttonhook, and put on her halter. I had meant to deal with her later, after I had let Kemp-Lore go, but in the changed circumstances I decided to do it straight away, while it was still light. Leading her out of the front door and through the gate, I jumped on to her back and rode her away up past the two cars hidden in the bushes and along the ridge of the hill.

A mile further on I struck the lane which led up to the Downs, and turning down that came soon to a gate into a field owned by a farmer I had often ridden for. Slipping off Button-hook I opened the gate, led her through and turned her loose.

She was so amiable that I was sorry to part with her, but I couldn't keep her in the cottage, I couldn't stable an elderly hunter in James's yard and expect his lads to look after her, I couldn't find a snap buyer for her at six o'clock in the evening; and I frankly didn't know what else to do with her. I fondled her muzzle and patted her neck and fed her a handful of sugar. Then I slapped her on the rump and watched my eighty-five quid kick up her heels and canter down the field like a two-year-old. The farmer would no doubt be surprised to find an unclaimed brown mare on his land, but it would not be the first time a horse had been abandoned in that way, and I hadn't any doubt that he would give her a good home.

I turned away and walked back along the hill to the cottage. It was beginning to get dark, and the little building lay like a shadow in the hollow as I went down to it through the trees and bushes. All was very quiet, and I walked softly through the garden to the back window.

He was still standing there. When he saw me he said quite quietly 'Let me out.'

I shook my head.

'Well at least go and telephone the company, and tell them I'm ill. You can't let them all wait and wait for me to come, right up to the last minute.'

I didn't answer.

'Go and telephone,' he said again.

I shook my head.

He seemed to crumple inside. He stretched his hands through the bars and rested his head against the window frames.

'Let me out.'

I said nothing.

'For pity's sake,' he said, 'let me out.'

For pity's sake.

I said, 'How long did you intend to leave me in that tack-room?'

His head snapped up as if I'd hit him. He drew his hands back and gripped the bars.

'I went back to untie you,' he said, speaking quickly, wanting to convince me. 'I went back straight after the programme was over, but you'd gone. Someone found you and set you free pretty soon, I suppose, since you were able to ride the next day.'

'And you went back to find the tack-room empty?' I said. 'So you knew I had come to no harm?'

'Yes,' he said eagerly. 'Yes, that's what happened. I wouldn't have left you there very long, because of the rope stopping your circulation.'

'You did think there was some danger of that, then?' I said innocently.

'Yes, of course there was, and that's why I wouldn't have left you there too long. If someone hadn't freed you first, I'd have let you go in good time. I only wanted to hurt you enough to stop you riding.' His voice was disgustingly persuasive, as if what he was saying were not abnormal.

'You're a liar,' I said calmly. 'You didn't go back to untie me after your show. You would have found me still there if you had. In fact it took me until midnight to get free, because no one came. Then I found a telephone and rang up for a car to fetch me, but by the time it reached me, which was roughly two o'clock, you had still not returned. When I got to Ascot the following day, everyone was surprised to see me. There was a rumour, they said, that I wouldn't turn up. You even mentioned on television that my name in the number frames was a mistake. Well . . . no one but you had any reason to believe that I wouldn't arrive at the races: so when I heard that rumour I knew that you had not gone back to untie me, even in the morning. You thought I was still swinging from that hook, in God knows what state . . . and as I understand it, you intended to leave me there indefinitely, until someone found me by accident . . . or until I was dead.'

'No,' he said faintly.

I looked at him without speaking for a moment, and then turned to walk away.

'All right,' he screamed suddenly, banging on the bars with his fists. 'All right. I didn't care whether you lived or died. Do you like that? Is that what you want to hear? I didn't care if you died. I thought of you hanging there with your arms swelling and going black . . . with the agony going on and on . . . and I didn't care. I didn't care enough to stay awake. I went to bed. I went to sleep. I didn't care. I didn't care . . . and I hope you like it.'

His voice cracked, and he sank down inside the room so that all I could see in the gathering dusk was the top of his fair head and the hands gripping the bars with the knuckles showing white through the skin.

'I hope you like it,' he said brokenly.

I didn't like it. Not one little bit. It made me feel distinctly sick.

I went slowly round into the front room and sat down again on the hay. I looked at my watch. It was a quarter past six. Still three hours to wait: three hours in which the awful truth would slowly dawn on Kemp-Lore's colleagues in the television studio, three hours of anxious speculation and stop-gap planning, culminating in the digging out of a bit of old film to fill in the empty fifteen minutes and the smooth announcement, 'We regret that owing to the – er – illness of Maurice Kemp-Lore there will be no *Turf Talk* tonight.'

Or ever again, mates, I thought, if you did but know it.

As it grew dark the air got colder. It had been frosty all day, but with the disappearance of the sun the evening developed a sub-zero bite, and the walls of the unlived-in cottage seemed to soak it up. Kemp-Lore began kicking the door again.

'I'm cold,' he shouted. 'It's too cold.'

'Too bad,' I said, under my breath.

'Let me out,' he yelled.

I sat on the hay without moving. The wrist which he had latched on to while we fought was uncomfortably sore, and blood had seeped through the bandage again. What the Scots doctor would have to say when he saw it I hated to think. The three warts would no doubt quiver with disapproval. I smiled at the picture.

Kemp-Lore kicked the door for a long time, trying to break through it, but he didn't succeed. At the same time he wasted a good deal of breath yelling that he was cold and hungry and that I was to let him out. I made no reply to him at all, and after about an hour of it the kicking and shouting stopped, and I heard him slither down the door as if exhausted and begin sobbing with frustration.

I stayed where I was and listened while he went on and on moaning and weeping in desolation. I listened to him without emotion; for I had cried too, in the tack-room.

The hands crawled round the face of my watch.

At a quarter to nine, when nothing could any longer save his programme, and even a message explaining his absence could scarcely be telephoned through in time, Kemp-Lore's decreasing sobs faded away altogether, and the cottage was quiet.

I got stiffly to my feet and went out into the front garden, breathing deeply in the clear air, with an easing sense of release. The difficult day was over, and the stars were bright in the frosty sky. It was a lovely night.

I walked along to the bushes and started Kemp-Lore's car,

turning it and driving it back to the gate. Then for the last time I walked round the cottage to talk to him through the window, and he was standing there already, his face a pale blue behind the window frames.

'My car,' he said hysterically. 'I heard the engine. You're going to drive away in my car and leave me.'

I laughed. 'No. You are going to drive it away yourself. As fast and as far as you like. If I were you, I'd drive to the nearest airport and fly off. No one is going to like you very much when they've read those letters in the morning, and it will be only a day or two before the newspapers get on to it. As far as racing goes, you will certainly be warned off. Your face is too well known in Britain for you to hide or change your name or get another job. And as you've got all night and probably most of tomorrow before the storm breaks and people start eyeing you with sneers and contempts you can pack up and skip the country quite easily, without any fuss.'

'You mean . . . I can go? Just go?' He sounded astounded.

'Just go,' I said, nodding. 'If you go quickly enough, you'll avoid the enquiry the stewards are bound to hold, and you'll avoid any charge they might think of slapping on you. You can get away to some helpful distant country where they don't know you, and you can start again from scratch.'

'I suppose I haven't much choice,' he murmured. His asthma was almost unnoticeable.

'And find a country where they don't have steeplechasing,' I finished.

He moaned sharply, and crashed his fists down on the window frame.

I went round into the cottage and in the light of Joanna's big torch unlocked the padlock and pushed open the door. He turned from the window and walked unsteadily towards me across the straw, shielding his ravaged face from the light. He went through the door, passed me without a glance, and stumbled down the path to his car; and I walked down the path behind him, shining the torch ahead. I propped the torch on top of the gate-post so as to leave my hands free in case I needed to use them, but there didn't seem to be much fight left in him.

He paused when he was sitting in his car, and with the door still wide open looked out at me.

'You don't understand,' he said, his voice shaking. 'When I was a boy I wanted to be a jockey. I wanted to ride in the Grand National, like my father. And then there was this thing about falling off . . . I'd see the ground rushing past under my horse and there would be this terrible sort of pain in my guts, and I sweated until I could pull up and get off. And then I'd be sick.'

He made a moaning noise and clutched his stomach at the memory. His face twisted. Then he said suddenly, fiercely, 'It made me feel good to see jockeys looking worried. I broke them up all right. It made me feel warm inside. Big.'

He looked up at me with renewed rage, and his voice thickened venomously.

'I hated you more than all the others. You rode too well for a new jockey and you were getting on too quickly. Everyone was saying "Give Finn the bad horses to ride, he doesn't know what fear is". It made me furious when I heard that. So I had you on my programme, remember? I meant to make you look a fool. It worked with Mathews, why not with you? But Axminster took you up and then Pankhurst broke his leg . . . I wanted to smash you so much that it gave me headaches. You walked about with that easy confidence of yours, as if you took your strength for granted, and too many people were getting to say you'd be champion one day . . .

'I waited for you to have a fall that looked fairly bad, and then I used the sugar. It worked. You know it worked. I felt ten feet tall, looking at your white face and listening to everyone sniggering about you. I watched you find out how it felt. I wanted to see you writhe when everyone you cared for said . . .

like my father said to all his friends . . . that it was a pity about you . . . a pity you were a snivelling little coward, a pity you had no nerve . . . no nerve . . .'

His voice died away, and his hollowed eyes were wide, unfocused, as if he were staring back into an unbearable past.

I stood looking down at the wreck of what could have been a great man. All that vitality, I thought; all that splendid talent wasted for the sake of hurting people who had not hurt him.

Such individuals could be understood, Claudius Mellit had said. Understood, and treated, and forgiven.

I could understand him in a way, I supposed, because I was myself the changeling in a family. But my father had rejected me kindly, and I felt no need to watch musicians suffer.

Treated . . . The treatment I had given him that day might not have cured the patient, but he would no longer spread his disease, and that was all I cared about.

Without another word I shut the car door on him and gestured to him to drive away. He gave me one more incredulous glance as if he still found it impossible that I should let him go, and began to fumble with the light switches, the ignition, and the gears.

I hoped he was going to drive carefully. I wanted him to live. I wanted him to live for years, thinking about what he had thrown away. Anything else would be too easy, I thought.

The car began to roll, and I caught a last glimpse of the famous profile, the eclipsed, exiled profile, as he slid away into the dark. The brake lights flashed red as he paused at the end of the lane, then he turned out into the road, and was gone. The sound of his engine died away.

I took the torch from the gate-post and walked up the path to the quiet cottage, to sweep it clean.

Forgiveness, I thought. That was something else again.

It would take a long time to forgive.

BLOOD SPORT

One

I AWOKE with foreboding. My hand closed in a reflex on the Luger under the pillow. I listened, acutely attentive. No sound. No quick surreptitious slither, no rub of cloth on cloth, no half-controlled pulse-driven breath. No enemy hovering. Slowly, relaxing, I turned half over and squinted at the room. A quiet, empty, ugly room. One-third of what for want of a less cosy word I called home.

Bright sunshine by-passed the thin pink curtains, spilling a gold slash on the faded brown Wilton. I didn't like pink. Also I didn't have the energy it would take to argue the landlord into changing to blue. After eight months I knew he never renewed anything until it had fallen to bits.

In spite of the prevailing calm the feeling of foreboding deepened and then identified itself and dissolved into a less threatening, more general state of gloom. Sunday morning, June 20th. The beginning of three weeks' leave.

I rolled back on to my stomach and shut my eyes against the sun, and took my hand six inches from the Luger, which was far enough, and wondered how long a man could sleep if he really put his mind to it. Even a man who never slept soundly to start with. Three weeks, the three obligatory overdue weeks could be got through more easily asleep.

Three millenniums of sleep lay under the pillow. The nine-millimetre equalizer, my inseparable friend. It went with me everywhere, to beaches, to bathrooms, to beds other than my own. It was there to save my life. Not to take it. I had lived through a lot of temptations, and I lived with that too.

The telephone bell put paid to the three weeks before they had gone half an hour.

''Lo,' I said blearily, balancing the receiver on the pillow.

'Gene?'

'Uh huh.'

'You haven't gone away then.' There was relief in the voice, the voice of my boss. I looked at my watch. Ten o'clock.

'No,' I said unnecessarily. He knew I wasn't going away. I didn't understand his relief. It was missing when he spoke again.

'How about a day on the river?'

He had a motor cruiser somewhere on the upper Thames. I'd never seen it. Hadn't been asked before.

'Invitation or order?' I said, yawning.

He hesitated. 'Whichever you'll accept.'

What a man. You did more for him than you believed you would, every time.

'Where do I go, and when?'

'My daughter will fetch you,' he said. 'She'll be there in about half an hour. Family party. Boating clothes. Come as you are.'

'Sure,' I said. Complete with stubble, Luger, and shorts. A riot. I never wore pyjamas. They slowed you up too much.

Boating clothes, I decided, were greyish brown cotton trousers and an olive green nylon jersey shirt. I carried the Luger with me in the left-hand pocket when the doorbell rang. One never really knew. But a look through the wide-angled spyhole showed it was only Keeble's daughter, as arranged. I opened up.

'Mr Hawkins?' she said hesitantly, looking from me to the dingy brass six screwed on to the solid dark stained wood.

'That's right,' I smiled. 'Come in.'

She walked past me and I shut the door, interested to notice that four flights of stairs hadn't left her breathless, as they did most visitors. I lived high up for that purpose.

'I was just finishing my coffee,' I said. 'Would you like some?'

'It's very kind of you, but Daddy said not to waste time, he wants to be off up river as soon as possible.'

Keeble's daughter was just like her photograph on Daddy's desk. Half woman, still at school. Short bouncy dark hair, and watchful dark eyes, a rounded body slimming down, a self-possessed touch-me-not expression, and an endearing gauceness in her present situation.

She looked cautiously round the sitting room, which neither she nor I nor anyone else would have classed as elegant living. The landlord's furniture was junk-shop stuff and I had made no effort to improve it. My total contributions to the scene were two rows of books on the shelves and in one corner a tin trunk of oddments which I had never bothered to unpack. A drawn-back curtain revealed the kitchen alcove and its entire contents: cupboard, refrigerator, sink, and cooker, all of them showing their age.

One went through the sitting room to the bedroom, through the bedroom to the bathroom, and through the bathroom to the fire escape. The flat had everything but a draw-bridge and a moat, and it had taken me weeks to find it. Only the tiny spyglass had been lacking, and the landlord had been furious when he finally noticed. I had installed it. It had cost me three months' rent in advance to convince him it wasn't there for the sole purpose of being out when he came.

I watched Keeble's daughter search for something nice to say about my living quarters and give up the struggle with a defeated shake of her young head. I could have told her that I had once had a better flat, a spacious comfortable first-floor front with a balcony overlooking a tree-dotted square. It had proved too accessible to unwanted guests. I had vacated it on a stretcher.

'I'll fetch my jacket,' I said, finishing the coffee. 'And then we'll go.'

She nodded, looking relieved, oppressed already by the emptiness of my home life. Five minutes of it had been enough, for her.

I went into the bedroom, picked the jacket off the bed, and transferred the Luger from my trousers into its built-in under-arm holster, fastening it there with a press stud on a strap. Then, coat over arm, I dumped the dirty coffee cup in the sink, pulled the curtain across the kitchen, opened the front door, and let myself and Miss Keeble out.

Four uneventful storeys down we emerged into the quiet sunlit Putney street, and she looked back and up at the solid old converted house. It needed paint and oozed respectability, exactly like its row of neighbours.

'I wasn't sure I'd come to the right place. Daddy just said the fourth house along.'

'He gives me a lift home, sometimes.'

'Yes, he said so.' She turned to the white Austin standing at the kerb and paused with the key in her hand. 'Do you mind if I drive?'

'Of course not.'

She smiled for the first time since she'd arrived, a quick flash-ing affair which verged on friendliness. She unlocked her door, climbed in, and reached over to unlatch the opposite one for me. The first thing I noticed as I bent to get in were the L plates lying on the back seat.

'When did you pass the test?' I said mildly.

'Well . . .' the smile lingered, 'as a matter of fact, yesterday.'

For all that, she drove very well, careful but confident, quiet with the gears though a bit heavy with the hand signals. She crept somewhat tentatively around the Chiswick roundabout and up the slope to the M4. The big blue motorway sign said no L drivers, and her nose twitched mischievously as we passed it.

'Did you come this way to fetch me?' I asked idly.

She edged into the slow lane and hit forty.

'Er, no. I live in a hostel with about sixty other girls in South Ken. Daddy just rang me and said as I'd got the car up in London this weekend I could collect you and meet him in Henley. Sort of spur of the moment thing.'

'I see.'

We came to the end of the fifty mile an hour limit and her foot went down with determination.

'Do I scare you?' The needle quivered on sixty-five.

I smiled wryly. 'No.'

'Actually . . .' Her hands gripped the wheel with the tension of inexperience. 'Actually, you don't look as if you'd scare easily.'

I glanced at her in surprise. I look ordinary. Quiet and ordinary. And very useful it is, too.

'Anyway,' she went on frankly, 'I asked Daddy about coming this way, and he said he guessed your nerves would stand it. He seemed to find it very funny, for some reason or other.'

'He has his own brand of humour.'

'Mm.' She drove on for several miles in silence, concentrating on the road. The speed dropped slowly down to fifty again, and I guessed she was finding the motorway not such pure fun as she'd imagined. The usual number of Sunday Jim Clarks were showing off in the fast lane and family outings with Grandma driving from the back seat were bumbling about in the slow. We went down the centre and pulled out bravely now and then to pass an airport bus.

Eventually, in thinner traffic after Windsor, she said, doubtfully, 'You do . . . er . . . work for Daddy?'

'Yes. Why not?'

'Well, no reason why not. I mean,' she looked embarrassed, 'I mean, I can't remember him ever asking anyone from work . . . well, he just doesn't usually, that's all.' She looked as if she wished she hadn't started.

'A kind thought,' I suggested; and wondered what he wanted. Not just to give me a sunny day out. As his daughter said, he didn't do that sort of thing.

We made it to Henley with the paint intact, and she parked neatly in a large gravelled enclosure by the railway station. Her hands trembled slightly as she locked the doors, and I realized that it must have been her longest drive, as well as her fastest.

'You drove beautifully,' I said sincerely. 'Like a veteran.'

'Oh.' She gave a laugh which was half a cough, and looked relieved and pleased. 'Well, thank you.' She would be more relaxed, I knew, on the way back, and less strung up when she got there. To give and to remove confidence were tools of my trade, and there was no union to say I couldn't use them on Sundays.

'*Flying Linnet* . . . that's our boat . . . will be somewhere along the bank,' she said. 'It isn't far.' She smiled again and gestured, 'That way.'

We walked down to the river and along the neatly built broad tarmac towpath, where half the town seemed to be out feeding the ducks. The sun sparkled on the dark green water and there was a queue at the boatyard for rowing boats and punts. There were gardens and lawns and seats, and a bowling green, and a playground with a slide and swings, all of them sprinkled with sunny Sunday faces and murmuring summer voices. Families and couples and groups: few alone. Three weeks alone, I thought bleakly. I could spend them beside the deep green river feeding ducks, and just jump in when I couldn't stand any more of it.

'There's Daddy,' said Keeble's daughter, pointing. The sun lay along her light brown arm and shifted in burnt toffee shadows on the curves of her orange tan dress. Too young for me, I thought inconsequentially. Or rather, I was too old. Aeons too old. Forty still lay a couple of years ahead, but I could have told Methuselah a thing or two.

Keeble had stepped ashore from one of the boats moored top to tail along the towpath and was walking towards us, hand outstretched, welcoming smile in face. My boss, except for an open-necked shirt, looked his usual weekday self, a short slightly chubby man with a mild manner and a faintly anxious expression. The light blue-grey eyes blinked freely as usual behind the unimpressive spectacles and as usual he had missed a patch while shaving. Premature baldness had made him look fifty at thirty-five, but far from regretting this, he believed it was the cause of his rapid promotion over well-thatched contemporaries. He may have been right. He looked harmless, cautious, unambitious, one of nature's safest plodders. It was eight years since he had inherited me along with the rest of the setup, and to discern the cutting brain behind the waffle had taken me two minutes flat.

'Gene,' he said. 'Glad you could come.' He pumped my hand up and down perfunctorily, the social gesture as meaningless to him as to me, and we exchanged smiles to match. For his daughter the warmth came from the heart. She kissed him affectionately on the cheek and his eyes held a glimmering pride I had never seen in him before.

'Well, Lynnie my love, you got here safely. Or did you let Gene do the driving?'

'Do me a favour,' she said. 'He didn't even flinch.'

Keeble flicked me an amused glance, and I repeated the compliment to her skill, with her father nodding his thanks to me over her head, knowing exactly why I said it.

They turned and began to walk back along the path, gesturing to me to come. Keeble's boat, the one they stopped at, was a graceful neat-looking fibre-glass cruiser with a cabin forward and a large open cockpit at the back, the decks spotless and the chromium shining. Sitting casually side by side on the pale blue plastic upholstery were a man and a woman, both of whom raised smiling faces at our approach and neither of whom got up.

Lynnie jumped down into the boat and kissed the woman, and Keeble stepped carefully after.

'Come aboard,' he said to me, and again in his tone there was a choice. An invitation or an order, whichever I would accept. I opted for the invitation, and embarked on more than the *Flying Linnet*.

'My wife Joan,' said Keeble, stretching a hand to the seated woman. 'Gene Hawkins, honey.'

Joan Keeble was a frail birdlike woman with a coyness of manner left over from the time when she was pretty. She twinkled her eyes at me, inviting admiration. I scraped some up, and exchanged the necessary platitudes about weather, boating and driving daughters. Keeble waded into this with a wave towards the man sitting beside her.

'You two haven't met . . .' he hesitated a fraction. 'Dave . . . Gene, this is Dave Teller.'

Teller stood up, shook hands economically, and said he was glad to know me. He wore a sloppy wrinkled pale blue shirt hanging out over patched cotton trousers, battered plimsolls on his feet, and a dirty old baseball cap on his head. American, well educated, prosperous, assured: the categories clicked over from habit in my assessing mind. Also he was a lean man nearing fifty, with a strong beaky nose, straightforward eyes, and a marvellous dentist.

Keeble offered no information beyond that bald introduction, but bustled about getting his ship ready to put to sea. His yell into the cabin for a certain Peter to come and help produced no results. I stuck my head through the door and saw a boy of about twelve engrossed in fitting a new roll of film into a small simple camera.

'Peter,' his father yelled.

Peter heaved a martyred sigh, scrambled the back of the

camera shut, and went out past me with his eyes down and his
fingers winding the knob. Surefooted, he stepped without looking on to the narrow side of the boat and from there to the
towpath.

'He'll fall in one day,' Lynnie said to the world in general.
Her brother didn't even hear. Still concentrating on his camera
with one hand he was slowly untying the rope from the mooring ring with the other, crouching down on the tarmac in his
clean black jeans and getting up with two large dusty patches on
the knees. Pointing his viewfinder at a passing formation of
ducks he clicked the shutter and with a serious, absorbed expression wound on the film.

Farther up the path Keeble and Teller were undoing the bow
rope, talking amicably in the sun. Lynnie and her mother
straightened the cushions and coiled the ropes and fussed
around over a lot of nothing, chatting trivialities. I wondered
what the hell I was doing there and felt out of contact with
everything around me. Not a new feeling, but recurring more
often. The two levels of living were growing farther apart. The
day-to-day social level had lost all meaning, and underneath,
where there should have been rock, had opened a void of shriv-
elling loneliness. It was getting worse. The present was bad
enough: the future an abyss. Only work brought my splintering
self into any sort of whole, and I knew well enough that it was
the work itself which had started the process. That and Caroline.
Or, to be more accurate, Caroline's husband.

'I say, hold this rope, will you?' Peter said. I took the wet
snake he offered. 'Hi,' he added, seeing me properly for the first
time, 'Who are you?'

'Anybody's guess,' I said with more truth than sense, and his
mother stared at me with astonishment and told him my name.

Keeble came back on board and started the engine. Teller
stood up on the small forward deck and cast off the bow rope
when Keeble told him, and Peter left it until almost too late to

leap on board with the stern. The camera bounced on the cord round his neck. 'Birthday present from Gran,' he said to Lynnie with pride. 'Super, isn't it.'

'You'll drop it in the river, if you aren't careful.'

'This is only my second film. I used the first one up on the boys at school. Do you think those ducks will come out all right?'

'I expect you had your finger over the shutter.'

'I've got a book in there.' He nodded to the cabin, expertly sifting out the affection behind her sarcasm and showing no resentment. 'It tells you about exposures and focuses. I think I'll just check what it says about sunny days. It was cloudy dull all week at school.'

I don't belong here, I thought. I wished I were asleep.

The *Flying Linnet* nosed upstream through a scatter of row-boats, Keeble at the wheel, Teller sitting forward still on the cabin roof, and Peter trying to get past Lynnie teasing him in the cabin doorway. Joan Keeble sat down on the wide seat across the back and patted the place next to her for me to join her. With an effort I did so, but after a minute or two, in the middle of apparently idle hostessy chat, she pulled me back to attention by trying delicately to find out who I was and why I had been invited, while not wanting to have me realize that she didn't know.

I could play that sort of game for ever. Inference on infer-ence. I didn't know the answer to why was I there, but that she needed to ask it, that indeed she had asked it, told me a great deal about non-contact between Keeble and his wife, and opened new doors on to Keeble himself. I knew then why he'd never before asked me home. It was one thing to employ a microscope, but another to put oneself under the lens. I thought it all the odder that he'd done it now.

As if he could feel my mind on the back of his neck he turned round and said, 'The lock's just ahead.' I stood up and joined him, and Peter gave up his struggle and went back to his duty with the stern rope.

'Marsh Lock,' Lynnie said, standing beside me and looking forward through the windscreen. 'Not an easy one, from this side, going upstream.'

When we got nearer I saw what she meant. The broad stretch of river narrowed abruptly to the lock gates on the left and the weir on the right, alongside. Baby whirlpools and trails of bubbles met us fifty yards away, with larger eddies and convolutions bubbling up as we went on. The boat tended to swing sideways under their power, and Keeble spun the wheel rapidly to keep her straight. Ahead of us water in tons tumbled over the weir, green and brown and splashing white, thundering down in great curving leaps, smelling of mustiness and mud.

A low wooden wall divided the lock approach from the turbulent weir water, and to the calm side of the barrier Keeble neatly steered his boat. Teller standing at the bow threw his rope over the hook on a mooring post there, and Peter slung a loop over a bollard at the stern.

I looked idly over the side of the boat, over the wall, up to the weir. Bouncing, tumbling, foaming, sweeping away back into the width of the river, the rough water looked superb in the sun. I felt the warmth and the fine spray mixed on my face and wondered whether if someone fell in there, he would ever come up.

The lock gates opened, the downcoming boats chugged out, and the *Flying Linnet* went in. Teller and Peter did their stuff mooring us to the side and Peter took a photograph of the boat in the lock. Water surged through the sluices in the upper gates, lifting us up, and in ten minutes we were going out of the lock on to another broad calm stretch of river, six feet higher than the one below.

'There are fifty locks on the Thames,' Keeble said. 'Lechlade is as far up as you can go except in a rowing boat, and that's about 300 feet above sea level.'

'Quite a staircase,' I commented.

'The Victorians,' he nodded, 'were a brilliant lot. They built them.'

Teller stood up on the foredeck holding the coil of rope, the peak of his baseball cap pointing forward like an attentive bird. I watched him, speculating, and Keeble followed the direction of my eyes and gave me only silence to work on.

Less than half a mile upstream from the lock we made an obviously pre-arranged stop at a riverside pub, Teller jumping ashore with his rope and fending the boat off the concrete edges as we drifted towards it. He and Peter tied expert knots, and everyone followed them ashore.

We drank sitting on a ring of uncomfortable metal chairs round a table with a sun umbrella spiked through its centre. Lynnie and Peter had Cokes and without consultation Keeble bought Scotch for the rest of us. Joan sipped hers with a pursed mouth and screwed eyes, as if it were a mite too strong for fragile little her, but I noticed she finished a long way first. Teller left his untouched for several minutes and then tossed it back in kingsized gulps. Keeble drank in pauses, revolving his glass in his hands and squinting through it at the sun. They were talking about the river, and other days on it, and other weather. On either side of us, round more umbrellas, sat more family parties much the same; Sunday morning drinks, Sunday lunch, Sunday snooze, *Sunday Express*, Sunday supper, *Sunday Night at the London Palladium* . . . safe little families in a sheltered routine, well intentioned and more or less content. Even Keeble fitted in. Whereas I . . . was apart.

'Drink,' Keeble said. 'You're on holiday.'

Faced with instant sharp curiosity from the rest of his family I meekly picked up my glass, still full when theirs were empty. It felt wrong to drink in the morning; it raised subconscious bells of alarm. I liked the taste of alcohol all right, but couldn't afford its effects. Alcohol encouraged you to put your trust in luck, and I was better off trusting a clear head. Consequently I sometimes didn't touch the stuff for weeks on end, and on that morning had had none for nearly a month.

Keeble watched me swallow the whisky, as vivid and familiar as a long-lost friend. The extent to which I was ever on holiday lay in the jacket across my knees, a pound of deadly mechanism in an under-arm holster; but it did seem most unlikely that I would need it on the Thames. When Teller ordered a refill, I drank that too. And then, since it was my turn, a third.

Peter lasted the course to three Cokes, and then wandered away with his camera poised, looking for excuses to use it. Next door a boatyard, like the one at Henley, was doing a roaring trade in punts. Four of the pub's more enthusiastic customers were having trouble stepping aboard, and Teller said chuckling, 'What's the fine for punting under the influence . . .?'

'A soaking,' Lynnie said. 'Silly nits.'

The punt pole waved recklessly as they set off, but the four men didn't fall in. The punt skidded ten feet up the river and hit the pub's landing stage with a thump that tumbled them into a leg-waving heap. I tried to laugh with everyone else and only succeeded in feeling more remote than ever.

We finished the drinks, re-embarked, and went up through the next lock, Harbour, to an unpopulated green-pasture stretch of river, where we moored for lunch. Peter swam, jumping off the boat repeatedly in glittering splashes, and Lynnie helped her mother in the cabin, preparing the food. Teller sprawled lazily on the back seat, and Keeble sat down with a Sunday newspaper and unfolded it, and I wearily began to wonder just when he would come to the point.

The point, however, was the newspaper. We had arrived.

'Read that,' he said, tapping a small paragraph on an inside page.

I read it.

'There is still no sign of Chrysalis, free in Kentucky, US, since Tuesday. Anxiety mounts for the safety of the £500,000 stallion, sire of this year's Derby winner, Moth.'

'Is this what you mean?' I asked, puzzled, making sure I'd read the right section. I had. He nodded vigorously.

'Didn't you know about it?' he asked.

'That Chrysalis had got lost? Yes, I suppose so. It was on all the news bulletins on Wednesday.'

'And it didn't mean a damn thing to you,' Teller said, with a trace of controlled and civilized bitterness under his smile.

'Well . . .'

'I have a share in that horse,' Teller said. 'A one-eighth share, 200,000 dollars worth.'

'Wow,' I said blankly. It seemed a lot of money to invest in one-eighth of a horse.

'What is more,' he said, sighing, 'I have spent all of last month negotiating the sale, and was lucky to beat out another syndicate that was bidding for him. And now as soon as he gets over there, this has to happen.'

'I'm sorry,' I said, conventionally polite.

'I can't expect you to understand.' He shook his head, excusingly. 'It isn't the money which matters, it's the horse. He's irreplaceable.'

'They'll find him.' I had no doubts of it, and I didn't care one way or the other.

'I am not so sure,' he said. 'And I would like you to get out there and look for him.'

For five seconds no one twitched a muscle, least of all me. Then Teller turned his head to Keeble and smiled his glossy smile. 'I wouldn't play poker with him,' he said. 'OK, I'll buy what you say about him being all that good.'

I glanced at Keeble and he gave me raised eyebrows, a tiny

shrug, and a slightly embarrassed expression. I wondered just how complete his testimonial had been.

Teller turned back to me. 'Sim here and I, we were in the same business, way back in World War II.'

'I see,' I said. And I did see. Quite a lot.

'It was just a war job for me, though,' he said. 'I got out of the Army in '47 and went back home to Pappy, and a couple of years later he died and left me his racehorses and a few bucks on the side.' The beautiful teeth flashed.

I waited. The story had hardly begun.

After a pause he said, 'I'll pay your fare and expenses, of course, and a fee.'

'I don't hunt horses,' I protested mildly.

'I can guess what you hunt.' He glanced again at Keeble. 'Sim says you're on vacation.'

I didn't need reminding.

'Chrysalis', he said, 'is the third stallion of international status to have disappeared in the last ten years.'

Two

THEY TRIED pretty hard in their subtle way, but it seemed ridiculous to me.

'You know about horses,' Keeble said. 'Your father trained them for racing.'

'There's the police,' I pointed out. 'Also the insurance company. Also every man, woman, and child with an eye for a horse in the state of Kentucky. And I presume there's a reward?'

Teller nodded.

'So why me?'

'No one found the other two.'

'There's a lot of land in America,' I said. 'They're both probably free on a prairie somewhere having a high old time siring herds of wild horses.'

Teller said grudgingly, 'The first one was found dead in a gully two years after he disappeared.'

'That's it, then.'

'But the second one . . . I bought that one too. I had a one-tenth share. This is second time around for me.'

I stared at him. 'Were any of the circumstances the same?'

Reluctantly he shook his head. 'No . . . except that they both got free. Allyx was never found. That's why I want something special done about Chrysalis.'

I was silent.

Keeble stirred. 'You've got nothing else to do, Gene. Why

not take your holiday in the States? What will you do with yourself, if you stay in Putney?'

His eyes had stopped blinking, as they always did when he
was intent. It was the surest guide I had to the complex calcula-
tions which sometimes lay beneath his most casual remarks. He
couldn't have guessed, I thought in alarm. He was a manipula-
tor but not clairvoyant. I shrugged and answered him on the
surface.

'Walk round Kew Gardens and smell the orchids.'

'They have no scent,' said Teller, pointing out the obvious.

'He knows that.' Keeble nodded, still unblinking. 'Any fruitless way of passing the time, is what he meant.'

'I guess you two operate on your own private wavelength,'
Teller said with a sigh. 'But I'd like you to come back with me,
Gene, and at least take a look. What's the harm in that?'

'And what's the good in it? It's not my sort of job.' I looked
away, down into the green water. 'And . . . I'm tired.'

They hadn't a quick answer to that. I thought it would have
been simple if all that was the matter with me was the straight-
forward tiredness of overwork, not the deadly fatigue of a
struggle I wasn't sure I could win. Chasing some crazy colt over
a thousand square miles didn't look like any sort of a cure.

Joan came out of the cabin into their defeated silence with a
bowl of salad and a string of bright fussing chatter. A folding
table was erected and the dishes put on to it, and we sat around
in the sun eating cold chicken and hot french bread. There was
a pleasant pink wine to drink and strawberries and cream afterwards, and Peter, still in wet bathing trunks despite orders from
his mother, took mouthfuls and photographs by turn. Lynnie,
sitting beside me, told Dave Teller an amusing story about the
finishing school she attended, her warm bare arm brushing
unselfconsciously against mine. I should have enjoyed that
placid Sunday picnic on the river. I tried to. I smiled and
answered when I was spoken to and concentrated carefully on

the taste and texture of what I was eating, and all that happened was that the fat black slug of depression flexed its muscles and swelled another notch.

At four o'clock, after dishwashing and dozing, we started back towards Henley. My refusal to go to America hadn't basic-ally disturbed Teller or Keeble an ounce. I concluded that whatever had prompted the suggestion it wasn't a burning con-viction that I and only I could find the missing horse. I put the whole thing out of my mind. It wasn't hard.

There was a punt in difficulties at the approach to Harbour Lock. Teller, again standing up on the bow with rope at the ready, shouted back to Keeble and pointed ahead. We looked, all of us, following his finger.

Where the river divided, going slowly into the left fork round the bend to the lock and fast on the right straight to the weir, a sturdy post in mid-stream bore a large notice, a single word: DANGER.

A girl, lying flat half in and half out of the punt with her arms round the post, was trying to tie up to it by passing a rope from one hand to the other, and making a poor job of it. On the stern, watching anxiously, punt pole in hand, stood a young man in a red-and-yellow shirt. He waved his arms when he saw us coming, and as Keeble throttled back and drifted near, he shouted across the water.

'Could you help us, sir?'

Since the punt was full in the weir stream with only the girl's slender arms keeping it from floating straight to destruction, he seemed remarkably cool. Keeble cursed about ignorant nitwits and edged nearer with his engine in slow reverse. The *Flying Linnet*, unlike the punt, was too big to go through this particu-lar weir, a long row of separately openable gates; but the sum-mer current was quite strong enough to crash her nastily against the thick concrete supports and pin her there for someone else humiliatingly to rescue.

Keeble shouted to the girl that we would tow them away, and to hand the mooring rope to me or Lynnie, whichever she could reach, as soon as we were nearer. The girl nodded, her arms still stretched forward round the big post, her long fair hair nearly brushing the water, her body quivering with the strain.

'Hold on,' Lynnie shouted urgently. 'Oh do hold on. Just a little longer, that's all.' She leaned over the side as if trying to shorten the few yards of water which still lay between, her worry and fright growing as we drew nearer. With the engine doing little more than tick over, the noise of the water on the far side of the weir began to fill our ears with its threat, but Keeble at any rate remained calm and sure of himself, an easy master of his boat and the situation. With six feet still to go the girl took one arm off the post and held out the rope towards Lynnie's groping hand. Then, disastrously she dropped it. Crying out, beating in big splashes on the water, she struggled to get her arm back round the post. Lynnie yelled to her to get hold of the rope again, it was fastened to the punt under her chest, to get hold of it again and hand it over. But the girl was now far too frightened either to listen or to let go of the post again, and the panic was rising to screams in her voice.

Out of the side of my vision I saw the young man start forward to help her, apparently at last realizing that their position was serious. The punt pole swung awkwardly in his hands, curved through the air in a clumsy arc, and hit Dave Teller on the head. With buckling knees the American fell forward off the bows and straight into the water.

I was up on the cabin roof, out of my shoes and into the river after him almost before any of the others realized what had happened. I heard Keeble's despairing voice shouting 'Gene' in the second before I went under, but I was thinking simply that speed was the only chance of finding Teller, since anything that sank in a river the size of the Thames was instantly out of sight. Algae made the water opaque.

Diving in as near to where he had gone as I could judge, I kicked downwards, arms wide. I was going faster than Teller, I had to be. I had a strong impression that the punt pole had knocked him out, that he was on a slow one-way trip to the bottom.

About eight feet down my fingers hooked almost immediately into cloth. Even with my eyes open I could see nothing and with my right hand I felt for his face while I tried to kick us both to the surface. I found his face, clamped his nose between my fingers and the heel of my hand on his mouth, and turned him so that I held his head against my chest. He didn't struggle; couldn't feel.

From that point on the rescue operation failed to go as per scheduled. I couldn't get back to the surface. The current underneath was much stronger, very cold, sweeping us downwards, clinging round our bodies with irresistible force. I thought; we'll hit the weir and be pinned there down deep, and that will be that. For a treacherous instant I didn't even care. It would solve all my problems. It was what I wanted. But not really with another life in my arms, for which I was literally the only hope.

My chest began hurting with the lack of air. When we hit the weir, I thought, I would climb my way up it. Its face might not be slippery smooth. It had to be possible . . .

There was a sudden tug as if some fisherman had us hooked. I felt us change direction slightly and then a tug again, stronger and continuing and stronger still. No miraculous rescue. It was the water had us, gripping tighter, sucking us fast, inexorably, into the weir. The sheer overwhelming weight and power of it made nonsense of human strength, reduced my efforts to the fluttering of a moth in a whirlwind. The seizing speed suddenly accelerated further still, and we hit. Or rather, Teller hit, with a jar which nearly wrenched him away from me. We spun in the current and my shoulder crashed into concrete and we spun again and crashed, and I couldn't get hold of any surface with my free hand. The tumbling and crashing went on, and the pain in my chest went deeper, and I knew I wasn't going to be climbing up any weir, I could only find it when it hit me, and when I reached for it it hit me somewhere else.

The crashing stopped, but the tumbling went on. My ears were roaring to bursting point. There was a sword embedded in my chest. The searing temptation came back more strongly just to open my mouth and be finished with it. But by my own peculiar rules I couldn't do that, not with someone else involved, not when what I was doing was in a way what I'd been trained for. Some other time, I thought lightheadedly, some other time I'd drown myself. This time I'll just wait until my brain packs up from lack of oxygen, which won't be long now, and if I haven't any choice in the matter, then I haven't any guilt either.

The tumbling suddenly died away and the clutching current relaxed and loosened and finally unlocked itself. I was only seconds this side of blackout and at first it didn't register: then I gave a feeble kick with legs half entwined round Teller and we shot upward as if on springs. My head broke the surface into the sun and air went down into the cramp of my lungs like silver fire.

The weir, the killing weir, was fifty yards away. Fifty yards *upstream*. We had come right through it under the water.

I took my freezing, stiffened fingers off Teller's face, and held his head up to mine, and blew into his flaccid mouth. The current, gentle again and comparatively warm, carried us slowly along, frothy bubbles bursting with little winks against our necks. I trod water with my legs, and held Teller up, and went on pushing into him all my used-up breath. He showed no response. It would be exceedingly inconsiderate of him, I thought resignedly, if he had died right at the beginning and I had gone to all that trouble for nothing.

There were shouts from the banks suddenly and people pointing, and someone came after us in a dinghy with an outboard motor. It puttered noisily by my ear and hands stretched over the side to grasp.

I shook my head. 'A rope,' I said, and breathed into Teller. 'Give me a rope. And pull slowly.'

One of the two men argued, but the other did as I asked. I wound the rope round my arm twice and held it, and when I nodded they let the boat drift away until we were a safe distance from its propeller and slowly began to pull us towards the bank. Teller got ten more of my ex-breaths on the way. They didn't seem to be doing him a bit of good.

The dinghy towed us out of the weir stream side of the river and landed on the same side as the lock. People appeared in a cluster to help, and there was little doubt it was needed, but even so I was loth to part with Teller until one large calm man lay on his stomach on the grass and stretched his arms down under the American's armpits.

'Don't worry,' he said. 'We'll go straight on with the breathing.'

I nodded, took my mouth away from Teller's and transferred his weight into the stranger's arms. He began to pull him out of the water as fast as he could. I put a steadying hand on Teller's chest and felt it heave suddenly under the clinging blue shirt. I hadn't enough breath left myself to tell the man who was lifting him, and while I was still trying to, Teller, half out, gave a choking cough and opened his eyes. There was some water in his lungs, racking him. The stranger pulled him even more quickly out on to the grass, and as his ankles bumped over the edge his returning consciousness flooded into a stark sort of awareness which had nothing to do with a release from drowning. Somewhere between a cough and a groan he said 'Jesus,' and again went completely limp.

Another couple of strong wrists hauled me up on to the bank in his wake, and I knelt there beside him feeling the reassuringly small swelling on the side of his head but anxiously listening to the dragging breath bubbling in his throat.

'Roll him over,' I said. 'Carefully . . . just so his tongue isn't choking him.'

We put him on his side and his breathing eased immediately, but I wouldn't let them pick him up and carry him up to the lock. Almost any injury was bound to be made worse by moving, and he'd been moved too much already. The calm man agreed and went briskly off to fetch a doctor.

The lock-keeper arrived along the towpath, followed at a rush by Keeble and all his family. Their faces were all strained with shock, and Lynnie had been crying.

'Thank God,' Keeble said, crouching beside me. 'You're both all right.' His voice held almost more incredulity than relief.

I shook my head. 'He's hurt, somewhere.'

'Badly?'

'Don't know . . . He crashed into the weir.'

'We didn't see you go over. We were watching . . .'

'They must have gone under,' said the lock-keeper. 'Through one of the gates. Those gates wind upwards, same as a sash window. We've got two of them a couple of feet open at the bottom today, with the river a bit full after all that rain.'

I nodded. 'Under.'

Dave Teller choked and woke up again, coughing uncontrollably through the puddle in his lungs, every cough jerking him visibly into agony. From his fluttering gesture it was clear where the trouble lay.

'His leg,' Keeble said. 'He's not bleeding . . . could he have broken it?'

The jar when he had hit the weir had been enough. I said so. 'We can't do anything for him,' said Keeble, watching him helplessly.

The crowd around us waited, murmuring in sympathy but

enjoying the disaster, listening to Teller coughing, watching him clutch handfuls of grass in rigid fingers. Not a scrap of use begging them to go away.

'What happened to the punt?' I asked Keeble.

'We towed it ashore. Lynnie got hold of the rope. Those kids were terribly shocked.' He looked round for them vaguely, but they weren't in the crowd. 'I suppose they've stayed back at the lock. The girl was nearly hysterical when you and Dave didn't come up.' A remembering bleakness came into his face. 'We towed them into the lock cut and moored there. Then we ran along to the lock to get the lock-keeper . . . and he was already down here.' He looked up across the river to the pretty weir. 'How long were you under the water?'

'A couple of centuries.'

'Seriously.'

'Can't tell. Maybe three minutes.'

'Long enough.'

'Mm.'

He looked me over objectively, boss to employee. One shoulder of my green jersey shirt was ripped in a jagged tear.

'Bruised,' he said matter-of-factly.

'The weir,' I agreed, 'has knobs on.'

'It's like a flight of steps under there,' said the lock-keeper solemnly. 'Going down from the top level to this one, you see. The current would have rolled you right down those steps, I reckon. In fact, it's a bleeding miracle you ever came up, if you ask me. There's some every year fall in this river and never get seen again. Current takes them along the bottom all the way to the sea.'

'Charming,' Keeble said under his breath.

Dave Teller stopped coughing, rolled slightly on to his back, and put his wrist to his mouth. His strong beaky nose stuck uncompromisingly up to the sky, and the wetness on his face wasn't from the Thames. After a while he moved his hand and asked Keeble what had happened. Keeble briefly explained, and the screwed-up eyes slid round to me.

'Lucky you were with us,' he said weakly, the smile in his voice making no progress on his face. He moved his hand apprehensively behind his ear, and winced when it reached the bump. 'I don't remember a thing.'

'Do you remember asking me to look for your horse?'

He nodded a fraction, slowly. 'Yuh. You said no.'

'I've changed my mind,' I said. 'I'll go.'

In the cabin of the *Flying Linnet* Keeble watched me slowly strip off my sodden clothes. I had never, as far as I remembered, felt so weak. I'd left half my muscles under the weir. Buttons would no longer come out of their holes.

'You heard what the man said,' Keeble remarked. 'It was lucky you were with us.'

I didn't answer.

'Make a note of it,' Keeble said. 'Stick around. You never know when you'll be needed.'

'Sure,' I said, refusing to acknowledge that I understood what he was talking about.

He wouldn't be deterred. 'You're like Dave's horse. Irreplaceable.'

My lips twitched. That was the crunch, all right. His job would be a little harder if he lost his head cook and bottle-washer. Personal regard didn't come into it.

I struggled out of my jersey. He handed me a towel, glancing non-committally at the marks of this and previous campaigns.

'I'm serious, Gene.'

'Yeah,' I sighed. 'Well . . . I'm still here.'

It was too much of an admission, but at least it seemed to reassure him enough to change the subject.

'Why are you going to the States?'

'Maybe I owe it to him.'

'Who? Dave?'

I nodded.

'I don't follow,' he said, frowning. 'Surely he owes you? If anyone owes anything.'

'No. If I'd been quicker, he wouldn't have gone in, wouldn't now have a smashed thigh. Too much whisky and wine and sleeping in the sun. I was much too slow. Abysmally, shamefully slow.'

He made a gesture of impatience. 'Don't be ridiculous, Gene. No speed on earth could have prevented an accident like that.'

I put the towel round my neck and started to take off my trousers.

'That accident', I said briefly, 'was attempted murder.'

He gazed at me, eyes blinking slowly behind the mild spectacles. Then he turned, opened the cabin door, and stepped up into the cockpit. I heard him shouting to Peter.

'Get out of that punt at once, there's a good chap. And don't let anyone else get in it. It's important.'

'Not even Lynnie?'

'Not even Lynnie.'

'I don't want to,' said Lynnie's voice in a wail from the cockpit. 'I never want to go in a punt again.'

She wasn't much her father's daughter. His mind was as tough as old boots. The chubby body which contained it came back into the cabin and shut the door.

'Convince me,' he said.

'The boy and girl have scarpered.'

He raised his eyebrows and protested. 'They were frightened.'

'They didn't stop to answer questions. They may quite possibly think Dave and I are dead, because they didn't even wait to make sure. I should say they never even intended to appear at any inquest.'

He was silent, thinking about it. The boy and girl had gone from the lock when we had eventually returned to it: gone unnoticed, leaving the punt behind. No one had given them a thought until after the doctor had splinted Teller's leg and seen him carried on a stretcher a hundred yards to an ambulance. When the doctor asked how the accident happened, the causes of it weren't around.

'We don't know,' Keeble said. 'They may very likely have come down the towpath and seen you were all right, and they might have dozens of personal reasons for not wanting to stay.'

I finished kicking my legs out of the clammy cotton trousers and peeled off my socks.

'The boy stood on the stern too long. He should have been helping with the rope.'

Keeble frowned. 'Certainly he seemed unconcerned, but I don't think he realized quite what a jam they were in. Not like the girl did.'

'The first time he moved, he hit Dave straight on the head.'

'Punt poles are clumsy if you aren't careful . . . and he couldn't have counted on Dave standing in so vulnerable a spot.'

'He'd been standing there most of the way, seeing to the bow rope.'

'The boy and girl couldn't know that.'

'He was certainly standing there when we approached the punt.'

'And,' Keeble said in a demolishing voice, 'no one would deliberately put themselves into so much danger just to bait a trap.'

I dried my legs and wondered what to do about my under-pants.

Keeble sighed down his nose and fluttered his fingers. 'No one except you.'

He reached into a locker and produced a bundle of clothes.

'Emergency falling-in kit,' he explained, giving them to me. 'I don't suppose anything will fit.'

As there was a mixture of his own cast-offs, which were too wide, and Lynnie's, which were too narrow, he was right. Everything, besides, was too short.

'In addition,' he went on, 'how did the boy and girl know we were on the river at all and would be coming down through Harbour Lock? How long did you expect them to wait there clinging to the post? How did they know exactly which boat to hail, and how did they avoid being rescued by any other boat?'

'The best accidents always look as if they couldn't possibly be anything else.'

'I grant you that,' he said, nodding. 'I just think that this one literally couldn't be set up.'

'Yes, it could. With a safe get-out, in that if it didn't work according to plan, if for instance Peter had been on the bows instead of Dave, they had no need to go into the act of yelling for help, because of course they wanted to make sure it was us before they started.'

'They were in danger,' Keeble protested.

'Maybe. I'd like to take a closer look at that post.'

'And there might have been other boats around, helping. Or watching.'

'If Dave never came within range of the punt pole they lost nothing but an opportunity. If other boats had been watching there would simply have been more people to cry accident. The girl was screaming and splashing and dramatically dropping her rope when the boy hit Dave. We were all watching her, not him. Any sized audience would have been doing the same.'

'And how could the boy and girl have known where Dave

would be this Sunday, in the first place? And why on God's earth should anyone want to kill him?'

I stepped into some aged grey trousers of Keeble's and found them a foot too generous round the waist. My boss wordlessly held out a short striped elastic schoolboy belt, which took care of the problem by gripping like a tourniquet.

'It was a simple accident, Gene. It had to be.'

The trousers ended four inches above my ankles, and the socks I slowly fumbled my way into made no effort to bridge the gap.

'Gene!' said Keeble, exasperated.

I sighed. 'You'll agree I'm a sort of specialist in arranging accidents?'

'Not usually fatal ones,' he protested.

'Not often.' And no more, if I could wriggle out of it. 'Just a general stage managing of events, so the victim believes that what has happened to him is the merest mischance.'

Keeble smiled. 'You've sprung more hares that way . . .'

'So,' I said reasonably, 'I'm apt to spot a rig-up when I see one.'

The smile half faded and changed into speculation.

'And no,' I said, 'I was not concussed in the recent boating party and I haven't got water on the brain.'

'Keep your telepathy to yourself,' he said uncomfortably. 'I just think you are mistaken.'

'OK, then I'll spend my holiday in Putney.'

He said 'No,' so vehemently, so explosively, that there was no subtlety left in the situation. From his naked alarm I saw unmistakably how much he understood of my depressed mental state and how convinced he was that I wouldn't survive three weeks of my own company. Shocked, I realized that his relief when I answered his telephone call had not been at finding me at home, but at finding me alive. He had dug me out on to the river to keep an eye on me and was prepared to send me off on any old wild goose chase so long as it kept me occupied. Then maybe, I supposed, he thought I would snap out of it.

'The blues', I said gently, 'have been with me for a long time.'

'Not like this.'

I had no answer.

After a pause he said persuasively, 'Three world class stallions disappearing . . . isn't that also the sort of accident you don't believe in?'

'Yes, it is. Especially when someone tries to get rid of the man who bought two of them.'

He opened his mouth and shut it again. I almost smiled.

'It was a craftsman's accident,' I said. 'It could hardly have been done better. All they didn't bargain for was interference from someone like me.'

He still didn't believe it, but as he was now happy that I should, since it meant that I would go to the States, he raised no more objections. With a shrug and a rueful smile he tossed me a darned brown sweater, which hung round me like a tent; and I picked up my own wet clothes and followed him out into the sunshine.

Peter and Lynnie both giggled at my baggy appearance, the nervous shock still sharp in their voices, especially Lynnie's. I grinned at her and ruffled her hair, and made as if to kick Peter overboard, and some of the tension loosened in their eyes. In another half hour they would have reached the compulsive talking stage and an hour after that they would be back to normal. Nice, ordinary kids, with nice, ordinary reactions.

I climbed wearily up on to the cabin roof and spread out my clothes to dry. My shoes were still there where I had stepped out of them, and absentmindedly I put them on. Then, standing up, I looked across to the weir, and back to the hefty post with its notice; DANGER, and at the innocent empty punt tied up behind the *Flying Linnet*: and I found myself thinking about the legend of the Sirens, the sea nymphs who sat on a rock near a whirlpool and with their pretty voices drew passing sailors towards them, to lure them to their death.

Three

THE PUNT had the name of the owner screwed on to the stern on a small metal plate. The lock-keeper, consulted, said that it came from a boatyard about a mile down the river, next to a pub; you couldn't miss it.

'That,' I murmured to Keeble, 'is where we had our drinks this morning.'

His eyelids flickered. He said to the lock-keeper, 'I suppose a lot of punts from there come up through your lock?'

'They sure do, on a fine Sunday like this,' he agreed.

'Did you happen to notice this one, with a girl and a young man in it? The girl had long fair hair, white trousers, and a pink shirt, and the boy was wearing tight pale blue jeans and a red-and-yellow check shirt.'

'I should say they came up before my dinner break. I can't remember anyone like that this afternoon.'

The lock-keeper eased the white-topped hat back on his head and eyed the boats lining up to go into the lock. He was a youngish man with an air of long-suffering patience, the occupational result, no doubt, of a life spent watching an endless procession of incompetence. People, he had said matter-of-factly, fell into his lock every day of the week. Near-drownings, however, were of no special interest to him: he too often had to deal with the unsaved.

'Would you know them again?' Keeble asked.

The lock-keeper shook his head decisively. 'Not a chance.

And if I don't get back to my lock there'll be a lot of bad tempers coming through the gates and as like as not we'll be fishing out another one . . .'

He gave me a sketchy farewell salute as one of the few who had gone down his weir and walked away, and strolled unhurriedly back to deal with his Sunday going home traffic problem.

'We may as well tow the punt back to the boatyard,' Keeble said thoughtfully. 'We've got to go down past there anyway, and they won't be able to spare anyone to come and fetch it on a busy day like this. And maybe they'll know where the boy and girl came from . . .'

And maybe they wouldn't, I thought: but even the most hopeless questions have to be asked.

'I'd like to look at the post,' I said.

Keeble was agreeable, but Lynnie and Peter and their mother were horrified when they found where we were proposing to go, and said they would wait on the bank. In a row, with anxious faces, they stood guard over the punt, while Keeble neatly manoeuvred the *Flying Linnet* upstream a little way through the downcoming cruisers, and then drifted gently across towards the post. I, standing on the stern seat, caught hold of the crossbar with its emphatic warning and clung on to it while Keeble put the boat into reverse against the drag of the weir stream.

Once the engine was thrusting hard enough to hold its own, so that the tension on my arms slackened, I knelt down on the seat and tried to do what the girl had been doing, to pass a rope round the post from one hand to the other. The tendency of the two-ton *Flying Linnet* to drift away couldn't have been much less to deal with than the weight of the punt, but even allowing also for the fact that my arms were longer and stronger, it was easy. I secured the rope and gave a thumbs up to Keeble, who stopped the engine. Then with one toe wedged and the narrow side of the boat under my pelvis, I shoved up the sleeves of the brown sweater and leaned down and over to inspect the scenery.

'For God's sake be careful,' Keeble said, his voice sharp over the noise of the weir.

I turned my head and laughed at him.

'We haven't any more dry clothes,' he pointed out, scowling. 'None that you can get into. If you fall in again you'll have to go home wet.'

Smiling, I turned back to the post. But feel and look how I might, there was nothing out of the ordinary about the square sturdy white-painted baulk of timber set rock-like up on end in the Thames' bed.

Keeble shrugged and said, 'I told you so,' and steered his boat back to the bank.

'How about fingerprinting the punt?' I said.

'You never let up.'

'You should be glad of it.'

The long line of past occasions when not letting up had led to a useful harvest rose up between us, and I saw his conviction waver.

'All right, Gene, if you're sure.'

'Get Raben to do it. He's the best.'

'All right. Tomorrow.'

'How about the police?'

He pursed his lips. 'It's not our usual territory. More theirs I agree. But they're not likely to take your theory seriously, or to act on it, unless we tell them what your job is . . . and impress them with it. No, I'm not in favour of that. We could just go along with this quietly on our own for a little while, I think.'

'So that if nothing turns up, we won't have made bloody fools of ourselves?'

All his facial muscles contracted for a second. 'You are not paid to turn your perceptions on your boss.'

'I probably am.'

'That's a point.'

The boat grounded gently against the bank, and I helped

294

Joan and Lynnie back on board. Peter, on his father's directions, stepped into the punt and handed him up the mooring rope, which Keeble fastened to the cleat on the *Flying Linnet*'s stern. Then, towing the punt, we took our turn into the lock, explained what we were doing to the lock-keeper, and cruised downstream to the pub and its next-door boatyard.

A flustered middle-aged boatman there was trying to cope with returning family picnic parties and a bunch of youths and girls who wanted to fill in the half hour before the pub opened at seven o'clock. The late afternoon sun shone redly on his big sweating face and his freckled bald head, and we had to wait while he juggled his customers precariously in and out of skiffs and punts and took their money and warned the young couples that it was an offence to be on the river without lights after dark and that the boatyard closed at nine-thirty anyway.

When Keeble at last had a chance he asked the boatman if he had seen the girl with fair hair and the boy in a red-and-yellow check shirt who had hired a punt that morning.

'Seen 'em? I suppose so, I've been here all day.'

'I mean, do you remember them?' Keeble said patiently.

'Where are they then?' The boatman looked round suspiciously.

'They've gone,' Keeble began.

'Then who's going to settle up?' said the boatman belligerently, this last problem looking to be just one too many for his temper.

'Oh, I will,' said Keeble soothingly. He took his wallet out of his back pocket and unfolded it to show the usual thickish wad. Keeble didn't have to live on Her Majesty's pay and worked from conviction, not need; his beer money represented a week's wage to me, and his boat a year's.

'How much do they owe you?' He handed over what the boatman asked and offered a fiver on top. 'I'd like to hire this punt for this evening and tomorrow,' he said. 'Is that all right?'

The boatman took the money without hesitation and made a few half-hearted efforts to appear cautious.

'Where'll you be taking it?'

'Henley,' Keeble said.

'You won't leave the cushions out if it rains?'

Keeble shook his head.

'All right then.' The boatman had already tucked the notes away. 'And you'll bring it back tomorrow?'

'Tomorrow afternoon,' Keeble agreed. 'Now, about those young people who took it this morning . . .'

Unexpectedly the boatman suddenly leered. 'I remember 'em,' he said, 'come to think of it, they was the two who had no business to be out together.'

'What do you mean?' Keeble asked.

'Well, see, this girl, she said like, what if her old man had put detectives on her, what would they say if she went off all day with him in a punt, and how she'd said she'd only come out as long as it was nothing anyone could use in a divorce. And the fellow in the check shirt turned round and said old money bags, meaning her old man, see, would never find out where they'd been, he was in France on business wasn't he, or somesuch, and then they took note that I was standing there hearing and they sort of nudged each other and shut up. But I reckon as they were off for a bit on the side see, and didn't want no one to catch 'em.'

'Exactly,' said Keeble to me with another touch of I-told-you-so.

'And very nicely done,' I agreed. 'Artistic.'

'You haven't seen them since this morning, I suppose?' Keeble said to the boatman. 'Do you happen to know how they got here?'

'Car,' said the boatman, waving an arm. 'They came from the car park back there.'

'Which car, do you know?'

He gave Keeble a pitying stare. 'Look, there's cars in and out all day, what with the pub and us. And I'm looking at the river, see, with my hands full an' all, and I couldn't tell you no one who's come and gone nor what they came in, but they must have come in a car, because they come in the morning, and there's no buses along here on Sundays before half-two in the afternoon.'

'Thank you anyway,' said Keeble, sighing. 'You've been very helpful.' He added another pound to his overpayment and the boatman's eyes swivelled rapidly from the pub to the clock over the boathouse door.

Still ten minutes until the bar opened. I proceeded to fill them.

'Did the young man, or the girl, or both of them, speak with any special type of accent?' I asked.

Since he spoke broad Berkshire himself, the boatman's hesitation was understandable. 'They talked', he said, considering, 'like they do on the telly.'

'Not much help,' Keeble commented.

'How do you lash the end of your punts' mooring ropes?' I asked.

'Eh?' said the boatman, puzzled.

'Do you lash the end of the ropes to stop them unravelling?'

'Oh, I get you. No, we splice 'em. Turn the ends back and sort of weave them in. Lashing's no good as it comes undone too easily.'

I unwound the punt's mooring rope from the *Flying Linnet*'s stern cleat. 'This one is coming undone, though.'

'Let's see that,' he said suspiciously, and I gave it to him. He twisted the frayed unravelling strands in his strong dirty fingers and hovered in what I guessed to be a fairly usual mixture of fury and resignation.

'These bleeding vandals . . . excuse me, ma'am,' he apologized to Joan. 'These so and sos, they tie up to a tree, see, or

297

something, and come they want to push on, they can't undo the knots if the rope's wet, and they just don't bother, they cut through the rope and off they go.'

'Does that often happen?'

'Every summer, we has this trouble now and then.' He pulled the rope up straight, measuring its length with his eye. 'There's a good four or five feet gone off this one, I shouldn't wonder. We've been talking of switching to chains, but they can get into holy terrors of knots, chains can. Here,' he added to Keeble, 'you'd better have another punt, one with a better rope.'

'This one will be fine,' Keeble said, fastening it on again. 'We'll see you tomorrow.'

He towed the punt down to Henley and right into the garage-like boathouse which kept the English summer off the *Flying Linnet*. The punt was secured alongside by Peter and his father and everyone disembarked along a narrow boardwalk carrying things like the remains from lunch, newspapers, bathing towels, and in my case, wet clothes and a loaded jacket, out through the boathouse and into Keeble's Rover, which was parked on a neat square of grass at the back.

Peter's main care was for his precious camera, again hanging round his neck on its cord.

'I suppose,' I said idly, 'you didn't happen to take a photograph up there by the weir? You didn't happen to get a shot of those people in the punt?'

He shook his head, blinking like his father.

'Gosh, no, I didn't. I don't suppose actually I would have thought of taking one, not when everything was happening, do you think? I mean, it would have looked a bit off if you and Mr Teller had been drowning and I was just standing there taking pictures and so on.'

'You'll never be a newspaperman,' I said, grinning at him.

'Wouldn't you have minded, then?'

'I don't think so.'

'But, anyway,' he said mournfully, 'I couldn't, you see, because I finished the film at lunch-time and I didn't have another one, so even if there had been a fire or something I couldn't have taken it.' He looked at his camera thoughtfully. 'I won't finish up any more films in the middle of the day, just in case.'

'A fire,' I agreed seriously, 'would anyway make a much better picture than just people drowning, which they mostly do out of sight.'

Peter nodded, considering me. 'You know, you're quite sensible, aren't you?'

'Peter!' exclaimed his mother in unnecessary apology. 'That's not the way to talk.' And she wasn't much pleased when I said as far as I was concerned he could say what he liked.

Keeble drove round to the station car park, where Lynnie and I transferred to the Austin.

'I'll ring in the morning,' Keeble said, standing half out of his respectable car.

'Right.'

'Take care of Lynnie.'

'I'll do that.'

Lynnie kissed her parents goodbye, but her father more warmly, and made a face at Peter as the Rover rolled away out of the gate. Then she climbed into the Austin, waited until I was sitting beside her, and stretched out her hand to the ignition.

She was trembling again.

'Shall I drive?' I said mildly, making it absolutely her own choice.

She put both her hands in her lap and looked straight out through the windscreen. Her face was pale above the orange dress.

'I thought you were both dead.'

'I know.'

'I still feel churned up. It's silly.'

'It's not silly. And I expect you're fond of Dave Teller.'

'He's sent us presents and things, since we were little.'

'A nice man.'

'Yes.' She sighed deeply and after a pause said calmly, 'I think it would be better, if you really don't mind, if you drive back.'

'Of course I will.'

We changed places, and went back to London with more cars passing us than we passed. At Chiswick roundabout I said I would drive her to her flat and go home by taxi, but with a sideways laughing glance she said no taxi would stop for me in her father's clothes, and that she was feeling better and could quite easily do the last lap herself: so I rolled round the few corners to Putney and stopped outside my own front door.

Summer dusk filled the quiet streets. No one about. Lynnie looked out of her window upwards at the tall house, and shivered.

'You're cold,' I said, concerned for her bare arms.

'No . . . I have a cardigan in the back . . . I was just thinking about your flat.'

'What about it?'

'It's so . . . empty.' She gave a half laugh, shrugging it off. 'Well, I hope you won't have nightmares, after today.'

'No . . .' I collected my things and got out of the car, and she moved over into the driver's seat.

'Will they have saved any dinner for you at the hostel?' I asked.

'Not a hope,' she said cheerfully. 'But I expect there'll be some cake and milk about, there usually is.'

'Would you care to eat with me? Not up there,' I added hastily, seeing the beginnings of well-brought-up suspicion. 'In a restaurant, I mean.'

'I've my mother to thank for my beastly mind,' she said unexpectedly. 'I really am rather hungry, and I don't see at all

why I shouldn't have supper in your flat, if you've got any food.'
And without more ado she got out of the car and locked it, and
stood expectantly beside me on the pavement.

'There are some tins,' I said, reflecting. 'Wait here just a
second, would you. I just want to have a look round the back.'

'Round the back?'

'For burglars,' I said sardonically. But I went to look, as
usual, at the powder-coated bottom flight of the fire escape. No
one had been up or down all day.

Lynnie climbed the stairs to the fourth floor as easily as
before, and having checked via a well-placed paper clip that my
door hadn't been opened since I had shut it that morning, I put
the key in the lock and let us in.

The green plastic lampshade in my sitting room scattered its
uncosy glare over the tidy room, switching the soft grey light
outside into sudden black, and evoking the forlornness of insti-
tution buildings on winter afternoons. It wouldn't be much
trouble, I thought, to go out and buy myself a red shade in the
morning, and see if it propagated rosy thoughts instead.

'Sit down,' I suggested. 'Are you warm enough? Switch the
electric fire on if you'd like it. I think I'll go and change, and
then we can decide about going out.'

Lynnie nodded, but took things into her own hands. When
I came out of the bedroom she had already investigated my
meagre store cupboard and had lined up a packet of soup, some
eggs, and a tin of anchovies.

'Soup, and anchovies on scrambled eggs,' she said.

'If you'd really like that,' I said doubtfully.

'I can't cook much else.'

I laughed. 'All right. I'll do the coffee.'

There were burnt specks in the eggs when she had finished,
which harmonized nicely with the scraped-off over-done toast
and the brown anchovy strips, and there had been a slight over-
emphasis on pepper.

'No one', she sighed, 'is going to marry me for my cordon bleu.'

There were plenty of other reasons why she'd be fending off suitors knee-deep in a year or two: a curvy figure, delicate neck, baby skin; the touch-me-not expression, the awakening social courage, the quick compassion. No one was going to care if she couldn't cook. But she wasn't secure enough to be told so at that moment.

'When were you seventeen?' I asked.

'The week before last.'

'You didn't waste much time passing the driving test.'

'I've been able to drive since I was eight. Peter can, too.' She finished her eggs and stirred two heaped teaspoonfuls of sugar into her coffee. 'I was hungry. Funny, that.'

'It's a long time since lunch.'

'A terribly long time . . .' She suddenly looked me straight in the face, which she had mostly been avoiding, and with devastating innocence said, 'I'm so glad you're alive.'

I turned a hopeless wince into a laugh. 'I'm so glad Dave Teller is.'

'Both of you,' she said. 'It was the worst thing in my whole life when you didn't come up.'

A child untouched by tragedy, I thought. A pity the world was such a rough place, would catch her by her pretty neck one day and tear her guts apart. No one ever escaped. To have got to seventeen unlacerated was merely a matter of luck.

When we had finished the coffee she insisted on doing the dishes, but when she hung up the tea towel I saw all her mother's warnings pour back, and she glanced at me and quickly away, and stood stiffly in the centre of the room, looking nervous and embarrassed.

'Why don't you have any pictures on your walls?' she said jerkily.

I gestured to the trunk in the corner. 'There are some in

there, but I don't like them very much. Not enough to bother with hanging them up . . . Do you know it's after ten? I'd better take you home or the hostel will shut you out.'

'Oh yes,' she said in great relief, and then hearing her own voice, added in confusion, 'I mean . . . I didn't know if you would think me very rude, dashing off as soon as we'd finished eating.'

'Your mother is quite right to tell you to be cautious,' I said lightly. 'Little Red Riding Hood couldn't tell a wolf from her grandmother . . . and you can never rely on a woodcutter turning up in the nick of time.'

The rigidity dissolved like mist. 'You do say some extraordinary things,' she said. 'As if you could read my mind.'

'I could,' I smiled. 'You'd better put that cardigan on. It will be cold outside.'

'OK.' She pulled a dark brown jersey out of her bucket-shaped holdall and put it on. I bent to pick up a clean folded handkerchief which had fallen out with it, and when she was ready, handed it to her.

'Thanks,' she said, looking at it casually. 'That's the one Peter found in the punt.'

'In the punt?'

'Yes, down a crack between two of the cushions. He gave it to me because it was too small for him, he said. Too cissy.'

'Did he find anything else?'

'I don't think so . . . I mean it isn't stealing or anything, is it, to keep her handkerchief? I'll give it to her of course if she comes back, but by the time Peter was sitting in the punt, they had been gone already for ages.'

'No, it's not stealing,' I reassured her, though technically it was doubtful. 'But may I have a look at it?'

'Of course.'

She gave it back and I unfolded it: a white square of thin gauzy material. In one corner, a stylized bear in a flat straw hat.

303

'Is that out of Walt Disney?' I asked.

She shook her head and said with surprise at my ignorance, 'Yogi Bear.'

'Who is Yogi Bear?'

'I can't believe it! Well, he's a character in a lot of cartoon films. Like Top Cat and Atom Ant and the Flintstones.'

'I've seen the Flintstones,' I agreed.

'Like them, then. The same people make Yogi Bear.'

'Do you mind if I keep it for a day or two?'

'Of course, if you really want to,' she said, puzzled. 'But it surely hasn't any value.'

Down in the street I said I might as well finish the job and drive her to her hostel.

'I'm really all right now,' she protested. 'You don't need to come.'

'Yes I do. Your father said to look after you, and I'm seeing you safe to your door.'

She raised her eyebrows and gave me a comical look, but compliantly went round to the passenger's seat. I started the car, switched on the lights, and started towards Kensington.

'Do you always do what Daddy tells you?' she asked, smiling.

She was feeling much surer of herself, I thought.

'Yes, when I want to.'

'That's a contradiction in terms.'

'So it is.'

'Well, what do you actually *do*? What does *anyone* do in the Civil Service?'

'I interview people.'

'What sort of people?'

'People who want jobs in Government departments.'

'Oh!' She laughed. 'A sort of Personnel Officer?'

'Sort of.'

'It sounds a bit drizz.'

'The sun shines occasionally.'

'You're pretty quick. We only made up drizz yesterday.'

'A very useful word.'

'Yes, we thought so, too. Covers a lot of things nicely.'

'Like wet boyfriends?'

She laughed. 'Actually, it's pretty drizz to *have* a wet boy-friend.' She pointed. 'The hostel's down there, but we have to drive around and find somewhere to park the car all night. One or two squares down here don't have meters yet.'

The nearest empty space was a good quarter of a mile from the hostel, so I walked her back.

'You don't need to . . .' she began. 'Well . . . don't say it. Daddy said.'

'Right,' I agreed.

She sniffed resignedly and walked beside me out of step, the leather bucket bag swinging and her flat shoes silent on the pavement. At the hostel's glossy black well-lit front door she came to a stop and hovered on one foot, her half anxious uncertain expression saying clearer than words that she wasn't sure how to part from me. I wasn't old enough for uncle terms or young enough for a casual contemporary brush-off. I worked for her father, but wasn't his servant. Lived alone, looked respectable, asked nothing: I didn't fit into any of the categories she had yet learnt how to deal with. I put out my hand and smiled.

'Goodnight, Lynnie.'

Her clasp was brief, warm, relieved.

'Goodnight . . .' There was a pause while she made up her mind to it; and even then it was little more than a breath. '. . . Gene.'

'I wish you,' I said, 'blind traffic wardens and foam rubber bumpers.'

'Goodnight.' The chuckle rolled spontaneously in her throat. 'Goodnight.' She turned on one toe and jumped the two steps up to the door, then looked over her shoulder and waved as she went inside.

Little Lynnie, I thought, whistling to a passing taxi, little Lynnie, right at the beginning of it. Flying half consciously, half unconsciously, the notice-me flags of the pretty young female; and it was no use pretending that she didn't make me hungry; that she wasn't absolutely what I would have liked as an oasis in my too continent life. But if I had learnt anything in thirty-eight years it was who not to go to bed with.

And, more drearily, how not to.

Four

THE BUTTRESS Life Offices on Thirty-Third Street were high on customer appeal on the sixth floor. On the fifth and seventh they tucked the computers and electric typewriters into functional plasterboard cubicles. I sat three inches deep in black leather and considered that of all American craftsmen, I admired their chair designers most: in no other country in the world could one sit on the same seat for several hours without protest from the sacro-iliac.

I had waited forty pleasantly cool minutes already. Long enough to discover that the rows of pot plants along the low wall dividing the forty-foot-square hall into five smaller bays were made of plastic. Long enough to admire the pinewood walls, the ankle-deep carpet, the carefully lowered ceiling with its inset lights. In each bay there was a large desk, with one large chair behind it, one at the side, one in front. Nearly all occupied. Dividing each bay neatly in two stood a second, smaller desk; for the secretary-receptionist with his back discreetly to his boss. In front of him, in each bay, the long black leather bench for waiting on.

I waited. There was still someone for the big man to see before me. Very sorry, said the secretary apologetically, but the schedule had been crowded even before Mr Teller's cable arrived. Could I possibly wait?

So why not? I had three weeks to spare.

The light was dim, and piped music poured over everything

like syrup. That and the built-in deadness of the acoustics made the earnest consultations going on at the five big desks completely inaudible to the waiting benches, while at the same time giving the customers a comforting illusion that they weren't alone in their troubles. Everyone, at the core of things, was alone. Just some more than others.

I hadn't slept all night after leaving Lynnie; but not her fault. It had been one long stupid struggle between a craving for oblivion and conviction that appeasing it wasn't so much morally wrong as a thoroughgoing defeat. I had never learnt to accept defeat. Obstinacy had given me what success I had had in my job, and it alone seemed to be keeping me alive, since all other props were as much use as toothpicks in an avalanche. Enthusiasm for finding Dave Teller's horse burned in me as brightly as wet coal dust: and the nation would hardly collapse if I left its employ.

Caroline had crowded like a flood-tide through my head and down my body. Caroline . . . whom I would have married, had it not been for the husband who would not divorce her.

Caroline had left him to live with me, and had felt guilty about it. A mess. An ordinary, everyday mess. Her fine passion had fretted away over six frustrating years of will-he won't-he; and to the end he wouldn't. Not that he'd ever got her back. In the year since she had left me she had returned to nursing and was working as a sister in a Nairobi hospital, impervious to come-back letters from either of us.

The sharp pain of her departure had dulled to the extent that I no longer felt it through every waking minute: it came stabbing back at longer and longer intervals. But when it did, I remembered her as she'd been at the beginning, and the hunger was pretty well unbearable. It was easy enough to find different girls to talk to, to work with, to take to bed: hard to find a match on all levels: and Caroline had been a match. In the past year, instead of receding, the loneliness had closed in. My work, of its nature, set me apart. And I had no one to go home to, to share with, to care for. The futility and emptiness had gone down to my roots, and nothing seemed to lie ahead but years and years more of what I was already finding intolerable.

The clients at the big desk stood up, shook hands, and left. The secretary ushered the man with the earlier appointment round into the presence. I went on waiting, without impatience. I was accustomed to it.

The punt, investigated in Henley that morning, had produced nothing but ten different sets of smudged fingerprints, of which the topmost and stickiest were Peter's. The Yogi Bear handkerchief was on its way round the manufacturers, in the distant hope that someone could tell where it had been sold. Dave Teller, briefly visited, had said wanly to charge everything to him. The Super VC 10 which lifted off at 3 PM British Summertime from Heathrow had landed at Kennedy at 3.10. Buttress Life closed its doors at 6, which gave it still a half hour to go. And outside in the canyon streets the hundred degree heatwave crept up a notch to a hundred and one.

My turn came round for the big desk. The big man, on his feet behind it, held out a large dry flabby hand and produced the sincere smile of the professional insurance man. Having settled me into the large comfortable chair alongside he sat down himself and picked up the cable discreetly placed to hand by the secretary. A polished chunk of wood sat on the desk between us. On it, neat gold letters facing me said helpfully: Paul M. Zeissen.

'We received this cable from Mr Teller,' he said. A slight, very slight undertone of disapproval.

I nodded. I had sent it myself.

'Our own investigators are experts.' He didn't like me coming: but he wouldn't want to lose the Teller policies. His politeness had effort behind it.

I smoothed him down, more from habit than anything else.

'Of course. Please think of me simply as an auxiliary. Mr

309

Teller persuaded me to come over because he has unfortunately broken a leg in England, and will be immobilized in hospital for a few weeks. He sent me very much on impulse, as a personal friend, to . . . kind of represent him. To see if there was anything I could do. There was no suggestion that he wasn't satisfied with your firm.' I paused delicately. 'If he criticized anyone, it was the police.'

Paul M. Zeissen's smile warmed up a fraction from within: but he hadn't risen to high executive status in his tough profession without disbelieving half that everyone said. That was all right with me. Half of what I'd said was true. Or half true, anyway.

'Mr Teller understands of course,' he said, 'that it is for our own sakes that we are looking for the horse?'

'Naturally,' I agreed. 'Mr Teller is also most anxious that you should succeed, as the horse is irreplaceable. He would infinitely prefer his return to any amount of insurance money.'

'A million and a half,' said Zeissen reverently.

'Worth more on the hoof,' I said.

He glanced at me with a first gleam of real welcome. Once he'd swallowed the firm's affronted pride, it was quite clear that they'd nothing to lose by letting me in.

'One of our best men, Walt Prensela, is in charge of the Chrysalis case,' he said. 'He'll give you the picture. He knows you're coming, I sent him a memo with a copy of the cable.' He pressed the switch on his desk intercom.

'Walt? We have Mr Hawkins from England here. Shall I have him come up to you now?'

The polite question was, as so often in American affairs, an equally polite order. The affirmative duly came. Zeissen flipped the switch and stood up.

'Walt's office is one floor up, number four seven. Anyone will direct you. Would you like to go up now?'

I would; and I went.

I'd expected to have to deal with the same ruffled feathers in four seven, but I didn't, because Walt had done his homework, though I wasn't sure of that at first. He greeted me with business-like casualness, shook hands, waved me to the spare chair, and sat down himself, all in five smooth seconds. Much my age, I judged, but shorter and a good deal thicker. His hands were square and powerful with nails so brief that the fingertips' pads seemed to be boiling over backwards. There were middle European origins in the bone structure of the skull, topped by roughly cropped wiry grey-brown hair, and his deep-socketed brown eyes were set permanently into the I-don't-believe-a-word-of-it expression of his boss downstairs, only more so.

'So, Gene,' he said, neither with nor without much friendliness, 'you've come a long way.'

'Dave Teller's idea, Walt,' I said mildly.

'Looking for horses . . . do you do much of that?' His voice was flat; uninformative.

'Practically none. How about you?'

His nostrils twisted. 'If you mean, was it I who didn't find the other two, then no, it wasn't.'

I tried a smile: didn't get one back.

He said: 'Buttress Life had to pay up for Allyx three years ago. One million six hundred and forty-three thousand seven hundred and twenty-nine dollars, give or take a nickel. Showman, the first one, was insured with another company.'

'Accident?' I murmured. 'Or design.'

He rubbed his left thumb over the top of the round-ended fingers, the first of a hundred times I saw that gesture.

'Now that you've come, design. Before, I wasn't sure.'

'I'm officially on holiday,' I protested. 'I came only because Teller asked me. You should read no meaning into it.'

He gave me a level, half sardonic stare.

'I checked you out,' he said, flicking at the copy of the cable, which lay on his desk. 'I wanted to know just what sort of limey busybody was being wished on to me.'

I didn't say anything, and he made a clicking noise at the side of his mouth, expressive of understanding, resignation and acceptance, all in one.

'A screener,' he said. 'How come Teller found you?'

'How come you found me?' I asked instead.

'I mentioned your name in two places,' he said complacently. 'The FBI, and the CIA. And got a positive reaction from both. A couple of useful pals there filled me in. It seems you're a major stumbling block in the way of the planting of spies in certain Government departments and places like biological warfare research laboratories; and you've passed on some useful warnings on that subject to our people at Fort Detrick. They say the other side have tried to deter you, a little roughly, once or twice.' He sighed. 'You have a clean bill with our boys. And how.'

'And with you?'

'They said you didn't like limelight.'

'It's all yours.'

'Just so as I stand in right with Buttress.'

My decisive nod satisfied him. If we found the horse, he was welcome to the handshakes.

'Fill me in, then,' I said. 'How did Chrysalis get lost?'

Walt glanced at his watch and checked it against the electric clock on the wall. The little box-like office had no windows, as the single glass panel faced out on to the corridor; and although it was cool and comfortable enough, it was no place to talk if one didn't have to.

'Five after six,' Walt said. 'Do you have any other engagements?'

'Know any good bars?' I suggested.

'A mind reader.' He raised his eyes to heaven. 'There's Dalaney's a block up Broadway.'

We stepped out of the air-conditioning into the sweltering street, up 30 degrees in two paces. With the humidity running also at 98 per cent, walking as little as a hundred yards left one damp to the skin. I never minded it: New York in a heatwave was always preferable to New York in a snowstorm, or anywhere hot to anywhere cold, for that matter. Cold seeped farther than into the bones; numbed the mind, drained the will. If the depression deepened towards winter, defeat would come with the snow.

Dalaney's was spilling out on to the pavement with a business convention let out of school. An oblong name tab sat on each neat Terylene lapel, a confident smile hid the anxiety behind every face; they stretched from the substantial group outside into the deep cool gloom of the bar. Pushing through them looked a problem; conversation in their company an impossibility.

'How about your hotel? Where are you staying?' Walt said.

'The Biltmore.'

Walt's eyebrows rose two clear inches.

'Teller's paying,' I said. 'He has an account there.'

'What did you do then? Save his life?'

'Six times,' I agreed, matching his sarcasm.

'He must really think,' Walt said reflectively, 'that you might get his horse back.'

'We,' I said.

'Nope. You. There's no trail. I've looked.'

A coloured cab driver in rolled-up shirt sleeves took us to the hotel, hot air blowing in gusts through the open window each time he accelerated. The city moved sluggishly under the brazen sun, and there was more rubbish than usual littering the streets.

'This is a filthy town,' said Walt, seeing it through my eyes. 'Give me Chicago.'

'Too cold,' I said automatically. 'Beautiful, but too cold. That freezing wind off the lake . . .'

'Are you guys from Chicago?' said the cab driver. 'I was born there, in the Loop.'

We talked to him about that. I drifted away into the disorientated state of not caring a jot about the cab driver, or Walt, or Dave Teller, or Caroline, or anyone on earth. We went up to my room in the Biltmore and I dragged through the host motions of ringing down for a bottle of Scotch and ice and seeing to heat, light and ashtrays. Walt loosened his tie and took a first appreciative swallow.

'You look pooped,' he said.

'Natural state.'

'I guess it's midnight already, to you.'

'I guess.'

There was a considerable drinking pause. Then he said, shifting his sturdy body in the white leather chair, 'Well, do you want to know about this horse, or don't you?'

'Sure.' The boredom in my answer came over shockingly strong, even to me. He looked faintly startled and then speculative, but when he spoke it was strictly business.

'They were taking him in a horse van from Kennedy Airport to Lexington, Kentucky. He'd spent the compulsory twenty-four hours immigration quarantine in the airport stable, along with six other horses which came over on the same flight. All normal at that time. They loaded Chrysalis and four others into the van, and drove westwards from New York on the Pennsylvania turnpike.'

'Time?' I asked.

'Left Kennedy 4 PM Monday. Last Monday, that is. A week today. Estimated Lexington midday Tuesday. Seven hundred miles.'

'Stops?'

'Yeah,' Walt said. 'Stops. That's where the trouble started.' He swirled the clinking ice round in his glass. 'They took their first meal stop at a diner near Allentown, about eighty-five miles from New York. There were four men in the van, two drivers and two grooms. Drivers in the cab, grooms in back with the cargo. At the first stop they took turns to eat, drivers first, grooms after. The drivers chivvied the grooms, and gave them too short a time to eat a good meal. There was an unfriendly argument.'

'They all say so?'

'Yeah. I've talked to all four, one at a time. They're all trying their hardest to pin the blame on the others. They left the diner and went about two hundred miles to their night stop at Bedford. That was no better. Far from cooling off, they had begun to scuffle.

'They turned off the turnpike on to the interstate highway – seventy – south of Pittsburg, and left that again at Zanesville, taking the south-west fork to Cincinatti. About fifty miles farther on they turned due south to cross the Ohio River into Kentucky, and go on through Paris and down the Paris Pike to Lexington.'

'I'll need to see it on a map,' I said.

He nodded. 'From Zanesville to Paris they took secondary routes, though all paved roads, of course. Right? Now it was in Ohio that the van was hi-jacked, and it was over the state border in Kentucky when it was found, which has caused a couple of arguments here and there.'

'Hi-jacked! That's the first I've heard of that.'

'It was hi-jacked by mistake for a truckful of liquor which was about twenty miles behind it along the road. The vans looked alike, same colour, same size, and neither of them had any large identifying signs.'

'How did it happen?'

'By that time, Tuesday morning, the drivers and grooms were all eating at the same time, though at each end of the lunch counter. They left the horses unguarded for a full quarter hour, and during that time someone simply drove off with the whole works.'

'Surely the drivers locked up, and took the keys, at least?'

'Oh sure. It was an expert job though. A direct wire contact from the battery terminals to the starter motor.'

'So then what?'

'When they found the van gone the drivers called the police but it wasn't until Wednesday morning that the van was found off the road and out of sight around a hill in Kentucky. But – no horses. The ramps were down, and all the horses had been let loose.'

'Deliberately.'

'Sure. Untied. All the halters were still in the van. Those racehorses were all free with no bridle or anything to catch them by. The Kentucky boys reckon the horses were let out to create a diversion, to get the cops off the tails of the hi-jackers by making them chase horses all over.'

'And it worked.'

'Yeah,' said Walt gloomily. 'The owner kicked up stink. All the horses were valuable, not only Chrysalis. But only Chrysalis was insured with Buttress.'

'Did they get all the others back?'

'Yeah. But Chrysalis has as good as disappeared off the face of the earth.'

'How do you know the hi-jackers meant to take the liquor truck?'

'The only thing they left in the cab of the horse van was a screwed-up scrap of paper. It was a note of the time the liquor company's truck made its daily run along that route.'

'Fingerprints?'

'Gloves. Even for writing the note.'

Walt had talked himself dry. I refuelled his glass and felt like sleep.

'What do you think?' he said.

I shrugged. 'It was Chrysalis they really wanted. The time-table note was the blind.'

'But why? Why should anyone want to steal a stallion? That's what's got us all floored. I don't know much about horses, I'm a false claims man really. I just got pitched into this between cripple cases, if you get me. But even I know that it's the stallion's name that brings in the stud fee. Say someone's stolen Chrysalis, what's the point? They can't advertise him for stud, so he isn't worth a dime. We figured someone might be nutty enough to want him all to themselves, like some world famous painting, but you can hide a painting quietly in a cellar, which you can't do with a horse. The whole thing don't make sense.'

I had my own views on that, but I said only, 'What happened to Allyx?'

'I only know about that from the files. I got the case out and looked it up this morning. Allyx was a French horse, apparently one of the best young sires in Europe. He was nine when he came over here, and already his get had won a list of races as long as your arm. Dave Teller was head of the syndicate which bought him; that's why he was insured with us, as we do all the Teller estate work. Allyx was delivered safely to the Teller stud farm. No trouble in transit that time. But he was there only four days. Then there was a fire in the stables one night and they took all the horses out of the barn and turned them loose into a small corral.'

'And when they came to fetch them – no horses?'

He nodded. 'There was a broken rail over the far side, which no one knew about. All the horses had got through it, including Allyx. They caught all the others, though some were free for days. No sign ever of Allyx. The company had to face that he probably got into the foothills of the Appalachian Mountains and maybe broke his neck, and in the end they had to pay up.'

'What about that fire?'

'There was apparently nothing suspicious about it at the

317

time. One of our very best men found no evidence of a fire being set. Still, stable fires can be started so easily . . . a cigarette butt in a pile of straw leaves no trace. This one didn't do much damage before they put it out. No question of kerosene, for instance. The whole chain of events was agreed to be accidental.'

I smiled thinly.

'What about Showman?'

Walt shook his head. 'I don't know how he got loose. But they found *him*. Dead, of course. He'd been dead some time, I think.'

'Where?'

'Oh, in the Appalachians. He came from that area, same as the others. But then Lexington has more stud farms than anywhere else in the States, so there's no significance in that really.'

'You went down to Lexington last week?'

He nodded. 'Flew there Wednesday, when Mrs Teller called us.'

'Mrs Dave Teller?'

'Uh huh.' Something moved obscurely in Walt's face. Dave's wife had made an impression. 'She's English, like you.'

'I'll go down there tomorrow,' I said. I watched him waver and decide not to tell me about her. Instead, he looked at his watch, put down his glass firmly, and stood up.

'Must be off,' he said. 'It's our anniversary, and my wife's fixed something special.'

'Give her my apologies for keeping you.'

'That's all right. It fitted in fine. I go home from Grand Central, right downstairs. A quarter of an hour to train time.'

I walked with him to the door.

'Walt . . . would you be free to come down to Lexington in the morning?' As he hesitated, I added, 'There's no point in my covering all the ground twice. I'd appreciate having you along.'

'Be glad to, Gene,' he said too politely, and I thought to hell with you Walt, to hell with everything on earth, including me, but I'm stuck with this horse nonsense for the next three weeks, and if I say go to Lexington, you go. I hid the violent moment of irritation in turning from him to open the door, and I understood his reluctance anyway, as who likes to be dragged down to do the same piece of work twice, especially under the critical eye of an imported limey busybody? He shook my hand. 'I'll call you in the morning,' he said, his feelings under better control than mine.

'Seven-thirty?'

'All right.' He loosened his jaw muscles into what looked like going to be a smile but didn't quite make it, sketched a salute with the thick-topped fingers, and ambled unhurriedly away down the passage.

I had dinner in the hotel restaurant. A steak. Never eat steak west of Nebraska, they used to say. The beef was bred on the prairie and walked eastwards to the markets: when it got to Nebraska it hit the corn belt and only after that was it fat enough to kill. New York steaks were mostly superb, but I didn't suppose they'd walked in through the New Jersey Tunnel. Long distance haulage took care of that . . . and whoever had removed Allyx and Chrysalis had had a haulage problem too. You couldn't ride a stallion along state highways. For one thing, they no longer took kindly to a saddle after years at stud, even if they had been reasonable to handle in the first place.

Nightclubs attract me like wet Mondays in Manchester, and apathy kept me from even reading the list of shows. I went straight upstairs after dinner to catch up on a lot of lost sleep and woke again infuriatingly at two, dead tired and with a restless brain.

From habit, the Luger lay under my pillow.

It was another long night.

Five

We flew down in the morning, Walt's puffed eyes showing that the anniversary had been duly celebrated, and mine feeling as if they'd been rolled in grit.

The two drivers, reached by telephone, met us by appointment in the entrance hall of a motel near the centre of Lexington, where Walt had stayed on his previous trip. He booked rooms for us both, and we took the drivers up to his, which proved a mile short of Biltmore standards but hot on cleanliness and Kleenex.

Walt switched on the air-conditioning, shuffled chairs around, and promised beer later. The drivers, very much on the defensive, went sullenly through the disastrous tale again, aware beyond any doubt that they should never have left the horses unwatched and were more than likely to lose their jobs. Nothing they said added much to what Walt had already told me.

'Do you know each other well?' I asked.

The thin birdlike one said they did.

'And the grooms. Do you know them? And do they know each other?'

'Seen them around,' said the heavy one. 'The lazy so and sos.'

The thin one said, 'One of them came from the Midway Farm.'

That was Dave Teller's. 'He came specially for Chrysalis. It's him ought to be blamed for the whole thing.'

'Did the boys know each other, before the trip?'

'Sure,' said the heavy one. 'Way they talked they both been in the horse game all their lives.'

Walt sniffed and nodded. He'd checked all this, his resigned face said. Routine.

To the drivers I said, 'I want you to think back, and make a list of all the cars and trucks you can remember seeing on the road, all the way from Kennedy to the place you lost the horses.'

They looked aghast and as if I were crazy.

'Look,' I said, 'on those turnpikes you sometimes see the same cars over and over. The ones going your way, that is. You see them at the rest stops, and maybe you start off first, and then they pass you, and then you see them again maybe stopped at another diner while you go on to the next one, and then they come past you again. Right?'

They nodded.

'So maybe you still remember some of the cars and trucks you saw on that trip? Especially any you saw on both days.'

They stared at me. The heavy one said, 'It's impossible. It was a week ago.'

'I know. Try, anyway. Think it over. See if you can remember any at all, between you. Then write them down and leave the list here for us, sometime this evening.'

I took out my wallet and tried twenty dollars each for size. It went down well enough. They said they would try.

'Don't invent anything,' I said. 'I'd rather pay for nothing than a lot of hogwash.'

They nodded and went, with the beer postponed to their return.

'What are you looking for?' Walt said curiously.

'Another horse van, I suppose.'

He thought it over. 'They could just have planned to rendezvous where the empty van was found. They didn't need to be seen on the road.'

'I don't think they can have been sure when they would be able to do the hi-jacking. They wouldn't know where the drivers would stop for meals. No good fixing a rendezvous in Kentucky if the opportunity came earlier, up near Wheeling.'

'They wouldn't want to drive too far with a hot truck,' Walt agreed. 'In fact, it was twenty-five miles, mostly back roads. They made straight for the hills, where it would take longest to round up loose horses.'

'Any tracks?'

'No tyre tracks of any use. The nearest road was gravel, dry and dusty this time of year. There were the tracks of the van going off the road round behind a hillock, but on the road itself they were just a jumble. Every car which passed raised a cloud of dust and wiped out all tracks which were there before.'

I grunted. 'Hoof prints?'

'Dozens of those. In all directions.'

'Back on to the gravel road?'

He shook his head resignedly. 'Impossible to tell. None on top of the van's tyre tracks, anyway. But we took a lot of soil samples, on the outside chance something would turn up later.'

'You did it pretty thoroughly.'

The smile almost came. 'A million and a half', he said briefly, 'is a lot of insurance.'

Midway Farm had prosperity printed on its gate posts, and I went through them alone, as Walt had said he felt the onset of a migraine headache.

A middle-aged Hungarian woman opened the door to me and in halting English asked me my business. Diagnosing her accent from long practice I replied in her own language, as it was simpler, and presently, having consulted in the drawing room, she showed me in there.

Dave's wife stood in the centre of a quarter acre of deep green carpet, surrounded by deep green walls, white paint, and tomato red upholstery. She flicked my card with one thumb and said, 'You're the man who fished Dave out of the river.'

'Yes,' I said, surprised.

'He telephoned me yesterday,' she explained. 'He says I am to trust you entirely.'

She was a slim small-boned creature with the rounded tight little bottom which comes from riding horses a great deal in early girlhood. Her jawline was delicately square, nose narrow, eyes wide and bright. Grey speckled the mouse-brown springy hair, and if she was wearing cosmetics one would have needed to be nearer than I was to be certain of it. Decisive assurance showed from every crisp gesture, and from her tone I gathered that taking her husband's word for things was not her habit.

'Sit down,' she said, pointing to a tomato chair. 'Drink?' It was two o'clock on a hot afternoon. 'Scotch,' she said without waiting for an answer, making it a statement, not a choice.

I watched her splash the pale golden liquid on to ice cubes in two tall glasses, and add a token drop of water. She came across and held out one of them with a graceful suntanned arm. A heavy gold chain bracelet loaded with fobs and charms clinked from her wrist, and into my nostrils floated a trace of 'Joy'.

I tasted the whisky. Hedges and Butler's Royal, I thought. Too fine and light for anything else. The flavour from one sip lasted a long time on my tongue.

'Eva says you speak Hungarian,' she said, moving away, picking up her own glass, and taking an adult swallow.

'Mm, yes.'

'She was most impressed.'

'I came about Chrysalis,' I began.

'Do you speak any other languages?' Her voice veered more to American than English and had the abrupt, inconsequential lurch of two drinks too many; but it didn't show in her face.

'German,' I said, raising a dutiful social smile.

The way I'd been taught languages, it took a week for a

smattering, three months for fluency, and two years to bring one
to the point of recognizing typical speech and thought patterns
when one heard them translated back into perfect English. In
one period of seven years, in my twenties, I'd been crammed
with German, Hungarian, and five Slavonic languages, from
Russian and Czech to Serbo-Croat. None of them was likely to
come in handy for finding stallions, and in any case they were
almost out of date. The new boys were learning Swahili, Arabic,
and Chinese.

'And French, I suppose?' she said.

'A little,' I agreed.

'Enough for the necessities of life, I expect.' Her expression
and emphasis gave the word necessities a precise meaning, which
wasn't food and drink.

'Absolutely,' I agreed, acknowledging her definition.

She laughed. Nothing frail or fine-boned about that.

'Chrysalis,' she said, 'is a right bloody nuisance. He wouldn't
have been my choice in the first place; that Purple Emperor
strain is as soft as an old man's pencil and he's passing it on, they
always do. Moth won the Derby in a shockingly bad year and if
anything had given him half a race he'd have folded like a wet
sheet.' She took a deep swallow. 'Do you know the first bloody
thing about horses?'

'What *is* the first bloody thing about horses?'

She gave me a startled stare which turned into an incredulous
laugh. 'The first bloody thing about horses is that they make
bloody fools of men.'

I smiled back spontaneously, amused by the contrast between
her robustness of thought and language and her delicacy of
frame.

'I'm going for a swim,' she said. 'Bring your drink.'

She mixed herself a new one in passing, and without looking
back crossed the green carpet, pulled open a sliding glass door,
pushed through the insect screen outside it, and walked with

rock-like steadiness across a paved terrace and on to a deep green lawn. Sighing, I got to my feet and followed her. The grass was thick and resilient, a different species altogether from English turf, and a sprinkler on one side threw diamond sprays around like water.

She stopped on another paved area round a kidney-shaped pool and unfastened some clips on her yellow dress, which came off in one piece, and left two more in view underneath. Her body was slender and well cared for, but not at all a young girl's. Middle to late forties, I thought: and the sort of woman who would have been uninteresting under thirty.

She slipped into the water and floated, and I watched the sun make watered silk ripples over her brown stomach.

'Come on in,' she said. 'There are plenty of swim suits in the hut.'

I smiled and shook my head, and sat down on one of the soft plastic pool-side chairs. She took her time, humming and splashing gently with her hands. The sun was hot, but not like in the city. I took my jacket off and felt heat baking into my skin through the white cotton shirt. Peacefulness gradually seeped in too. I was in no hurry for her to rejoin me, which she presently did, the water drops shining singly on her oiled skin.

'You've hardly touched your drink,' she observed accusingly. 'Surely you're not one of those soft buggers who can't hold their liquor?' She picked up her own glass and went on proving that she, at any rate, wasn't.

'Chrysalis . . .' I began.

She interrupted immediately. 'Do you ride?'

'I can,' I said, 'but I don't.'

'Why not?'

'I haven't a horse. Nor a kingdom to give for one.'

'Drink your whisky,' she said, smiling.

'In a while.'

'Then strip off and get in the pool.'

I shook my head.

'Why not?'

'I like it as I am.' And I had too many bruises, from the weir.

She shrugged, half annoyed. 'Don't you do any bloody thing?'

'How many people knew at what hour Chrysalis would leave Kennedy Airport?'

'God,' she said, 'you're a bloody bore.'

'Don't you want the horse back?'

'No,' she said vehemently, 'as far as I'm concerned, we'd be far better off with the insurance.'

'Two hundred thousand dollars', I agreed, 'is a heck of a gamble. Supposing he never sired another like Moth?'

'There's no stopping Dave, when he's set his mind on something.' She sat on the edge of a full-length chair bed and smoothed cream on to her face from a dusky pink tube. 'And he had meant to sell off a bit of that, when he got back. God knows what will happen now he's strung up in those goddam pulleys.'

'He'll be home in about four weeks.'

'Yeah. So he said.' She lay down flat and closed her eyes. 'I told him to take his time. It's too bloody expensive being ill over here.'

Five quiet minutes passed. A single jet plane flew across, a silver streak so high up one couldn't hear it until it had gone. The air was still. The oiled brown body in the yellow bikini took in a hefty dose of ultra violet and the ice cubes melted in the drinks.

'Take your clothes off, for God's sake,' she said, without opening her eyes. 'Or are you ashamed of that pink-white slug of a body the English usually bring over here?'

'I'd better be going.'

'Do what you damn well like.' She fluttered a lax wrist in a double gesture which said, equally well, stay or goodbye.

I stood up and walked over to the hut, a large beautifully

made pinewood structure with a protruding front roof, for shade. Inside were a bathroom and two changing rooms, and in the tiny lobby some shelves in a cupboard held bright-coloured towels and swimsuits. I took a pair of blue shorts and put them on. The bruises on my legs very nearly matched. I left my shirt on, picked up a towel for a pillow, and went back and lay down on the next bed to hers.

She merely grunted with her eyes still shut, but after another minute she said, 'If you want to know about the timetable for Chrysalis, you'd better ask Sam Hengelman in Lexington. He fixed the van. He runs a private service from here. Dave called me and told me the date the horse was being shipped over, and I called Sam Hengelman. And he took it from there.'

'Who else did you tell the shipping date to?'

'It wasn't any goddam secret, for God's sake. I called six or seven of the syndicate to let them know. Dave asked me to. Half Kentucky knew about it, I guess.'

She suddenly sat up straight and opened her eyes.

'Why the hell does it matter how many people knew when Chrysalis was coming? It wasn't him the hi-jackers wanted. They simply made a balls of it and took the wrong truck.'

'Supposing they got just what they wanted?'

'Were you born yesterday? The blood-line is what breeders pay stud fees for. Chrysalis isn't worth a sou to anyone, if they can't use his pedigree. No one's going to even send a decent mare to a stallion someone just happens to have handy, which has no name in the stud book, no history, and no papers; let alone pay fifteen thousand dollars for the privilege.'

'Buttress Life have been looking for an insurance swindle.'

'They can look till they're blue in the face.' She picked up her glass, swallowed, and grimaced. 'This drink's as warm as that pool and just as sodden. Mix me another, will you?' She held out the glass to me and I unwound myself from the bed and took it and my own back into the house. I mixed her the same size dose as before, concocted a different one for myself, and took them both back, the ice clinking coolly as I walked.

'Thanks.' She sank almost half. 'That's better.'

I stood beside the pool and put one toe in the water. It was blood warm, or more.

'What's the matter with your legs?' she said.

'The same as your husband's, only mine didn't break.'

'What's under the shirt?'

'The sun's too hot. I can do without a sunburn.'

'Yeah.' She lay flat again. 'Pink-white slug.'

Smiling, I sat down on the edge of the pool with my back towards her and dangled my feet in the water. I ought, I supposed, to go away and do something more useful, like interviewing Sam Hengelman. But Walt would no doubt have thought of that, and done it, since his threatening migraine would only have lasted until the car we had rented had taken me out of sight. Walt and Dave's wife hadn't exactly clicked.

'Mr Hawkins,' she said from behind me.

'Mm?'

'What do you do for a living?'

'I'm a civil servant.'

'With this?'

There was a sharp metallic click, the one sound guaranteed to raise the hairs on my neck as if I'd never left the jungle.

'Do you know what you're doing with that thing?' I asked, as conversationally as I could.

'Yes.'

'Then put the safety on.'

She didn't answer, and I stood up and turned round, and looked straight into the barrel of my own gun.

I deserve it, I thought. Slow, careless, and stupid. I was anything one cared to mention.

She was sitting with her legs curled underneath her, the Luger lodged unwaveringly in her fist. The gap between us, five yards at least, was too great for anything constructive in the way of action, so I simply stood still.

'You're a cool bastard, I'll say that for you.'

'You won't shoot me,' I said, smiling.

'Why not?'

'I'm not insured for a million and a half.'

Her eyes widened. 'Does that mean that you think that I . . . I . . . *shot Chrysalis?*'

'It's possible.'

She stared. 'You're a goddam fool.'

'So are you, if I may say so. That gun goes off very easily.'

She looked down at it vaguely and before I could stop her she threw it away from her on to the paving stones. The jar as it hit the ground inevitably fired it. Flame streaked out of the barrel, and the bullet smashed through the whisky glass which stood on the ground beside her long chair, nine inches from her body.

It took her a second to realize what had happened, then she shuddered heavily and put her hands over her face. I walked across to fetch the gun, and put the safety on, and then perched on the bed facing her.

'Games,' she said in a shattered voice. 'What do I have but games? Bridge and golf. All games.'

'This too?' I put the Luger back in the under-arm niche and buttoned the strap.

'I just thought I'd make you sweat.'

'Why?'

'That's a bloody good question. A bloody good question. All games. Life is all bloody games.'

'And we're all poor bloody losers,' I agreed sardonically.

She put her hands down and looked at me. Her eyes were dry, but half her assurance had drained away.

'It was only a game. I didn't mean you any harm.'

She thought she was telling the truth, but I'd met too many

of the tricks the unconscious mind gets up to. Perhaps because I'd saved her husband, or was looking for his horse, or merely represented some obscure form of male challenge, she'd had an undoubted urge to destroy me. And she was a very troubled lady in far more obvious ways than that.

'Give me your drink,' she said abruptly.

'I'll get you some more whisky,' I said.

'Yours will do,' she insisted.

I gave her the glass, but one sip was enough. Dry ginger ale. On the rocks.

'Do you cheat all along the line?'

'Whenever it's kinder, or safer, or gets better results.'

I walked away across the lawn and brought her back another glass. She took a moderate pull and put it down amid the ruins of the first one.

'Stay to dinner,' she said. She made it a casual suggestion rather than a warm invitation, and I answered her need, not her tone.

'All right.'

She nodded briefly and flattened herself face down, to roast her back. I lay with one arm over my eyes to shield them from the direct sun, and thought about all the things she hadn't asked, like how was Dave when I saw him and how bad was the broken thigh.

After a while she went back to floating.

'Come on in,' she called.

I shook my head.

'Don't be so prissy,' she said. 'I'm not a swooning virgin. If your legs are like that, the rest of you must be the same. Take that bloody shirt off and give yourself a break.'

It was indeed very hot, and the clear blue water looked good. I sighed, stood up, took the shirt off, and slid down into the pool. Its lukewarm antigravitational gentleness unlocked knots and tensions in my nerves and muscles that I hadn't even realized were there, and I swam and floated tranquilly for nearly an hour. When finally I hauled myself out over the edge she was smoothing on another coating of oil. Her whisky glass was empty.

'Is Dave in that state too?' she asked, eyeing me.

'Pretty much.'

She grimaced slightly and said nothing when I put my shirt back on.

The sun had begun to lose its height in the sky and shadows were fanning out from the trees. A golden sheen lay on the big cream colonial-type house across the green lawn. The pool water stilled, and the quietness of the place crept subtly into all the senses.

'It's so beautiful here,' I said. A banal enough phrase for the promise of peace.

She looked round casually. 'I suppose it is. But we're moving, of course.'

'Moving?'

'Yes. To California.'

'Moving the stud? Horses, and everything?'

'That's right. Dave's just bought a farm down near Santa Barbara, and we're moving over there in the fall.'

'I would have thought you were settled here for life. Wasn't this Dave's father's place?'

'Oh no. We moved here about ten years ago. The old farm was on the other side of Lexington, out on the Versailles Road.'

'California is a long way,' I commented. But she didn't respond with a reason for the move, and after a pause I said, 'If it wouldn't be much trouble to you, I'd like very much to see the horses and stables you have here.'

She narrowed her eyes. 'Business or pleasure?'

'Both,' I smiled.

She shrugged. 'Help yourself. But get me another drink first.'

A pool-side icebox, I reflected, would save a lot of walking: but maybe she still needed the illusion that she didn't drink in the afternoon. I fetched her a refill, changed into my clothes, and found her still face down in the bikini.

'Say I sent you,' she said.

Before I could move, however, Dave rang from England, and Eva brought a portable telephone out and plugged the long cord into a socket in the hut. Dave's wife made three or four unanxious inquiries about her husband's condition, and then said, 'Yes, he's here right now.' She held out the receiver to me. 'He wants to talk to you.'

'Gene?' His voice was as clear as if he'd been in Lexington, and much stronger than it had been the previous morning.

'Hi,' I said.

'Look fella, Sim and I want you back here for a conference. Can you get a plane tomorrow?'

'But the fare . . .' I protested mildly.

'To hell with the fare. You've got a return ticket.'

'All right.'

'You haven't found the horse yet?'

'No.'

'Do you think you will?'

'I don't know yet.'

He sighed. 'See you Thursday, then,' and the line went dead.

The stables lay some distance away on the far side of the house. I walked round there and was shortly talking to the stud groom, Chub Lodovski, a large good-natured man with slow speech, a bird head, and great ham-like hands. He showed me round the whole setup with unlimited patience and an obvious pride in his job. The state of the place was his testimonial. The mares and foals ate peacefully in neatly railed paddocks reached by impeccable narrow drives with sharply cut grass edges. The stallions lived in a short row of six large airy box-stalls in a spacious barn, with a wooden railed exercise paddock in front, flanked by two high-walled mating compounds.

Only five of these stalls were occupied. The vacancy was for Chrysalis.

'Is this where you kept Allyx?' I asked.

'That's right. Second stall from the end. He was only in it four days.'

'And where was the fire?'

He frowned. 'It started in some straw one night, just about here.' We were fairly central. 'It wasn't much. Mostly smoke.'

'And you turned the horses out into the exercise paddock in front here?'

'That's right. Just as a precaution. But one of those doggone animals got scared and broke a rail on the far side, and the whole bunch got out across that stretch of grass on to that dirt road over there. We never did find Allyx. There hasn't been sight nor sound of him since.'

We talked for a while about the search they'd made next morning, but, Lodovski said, the whole of Kentucky was plastered with horses, and no one thought much about it if they saw one loose, and although a reward had been offered, and the insurance people had swarmed around like bloodhounds, they'd never found him.

'And now Chrysalis,' I sighed sympathetically.

'Sure. And they say lightning never strikes in the same place twice!'

He was moderately upset that the stud looked like losing another major attraction, but it wasn't his money that was involved, and besides that he was proud enough of the stallions remaining in residence. I asked him if he'd ever been to California.

'The farm's moving out there, did you know?' he said.

'Are you going, yourself?'

'Mebbe, mebbe not. Depends on the missus, and she can't

make up her mind.' He grinned comfortably and accepted the note I gave him with dignity.

When I got back to the pool Dave's wife had got her dress on again and Eva was brushing the splinters of whisky glass into a dustpan, which she carried carefully away across the lawn.

'Well, what did you think of the place?'

'The horses all looked very well. The stallions especially.'

'So would you, if all you had to do was . . .' she began, and then stopped and shrugged. 'So would you.'

Apart from an occasional 'bloody' which crept in from habit, that was the last of her verbal squibs for the day. But my lack of scandalized reaction didn't have the same effect on her drinking, and she kept up a slow but steady intake right through dusk and dinner. Her mental brakes remained half on, half off, as before.

Over thick slices of rare beef she said, 'Are you married?'

'No.' I shook my head.

'Divorced?'

'No,' I said. 'I've never been married at all.'

'Are you queer?' she asked, as simply as if she'd said, 'Are you comfortable?'

I smiled slightly. 'No.'

'Then why aren't you married?'

'I haven't found anyone who will marry me.'

'Don't be ridiculous. You must have women lying down for you in droves.'

'It's not the same thing.'

She looked at me broodingly over the rim of her glass. 'So you live all alone?'

'That's right.'

'No parents?'

'They're both dead,' I said. 'And I've no brothers, no sisters, no uncles, aunts, or cousins.' I smiled. 'Anything else?'

'Stay the night.'

She said it abruptly, as if it came from a deeper level than her fairly harmless interrogation, and there was an element of surprise and alarm on her face afterwards.

'I'm sorry,' I said matter-of-factly, 'but I can't.'

She looked at me without expression for about ten seconds.

'I have a mother,' she said. 'And sisters, and brothers, and dozens of relations. And a husband, and a son, and all this.' She waved a hand around the millionaire bracket walls. 'I have everything.' Her eyes filled with tears, but she went on looking straight across the table, without blinking.

'I have . . . bloody . . . everything.'

Six

THERE WAS an envelope from Walt in my room at the motel containing a short note and a list.

> Gene,
> This is all the drivers came up with. I think it's safe to bet that they actually did see these vehicles. The top three, they both remembered. The others, only one of them remembered. No horse vans, though.
> Walt

The list read:

'Impala, lilac, two years old, California number plates. Passengers included a fat child who made faces out of the rear window. Both days.

Grey station wagon trailing a load of furniture. Both days.

Dark green Ford Mustang, Nevada plates. Young couple, no description. The horse van drivers remember this one because they were discussing whether the Mustang was a good car or not. Second day only.

White convertible: young woman with blond hair wound on rollers. Second day only.

Army green pick-up truck with white lettering on the doors. Second day only.

The pick-up, one of the drivers thinks, was probably on

Inter-state 70, after Zanesville and before they turned off south. He doesn't remember clearly.'

I read the list through three times while I dressed. The load of furniture looked the most promising, but none of it exactly inspired.

Walt, driving to the airport in the morning, damped even the furniture.

'It was only one of those Snail Express trailers.'

'Like the U-Haul,' I said.

'That's right. "Carry your house on your back, but let us take the weight",' he said, quoting the Snail Express advertising slogan. 'The drivers said it wasn't big enough to put a horse in.'

There were furniture trailers of all sizes all over the country: people moving house hired one at their old home, loaded up, and drove off to the new, maybe six states away. There they unloaded and simply left the trailer in a local depot, from where the haulage firm hired it to the next removing client. The bright orange U-Haul trailers and the aluminium and blue ones of the Snail Express were as frequent on the roads as the Greyhound buses.

'How about the pick-up?' I asked.

'Much too small for a horse,' Walt said gloomily.

He came back with me to New York and rubbed his thumb continuously over the finger pads while I went through the file we had made on the case.

There was a batch of photographs of the missing horse, mostly taken from stud book advertisements, by the look of them. Not a very remarkable creature on paper, I thought.

Sam Hengelman had sent his two most careful drivers to fetch Chrysalis. He had had a call from Mrs Teller informing him of the date fixed for the horse to fly over, and also a cable from England when he was on his way. Hengelman had telephoned Kennedy Airport and been told the horses would be through the twenty-four hour immigration regulations at noon,

Tuesday. He had sent the van as soon as he got the cable, on Sunday. There was, he agreed, a system like the U-Haul in operation among horse vans, to avoid the need for long empty journeys, but some folks liked personal service, and Mr Teller was one of them.

The Buttress Life Insurance covered transport. Sam Hengelman had not had to take out a policy for the trip, and neither stood to lose nor gain from the hi-jacking.

Both drivers had clean records going way back.

Both grooms had been in their present jobs for more than three years. One of them came from Midway Farm; the other from another farm which had a horse coming in on the same trip.

An interview with Mrs Eunice Teller had produced no helpful information.

I shut the folder with a smile, and gave it back to Walt.

'How about checking with Snail Express, on the off-chance?'

He looked sceptical. 'The drivers said the trailer wasn't high enough.'

'They're used to thinking in terms of ordinary horse vans. And they were looking down, from their cab. You could squeeze a racehorse into a box about seven feet by four, by six feet high, if you were ruthless enough. Find out how many trailers that size or larger Snail Express had out last Monday or Tuesday, which might conceivably have been on the turnpike.'

'All right,' he said expressionlessly. 'If you say so.'

With the time lag working in reverse it was 3 AM Thursday morning when I landed at Heathrow, and 12 before I walked into Dave Teller's room in a Reading hospital. Flaming June had come and gone: it was raining again.

If one discounted the ropes, pulleys, slings, and plaster suspending his leg in mid air, the patient looked healthy enough. He greeted me without fuss, the direct eyes steady and bright.

'Tiring trip?'

'So so.'

'You've eaten?' He waved vaguely at a collection of chocolates and grapes.

'I had breakfast over Ireland, at two o'clock.'

He laughed, eased himself on the pillows, and stretched out a hand for a cigarette.

'How's my wife?'

'Very well.'

He lit his cigarette and flicked shut the lighter.

'What was she doing, when you called?' His apprehension was pretty well concealed.

'Sunbathing. Swimming. There's a heatwave coast to coast.'

A couple of muscles relaxed in his forearm and he inhaled deeply. 'She gave you a drink . . . I hope?'

'Sure. And a swim. And I stayed to dinner.'

He looked at me directly for some time without speaking. Then he said merely, 'A good one?'

'Very, thank you. And I saw your horses. Chub Lodovski showed me round.'

He talked much more naturally about the horses: no problems there.

'I hear you're moving to California,' I said, after a while.

The tenseness instantly came back; the small give-away tightening of eye, neck, and respiratory muscles that I looked for every day in my job, and couldn't be blind to in my friends.

'Yes,' he said, tapping off ash. 'Eunice loves the ocean, and in Kentucky we're as far from it as can be . . . and of course, the horse breeding business in California is every bit as profitable. We will do very well out there, I've no doubt.'

Eunice would take her problems right along with her, I thought: though with a bit of luck they would recede for a year or two. Perhaps Teller considered the upheaval worth it.

'What's the new place like?' I asked.

'It's good land, pretty well irrigated. And the stable and general layout are as good as Midway. Better even, in some respects. It's Davis L. Davis's old place.'

I looked blank, and he explained. 'Made his money out of roadside hamburger stands. Well, he died early this year, and last month they held a dispersal sale of his brood mares and stallions, to divide up his estate for inheritance. I put in a bid for the farm to his executors before I came over here this time, and they wrote me a week or so back to say they're accepting it. The contracts are in hand right now, but I don't foresee any difficulties. I'm sure glad to have got it settled at last.'

'At last?'

'Been looking for a farm in southern California for over a year now, but there were too many snags to most of them. Eunice and I took a trip over in March of this year, and we saw the Davis farm then, and liked it. So . . .' He waggled his fingers to finish the sentence.

The door opened and Keeble came in, mild spectacles reflecting the pallid light from the window, eyes blinking rapidly, and the usual patch of bristle growing grey where he had short-sightedly missed with the razor. He said hellos all round and settled himself comfortably into the spare armchair.

'Well, how's it with the States?' he said: and I told them everything Walt had told me. They thought it over for a while in silence.

'So what do you think now?' Keeble said.

I glanced doubtfully at Teller, but he tapped ash off his cigarette and remarked simply, 'Sim says you were convinced I was pushed into the river on purpose. I guess what he's asking you is, have you changed your mind?'

'No, I haven't.'

Keeble and Teller looked at each other. Then Teller said, sighing, 'We've come up with one or two things which makes it almost certain you are right.'

Keeble nodded. 'I went to Dave's hotel in London to collect his luggage and pay his bill, and explained where he was if anyone wanted him. The young man at the reception desk asked me if the lady journalist from *Stud and Stable* had found Dave all right on Saturday. She had, he said, been most insistent, owing to a deadline on the magazine, and he had given her my address and telephone number, which Dave had left with him in case he was wanted hurriedly in connection with Chrysalis.'

'And that', I remarked, 'is how boy and girl knew where to find you.'

'Quite,' Keeble agreed. 'From the house to the river was no doubt a simple piece of following. Incidentally, I checked with *Stud and Stable*. They didn't want Dave, and their deadline is the first day of each month.'

'Nice,' I said.

Keeble took an envelope from his pocket and fished out some three by three inch black-and-white photographs. 'These are Peter's snaps,' he said. 'Take a look.'

I took them from him and looked. The ducks had come out splendidly; better than one of Lynnie, who had been moving. The picnic lunch was there, and the *Flying Linnet* in Marsh Lock, and one of Dave Teller standing on the bows, and a rather grim one of myself staring down into the water. There was one of the four men fallen in a heap in the punt at the hotel where we'd had our morning drinks, and another, taken with the photographer's back to the river, of Keeble, Joan, Dave, Lynnie, and myself sitting round the little table under the sun umbrella, with glasses in our hands.

Keeble waited without blinking. With this in mind I started through the pile again, and found what he had seen. I looked up at him. He nodded, and from an inside pocket produced a magnifying lens, which he threw over to me. With the help of that, the two figures were clear. A girl with long hair and white trousers, a young man with pale trousers and a check shirt, standing side by side in the background of the photograph of us all drinking at the pub.

'It's them,' I nodded.

'Yes,' Keeble agreed. 'They were there in the morning. So I'll grant you they could have followed us by car from Henley . . . you can see the river from several places along that road . . . and also that they saw Dave standing on the bows when we left Henley and when we left the pub. And possibly also when we arrived at the pub, and at Marsh Lock. They would know there was a good chance of him being there again when we came back through Harbour.'

I smiled. 'And the five feet which was missing from the punt's mooring rope had been used to tie it securely to the Danger post while they waited for us.'

'I agree,' Keeble said. 'We took that punt right out of the water after you'd gone on Monday, and we found that the cleat for the stern rope had been unscrewed from the stern, and screwed on again under the water line at the bow end.'

'So both mooring points were at one end,' Teller said. 'The safe rope was under water all the time, hidden by the punt itself and the girl's body and arms. And, of course, we weren't looking for anything like that at the time, so we'd never have seen it.'

Keeble finished it. 'Once they'd got the visible rope safely in Joan's hands, and we were all looking anxiously for you and Dave to surface, the girl had only to pull some sort of quick release knot, and the punt was free. So I'll agree, Gene, that that was an accident which could be staged, and was staged, and you were right and I was wrong. Which, I seem to remember vaguely, has happened once or twice before.'

He smiled at me with irony, and I reflected that there were few superior officers who would say that sort of thing so utterly ungrudgingly.

A nurse clattered in with Teller's lunch, which proved to be chicken salad and tinned mandarin oranges. The patient poured the oranges on to the salad and ate the combined course with resignation.

'The food is lousy,' he said mildly. 'I've forgotten what a good steak looks like.'

We watched him eat without envy, and I asked Keeble if he'd had any results with the handkerchief.

'Only negative ones. None of the Yogi Bear concessionists in this country imported it. They say, from the material and the sort of paint used for the bear, that it was probably made in Japan. And some of them had doubts it was done by the Hanna-Barbera artists. Not well enough drawn, they said.'

'I'll take it back to the States and try there,' I said. 'After all, boy and girl were almost certainly American.'

Teller raised his eyebrows with his mouth full.

'The boy shouted "Can you help us, sir," and that "sir" comes a great deal more commonly from Americans, than from the English. Also, the boatman said their accent was "same as on the telly" and there's as much American as English on our television.'

'The same argument might apply to public school-boys,' Keeble said casually. 'But they were Americans, I agree.'

'So all we need to know now, apart from who were they,' I said to Teller, 'is why they wanted you dead.'

No one had any constructive ideas on that point. Teller drank his coffee and a maid in a green overall came to take the tray.

'You're guarding against them having another go?' I said to Keeble, watching the maid's back disappear through the door.

Keeble followed my eyes. 'All precautions,' he nodded. 'The works. I got the Radnor-Halley Agency. Only the best for Dave!'

'They won't let me open any packages,' Teller complained. 'I think they take them outside, dunk them in a bucket, and wait for the ticking to start. And the only chocolates I have were bought by Sim personally. You'd never believe the half of what goes on in here.'

I laughed. 'It's when you get out of here you'll notice it.'

'He'll stay here till you've wrapped it up,' remarked Keeble; and he wasn't joking.

I stared. 'I'm in anti-infiltration, remember? Not the CID.'

'Oh sure. But the same motivation, I imagine. Just let your hunter instincts loose . . . and tell us what you plan to do next.'

I stood up restlessly and went to the window. It was still raining. Two nurses ran from one building to another, clutching capes around them and skitting mud up the backs of their stockings. Useful people, nurses. Needed people. Constructive, compassionate, tough people . . .

'Well?' said Keeble, behind me.

I turned round and leaned against the wall. 'How's the exchequer?'

Teller answered, 'Look, Gene, I've enough to launch a minor space programme. And as I said before, if it weren't for you I wouldn't be here at all. So spend what you need to, and I'll pick up the chits.'

'Right . . . then I think it would be best to let the Radnor-Halley Agency deal with anything which crops up here . . . I suppose they did the handkerchief inquiry?'

Keeble nodded.

'And I'll go back to the States tomorrow. I can't believe the attempted murder isn't tied in with the horse theft, so the springboard for everything must be in America. Unless some Irish fanatic disapproves of you skimming off the cream of British bloodstock!'

'Is Chrysalis Irish, then?' Keeble asked seriously.

'Irish-bred dam,' I said. 'That's all. His sire was Purple Emperor, in the Read Stud at Newmarket.'

'How do you know?' Teller asked, surprised.

'I looked it up,' I said briefly. 'Also his markings. And that is important.' I paused. 'Whoever took Allyx and Chrysalis knew a lot about horses. Allyx was one of six stallions loose in a paddock at night. Chrysalis was one of five horses in a horse box. Yet each time the right horse was singled out for removal. We have to believe it was the right horse, not just chance, because each time it was by far the most valuable one of the collection which disappeared. Well . . . Chrysalis is a dark bay with no distinguishing marks. No socks, no blaze, no star. One colour all over. And Allyx was exactly the same. There are literally thousands of horses like that.'

The two men didn't stir.

I went on, 'This means that if we ever do find Chrysalis, there will be an enormous problem of identification. English horses have no tattooed numbers, like American.'

'Christ,' Teller said.

'I wouldn't know him if he came up and ate sugar out of my hand. Would you?' He shook his head. I went on, 'The only people at all likely to be able to pick him out for us with any certainty are those who handled him in England. And that's where we hit a very big snag. The stud groom at Read's died of a heart attack two months ago and the new man couldn't be sure of knowing Chrysalis again. Read himself is too short-sighted, apparently, to be of any help. This means we have to go back nearly five years, to the season when Chrysalis last raced. To his owner at that time, and his trainer. Though the only one I'd pin any faith on would be the lad who looked after him. And it's the lad, I think, who we'll need to take to the States, if we find a horse which might be Chrysalis.'

'We could easily find out who the lad is,' Keeble nodded, 'and shunt him over.'

'His name is Sam Kitchens, and he'll be at Ascot at this moment, as one of his horses is running in the four-thirty. It's Gold Cup day today.' I smiled faintly. 'I thought I might just drift along to the races when I leave here.'

'Just tell me,' Teller said in a small voice, 'how and when you found out all this?' He spread his fingers. 'I only ask.'

'I spent an hour this morning at the British Bloodstock Agency . . . I was practically camped on their doorstep at nine o'clock. And then I did some telephoning. That's all.'

'When do you sleep, fella?'

'Between meals. Very bad for the appetite.'

'He's mad,' Teller said to Keeble.

'You get used to it,' Keeble assured him. 'The first eight years are the worst.'

'And this is the guy you'd trust your daughter to?'

'Hm,' said Keeble. 'We haven't mentioned that.'

'What?' I said suspiciously.

'We'd . . . er . . . like you to take Lynnie back with you, to the States,' Teller said. 'She's going to visit with Eunice for a while.'

I glanced at Keeble and saw that he knew what I was inevitably thinking: that Eunice's special need for company was more compelling than the rest of Lynnie's finishing-school term.

'I'd be glad to,' I said to them both with formality. 'On a slow boat via New Zealand, if you like.'

'She's too young for you,' said Keeble, without anxiety.

'She is indeed.' I pushed myself away from the wall and stood upright. 'Where will I collect her?'

Keeble handed me an envelope. 'Air tickets for you both. She'll be at the Victoria Air Terminal at eight-thirty tomorrow morning. Is that all right?'

I took the tickets and nodded. 'Can I have the handkerchief?'

He obligingly produced it, in another envelope. I put that and the air tickets away, and picked up Peter's snaps. Holding the negatives up to the light I singled out the drinking group and put it in my wallet.

'I'll get it blown up tomorrow in New York,' I said. 'Then

it'll only be a matter of sifting through two hundred million inhabitants.'

Drizzle was wilting the fluffy hats when I got to Ascot, but the turf looked greener for it, and the horses glossier. I spotted the trainer I wanted and walked across to where he was talking to a large woman in a creased pink dress under a dripping pink umbrella. He caught sight of me over her shoulder, and I watched the initial memory-jog pass through mind-search to recognition. He smiled warmly at his success.

'Gene Hawkins.'

The large woman turned round, saw she didn't know me, decided she didn't want to, and departed.

'Mr Arkwright.' We shook hands, and I thought how little age had changed him. Still the upright, brisk, grey-headed neighbour from my father's days in Yorkshire.

'Come and have a drink,' he said, 'and let's get out of this rain.' There were misty beads of water fuzzing his tall grey hat. 'Though it's much better than it was an hour ago, isn't it?'

'I've only just come.'

He led the way up the staircase into the balcony bar and ordered vodka and tonic. I asked if I could have the tonic without the vodka and he remarked that my father, an enthusiastic alcoholic, would have turned in his grave.

'What are you doing now then?' he said, sipping the clear fizzy mixture. 'Still in the Civil Service?'

'Yes,' I nodded. 'But I'm on leave at present.'

'It always seemed rum to me, you doing something so . . . so tame,' he said. 'Considering the sort of boy you were.' He shrugged. 'Never would have thought it. Your old father always thought you'd do something in racing, you know. You rode well enough, you knew your way around. Can't understand it.' He looked at me accusingly. 'Those two years in the Army did you no good.'

I smiled. 'It was while I was in the Army that they offered me this job.'

'Safe, I suppose,' he said, making allowances. 'Prospects, pension, and all that.'

'Mm,' I said non-committally. 'Actually, I really came here today to see you, to ask you about Chrysalis.'

'Have they found him, do you know?' he said.

'Not yet, no. The American who bought him is a friend of my boss, and they've asked me, as I know you, to see if you would do them a favour.'

'If I can,' he said promptly. 'If I can.'

'Their problem is', I explained, 'that if and when a loose horse is found, especially if he's some distance from where he was lost, how are they to be sure it is Chrysalis.'

He looked startled and then amused. 'That certainly is a problem. But Chrysalis hasn't been in my yard since . . . let's see . . . four years last October. I don't know whether I'd be certain of him, not absolutely certain, if I saw him, for instance, among twenty others rather like him. And you'd want it to be more positive than that.'

'Yes,' I agreed. 'Actually I rang your home this morning and your secretary said I'd find you here. And he also said Chrysalis's old lad would be here. Sam Kitchens. Would you mind if I had a word with him?'

'That's right, he came with Milkmaid for the four-thirty. No, I don't mind, you ask him what you like.'

'Mr Dave Teller, who bought Chrysalis, wonders whether you would let Sam Kitchens go over to the States for a few days, if and when the horse turns up, to identify him. Mr Teller will pay his fare and expenses.'

Arkwright laughed. 'Sam will like that. He's not a bad chap. Pretty reliable.'

'Then if he's needed, you'll get a cable saying which flight he's to go on, and so on. Will that be all right?'

He nodded. 'You tell the American I'll let him go.'

I thanked him. 'They'll be very grateful.' I bought him another vodka and tonic and we talked about horses.

Sam Kitchens walked his fair young Milkmaid around the parade ring and I risked ten bob on her, but she turned out to be a cow. I joined Arkwright while he ran his hand down the filly's legs and listened to the jockey explaining forcibly that it wasn't down there that the trouble lay, but up in her pea-sized brain.

Lads usually resent criticism of their charges, but from his expression Kitchens, a short stocky man of about thirty, held much the same view. I asked him, after introductions from Arkwright, whether he would know Chrysalis again with enough certainty to testify if necessary in a court of law.

'Sure,' he said without hesitation. 'I'd know the boy. I had him three years. Sure, I'd know him. Maybe I couldn't pick him out of a herd, now, but I'd know him close to. The way his hide grows, and little nicks in his skin, I wouldn't have forgotten those.'

'That's fine,' I said, nodding. 'Was there . . . is there . . . anything special about him, which might help someone who'd never seen him before to recognize him?'

He thought it over for several minutes. 'It's four years. More, nearly five, see. The only thing I remember is, we had trouble with his off hind hoof. It was thin, used to crack at the same place every time. But the stud he went to might have cured it, as he wasn't racing any more. Or he might just have grown out of it, being older now.' He paused. 'Tell you something, he liked sardines. He's the only horse I know of who had a taste for sardines.'

I smiled. 'That's pretty odd. How did you find out?'

'Took my tea into his box once. Sardines on toast. I put it down for a minute on the window sill, and when I looked round he'd scoffed the lot. It tickled me, it did. I used to share a tin-ful with him sometimes, after that. He always liked them.'

I stayed for the last race and picked another loser. I would have made a lousy trainer, anyway.

Seven

I REACHED the Air Terminal at eight-fifteen, but Lynnie was there first.

'I couldn't sleep much,' she said. 'I've never been to America before.'

I'd been to America a dozen times. I hadn't slept much either.

Lynnie's clothes, a deep pink shiny PVC raincoat over the orange tan dress, were having an anti-soporific effect on everyone in sight. Resisting an urge to grope for dark glasses I felt an uncommon lift to the spirits, which lasted to mid Atlantic. There Lynnie went to sleep and a strong wave of non-enthusiasm for finding Chrysalis invaded my mind like one enormous yawn. I wouldn't mind, I thought idly, I really wouldn't mind lazing around that swimming pool with Eunice and Lynnie, doing nothing at all but drink in sunshine, peace, Scotch, and an uninterrupted view of two well-shaped females in bikinis. Peace most of all. Lie like a log, and not think, not feel. And sleep. Sleep for sixteen hours a day and mindlessly laze away the other eight: a programme as near to death as dammit. A very small step from there to eternity, to make the peace permanent . . .

'What are you thinking about?' Lynnie said.

She had opened her eyes and was watching my face.

'Heaven,' I said.

She shook her head slightly. 'Hell, more like.' She sat up briskly. 'How long before we land?'

'About an hour.'

'Will I like Mrs Teller?'

'Haven't you met her before?' I asked.

'Once, when I was little. I don't remember her.'

I smiled. 'She isn't easy to forget.'

'Exactly,' Lynnie said. 'There's something odd about me going to stay with her. Of course I said I'd love to, and who wouldn't go off on any trip to get away from school, let alone a super one like this, but I distinctly think that Daddy and Mr Teller have an ulterior motive and I want to know what it is.'

'They want her to have company, to stop her drinking too much alone.'

'Wow!' She looked surprised. 'You're not serious?'

'They didn't say so. I'm only guessing.'

'But I can't stop her drinking,' she protested.

'Don't try. She doesn't get drunk. And you'll like her all right, as long as your ears don't fall off.'

She laughed. 'My mother wouldn't approve of her?'

'Quite likely not.'

'I expect that's why I've only met her once.' She grinned at me mischievously without a shred of self-consciousness, Joan's influence waning visibly with every hundred miles.

It was late morning, local time, when we checked in at the Biltmore. From there Lynnie departed on foot for a private tour of New York, and I cabbed down town to Buttress Life. The heatwave was still in position, the air still saturated. Lethargy and haze hung over the city, and buildings shivered like mirages through the blue exhausts of the cars. Once over the Buttress building's threshold the temperate zone took over: I rode up to the seventh floor with the humidity in my clothes condensing into water, and sagged damply into Walt's spare chair in four seven.

'Good trip?' he said. 'You look . . .' he hesitated.

'Yeah,' I said. 'Pooped.'

He smiled. It was worth waiting for. There's a load to be read in a smile, and Walt's was a good one.

'How's it with the Snail Express?' I asked.

He picked a list off his desk. 'They were very cooperative. Only trouble is, they had about thirty-five trailers out on those dates which just might have been going west on the turnpike.' He handed me the paper sympathetically. 'It was a pretty long shot, of course.'

'Hm.' I looked at the list of names and addresses, and at my watch. 'I think we'd better check them.'

'I had a feeling you'd say that.' A touch of gloom.

I smiled at him. 'I'll start it, if you like. Do you know where we can get good enlargements of a snapshot done quickly?' He nodded and mentioned a name, and I gave him the negative. 'The top left-hand corner. A couple. Man and girl.' He nodded again. 'And there's this handkerchief.' I produced it. 'Would you mind making a tour of all the offices on this floor, and perhaps the fifth as well, and finding out what everyone associates with it?'

Walt took the small white square curiously.

'Yogi Bear,' he said. 'What's the point?'

'It belonged to a girl who may know more than she ought about Chrysalis. The girl on the negative.'

'Find her, find the horse?' He was half incredulous, a fraction excited.

'Maybe.'

'Right then,' he said at the door. 'See you.'

I studied the list. Snail Express had done their best. Most names had two addresses, the old and the new. All were followed by a place and a date, the depot where the trailer had been checked in after its trip. There were several telephone numbers for the eastern addresses, a few for the west.

Working stolidly down the list, with long pauses while new inhabitants went to find the new telephone numbers of the old,

I said I was calling from Snail Express, wanting to know that the service had been satisfactory, or if the customers had any suggestions or complaints. I listened to more praise than criticism, and eventually checked off twenty-seven genuine hirings.

Walt came back while I was biting the end of one of his pencils and wondering what to do next. It was three o'clock. He'd added lunch to his itinerary but he carried a large white package, which he opened carefully. Six enlargements of the corner of Peter's negative. Various sizes, from postcard to nine by seven. The faces were clearest on the smallest print, too fuzzy on the largest.

'He says he'll run off as many as you want by this evening, if you let him know at once.'

'Ask him for six, then. Postcard size.'

'OK.' He picked up the receiver, pressed the buttons, and asked.

The boy and girl stood side by side, their heads turned slightly to the left, towards where we had sat under the sun umbrella. Their faces were calm, good-looking, and somewhat alike. The boy's hair was darker. They were of almost the same height. The checks of the boy's shirt stood out clearly, and one of its buttons was either undone or missing. The girl had a watch with an extra wide strap on her left wrist. She hadn't been wearing it while she hung on to the post.

'All-American kids,' Walt commented. 'So what?'

'So how did you get on with the handkerchief?'

Walt produced it. A little limper, a little grubbier than before.

'Fifteen Yogi Bears, ten don't-bother-me-nows, six lewd suggestions, and one Yellowstone Park.'

'One where?'

'Yellowstone Park?'

'Why Yellowstone Park?'

'That's where Yogi Bear lives. At least, it's called Jellystone in the cartoons, but it's Yellowstone really.'

'Real live bears still in Yellowstone?'

'Oh sure.'

'A natural beauty spot . . . holiday place, isn't it?' I remembered vaguely.

Walt nodded.

'With souvenirs?' I suggested.

'Great lot of help that would be to us.'

I agreed. It would only narrow the field down to one of the thousands who'd been to Yellowstone sometime, or one of the other thousands who knew someone who'd been to Yellowstone sometime. But I remembered a Jamaican would-be assistant to the Biological Warfare Defence Laboratory at Porton who'd been turned down because of a Russian-made bust of Castro in his bedroom. Souvenirs sometimes had their uses.

'The handkerchief probably came from Japan. Do you have a leg-man who can check who imported it, and where it was sold over here?'

'Leg-man?' Walt echoed dismally. 'That's me.' He put the handkerchief away in its envelope, chased up a few answers on the telephone, and heaved himself reluctantly to his feet. 'I may as well go see a man about a Yogi, then. How're the trailers?'

'Twenty-seven are OK. Of the other eight, five don't answer, and three have no telephone.'

I tried two of the non-answerers yet again. Still no reply. Walt looked through the shorter list I'd made of the unchecked.

'They sure went all over, didn't they?' He said, 'Nebraska, Kentucky, New Mexico, California, Wyoming, Colorado, Texas, and Montana. Just don't ask me to leg it around all those places!' He drifted out of the door and his solid footsteps diminuendoed down the passage.

I went on trying the numbers now and then. After two hours I had crossed Texas off the list, bitten the end right off Walt's pencil and started on it an inch farther down, decided I couldn't work many days in his rabbit hutch of an office, and wondered how Eunice was making out beside her pool.

The telephone buzzed.

'Are you staying at the Biltmore again?' Walt said.

'Yes.'

'Meet me in the bar there,' he suggested. 'I'm nearer there than to you.'

'Sure,' I said. 'I'm on my way.'

Lynnie wasn't back. I left a message at the desk for her and joined Walt. His pale blue suit looked as if it had just come out of a spin dryer and there was a damp translucent look to his skin. Repentant, I bought him a large Scotch on the rocks and waited until he had it where it would do most good. He sighed, rubbed the back of one wrist across his eyes, fished a crumpled piece of paper out of his pocket, and spread it open on the bar.

'To start with,' he said disgustedly, 'it's not Yogi Bear.'

I waited in sympathetic silence and beckoned to the barman for a refill. On the paper a list of about eight souvenir manufacturers and distributors had been crossed out, a single line through each. The top lines were neat and straight, the last three a great wild slash across the paper. Walt had had a very bad day.

'The handkerchief came from Japan, like you said.' He took a swallow of his second drink and began to revive. 'Several of the firms phoned their west coast offices for me. No dice. It seems as if at least half of the souvenirs sold in the west are made in Japan, but all these Yogi Bear concessionists say that this isn't Yogi Bear at all, it's the wrong shaped head.'

He pulled out of the by now battered envelope a very bedraggled-looking handkerchief and looked at it with loathing.

'If it was sold at or near Yellowstone Park, it could have come from any two-bit import business. As it's not Yogi Bear, no one will have had to pay commission to use the picture, and there isn't any way that I know of finding who brought it into the country and who sold it to where.'

After ten seconds I suggested diffidently, 'We could start from the other end.'

He glared at me incredulously. 'Are you plumb nuts? You can't mean what I think you mean.'

The rocks in my drink had melted to pebbles. I tasted the drowned whisky and put the glass back on the bar.

I said, 'One of the Snail Express trailers was checked in at Rock Springs, Wyoming. It's still there: they haven't had another customer for it yet. I've asked them to hold it until I've had a look at it.'

'Why that one? Why that one particularly?' Walt asked. Irritation only half repressed sharpened his voice.

'Because it's one of the three with no phone number. Because it's in the same state as Yellowstone. And because it gives me an itch.'

'Yellowstone is clear across Wyoming from Rock Springs,' he said. 'Must be four hundred miles.'

'Three hundred. I looked at the map.'

He drank and rubbed his thumb over his fingers much faster than usual. Tired lines had appeared round his eyes.

'I think it's a futile waste of time,' he said abruptly.

'I've time to waste.'

'And I haven't.'

He put the glass down with a thump, reached into an inner pocket and brought out another white package which he tossed down in front of me.

'These are your photographs.'

'Thanks.'

The look he gave me was a long way from the smile of that morning. I wondered whether I would have let him go looking for answers if I'd known he was short on stamina, and decided I probably would. He hadn't given up half way: only at the end.

Lynnie appeared in the bar doorway in her orange dress and the tired-looking men there straightened their spines in a hurry.

She wouldn't come in. I eased Walt with me across the heavy carpet and introduced him to her in the hall outside. He made only a few perfunctory remarks and left in a short time with a glowering face and solid back.

'Whatever's bitten him?' said Lynnie, looking after him.

'He's had a tiring day and he's going home to his wife.'

She looked at me quickly, half laughing. 'Do you always know what you're saying?'

'Frequently.'

She chuckled. 'Anyway, you look a lot tireder than he does.' We started to walk over to the desk to collect our keys.

'That's most encouraging.'

'What shall we do this evening? Or do you want to sleep?' She was unselfish enough to keep anxiety entirely out of her voice, but when I said we'd go wherever she wanted there was an extra bounce in her stride. She decided on a two-hour taxi ride to everywhere in the city she'd ever heard of that she hadn't managed to see that afternoon, followed by dinner in a second-floor glass-walled restaurant, looking down and across the lights of Broadway and Times Square. At eleven-thirty, when we got back to the Biltmore, she was still wide awake.

'What a fabulous, fantastic day,' she said in the lift.

'Good.'

'I'll remember it as long as I live.'

I smiled at her enthusiasm. It was a thousand years since I'd been as happy as that, but sometimes I could still imagine how it felt. That evening it had been quite easy.

'You are far from drizz,' she said, contentedly grinning.

'You'd be no great drag to be stuck in a lift with yourself.'

But the lift stopped unimaginatively at the eighth floor as scheduled and we walked along to our rooms. Her door was opposite mine.

I kissed her cheek. 'Goodnight, little Lynnie.'

Her brown eyes smiled serenely back. 'Goodnight, Gene. Sleep well.'

'You too,' I said. 'Kentucky first stop in the morning.'

It took four more days to find the girl in the photograph, though maybe I could have done it in two if it hadn't been for Lynnie. Privately aware that it wasn't necessary for me to do the job myself I dredged up a cast iron-sounding reason for having to accompany her to Lexington, and we flew down via Washington, which involved another quick taxi tour instead of a lengthy wait at the airport. Lynnie didn't intend to miss a thing.

Eunice met us at Lexington airfield and drove us to Midway, and after a prawn and avocado lunch lent me her car to go on my errand. I greased Chrysalis's ex-groom into going with me with twenty dollars of his employer's money, and took him off to Sam Hengelman's. The horse van, Sam said out of the corner of his mouth as he watched an old movie on a cyan-heavy colour set, was still in care of the police department. If I wanted to look at it, go talk to them.

At the police department a state trooper listened to what I had to say, said 'Yeah,' several times, consulted higher authority, and sorted out some keys. Higher authority turned out to be a good-looking detective in his twenties, and we all four repaired to the parking lot behind the police building, where the horse van stood in one corner.

Chrysalis's lad pointed out the stall the stallion had inhabited, and the state trooper came up with a successful conclusion to the expedition: four long shining bay hairs.

'From his mane,' said the groom authoritatively.

The detective kept two for the State and sent off the other two special delivery to Walt at Buttress Life, and the groom and I drove back to Midway.

Eunice and Lynnie were both in the pool, and the rest of the day and night came close enough to my daydream on the plane, except that the sixteen hours' sleep shrank to six, but even that was spectacular by recent standards.

When Lynnie said over large cups of breakfast coffee the next morning that she wished I wasn't going, I very nearly didn't. If I'd stayed, Buttress Life would have paid the insurance and a load of grief would never have happened. Yet if I could go back to that cross-roads moment again I know I would inevitably make the same decision. Once a hunter, always a hunter: the inner compulsion hadn't loosened its grip: the quality they'd hauled me out of the Army for was too basic in my nature, and being what I was, what I am, slopping out of the chase was impossible. Keeble had known, I admitted wryly, that he had only to get me hooked.

'I must go,' I said, 'if I'm to find the horse.'

'Damn the horse,' Lynnie said.

I laughed at her. 'You've learnt quickly.'

'I like Eunice,' she said defensively. 'She doesn't shock me.'

I gathered from that that she certainly did, but that Lynnie would never admit it.

'But you will come back here? Before you go home, I mean?'

'I expect so,' I said.

She fiddled with her coffee cup, looking down. 'It's only a week since I picked you up at your flat, last Sunday.'

'And you've aged a year.'

She looked up quickly, startled. 'Why did you say that?'

'It was what you were thinking.'

'I know,' she said, puzzled, 'but I don't know how you do.'

'Crystal set in the attic. Intermittent though, unfortunately.'

'Just as well, if you ask me.' There was a healthy mockery on her laughing face. 'How would you like to be tuned in permanently to Eunice?'

Eunice herself trailed through the doorway at that moment wearing an electric blue wrapper and a manageable hangover.

With both still in place, after two cups of coffee and a cigarette, she trundled Lynnie and me to the airport.

'Goodbye, you son of a bitch,' she said to me, as I stood beside her window. 'I guess you can come back any time you want to.'

Lynnie glanced at her sharply, with sudden speculation: growing up in front of one's eyes. I smiled goodbye to them both and walked away into the airport. From there I bus-stopped a thousand miles to Denver, and chartered a twin-engined Piper from a local firm for the last two hundred to Rock Springs. The pilot chewed his nails savagely beside me all the way as if he were a dedicated auto-cannibal, and I arrived feeling sick.

On the hot late Sunday afternoon the little desert town looked lifeless. Shimmering air rose endlessly over the dump of abandoned rusting motor cars, a Greyhound bus rolled past with passengers staring like fish through its green glass windows, and sprinklers on the richer front lawns kept the parching heat at bay. At the bus station I learnt that old man Hagstrom's boy was the agent for Snail Express, but when I found old man Hagstrom, fanning himself in a rocker on the front porch of his small frame house, he said that his boy was out calling.

Hagstrom himself seemed to be glad to have company and told me to go inside and bring two beers out of the icebox. The icebox was in the living room, just through the screen door. It was a shambles of a room with sagging broken-spring chairs, dirty worn-out rag rugs, a scattered assortment of cups, glasses, and bottles, all unwashed, and a vast new television. I took the beer out on to the porch, sat on the top step, and drank from the bottle, like my host.

The old man rocked, scratched himself, drank, and said vaguely that his boy would be right along, I could bet on it. I looked up and down the hot empty street. There were other shapes rocking gently in the shade of the porches, half invisible because many had the insect screens round the outside rails. From behind them they watched the world go by: only thing was, the world rolled past in automobiles and didn't stop to talk.

Two beers later, while old man Hagstrom was telling me how he personally would have dealt with the Saigon situation in '67, his boy rolled up in a pockmarked Chrysler. His boy was literally a boy, not more than eighteen: old man Hagstrom's grandson. He rubbed his hands down his grease-marked T-shirt and jeans, and held one out to me with as easy going a welcome as his grandfather's. I explained what I wanted.

'Sure you can look at the trailer,' he said, amiably. 'Now?'

'If you don't mind.'

'You're welcome.'

He waved me into his baking car and whirled it casually round a few corners, drawing up with a jerk outside a rickety-looking gate set in a head-high wall. Through the gate, in a dusty area, stood four Snail Express trailers, all different sizes.

'That one,' I said, pointing to the largest.

'Came in last Saturday. I think. I'll look it up.' He unlocked a small brick-built office on one side, and I followed him in. Hot enough in there to please Satan.

'That's right, Saturday,' he said, consulting the ledger. 'Came from New York State, renting charge paid in advance for one week. The week wasn't up until Monday.'

'Do you remember who brought it here?'

'Uh, let's see. Oh yes. An old guy. Can't remember much about him. He had white hair, I guess.'

'What sort of car did he have, to pull the trailer?'

'I helped him unhitch . . . a station wagon, I think. Grey, mebbe.'

'It wasn't these two?' I showed him the photograph.

'Nope.' He was definite. As far as he knew, he'd never seen them. Had I asked his grandfather? I had.

He said he'd swept out the trailer, but I could look inside if I wanted to.

'Why did you sweep it?' I asked.

'Usually do. It was pretty clean already, though.'

I looked anyway. There were no bay hairs. Nothing at all to suggest that Chrysalis had ever been squeezed into it. The only suggestive thing about it was the way it was built: the roof opened outwards right along the centre line, to make the loading of tall objects easier. It had been worrying me that Chrysalis would not have walked into a tiny dark trailer: but one open to the sky was a different matter.

Old man Hagstrom's boy obligingly dug out the Hertz agent, who rented me an air-conditioned black Chevrolet with only five thousand on the clock. Overnight I added three hundred and thirty-four more, and drove into Gardiner for breakfast.

The road there had led through Yellowstone Park itself where the dawn had crept in mistily between the pine trees, and glimpses of lakes had looked like flat puddles of quick-silver. I had seen an ugly great moose, but no bears. Yogi was asleep.

I spent all morning walking round the town. None of the shops were selling the handkerchief, or had ever stocked any like it. The photograph produced no reactions at all. After a toasted bacon, tomato, and lettuce sandwich at a lunch counter I left Gardiner and went fifty-four miles to West Yellowstone.

The afternoon's trudge produced exactly the same absence of results. Hot, tired, and frustrated, I sat in the Chevrolet and wondered what to do next. No trace of Chrysalis in the trailer, even though it seemed likely it was the one the drivers had seen. No matching handkerchiefs at Yellowstone Park. Walt had been right. The trip was one pointless waste of time.

I thought of the long forest drive back through the park, the canyon gradients at midway, and the final hundred miles of desert to Rock Springs, and decided to put it off until the next day. Sighing, I found the best-looking motel and booked the best room they had, stood under the shower until the day's aches had run down the drain with the dust, and stretched out for a couple of hours on the kingsized Slumberland.

The waitress who brought my steak at dinner was large, loosely upholstered, kind-natured, and with an obvious conviction that a man alone liked a bit of gossip. I wanted her to go away and let me eat in peace, but custom was slack and I learnt more than I cared about her complicated home life. In the end, simply to stop the flow, I pulled out the crumpled handkerchief and asked if she knew where I could get a new one like it.

She thought 'the girls' might know, and went off to ask them. Relieved, I finished my steak. Then she came back and doubtfully put the white square down beside me on the table-cloth.

'They say you might get one in Jackson. They do have bears on ashtrays and things down there. Down in the Tetons. A hundred, hundred-fifty miles. It's a holiday town, Jackson.'

I'd driven straight through Jackson the night before on the way up from Rock Springs, and seen only a small western town fast asleep. When I went back on the Tuesday morning it was buzzing with holiday-makers and local inhabitants, dressed all alike in cowboy clothes. Dude ranch country, I learnt. The main street was lined with souvenir shops, and the first one I went into had a whole pile of small white handkerchiefs with bears on.

Eight

THE GIRL in the punt opened the ranch house door, walked halfway to meet me from the car, and greeted me with professional instant welcome.

'Mr Hochner? How nice to have you with us.'

'I'm glad you could take me at such short notice, with the Fourth coming up next weekend.' I shook her hand, putting a slight touch of German accent into my voice because it was easier for me than American if I had to keep it up for any length of time. It didn't seem altogether wise to be English.

'We're seldom full this early in the season.' She smiled as far up her face as her cheek bones while her eyes skimmed my clothes, car, and luggage. Only a hotel keeper's check-up: it hadn't occurred to her that she'd seen me before.

'I'll show you straight to your cabin, if you like? Then you can freshen up and come along here to the ranch house for dinner later on. There will be a bell, to let you know when.'

I parked the car, and carrying my two suitcases, the old one and the new one from Jackson, followed her along a grassy woodland track towards one of several small log cabins scattered among the trees.

She was tall and strong, and older than she had seemed on the river: twenty-six or twenty-seven, I guessed. The fair hair no longer hung childishly loose, but was combed up into a round topknot, leaving her neck cool and uncluttered. She wore dark blue Levis instead of the white trousers, but the pink shirt on top looked identical. One of the storekeepers in Jackson, the fifth I tried, had known her immediately when I had artistically let the photograph drop face up in front of him as I took money for a local map out of my wallet.

'Yola Clive,' he said casually, picking it up. 'And Matt. Friends of yours?'

'I'd thought of looking them up,' I agreed, sorting out bills. 'How do I get there, do you know? I haven't been to their place before.'

He obligingly gave me clear directions for a fifteen-mile drive, finishing, 'and the High Zee Ranch is the only place along there, so you can't miss it. But if you're planning on staying, I'd give them a call and make a reservation. It's a mighty popular place they run.'

'I sure will,' I said: and I did. I also bought some Levis and shirts and a pair of riding boots, and the suitcase to put them in. In cowboy country guns passed without comment: I added a heavy black tooled-leather belt with a silver buckle, and the clerk didn't show any surprise at my wanting to make sure that the small-of-the-back holster I sometimes used would slot on to it.

Jackson preserved its own wild western flavour to the extent of a small authentic stage coach waiting in front of the drug store: but the sleepy disillusioned horses between the shafts looked a poor prospect against galloping redskins. Broad raised boardwalks edged with hitching rails ran along in front of the stores in the short main street, though the mud they had been built to avoid had long been metalled over. Motels with signs saying 'air-conditioning and central heating' were called 'Covered Wagon' and 'Rustlers' Hideout'. Jackson was an uneasy mixture of evolution and make believe, and clearly a success.

I sat in the sun on a hitching rail most of the afternoon: did a bit of thinking, and made two calls to Walt at Buttress Life.

Yola Clive led me round a neat stack of sawn logs, up two

steps, across a minimal porch and through a screen door and a
wood door into the cabin.

'Bathroom through there,' she said, pointing. 'And you'll
probably need to light the stove in the evenings. The snows only
melted here two or three weeks ago, and the nights are cold.'
She smiled briefly and indicated a small tubful of a crumbly mixture which stood beside the squat black stove. 'Light the logs
with two or three handfuls of that.'

'What is it?' I asked.

'Pep,' she said. 'A mixture of diesel oil and sawdust.' Her
eyes glanced professionally round the room, checking that
everything was in order. 'There's an ice machine out back of the
kitchen, if you want to make drinks. Most guests bring their
own liquor . . . We don't sell it ourselves. I expect you'll want to
go riding tomorrow. We usually fix that up over dinner.' The
half smile came and went, and Yola walked quietly away along
the track.

Sighing, I investigated my quarters. There had been a reasonable compromise between age-old materials and modern
construction, resulting in a sturdy two-roomed cabin with a
pitch roof and varnished tree trunk walls. Two single beds stood
on the polished wood floor in the main room, covered with
patchwork quilts. A curtain across a half-shelved recess acted as
closet, and the two upright chairs and the table were all home-
built. So, too, I discovered, were the towel rail, stool, and shelf
in the bathroom. But the backwoods stopped short of the
plumbing: and the lighting was ranch-generated electric.

I unpacked on to the shelves and hangers, and changed from
town clothes into Levis and a blue-and-white check shirt. The
complete vacationer, I thought sourly: and buckled the gun belt
round my waist.

After that for an hour I sat on the porch and looked at the
view, which was good enough for a chocolate box. The Teton
range of the Rocky Mountains stretched north and south, with

dark green pine forests washing up from the valley to meet spot-less snowcapped peaks. Along the bottom ran a sparkling thread of blue and silver, a tributary to the upper reaches of the one thousand-mile Snake River: and between the river and the woods on whose edge my cabin stood, a wide stretch of sage brush and scrub was dotted with yellow weed-like flowers.

The woods around the cabin stood on the lower slopes of another ridge of peaks which rose sharp and high behind the ranch, shutting it in, close and private. The stream ran right along, in and out, but the only road into the narrow valley stopped dead in the parking area of the High Zee.

A bell clanged loudly up at the ranch house. I went back into the cabin and put on a sloppy black sweater which hid the Luger and looked reasonable at nine thousand two hundred feet above sea level, though the still persisting heatwave was doing a good job in the mountains too. Walking slowly along the dusty grass track I wondered if Matt Clive would know me. I certainly had no clear memory of his face on the punt, though I now knew it well from the photograph. It was unlikely, since his full attention must have been concentrated on Dave Teller, that he had taken much notice of me; but he might possibly have a sharper impression than Yola, as I had been closer to him when I went in after Dave.

I needn't have wondered. He wasn't there.

Yola sat at one end of a long golden wood table flanked by chattering well-dug-in ranch guests. Family groups, mostly, and three married couples. No singles except me. A bright well-coiffured mother invited me to sit beside her, and her hearty husband opposite asked if I'd had a long drive. On the other side of me a small boy told his parents loudly that he didn't like stuffed pancakes, and every face round the table looked sun-burned, vital, and overflowing with holiday spirits. I battened down a fierce urge to get up and go out, to get away from all that jollity. I didn't see how I was ever going to make the effort to look as if I were enjoying myself.

By the end of the meal it felt as if my smile were set in plaster, rigid and mechanical to the extent that my face ached with producing it. But the hearty man opposite, Quintus L. Wilkerson III, 'Call me Wilkie,' seemed pleased to have a practically non-speaking audience, and made the most of it. I endured a splash by splash account of his day's fishing. His wife Betty-Ann had ridden to the lake with him, and then gone on into the hills in a party containing her two children, Samantha and Mickey. I heard about that too, from all three of them. They asked me to ride with their party the next day, and I wrenched my tongue into saying I'd be glad to.

I lasted out the coffee. The Wilkersons promised to see me at breakfast, and Yola asked if I were comfortable in the cabin.

'Thank you, yes.' Remembering the German accent. Smile.

'That's fine,' she said brightly, her eyes sliding past. 'Ask if there's anything you need.'

I walked stiffly out of the ranch house and along the dark track to the empty cabin; leaned wearily against one of the posts holding up the porch roof and looked at the row of peaks glimmering palely in shifting moonlight, with streaky cloud across the sky. My head ached with a feeling of compression, as if my brain wanted to expand and fill up with air.

How could I go on like this, I thought. Dinner had been about as much as I could manage. I didn't know what to do about it. No use praying: no faith. If I went to a doctor I'd get a bottle of tonic and a homily about pulling myself together. There was absolutely nothing to be done but endure it, and go on with that until it got better. If I could only convince myself that it would in the end get better, at least I would have something to cling to.

Somewhere in the valley a stallion shrieked.

Maybe it was Chrysalis. If he wasn't actually on the High Zee

Ranch I thought the chances very high that he was somewhere near. Maybe Keeble did know what he was doing sending me to find him, because it was evident that I could still function normally on the work level: concentration acted like a switch which cut out the personal chaos. If I concentrated twenty-four hours a day, life would be simple.

One trouble with that. It was impossible.

The ranch held upwards of a hundred and twenty horses. About forty of them were penned in a big corral near the main ranch house, saddle horses for the ranch guests to ride.

Breakfast had been early, but the fitting of guests to horses took some time, even though everyone except me had been there two or three days and knew which animal they wanted. The head wrangler asked me if I could ride, and if so, how well.

'I haven't been on a horse for nine or ten years,' I said.

He gave me a dead quiet one with U-shaped hocks. The western saddle seemed like an armchair after the postage stamp I'd been teethed on: and there were no new-fangled things like buckles for raising and lowering stirrups. The head wrangler unlaced the thong holding the three-inch-wide leathers to the saddle, slid them down two or three holes, and laced them up again. Good soft leather, which could go all day and not rub the horse.

Over to one side of the ranch house, past its green watered lawn, there was a smallish sturdily railed paddock of not more than an acre. I'd spent all breakfast looking out of the window at the seven horses in it. Three mares, two small foals, two stallions. Both the stallions were bays, but one had a white blaze and was no thoroughbred.

'What are those horses over there?' I asked the wrangler, pointing.

He paused a second while he worked out how to put it delicately to an ignorant dude, and foreigner into the bargain, and then said, 'We breed most of the horses, on this ranch.'

'Oh, I see,' I said. 'Do you have many stallions?'

'Three or four. Most of these', he glanced round the patiently waiting mounts, 'are geldings.'

'That's a nice-looking bay,' I commented.

He followed my eyes over to the small paddock again. 'He's new,' he said. 'A half-bred Matt bought in Laramie two or three weeks back.' There was disapproval in his tone.

'You don't like him?' I said.

'Not enough bone for these hills,' he said briefly, finishing the second stirrup. 'Now, is that comfortable?'

'Fine,' I said. 'Thank you.'

He nodded with casual friendliness and went to see to someone else. The wranglers differed from the dudes only in the matters of age and dress. They were all boys or young men between eighteen and thirty, several of them college boys working their vacation. The dudes were either parents or children; scarcely one in the twenties. No one, Betty-Ann Wilkerson told me knowledgeably, called cowboys cowboys anywhere except in films. Cowhand was possible, but the right word was wrangler. There were no cattle on the High Zee. The wranglers herded the horses, and the horses were there for the dudes to ride.

In the matter of clothes the wranglers were less flamboyant, less well pressed, altogether dustier. They had been up since five-thirty and other people's holidays were their hard work.

'They turn the horses out on the hills every night,' Wilkie explained, 'and go up and herd them down in the morning.'

We set off from the ranch in two parties, about twelve guests and two wranglers in each. Down over a flat wooden bridge across the narrow river, and up into the main Teton range opposite. Wilkie rode in front of me and Betty-Ann behind as we wound upwards through the woods in single file; and neither of them tired of talking.

'They turn the horses out on the hills over here because there isn't enough pasture in the valley to feed them.' Wilkie turned half round in his saddle to make sure I could hear. 'They go miles away, most nights. The wranglers fix a bell on to some of them, like cowbells in Switzerland, so that they can find them in the morning. The ones they put bells on are the sort of natural leaders, the horses other horses like to be with.' He smiled heartily. 'It's sure difficult to see them sometimes, with the sun shining through the trees and making shadows.'

What he said was true because we passed a group of three in a hollow later on, and I didn't see them until one moved his head and clinked his bell.

'They only bring in the number they need,' Betty-Ann filled in. 'They just leave the rest out, and maybe bring some of them in tomorrow, if they come across them first.'

'So sometimes a horse could be out for a week at a time?' I suggested.

'I guess so,' Wilkie said vaguely. He didn't really know. 'Of course, if they want one particular horse, the wranglers will go right up the mountain to find him, I do know that.'

'Anyone who can ride well enough can go up with the wranglers in the morning,' Betty-Ann said. 'But they *canter* up and down here instead of walk.'

The path was steep and also rocky.

'These horses are born to it, honey,' said Wilkie kindly. 'Not like the riding school horses back home.'

At eleven thousand feet the path levelled out on to a small tree-shaded plateau overlooking a breathtaking pine-wooded valley with a brilliant blue lake in its depths. The cameras came out and clicked excitedly. The chattering voices exclaimed over an order of beauty that demanded silence. And eventually we rode down again.

Yola asked me at lunch if I had enjoyed my morning, and I said without difficulty that I had. The Wilkerson children were calling me Hans and asked me to swim in the stream with them in the afternoon. Wilkie clapped me heartily on the shoulder and told me I was a good guy, and Betty-Ann had irritatingly begun looking at me in a way which would change her husband's mind about that instantly, if he noticed.

I left the lunch table last and whisked away a large slice of bread in a paper napkin. Alone in my cabin I unpacked some specially acquired groceries, filled one pocket with sugar cubes, and on the bread scooped out a whole tin of sardines. With the bread still held in the napkin I walked down through the sage brush and along to the mares' and foals' paddock, reaching it on the far side from the ranch house.

There I offered sugar in one hand and sardines in the other. The mares came and sniffed, and all chose sugar. The foals chose sugar. The bay with the white blaze chose sugar. The dusty half-bred that Matt bought two or three weeks ago in Laramie came last, less curious than the rest.

He sniffed at the sardines and raised his head with his ears pricked, staring across at the high Tetons as if hearing some far-off sound, smelling some distant scent. His nostrils quivered gently. I looked at the splendid lines of bone in the skull, the gracefully slanted eye, the perfect angle of head on neck. He had the crest of a thoroughbred stallion, and the hocks of a racehorse.

He bent his head down to the sardines and ate the lot.

Yola and Matt Clive lived in a cabin of their own, separate from the main ranch house, which contained only the dining room, kitchens, sitting room, and wet day games room for the guests.

Yola backed an olive-drab pick-up with small white lettering on its doors out of a shady carport beside her cabin, and drove away down the dusty road. I stared after her, half amazed, half smiling. Full marks to the horse van drivers, I thought. They'd seen both the Snail Express van and the pick-up. They must have seen them both several times, but even so, they'd remembered.

Guests were allowed to use the telephone, which was located in the Clives' cabin. I strolled over there, knocked on the door, and found the place empty. Not locked, though in this case there was a key. There were no locks on any of the guest cabin doors: one could only bolt them on the inside, with a simple wooden wedge slotted into the latch.

A quick tour of the Clives' cabin revealed two separate single bedrooms, living room, kitchen, bathroom, and office. I planted three hypersensitive listening devices as invisibly as possible, and unhurriedly left.

After that I climbed into the Chevrolet and drove myself back to Jackson, where the telephone was more private. My call to Buttress Life lasted a long time, and Walt's contribution to the second part of the conversation consisted of gasps and protests of 'You can't.'

'Listen, Walt,' I said in the end. 'We're not policemen. I imagine your company would settle for the property back and no questions asked? And my brief is to restore Chrysalis to Dave Teller. Just that. Nothing more. If we start things the way you want, we'll end up with a lot of smart lawyers and most probably a dead horse.'

There was a long pause. 'All right,' he said slowly. 'OK. You win.'

He wrote down a long list of instructions. 'This is Wednesday,' I said, thinking aloud. 'Sunday morning. That gives you three clear days. Should be enough.'

'Only just.'

'Never mind,' I said soothingly. 'You can do most of it sitting down.'

Walt wasn't amused. 'And you, what exactly will you be doing?' he asked sarcastically.

'On a dude ranch,' I said reasonably, 'one dudes.'

At the Post Office I mailed off to him by express delivery six hairs from the mane of the sardine horse, and motored back to the grim business of acting the holiday I'd feared from the start.

The three days seemed eternal. Riding took up the mornings and most afternoons and that was the best of it. Meals continued to be a desperate trial. The nights were long. I wished that Lynnie could have come with me, because in her company the depression seemed to retreat, but she was Eunice's crutch, not mine. And her father, trust me as he might, would have found it hard to believe I would only ask for her daytime closeness. And maybe I couldn't have done it. So no props. No props at all.

Yola ran the ranch with a sort of super-efficiency which looked easy, juggling staff and guests into harmony without a single wrinkle of anxiety and without any show of aggression. The fair hair continued to be worn tidily on top. Her clothes were jeans and shirt and soft flat shoes. No boots: no masculinity. She radiated friendliness and confidence, and her smile never once reached her eyes.

She didn't go riding with her guests, and I never sat next to her at meals because most of the husbands and many of the wives conducted a dignified scramble for her favours, but on Thursday evening, when with several others I was drinking after-dinner coffee out in the open on the long porch, she dropped gracefully down into the empty chair beside me, and asked if I were enjoying my holidays, and was finding my cabin comfortable.

I answered with half-true platitudes, to which she half listened.

'You are young,' I said next, with great politeness, 'to own so beautiful a place.'

She replied to this small probe with frank ease. 'It belonged to my grandfather and then to my mother. She died a year or two back.'

'Has it always been a dude ranch? I mean, it seems a bit hilly for cattle . . .'

'Always a dude ranch,' she agreed. 'My grandfather built it about forty years ago . . . How did you hear of us?'

I glanced at her unhurriedly, but she was merely curious, not suspicious.

'I asked in Jackson for somewhere good and fairly quiet, out in the mountains.'

'Who recommended us?'

'Just a man in the street.'

She nodded, satisfied.

'What do you do in the winter?' I asked.

There was a flicker in the eyes and a quick private smile on the mouth: whatever she did in the winter pleased her more than hotel keeping.

'We move down south. Snow completely blocks this valley from November through March. Most years it's May before we come back . . . We usually open the ranch the second week in June, but the canyons are often impassable then.'

'What do you do with the horses?'

'Oh, they go down to the plain, on a friend's ranch.'

Her voice was as strong and capable as the rest of her. I watched her eyes slide round towards the paddock with the mares and foals, and pause there calmly, and return to me. Expressionless.

I smiled her a force five version of an adults-only smile, and asked if she ever found it lonely, so far out in the wilds. To this mild but unmistakable come-on there was no reaction beyond a crisp shake of the head. I was the only man there not guarded by a watchful wife: Yola wasn't in the least bit interested.

I complimented her on the ranch food, and on the helpfulness of the wranglers. She said she was glad I was pleased. I yawned and apologized, and said it must be all the fresh air . . . she'd heard it all dozens of times a year, said everything she'd said so often that she no longer had to think. No use on this occasion using any jolting technique to force out an unguarded phrase: jolting her was roughly the last thing I wanted to do.

After a while I stood up lazily and said I would turn in, and she gave me the usual meaningless half-way-up smile. She hadn't really seen me at all: wouldn't remember me in another month. Unless I inadvertently gave her cause.

The three bugs in her cabin worked on the audio-switch principle: any noise, and speech especially, which they picked up, automatically started the recording machine which occupied the back half of the ordinary-looking transistor radio standing beside my bed. But there was little to overhear. Yola slept alone, and apart from one evening when she invited four of the guests in for a drink, the only conversations were telephone calls.

In my cabin each evening, warming by the squat black stove, I played back the day's 'take'. Nearly all the calls were to do with business: grocery orders, laundry, blacksmith's supplies, and future bookings. But one call, on Friday evening, was worth all the trouble.

'Uncle Bark?' Yola's voice said, low and clear. One of the bugs was behind a picture of drooping roses on the wall over the telephone table.

'. . . honey.' The occasional word escaped from the receiver in return, but Yola must have been holding it close to her ear.

'Sure. Everything's fine here,' she said. 'Absolutely no kind of trouble.'

'. . . Matt? . . .'

'That's what I called about, Uncle Bark. Matt wrote me he's having to give up in Europe. He says he can't get near to you-know-who, they've got him holed up as tight as Fort Knox. So I guess we'll just have to keep everything under wraps for a while longer.'

'. . .'

'It sure is a nuisance, yeah. But as long as we get him to you before the snows come again . . .'

'. . .'

'How can we? You know it isn't built for that.'

'. . . stay . . .'

'We certainly can't send him down to Clint's with the others. We'd waste a whole year and he might break a leg or something.'

'. . . desert.'

'We don't want him at Pitts, it isn't built for it. But there's a good long time for Matt to arrange something.'

'. . . hadn't started.'

'Yeah, I'm sure you would. But it's too late now. How were we to know that something so goddam stupid would happen? Matt will probably be home sometime tomorrow. I'll have him call you.'

She put down the receiver soon after that: and I wound back the tape and played the conversation over again. Two unsubstantial points emerged. If Dave Teller had been too obviously guarded, Matt would have realized that the punt episode was not considered to be an accident. And the something 'goddam stupid' which had somewhere or other upset the Clives' original plans might be that I'd been there to fish Dave out of the river, or might be something else quite different; something which had made the removal of Dave necessary in the first place. The horse had been stolen on June 15th, Tuesday, and Yola had asked the London hotel for Dave's weekend address on June 19th, Saturday. So what, if anything, had happened in the four days between? Something goddam stupid . . .

I told Yola after breakfast on Saturday morning that I had enjoyed my stay immensely and would be leaving the following day. She smiled the regulation smile without clearly focusing, and thanked me for letting her know.

'So if I could have my bill at breakfast tomorrow?' I suggested.

'Sure,' she said. 'But you can't stay over Monday for the Fourth?'

'I'm afraid not.'

She nodded, not caring one way or the other. 'I'll get it ready for you, then.'

The Wilkersons exclaimed over my going. 'You'll miss the barbecue,' Samantha said. 'And the float trip down the river.'

A local man took parties down the fast-flowing Snake on black inflated rubber raft dinghies: one of the area's attractions, like the rodeo and the ski lift. The Wilkersons had asked me to join them. 'Maybe I'll come back next year,' I said. And maybe I wouldn't.

I looked after the children that afternoon while Betty-Ann went to the hairdresser and Wilkie drove to a distant lake for the fishing. They swam in the stream, where I refused to join them in case my head in the water jogged Yola's sleeping memory, and we fed sugar and handfuls of grass through the rails to the leggy foals in the little paddock. The rails were solid young tree trunks dove-tailed and nailed into even sturdier posts, and the gate was just as substantial. Its hinges were bolted through the gatepost, and a heavy padlock fastened it through two strong hasps. None of this strength was new.

Samantha and Mickey didn't think much of the sardine bay.

'Too spindly,' Mickey said. 'His legs would snap if he went up the mountain.' I looked across at the Teton range, the tops shining white in the hot sun. The surefooted born-to-it ranch horses picked their way easily up and down the steep rocky paths over there, through the woods growing with flat huckleberry leaves, across the screes left from landslips, and on to the bare stony patches above the snow line.

'Why don't you stay till Monday night?' said Mickey. 'If you go tomorrow, you'll miss the fireworks.'

Nine

AT ONE o'clock, early Sunday morning, I stood on the porch of my cabin waiting for my eyes to dilate, and listening to the night.

A slight wind, riffling the trees. A car horn, very distant. The faint hum of the electric generator in its special house. No sound from Yola's cabin. None all evening. Matt hadn't yet come home.

With some misgivings I had left my riding boots in the cabin, and wore only thin rubber-soled plimsolls, with a pair of socks on top. I walked quietly through the sage brush on the long way round to the little paddock, the spicy fragrance rising into my nose as I disturbed the silver-grey leaves. The half moonlight was enough to see by without a torch and streaky clouds made shifting shadows across the ground: it couldn't have been better if I'd sent in an order.

The padlock's strength was illusory. It had a simple lever movement inside which took me less than five minutes to fiddle open. No one could have heard the click of success. Nor the tiny squeak of the gate opening. I slipped through and distributed sugar to the mares and foals. The bay with the white blaze greeted this with a trumpeting whinny; but no lights went on in Yola's cabin or the wranglers' bunkhouse.

The sardine horse flared his nostrils at me but ate the sugar and let me slip over his head the simple rope halter I had come armed with. I spent some time rubbing his nose and patting his neck, and when I walked towards the gate he came with me docilely enough. I opened the gate and led him through, and the mares and foals quietly followed, their unshod hooves making dull little clops on the loamy ground.

The gentle procession went slowly across towards the river, over the flat bridge with hollow thuds, and up into the darkness of the pine woods. The mares soon stopped to graze, and the foals with them, but the bay stallion with the blaze suddenly realized he was free again, and crashed past me at high speed, squealing and cantering up the path and making as much noise as a train-load of football supporters. Anxious, heart-quickened moments passed: but still no reaction from below.

The sardine bay tugged hard to follow. I soothed him and steadied him, and we presently walked on. He picked his way too cautiously over the stones and corners of rocks sticking up in the narrow path, but I couldn't hurry him without risk; my neck prickled at the thought of being slung into a Wyoming jail for horse stealing; but it was nothing to the fear I had that Mickey might be right about those spindly legs.

In places all the way up the width of the path dwindled to two feet, with a wall of rock on one side and a steep slope on the other. Riding along them by day one simply had to trust that one's horse wouldn't tumble over the edge, as nothing could then have stopped a rock-strewn descent of two or three hundred feet. At these points there wasn't room to walk side by side with a horse one was leading: I inched up the path ahead of him, and slowly, cautiously, he put his feet delicately down between the bigger stones, and scrunched after me.

Two or three times we passed small groups of horses from the ranch, the cow bell clanking gently round the neck of the leader and betraying their presence. Their dark shapes melted into the jumbled background of woods and rocks, and the moonlight picked out only an eye, a rump, a swishing tail. The wranglers found them each morning by tracking, as the bells were only audible for a furlong. I'd had a long talk with one of the boys about tracking, and he'd shown me how they did it. They were going to be able to follow my way up the mountain as clearly as if I'd given them directions, and to tell the time I went by the amount of dew which formed in the hoof prints. The boy had shown me hoof prints, told me how many horses had gone by and when, and all I had seen were some scattered dusty marks. They read the ground like a book. If I tried to obliterate the sardine horse's hoof prints, I obliterated also any chance of the Clives believing he had wandered off by accident. The fuzzy outline of plimsolls under socks was, I hoped, going to pass unnoticed: nothing less was worth the discomfort of wearing them on such jagged going.

It took two hours to reach twelve thousand feet and to come to the end of the tracks I'd learnt in the past four days. From there it was a case of trusting my own nose. The drifting streaks of cloud made black shadows like pits across the rocks and several times I stood still and felt ahead with one toe to make sure that the ground was in fact still there, and I was not stepping straight off a precipice. The moon itself, and the cold mountain air moving against my right cheek, kept me going in the right general direction, but the dotted-line trail I had studied on the map proved more optimistic than actual.

The horse's legs stood up to it remarkably well. Mine had already had enough. Mountaineering was not among Civil Service requirements.

The peak of the Grand Teton rose to thirteen thousand seven hundred feet. The summit loomed very close. Patches of snow, half melted, exposed black-looking banks of scree. I came suddenly across a narrow trail winding past them like an eel: people had walked along there recently, scraping into the snow. I had, with some luck, come the right way. The cold bit down under my black jersey and through the thin shirt underneath, and I wished I had had the sense to bring gloves. But it couldn't be a great deal farther: through the short canyon pass, and out the other side. I looked at my watch. The climb had taken nearly three hours and I was late.

It was darker in the canyon, but also invisible from the valley below. I took the small torch out of my jeans pocket, and shone it in front of my feet. Because of that, the whole expedition came unstuck.

A man suddenly rounded a corner a short way ahead and stood foursquare in the centre of the trail. Startled even more than I was, the horse backed instantly away, tore the rope out of my hand, pulled me flat over as I tried to hang on, and skipped sharply away along a narrow ridge branching off to the left.

Sick and furious I got back on my feet and turned to go after him. The man took a tentative step down the trail and called out.

'Gene?'

It was Walt.

I bit my tongue literally to stop the rage in my mind from spilling over him. There wasn't time for it.

'I saw you coming. The light,' he explained. 'I thought I'd come along to meet you. You're later than you said.'

'Yes.' I shut my mouth. There was half a million pounds loose in a death trap. My responsibility, and my fault.

The moon pushed out a feeble twenty watts. I couldn't see the horse. The path he had taken in panic was a ledge eighteen inches wide with sheer rock on the left and a fierce slope of scree on the right. A gradient so steep that it was as dangerous as a straight-down drop: and in its black invisible depths there would be the usual big slabs with upjutting edges.

'Stay here,' I said to Walt. 'And keep quiet.'

He nodded without speaking, understanding that the situation was beyond apology. His instructions had been expressly to wait for me at one arranged spot.

The ledge was thirty feet long with a bend to the left. I

walked along it slowly, not using the torch, my left hand trailing along the rock wall, the grey light just enough to show the crumbly uneven outer edge.

After thirty feet the ledge widened into a saucer-shaped bowl three quarters surrounded by towering rocks. The sloping floor of the bowl led directly into the sharper slope of the scree. On the floor of the bowl, patchy snow and rough black pebble.

The horse was standing there, sweating. Quivering in every rigid limb. There was no way out except back along the ledge.

I stroked his muzzle and gave him four lumps of sugar, speaking gently to him in a voice much calmer than my feelings. It took ten minutes for the excessive tension to leave his body, and another five before he would move. Then I turned him carefully round until he was facing the way he had come.

Horses react instantly to human fear. The only chance I had of getting him safely back was to walk round there as if it were a broad concrete path across his own stable yard. If he smelt fear, he wouldn't come.

Where the ledge began, he baulked. I gave him more sugar and more sweet talk. Then I turned my back on him and with the halter rope leading over my shoulder, walked slowly away. There was the faintest of protesting backward tugs. Then he came.

Thirty feet had never seemed so interminable. But an animal's sixth sense kept him from putting a foot over the edge, and the slithering clop of his hooves on the broken ground came steadily after me all the way.

Walt, this time, made no sound at all. I came across him standing motionless several yards up the intended trail and he turned without speaking and went on ahead.

Less than half a mile farther the path descended and widened into a broad sweeping basin: and there, where Walt had been supposed to meet me, waited another man, stamping his feet to keep warm.

Sam Kitchens. Holding another horse.

With a powerful torch he inspected every inch of the one I'd brought, while I held his.

'Well?' I said.

He nodded. 'It's Chrysalis all right. See that tiny scar up there, under his shoulder? He cut himself on a metal gate post one day when he was a two-year-old and a bit full of himself. And these black dots, sort of freckles, along that patch of his belly. And the way his hide grows in a whirl just there inside his hock. He always had clean legs. There's a mark or two on them now that wasn't there when I had him. But apart from knowing him from his general shape, like, I'd certainly swear to those other things in any court you'd like to mention.'

'Was the cut from the gate post bad enough to be treated by a vet?'

He nodded. 'Five or six stitches.'

'Good,' I said. 'Then off you go with him. And take good care.'

Sam Kitchens grinned. 'Who'd have thought I'd have seen him again up the Rocky Mountains in the middle of the night? Never you mind, I'll take care all right.'

He turned Chrysalis expertly round, clicking his tongue affectionately, and began the mile-long walk down to the Teton camping ground, to where he and Walt and Sam Hengelman had come in a horse box.

Walt said, 'It's too late for you to go back. Come with us.'

I shook my head. 'I'll meet you in Idaho Falls as we arranged.'

Walt moved uncomfortably. 'It's not safe to go back.'

'I'll be fine. You just get the two Sams cracking. They've got to be well on their way before dawn. They've got that bill of sale?'

Walt nodded, looking at the big mountain pony beside me.

'He cost five hundred dollars. One bay horse, no markings,

entire, aged seven or eight. As ordered. That's what the bill of sale says, and that's what we've got in the van, if anyone asks. Sam Kitchens chose it. Said it was as near as you would get, without actually paying thousands for a blood horse.'

'This one looks fine. See you, then, Walt.'

He stood in silence while I levered myself on to the new horse's bare back and gathered up the reins. I nodded to him, turned away, and started back up the trail to the canyon.

Late, I thought. Almost too late, now. The wranglers would be high up in the hills by six, rounding up the horses. Dudes rode as usual on Sunday mornings. It was already five, and the first greyness of dawn had crept in as the moon faded. If they saw me out so early, I was in trouble.

At a jog trot, his sturdy legs absolutely at home on the terrain, the new horse took me back up into the canyon, past the fearful little ridge that Chrysalis had taken, and out on to the Clive valley side of the Tetons. From there down I looked out for a bunch of High Zee horses, but I was well below the snow line before I heard any of the bells.

There was a little group in a tree-filled hollow. They moved away at my approach, but slowly, and when I was among them and stopped, they stopped also. I slid off the horse I was riding, threaded my fingers through the mane of one of the High Zee group, and transferred the bridle from one to the other. Then, leaving Dave Teller's five-hundred-dollar purchase free on the hill, I pointed my new mount's nose homewards, and gave him a kick.

He knew the way, and he consequently could go much faster. The Wilkersons had told me the wranglers cantered down those steep rocky inclines, but until I did it I hadn't imagined what a hair-raising business it would be. The horse put his feet where I would have said no man could balance, let alone a quadruped, and when I turned him off the regular path he hardly slackened his pace. We went headlong downwards through pines and alders and groves of silver-trunked dead trees, back to the thicker woods with patches of grass underfoot, and more under-growth of huckleberry and sapling. There was one sticky incline of black bog where a mountain stream had spilled out sideways on to a slope of earth, but my pony staggered across it, tacking downwards, sinking in to his knees at every step. Farther on, he crossed the tumbling stream itself, picking his way through a mass of underwater rocks, and lower still he went straight down a bare pebbly slope where the normal path ran from side to side in easier zigzags. Whippy branches caught at us under the trees, but I laid my head flat beside his ears, and where he could go, I went too.

The gentle dude rides had been no preparation for this reck-less descent, and the one or two point-to-points I'd tried in my teens were distant memories and milksop stuff in comparison. But skills learnt in childhood stay for ever: balance still came instinctively. I didn't fall off.

We kept up the pace until there was less than a mile to go, then I veered the pony along to the right, up along the valley and away from the bridge to the ranch.

The wranglers would no doubt follow him up there to round him up, but I hadn't time to do the whole detour on foot. It was too light and too late to get back into the ranch across the bridge. I was going to have to cross the stream higher up and go down to my cabin through the woods on the far side.

I slid off the pony nearly half a mile upstream, and took off the bridle. The rough brown hide was streaked dark with sweat, and he didn't look at all like an animal who had spent a peace-ful night grazing. I gave him a slap and he trotted away, wheel-ing round and upwards, back on to the hill. With luck the wranglers wouldn't find him until he'd cooled down, especially as it wouldn't be him they'd be looking for.

I could hear the panic going on down by the ranch house as soon as I stepped cautiously out of the woods and began the freezing cold traverse of the stream. The stones dug into my bare feet, and the water splashed my rolled-up trouser legs. But as I couldn't from where I was see any of the buildings, I trusted that no one there could see me. The shouts came up clearly, and then the thud of several horses cantering across the bridge. By the time I was across the stream and sitting down to put on my shoes again, they were going up towards the woods, and I could see them. Six wranglers, moving fast. If they looked back, they could see my head and shoulders sticking up out of the stretch of sage brush.

A hundred yards of it between me and the safety of the trees on the ranch-house side of the valley. I lay down flat on the ground for a few exhausted minutes, looking up at the dawn-filled sky: a high clear pale blue taking over from grey. The tracks of the mares and foals and both the stallions led straight uphill. I gave the wranglers time to go some way after them, and then quietly got to my feet and slipped unhurriedly across the sage brush and down through the trees to my cabin.

It was ten past six. Broad daylight.

I pulled off my filthy sweaty clothes and ran a deep hot bath. Tiredness had gone down to the bone, and the water tingled like a friction rub on my skin. Relaxing, reviving, I stayed in it for half an hour.

The tape played back for me the heavy knocking on Yola's door and the head wrangler telling her that the mares and stallions were out.

'What do you mean, out?'

'The tracks lead down to the bridge. They're out on the hills.'

'What?' Yola's voice screeched as the full meaning hit her. 'They can't be.'

'They sure are.' The wrangler's voice was much calmer. He didn't know the size of the disaster: wasn't in the game. 'But I can't understand it. The padlock was fastened like you said it must be, when I checked around yesterday evening.'

'Get them back,' said Yola sharply. 'Get them back.' Her voice rose hysterically. 'That new stallion. Get him. Get him back.'

There were sounds after that of drawers being pulled roughly open, and a door slamming, and silence. Yola was out looking for Chrysalis. And, Chrysalis was on his way to Kentucky.

The ranch guests knew all about it, at breakfast.

'What a fuss,' Wilkie said. 'You'd think they'd lost the deeds to a goldmine.'

They had.

'I'm glad they found the dear little foals anyway,' Samantha said.

'They've found them?' I asked. The small paddock was still empty.

'They've put them in the barn,' agreed Mickey. 'With their mothers.'

'Someone left the gate unlocked,' Betty-Ann told me. 'Isn't it a shame? Yola's obviously in a fearful state.'

Yola had been in the dining room when I strolled in to breakfast, standing silent and rigid by the kitchen door, checking that all the guests were there, looking for signs of guilt.

Poise had deserted her. The hair was roughly tied with a ribbon at the nape of her neck and the lipstick was missing. There had been no professional reassuring smiles. A muscle twitched in the strong jaw and she hadn't been in control of the wildness in her eyes.

I ate a double order of bacon and buckwheat hot-cakes with maple syrup, and drank three cups of coffee.

Betty-Ann opposite me lit a cigarette and said did I have to leave, couldn't I stay another few days. Wilkie gruffly said they shouldn't try to keep a feller. Wilkie had cottoned on, and was glad to see me go.

Strong footsteps came into the room from the door behind me. Betty-Ann looked over my head and her eyes widened.

'Why hello there,' she exclaimed warmly, transferring her attentions. 'How good to see you.'

Wilkie, I thought in amusement, should be used to it by now. But the Wilkersons' problems blinked out of my mind for ever when someone else called the new man by his name.

Matt.

Matt Clive spoke from behind my shoulder; a drawling bass voice under strict control.

'Listen folks. I guess you know we've had a little trouble here this morning. Someone let out the mares and horses from their paddock over there. Now if it was any of you kids, we'd sure like to know about it.'

There was a short silence. The various children looked uncomfortable and their parents' eyebrows peaked into question marks.

'Or if anyone knows that the gate wasn't properly fastened yesterday at any time?'

More silence.

Matt Clive walked tentatively round the long table, into my line of sight. About Yola's age, Yola's height. Same jawline. Same strong body, only more so. I remembered the two bedrooms in their cabin: the ringless fingers of Yola's hand. Yola's brother, Matt. I drank my coffee and avoided meeting his eyes.

One or two of the guests laughingly mentioned rustlers, and someone suggested calling in the police. Matt said they were seriously thinking of it. One of the stallions was quite valuable. But only, of course, if it was absolutely certain that none of the guests had left the gate open by accident.

Sympathetic murmurs were all he got. He might indeed be brave enough, or desperate enough, to call in the police. But if he did, they wouldn't recover Chrysalis, who should by now be hundreds of miles away on a roundabout route, accompanied by a strictly legal bill of sale.

Matt eventually went away, trailing a thunderous aura and leaving the guests unsettled and embarrassed.

I asked the girl who waited at table if she could fetch my account for me, as I wanted to pay up before leaving, and after an interval she returned with it. I gave her cash, and waited while she wrote a receipt.

The Wilkerson family said their goodbyes, as they were hoping to go riding if any of the wranglers had come back from searching for the missing horse, and I walked unhurriedly back to my cabin to finish packing. Up the two steps, across the porch, through the two doors, and into the room.

Yola came out of the bathroom carrying a rifle. The way she handled it showed she knew how to use it. Matt stepped from behind the curtained closet, between me and the way out. No rifle for him. A shotgun.

I put on the puzzled act, German accent stronger.

'Excuse me. I do not understand.'

'It's the same man,' Matt said. 'Definitely.'

'Where's our horse?' said Yola furiously.

'I do not know,' I said truthfully, spreading my hands out in a heavy shrug. 'Why do you ask such a question?'

Both the guns were pointing steadfastly my way.

'Excuse me,' I said, 'I have my packing to finish. I have paid the bill. I am leaving this morning.'

'You're not going anywhere, friend,' Matt said grimly.

'Why not?'

'You get that horse back here, and then you can go. Not before.'

He was going to have a fine old time if he intended to keep a prisoner silent indefinitely on a ranch full of holiday guests.

'I can't get him back,' I said. 'I don't know where he is.

Several friends of mine, however, do know where I am. They will be expecting me to be leaving here this morning.'

They stared at me in silent fury. Children in crime, I thought, for all their ingenuity. They had walked straight in with their guns without thinking clearly through. They were, however, lethal children, ruled by impulse more than reason.

I said, 'I am unlikely to go around saying "I stole a horse from the Clives." If you do nothing, and I now drive safely away, you may hear no more of it. That's the best I can offer. You will not, whatever you do, recover the horse.'

The only sensible course open to them was to let me go. But Yola's finger tightened on the trigger, and I reluctantly decided it was time for the Luger. Watching her, I saw a split second too late in the looking glass that Matt had taken a step behind me and was swinging his gun butt like a bludgeon.

He caught me solidly across the back of the skull and the patchwork quilt on the bed dazzled into kaleidoscopic fragments in my glazing eyes as I went down.

Ten

WHEN I woke up it was pretty clear that I wasn't intended to be a hostage, but a corpse.

The cabin was full of smoke, and small flames rose in a long uneven swathe across the floor. I couldn't remember anything at first. Looked at the scene muzzily, half sitting up, my head dizzy and splitting with pain. The Clives, I thought. They'd emptied the whole tub of pep out into a straggling line, and set it alight. Sawdust and diesel oil burning slowly and billowing out unbreathable gases.

They'd laid me against the stove so that it would seem as if I'd fallen and hit my head on it. The empty pep tin rolled away from my foot as I tried to get up, and my hand brushed against a cigarette and a book of matches.

Most deaths in fires weren't caused by burns but by asphyxia. The cabin wouldn't burn down from fire on the floorboards: fire never burnt downwards, only up. The Clives were staging my exit for no better motive than revenge. And as an accident it was one of their poorer efforts.

Having staggered its way through those useless random thoughts, my brain cleared enough for me to decide it was high time to move if I was going to do anything about living. And I supposed I would have to.

I stumbled on to my feet, pulled the quilt off one of the beds, tottered into the bathroom with it and soaked it under the taps in the bath. Smoke was well down in my lungs, thick and choking. It's bloody stupid, I thought groggily, it's damn bloody stupid that boy-and-girl keep trying to shove me where I want to go, and I keep trying not to let them. Ridiculous. Ridiculous . . .

I found myself on my knees, half unconscious. The bath water still running. Pulled myself up a little, hauled out the dripping quilt, flung it over the worst of the fire. Silly, I thought. Much better to go out of the door. Tried that. Damn thing was stuck.

Window, then. Stuck.

Wrapped my hand in the curtain and pushed it through one of the panes of glass. Some air came in. The insect screen stopped more.

Down on my knees again. Terribly dizzy. A black hell in my head. Smelt the quilt burning, lifted it off one lot of fire, and on to the next. Damped it all out into a smelly black faintly smouldering path and felt old and weak from too much scrambling up and down mountains and deeply ill from the crash on the brain and too much smoke.

Opened the front of the fat black stove. Shapleigh, it said. Gradually the smoke began to clear away up its stackpipe while I lay in a poor state beside the cabin door and breathed the fresh air trickling in underneath.

Several eras later I stopped feeling like morgue material and the hammer in my head died to a brutal aching throb. I began to wonder how long it would be before Matt and Yola returned to make their horrified discovery of my death, and wearily decided it was time for action.

I stood up slowly and leaned against the door. They'd fastened it somehow from the outside, in spite of there being no lock: and it was simple enough to see when one's eyes weren't filled with smoke. The screen door opened outwards, the wooden door inwards. A small hook leading in through the latch was holding the two together. I pushed it up, and it slid away as the inner door opened.

My wallet lay on the table, not in my pocket. They'd been looking. Nothing for them to find, except their own photograph. They'd taken that. But they hadn't searched very far: the Luger was still in its holster at my back, under my outhanging shirt. I checked the magazine – still loaded – and put it back in place.

The only other thing I really wanted to take with me was my radio. I squashed down its extended antenna aerial and shoved it into my old suitcase on top of the things I'd packed before breakfast. Then, picking it up and fighting down the whirling chaos which resulted, I opened the screen door. Behind me the cabin lay in a singed shambles. Ahead, the comparatively short walk to the car seemed a marathon.

I might have made it in one if I hadn't felt any worse: but at the end of the woodland track, when all that was left to go was the open expanse of the car park, a wave of clammy sweating faintness seethed through me and I dropped the suitcase and leaned against a tree, waiting weakly for it to pass.

Yola came out of the kitchen door and saw me. Her mouth fell open, then she turned on her heel and dived back into the ranch house. For the rifle. Or for Matt. My hand closed on the pistol at my back, but I was very loath to use it. Too many explanations to authority would be involved, and I preferred to avoid them at this stage.

'Hello,' said a cheerful voice behind me. 'We thought you'd gone ages ago.'

I turned my wonky head and let my hand fall away from the gun. Mickey and Samantha were coming down the track from the branch which led to the Wilkersons' cabin.

'And I thought,' I said, 'that you'd gone riding.'

'The wranglers haven't brought in enough horses,' Mickey explained sadly.

'Are you sick or something?' asked his sister, coming to a halt. and staring up into my face.

'A bit,' I admitted. 'I'd be awfully glad if you'd carry my suit-case for me, across to that black car.'

'Sure,' said Mickey importantly, and Samantha took my hand in motherly solicitude. With one child at each side I completed the trip.

It was the rifle Yola fetched. She stood with it stiffly in her hands and watched the children put the suitcase in the car and stand close to my window while I started the engine. An acci-dental drowning, an accidental smothering she could manage: but three public murders by shooting were outside her range. Just as well. If she'd lifted that rifle towards the children, I would have shot her.

'Bye,' they said, waving. Nice kids.

'Bye.'

I released the brakes and rolled away down the drive in a plume of dust, accelerating fast as soon as I hit the metalled road, and taking the main branch down to Jackson. If Yola thought of following in the pick-up, she didn't do it fast enough. Repeated inspection in the mirror showed no Clives chasing on my tail. The only things constantly before my eyes were bright dancing spots.

Through Jackson I turned north and west on the winding road to Idaho Falls. Along there the Snake River and the Pal-lisades Reservoir, sparkling blue against the dark pines, were stunningly beautiful. But my several stops weren't for appreci-ation: the cold sweating waves of dizziness kept recurring, like twenty-two over seven. I drove slowly, close to the side, never overtaking, ready to pull up. If I hadn't wanted to put a hun-dred miles or so between me and the Clives, I wouldn't have started from Jackson. Most of the time I wished I hadn't.

Walt was pacing the motel lobby like a frenetic film producer when I finally showed up at five-thirty in the afternoon.

'You are four-and-a-half hours late,' he began accusingly. 'You said . . .'

'I know,' I interrupted. 'Book us some rooms. We're staying here.'

He opened his mouth and shut it tight.

'I'm sorry,' I said, softening it, 'but I feel ill.'

'What's the matter?'

'Concussion.'

Walt gave me a searching look, booked the rooms, and even went so far as to carry my suitcase. I lay straight down on the bed, and he sat in an easy chair in my room and rubbed his fingers.

'Do you need a doctor?' he said.

'I don't think so. It's not getting any worse.'

'Well . . . what happened?'

'I'll give you some free advice,' I said. 'Don't ever let Matt Clive come within bashing distance of your head.'

The dizziness wasn't so bad lying down.

'Do you want a drink?' he asked.

'No . . . Let's listen to a tape recording instead.' I told him how to open the back of the radio and to rewind the reels.

'Neat little job,' he commented. 'Where did you get it?'

'Had it specially made, two or three years ago.'

Walt grunted, and switched on. The head wrangler banged on Yola's door and told her that the mares and stallions were out. Walt's face lifted into a half grin.

The recorder played twenty seconds of silence after each take, and began again at the next sound. The next piece was very short.

'Yola?' A man's voice, very loud. 'Yola! Where the hell is everybody?' A door slammed. Silence.

'That's Matt Clive,' I told Walt. 'He came back before breakfast.'

The voices began again. Yola speaking, coming indoors.

'. . . say the tracks go straight up the hill, but he turned back at the high patch of scree and came down again.'

That was a bit of luck.

'They'll just have to go on looking,' Matt said. 'Yola, for God's sake, we can't lose that horse.' His voice was strained and furious. 'I'll go over to the house and see if any of those kids had a hand in it.'

'I don't think so. Not a darned one of them looks nervous.'

'I'll try, anyway.' His footsteps receded.

Yola picked up the telephone and made a call.

'That you, Jim? Have you seen any horse vans coming through Pikelet since last night? . . .

'Well no, I just wondered if you'd seen one. Not this morning, early? . . .

'No, it was just a chance. Sure. Yeah. Thanks anyway.' She put down the receiver with a crash.

Walt raised his eyebrows. 'Pikelet?'

'Couple of shops and a filling station where the Clives' own road joins the main road to Jackson.'

'Just as well we didn't . . .' he began, and then changed it to, 'Is that why you insisted on the long way round?'

'Partly,' I agreed. 'I wanted it to look as if Chrysalis had gone off by himself. I wanted to avoid them realizing he'd been deliberately stolen. Keep them guessing a bit, give us time to get well clear.'

The tape began again. Matt came back running.

'Yola. That man. That damned man.'

'What man?' She was bewildered.

'The man that pulled Teller out of the river. How long has he been here?'

Yola said almost in a whisper, 'Here?'

Matt was shouting. 'Here. Having breakfast. Staying here, you stupid bitch.'

'I don't . . . I don't . . .'

'I saw him at Reading too,' Matt said. 'He called to see Teller in the hospital. They let him in past all the watchdogs. I saw him looking out of the window. How the hell did he get here? Why in God's name didn't you spot him, you stupid, stupid . . . He's the one that's taken the horse. And I'll damn well make him bring it back.'

'How?' Yola said, wailing.

'Excuse me,' said the voice of the girl who waited at table. 'Excuse me, Miss Clive. Mr Hochner wants his bill.'

'There on the desk,' Yola said.

'Which is Hochner?' Matt, urgent.

'The German in cabin three.'

'Where was he sitting at breakfast? What does he look like?'

'He had his back to the door from the hall,' the girl said. 'He's wearing a blue-and-white check shirt, and he's quite tall and has dark brown hair and a tired sort of face.'

'Give him the bill then,' Matt said, and waited until she had gone. 'Hochner!' The voice was almost incoherent with rage. 'How long has he been here?'

'Since . . . Tuesday.' Yola's voice was faint.

'Get your rifle,' Matt said. 'If he won't give us that horse back . . . I'll kill him.'

There were small moving-about sounds, and the tape went quiet. The time they had spent in my cabin telescoped into twenty seconds of silence; and the recording began again.

'He was right, Matt,' Yola said. 'We should have let him go.' Her voice had gone quiet with despair, but Matt's still rode on anger.

'He had his chance. He should have told us what he'd done with Chrysalis.'

After a pause Yola said, 'He wasn't going to do that. He said so. Whatever you do, he said, you won't recover the horse.'

'Shut up,' Matt said violently.

'Matt.' A wail in her voice. 'He was right. We won't recover the horse and his friends will come looking for him, like he said.'

'They'll only find an accident.'

'But they won't believe it.'

'They won't be able to prove any different,' Matt insisted.

After another pause Yola said almost without emotion, 'If he got the horse clean away . . . if someone else has him now, and he's on his way back to Teller . . . they'll know we had Chrysalis here. We'll be arrested for that.'

'Hochner wasn't going to say he'd stolen the horse from here.'

'But you wouldn't listen.' Yola suddenly flared into anger of her own. 'He was right all the time. We should have let him go. We'd have lost Chrysalis . . . but this way we're in terrible trouble, they'll never believe he died by accident, we'll have the whole FBI here and we'll end up . . . we'll end up in . . .'

'Shut up,' Matt said. 'Shut up.'

'He might not be dead yet . . . can't we go and stop it?' Her voice was urgent, beseeching.

'And have him accuse us of attempted murder? Don't be such a fool. No one can prove it isn't an accident, can they? Can they?'

'I suppose not . . .'

'So you leave him, Yola. You just leave him. He had his chance. I gave him his chance . . . You just wait for some of the guests to see the smoke and come and tell you, like we said. Don't you try going up there. Just don't try it.'

'No . . .'

'And I'm going back on the mountain with the wranglers. Chrysalis went across the bridge. His tracks are there. Well . . . I'm going tracking. Mr Clever Hochner might be bluffing all along the line. He might have Chrysalis tied to some tree up there, and he might not have told anyone where he is, and no one will come asking.' He convinced himself that this view of things was reasonable, and in the end Yola halfway agreed.

'We'll have to tell Uncle Bark,' she said finally.

There was a blank pause while they considered this.

'He'll blow his top,' Matt said gloomily. 'After all that planning.'

'He'll have to know,' Yola said.

'I'll call him this evening, if we have to. But we might have found Chrysalis by then.'

'I sure hope so . . .'

Matt went away then on his search, and presently, after Yola had left to go back to the ranch house, there was continued silence on the tape.

Walt switched the recorder off and looked across at me with a complete absence of expression.

'What did they do?'

I told him.

'Would it have passed as an accident?'

'I expect so. Neat little picture: man lighting cigarette, throws match absentmindedly in tub of pep instead of waste basket, panics, spills the stuff, steps wildly back from flames, trips over stove and knocks himself out. Bingo.'

'Do you smoke, though?'

'Sometimes. They used my own pack from the bed-side table. And my own matches. It was impulsive, unpremeditated. They just looked round and used what came to hand. They're quite good at it.'

'Lucky you woke up in time,' Walt said.

'I suppose so.' I shut my eyes and wondered how he would react if I asked him to go out for some codeine.

'I've worked with one or two people like you before,' he said. 'And I can't say I like it.'

'Thanks,' I said sardonically. No pills.

'With your kind,' he said, 'dying comes easy. It's living takes the guts.'

I opened my eyes. He was watching me steadily, his sober face removing any possibility that he was intending to be funny.

'How are you on guts?' he asked.

'Fresh out.'

He sighed deeply. 'That figures.'

'Walt . . .' I began.

'It struck me first last night, on the mountain. You were sure anxious about Chrysalis, but you didn't give a goddam about falling off the top yourself. It made me freeze just to watch you leading him along that ledge . . . and you came back as calm as if it had been your own yard.'

He was apologizing, in his indirect way, for his startling appearance on the path.

'Walt,' I said, half smiling. 'Will you go get me something for a headache?'

Eleven

EUNICE, LYNNIE, Sam Kitchens, and stud groom Chub Lodovski leaned in a row on the rail of the stallions' paddock at Midway and watched Chrysalis eat Kentucky grass with opinions varying from Lodovski's enthusiasm to Eunice's resignation.

The half-a-million pounds' worth looked none the worse for his trip up the Tetons. Better than on the ranch, as Sam Kitchens had removed all the Wyoming dust from his coat on the journey back, and the bay hide shone with glittering good health in the sunshine. There wasn't, Lodovski assured me, the slightest chance of his going missing again.

Batteries of photographers and pressmen had come and gone: the stallion had been 'found' straying on the land of a friend of Dave Teller's about thirty miles from where he had disappeared. All the excitement was over.

I walked back to Dave's house with Eunice and Lynnie, and Eunice poured me a drink which was four-fifths whisky and one-fifth ice.

'Who put you through what meat grinder?' she said. 'You look like a honeymoon couple on the tenth night.'

Sam Hengelman had driven into Midway with Chrysalis at lunchtime (Tuesday). I had flown to New York with Walt the day before, and had just back-tracked to Lexington, in time to catch the tail end of Eunice interviewing the press. Several of that hard-bitten fraternity had tottered out past me with poleaxed expressions and Lynnie had been halfway through a fit of giggles.

I made inroads into the hefty drink.

'I could do with a good long sleep,' I admitted. 'If you could give me a bed? Or there's the motel . . .'

'Stay here,' Eunice said abruptly. 'Of course you're staying here.'

I looked from her to Lynnie. I couldn't stay in the house with one alone: perfectly proper with both. Silly.

'Thanks, then. And I must call Dave, in England.'

Dave, still in hospital, sounded incredulous.

'I heard it on a news flash, not half an hour ago,' he said. 'Chrysalis just plain turned up.'

'He sure did,' I said dryly.

'Where had he been?'

'It's a long story,' I said, 'and wires have ears. But the expenses stand right now at somewhere near six thousand three hundred dollars. Is that enough for you, or do you want to go on for some answers?'

'To what questions, fella?' He sounded uncertain.

'To why Chrysalis was hi-jacked, and why you fell in the river. And another thing: do you want Allyx back?'

'For God's sake . . . do you know where he is?'

'No. But maybe I could find him. However, if I do, and we get as positive an identification as on Chrysalis, the insurance money on Allyx will have to be repaid to Buttress Life. That will be the equivalent of buying him all over again. He's three years older now, and you'll have lost three crops of foals. He may not be a good proposition for you or your syndicate any more. In which case you might prefer not to have him found. It's up to you.'

'Jeez,' he said.

'Will you think it over, and call back?' I suggested. 'Your wife and Lynnie are filling me up with food and drinks, and I guess

I'll be staying here tonight. But if you want me to go on, will you clear it with Keeble? I'm due back at my desk at nine AM next Monday morning, and I might not make it.'

'Sure,' he said, somewhat weakly, and I handed the receiver to Eunice.

'How's it going, honey?' she said, and I took a good swallow, put my head back on the chair, and listened to her long-married-wifely conversation with my eyes shut.

'Don't ask me how he did it, Dave, I don't know. All I know is he rang from New York yesterday afternoon and asked me for the name of any close friend of ours who was influential and respected, preferably high up in horsebreeding circles, and whose word would be taken as gospel by the press. So, after a rake around I said I guessed Jeff Roots fitted the bill; and lo and behold Chrysalis turned up on Jeff's land this morning . . . Yeah, the horse is as good as new; wherever he's been they've treated him right . . . Look, Dave, surely enough's enough? I heard what Gene said about finding Allyx. Well, don't do it. We need Allyx like a dose of clap. And your boy here is no goddam Hercules, a puff of wind would knock him off, the way he's come back . . . Lynnie's fine, sure. We're taking a trip tomorrow out to California. I'll measure up the curtains for the new place, things like that, and Lynnie can have some days on the beach and maybe try some surfing with those de Vesey boys. So look, why don't we take Gene with us, huh? . . . Sure, I've made reservations at The Vacationer in Santa Barbara . . . they're bound to have another room . . .'

I listened to her plans with disappointment. If I wanted to laze anywhere, it was right where I was, on the Midway Farm. By the peaceful pool in the quiet green garden, sleeping, drinking, and looking at Lynnie.

Eunice put down the receiver, and we had dinner, and late in the evening Dave rang through again.

'Gene?' he said. 'Now listen, fella. Apart from curiosity, is there any good reason for finding those answers you talked about?'

'Forestalling repetition,' I said promptly.

'No more stolen stallions and no more attacks on me?'

'That's right.'

There was a pause.

'I'll buy the answers, then,' he said. 'If you can get them. And as for Allyx . . . if you think there's any chance of finding him alive and vigorous, then I guess I'm morally obliged to give you the go-ahead. I'd have to syndicate him all over again, of course. He'll be twelve now. That would give him only about six to eight more years of high potency . . . But his get from before his disappearance are winning all over Europe. Business-wise I'm not too happy about those three lost years. But blood-wise, it would be criminal not to try to get him back.'

'All right,' I said. 'I'll see what I can do.'

'What you spent on finding Chrysalis is less than his fee for covering a single mare. You've a free hand again for Allyx.'

'Right,' I said.

'Sim Keeble says you've got seven days' extension of leave. Something about it being due to you anyway, from a week you were entitled to at Christmas and didn't take.'

'I'd forgotten about that.'

'I guess I could fix it with him for more, if the extra week isn't enough.'

'If I haven't finished by then I'll have failed anyway, and might as well go home.'

'Oh.' He sounded disappointed. 'Very well, we'll leave it like that for the present.' He cleared his throat. 'Eunice didn't seem to think you looked too well.'

'The boy on the punt who knocked you out did the same thing for me.'

'Gene!' His voice was shocked.

'Yeah. Don't tell my boss I'm that incompetent. Though come to think of it, he knows.'

He laughed. 'When you find that boy again give him a one-two from both of us.'

'Sure,' I said. But I'd been taught my job by cerebral people who didn't reckon a screener would ever have to fight for his life, and by the time I proved them wrong I was too old to become expert at boxing or judo, even if I'd liked the idea, which I didn't. I had learnt instead to shoot straight, and the Luger had in the past three years extricated me unharmed from two sticky situations. But in a stand-up hand-to-hand affair with that young bull Matt Clive I would be a five hundred to one loser, and 'giving him a one-two from both of us' in any physical sense was a very dim possibility indeed.

'Keep in touch, fella,' Dave said.

'Sure,' I answered again, meaning it as little: and we rang off.

Curled opposite in a tomato armchair, Eunice said gloomily, 'I gather we're stuck with that bloody Allyx.'

'Only if we find him.'

'Oh, you'll do that, blast you.' Her bitterness was so marked that Lynnie stared at her. Too young to understand, I thought, that it wasn't me particularly that Eunice wanted to hurt, but life in general.

They went upstairs shortly afterwards murmuring about California in the morning, and I switched off the light and sat in near darkness, finishing the fourth of Eunice's massive ideas on drink and working out the questions I would ask the next day. I could find Allyx on paper, if I were lucky: but he could hardly turn up loose after three years. Three weeks had been strictly the limit. The whole thing might have to be more orthodox, more public. And I wouldn't again, I decided mildly, put myself within accident reach of the murderous Clives.

After a while I deserted the last half of the drink and wandered upstairs to the spacious air-conditioned room Eunice had given me. With a tired hand I switched on the light inside the door, and yellow pools in frilly shades shone out on brown and gold and white furnishings.

One splash of jarring bright pink. Eunice herself, in a fluffy trimmed wrapper, was lying on my bed.

I walked slowly across the thick white carpet and sat beside her on the white spotted muslin coverlet.

'What do you want?' I said gently.

'What do you think?'

I shook my head.

'Does that mean no?' Her voice was abruptly matter of fact.

'I'm afraid it does,' I said.

'You said you weren't queer.'

'Well . . . I'm not.' I smiled at her. 'But I do have one unbreakable rule.'

'And that is?'

'Not to sleep with the wives . . . or daughters . . . of the men I work for.'

She sat bolt upright so that her face was close to mine. Her eyes had the usual contracted pupils of the quarter drunk.

'That includes Lynnie,' she said.

'Yes. It does.'

'Well, I'll be damned. You mean that night you spent in New York with her you didn't even try . . .'

'It wouldn't have been much good if I had,' I said, half laughing.

'Don't you believe it. She never takes her eyes off you, and when you were away she talked about nothing else.'

I stared at her in real surprise. 'You must be wrong.'

'I wasn't born yesterday,' she said gloomily. 'She has two photographs of you as well.'

'What photographs?' I was staggered.

'Some her brother took. That day on the river.'

'But she shouldn't . . .'

'Maybe she shouldn't,' Eunice said dryly. 'But she does.' She swung her legs carelessly around to sit on the edge of the bed beside me and I saw that for someone bent on seduction she had come well wrapped up.

'You expected me to say no,' I said.

She made a face. 'I thought you might. But it was worth a try.'

'Eunice, you're nuts,' I said.

'I'm bored,' she said explosively, and with an undoubted depth of unbearable truth.

'That puts me into the golf and bridge category.'

She was still playing games.

'At least you're goddam human,' she said, her mouth cracking into a smile. 'More than you can say about most men.'

'What do you like best about moving to California?' I asked.

She stared. 'Your mind's like a bloody grasshopper. What has that to do with sex?'

'You tell me, and I'll tell you.'

'For God's sake . . .' But she made some effort at concentrating, and in the end came up with the answer I had been most expecting.

'Fixing up the rooms, I guess.'

'You did all these . . .' I waved my hand around, embracing the house.

'Yeah, I did. So what?'

'So why don't you start in business, doing it for other people?'

She half laughed, ridiculing the idea, and half clung to it: and I knew she'd thought of it in the past, because I hadn't surprised her.

'I'm no bloody genius.'

'You have an eye for colour. More than that: for mood. This is the most comforting house I've ever been in.'

'Comforting?' she said, puzzled.

'Yeah. Laugh, clown, laugh. That sort of thing. You can fill other people even though you feel empty yourself.'

Tears welled up in her grey-green eyes, and she shut the lids. Her voice remained normal.

'How do you know?'

'I know.'

After a pause, she said, 'And I suppose what it has to do with sex is that interior decorating would be a suitable sublimation for a middle-aged woman whose physical attraction is fading faster than her appetite . . .' The bitterness came from long acquaintance with the jargon and its point of view.

'No,' I said mildly. 'The opposite.'

'Huh?' She opened her eyes. They were wet and shiny.

'Playing games is easier than working.'

'Spell it out,' she said. 'You talk in goddam riddles.'

'Sex . . . this sort of casual sex . . .' I patted the bed where she'd lain, 'can be a way of running away from real effort. A lover may be a sublimation of a deeper need. People who can't face the demands of one may opt for passing the time with the other.'

'For Christ's sake . . . I don't understand a bloody word.' She shut her eyes and lay flat back across the bed.

'Thousands of people never try anything serious because they're afraid of failing,' I said.

She swallowed, and after a pause said, 'And what if you do bloody fail? What then?'

I didn't answer her, and after a while she repeated the question insistently.

'Tell me what you do if you fail?'

'I haven't got that one licked myself, yet.'

'Oh.' She laughed weakly. 'Oh God. The blind leading the blind. Just like the whole bloody human race.'

'Yeah.' I sighed and stood up. 'We all stumble along in the dark, and that's a fact.'

'I don't know if you'll believe it, but I've been utterly bloody faithful to Dave . . . except for this . . .'

'I'm sure of it,' I said.

She got to her feet and stood swaying slightly.

'I guess I'm tight.'

'Better than loose,' I said smiling.

'For God's sake, spare me goddam puns at one o'clock in the morning. I suppose if you're looking for that so and so Allyx there's no chance of you coming to California?'

'I wish there were.'

'Goddam liar,' she said vaguely. 'Goodnight.'

She made straight for the door and didn't look back.

I drove them to the airport in the morning. Eunice had lent me her car and the house for as long as I needed them, and had passed off her overnight visit with one sarcastic dig at breakfast.

'Better undersexed than sorry.'

'What?' said Lynnie.

'Eunice is offering a solution to the population explosion,' I explained.

Lynnie giggled. Eunice showed me a double row of teeth and told me to pass the cream.

When I'd seen them off I followed a local road map and Eunice's inaccurate directions, and eventually arrived at the Perry Stud Farm, home of Jefferson L. Roots, chairman, among other things, of the Blood-horse Breeders' Association. A houseboy in a spotless white coat showed me through the house and on to the patio: a house made of large cool concrete boxes, with rough-cast white walls and bare golden wood floors. The patio was shaded by a vine trained across a trellis. There was a glass and metal table, and low comfortable lounging chairs around it. From one of these Jeff Roots extricated himself and held out a welcoming hand.

He was a thick man with a paunch which had defied health

farms, and he worried about his weight. His manner had the gentle, deprecating ease of the really tough American; the power was inside, discernible but purring, like the engine in a Rolls. He was dressed in a tropical-weight city suit, and while I was there an efficient girl secretary came to remind him that time and his connection to Miami would wait for no man.

'A drink?' he suggested. 'It's a hot day already. What would you like?'

'Lime juice?' I asked. 'Or lemon.'

I got lime, squeezed fresh on to crushed ice. My host drank sugar-free tonic water and made a face over it.

'Just the smell of french fries and I'm a size larger in shirts,' he complained.

'Why worry?' I said.

'Ever heard of hypertension?'

'Thin people can have it too.'

'Tell that to the birds . . . or rather, tell it to my wife. She starves me.' He swirled his glass gloomily, ice and lemon rising perilously to the rim. 'So, anyway, Mr Hawkins, how can I help you today?'

He pushed a folded newspaper across the table and pointed at it with an appreciative smile.

'Chrysalis cocooned,' the headlines said. And underneath, in smaller letters, 'High price stallion loses liberty, corralled at Perry, reshipped to Midway. And are the mares there glad, or are they? Our tip is syndicators breathe again.' There was a picture of Chrysalis in his paddock, some mention of Dave's leg, and a few snide remarks about the police and the local horse folks who hadn't been able to spot a million dollars at ten paces.

'Where did you rustle him up from?' Roots asked. 'Sam Hengelman wouldn't say. Most unlike him.'

'Sam was an accessory to a conjuring trick. A little matter of substitution. We left a horse and took a horse . . . I guess he didn't want to talk himself into trouble.'

'And naturally you paid him.'

'Er, yes,' I agreed. 'So we did.'

'But I gather from your call that it's not about Chrysalis that you want to see me now?'

'No. It's about Allyx.'

'*Allyx?*'

'Yes, the other stallion which . . .'

'I know about all that,' he interrupted. 'They turned the whole state upside down looking for him and they found just as much trace as they did of Chrysalis.'

'Do you by any chance remember, ten years ago, another horse called Showman?'

'Showman? Showman? He got loose from a groom who was supposed to be exercising him, or something like that, and was killed in the Appalachians.'

'How certain was the identification?'

He put his tonic water down carefully on the table.

'Are you suggesting he's still alive?'

'I just wondered,' I said mildly. 'From what I've been told, they found a dead horse two years after Showman vanished. But although he was in a high state of decomposition, he'd only been dead about three months. So it easily might *not* have been Showman, just somewhat like him in colour and size.'

'And if it wasn't?'

'We might just possibly turn him up with Allyx.'

'Have you . . .' he cleared his throat. 'Have you any idea where they . . . er . . . might be . . . turned up?'

'I'm afraid not. Not yet.'

'They weren't . . . wherever you found Chrysalis?'

'No. That was only a shipping station, so to speak. Chrysalis was intended to go on somewhere else.'

'And at that somewhere else, one might find . . .?'

'There's a good chance, I think.'

'They might have been shipped abroad again. Down to Mexico or South America.'

'It's possible; but I'm inclined against it, on the whole.' Uncle Bark, whoever he was, lived somewhere in the States. Yola had not needed to call the overseas operator to get through to him, on the telephone. She hadn't even made it person to person.

'The whole thing seems so extraordinary,' Roots said, shaking his head. 'Some nut going around stealing stallions whose value at once drops to zero, because he can't admit he's got them. Do you think some fanatic somewhere is conducting experiments? Trying to produce a super-horse? Or how about a criminal syndicate all getting their mares covered by bluest blood stallions at donkey prices? . . . No, that wouldn't work, they'd never be able to sell the foals for stud, they wouldn't be able to cash in on the blood lines . . .'

'I think it's a good deal simpler than either of those,' I said, smiling. 'Much more down to earth.'

'Then what?'

I told him.

He chewed it over and I drank my lime juice.

'Anyway,' I said. 'I thought I'd try along those lines, and see if it leads anywhere.'

'It's fantastic,' Roots said. 'And I hope to God you're wrong.'

I laughed. 'Yes, I can see that.'

'It'll take you months to plough through all that work yourself . . . and I don't suppose you have too close a knowledge of the thoroughbred scene over here . . . so why don't I get you some help?'

'I'd be very grateful.'

There was an outside extension telephone close to his chair. He lifted the receiver and pressed buttons. I listened to him arranging with the publishers of a leading horse journal for me to have the run of their files and the temporary services of two long-memoried assistants.

'That's fixed, then,' he said, standing up. 'The office is on North Broadway, along in Lexington. I guess you'll let me know how you make out?'

'I certainly will.'

'Dave and Eunice . . . they're great guys.'

'They are.'

'Give her my best,' he said, looking at his watch.

'She's gone to California . . .'

'The new place?'

I nodded.

'Crazy idea of Dave's, moving to the coast. The centre of the bloodstock industry is right here in Lexington, and this is the place to be.'

I made the sort of non-critical, non-committal noise in my throat necessary on such occasions, and Jeff Roots thrust out a rounded hand.

'I have this stockholders' meeting in Miami,' he said, apologetically, and he walked with me through the house to where his secretary waited in a Cadillac parked beside Eunice's Toronado Oldsmobile.

At the newspaper offices, I found, anything Jeff Roots wanted done was done whole-heartedly and at the double. My two temporary assistants proved to be an elderly man who spent most of his time compiling an annual stallion register, and a maiden lady in her fifties whose horse face and crisp masculine voice were easy to take, as she had an unexpectedly sweet smile and a phenomenal memory.

When I explained what I was looking for they both stared at me in dumb-struck silence.

'Isn't it possible?' I asked.

Mr Harris and Miss Britt recovered themselves and said they guessed so.

'And while we're at it, we might make a list of anyone whose name or nickname might be Bark. Or Bart, perhaps; though I think it's Bark.'

Miss Britt promptly reeled off six names, all Barkleys, living in and around Lexington.

'Maybe that's not such a good idea,' I sighed.

'No harm in it,' Miss Britt said briskly. 'We can make all the lists simultaneously.'

She and Mr Harris went into a huddle and from there to the reference room, and were shortly up to their elbows in papers and books. They told me to smoke and wait, which I did all day.

At five o'clock they came across with the results.

'This is the best we can do,' Miss Britt said doubtfully. 'There are well over three thousand stallions at stud in the States, you see. You asked us to sort out any whose fees had risen steadily over the past eight or nine years . . . there are two hundred and nine of them.' She put a closely typed list in front of me.

'Next, you wanted the names of any stallions who had been conspicuously more successful at stud than one would have expected from their own breeding. There are two hundred and eighty-two of those.' She gave me a second sheet.

'Next, you wanted to know if any of this year's two-year-olds had proved conspicuously better at racing than one would normally have expected from their breeding. There are twenty-nine of those.' She added the third list.

'And lastly, the people who could be called Bark . . . thirty-two of them. From the Bar K Ranch to Barry Kyle.'

'You've done wonders,' I said sincerely. 'I suppose it's too much to hope that any one farm is concerned on all four lists?'

'Most of the stallions on the first list are the same as those on the second. That stands to reason. But none of the sires of the exceptional two-year-olds are on either of the first two lists. And none of the two-year-olds were bred by any of the Barks.' Both

416

of them looked downcast at such negative results after all their work.

'Never mind,' I said. 'We'll try another way tomorrow.'

Miss Britt snorted, which I interpreted as agreement. 'Rome wasn't built in a day,' she said, nodding. Mr Harris seemed to doubt that this particular Rome could be built at all with the materials available, but he turned up uncomplaining at nine the following morning, and they both dived in again, on new permutations.

By noon the first two lists had been reduced to twenty. We all adjourned for a sandwich. At two the searching began again. At three ten Miss Britt gasped sharply and her eyes went wide. She scribbled quickly on a fresh piece of paper, considered the result with her head on one side, and then looked across to me.

'Well . . .' she said. 'Well . . .' The words wouldn't come.

'You've found them,' I said.

She nodded, only half believing it.

'Cross-checking them all by where they raced, their years of purchase, their markings and their approximate ages, as you asked . . . we came up with twelve possibles which appeared on the first two lists. And one of the sires of the two-year-olds fits your requirements and comes from the same farm as one of the first twelve. Er . . . do you follow me?'

'On your heels,' I said, smiling.

Mr Harris and I both joined her and looked over her shoulder at what she had written.

'Moviemaker, aged fourteen years; present stud fee ten thousand dollars.

'Centigrade, aged twelve years; this year's stud fee fifteen hundred dollars, fee next year twenty-five hundred.

'Both standing at Orpheus Farm, Los Caillos.

'The property of Culham James Offen.'

Moviemaker and Centigrade: Showman and Allyx. As clear as a frosty sky.

Stallions were normally booked for thirty to forty mares each breeding season. Forty mares at ten thousand dollars a throw meant four hundred thousand dollars every year, give or take a live foal or two. Moviemaker had cost one hundred and fifty thousand dollars at public auction ten years ago, according to Miss Britt's researches. Since then Offen had been paid somewhere near two-and-a-half million dollars in stud fees.

Centigrade had been bought for a hundred thousand dollars at Keneland sales. At twenty-five hundred a time he would earn that hundred thousand next year alone. And nothing was more likely than that he too would rise to a much higher fee.

'Culham James Offen is so well regarded,' Miss Britt said in consternation. 'I simply can't believe it. He's accepted as one of the top rank breeders.'

'The only thing is, of course,' said Mr Harris, regretfully, 'that there's no connection with the name Bark.'

Miss Britt looked at me and her smile shone out sweet and triumphant.

'But there is, isn't there? Mr Harris, you're no musician. Haven't you ever heard of Orpheus in the Underworld . . . by Offenbach?'

Twelve

WALT SAID 'For God's sake' four times and admitted Buttress Life might be willing to send him from coast to coast if Allyx were the pot of gold at the end of the rainbow.

'Los Caillos is a short distance north-east of Los Angeles,' I said. 'I thought of staying a bit farther north, on the coast.'

'If you like.'

'Come to The Vacationer, Grand Beach, Santa Barbara, then. I'll meet you there tomorrow.'

He repeated the address. 'Who's paying?' he said.

'Buttress Life and Dave Teller can fight it out between them. I'll put the motel on Teller's expenses. Can you wring the fare out of your office?'

'I guess so.' His sigh came wearily over the wire. 'My wife and kids aren't going to like it. I was fixing to take them on a picnic this Sunday.'

'Postpone it a week,' I suggested.

'It's been postponed twice already, on your account.'

'Oh.'

After a short pause, he said, 'Around six, tomorrow, local time. That do?'

'That would do very well.'

'See you,' he said briefly, and put down his receiver with a crash. I returned the Teller instrument more kindly to its cradle and surveyed the green and tomato room.

Nothing to do.

Mixed a drink with precision, and drank it. Wandered down to the pool, thought about a swim in the dusk, and couldn't be bothered to undress. Went back to the house, and ate a dinner cooked and served by Eva, who chattered so long in her pleasure at having someone to speak to in her own language that I heartily regretted I'd ever used it. Wished desperately she would stop and go away, and when at last she did, that was no good either.

Tried to read and turned six pages without taking in a word. Wandered restlessly again into the black velvet deep green garden, and sat in one of the chairs by the pool, looking at darkness inside and out. Unreasonable, I thought drearily, that I shouldn't have recovered normally from losing Caroline, that I didn't value the freedom other men envied, that I couldn't be content with all I had: cruel that depression was no respecter of status or achievement and struck so deep that no worldly success could alleviate it.

Great fame, universal honour, droves of personal friends had demonstrably failed to save a whole string of geniuses from its clutches, and every year it bagged its thousands from unimportant people like me who would never see their name in print or lights, and didn't necessarily want to. Probably depression was an illness as definite as jaundice, and one day they would inoculate babies against it. I supposed I could count myself lucky not to have had it in its acute form, where its grey-black octopus tentacles reached out and sucked into every corner of the spirit until quite quickly life became literally unbearable, and the high jump suddenly presented itself with blinding clarity as the only logical, the only possible relief.

I wouldn't come to that day, if I could help it. I would *not*.

The Vacationer was right down on the beach, with the sound of the bright blue Pacific creeping in a murmur under the transistors, the air-conditioning, the civilized chatter, the squalling of children, and the revving of cars. There were no ocean rooms left. Walt and I, next door to each other, overlooked the parking lot.

Eunice and Lynnie were out when I arrived and still out when Walt checked in at six, but they were back when I went down with him for a drink before dinner. I had left a note at the desk for Eunice, but I hadn't told Walt she would be there. He stopped dead in his tracks when he saw her sitting with Lynnie, and turned on me a narrow-eyed composite glance of dislike and anger. If I'd told him she was to be with us, he wouldn't have come: he knew that I knew it. He was entitled to his rage.

Eunice was, however, the wife of a very good client of his firm. He swallowed his feelings like a pill, and chased them down with a double bourbon in silence. Eunice and Lynnie were on frosted-looking daiquiris and happy with it. They both looked marvellous, with honey-brown skin and a languorous and sun-filled way of moving. Eunice wore fluorescent green with bits of gold at anatomical points like ears, wrists, and feet. Lynnie had acquired a locally grown hot pink-orange tunic, and the few straps of her sandals seemed to be made of polished semi-precious stones. Even Walt, after a while, couldn't take his eyes away from them for long.

We had dinner outside, under a trellis lit by hundreds of tiny multi-coloured lights, on a shallow terrace which led directly out on to the sand. Eunice's language was for once as soft as the sea breeze, and consequently as a social evening it developed into a reasonable success.

Over the coffee I asked Eunice with a casualness which drew a piercing glance from Walt, 'Have you by any chance heard of a racehorse breeder called Culham James Offen?'

'Heard of him,' she said. 'Of course I have. Everyone has.'

'I haven't,' Walt said flatly. One couldn't expect complete capitulation. He was doing very well.

'I mean, everyone in the bloodstock world would have heard

of him,' Eunice explained without obvious patience. 'He has that terrifically successful stallion Moviemaker. And Dave says one ought to think of sending mares to another one of his, Centigrade . . . The first crop of foals is winning two-year-old races this season all over the place. But quite apart from that,' she smiled broadly, 'I guess we'll be seeing a good deal of him from now on.'

'Er . . . why?' I asked diffidently.

'Our new place is right next to his.'

Walt's mouth fell open and I stopped stirring my coffee.

'What did you say?' I said, feeling my eyes go blank, as I knew they always did under shock.

'Our new place, where we're moving to, is right across the road from Offen. We can see his paddocks from our bedroom windows.' I gaped in fascination at Eunice while she outlined in such blissful ignorance the reason for the attempted murder of her husband. He himself had told me that the executors of the late Davis L. Davis had accepted his tender for the farm only recently, during the week before our momentous trip on the river. So the something 'goddam stupid' which had happened to Yola and Matt Clive's scheme was that they had discovered that of all the people on earth it was to be Dave Teller who was to be Offen's new close neighbour. They had discovered it *after* they'd hi-jacked the horse, or they wouldn't have gone ahead with the plan.

'Why are you laughing?' Eunice asked, frowning. 'What's so funny?'

'It's not funny,' I agreed, straightening my face, 'Far from it. Do you know Culham James personally?'

'Not yet. Does it matter?' She still looked puzzled.

'It would be wiser not to make close friends with him in too much of a hurry.'

'Why not?'

'Might prove a prickly flower.' I had a mental vision of Dave looking out of his bedroom window day after day, looking over to the paddocks where Showman and Allyx were let out to graze. He might never have recognized them. But also he might. Culham James simply couldn't take the risk. Yola and Matt had flown immediately to England to dispose of Dave a long way from the real scene of danger.

While Allyx remained at Orpheus Farm and Dave continued making active plans to move alongside, the explosive situation would still exist. Though Matt Clive might have given up temporarily, I fervently hoped that Radnor-Halley wouldn't let their vigilance slide a millimetre. A call to Keeble would be wise . . . even at California–London rates.

'I'm going for a walk on the shore,' said Lynnie, kicking off the pebbly sandals. 'Who's coming?'

I beat Walt to it by quicker reflexes, and collected a grim look from him as I left him alone with Eunice. Lynnie remarked on it, grinning as we ambled silently away on the trickling sand.

'He's put off by the bloodies,' I explained. 'That's all.'

'She says it less often over here,' Lynnie commented. 'And she doesn't drink, except one or two before lunch, until after we've changed in the evening. Why is that, do you think?'

'She's escaped from the Lexington cage.'

'That heavenly house . . . a cage?'

'Uh huh.'

'The new one isn't half so beautiful,' she protested.

'It will be, when Eunice has finished. And then the walls will close in again.'

'Another cage, do you mean?' She sounded uncertain.

'Another cage,' I agreed.

'Life can't be just escaping from one cage and ending up in another,' she said explosively, repudiating violently so bleak a vision.

'Everyone lives inside bars,' I said. 'The trick is not to want to get out.'

'Stop it,' she said in distress. 'I don't want to hear that.'

'They used to keep linnets as pets,' I said. 'But there aren't any linnets in cages any more. Budgerigars instead. You'll be all right, little linnet.'

'I never know when you're being serious.'

'Always.'

'But half the time what you say is so . . . so crazy.'

'Life is serious, life is crazy. Anything crazy is serious, and everything serious is crazy . . . I'll race you along to that beach hut.'

She beat me to it in her bare feet, and leaned against the rough wooden wall laughing and getting her breath back while I tipped half-a-ton of sand out of my shoes. We walked on a little farther, and then sat down in the warm night and looked out across the shadowy peaceful ocean. No land between us and Japan, half a world away.

'Did you come out here to be with . . . us, or to find Allyx?' she said.

'Both.'

She shook her head. 'You brought Walt. That makes it to find Allyx.'

'Walt would have chosen to stay somewhere else,' I said, smiling. 'So California for Allyx, Santa Barbara for you. Satisfied?'

She murmured something unintelligible, and we sat in silence while she scuffed sand into a heap with her toes.

'Will you find him, do you think?' she asked in the end.

'Allyx? We might do.'

'When, roughly?'

'I don't know. Tomorrow, maybe.'

'And then . . . you'll go home?'

'I guess.'

'Back to an office . . .' She swept out an arm, embracing the wide sky. Back to an office, I thought coldly: and to the perpetual digging into people's privacy, to the occasional snaring of

424

a bent applicant, to drizzle, to Putney, to the vacuum of the flat. To, in short, my normal life. The trick was not to want to slip through the bars.

'What are you going to do, now that you've left school?' I asked.

She sucked in a breath. 'After this, all the old things seem horribly dreary.'

'They'll soon give Dave a walking plaster . . .'

'I *know*,' she wailed. 'Don't think I don't know. I was supposed to be starting a secretarial course in September . . . I utterly don't want to, any more. Why can't everyone just live on the beach and be warm all the time . . .' She rocked with her arms laced round her bent-up knees.

'Not enough beach.'

She giggled. 'You are just about the least romantic man alive. Comes of being a civil servant, I suppose. Like Daddy.'

In time we walked back along by the edge of the sea and paused when we came level with the motel. She put her hand on my arm and simply stood there waiting. I kissed her forehead, and then her nose, and finally her mouth. It was all very gentle, and utterly unnerving.

'This is no good,' I said, taking my hands from her shoulders. 'No good at all.'

'I've been kissed before,' she said anxiously. 'I really have.'

'That isn't what I meant,' I said, half laughing. 'You'd qualify for a diploma. No . . . it's just, little Lynnie, that we're a long way from home . . . and I never kiss brunettes more than once on a Friday.' I turned away towards the motel and jerked my head for her to follow. The best resolutions in the world would come a cropper faced with something like Lynnie, and immediate flight was the only course. It didn't seem to be popular with Lynnie herself, but I couldn't help that. I walked her briskly up the beach and made a joke about what Walt would be saying to Eunice, and we arrived in reasonable order to find that it was nothing: they were sitting across the table from each other in a miles-apart silence. Eunice gave us a long cool look and Walt one of disillusion, and Lynnie quite unnecessarily blushed, confirming their obvious suspicions. The harmless little walk hadn't been a good idea from any one of four points of view.

Walt and I drove quietly into Orpheus Farm the following morning. He did the talking: a thoroughly professional piece of work, insurance patter at the double. A survey for new fire regulations, he glibly explained, necessitated us seeing over the entire establishment.

We saw. Every stall in every barn, every hay loft, every straw bale, every inch. We saw Moviemaker. We saw Centigrade. We made a great many notes.

Culham James Offen himself escorted us round the coolest barn containing his four prize stallions. A great deal of self-satisfaction sat on his shoulders like an impervious duck's-back mantle. I considered this with uneasy suspicion.

Uncle Bark was not only a man in his fifties with white hair, but he had a grey station wagon in a third of his large garage. I saw Walt giving it a sidelong glance. Undoubtedly it was Uncle Bark who had delivered the Snail Express trailer to old Hagstrom's boy at Rock Springs; and very likely Uncle Bark who had followed Sam Hengelman's van along the turnpike. Impossible to prove, though, at this distance.

The colour of his hair was premature. Very few wrinkles marked the smooth suntanned face, from which white eyebrows stood out like a bracket of snow, nearly meeting over the nose. His eyelashes were also white, but the albino non-pigmentation stopped short of the eyes: not pink, but a clear pale blue.

He carried his head stiffly on a thick muscular neck, and the large body beneath the airy white shirt looked solid more than soft. Not a man to ignore in any company. A physique which teamed naturally with success: and success had given him an arrogance of expression where a decent humility would have been more fitting.

The whole farm had the high gloss of money-no-object. Mathematically precise white-painted wood railings ringed the paddocks, and the approach to the Spanish-style house was land-scaped with watered lawns and palms and an occasional bed full of spiky red flowers with sharp purplish leaves. We didn't pene-trate the house: Walt's fire insurance only stretched to the stabling.

After we'd seen the stallions Offen handed us over to his stud groom, a fair, surprisingly young man he called Kiddo, who had a drawling western voice and an air of having been born with-out urgency. Every second word was 'uh', and his walk was thirty-two frames a second; slow motion.

'Been here long?' I asked him, as he pointed out the spotless foaling stalls.

'Five or six months,' he said, showing no resentment at a per-sonal question; good natured, unsuspicious, no sign of nerves.

'You must be good, to get a job like this so young,' I con-gratulated him.

After a pause he said, 'I got a feeling for horses, see? Mares, they foal down nearly always at night. Comes from having to give birth in the dark out in the wild, you understand?'

'Why in the dark?' asked Walt, puzzled.

Another pause. Not for a deliberate choice of what or what not to say, I realized, but just a moment of waiting while the instinctive knowledge coalesced into words.

'They drop 'em by day, some hungry hyena comes along and kills the foal in the first half hour. Foals, now, they're readier to run at birth than most other critturs, but you've got to give 'em a half hour to dry off.'

'But they don't have to run, here,' Walt protested.

'Nature don't know that,' Kiddo pointed out reasonably. 'Another thing, mares mostly drop their foals pretty quick.

Don't take some of them no time at all. And then, see, I always know when a mare's ready, and most often I go to the stall and make sure she's doing all right.'

'How do you know?' I asked, fascinated.

A much longer pause. Then he said, 'I don't know how I know, I got a feeling for it. I just wake up some nights and think, that Rose is about ready, and I go on out to her, and maybe there she is, not needing a bit of help, or maybe with the cord round the foal's neck, strangling it. I bin with horses, see, all my life.'

'Where were you before you came here?' I asked.

'Uh . . . all over. Had a job in Lexington a while back, but they said I didn't keep good time turning up at work.' He grinned suddenly, a big mischievous lighting-up of the passive patient face. 'Then . . . uh . . . I was with a feller in Maryland . . . he had a barn was falling down and honeysuckle breaking his fences and creeping into his windows, but he sure had some pretty mares and one of them was the dam of the horse who won the Preakness a year back. Though I don't go to the races, myself.'

'Where after Maryland?' I asked.

'Uh . . . here. I seen this ad in the *Blood Horse*, and I wrote. It was a joke, mostly. I never expected to hear a word, knowing this was a big place and everything. But Mr Offen, it seems he didn't want no great business man, just someone with a feeling for the mares . . . and he's keeping me on, he says, though there was two before me he let go after they'd been here a month.'

It didn't seem to worry him. He had the God-will-provide nature which doesn't understand anxiety and never stores up winter nuts. Not that he had any need to. His 'feeling for mares' was in fact priceless: he would probably never cash in on it as he could but he'd never want for a job.

Kiddo watched us go in the same calm friendliness with which he'd shown us round. Walt and I agreed on the way back to Santa Barbara that he was only potentially an opponent. Loyalty might be given to Offen if he demanded it, but at present Kiddo had no idea what was going on.

'Unless,' Walt said thoughtfully, 'he's a brilliant actor.'

I shook my head. 'He wasn't acting. None of the signs.'

Walt looked at me curiously, taking his eyes too long off the road. 'Can you always tell?'

I smiled. 'That's one of those unanswerable questions. I've a feeling for it, like Kiddo with his mares. But if it lets me down sometimes, how am I to know?'

'You'd know soon enough when secrets started leaking to the other side,' Walt pointed out. 'Have you ever passed as clear anyone who turned out to be a spy?'

'Yes.'

'How often?'

'Once.'

'In your first year, I suppose,' Walt said with mild sarcasm.

'In my second year. He was the first serious spy I had to deal with, and I didn't spot him. The counter-espionage chaps turned him up six months later when he'd done a good deal of damage, and the press made the usual scathing remarks about the feebleness of our screening system.'

'Which you took to heart,' Walt said dryly.

'I guess so.'

He drove a mile and then said, 'And now you're so good at it that they beat you up. What do you think about things when that happens?'

'That there's a big fish coming down the pipeline and they want me out of the way.'

'So you look all the harder.' A statement, not a question.

'You might say so. Yes.'

'They'll kill you one of these days.'

I didn't answer. Walt flicked a glance sideways and sighed. 'I suppose you don't care.'

429

'There are a lot of others in the department.'

Walt drove into Santa Barbara without another word, where we joined Eunice and Lynnie in the terrace restaurant for lunch. They had, they said, bought that morning the big bright dangling earrings which swung with every turn of their heads. Lynnie's were scarlet, Eunice's acid green; otherwise identical. Still friends, I thought in some relief. Still in harmony. Whether Eunice would do a small chore for me was, however, another matter.

We had clam chowder with shrimp to follow, and Lynnie said with all this seafood she'd be growing fins. During coffee, when she stood up restlessly and said she was going down to the sea, it was Walt, after a pause, who said he would go with her. She looked at me questioningly, worriedly, and then turned and walked quickly off with him, talking a good deal too brightly.

'Don't you hurt that child,' Eunice said fiercely.

'I don't want to.'

'You're too bloody attractive.'

'Yeah. Charm the birds off the trees,' I agreed sardonically. 'Little wives spill their husbands' secrets into my bloody attractive ears.'

She looked shocked. Quite a change, I thought, from dishing it out.

'You mean you . . . *use* it?'

'Like a can opener. And as a catalyst. Who doesn't? Salesmen, politicians, actors, women, all using it like mad.'

'For God's sake . . .' Her voice was faint, but she was also laughing.

'But not on Lynnie,' I added wryly.

'You didn't need to, I guess. Dragging Dave out of the Thames was a lot more effective.'

I watched Lynnie's and Walt's backs as they reached the tide line.

'So that's why . . .?' I said, almost to myself.

'Hero worship,' Eunice said with barbs. 'Does it give you a kick?'

'Like a mule's in the stomach . . .'

She laughed. 'It's not that you're so madly handsome in any obvious way.'

'No,' I agreed with truth, 'I'm not.'

She looked as if she were going to say more and then thought better of it. I jumped straight in while her mind was still half flirting, knowing, and despising the knowledge, that in that mood she was more likely to do what I asked.

'Has Lynnie still got those photographs of me?'

'Don't worry,' she said sarcastically. 'In a fire, she'd save them first.'

'I'd like Culham James Offen to see them.'

'You'd like *what*? What are you talking about?'

'About you and Lynnie driving over to pay a neighbourly call on Culham James this afternoon, and easily, dearest Eunice, you could tell him about me pulling Dave out of the Thames, and Lynnie could show him my photograph. Especially the one of me sitting by a table outside a pub. That group of all of us.'

She gaped and gasped, and then started thinking.

'You really can't be as pleased with yourself as all that . . . so for God's sake, why?'

'An experiment.'

'That's no answer.'

'Earning my keep at The Vacationer.'

A look of disgust turned down her mouth.

'Finding that bloody horse?'

'I'm afraid so.'

'You don't mean . . . surely you can't mean that Offen has anything to do with it?'

'I'd like to make sure he hasn't.'

'Oh, I see. Well, I guess that's not much to ask. Sure. I'll get Lynnie to come with me.'

431

'And tell him I'm looking for Allyx.'

She gave me a straight assessing stare, and said, 'How about Chrysalis?'

'Whatever you like. Say that Dave employed me to get him back.'

'I don't know why I'm doing it.'

'More interesting than golf?' I suggested.

'Is it a game?' She was sceptical.

'Well . . . like hunting bears,' I smiled.

'Oh, yes.' She nodded sardonically. 'A sport.'

Thirteen

I PARKED a hired car in some scrub off the road leading to Orpheus Farm, and smoked a rare cigarette. The fierce afternoon sun roasted through the metal roof and a water mirage hung in a streak over the dry road. A day for lizards to look for shade. They'd run out of air-conditioned heaps at the hire firms: I'd had to take one of those old-fashioned jobs where you breathed fresh air by opening the window. The air in question was as fresh as last week's news and as hot as tomorrow's.

At five past four Eunice and Lynnie passed unseeingly across my bows, heading back to Santa Barbara. I finished the cigarette and stubbed it out carefully in the flaked chromium ashtray. I looked at my fingernails for ten minutes. No special inspiration. At half past four I started the car, pointed its nose towards Orpheus, and went to call on Uncle Bark.

This time I drove straight up to the house and rang the ornate bell. A houseboy came: all on the same scale as at Jeff Roots's. When he went to find Culham James I followed quietly on his heels, so my host, even if he had meant to, had no chance to say he was out. The houseboy opened the door on to a square comfortable office-sitting room and Culham James was revealed sitting at his desk with a green telephone receiver to his ear.

He gave the houseboy and myself a murderous glare between us which changed to reasonable affability once he'd got control of it. 'I'll call you later,' he said to the telephone. 'A Mr

Hawkins has this minute arrived . . . that's right . . . later then.'
He put down the receiver and raised his eyebrows.

'Did you miss something this morning?' he asked.

'No . . . should we have done?'

He shook his head in mild annoyance. 'I am merely asking
the purpose of this return visit.'

'My colleague and I wanted answers to one or two extra
questions about the precautions you take against fire, especially
as regards those two exceptionally valuable stallions . . . er . . .
Moviemaker and Centigrade.'

Under his suntanned face, behind the white bracket of eyebrows, Culham James Offen was beginning to enjoy a huge
joke. It fizzed like soda water in his pale blue eyes and bubbled
in his throat. He was even having difficulty in preventing himself from sharing it: but after a struggle he had it nailed down
under hatches, and calm with a touch of severity took over. We
went solemnly through the farce of fire precautions, me leaning
on his desk and checking off Walt's solid-sounding inventions
one by one. They mostly had to deal with the amount of super-
vision in the stallions' barn at night. Whether there were any
regular patrols, any dogs loose on watch, any photoelectric
apparatus for detecting opacity, such as heavy smoke?

Offen cleared his throat and answered no to the lot.

'We have the extremely expensive and reliable sprinkler system which you saw this morning,' he pointed out. 'It is thoroughly tested every three months, as I told you earlier.'

'Yes. Thank you, then. I guess that's all.' I shut my notebook.
'You've been most helpful, Mr Offen.'

'You're welcome,' he said. The joke rumbled in his voice, but
was coloured now with unmistakable malice. High time to go, I
thought: and went.

When I got back to The Vacationer some while later I found
Eunice and Lynnie and Walt sitting in a glum row behind empty

glasses. I flopped into a chair opposite them and said, 'Why the mass depression?'

'You're late,' Walt said.

'I told you not to wait for dinner.' I caught a passing waiter on the wing and arranged refills all round.

'We were considering a search party,' Eunice said.

I looked at all three of them more carefully. 'You've been comparing notes,' I said resignedly.

'I think it's terrible of you . . . *wicked*,' Lynnie burst out. 'To have made me go and deliberately . . . *deliberately* . . . put you in such frightful danger.'

'Lynnie stop it. I wasn't in any danger . . . here I am, aren't I?'

'But Walt said . . .'

'Walt needs his brains seen to.'

Walt glared and compressed his mouth into a rigid line. 'You didn't tell me you'd arranged for Offen to know you were the man who took Chrysalis. And you didn't tell me the Clives had tried to kill Mr Teller.'

'And you didn't tell *me*,' Eunice added, 'that the couple in the background of the photograph Lynnie showed Culham Offen had tried to kill you too.'

'Or you'd never have let Lynnie show it to him?'

'No,' she said slowly.

'Just as well I didn't.'

'And you deliberately misled me by saying you wanted to clear Offen. It wasn't true.'

'Er . . . no. But I did want you to behave naturally with him. And anyway, why all the fuss?'

'We thought . . .' Lynnie said in a subdued voice. 'We almost thought . . . as you were gone so long . . . that you . . . that they . . .'

'They didn't,' I pointed out obviously, smiling.

'But won't you please explain why?' Lynnie said. '*Why* did you want me to give you away like that?'

'Several reasons. One was to make Dave safer.'

'I don't see how,' Eunice objected.

'By letting Offen know, and through him the Clives, that we could prove the Clives were in England and beside the Thames on the day of Dave's accident. Murder by accident is only a good idea as long as there's no apparent motive and the murderers have no apparent connection with the victim. We've shown them that we know their motive and their connection, and they must now be aware that if Dave were killed they would be the first suspects. This makes it less likely they will try again.'

'Crikey,' Lynnie said, 'Go on.'

'When Walt and I went to Orpheus Farm this morning saying we were making a survey for new fire precautions, Offen wasn't worried. He didn't know me from Adam then, of course. It was before you showed him my photograph. But he showed no anxiety at all about two strangers turning up on a pretext that he didn't even bother to check. None of the edginess one might have expected if he'd just had one stolen horse pinched back from him, and was in possession of two others standing in his barn. I didn't like it. It didn't feel right.'

'He hasn't got them,' Eunice said with relief. 'I was sure it couldn't possibly be right that Culham Offen would steal horses. I mean, he's *respected*.'

Walt and I exchanged a glance of barely perceptible amusement. To be respected was the best cover in the world for fraud. Fraud, in fact, could rarely exist without it.

'So,' I said, 'I thought it would be helpful if he knew for certain that I was especially interested in Moviemaker and Centigrade, and that I wasn't in fire insurance, but was the man he had to thank for losing Chrysalis. When I went back, after you two had left, he still wasn't worried. On the contrary, he was enjoying the situation. It amused him enormously to think that

I believed I was fooling him. I asked him a lot of questions about the security precautions surrounding Moviemaker and Centigrade, and he was still completely untroubled. So,' I paused, 'it's now quite clear that the two horses standing in his barn called Moviemaker and Centigrade are in actual fact exactly what he says: Moviemaker and Centigrade. He isn't worried about snoopers, he isn't worried about me making clumsy preparations to steal them. He must therefore be confident that any legal proceedings will prove the horses to be the ones he says they are. He'd ambush me if I tried to steal them, and have me in real deep trouble, which would be to him some small compensation for losing Chrysalis.'

Walt nodded briefly.

Eunice said obstinately. 'I think it only proves that you're barking up the wrong damn tree. He isn't worried simply because he isn't guilty of anything.'

'You liked him?'

'Yes,' she said. 'He was bloody sweet.'

Lynnie nodded. 'I thought so too.'

'What did he say when you showed him the photographs?'

'He just glanced at them at first,' Lynnie said. 'And then he took them over to the window. And then he asked me who had taken them, and where, and when. So I told him about the day on the river, and about you and Dave going under the weir . . .'

At the side of my vision Eunice gave me an I-told-you-so smile.

'. . . and he said one or two nice things about you,' Lynnie finished. 'So I told him you came over here to look for Chrysalis, and somehow or other you found him.'

'He asked where you found him,' Eunice nodded. 'But we didn't know. I said you were now trying to find Allyx, and it certainly didn't worry him. I'm sure you must be wrong.'

I smiled at her. She didn't want the horse found, and as an ally she was as reliable as thin ice on a sunny day. I didn't intend to tell her anything in future which I wasn't prepared to have passed on to Offen. Like most law-abiding citizens she had not grasped that a criminal mind didn't show, that an endearing social manner could co-exist with fraud and murder. 'Such a *nice* man,' the neighbours say in bewilderment, when Mr Smith's garden is found to be clogged with throttled ladies. 'Always so pleasant.'

Eunice, propelled by a strong semi-conscious wish for him not to have Allyx, might tell Offen anything, simply because she couldn't visualize a 'sweet' man being deadly. She might also tell him anything propelled by the same impulse which had made her point a gun at me.

'Let's have dinner,' I suggested; and Eunice and Lynnie went away to freshen up.

Walt looked at me thoughtfully, then raised his eyebrows.

I nodded. 'I put a bug on the underside of his desk, two feet from the telephone. I was late back because I was listening. He called Yola and told her about my visit but there wasn't much else. I left the set hidden, and came back here.'

'Do you mean it, that those two horses really are Moviemaker and Centigrade?'

'Sure. He bought them, remember. Openly. At bloodstock sales. And obviously he's kept them. I suppose he never could be certain that some ex-owner would turn up for a visit. Those horses will have been tattooed inside their mouths with an identity number when they first began to race. They have to be, over here, don't they? It'll be quite easy to establish that they're the right two.'

'You don't think Mrs Teller's right . . . that he never had Showman and Allyx after all?'

'I'll play you his call to Yola some time. He had the foresight to whisk those horses away from Orpheus when we got Chrysalis. He was more or less waiting for something like our visit this morning. No flies on Culham James, I'm afraid. Er . . .

Walt, did you give Eunice and Lynnie any details about our jaunt in the Tetons?'

He looked uncomfortable. 'I was annoyed with you.'

'What exactly did you tell them?'

'Not much. I was horrified at Lynnie having shown Offen that picture of the Clives, and when Mrs Teller said you'd planned it I said you must be mad, they'd tried to kill you once already.'

'And you told them how?'

He nodded, not meeting my eyes.

'Did you tell them about the bugs and the wireless set?'

'No.'

'It's important, Walt.'

He looked up. 'I didn't mention them.'

I relaxed. 'How about our mountain walk?'

'No details.'

'Place?'

'I'm pretty sure I mentioned the Tetons.'

Nothing there that would hurt.

'How much did you say about Showman and Allyx?'

'I told them that you'd worked out through the stud books that Offen must have them.'

'Did you say the words "Uncle Bark"?'

He shook his head. 'I'd forgotten about that.'

I sighed. 'Walt. Mrs Teller doesn't want Allyx found any more than she wanted Chrysalis. Let's not entrust the state of the nation to the Indians.'

He flushed a little and compressed his mouth. Eunice and Lynnie came back shortly after, and, though we all four had dinner together it proved a taciturn and not over-friendly affair.

Walt rode up to my room for a conference after the coffee.

'How do we find them?' he said, coming bluntly to the point and easing himself simultaneously into the only armchair.

'They've made us a gift of them, in one way,' I said thought-fully. 'We can send a bunch of lawyers in to query Moviemaker and Centigrade's identity, and get it established beyond doubt that the two Offen showed us are in fact those two horses. He'll be keen for them to do it: and once he's done it, he'll be stuck with them. We will meanwhile do another little vanishing trick with the other two and start our own identification parade on our ground. Once they are established as Allyx and Showman, Offen cannot possibly claim them back.'

'Two objections,' Walt said. 'We don't know where Allyx and Showman are. And if we find them, why not get lawyers into the act right away? Why go to all the danger and trouble of taking them?'

'Same as Chrysalis,' I pointed out. 'The first sign of any real trouble, and they'd be shot. It's not illegal to kill a horse and whisk it smartly off to the dog food people. And vastly more difficult to identify a dead one. Impossible, I'd almost say, for the degree of certainty we need here.'

'Even if we take them, and establish their identity, and every-thing goes smoothly, Offen will still be raking in those colossal stud fees of half a million dollars a year, because we'd never be able to prove that for the past ten years Showman has been sir-ing every foal that's down in the book as Moviemaker's . . .'

I smiled. 'We'll do something about that, once we've sorted out the rest.'

'Which brings us back to square one,' Walt said flatly. 'Where the hell do we start?'

I perched on the window sill and looked down sideways into the brightly lit car park. Coloured bulbs on the face of the motel raised rainbow shimmers on glossy hard tops and struck me as a deeply melancholy commentary on human achievement. Yet I wouldn't have wanted to live without cars or electricity . . . if I'd wanted to live. My room was only two floors up, with none above. Too near the ground. I'd known of a woman who'd jumped from five and bungled it. A gun was better . . .

'Well?' Walt said insistently.

'I'm sorry . . .?' I said vaguely, turning my head back to him.

'Where do we look?'

'Oh . . . yes.'

'On the ranch?'

'Very doubtful, don't you think? They must know that's the first place we'd think of.'

'There's a lot of land there,' he said. 'And a lot of horses to lose them in.'

I shook my head. 'They'd have to keep them in a paddock close to the house. All the rest of the ranch is well named Rocky Mountains, and they couldn't turn them loose for fear of them breaking a leg. We'd better check, though.' I stared unseeingly at the carpet. 'But I guess the horses are with Matt. Offen is at Orpheus Farm, and Yola is tied to the ranch seeing to about thirty guests, so where's Matt?'

'Where indeed,' Walt said gloomily.

'He and Yola don't spend their winters on the ranch because the valley is blocked by snow. She told me that they go south . . . On one of those telephone calls she told Offen they couldn't keep Chrysalis at a place called Pitts, because it wasn't suitable. But that was when they didn't know we were after them . . . when it wasn't an emergency.'

'So somewhere south of the Tetons we find this Pitts, and Matt and the horses will be waiting for us?'

'Yeah.' I smiled briefly. 'Sounds too easy.'

'Easy!' Walt said.

'They must leave a forwarding address for mail,' I pointed out. 'They live a conventional law-abiding life with a longstanding business to give them obvious legal means of support. There must be dozens of people in Jackson who know their winter address.'

'Our Buttress agent could get that, then. First thing in the morning.'

'Fine.'

Walt levered himself out of the armchair and hesitated.

'Come along to my room,' he said. 'I've got a bottle.'

I wasn't sure that I wanted to, but he smiled suddenly, wiping out all resentments, and one didn't kick that sort of olive branch in the teeth.

'Be glad to,' I said.

The smile went deeper and lasted along the passage to his room, which was almost identical to mine. The window looked out on the same cars from a slightly different angle, and he had two armchairs instead of one. There was a bottle of Old Grandad on a round tray with glasses and a water jug, and on his bedside table stood a leather-framed photograph. I picked it up idly while he went to fetch ice from the machine along the passage. Walt with his family. A good-looking woman, a plain girl in her early teens, a thin boy of about ten: all four of them smiling cheerfully into the lens. He came back as I was putting them down.

'I'm sorry about the picnic,' I said.

'Next week will do just as well,' he said. 'We've got the whole of the summer, I guess.'

We sat in the armchairs, drinking slowly. I didn't like bourbon much; but that wasn't the point. He talked casually about the split-level ranch-type house they'd moved into the year before, and how his daughter got along just fine with the folks next door, and how they'd had trouble with the boy's health, he'd had rheumatic fever . . .

'How about your own future, with Buttress Life?' I asked.

'I've gotten about as high as I'll get,' he said with surprising honesty. 'There's only one more step up that I really want, and that's to chief investigator, claims division, and that'll come along next year when the present guy retires.'

He poured more drinks, rubbed his thumb slowly over the round fingertips, and said Amy and the kids were asking him for a pool in their back yard, and that Amy's mother was a problem since Amy's father died last fall, and that he hadn't caught a single ball game last season, he'd been that busy . . .

We sat for more than an hour without mentioning the horses once. He yawned finally and I uncurled myself from the soft chair, putting down the third time empty glass. He said goodnight sleepily with easy friendliness and, for the first time since I'd known him, without tension. Back in my own room, undressing, I wondered how long it would last. Until I made the next unpopular suggestion, I supposed. I didn't know whether to envy him his enclosing domesticity or to feel stifled by it. I did know that I liked him both as a man and as a working companion, moods and all.

The Buttress Life agent in Jackson came through with the Clives' winter address within twenty minutes of Walt calling him: 40159 Pittsville Boulevard, Las Vegas, Nevada.

I remembered Yola's smile at the thought of winter. Las Vegas explained it. Yola liked to gamble.

'What now?' Walt said.

'I'll go on out there and take a look.'

'Alone?' There was a certain amount of anxiety in his voice, which I interpreted as a desire not to be left in Santa Barbara with Eunice.

'We need you here,' I said placatingly. 'And don't tell her where I've gone.'

He gave me a sharp glance. 'I won't.'

We drove in the hired car out to Orpheus Farm, where I showed him where I'd hidden the radio tape recorder between three rocks, with its aerial sticking up through the branches of a scrubby bush. The nearest neatly railed paddock was only feet away; the house, about four hundred yards. We picked up the radio and parked a short distance down the road.

'Supposing he sees us?' Walt said, watching me wind back the reel.

'He'll only think we're watching the farm routine, to know when to pinch Moviemaker. The radio will pick up the bug in his office from at least a quarter mile, but it gets fainter after that. It has to work on the air-vibration system. Not such a good amplification as electricity. Do you ever use them?'

'Bugs?' He shook his head. 'Not often. Cameras with telescopic lenses are better. Catch the claimants walking around on their paralysed legs.' Satisfaction echoed in his voice. Like me, a rogue hunter to the bone.

Smiling to myself, I switched on. Cutting in and out, Culham James' various conversations filled three-quarters of an hour of tape time, but nothing he said was of any use to us. I rewound the reels again and we put the radio in among the rocks, Walt agreeing that he would come back after sunset and listen to the day's take.

He drove me then to the Los Angeles airport, where I hopped on a plane to Las Vegas, arriving mid afternoon. The desert hit like a gust from an oven when they opened the plane doors, and from a nearby building the usual lighted numbers proclaimed to the populace that in the shade, if they could find any, it would be 108.

The air-conditioning at the edge of town motel I booked into was turning itself inside out under the strain, and the Hertz man who presently took my money admitted that this was a little old heatwave, sure thing. Had to expect them, in July. The inconspicuous Pontiac he hired me was this time, however, a cooled one. I drove around for a while to get my bearings, and then took a look at Pittsville Boulevard.

The high numbers ran two miles out of the town, expensive-looking homes along a metalled road with the desert crowding in at their rear. The Clives' house was flanked by others on both sides: not near enough to touch, but too near for the invisible stabling of stallions. The place on Pitts wasn't suitable, as Yola had said.

It was low and white, with a flat roof and a frame of palms and orange trees. Blinds and insect screens blanked out the windows, and the grass on each side of the drive was a pale dry biscuit colour, not green watered like its neighbours. I stopped the car in the roadway opposite and looked it over. Not a leaf moved under the bleaching sun. Ten minutes ticked away. Nothing happened in the street. Inside the car, with the engine stopped, the temperature rose like Christmas prices. I started up again, sucked in the first cold blast from the air-conditioner, and slid on along the way I was heading.

A mile past the Clives' house the metal surface ended, and the road ran out across the desert as a dusty streak of gravel. I turned the car and went back, thinking. The comparative dead-endedness of Pittsville Boulevard explained the almost total lack of traffic past the Clives', and also meant that I couldn't drive past there very often without becoming conspicuous to the neighbours. Keeping a check on an apparently empty house, however, wasn't going to get me much farther.

About five houses along on the town side of the Clives' there was another with water-starved brownish grass. Taking a chance that these inhabitants too were away from home I rolled the Pontiac purposefully into the palm-edged driveway and stopped outside the front door. Ready with some of Walt's insurance patter, I leant on the bell and gave it a full twenty seconds. No one came. Everything was hot, quiet, and still.

Strolling, I walked down the drive and on to the road. Looking back one couldn't see the car for bushes. Satisfied, I made the trip along to the Clives', trying to look as if walking were a normal occupation in a Nevada heatwave: and by the time I got there it was quite clear why it wasn't. The sweat burnt dry on my skin before it had a chance to form into beads.

Reconnoitring the Clives' place took an hour. The house was shut up tight, obviously empty. The window screens were all securely fastened, and all the glass was covered on the inside with blinds, so that one couldn't see in. The doors were fastened with safe-deposit locks. The Clives had made casual breaking-in by vagrants nearly impossible.

With caution I eased round the acre of land behind the house. Palms and bushes screened a trefoil-shaped pool from being overlooked too openly by the neighbours, but from several places it was possible to see the pools of the flanking houses some sixty yards away. Beside one of them, reminding me of Eunice, a woman in two scraps of yellow cloth lay motionless on a long chair, inviting heatstroke and adding to a depth of suntan which would have got her reclassified in South Africa. I moved even more quietly after I'd seen her, but she didn't stir.

The rear boundary of the Clives' land was marked by large stones painted white, with desert scrub on the far side and low-growing citrus bushes on the near. From their windows, brother and sister had a wide view of hills and wilderness; two miles down the road neon lights went twenty rounds with the midday sun, and the crash of fruit machines out-decibelled the traffic. I wondered idly how much of Uncle Bark's illicit proceeds found their way into Matt and Yola's pocket, and how much from there vanished into the greedy slot mouths in Vegas. The stud fees went around and around and only Buttress Life were the losers.

On the way back to the motel I stopped at every supermarket I came to, and bought two three-pound bags of flour from each.

From a hardware store I acquired a short ladder, white overalls, white peaked cotton cap, brushes, and a half-gallon can of bright yellow instant-drying paint.

Fourteen

WALT LISTENED to what I had to say in a silence which hummed down the telephone wires more eloquently than hysterics.

'You're crazy,' he said at last, sounding as if he seriously meant it.

'Can you think of anything else?'

After a long pause he said grudgingly, 'Nothing quicker.'

'Right, then. I'll fix everything this end and give you a call in the morning. And let's hope it works.'

'What if it doesn't?'

'Have to try something else.'

Walt grunted gloomily and hung up.

I spent an hour at the airport, and then went back to the motel. The evening oozed away. I played some roulette without enthusiasm and lost backing black against a sequence of fourteen reds; and I ate a good steak listening to a girl singer whose voice was secondary to her frontage. After that I lay on my bed for a while and smoked, and kept the blues from crowding in too close by thinking exclusively of the job in hand.

At two I dressed in a dark green cotton shirt and black jeans, went downstairs, stepped into the car, and drove along Pittsville Boulevard to 40159. The town itself was wide awake and rocking: the houses along Pitts were dark and silent. With dimmed lights I rolled quietly into the Clives' driveway and stacked the bags of flour close to the front door. Then, holding the car door

447

but not shutting it, I eased the Pontiac back along the road and parked it in the driveway of the same empty house that I had used in the afternoon. Again, not wanting any neighbours to remember hearing a car door slam, I left it ajar, and walked back to the Clives'.

The night was warm and gentle with a deep navy blue sky and stars like fluorescent polka-dots. Two miles away the blazing lights of Vegas raised a bell-shaped orange glow, but among the palms and orange trees the shadows were thick and black and comfortably concealing.

The Clives' was only the latest of a great many houses I had broken into. My short cuts to truth were scandalous by all public and private standards, and Keeble rarely asked how I got my information: and as I would have had the press, the police, and public opinion all balefully against me if I'd ever been caught, A gag on eggs would have been clumsy in comparison. Law-abiding citizens never knew I'd been their guest. For the Clives', however, I had alternative plans.

Wearing surgeons' rubber gloves, and with my shoes stuck through my belt to the left of the Luger, I worked on the lock on the back door, and after not too bad a time, considering its complexity, the two sets of tumblers fell sweetly over, and the house was mine.

Inside, the air was stale and still, and dust sheets draped the furniture, looking like pale boulders in the dim light of my torch. The rear door opened into a spacious hall which led straight through to the front. I walked across, unbolted and unfastened the front door, brought in the bags of flour, and left the door ajar, like the one I'd come in by: the value of always being prepared for instant flight had been drummed into me by an ex-burglar who had once neglected it.

I went into the bedrooms. Large separate single-bedded rooms again for Yola and Matt, and a guest bedroom, with a bathroom to each. I pulled all the covers off the furniture and flung on to the floor everything they had left in the chests and closets. Over the resulting mess in each room I shook six pounds of self-raising flour.

In the kitchen I emptied on to the floor a packet of soap flakes, a packet of rice, some cereal and four pounds of brown sugar, which were all lying handy in the pantry. I unlocked the pantry window and unfastened its outer screen, leaving both open: and as an afterthought tumbled some canned fruit off the shelf beneath it, to show that the intruder had come in that way.

In the spacious living room I again removed all the covers, put every ornament and small loose object in a heap on the floor, and flung flour over them and around the whole place. A smaller cosier room, facing the road, contained a desk full of papers, two large bookshelves, and a well-filled sewing box. Together the jumbled contents made a splendid ankle-deep mess on the floor. Pounds of flour fell over everything like snow.

It was while I was tearing open the last bag, ready for a final scatter round the hall, that I heard the distant police siren. Frozen, I doubted for a second that it was for me: then considered that either a too watchful neighbour had seen my torch in chinks through the blinds, or else that the Clives' complicated locks weren't their only protection, and that they had a direct burglar alarm line to the police.

Without wasting much time I shut the front door and heard the lock engage. Emptied the last bag of flour over a plastic flower arrangement on a table in the hall. Flitted through the rear door and clicked it shut behind me. Thrust the torch into my pocket.

The siren wailed and stopped at the front of the house. Doors slammed, men shouted, boots ran. Someone with a megaphone urged me to come out with my hands on my head. The edges of the house were outlined by a spotlight shining on its front.

With bare seconds to spare before the first uniform appeared in silhouette around the corner I reached the nearest of the bushes flanking the trefoil pool and dived behind it. Being quiet enough was no problem, as the law were making an intimidating clatter all around the house, but staying invisible was more difficult. They brought another spotlight round to the rear and shone it full on the house. The shuttered windows stared blindly and unhelpfully back, reflecting the glare almost as far as my cover.

Lights appeared in neighbouring houses, and heads stuck like black knobs out of the windows. I eased gently away past a few more bushes and thought I was still a great deal too close to a spell in the zoo.

A shout from the side of the house indicated that they had found the open pantry window. Four troopers altogether, I judged. All armed to the teeth. I grimaced in the darkness and moved another few yards with less caution. I wasn't going to give them any forefinger exercise if I could help it, but the time was running out.

They were brave enough. One or more climbed in through the window and switched on the light. I more rapidly crossed the last stretch of garden, stepped over the white-painted stones, and headed straight out into the desert.

Five steps convinced me I needed to put my shoes on. Ten steps had me certain that the only vegetation was prickly pear, and close-ranked, at that. I should imagine I impaled myself on every one in the neighbourhood.

Back at the Clives' they had temporarily stopped oohing and ahing over the mess, and were searching the grounds. Lights moved round the next-door houses as well. If they went five along and found the car, things would get very awkward indeed.

I had meant to be safely back in my motel long before I called the police early in the morning to say that I was a civic-minded neighbour who had just seen a prowler coming out of the Clives' . . .

When they showed signs of shining the light out towards where I was stumbling along I lay down flat on the ground and listened to the thud of my heart. The spotlight beam flickered palely over the low scrubby bushes and outlined the flat spiky plates of the prickly pears, but in the shifting uneven shadows that they threw, I reckoned I must be just another clump. There was a good deal of shouted discussion about whether it was necessary to take a look-see in the desert, but to my relief no one came farther out than the boundary stones. Gradually, frustrated, the dazzle and commotion retreated and died away.

The lights inside the Clives' house went out. The police car drove off. The neighbours went back to bed. I got to my feet and brushed off the surplus of dry sandy earth. What with that and flour dust even the blindest cop would have little difficulty in buttoning me on to the crime.

With more care than on the outward trip I headed back towards the houses, but at an angle I hoped would bring me near the car. The sooner I beat it from that little neck of the woods, the better . . .

I stopped dead.

How might one catch a prowler? Just pretend to go away, and wait somewhere down the road, and when he thought everything was safe, he'd come carelessly along and fall into your waiting hands like a ripe plum.

I decided not to drive back towards Las Vegas from that quiet cul-de-sac. Just in case.

At the fifth house along, everything was quiet. I cat-footed through the grounds, around the house, and took a distant look at the car. Still there. No trooper beside it. I stood in the shadows for longer than was probably necessary, then took a deep breath and risked it. I completed the steps to the car and peered in through the window. Empty. Made a quick cautious tour of the row of spiky low-growing palms hiding it from the road.

Nothing. No irate shouts. All quiet. Car undiscovered.

Sighing with relief, the vision of the malicious Clives dancing at my trial fading a little, I pulled wide the already open door and folded like an understuffed rag doll into the driving seat. For five minutes I did nothing more energetic than to breathe freely, and enjoy it.

There remained, however, the problem of telephoning Walt: and I chewed it over thoughtfully while absent-mindedly pulling prickly pear needles out of my legs.

I was a fair hand at wire tapping, when I had the kit: but it was in Putney. No doubt there would be a telephone in the empty house alongside. But I wasn't sure that I wanted to risk this house too being directly connected to the police, if that was what had happened at the Clives'. On the other hand, I had been in the Clives' house twenty minutes before the police showed up. Yet they might be quicker, on a second call.

After half an hour I pulled on the rubber gloves, climbed out of the car, and picked the front door lock. It turned all right, but unfortunately the prudent householders had also used bolts. Always a toss-up which door of the house people bolted. I walked round to the rear, and let myself in. There was a telephone on a table in the hall. I walked over to it, then turned, retraced my steps, left the door ajar, went round to the car, started up, and drove quietly away in the dead end direction, not stopping until I was off the metalled road on to the gravel, and round a couple of bends. I switched off the light and smoked a cigarette.

Another half hour passed. No lights went on along by the houses; no police sirens, no disturbances at all. I drove gently back, parked in the same spot as before, went round into the house, and called up Walt.

He wasn't amused at being woken at 5 AM.

'A slight change of timing,' I said apologetically. 'The police have already seen the mess.'

He drew in a sharp breath. 'They didn't catch you!'

'No.' No point in telling him how close it had been: he hadn't approved of my going in at all.

'I suppose you want me to come now, then?' he said, with resignation.

'Yes, please. As soon as you can. Leave the car keys at the inquiry desk at Los Angeles airport, and I'll pick them up. The helicopter pilot I've engaged at Las Vegas is Michael King. He's expecting you. Just ask for him. The helicopter radio will pick up the frequency of the bug I've got with me, so you won't need to bring my recorder. Was there anything on the tape today?'

'Yesterday,' Walt corrected. 'Not much. I went over after dinner last night and ran it through. Offen had a friend over. There was two hours of just ordinary yapping. I didn't get back here to bed until one.'

'When this is over you can sleep for a fortnight.'

'Yeah?' he said sarcastically. 'Tell it to the marines.'

He put down his receiver with less of a crash than usual. Smiling, I took out a five-dollar bill and left it stuck half under the telephone. Then I let myself out, relocked the door behind me, and went back to the car.

Three hours uneventfully went by. Night changed to day. The air temperature began its morning climb. A few energetic birds sang: and I smoked another cigarette.

Soon after eight a patrol car went up the road, siren fortissimo. Pittsville Boulevard woke up. I eased out of the car, walked carefully down towards the road, and tucked myself invisibly between a palm and a bush, from where I had a clear view of everyone driving up towards the Clives'.

From along the road I could hear several excited voices, most of them children's: and a small boy and a girl came past close to me doing an Indianapolis on their tricycles.

Several cars drove down from the houses, all with men alone, going into Las Vegas. One woman followed. Three women came the other way, all looking eager. At nine-thirty two men drove in from Vegas, one of them adjusting a large folding camera: the local press.

An hour later a quiet-engined helicopter drifted over and landed out of sight behind a fold of hill.

At ten-fifty the hawk came to the lure.

A sky blue convertible Ford, with the hood down. Matt, driving fast, hunched with anger. Youth, strength, and fury, knotted into one callous personality. Even in a speeding car the impression came across with the solidity of a shockwave. Standing on his brakes flamboyantly late, he screeched down from sixty to nil outside his own house, scattering children like pigeons.

Satisfied, I got stiffly to my feet and went back up the drive to the car. There I removed from the boot the white overalls, white cotton gloves and a cap, and put them on, along with a pair of sunglasses. With a screwdriver from the tool kit I opened the tin of paint and gave the oily yellow contents an encouraging stir; cleaned and replaced the screwdriver, and rested the paint lid gently back on the tin. Then, picking it up by its handle with my right hand, and carrying brushes and ladders with my left, I strolled out on to the road, and along to the Clives'.

Matt's Ford stood at the door at a crooked angle to the patrol car. A good many people were still standing around, staring and gossiping in the sun. I meandered slowly through them and took a closer look at the blue convertible, and then withdrew discreetly to the edge of the proceedings.

Taking the bug out of my pocket, I talked to Walt, hoping he could hear. He couldn't answer: it was strictly one-way traffic on the midget transmitter.

'Do you read me, Walt? This is Gene. Our young friend came in his own car, not a hired one or a taxi. His name is on the registration. Pale blue new Ford convertible, at present with the top down. Grey upholstery. Nevada plates, number 3711–42.

I'll do the paint if I possibly can, though he may deal with it, of course; and I'll put this bug in the car. When he starts up, you'll hear him. Good luck. And for God's sake don't lose him.'

Indirectly, vaguely, I again approached the car. No one took any notice. I was merely one of the time-passing onlookers, a workman who wasn't working. Several of the children and some of their mothers had seen the state of the well-floured rooms, and thought it a dreadful shame. I leaned my ladder against the rear wing of the blue convertible, put the brushes and paint pot down casually on the flat surface of the boot, and mopped not too imaginary sweat off my face and neck.

Some of the blinds in the Clives' house had been raised, so that in places one could see into the house. No one was looking out. I stretched a hand over the side of the car with the bug in my palm, and felt its sucker cling snugly under the glove shelf.

Still no faces at the windows.

I said to the nearest little boy, 'Someone told me the intruder got in through the pantry window, round that corner.'

'No kidding?' he said, his eyes wide.

'Sure thing.'

He told his mother. They went to look. Nearly everyone followed them, especially as someone nudged the press photographer, who said he would take a picture.

I took a last comprehensive look at the windows, turned to walk away, and with a quick backward flip of a gloved hand, tipped over the can of paint. The lid came off. The can rolled slowly across the flat top of the boot and clanked heavily to the ground. The result was a bright broad spreading pool of yellow on blue, and a proper lake on the gravel.

I was out on the road when the first child saw it and ran after me.

'Your paint's tipped over, mister.'

'Yeah, I know. Don't touch it. Don't let anyone touch it, huh? I'm just going to fetch the stuff to get it off.'

He nodded importantly and ran back, and I made it safely along to the hired car, and drove away in peace towards Las Vegas, taking off the useful cap and gloves as I went. Back at the motel I showered, changed, packed, and paid my account; drove to the airport and returned the car to the Hertz agent: kept a very wary eye open in case Matt Clive had decided to travel by air; ate a much needed sandwich, and caught the first plane out to Los Angeles.

When I collected the car keys at the inquiry desk, there was a note from Walt as well.

You're one great crazy guy. And don't think I don't realize what you risked. If you're reading this, I guess you've made it, and aren't behind bars. My pal in the CIA told me you could be relied on to do mad things, and boy, he was right. What do you use for nerves? Count me strictly out, next time.
Walt.

Surprised, and not ungrateful that he should have bothered, I slipped his letter into my pocket and drove into the city to look for a good place for tape recorders. I managed in the end to hire for one week an elaborate recorder which would play at the ultra slow fifteen-sixteenths of an inch per second, the speed of my own, and with it sitting on the passenger seat beside me, pointed my nose towards Orpheus Farm, Los Caillos. Then I removed the full reel from the radio recorder and fixed it up with another: no one appeared to have disturbed it in its bush and boulder hiding place, and as far as I could tell, no one saw me come and go.

Lynnie and Eunice were just walking up from the beach when I got back to The Vacationer: but they both greeted me with ten degrees of frost and went straight on past, murmuring that they guessed they would see me at dinner.

Slightly puzzled, shrugging, I carried my bag and the recorder up to my room, rewound the tape I had collected, and started it to run through while I took off my city suit and turned the air-conditioning to high.

Yola rang up, in great agitation. The houseboy answered, and went to tell Offen, who was still in bed. By great good fortune the houseboy neglected to go back to replace the downstairs receiver when Offen lifted the bedroom extension, and the bug in consequence had picked up the whole conversation.

'I've had a call from the cops in Vegas . . .'

'Don't shout, Yola. I'm not deaf.'

She didn't listen. 'Some vandals have wrecked the house at Pitts.' She really minded: there was grief as well as anger in her voice.

'How do you mean, wrecked?'

'They say everything in the house has been thrown on the floor, and flour and sugar and stuff have been tipped over everything. They want to know what's been stolen, they want me or better Matt to go down there and deal with it . . . and I can't, Uncle Bark, I simply can't. We've got thirty-two people in, and I can't possibly get away. Matt will have to go.'

'But Matt . . .'

'Sure,' she wailed. 'Do you think I don't *know*? But he'll have to. Those horses won't die if he leaves them for a few hours. It's much farther for me, I'd be away at least two days. It's *hopeless*. Everything's gone wrong since we took that damn Chrysalis.'

'And if you remember,' Culham James said tartly, 'that was your and Matt's idea. I always said it was too soon after the last one. You and Matt have been too greedy ever since you found out.'

'Relatives ought to share their good luck, not to keep it to themselves.'

'So you're always saying.'

Nothing like a little blackmail to cement a family together,

I thought in amusement. Offen had been happy with his half million a year, it seemed: but Matt and Yola, stumbling on the honey pot, had been in a hurry for more. Impulsive, ingenious, greedy Clives; if they had only been content with a share from Showman and Allyx, Offen would never had been found out.

Yola glossed over the longstanding squabble and returned to the current disaster. 'I didn't get Matt's number. What is it?'

'I haven't got it here, it's in my book downstairs . . .'

'Well look, will you call him? Tell him to get right on over, the cops will be there waiting. Tell him to call me from there and tell me what gives . . . I can't bear it if those bastards have stolen my mink wrap . . . and there's all that money in the safe . . .'

'Better face up to it that it's gone,' Offen said, with the tiniest trace of malice.

'They might not have had time,' Yola said. 'The alarms go off when anyone goes in the den, and there isn't supposed to be time for anyone to find the safe and open it before the cops get there. We paid enough for it . . .'

It had been their bad luck that by the merest chance I had left the den until last.

Yola disconnected, and after the twenty-second gap on the tape, Uncle Bark called up Matt from the downstairs telephone. Matt's comments were mostly inaudible though detectably explosive. He agreed to go to the house, but nothing Offen said gave any clue as to where Matt was at that moment. It appeared only that he was somewhere within a reasonable radius of Las Vegas, as he was going to be able to drive there, see to things at the house, and get back in time to feed the horses in the evening: which narrowed it down to somewhere in an area of roughly a hundred and fifty thousand square miles. A pocket handkerchief.

A brief telephone conversation of no interest followed and then, presumably in the afternoon, Offen had switched on his television set to watch a racing programme. As far as I could tell from spot checks, it had used up the whole of the rest of the four-hour playing time.

Sighing, I switched off, and went downstairs. Lynnie and Eunice, dressed in dazzling colours, were drinking daiquiris and watching the Pacific sunset. I got another cool welcome and monosyllabic replies to my inquiries about their day.

Finally Eunice said distantly, 'Did you have a good time in San Francisco?'

I blinked. 'Yes, thank you.'

They relapsed into a longer silence which was broken only by a waiter coming to tell me I was wanted on the telephone.

It was Walt.

'Where are you?' I said.

'Las Vegas airport.'

'How did it go?'

'You can relax,' he said comfortably. 'The horses are on a small farm in a valley in Arizona, out beyond Kingman. We landed there and I asked around some. Seems the couple who own the farm don't make much of a living, but last week they said a friend was giving them a trip to Miami, and a young fellow would be looking after the place while they were away.'

'That's great,' I said with emphasis.

'The paint made it easy. We heard him yelling blue murder when he saw it, but I guess it had dried on by then and he couldn't get it off, because it was way past midday, and I'd begun to worry that he'd gone already and we hadn't heard him or that they'd picked you up planting the bug . . . anyway, we took off when his engine started, and the yellow splash was easy to see from a height, just as you said. He went right through Las Vegas and out on to the Hoover Dam road and across into Arizona. I kept the binoculars on him and we never flew near enough for him to notice us, I'm certain of that. He went up a winding graded road into the hills south-east of Kingman, and that was it.'

'You've done marvels.'

'Oh, sure. It was simpler than we were prepared for, though. You could hear the bug pretty clearly through the helicopter's headsets as high as two thousand feet, and we could have followed him in the dark if we'd had to, especially as he had his radio on for most of the way. We could hear music and news broadcasts now and then.'

'Are you coming back tonight?'

'Yeah, there's a plane in a half hour from now. But it'll be better than midnight when I get in.'

'I'll be awake,' I said. 'And just by the way, Walt, what did you tell Eunice and Lynnie I was doing in San Francisco?'

He cleared his throat. 'I said you had some unfinished business there.'

'What sort of business?'

'Uh . . . like . . . er . . . female.'

'Thanks,' I said sarcastically. 'You're a right pal.'

Something very like a laugh lingered in my ear as I disconnected.

Fifteen

LYNNIE AND Eunice talked brightly to each other over dinner and I sat making plans for the next day and didn't listen. Politely after coffee we parted for the night, and at eleven I drove out to Orpheus with a fresh reel for the receiver in the rocks, and brought back the one I had fitted earlier.

Walt came back into my room as I was running it through, and we both listened to Culham James Offen talking to Matt and then to Yola.

Yola was a better bet from our point of view, because her angry feminine voice scattered higher sound waves out of the receiver, and one could imagine Uncle Bark holding it inches away out of deference to his eardrums.

He was doing his best to soothe her. 'Matt says it could have been worse; some of these vandals have thrown molasses and preserves and even sewage around in people's houses . . .'

'He says the whole place is *covered* in flour . . . it'll take weeks to clear up.'

'It'll vacuum quite easily, won't it? It's not sticky and it doesn't stain.'

But she couldn't be consoled, even when he reminded her that the money was safe, and that her mink wrap hadn't been stolen.

'But Matt says', she wailed, 'that it was *white*.'

'Flour will shake out . . . and might even clean it.'

'You don't understand.'

'Sure I do, Yola,' he said patiently. 'You feel like it was you who was assaulted, not your house. You feel dirty and furious and you'd like to kick the bastards who did it. Sure, I know. We had thieves in here once, when your Aunt Ellen was alive. They stole all her rings, and she said it was like being raped.'

They talked about the break-in for a good while longer, and Walt raised an eyebrow and remarked that I seemed to have gotten reasonable revenge for that clap on the head.

We were both yawning by the time Offen was through for the evening. The last half hour consisted of him telling his houseboy his plans and requirements, and none of these betrayed any anxiety or uncertainty. Culham James was confident, and I was glad of it. Worried men patrol their defences.

Walt went off to bed, and although I hadn't slept at all the previous night I woke again after only three hours. The coloured lights on the outside of the motel threw prismatic reflections on the ceiling. I stared up at them, trying to make patterns and shapes, trying any silly ruse to stop my mind from nose-diving into the pit. The tug of the unfinished chase was very faint, and whether Allyx and Showman ever sired another foal seemed a matter of supreme unimportance. Fraud, theft, attempted murder . . . who cared?

I had left the Luger in its belt holster across the room on a chair. Neither the Clives nor Offen were likely to come creeping through the night to do me in, and my usual enemies were six thousand miles to the east. The only danger lay in myself, the deadliest enemy of the lot. The theory that going to bed with the gun out of reach would lessen its magnetic temptation was proving a dreary flop.

One more day, I thought in the end. Anyone could manage just one more day. If you said that firmly enough every night, one might even finish the course.

Dawn crept up on the coloured bulbs and washed them out.

I took a shower and shaved, and admitted that I had seen healthier-looking men than the one in my reflection.

Walt came along to my room when I was midway through orange juice and coffee at eight-thirty. 'What you need,' he said, eyeing this, 'is some good solid food.'

'I don't feel hungry.'

His eyes slid to my face and away. 'Come on down and eat with me.'

I shook my head. 'I'll wait for you.'

He wouldn't go alone. He ordered hot-cakes and eggs and coffee from room service, and we got straight down to business while he demolished them.

'It'll take two and a half days for Sam Hengelman to get to Kingman,' I said.

He nodded with his mouth full.

'He was starting early this morning,' I went on, 'I called him last night, after you'd been through from Las Vegas. He's driving the van himself, and he's coming alone. That means his journey time will be longer, but it seemed better that way from the secrecy point of view.'

'Did you tell him it was another snatch?' Walt said doubtfully.

I smiled. 'I engaged him to come and collect a horse belonging to Dave Teller. He asked if we were likely to be collecting this one in a lonely place at night, and I said yes, we probably would.'

'And he didn't back out?'

'He merely remarked that he had no great objection to an easy buck if I would assure him he couldn't go to jail for it.'

Walt wiped errant egg off his chin. 'And could he?'

'I couldn't tell him it was impossible. Odds of a thousand to one, I said. He said a thousand bucks against one chance of going to jail wasn't enough.'

Walt laughed. 'So how much is he coming for?'

'Fifteen hundred, plus the normal hiring fee, plus expenses.'

'Not bad for one week's work.' He paused, stirring sugar, then said tentatively, 'What do you get out of this yourself?'

'Me?' I said in surprise. 'I've no idea. Three weeks' heatwave instead of the English summer . . .'

'Didn't you negotiate a fee?'

'No.'

'How come?'

'It didn't occur to me.'

His face crinkled into a mixture of emotions with what appeared to be amazement and pity coming out on top.

'How about you?' I said.

'I'm not on vacation,' he pointed out. 'I get a pretty good salary, and also a cut of everything I save the company.'

'So Chrysalis has been worth the extra work?'

'At a million and a half, are you kidding?' Walt looked at me earnestly. 'Look, Gene, I'm going to give you one half of that cut . . .'

'No,' I said, interrupting. 'I don't want it.'

'You know darned well I wouldn't have found that horse, not in a million years. Nor got him back alive so quickly. And as for these other two . . .'

'You keep it for your kids,' I said. 'But thanks, anyway.'

He would have gone on insisting, but I wouldn't listen, and after two attempts he gave it up. In the back of my mind, as I outlined what I suggested we should do next, there lingered a bitter suspicion that I hadn't accepted his gift because it would be a selfish waste if I didn't stick around to spend it. I had rejected any strings of conscience tying me to life. The death-seeking force was up to another of its tricks.

'A pincer movement, I think,' I said. 'Or rather, a simultaneous attack on two fronts.'

'Huh?'

'Keep Culham James Offen's attention riveted on the

Moviemaker and Centigrade he has on his farm while we spirit away the others.'

'Er, quite,' Walt agreed.

'You can take Offen,' I said.

'And you take the horses?'

I nodded. Walt considered what might happen if we exchanged roles, and didn't argue.

'What are the chances of finding out which company Matt insures the Las Vegas house with?'

Walt thought about it. 'Our agent there might be able to. But why?'

'I . . . er . . . would rather take those horses when I know Matt is safely away.'

Walt smiled.

'So,' I went on, 'it shouldn't be too difficult to get him to go back to the house on Pitts. Say for instance his insurance company required him to make an inspection of his security arrangements and sign some document or other, before they would renew full cover? We know from the telephone calls to Offen that Matt and Yola have a safe in the den with a lot of money in it. Matt won't want to be uninsured for more than a minute, after having one break-in already.'

'We couldn't ask his company to do that . . .' Walt paused and looked at me with suspicion.

'Quite right,' I nodded. 'You can. You know all the jargon. As soon as we hear from Sam Hengelman that he has reached the Arizona border, you can start the spiel on Matt.'

'From here?'

'Yes. Ask him what time would be convenient for him, but try to manoeuvre him into coming late in the afternoon or early evening, say six or seven. Then it would be dark when he got home, and late, which should hamper him a bit when he finds the horses are gone . . . he might even stop off in Las Vegas for a couple of hours at the tables.'

Walt said thoughtfully, 'I reckon I'd better go to the house on Pittsville and meet him.'

'No,' I said abruptly.

He looked at me. 'You'd thought of it?'

'You are not going anywhere near Matt Clive.'

'And why not?'

'You want a split skull or something?'

'Like webbed feet.' The smiled hovered. 'All the same, what is Matt going to do when he arrives at his house and no insurance man turns up? What would you do? Call the company, I guess. And then what? He discovers no one in the company knows anything about him having to come back to the house, and he starts thinking like crazy. And if I were him I'd call the local cops and get them whizzing out to the farm for a look-see. You didn't see the road there from Kingman. But I did. There are no turnings off it for the last ten miles to the farm. What if you met the cops head on, you and Sam Hengelman and two stolen horses?'

'He wouldn't risk calling in cops.'

'He might reckon that if he was losing everything anyway, he'd make sure you went down as well. And I mean down.'

Every instinct told me not to let Walt meet Matt Clive.

'Suppose he won't make a late appointment?' he said. 'When I grant most of the company would have gone home, and it would be more difficult to check. Suppose he insists on three in the afternoon, or even the next morning? Do you want to snatch those horses by day?'

'Not much. But it would take him at least two hours each way. Add an hour for waiting and checking. Even if he called the police, it wouldn't be for three hours after he left home. We'd have been gone with the horses for two of those.'

Walt obstinately shook his head. 'The limits are too narrow. A horse van won't be liable to do better than thirty miles an hour on the farm road, if that much. You have to go into Kingman, which is in the opposite direction from Kentucky, and then round and across Arizona . . . there aren't too many roads in that state, it's mostly desert. The police could find you too easily.'

'Down through Phoenix . . .'

'The road to Phoenix twists through mountains, with hairpin curves most of the way.'

'I don't want you walking into an empty house with Matt Clive.'

He looked at me without expression. 'But you would go. If he didn't know you, I mean.'

'That's different.'

'How?' he said, half insulted, half challenging.

I looked at him sideways. 'I bet I can run faster than you.'

His forehead relaxed. 'You're in pretty good shape, I'll give you that. All the same, I'm going to Las Vegas.'

He'd manoeuvred me into not being able to persuade him against it on the grounds of safety; and from all other points of view it was a good idea. Against my instinct I agreed in the end that he should go.

'I'll drift on out tomorrow and look at the farm beyond Kingman,' I said. 'I suppose you couldn't see whether there were any other horses there besides the two we're after?'

He looked startled. 'You mean there might be another identification problem?'

'Perhaps. Though I'd say it's certain our two have Moviemaker's and Centigrade's stud book numbers tattooed inside their mouths. They would have to, to satisfy visiting grooms, for instance, that their mares were being mated with the right stallion. But I've never seen them . . . Showman and Allyx. If there are other horses there, it'll simply mean going round peering into all their mouths until I find the right ones.'

Walt raised his eyes to heaven. 'You make everything sound

so darned easy. Like it's only five miles to the top of Everest, and everyone can walk five miles, can't they?'

Smiling, I asked him for precise directions to the farm, and he told me.

'And now this end . . .' I said. 'How many strings can you pull with the Los Angeles fraud squad?'

'Not many,' he said. 'I don't know anyone out there.'

'But with Buttress Life behind you?'

He sighed. 'I suppose you want me to go and dip my toes in the water?'

'Jump right in,' I agreed. 'Talk your way to the top chap, and tell him Buttress Life suspect that Moviemaker and Centigrade are Showman and Allyx. Get everything nicely stirred up. Make Offen prove beyond any doubt that the two horses at Orpheus literally are Moviemaker and Centigrade.'

He nodded. 'OK. I'll start this morning. Have to go a little carefully, though, or Offen will come up so fast with a libel suit that we'll wonder what hit us.'

'You must be used to ducking.'

'Yeah.'

I gave him the page Miss Britt had written out for me in Lexington.

'Here are the figures. No one can question these, not even Offen. You might find them useful in getting the law moving.'

He tucked the paper into his pocket and nodded, and shortly after, with the habitual martyred sigh, levered himself out of his chair and ambled on his way.

I sat and thought for a while but got nowhere new. There was going to be little else for me to do but wait and watch for the next few days while Sam Hengelman rolled his way two thousand miles across the continent.

When I went down to lunch I found Eunice and Lynnie sitting in cool bright dresses under the dappled shade of the sea-facing terrace. Their hair was glossy and neat, their big earrings gently swinging, their legs smooth and tanned, the whites of their eyes a detergent white.

They didn't get the lingering scrutiny they deserved. With them, equally crisp, equally at ease, sat Culham James Offen, Uncle Bark.

All three seemed a scrap disconcerted when I folded myself gently on to the fourth chair round the low table on which stood their long frosted drinks.

Offen and I nodded to each other. There was still in his manner the superior, self-satisfied amusement he had treated me with at his house. Reassuring. Lynnie smiled, but with a quick sidelong glance at Eunice to make sure such treachery hadn't been noticed. Eunice had on an 'I-am-your-employer's-wife' face, which didn't wipe from my mind, nor hers, I imagine, the memory of the fluffy pink wrapper.

'We thought you'd gone to LA with Walt,' Lynnie said.

Eunice gave her a sharp glance which she didn't see. 'We ran into Mr Offen in the lobby here, wasn't that extraordinary?'

'Extraordinary,' I agreed.

Offen's white eyebrows went up and down in an embarrassment he couldn't entirely smother.

'It sure has been a pleasure,' he said, 'to get to know you folks better.' He spoke exclusively to Eunice, however.

She had warmed again to the charm he had switched on for her, and gave me the tag end of a scornful glance. How could I, she inferred, imagine this nice influential citizen could be a crook.

'How are Matt and Yola these days?' I said conversationally.

Offen visibly jumped, and a blight fell on the party. 'Such charming young people,' I said benignly, and watched Eunice remembering what had happened to Dave, and also perhaps what Walt had told her about their attack on me. 'Your nephew and niece, I believe?'

Offen's pale blue eyes were the least impressive feature in his tanned face with its snow-white frame. I read in them a touch of wariness, and wondered whether in prodding Eunice to face reality I had disturbed his complacency too far.

'They would sure like to meet you again,' he said slowly, and the heavy ill-feeling behind the words curdled finally for Eunice his milk-of-human-kindness image.

'Are you expecting them within the next few days?' I asked, dropping in the merest touch of anxiety.

He said he wasn't, and his inner amusement abruptly returned. I had succeeded in convincing him I would be trying to remove his horses from Orpheus pretty soon now; and shortly afterwards he got purposefully to his feet, bent a beaming smile on Eunice, a smaller one on Lynnie and a smug one on me, and made an important exit through the motel.

After a long pause Eunice said flatly, 'I guess I was wrong about that guy being sweet.'

We ate an amicable lunch and spent the afternoon on the beach under a fringed umbrella, with the bright green-blue Pacific hissing gently on the sand. Out on the rollers the golden boys rode their surfboards, and flat by my side little Lynnie sighed to the bottom of her lungs with contentment.

'I wish this could go on for ever,' she said.

'So do I.'

Eunice, on the other side of Lynnie, propped herself up on one elbow. 'I'm going to take a dip,' she said. 'Coming?'

'In a minute,' Lynnie said lazily, and Eunice went alone. We watched her tight well-shaped figure walk unwaveringly down to the water, and Lynnie said what I was thinking. 'She hardly drinks at all now.'

'You're good for her.'

'Oh sure.' She laughed gently, stretching like a cat. 'Isn't this heat just gorgeous?'

'Mm.'

'What are all those scars on you?'

'Lions and tigers and appendicitis.'

She snorted. 'Shall we go in and swim?'

'In a minute. What did you and Eunice and Offen say to each other before I arrived?'

'Oh . . .' She sounded bored. 'He wanted to know what you were doing. Eunice told him you and Walt were cooking something up but she didn't really know what. And . . . er . . . yes . . . he asked if Walt was really an insurance man, and Eunice said he was . . . and he asked other things about you, what your job was and so on, and why you were out here with us . . .'

'Did Eunice tell him I got her to show him that photograph on purpose? Did she tell him that I was certain that the horses he has at Orpheus Farm are Moviemaker and Centigrade?'

Lynnie shook her head.

'You're quite sure?'

'Yes, absolutely. Would it have been a nuisance if we had?'

'A fair way to being disastrous.'

'Don't worry then. He was only here about a quarter of an hour before you came down, and all Eunice said was that you were er . . . er . . . well her actual words were, some dim bloody little office worker on vacation.' Lynnie laughed. 'She said her husband had been grateful to you for saving his life and was paying your bill here, and that all you seemed to be interested in at present was a girl up in San Francisco.'

I looked down to where Eunice's head bobbed in the surf and wondered whether she'd given him perfect answers from design or bitchiness.

'What's she like?' Lynnie said.

'Who?'

'The girl in San Francisco.'

'You'd better ask Walt,' I said, turning my head to look at her. 'He invented her.'

She gasped and laughed in one. 'Oh good! I mean . . . er . . . then what were you really doing?'

471

'Ah, well,' I said. 'Now that's something I'd hate Eunice to have told Culham Offen.'

She lay looking back at me steadily for several seconds. So much more assurance, I thought idly, than on that day on the river, when she had still been a child.

'Is that why you've told us practically nothing? Don't you trust her?'

'She's never wanted the horses back.'

Lynnie blinked. 'But she wouldn't . . . she wouldn't have ruined on purpose what you're trying to do. After all, you're doing it for her husband.'

I smiled and she sat up abruptly and put her arms round her knees.

'You make me feel so . . . *naive*.'

'You', I said, 'are adorable.'

'And now you're laughing at me.'

I wanted impulsively to say that I loved her, but I wasn't sure that it was true. Maybe all I wanted was an antedote to depression. She was certainly the best I'd found.

'I'm going away again in the morning,' I said.

'To San Francisco?'

'Somewhere like that.'

'How long for?'

'Two nights.'

'This is your last week,' she said, looking out to sea.

The thought leapt involuntarily, *if only it were* . . . I shook my head abruptly, as if one could empty the brain by force, and climbed slowly up on to my feet.

'There's today, anyway,' I said, smiling. 'Let's go and get wet.'

Walt came back at seven with dragging feet and a raging thirst.

'Those detectives from the DA's office will scalp me if they find out we're only using them,' he said gloomily, up in my room. 'Two of them have agreed to go out to Orpheus Farm tomorrow, and I'm meeting them on the LA road to show them the way. Day after tomorrow, some guy from the bloodstock registry office is going out. I got the DA's office to call him and fix it.'

'Couldn't be better.'

Walt recharged his batteries with Old Grandad and said, 'So what's new with you?'

'Offen came here on a fact-finding mission.'

'He did *what*?'

'Came looking for answers. Got some real beauties from Eunice which won't help him any, and went away believing we'd be back on his doorstep pretty soon.'

'I guess', Walt said, 'that he wanted to know if we'd called it off and gone home, and whether it was safe to bring those horses back again. It's days since he saw any sign of us. Must have been like sitting on an H-bomb with a tricky firing pin.' He swallowed appreciatively and rolled his tongue over his gums. 'He'll get all the action he wants, tomorrow.'

When he plodded tiredly off to shower before dinner, I telephoned Jeff Roots.

'How was Miami?' I said.

'Hot and horrible, and I gained four pounds.'

Commiserating, I thanked him for his help with the newspaper files and told him that owing to Miss Britt we had found the two stallions.

'I wish I didn't believe it. Are you certain?'

'Yes.'

His sigh was heartfelt. 'We'd better start proceedings . . .'

'I've . . . er . . . already started them. We may in a day or two have two horses on our hands which will need to be stabled somewhere eminently respectable while their identity is being investigated. Owing to the length of time they've been lost, it may take a couple of months to re-establish them. Where would you think it would be best to put them?'

After a pause, he said, 'I suppose you're asking me to have them here?'

'Not really,' I explained. 'Too much of a coincidence after Chrysalis, perhaps. I'd thought rather of a more official place . . . I don't know what you have.'

'I'll think of something.' He coughed slightly. 'There won't be anything illegal about their recovery?'

'No more than for Chrysalis.'

'That's no answer.'

'There shouldn't be any trouble with the police,' I said.

'I guess that'll have to do,' he sighed. 'When do I expect them?'

'If all goes well, they should reach Lexington on Sunday.'

'And if all doesn't go well?'

'You'll have no problem.'

He laughed. 'And you?'

'One more won't matter.'

Sixteen

FOR MOST of thirty hours I sat in the mountainous Arizona desert and looked down at Matt Clive leading a boring life.

Like his sister, he was capable, quick, efficient. He watered the stock and mended a fence, swept out the house and fed the hens; and spent a great deal of time in the largest barn on the place.

I had found myself a perch among the rocks on the east-facing side of the valley, half a mile off the dusty road to the farm. At nearly three thousand feet above sea level the heat was bearable, though the midday sun blazed down from nearly straight overhead, and eggs would have fried on the sidewalks if there had been any. Desert plants were designed to save themselves and no one else: at my back grew a large agave, its central stem rising six feet high with flat outspreading flowers turning from red to brilliant yellow. For leaves it had razor-sharp spikes springing outwards from the ground in one large clump. Stiff; angular; not a vestige of shade. The spindly buckhorn and the flat devil's fingers would have been pretty useless to a midget. I folded myself under the overhang of a jagged boulder and inched round with the meagre shade patch until the sun cried quits behind the hill.

Showman and Allyx had to be in the big barn: though I saw no sign of them, nor of any other horses, on the first afternoon.

By air to Las Vegas and hired car to Kingman had taken me all morning, and at the last fork on the way to the farm I'd had to decide whether to risk meeting Matt head on on the road or to walk ten miles instead. I'd risked it. Ten miles there was also ten miles back. The car had bumped protestingly off the road two miles short of his farm, and was now out of sight in a gulley.

Binoculars brought every detail of the meagre spread up clear and sharp. The small dilapidated house lay to the left, with the big barn on the right across a large dusty yard. Along most of a third side of the rough quadrangle stretched an uneven jumble of simple stone buildings, and behind those the rusting guts of two abandoned cars lay exposed to the sky.

Maintenance was at a minimum: no endemic prosperity here. The owners scratched for a living in a tiny valley among the Arizona hills, existing there only by courtesy of the quirk of rock formation which had brought underground water to the surface in a spring. The small river bed was easy to follow from where I sat: grass and trees circled its origin, sparse paddocks stretched away to sagging fences on each side of its upper reaches, a corn patch grew beside it near the farm buildings, and lower down it ran off into the desert in a dry wide shallow sandy trough. Heavy rain would turn it every time into a raging torrent, as destructive as it was vital. High behind the house, dominating the whole place, a huge onion-shaped water storage tank sat squatly on top of a spindly looking tower.

Mile after mile of plain dark poles stretched along the road to the farm, carrying an electric cable and a telephone wire, but civilization had fallen short of refuse collection. A sprawling dump at one side of the big barn seemed to consist of a brass bedstead, half a tractor, a bottomless tin bath, the bones of an old wagon, a tangled heap of unidentifiable rusting metal, and roughly fifty treadless tyres of varying sizes. Filling every crevice among this lot were bottles and empty food cans with labels peeling and jagged lids mutely open like mouths. Over the top the air shimmered with reflected heat.

Matt had already spent at least a week in this ugly oasis. Walt

476

shouldn't find it too hard to persuade him to make an evening visit to Las Vegas.

I watched until long after dark. Lights went on and off in the house, and Matt moved about, visible through the insect screens because he didn't draw any curtains. If, indeed, there were any.

Cautiously at some time after one o'clock, when all the lights on my side of the house had been out for more than two hours, I picked my way down to the farm. The night was still warm, but as the only light came from the stars it was black dark on the ground, and with agave clumps in mind I reckoned my torch held lesser risk.

I reached the farmyard. Nothing stirred. Quietly, slowly, I made the crossing to the barn. Matt in the house slept on.

No padlocks: not even bolts. There weren't any. The wide door of the barn stood open; and with this invitation, I went in. Inside, the barn was divided into six stalls along one side, with feed bins and saddlery storage racks along the other. Here and everywhere else dilapidation and decay were winning hands down: everything my torch flicked over looked in need of help.

Four of the stalls were empty, but in the two central ones, side by side, stood two horses. Gently, so as not to frighten them, I went over, talking soothingly in a murmur and shining the torch beam on the wall in front of their heads. Their eyes in the dim light rolled round inquiringly, but neither gave more than a single stamp of alarm.

The first one tried to back away when I shone the torch into his mouth: but an exceedingly strong-looking head collar and a remarkably new chain kept him from going more than a few feet. I ran my hand down his neck and talked to him, and in the end got my inspection done. The tattooed mark, as often, was none too clear: but discernibly it was 752:07. The registration of Moviemaker.

The tattoo on the second horse was more recent and also clearer: the registration number of Centigrade.

Satisfied, I gave them each a friendly slap, and with great care left the barn. Matt still slept. I hesitated, thinking that enough was enough, but in the end went down to the end of the farmyard to take a quick look through the other buildings. In one only, a deep narrow garage, was there anything of interest: a car.

It was not Matt's pale blue convertible, but a tinny black saloon three or four years old. My flashlight picked out a piece of paper lying on the passenger seat, and I opened the door and took a look at it. A copy of a work sheet from a garage in Kingman. Customer's name: Clive. Work required: Remove yellow paint from Ford convertible. Further instructions: Complete as soon as possible.

I put the paper back on the seat and shone the light over the dashboard. A small metal plate screwed on to it bore the name of the garage in Kingman: Matt had rented this car while his own was being cleaned.

Outside, everything was still, and feeling like a shadow among shadows I went quietly out of the farmyard and along the dusty road towards Kingman. It seemed a lot farther than two miles to the flat stones I had left one on top of the other as a marker, and even after I had reached them it took me quite a while to find the hidden car and get it back on to the road.

It was well after three when I called Walt. He sounded resigned, but he'd known it would be some time in the night.

'Are they there?' he said.

'They are. They're quite unguarded, and there's only Matt on the place. How about things your end?'

'Oh.' Amusement crept in. 'Offen was full of offended dignity. Didn't know how anyone could suggest he was engaged in fraud; that sort of thing. It didn't impress the DA's squad at all, because they get that sort of bluster every time. Made them all the keener, if anything. They had quite a long session with him, all fairly polite but definitely needling. Artists, they are. From our point of view Offen said nothing significant except for one

478

little gem. The DA's guys asked to see the stud groom. That's Kiddo, remember? The one who told us about the mares foaling at night?'

'I remember,' I said.

'Well, it seems it's a slow time around studs just now, and Kiddo went off on vacation the day after our first visit.'

'He didn't say anything about that when we were there.'

'He sure didn't. Offen says Kiddo will be back in three weeks. By then, I guess, he expects to have had Moviemaker and Centigrade identified as themselves, and then when the dust has settled he can bring Showman and Allyx quietly back, and it'll be safe for Kiddo to return. I guess Offen didn't know which way he'd jump, and booted him off out of trouble.'

'I'm sure you're right,' I said. 'Anything interesting on the tape?'

'I've been listening to that damned machine until I'm bored to death with it,' he said wearily. 'Today's run was mostly the DA's men talking to Offen, so I heard all that twice over. He then called both Yola and Matt and told them about it, and he sounded pretty pleased with the way things were going. I'd say Matt was a mite annoyed at having to stay where he is: Offen was telling him not to be stupid, what was a week or two with so much at stake. Also Yola must be wanting Matt back, because Offen smoothed her down with the same spiel.' Walt paused and cleared his throat. 'What would you say is the relationship between Matt and Yola?'

Smiling into the receiver I said, 'Such thoughts, Walt, from you!'

'It's possible . . .' he said uncomfortably.

'It sure is. But there's nothing to indicate it except for their not being married.'

'Then you don't think . . .?'

'I'd say they're certainly centred on each other, but how far it goes I couldn't guess. The only time I've seen them together they've had their hands full of punts and guns.'

'Yeah . . . well, maybe crime is how it takes them.'

I agreed that it probably was, and asked him if he'd got Matt set up for the insurance meeting.

'I sure have,' he said with satisfaction. 'I called him this afternoon. It must have been soon after he'd been talking to Offen, I guess, because he seemed to be glad enough to be given a reason for going to Las Vegas. I suggested six PM which sounded all right, but he himself asked if I could make it later.'

'He'll probably want to feed the horses about then, when the day gets cooler,' I said. 'And those horses would come first.'

'Yeah. At three million for two, they sure would. It beats me why he doesn't guard them every minute.'

'Against what?' I said.

'You got a point,' he conceded. 'Only us. And we're obviously concentrating on the two at Orpheus. Right?'

'Right.'

'Anyway, Matt said could I make it later than six, and we agreed in the end on nine. That should mean he'll take that gander at the roulette tables on his way home, and maybe give us most of the night to get the horses clear.'

'Good,' I said. 'That's fine. But Walt . . .'

'Yes?'

'Take care.'

'Go teach your grandmother,' he said, and I smiled wryly and asked him if he'd heard from Sam Hengelman.

'Sure, he called this evening, like you asked. He'd reached Santa Rosa in New Mexico and he was going on to Albuquerque before stopping for the night. He said he'd be in Kingman by four or five tomorrow afternoon . . . today, I suppose, technically . . . and he'll meet you at the Mojave Motel. I told him the return trip wouldn't be starting before eight, so he's going to take a room there and catch a couple of hours' sleep.'

'Thanks, Walt, that's great,' I said.

'We're all set, then?' There was a hint of unease in his voice, and it raised prickles again in my early warning mechanism.

'You don't have to go to Las Vegas,' I said reasonably. 'We've time enough without it.'

'I'm going,' he said. 'And that's that.'

'Well . . . all right. I think we could do with a checkpoint, though, in case anything goes wrong. Let's say you wait in the lobby of the Angel Inn from eight to eight-thirty tomorrow evening. That's where I stayed. It's right on the edge of Las Vegas, but it's an easy trip to Pittsville Boulevard. I'll call you there sometime during that half hour; and if I don't, you stay put, and don't go out to Matt's house.'

'OK,' he said, and although he tried, there was distinct relief in his voice.

We disconnected, and I ate a sandwich and drank coffee at an all-night lunch counter at the bus station before returning to my hired car and pointing its nose again towards the farm and the hills. The two flat stones came up again in the headlights, and re-stowing the car in its former hiding place, I finished the journey on foot.

Back in the shelter of the same jagged rock I tried for a time to sleep. There was still an hour or more before dawn, and the sun wouldn't be too hot for a while after that, but in spite of knowing that I'd get no rest at all during the following night, my brain stayed obstinately awake. I supposed an inability to sleep on open ground surrounded by cacti and within yelling distance of a man who'd kill me if he had a chance could hardly be classed as insomnia in the ordinary way: but I had no illusions. That was precisely what it was. The restless, racing thoughts, the electrical awareness, the feeling that everything in one's body was working full steam ahead and wouldn't slow down; I knew all the symptoms much too well. One could lie with eyes shut and relax every muscle until one couldn't tell where one's arms and legs were, and still sleep wouldn't come. Breathe deeply, count all the sheep of Canterbury, repeat once-learnt verses; nothing worked.

The sun came up and shone in my eyes. Inching out of its revealing spotlight I retreated round the side of the rock and looked down to the farm through the binoculars. No movement. At five-thirty Matt was still in bed.

I put down the glasses and thought about a cigarette. There were only four left in the packet. Sighing, I reflected that I could easily have bought some in Kingman, if I'd given it a thought. It was going to be a long day. All I'd brought with me beside the binoculars was a bottle of water, a pair of sunglasses, and the Luger in my belt.

At seven-thirty Matt came out through the rickety screen door of the house, and stood in the yard stretching and looking around at the cloudless cobalt blue sky. Then he went across to the barn and poked his head briefly inside.

Satisfied that the gold was still in the bank, he fetched buckets of water and joined it for long enough to muck out the stalls and see to the feed. After a time he came out with a barrowful of droppings and wheeled it away to empty on the far side of the barn, out of my sight.

The hens got their grits, and the calves in a near compound their ration of water, and Matt retired for his breakfast. The morning wore on. The temperature rose. Nothing else happened.

At noon I stood up for a while behind the rock to stretch my legs and restore some feeling to the bits that were numb from sitting. I drank some water and smoked a cigarette, and put on the sunglasses to circumvent a hovering glare headache: and having exhausted my repertoire except for a few shots from the Luger, folded myself back into the wedge of slowly moving shade, and took another look at the farm.

Status quo entirely unchanged. Maybe Matt was asleep, or

telephoning, or watching television, or inventing systems for his trip to Las Vegas. He certainly was not doing much farming. Nor did he apparently propose to exercise the horses. They stayed in their stalls from dawn to dusk.

By two I knew intimately every spiny plant growing within a radius of ten feet of my rock, and found my eyes going far oftener to the broad sweep of desert on my left than to the dirty little farm below. The desert was clean in its way, and fierce, and starkly beautiful. All hills and endless sky. Parched sandy grey dust and scratchy cactus. Killing heat. A wild, uncompromising, lonely place.

When I first felt the urge just to get up and walk away into it I dragged my eyes dutifully back to the farm and smoked the second cigarette and thought firmly about Matt and the horses. That only worked for a while. The barren country pulled like a magnet.

I had only to walk out there, I thought, and keep on going until I was filled with its emptiness, and then sit down somewhere and put the barrel of the Luger against my head, and simply squeeze. So childishly easy; so appallingly tempting.

Walt, I thought desperately. I couldn't do it because of Walt and the unfinished business we were embarked on. The horses were there in front of me, and Walt and Sam Hengelman were on their way. It was impossible just to abandon them. I hit my hand against the rock and dragged my mind back to the farm and the night ahead. And when I'd gone through that piece by piece I concentrated one at a time on Yola and Offen, and Eunice and Dave Teller, and Keeble and Lynnie, trying to use them as pegs to keep me believing that what I did mattered to them. That anything I did mattered to anybody. That I cared whether anything I did mattered to anybody.

My hand had been bleeding. I hadn't even felt it. I looked dispassionately at the scraped skin, and loathed myself. I shut my eyes, and the desolation went so deep that for an unmeasurable age I felt dizzy with it, as if I were in some fearful pitch black limbo, with no help, no hope, and no escape. Spinning slowly down an endless shaft in solitary despair. Lost.

The spinning stopped, after a while. The internal darkness stayed.

I opened my eyes and looked down at the farm, only half seeing it, feeling myself trembling and knowing that there wasn't much farther to go.

Matt came out of the house, walked across the yard, took a look into the barn, and retraced his steps. I watched him in a disorientated haze: those horses in the barn, what did they matter? What did anything matter? Who cared a sixpenny damn about blood lines, it would all be the same in a hundred years.

Dave Teller cared.

Let him.

Dave Teller cared a ten-thousand dollar damn what happened to them.

Crystal clear, like distilled water logic, it occurred to me that I could give us both what we wanted if I postponed my walk into the desert until later that night. I would pack the horses off with Hengelman, and instead of driving back to Kingman after him, I would set off on foot, and when it was nearly dawn, and everything looked grey and shadowy, and the step would be small . . . then . . .

Then.

I felt, immediately after making this firm decision, which seemed to me extremely sensible, a great invasion of peace. No more struggle, no more fuss. My body felt relaxed and full of well-being, and my mind was calm. I couldn't think why such an obvious solution hadn't occurred to me before. All the sweat and sleeplessness had dissolved into a cool, inner, steady light.

This stage lasted until I remembered that I had once been determined not to reach it.

After that, creeping in little by little, came the racking conviction that I had merely surrendered, and was not only despicable but probably insane.

I sat for a while with my head in my hands, fearfully expecting that with the false peace broken up and gone, back would come the shattering vertigo.

It didn't. There was only so great a tiredness that what I'd called tiredness before was like a pinhead on a continent. The dreary fight was on again; but at least I'd survived the bloodiest battle yet. Touched bottom and come back. I felt that after this I really could climb right out, if I went on trying.

A long way to go. But then, I'd have all the time I needed.

Seventeen

I HAD cramp right down both legs. Matt came out of the house and I woke up to find that the shade patch had moved round while I hadn't. When he went into the barn I started to shift the necessary two yards and found my muscles in knots.

The shade wasn't much cooler, but much better cover. I sat in it waiting for Matt to come out of the barn and for my legs to unlock. What they needed was for me to get to my feet and stamp about: but if Matt caught sight of anyone moving so close to him the whole project would lie in ruins.

He fetched water for the horses, for the calves, and for the hens. I looked at my watch, and was horribly startled to see it was nearly six. It couldn't be, I thought; but it was. Four hours since I last checked. Four hours. I shivered in the roasting air.

Matt brought the empty muck barrow around and into the barn, and came out with it filled. For the whole afternoon I'd fallen down on the surveillance, but looking back I was fairly sure nothing had changed at the farm. Certainly at this point things were as they had been: Matt had no helpers and no visitors, and when he left for Las Vegas the horses would be alone. For that piece of certainty I had been prepared to watch all day, and a poor job I'd made of it.

Matt shut the barn door and went into the house. Half an hour later he came out in a cream-coloured jacket and dark trousers, a transformation from his habitual jeans and a checked shirt. He opened the doors of the shed containing the car, went inside, started up, and drove out across the yard, round the bend on to the road, and away over the desert towards Kingman.

Satisfied, I finally got to my feet. The cramps had gone. I plodded tiredly off to the two-mile distant hidden car, and wished the night was over, not beginning. I hadn't enough energy to lick a stamp.

Matt's dust had settled when I followed him along the empty road, but when I got into Kingman he was still there. With shock I saw him standing outside a garage I was passing, and I drew into the kerb fifty yards on and looked back. The black saloon he had hired and his own blue Ford were both standing there in the forecourt. An overalled girl attendant was filling the Ford's tank from the pump, and Matt was looking in snatches at his watch and exhibiting impatience. Seven-twenty; and a hundred miles to Las Vegas. He would be a few minutes late for his appointment with Walt.

Slumping down in my seat I fixed the driving mirror so that I could watch him. He paid the girl for the petrol and hopped into his car over the top, without opening the door. Then he pulled out on to the road, turned in my direction, and went past me with his foot impressively on the accelerator. I gently followed for a while at a respectable distance, content to keep him only just in sight, and turned back to the town once he was conclusively topping the speed limit on Route 93 to Las Vegas.

Outside the unprosperous-looking Mojave Motel Sam Hengelman's horse van took up a sixth of the parking space. Inside, they told me that he had arrived at four-thirty and was along in Room 6, sleeping. I left him to it, because we couldn't move anyway until I'd phoned Walt at eight, and went into the bus station for some coffee. It came in a plastic carton out of an automat, black but weak. I drank it without tasting and thought about some food, but I wasn't really hungry enough to bother, and I was too dirty and unshaven for anywhere good. Until after eight I sat on the bus station bench staring into space, and then used the bus station telephone to get through to Walt.

He came on the line with little delay.

'How's things?' he said.

'Matt left Kingman for Las Vegas at seven-thirty, so he will be a little late.'

'Left Kingman?' Walt sounded surprised.

I explained about Matt changing cars.

'I suppose his Ford wasn't quite ready when he got there. Anyway, he's coming in that, not the hired one.'

'Are you all right?' Walt said hesitantly.

'Of course.'

'You don't sound it.'

'Sam Hengelman's here,' I said, ignoring him. 'He's asleep along at the Mojave Motel. We'll start as soon as I get back there and wake him up.'

'It's all safe at the farm?' He seemed anxious.

'Deserted,' I assured him. 'Has been all yesterday, all last night, and all today. No one around but Matt. Stop worrying. You just see Matt and put on your act, and then head straight back to Santa Barbara. As soon as Sam's clear of the area I'll follow you. See you for breakfast about twelve hours from now.'

'Right,' he said. 'Well . . . keep your nose clean.'

'You too.'

'Sure thing. It's not me that's nuts.'

The line clicked clear before I found an answer, and it left me with a vague feeling that there was more I should have said, though I didn't know what.

I knocked on Sam's door at the motel, and he came sleepily stretching to switch on the light and let me in.

'With you in a minute,' he said, reaching for his shoes and looking round for his tie.

'Sam, you don't have to come.'

'Eh?'

'Go back to sleep. I'll go and fetch the horses. That way you won't be so involved.'

He sat on the edge of the bed looking down at the floor. 'I'm still driving them to Lexington?'

'Unless you want out. Leave the van, and fly home.'

'Nope.' He shook his head. 'A bargain's a bargain. And I may as well come all the way. That van's none too easy in reverse . . . don't know that you could handle it.'

I half smiled and didn't argue. I'd wanted him with me, but only willingly, and I'd got that. He knotted his tie and brushed his hair and then took a sidelong glance at my own appearance, which fell a ton short of his. He was a fleshy man of about fifty, bald, pale-skinned, and unexcitable. His nerves, I thought, were going to be at least equal to the evening's requirements.

'Let's go, then,' he said cheerfully. 'I paid in advance.'

I followed him across to the van and climbed up into the cab. Sam started the engine, told me he'd filled up with gas when he'd first reached Kingman, and rolled out south-east on the road to the farm. His broad face looked perfectly calm in the glow from the dashboard, and he handled his six-stall horsebox like a kiddicar. He went eight miles in silence, and then all he said was, 'I'd sure hate to live this far from town, with nowhere to get a beer.'

We passed the third of the three side roads and started on the last ten uninhabited miles to the farm. Three miles farther on Sam gave an alarmed exclamation and braked from his cautious thirty to a full stop. 'What is it?' I asked.

'That gauge.' He pointed, and I looked. The needle on the temperature gauge was quivering on red.

'Have to look see,' he grunted, and switched off the engine. My thoughts as he disappeared out of the cab were one enormous curse. Of all hopeless, dangerous places for his van to break down.

He came back and opened the door my side. I jumped down beside him and he took me round to show me the exhaust.

'Look,' he said unnecessarily. 'Water.'

Several drops slid out, glistening in the light of his torch.

'Gasket,' he said, putting into one word the enormity of the disaster, and what he thought of fate for trapping us in it.

'No water in the radiator,' I said.

'Right.'

'And if we go on, the engine will seize up.'

'Right again.'

'I suppose you don't carry any extra water in the van?'

'We sure do,' he said. 'Never travel without it.'

'Can't we pour some in the radiator . . .?'

'Yeah,' he said. 'We can. There's two gallons. We can pour in a quarter, and go three miles maybe before it's all leaked out, and then another quarter, another three miles. Four quarts, twelve miles. And that's it.'

Thirteen miles out from Kingman. We could just about get back. Seven to the farm. We could refill the radiator at the farm, but Sam couldn't set out on his two thousand-mile journey with a stolen cargo in a van emptying like a dry dock.

'There's an extra gasket, of course,' he said.

'A spare one?'

'Sure. Always carry a full set of spares. Never know where you're going to need them. Universal joints, big ends, carburettors, I carry them all. Anyone with any sense does that.'

'Well,' I said in relief, 'how long will it take you to fit the spare?'

He laid the engine bare and considered it in the torch light.

'Cylinder head gasket. Say three hours.'

'*Three hours!*'

'Won't take much less,' he said. 'What do you want to do?'

I looked at my watch. Eight-fifty. Three hours made eleven-fifty; and if we then went on to the farm and picked up the horses we couldn't be back through Kingman until one-fifteen.

Matt would reach Pittsville Boulevard by nine-thirty, and finish his insurance business long before ten. If he drove straight home again he would be on the farm road at midnight. If Sam changed the gasket, so would we.

If Matt stopped to play the tables, he would be at least an hour later. His clothes had suggested he would stop. But whether for one hour or six, there was no way of telling.

'Change the gasket,' I said abruptly. 'Then we'll see.'

Sam nodded philosophically. It was what he would have done in any case if the van had broken down anywhere else, and without more ado he sorted out what he wanted and started unscrewing.

'Can I help?' I said.

He shook his head and clipped his torch on to a convenient spar to give a steady working light. There seemed to be little haste in his manner, but also no hesitation and a good deal of expertise. The heap of unplugged parts grew steadily on a square of canvas at his feet.

I walked away a few steps and felt for the cigarettes. Two left. I'd still forgotten to buy more. The smoke didn't help much towards making the next decision: to go on, or to go back.

I'd already gambled on Matt staying to play. If it had been Yola, I would have felt surer that it would be for most of the night: but her brother might not have the fever, might only want a short break in his boring stint with the horses. How short? How long?

The decision I came to, if you could call it that, was to wait and see what time Sam restarted the engine.

The night, outside the bright pool by the van, was as dark as the one before. The stars glittered remotely, and the immensity of the American continent marked their indifference to the human race. Against such size, what did one man matter? A walk into the desert . . .

Carefully I pinched out the end of my cigarette and put the stub in my pocket. A good criminal, I thought wryly: I'd always been that. I had a job to do, and even when I'd finished it, I was going for no walks into the desert. I was going back to Santa Barbara, to have breakfast with Walt and Eunice and Lynnie. The prospect at that moment seemed totally unreal, so far were the Arizona hills from the lush coast, so far had I been into the wasteland inside me.

I went back to Sam and asked how it was going. He had the cylinder head off and was removing the cracked gasket.

'So, so,' he said calmly. 'I'm breaking the record.'

I did my best at a smile. He grunted, and said he could do with a cup of coffee, and I said so could I. We hadn't brought any.

He worked on. The air was still warmer than an English summer and he wiped sweat off his bald forehead with the back of a greasy hand. The light shone on his thick stubby fingers, and the click of his spanners echoed across the empty land. The hands on my watch went round in slow fractions. The gasket was wasting the night. And where was Matt?

After two hours Sam's spanner slipped on a nut and he cursed. In spite of his calm, the tension wasn't far from the surface. He stopped what he was doing, stretched upright, took three deep breaths and a look at the night sky, and waited for me to say something.

'You're doing fine,' I said.

He sniffed. 'What'll happen if they catch us here?'

'We won't get the horses.'

He grimaced at my non-answer and went back to his task. 'What have you been doing all day?'

'Nothing. Sitting still.'

'You look half dead,' he commented. 'Pass me those two washers, will you?'

I gave him the washers. 'How much longer?'

'Can't say.'

I stifled the urge to tell him to hurry. He was going as fast as he could. But time was ticking away, and the postponed decision had got to be made. Turning my back on the tugging desert I climbed up to sit in the cab. Eleven-twenty. Matt could be a bare quarter of an hour out from Kingman. Or glued to the green baize and the tricky numbers in Las Vegas.

Which?

For a long half hour I looked out of the back windows while no helpful telepathic messages flowed through them. A straight-forward gamble, I thought. Just decide if the winnings were worth the risk.

An easier decision if I'd come alone: but if I'd come alone I couldn't have mended the gasket.

At eleven-forty Sam said gloomily that he was having to fix the water pump as well. It was sticking.

'How long?'

'Another twenty minutes.'

We stared at each other in dismay.

'Go on then,' I said in the end. There was nothing else to do.

I left the cab and walked restlessly a short way back along the road, fearing every second to see Matt's headlights and wonder-ing how best to deal with him if we had to. I was all for stealing from him what wasn't his, but not for damaging his skin. He, however, would have no such inhibitions. There would certainly be blood. Not fair to make it Sam's.

At two minutes past midnight he called out that he had finished, and I walked quickly back to join him. He was pouring water into the radiator, and screwed on the cap as I came up.

'It should be OK now,' he said. His hands were covered in

grease and his big body hung tiredly from the shoulders. 'Which way do we go?'

'On.'

He nodded with a wide slicing grin. 'I figured you'd say that. Well, I guess that's OK by me.'

He swung up into the cab and I climbed in beside him. The engine started sweetly at first try, and switching on his headlights, he released the brake and eased away along the road.

'If anyone catches us here from now on,' I said, 'duck.'

'Yeah?'

'Yeah.'

'Tell you something,' he said comfortably. 'I swing a mean left hook.'

'The chap we'd be taking on goes for the head. But with a club of some sort in his fist.'

'Nice guys you play with,' he said. 'I'll remember that.'

We covered the remaining distance at a good speed and in silence. The horsebox crept round the last corner and its headlights flickered over the farm ahead. I put my hand on Sam's arm, and he braked to a halt a short way from the yard.

'Switch off, would you? Lights too,' I said, and jumped quickly down from the cab to wait a few precious seconds until my eyes and ears got used to silence and dark.

No lights in the house. No sound anywhere except the ultra-faint ringing vibrations of limitless air. The calves and hens were asleep. The horses were quiet. I banged on the cab door and Sam switched his headlights on again before climbing down to join me. The bright shafts lit up the back of the house and wouldn't shine straight into the horses' eyes when I led them from the barn. Over on the shadowy side of the yard the open doors of the shed where Matt had kept his car yawned in a deep black square. The jumbled rubbish dump just in front of us threw surrealistic shadows across the dusty ground, and its smell of decay brushed by our noses.

Sam swept it all with a practised glance. 'Not much of a place.' His voice was as low as a whisper.

'No . . . If you'll unclip the ramp, I'll go fetch the horses. One at a time, I think.'

'OK.' He was breathing faster and his big hands were clenched. Not used to it, after all.

I hurried down towards the barn. It wasn't far; about forty yards. Now that we were totally committed my mind raced with urgency to be done, to be away, to be safely through Kingman before Matt came back. He could have been on the road behind us, be rushing at this moment across the desert to the farm . . .

What happened next happened very fast, in one terrifying cataclysmic blur.

There was an urgent shout behind me.

'Gene!'

I turned, whirling. There were two sets of headlights where there should have been one.

Matt.

The voice again, yelling. 'Gene! Look out.' And a figure running down the yard towards me.

Then there was a roar behind me and I turned again and was met full in the eyes by the blinding glare of two more headlights, much closer. Much closer.

Moving.

I was dazzled and off balance and I'd never have got clear. The running figure threw himself at me in a rugger tackle with outstretched arms and knocked me over out of the way, and the roaring car crashed solidly into the flying body and left it crumpled and smashed and lying on top of my legs.

The car which had hit him turned in a wide sweep at the end of the yard and started back. The headlights lined themselves up like twin suns on their target and with a fraction of my mind I thought it ironic that now when I'd decided not to, I was going to die.

Half sitting, half kneeling, I jerked out the Luger and pumped all of its eight bullets towards the windscreen. I couldn't see to aim straight . . . my eyes were hurting from the glare . . . Not that bullets would do any good . . . the angle was wrong . . . they'd miss the driver . . . By the time I fired the last one the left headlight was six feet away. I uselessly set my teeth against the mangling, tearing, pulping collision . . . and in the last tenth of a second the straight line wavered . . . the smooth side of the front wing hit the back of my shoulder, the front wheel ran over a fold of my shirt, and the rear wheel gave me a clear inch.

Almost before I realized it had missed me, the car crashed head on into one of the buildings at my back with a jolting screech of wood and metal. The bodywork crumpled and cracked. The stabbing lights went black. The engine stopped. Air hissed fiercely out of a punctured tyre.

Gasping, dreading what I would find, I leaned over the heavy figure lying on my legs. There were more running footsteps in the yard, and I looked up hopelessly, unable to do any more. I'd used all the bullets . . . none left.

'You're alive!' The voice came from the level of my ear, the man kneeling. Sam Hengelman. I looked at him in a daze.

'I thought . . .' I said, with no breath, '. . . this was you.'

He shook his head. 'No . . .'

He helped me raise and turn the man who'd saved me; and with sickness and unbearable regret I saw his face.

It was Walt.

We laid him on his back, in the dust.

'Look in the car,' I said.

Sam lumbered silently to his feet and went away. I heard his footsteps stop and then start back.

Walt opened his eyes, I leaned over him, lifting his hand, feeling with surging hope for his pulse.

'Gene?' his voice mumbled.

'Yes.'

'He didn't come.'

'Didn't . . .?'

'Came to help you . . .'

'Yes,' I said. 'Thanks, Walt . . .'

His eyes slid aimlessly away from my face.

'Christ,' he said distinctly. 'This is it. This is . . . really . . . it.'

'Walt . . .' His hand was warm in mine, but it didn't move.

'Sod it,' he said. 'I wanted . . . I wanted . . .'

His voice stopped. There was no pulse. No heartbeat. Nothing. Nothing at all.

I put gently down on the ground the warm hand with the rounded fingertips, and stretched out my own, and shut his eyes. It should have been me lying there, not Walt. I shook with sudden impotent fury that it wasn't me, that Walt had taken what I'd wanted, stolen my death . . . It would have mattered so little if it had been me. It wouldn't have mattered at all.

Walt . . . Walt . . .

Sam Hengelman said, 'Is he dead?'

I nodded without looking up.

'There's a young guy in the car,' he said. 'He's dead too.'

I got slowly, achingly, to my feet, and went to look. The car was a blue Ford convertible, and the young guy was Matt.

Without caring, automatically, I took in that the car had smashed the right-hand door of the garage shed and ploughed into the wall behind it. Most of the windscreen was scattered in splintered fragments all over the inside of the car, but in one corner, where some still clung to the frame, there was a finger-sized hole.

Matt was lying over the steering wheel, his arms dangling, his eyes open. The skull above the left eyebrow was pierced and crumpled inwards, and there was blood and hair on the chromium upright which had held the windscreen. I didn't touch him. After a while I went back to Walt.

'What do we do?' Sam Hengelman said.

'Give me a moment . . .'

He waited without speaking until eventually I looked up and down the yard. Two sets of headlights still blazed at the way in.

'That's Walt's car up there?'

'Yeah. He drove up with the devil on his tail and jumped out and ran down after you . . .'

I turned the other way and looked at the dark garage.

'The young guy must have been in there all the time, waiting for us,' Sam said. 'He came roaring out and drove straight at you. I couldn't have stopped him . . . too far away. Walt was halfway down the yard . . .'

I nodded. Matt had been there all the time. Not in Las Vegas. Not on the road. Lying in ambush, waiting.

He hadn't passed us on the road, and there was no other way to the farm. He must have gone back ahead of us. Turned round on the road to Las Vegas and driven back through Kingman while I was sitting in the bus station waiting to telephone Walt.

But why? *Why* should he have gone back? He hadn't seen me following him, I'd been much too far behind, and in any case I'd left him once he was safely on the highway.

It didn't matter why. It only mattered that he had. Sam Hengelman looked down at Walt and summed up the mess we were entangled in.

'Well . . . what the heck do we do now?'

I took a deep breath.

'Will you fetch that torch of yours?' I asked, and he nodded and brought it from his van. I went with it over to the Ford, and took a longer, closer look. There wasn't much to see that I hadn't seen before, except for a bottle of bourbon that had been smashed in the impact. The neck and jagged top half lay on the floor to Matt's right, along with several smaller pieces and an uneven damp patch.

I walked into the garage and looked at the Ford from the front. It wouldn't be driving anywhere any more.

The big torch lit up clearly the interior of the deep shadowy garage. Quite empty now, except for a scatter of cigarette stubs against the left-hand wall. Matt had been smoking and drinking while he waited. And he'd waited a very long time.

The bullet hole faced me in the windscreen and left me with the worst question unanswered.

I'd have to know.

I stood beside Matt and went over every inch of his body down to the waist. He'd taken off the cream-coloured jacket and was wearing the checked shirt he'd worked in. There were no holes in it: no punctures underneath. His head was heavy. I laid it gently on the steering wheel and stepped away.

None of the bullets had hit him. They'd only smashed the windscreen and blinded him, and he'd slewed a foot off course and run into the wall instead of me, and his head had gone forward hard against the slim metal post.

Slowly I returned to where Sam Hengelman stood beside Walt. He drooped with the utmost dejection and looked at me without hope.

'Did you unclip the ramp?' I asked abruptly.

He shook his head. 'Didn't have time.'

'Go and do it now. We're taking the horses.'

He was aghast. 'We can't!'

'We've got to. For Walt's sake, and your sake, and Dave Teller's sake. And mine. What do you propose? That we call the police and explain what we were all doing here?'

'We'll have to,' he said despairingly.

'No. Definitely not. Go and let down the ramp.'

He hesitated unbelievingly for a few seconds, and then went and did as I asked. The horses stood peacefully in the barn, apparently undisturbed by the racket, the shots, and the crash.

I untied the nearest, Showman, and led him quietly up the yard and into the van.

Sam watched me in silence while I tied him into one of the stalls.

'We'll never get away with it.'

'Yes we will,' I said, 'as long as you take these horses safely back to Lexington and never tell anyone, anyone at all, what happened here tonight. Blot it out of your mind. I'll let you know, when you get back, that you've nothing to worry about. And as long as you tell no one, you won't have.'

The broad fleshy face was set in lines of anxiety.

'You've collected two horses,' I said matter-of-factly. 'An everyday job, collecting two horses. Forget the rest.'

I returned to the barn, fetched Allyx, and loaded him up. Sam still hadn't moved.

'Look,' I said. 'I've . . . arranged . . . things before. There's a rule where I come from – you take a risk, you get into a mess, you get out.' He blinked. 'Walt threw himself in the way of that car,' I said. 'Matt didn't intend to kill *him* . . . You didn't see a murder. Matt drove straight into the wall himself . . . and that too was an accident. Only two automobile accidents. You must have seen dozens. Forget it.' He didn't answer, and I added brusquely, 'The water can's empty. You can fill it over there.'

With something like a shudder he picked up the container and went where I pointed. Sighing, I checked that he had brought three days' fodder for the stallions, which he had, and with his help on his return, shut the precious cargo up snugly for their long haul.

'You don't happen to have any gloves around?' I asked.

'Only an old cotton pair in the tool kit.'

He rooted about and finally produced them, two filthy objects covered with oil and grease which would leave marks on everything they touched, as tale-bearing as fingerprints. I turned them inside out and found they were thick enough to be clean on the inside. Sam watched wordlessly while I put them on, clean side out.

'OK,' I said. 'Will you turn the van, ready to go?'

He did it cautiously as far away from Walt as he could, and when he'd finished I stepped with equal care into the car Walt had come in, touching it as little and as lightly as possible, and drove it down into the yard, stopping a little short of the screen door to the house. There I switched off the engine and lights, put on the brake, and walked back to talk to Sam where he sat in his cab.

'I've three jobs to do,' I said. 'I'll be back as quick as I can. Why don't you just shut your eyes for a couple of minutes and catch a nap?'

'You're kidding.'

I concocted a replica of a smile, and a fraction of the tension in his face unwound.

'I won't be long,' I said, and he nodded, swallowing.

With his torch I surveyed the yard. The Luger was an automatic pistol, which meant it threw out the cartridge after each shot. No one would find the spent bullets, but eight shiny metal shells scattered near Walt's body were something else. Seven of them winked in the light as I inched the torch carefully round, and I collected them into my pocket. The eighth remained obstinately invisible.

The ejection slot had been on the side of the gun away from Walt, but the cases sometimes shot out straight upwards instead of sideways, and I began to wonder if the eighth could possibly have travelled far enough over to be underneath him. I didn't want to disturb him: but I had to find the little brass thimble.

Then, when I'd decided I had no choice, I saw it. Bent and dusty, partly flattened, no longer shining. I picked it up from the spot where I had been half-lying in the path of Matt's car. He had run over it.

After that I attended to the ground itself. Tyre marks didn't show on the rough dusty surface, but the hoof prints did to some extent. I fetched a broom of twigs from the barn and swept them out.

The garage was next. I punched through into the car the remaining corner of the windscreen with its significant bullet hole, and I picked up every one of the cigarette stubs which told where and how long Matt had waited. They went into a trash can standing a few yards along from the house door.

Matt hadn't locked the house when he went out. I went in to look for one essential piece of information: the address of the place, and the name of its owner. The torchlight swept over the threadbare covers and elderly furniture, and in one drawer of a large dresser I found what the farmer used for an office. The jumble of bills and letters gave me what I wanted. Wilbur Bellman, Far Valley Farm, Kingman. On the scratch pad beside the telephone, Matt had written a bonus. In heavy black ballpoint were the simple words: 'Insurance 9 PM.'

Before leaving I gave the big dilapidated living room a final circuit with the torch and the beam flickered over a photograph in a cardboard folder standing on a shelf. Something about the face in it struck me as familiar, and I swung the torch back for a second and closer look.

The patient passive face of Kiddo smiled out, as untroubled as it had been when he told Walt and me about Offen's mares. Loopy unformed writing straggled over the lower half of the picture. 'To Ma and Pa, from your loving son.'

If Offen had sent his stud groom to Miami to join his parents, Kiddo's loyalty to his employer was a certainty. I almost admired Offen's technique in furnishing himself in one throw with an obscure hideout for the horses and a non-talking employee.

After the house there remained only Walt. Nothing to do but to say goodbye.

I went down on my knees beside him in the dust, but the

silent form was already subtly not Walt. Death showed. I took off one glove and touched his hand: still warm in the warm air, but without the firmness of life.

There was no point in saying to him what I felt. If his spirit was still hovering somewhere around, he would know.

I left him lying there in the dark, and went back to Sam.

He took one slow look at my face and said in an appalled voice, 'You're not leaving him there?'

I nodded, and climbed up beside him.

'But you *can't* . . .'

I simply nodded again, and gestured to him to start up and drive away. He did it with a viciousness that must have rocked the stallions on their feet, and we went back to Kingman without speaking. His revulsion at what I had done reached me in almost tangible waves.

I didn't care. I felt only one grim engulfing ache for the man I'd left behind.

Eighteen

LYNNIE PUT her brown hand tentatively on mine and said, 'Gene . . . what's the matter?'

'Nothing,' I said.

'You look worse than you did when you came back with Chrysalis. Much worse.'

'The food doesn't agree with me.'

She snorted and took her hand away. We were sitting on the sea terrace, waiting for Eunice to come down for dinner, with the sun galloping the last lap to dusk and the daiquiris tinkling with civilized ice.

'Is Walt back yet?' Lynnie said.

'No.'

'He's a funny man, isn't he?' she said. 'All moods and glum looks, and then suddenly he smiles, and you realize how nice he is. I like him.'

After a pause I said, 'So do I.'

'How was San Francisco?' she asked.

'Foggy.'

'What's the matter?'

'Nothing.'

She sighed and shook her head.

Eunice arrived in a cloud of yellow chiffon and clanked her gold bracelet as she stretched for her drink. She was cheerful and glowing; almost too much to bear.

'Well, you son of a bitch, when did you crawl in?'

'This afternoon,' I said.

'So what's new?'

'I've given up trying to find the horses.'

Eunice sat up straight with a jerk. 'For crying out loud!'

'I'll be starting home soon. Tomorrow evening, I expect.'

'Oh no,' Lynnie said.

'Oh, yes, I'm afraid so. The holidays are over.'

'They don't look as if they've done you much good,' Eunice observed. 'So now how do you deal with it?'

'With what?'

'With flopping. With not making out.'

I said wryly, 'Look it smack in the eye and dare it to bite you.'

'It probably will,' said Eunice sardonically. 'It'll chew me to bloody bits.' She drank the second quarter of her drink and looked me thoughtfully over. 'Come to think of it, it seems to have done that to you already.'

'Maybe I'll take up golf.'

She laughed, more internally relaxed than I'd ever seen her. 'Games', she said, 'are a bore.'

When they went in to eat I couldn't face it, and drove off instead to fetch the tape recorder from the rocks at Orpheus Farm. The short journey seemed tiresomely long. It had been nearly four hundred and fifty miles back to Santa Barbara from Kingman, and neither bath, shave, nor two hours flat on the bed seemed to have had any effect.

Back in my room at The Vacationer I listened to the whole of the tape's four-hour playing time. The first conversations, two or three business calls, were from the previous morning, after Walt had put in a new reel. Then there was almost an hour and a half of an interview between Offen and a man from the Blood-stock Registry Office. They had already been out to see the horses, and Offen was piling proof on proof that the horses in his barn were veritably Moviemaker and Centigrade. A groom who had cared for Centigrade during his racing days was asked in to sign a statement he'd made that he recognized the horse and would if necessary swear to its identity in any inquiry.

The bloodstock man apologized constantly that anyone should have doubted Offen. Offen enjoyed the scene, the joke rumbling like an undertone. After they'd gone he laughed aloud. I hoped he'd enjoyed it. He wouldn't be laughing much for a long time to come.

Next on the tape was a piece of Offen giving his houseman instructions for replenishing the drink stocks, then an hour's television programme. And after that, Matt telephoned.

I couldn't hear his voice at all, only Offen's replies, but they were enough.

'Hello, Matt . . .

'Slow down, I'm not taking this in. Where did you say you were? . . .

'What are you doing on the road to Las Vegas? . . .

'Well, I can see the house must be insured . . .

'You found *what* under the glove shelf? . . .

'How do you know it's a homer? . . .

'All these minute transmitters are a mystery to me . . .

'Who could have put it there? . . .

'I don't follow you. What was that about yellow paint? . . .

'But the police said it was vandals . . .

'All right, Matt, don't shout. I'm doing my best. Now let's get this clear. You were fumbling for a pack of cigarettes and you dislodged this . . . thing. Bug, whatever you said. And you're worried now that Hawkins and Prensela put it in your car, and that they used that and the yellow paint to follow you, so that they know where you've been staying, or maybe. Is that right? . . .

'Matt, I think you're blowing this thing up too big . . .

'But did you actually *see* a plane following you? . . .

'Well, yes, sure, if you think you should go back, go back. The horses are far more important than the insurance on the house. But I think you're wrong. Hawkins and Prensela have been concentrating on Moviemaker and Centigrade here, they've stirred up the DA's office from LA and the bloodstock registry, and it's been a three-ringed circus here for the last couple of days. They wouldn't have been trying to find any horses anywhere else, because they're sure they're here in the barn . . .

'Well, I don't *know* who could have planted the bug . . .

'Yeah. All right. Go on back, then . . .

'Call me in the morning . . .

'Goodnight, Matt.'

The receiver went down, and for a few seconds there were the indistinct noises of Offen going over the conversation again in his mind, punctuating it with 'umphs' and small doubtful grunts.

I switched the tape off temporarily and thought bitterly about Matt finding the bug. I hadn't had a chance to remove it: on my first night visit to the farm the car in the garage had been the one he'd hired while his own was being cleaned of paint. But neither had I looked upon it as a very great hazard, because the little capsules were light and clung tightly. It had been long odds against him groping for cigarettes while driving in the dark, and dislodging it. I hadn't taken it into account.

Sometime on his way back to the farm it must have struck him that the insurance appointment might be phoney; that if we had tricked him into going to Las Vegas once already, we might be tricking him again. If we'd got him out of the way, it could only be to take the horses. So he'd wait; in the dark, ready to spring.

He must have begun to think, when he'd sat out the three hours it took to mend the gasket, that Uncle Bark was right and he was wrong: but all the same he'd gone on waiting. And, in the end, we had come.

I switched the tape on again for the rest. The whole night

had been telescoped into the few seconds' silence, because when Offen made his next call it was clearly morning.

'Yola, is that you?'

A faint clacking reached the bug. Yola's higher-pitched voice disturbed more air.

'Have you heard from Matt?'

'. . .'

'No, he said he'd call me this morning, and he hasn't. I can't get any answer from the farm.'

'. . .'

'Well, not really. He called me last night because he had some crazy idea Hawkins had traced the horses . . .'

A loud squawk from Yola.

'Something about a listening bug and yellow paint.'

Yola talked for some time and when Offen answered he sounded anxious.

'Yeah, I know he found the first one when we thought that was impossible . . . do you really think Matt may be right?'

'. . .'

'Yola, that's right out. Why don't you go yourself?'

'. . .'

'Close the ranch then. Send them all home.'

'. . .'

'Look, if you're right, if Matt's right . . . say when he went back last night the DA's men were sitting there waiting for him? Say they're sitting there right now, waiting for me to turn up and see why Matt doesn't answer his calls? No, Yola, I'm not walking into that farm and find I have to answer questions like what am I doing there, and what are those two horses in the barn, with Moviemaker and Centigrade's registrations tattooed inside their lips? I'm not going.'

'. . .'

'Matt may be off on some plan of his own.'

'. . .'

'No. I'll give him today. If I haven't heard from him by morning I'll . . . well, I'll think of something.'

Yola's final remark was loud, and I heard it clearly. Full of anxiety, full of anguish.

'If anything's happened to Matt . . .'

The end of the tape ran off the reel, and I switched off the recorder. For Yola, as for Walt's wife, life would never be the same again.

I went to bed and lay awake, feeling feverish from lack of sleep. Relaxed every limb, but my mind would have none of it. It was filled too full, as it had been all day, of a picture of Walt still lying on his back in the farmyard. The sun had risen and blazed on him, and set again. He would have no shelter until tomorrow. I couldn't sleep until he had. I tried to, but I couldn't.

On my way back to Santa Barbara I'd stopped for coffee and a handful of change, and I'd telephoned to Paul M. Zeissen in the Buttress Life office on Thirty-Third Street. It had been nearly 6 PM New York time. Zeissen was preparing to go home for the weekend. I was a little worried, I told him, about Walt. He had gone to do some life insurance business on a farm in Arizona, and I hadn't heard from him since. Zeissen and I talked it over for a few minutes in unurgent civilized tones, and arranged finally that if I hadn't heard from Walt by morning, Buttress Life would ring the Arizona State Police in Kingman, and ask them as a favour to go out to the farm, just to check.

In the morning I would ring Zeissen at his home. By noon, perhaps, the Kingman police would reach the farm. They would read the story: insurance salesman arrives for appointment, gets out of car. Matt Clive, hurrying back to meet him, swings into the yard, sees a dark figure too late, hits him, runs straight on into the wall because judgement suspended by horror at collision. Matt, with whisky inside him, and a bottle in the car. Inside the house the 9 PM insurance appointment written in Matt's hand. And nothing else. No horses. No suggestion of visitors. No sign that it could have been anything but a tragically unlucky accident.

Matt had been good at accidents.

So was I.

I lay on my stomach on the beach all morning while Lynnie sat beside me and trickled sand through her fingers. Eunice had gone to Santa Monica, down the coast.

'Are you really going home this evening?' Lynnie said.

'First hop, yes.'

'Would you mind . . . if I came with you?'

I stirred in surprise.

'I thought you wanted to stay here for ever.'

'Mm. But that was with you . . . and Eunice. Now you're going . . . and Eunice hasn't been here much this week, you know. I've spent ages all on my own, and there isn't that much to do on a beach, when you do it every day . . .'

'Where had Eunice been?'

'Santa Monica, like now. There's some place there she spends all her time in, where they import vases and bits of sculpture and expensive light fittings, and things like that. She took me there the day before yesterday . . . I must say it's pretty gorgeous. Marvellous fabrics, too.'

'She might feel hurt if you just pack up and leave her.'

'Well, no. I mentioned it to her before she went this morning, and honestly I think if anything she was relieved. She just said if I really wanted to go, OK, and she would probably be moving down to Santa Monica in a day or two anyway.'

'If you really want to, then. I'm catching the night flight to Washington . . . I've a visit to make in Lexington tomorrow morning. After that, back to New York, and home.'

'You don't mind if I tag along?' She sounded a scrap uncertain.

'Come to think of it,' I said, 'you can wake me at the stops.'

We had a sandwich for lunch which I couldn't eat, and at two the girl from the reception desk came to say I was wanted on the telephone. Paul M. Zeissen told me in a suitably hushed voice that the Arizona police had been most co-operative and had gone to Bellman's farm as asked, and had found Walt dead. I made shocked noises. Zeissen said would I pack Walt's things and send them back? I said I would.

'I suppose,' he suggested diffidently, 'that you and he had not completed your other business?'

'The horses?'

'One horse. Allyx,' he said reprovingly. 'Showman was insured with another company.'

'Oh . . . yes. Allyx should be in circulation, safe and authenticated within a month or so. I expect the Bloodhorse Breeders' Association will be getting in touch with you. Walt worked very hard at this, and it was entirely owing to his efforts that Buttress Life will be recovering most of the million and a half it paid out.'

'Where did he find the horse?'

'I can't tell you. Does it matter?'

'No . . .' he said thoughtfully. 'Goods back, no questions asked . . . we work on that principle, the same as any other company.'

'Right then,' I said. 'And you'll of course pay his commission to his widow?'

'Uh . . . of course. And naturally Walt had insured his life with us . . . Mrs Prensela will be well provided for, I feel sure.'

Provided for. Money. But no Walt. No picnic.

I said goodbye to Zeissen and went slowly back to Lynnie. When I told her Walt was dead, she cried for him.

Upstairs, when I packed his clothes, I lingered a good while over the framed photograph of him with Amy and the kids, and in the end put it in my suitcase, not his. It could hardly be the only photograph his wife would have of him, and I didn't think she'd worry much if it didn't return with his baggage.

Eunice came back tired and abstracted from Santa Monica, and after absorbing the shock of Walt's death was unaffected when Lynnie told her over early dinner that she was going home with me.

'Much better to travel with a man to look after you, honey,' she agreed absent-mindedly: and then, giving me a more characteristic sharp glance, added, 'Don't let him get up to any tricks.'

Lynnie sighed. 'He wouldn't.'

'Huh,' she said, but without conviction, and then asked me, 'Will you be seeing Dave when you get back?'

I nodded. 'Very soon after.'

'Tell him then, will you, that I've found a darling little business in Santa Monica. They're looking for a partner with some capital, to open another branch, and if the accounts are right I'd like to do it. I'll write to him, of course, but you could explain . . . I guess you could explain better than anyone.'

'I'll explain.'

She said she was too tired to come all the way back to Los Angeles to see us off, and we said goodbye to her in the lobby, where she kissed Lynnie and then me on the cheek with a quite surprising strength of feeling.

Lynnie said, as we drove away, 'I'll miss her. Isn't that extraordinary. I'll really miss her.'

'You'll come back.'

'It won't be the same . . .'

I returned the hired car to the Hertz agent at the airport, we caught the plane to Washington, and I made up on parts of the way for the three nights without sleep. Lynnie said at Lexington that she could quite see why I needed someone to wake me at the stops.

We went in a taxi to Jeff Roots's house and his teenage

daughters took Lynnie off for a swim in the pool while I sat with him under his vine-covered trellis and thought how cool and substantial he looked in his bright open-necked Sunday shirt.

'Sam Hengelman should reach Lexington some time this afternoon or early evening,' I said. 'He'll call you to know where to take the horses.'

'That's all fixed,' Roots nodded.

'Would you give him a message from me?'

'Sure.'

'Just tell him everything's OK: that I said so.'

'Sure. You are, aren't you, one hundred per cent certain that those two definitely are Showman and Allyx?'

'One hundred per cent. There isn't the slightest doubt.'

He sighed. 'I'll get the identification started. Though who is to know Showman after ten years? A bay with no markings . . . and only a four-year-old when he came from England.' He paused, then said, 'Have you any suggestions as to how we can start prosecuting Offen for fraud and theft?'

I shook my head. 'I'm not a policeman. Not interested in punishment, only prevention.' I smiled briefly. 'I came to get the horses back. Nothing else. Well . . . they're back. I've done what I was engaged for, and that's as far as I go.'

He eyed me assessingly. 'Do you want Offen to go on collecting huge stud fees, then?'

'He won't,' I said. 'Not if someone starts a quick rumour immediately that both Moviemaker and Centigrade have been suffering from an obscure virus which will certainly have affected their virility. Owners of mares can be quietly advised to insist they don't pay any stud fees until the foals have shown their quality. After that . . . well, Offen does legally own Moviemaker and Centigrade, and he's entitled to the fees they earn on their own merits.'

'You're extraordinary,' he said. 'Don't you want to see Offen behind bars?'

'Not passionately,' I said. Offen had enjoyed his prestige almost more than his income. He would be losing both. And Yola . . . she was going to have to work hard, without Matt, and probably without the expensive house on Pitts. Bars seemed superfluous.

He shook his head, giving me up as a bad job. 'We'll have to prosecute, I'm sure of it. I'll have to get the lawyers to see about it.'

He called the houseman to bring our drinks, and merely sighed when I said I'd as soon share his sugar-free tonic.

We sipped the well-iced innocuous stuff and he said again that Offen would have to be prosecuted, if only to provide a reason for Allyx and Showman having disappeared for so many years, and to account for tattoo marks inside their mouths.

'I can see you would think that,' I said. 'I also think you'll have a terrible job proving that any of the mares booked to Moviemaker and Centigrade were actually covered by Showman and Allyx. I didn't find Showman and Allyx on Offen's farm. I doubt if anyone would testify that they were ever there. Certainly Offen would deny it, and go on denying it to the bitter end. It's his only hope.' I paused. 'I did manage to get some tape recordings, but unfortunately, even if they could be used as evidence, they are inconclusive. Offen never mentioned Showman or Allyx by name.'

Roots stared gloomily into space.

'This makes it difficult,' he said. 'What you are in fact saying is that we know Offen switched the stallions, because of the tattoo marks, but no one will be able to prove it?'

I looked down to where Lynnie was jumping into the pool in a big splash contest with Roots's daughters. Her lighthearted laughter floated up, carefree and very young.

'I wouldn't try,' I said. 'Rightly or wrongly I decided to repossess the stolen goods by stealing them back. First, so that Offen would have no chance of destroying them. Second, so that there shouldn't be years of delay while lawyers argued the case, years of the stallions standing idle, with their value diminishing day by day and their blood lines wasting. Third, and most important, that there should be no chance of Offen getting them back once the dust had settled. Because if he had any sense he would swear, and provide witnesses to swear, that the horses in dispute were two unraced halfbred animals of no account, and he'd explain the tattoos on their lips by saying he'd used them to try out some new type of ink. What more likely, he would say, than that he should repeat the numbers of his two best horses? He could make it sound a lot more reasonable than that he should have stolen two world famous stallions and conducted a large-scale fraud. He has great personal charm.'

Roots nodded. 'I've met him.'

'Showman and Allyx were being looked after by Offen's nephew,' I said. 'Offen can say he'd lent him two old nags to hack around on, and he can't imagine why anyone would want to steal them.'

'He could put up an excellent defence, I see that,' he admitted.

'His present stud groom is innocent,' I added. 'And would convince anyone of it. If you leave things as they are, Offen won't get Allyx and Showman back. If you prosecute him, he may.'

He looked shattered, staring into his glass but seeing with experienced eyes every side of the sticky problem.

'We could try blood tests,' he said at last.

'Blood tests?'

'For paternity,' he nodded. 'If there is any doubt about which horse has sired a certain foal, we take blood tests. If one disputed sire's blood is of a similar group to the foal's, and the other disputed sire's is different, we conclude that the foal was sired by the similar sire.'

'And like in humans,' I asked, 'you can tell which horse could *not* have sired which foal, but you couldn't say which, of a similar blood group, actually did?'

'That's right.'

We thought it over. Then he said cheerfully, 'If we can prove that none of the so-called Moviemaker foals could in fact have been sired by Moviemaker, but could all have been sired by Showman, we'll have Offen sewn up tight.'

'Couldn't he possibly have made sure, before he ever bought Moviemaker, that his and Showman's blood groups were similar? I mean, if he's a breeder, he'd know about blood tests.'

Roots's gloom returned. 'I suppose it's possible. And possible that Centigrade and Allyx are similar too.' He looked up suddenly and caught me smiling. 'It's all right for you to think it's funny,' he said, wryly matching my expression. 'You don't have to sort out the mess. What in God's name are we going to do about the Stud Book? Moviemaker's . . . that is, Showman's . . . get are already siring foals, in some cases. The mix-up is in the second generation. How are we ever going to put it straight?'

'Even if,' I pointed out, trying hard to keep the humour out of my voice and face, 'even if you prove Moviemaker couldn't have sired the foals he's supposed to have done, you can't prove Showman *did*.'

He gave me a comically pained look. 'What other sire could have got such brilliant stock?' He shook his head. 'We'll pin it on Offen in the end, even if we have to wait until after Showman and Allyx have been re-syndicated and their first official crops have won as much stake money as all the others. Offen wouldn't be able to say then that they were two halfbred nags he'd given his nephew to hack around on. We'll get him in the end.'

'The racing scandal of the year,' I said smiling.

'Of the year? Are you kidding? Of the century.'

*

Lynnie and I flew from Kennedy that night on a Super VC 10, with dinner over Canada at midnight and breakfast over Ireland three hours later. I spent the interval looking at her while she slept beside me in her sloped-back chair. Her skin was close textured like a baby's, and her face was that of a child. The woman inside was still a bud, with a long way to grow.

Keeble met us at Heathrow, and as usual it was raining. Lynnie kissed him affectionately. He went so far as to shake my hand. There was a patch of stubble on his left cheek, and the eyes blinked quickly behind the mild glasses. Santa Barbara was six thousand miles away. We were home.

Keeble suggested a cup of coffee before we left the airport and asked his daughter how she'd enjoyed herself. She told him non-stop for twenty minutes, her suntan glowing in the grey summer morning and her brown eyes alight.

He looked finally from her to me, and his face subtly contracted.

'And what have you been doing?' he said.

Lynnie answered when I didn't. 'He's been with us on the beach a good deal of the time,' she said doubtfully.

Keeble stroked her arm. 'Did you find the horses?' he asked.

I nodded.

'All three?'

'With help.'

'I told Dave I'd drop you off at the hospital when we leave here,' he said. 'He's still strung up, but he hopes to be out next week.'

'I've a lot to tell him, and there's a lot he'll have to decide.' The worst being, I thought, whether to carry on with his move alongside Orpheus Farm, or to disappoint Eunice in her new-found business. Nothing was ever simple. Nothing was easy.

'You don't look well,' Keeble said abruptly.

'I'll live,' I said, and his eyes flickered with a mixture of

surprise and speculation. I smiled lopsidedly and said it again,
'I'll live.'

We stood up to go. Instead of shaking hands Lynnie suddenly put her arms round my waist and her head on my chest.

'I don't want to say goodbye,' she said indistinctly. 'I want to
see you again.'

'Well,' I said reasonably. 'You will.'

'I mean . . . often.'

I met Keeble's eyes over her head. He was watching her
gravely, but without disquiet.

'She's too young,' I said to him, and he knew exactly what
I meant. Not that I was too old for her, but that she was too
young for me. Too young in experience, understanding, and
wickedness.

'I'll get older,' she said. 'Will twenty-one do?'

Her father laughed, but she gripped my arm. 'Will it?'

'Yes,' I said recklessly, and found one second later that I really
meant it.

'She'll change her mind,' Keeble said with casual certainty.

I said, 'Of course,' to him, but Lynnie looked up into my
eyes and shook her head.

It was late afternoon when I got back to the flat. The tidy,
dull, unwelcoming rooms hadn't changed a bit. When I looked
at the kitchen I remembered Lynnie making burnt scrambled
egg, and I felt a fierce disturbing wish that she would soon make
some more.

I unpacked. The evening stretched greyly ahead.

I sat and stared vacantly at the bare walls.

If was a grinding word, I thought. If Sam Hengelman had
taken longer to mend that gasket, Walt would have found us on
the road and would have stopped us going to the farm. If Sam
had mended it faster, we'd have reached the farm well before
Walt, and Matt would have killed me, as he'd meant.

If I hadn't decided to recover the horses by stealing them,

Walt would be alive. They might collectively be worth nearly five million dollars, but they weren't worth Walt's life.

I wished I'd never started.

The grey day turned to grey dusk. I got up and switched on the light, and fetched two objects to put on the low table beside my chair.

The Luger, and the photograph of Walt with his wife and kids.

The trouble with being given a gift you don't really want is that you feel so mean if you throw it away. Especially if it cost more than the giver could afford.

I won't throw away Walt's gift. Even if Lynnie changes her mind, I'll survive.

Tired beyond feeling, I went to bed at ten. I put the Luger under the pillow, and hung the photograph on the wall.

And slept.

IN THE FRAME

My thanks to two professional artists, Michael Jeffrey of Australia and Josef Jira of Czechoslovakia, who generously showed me their studios, their methods, their minds and their lives.

Also to the many art galleries whose experts gave me information and help and particularly to Peter Johnson of Oscar and Peter Johnson, London SW1, and to the Stud and Stable Gallery, Ascot.

for Caroline
sound asleep

Alice Springs

Perth

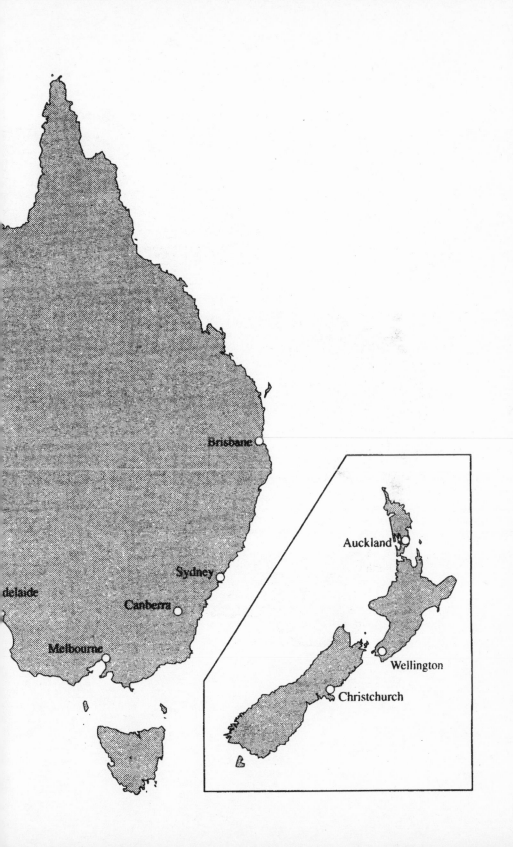

Introduction

In the Frame was conceived in Czechoslovakia, incubated in Australia and New Zealand and written in England.

We (my wife, Mary, and I) were with the remarkable lady burns-specialist doctor who translates my books into the Czech language in her spare time, when she had business to attend to with a painter friend of hers. She took us briefly to his studio, where our eyes and emotions were bombarded by massed canvases of extraordinary passion and vigorous jumbled colour, chiefly on the subject – if deciphering were possible – of the feeding of the multitude with five fishes. As the painter spoke no English nor we a word of Czech, asking for meaning was impracticable, especially as (according to my translator) he couldn't explain them to her either.

We visited her apartment and found another of his paintings on her wall: again the fishes, the thick brilliant and dark colours, the unfathomable urgent mysterious message.

I began unexpectedly to want to write about a painter, and I asked if we could go back and watch him work. To my translator's surprise he agreed, and for two fascinating silent hours the three of us watched him sticking paint on to canvas with a sort of violent divine energy, using brushes, fingers and even at one point his elbow to satisfy his vision.

I came away shaken. I couldn't imagine being *him*. I needed a less driven artist for my protagonist. I thought I could manage a painter of horses.

Later that year we went to Australia and New Zealand on a book-promotion tour, and there – arranged in advance – I met Michael Jeffrey, one of Australia's foremost horse painters. He, too, generously let me into his studio and gave great advice about the use and mixing of colours.

Back home in England, Mary and I read books about the chemical composition of oil paints and how they adhere to wood and canvas, and we filled our sunroom with easels, linseed, turps and other tools of the trade. Primed by this little knowledge, I put Charles Todd to paper as a painter of horses, alongside the flamboyant abstract genius of his long-time friend, Jik.

Mary finally painted a horse. Its neck was too long. We both learned we were never destined to be artists ourselves, but, nevertheless, *In the Frame* taught us a lot about Art.

One

I STOOD on the outside of disaster, looking in.

There were three police cars outside my cousin's house, and an ambulance with its blue turret light revolving ominously, and people bustling in seriously through his open front door. The chill wind of early autumn blew dead brown leaves sadly on to the driveway, and harsh scurrying clouds threatened worse to come. Six o'clock, Friday evening, Shropshire, England.

Intermittent bright white flashes from the windows spoke of photography in progress within. I slid my satchel from my shoulder and dumped both it and my suitcase on the grass verge, and with justifiable foreboding completed my journey to the house.

I had travelled by train to stay for the weekend. No cousin with car to meet me as promised, so I had started to walk the mile and a half of country road, sure he would come tearing along soon in his muddy Peugeot, full of jokes and apologies and plans.

No jokes.

He stood in the hall, dazed and grey. His body inside his neat business suit looked limp, and his arms hung straight down from the shoulders as if his brain had forgotten they were there. His head was turned slightly towards the sitting-room, the source of the flashes, and his eyes were stark with shock.

'Don?' I said. I walked towards him. 'Donald!'

He didn't hear me. A policeman, however, did. He came

swiftly from the sitting-room in his dark blue uniform, took me by the arm and swung me strongly and unceremoniously back towards the door.

'Out of here, sir,' he said. 'If you please.'

The strained eyes slid uncertainly our way.

'Charles . . .' His voice was hoarse.

The policeman's grip loosened very slightly. 'Do you know this man, sir?' he asked Donald.

'I'm his cousin,' I said.

'Oh.' He took his hand off, told me to stay where I was and look after Mr Stuart, and returned to the sitting-room to consult.

'What's happened?' I said.

Don was past answering. His head turned again towards the sitting-room door, drawn to a horror he could no longer see. I disobeyed the police instructions, took ten quiet steps, and looked in.

The familiar room was unfamiliarly bare. No pictures, no ornaments, no edge-to-edge floor covering of oriental rugs. Just bare grey walls, chintz-covered sofas, heavy furniture pushed awry, and a great expanse of dusty wood-block flooring.

And on the floor, my cousin's young wife, bloody and dead.

The big room was scattered with busy police, measuring, photographing, dusting for fingerprints. I knew they were there; didn't see them. All I saw was Regina lying on her back, her face the colour of cream.

Her eyes were half open, still faintly bright, and her lower jaw had fallen loose, outlining brutally the shape of the skull. A pool of urine lay wetly on the parquet around her sprawled legs, and one arm was flung out sideways with the dead white fingers curling upwards as if in supplication.

There had been no mercy.

I looked at the scarlet mess of her head and felt the blood draining from my own.

The policeman who had grabbed me before turned round from his consultation with another, saw me swaying in the door-way, and took quick annoyed strides back to my side.

'I told you to wait outside, sir,' he said with exasperation, stating clearly that my faintness was my own fault.

I nodded dumbly and went back into the hall. Donald was sitting on the stairs, looking at nothing. I sat abruptly on the floor near him and put my head between my knees.

'I . . . f . . . found . . . her,' he said.

I swallowed. What could one say? It was bad enough for me, but he had lived with her, and loved her. The faintness passed away slowly, leaving a sour feeling of sickness. I leaned back against the wall behind me and wished I knew how to help him.

'She's . . . never . . . home . . . on F . . . Fridays,' he said.

'I know.'

'S . . . six. S . . . six o'clock . . . she comes b . . . back. Always.'

'I'll get you some brandy,' I said.

'She shouldn't . . . have been . . . here . . .'

I pushed myself off the floor and went into the dining-room, and it was there that the significance of the bare sitting-room forced itself into consciousness. In the dining-room too there were bare walls, bare shelves, and empty drawers pulled out and dumped on the floor. No silver ornaments. No silver spoons or forks. No collection of antique china. Just a jumble of table mats and napkins and broken glass.

My cousin's house had been burgled. And Regina . . . Regina, who was never home on Fridays . . . had walked in . . .

I went over to the plundered sideboard, flooding with anger and wanting to smash in the heads of all greedy, callous, vicious people who cynically devastated the lives of total strangers. Compassion was all right for saints. What I felt was plain hatred, fierce and basic.

I found two intact glasses, but all the drink had gone.

Furiously I stalked through the swing door into the kitchen and filled the electric kettle.

In that room too, the destruction had continued, with stores swept wholesale off the shelves. What valuables, I wondered, did thieves expect to find in kitchens? I jerkily made two mugs of tea and rummaged in Regina's spice cupboard for the cooking brandy, and felt unreasonably triumphant when it proved to be still there. The sods had missed that, at least.

Donald still sat unmoving on the stairs. I pressed the cup of strong sweet liquid into his hands and told him to drink, and he did, mechanically.

'She's never home . . . on Fridays,' he said.

'No,' I agreed, and wondered just how many people knew there was no one home on Fridays.

We both slowly finished the tea. I took his mug and put it with mine on the floor, and sat near him as before. Most of the hall furniture had gone. The small Sheraton desk . . . the studded leather chair . . . the nineteenth-century carriage clock . . .

'Christ, Charles,' he said.

I glanced at his face. There were tears, and dreadful pain. I could do nothing, nothing, to help him.

The impossible evening lengthened to midnight, and beyond. The police, I suppose, were efficient, polite, and not unsympathetic, but they left a distinct impression that they felt their job was to catch criminals, not to succour the victims. It seemed to me that there was also, in many of their questions, a faint hovering doubt, as if it were not unknown for householders to arrange their own well-insured burglaries, and for smooth-seeming swindles to go horrifically wrong.

Donald didn't seem to notice. He answered wearily, automatically, with long pauses sometimes between question and answer.

Yes, the missing goods were well insured.

Yes, they had been insured for years.

Yes, he had been to his office all day as usual.

Yes, he had been out to lunch. A sandwich in a pub.

He was a wine shipper.

His office was in Shrewsbury.

He was thirty-seven years old.

Yes, his wife was much younger. Twenty-two.

He couldn't speak of Regina without stuttering, as if his tongue and lips were beyond his control. She always s . . . spends F . . . Fridays . . . working . . . in a f . . . friend's . . . flower . . . shop.

'Why?'

Donald looked vaguely at the Detective Inspector, sitting opposite him across the dining-room table. The matched antique dining chairs had gone. Donald sat in a garden armchair brought from the sunroom. The Inspector, a constable and I sat on kitchen stools.

'What?'

'Why did she work in a flower shop on Fridays?'

'She . . . she . . . I . . . likes . . .'

I interrupted brusquely. 'She was a florist before she married Donald. She liked to keep her hand in. She used to spend Fridays making those table arrangement things for dances and weddings and things like that . . .' And wreaths, too, I thought, and couldn't say it.

'Thank you, sir, but I'm sure Mr Stuart can answer for himself.'

'And I'm sure he can't.'

The Detective Inspector diverted his attention my way.

'He's too shocked,' I said.

'Are you a doctor, sir?' His voice held polite disbelief, which it was entitled to, no doubt. I shook my head impatiently. He glanced at Donald, pursed his lips, and turned back to me. His gaze wandered briefly over my jeans, faded denim jacket, fawn polo-neck, and desert boots, and returned to my face, unimpressed.

'Very well, sir. Name?'

'Charles Todd.'

'Age?'

'Twenty-nine.'

'Occupation?'

'Painter.'

The constable unemotionally wrote down these scintillating details in his pocket-sized notebook.

'Houses or pictures?' asked the Inspector.

'Pictures.'

'And your movements today, sir?'

'Caught the two-thirty from Paddington and walked from the local station.'

'Purpose of visit?'

'Nothing special. I come here once or twice a year.'

'Good friends, then?'

'Yes.'

He nodded non-committally. Turned his attention again to Donald and asked more questions, but patiently and without pressure.

'And what time do you normally reach home on Fridays, sir?'

Don said tonelessly, 'Five. About.'

'And today?'

'Same.' A spasm twitched the muscles of his face. 'I saw . . . the house had been broken into . . . I telephoned . . .'

'Yes, sir. We received your call at six minutes past five. And after you had telephoned, you went into the sitting-room, to see what had been stolen?'

Donald didn't answer.

'Our sergeant found you there, sir, if you remember.'

'*Why?*' Don said in anguish. 'Why did she come home?'

'I expect we'll find out, sir.'

The careful exploratory questions went on and on, and as far as I could see achieved nothing except to bring Donald ever closer to all-out breakdown.

I, with a certain amount of shame, grew ordinarily hungry, having not bothered to eat earlier in the day. I thought with regret of the dinner I had been looking forward to, with Regina tossing in unmeasured ingredients and herbs and wine and casually producing a gourmet feast. Regina with her cap of dark hair and ready smile, chatty and frivolous and anti-blood-sports. A harmless girl, come to harm.

At some point during the evening her body was loaded into the ambulance and driven away. I heard it happen, but Donald gave no sign of interpreting the sounds. I thought that probably his mind was raising barriers against the unendurable, and one couldn't blame him.

The Inspector rose finally and stretched the kinks caused by the kitchen stool out of legs and spine. He said he would be leaving a constable on duty at the house all night, and that he would return himself in the morning. Donald nodded vaguely, having obviously not listened properly to a word, and when the police had gone still sat like an automaton in the chair, with no energy to move.

'Come on,' I said. 'Let's go to bed.'

I took his arm, persuaded him to his feet, and steered him up the stairs. He came in a daze, unprotesting.

His and Regina's bedroom was a shambles, but the twin-bedded room prepared for me was untouched. He flopped full-length in his clothes and put his arm up over his eyes, and in appalling distress asked the unanswerable question of all the world's sufferers.

'*Why?* Why did it have to happen to *us?*'

I stayed with Donald for a week, during which time some questions, but not that one, were answered.

One of the easiest was the reason for Regina's premature return home. She and the flower-shop friend, who had been repressing annoyance with each other for weeks, had erupted into a quarrel of enough bitterness to make Regina leave at once. She had driven away at about two-thirty, and had probably gone straight home, as it was considered she had been dead for at least two hours by five o'clock.

This information, expressed in semi-formal sentences, was given to Donald by the Detective Inspector on Saturday afternoon. Donald walked out into the autumnal garden and wept.

The Inspector, Frost by name and cool by nature, came quietly into the kitchen and stood beside me watching Donald with his bowed head among the apple trees.

'I would like you to tell me what you can about the relationship between Mr and Mrs Stuart.'

'You'd like *what?*'

'How did they get on?'

'Can't you tell for yourself?'

He answered neutrally after a pause. 'The intensity of grief shown is not always an accurate indication of the intensity of love felt.'

'Do you always talk like that?'

A faint smile flickered and died. 'I was quoting from a book on psychology.'

'"Not always" means it usually is,' I said.

He blinked.

'Your book is bunk,' I said.

'Guilt and remorse can manifest themselves in an excess of mourning.'

'Dangerous bunk,' I added. 'And as far as I could see, the honeymoon was by no means over.'

'After three years?'

'Why not?'

He shrugged and didn't answer. I turned away from the sight

of Donald and said, 'What are the chances of getting back any of the stuff from this house?'

'Small, I should think. Where antiques are involved, the goods are likely to be halfway across the Atlantic before the owner returns from his holidays.'

'Not this time, though,' I objected.

He sighed. 'Next best thing. There have been hundreds of similar break-ins during recent years and very little has been recovered. Antiques are big business these days.'

'Connoisseur thieves?' I said sceptically.

'The prison library service reports that all their most requested books are on antiques. All the little chummies boning up to jump on the bandwagon as soon as they get out.'

He sounded suddenly quite human. 'Like some coffee?' I said.

He looked at his watch, raised his eyebrows, and accepted. He sat on a kitchen stool while I fixed the mugs, a fortyish man with thin sandy hair and a well-worn grey suit.

'Are you married?' he asked.

'Nope.'

'In love with Mrs Stuart?'

'You do try it on, don't you?'

'If you don't ask, you don't find out.'

I put the milk bottle and a sugar basin on the table and told him to help himself. He stirred his coffee reflectively.

'When did you visit this house last?' he said.

'Last March. Before they went off to Australia.'

'Australia?'

'They went to see the vintage there. Donald had some idea of shipping Australian wine over in bulk. They were away for at least three months. Why didn't their house get robbed *then*, when they were safely out of the way?'

He listened to the bitterness in my voice. 'Life is full of nasty ironies.' He pursed his lips gingerly to the hot coffee, drew back, and blew gently across the top of the mug. 'What would you all have been doing today? In the normal course of events?'

I had to think what day it was. Saturday. It seemed totally unreal.

'Going to the races,' I said. 'We always go to the races when I come to stay.'

'Fond of racing, were they?' The past tense sounded wrong. Yet so much was now past. I found it a great deal more difficult than he did, to change gear.

'Yes . . . but I think they only go . . . went . . . because of me.'

He tried the coffee again and managed a cautious sip. 'In what way do you mean?' he asked.

'What I paint,' I said, 'is mostly horses.'

Donald came in through the back door, looking red-eyed and exhausted.

'The Press are making a hole in the hedge,' he said leadenly.

Inspector Frost clicked his teeth, got to his feet, opened the door to the hall and the interior of the house, and called out loudly.

'Constable? Go and stop those reporters from breaking into the garden.'

A distant voice replied 'Sir', and Frost apologized to Donald. 'Can't get rid of them entirely, you know, sir. They have their editors breathing down their necks. They pester the life out of us at times like these.'

All day long the road outside Donald's house had been lined with cars, which disgorged crowds of reporters, photographers and plain sensation-seekers every time anyone went out of the front door. Like a hungry wolf pack they lay in wait, and I supposed that they would eventually pounce on Donald himself. Regard for his feelings was nowhere in sight.

'Newspapers listen to the radio on the police frequencies,'

Frost said gloomily. 'Sometimes the Press arrive at the scene of a crime before we can get there ourselves.'

At any other time I would have laughed, but it wouldn't have been much fun for Donald if it had happened in his case. The police, of course, had thought at first that it more or less had, because I had heard that the constable who had tried to eject me forcibly had taken me for a spearheading scribbler.

Donald sat down heavily on a stool and rested his elbows wearily on the table.

'Charles,' he said, 'if you wouldn't mind heating it, I'd like some of that soup now.'

'Sure,' I said, surprised. He had rejected it earlier as if the thought of food revolted him.

Frost's head went up as if at a signal, and his whole body straightened purposefully, and I realized he had merely been coasting along until then, waiting for some such moment. He waited some more while I opened a can of Campbell's condensed, sloshed it and some water and cooking brandy into a saucepan, and stirred until the lumps dissolved. He drank his coffee and waited while Donald disposed of two platefuls and a chunk of brown bread. Then, politely, he asked me to take myself off, and when I'd gone he began what Donald afterwards referred to as 'serious digging'.

It was three hours later, and growing dark, when the Inspector left. I watched his departure from the upstairs landing window. He and his attendant plain-clothes constable were intercepted immediately outside the front door by a young man with wild hair and a microphone, and before they could dodge round him to reach their car the pack on the road were streaming in full cry into the garden and across the grass.

I went methodically round the house drawing curtains, checking windows, and locking and bolting all the outside doors.

'What are you doing?' Donald asked, looking pale and tired in the kitchen.

'Pulling up the drawbridge.'

'Oh.'

In spite of his long session with the Inspector he seemed a lot calmer and more in command of himself, and when I had finished Fort-Knoxing the kitchen-to-garden door he said, 'The police want a list of what's gone. Will you help me make it?'

'Of course.'

'It'll give us something to do . . .'

'Sure.'

'We did have an inventory, but it was in that desk in the hall. The one they took.'

'Damn silly place to keep it,' I said.

'That's more or less what *he* said. Inspector Frost.'

'What about your insurance company? Haven't they got a list?'

'Only of the more valuable things, like some of the paintings, and her jewellery.' He sighed. 'Everything else was lumped together as "contents".'

We started on the dining-room and made reasonable progress, with him putting the empty drawers back in the sideboard while trying to remember what each had once contained, and me writing down to his dictation. There had been a good deal of solid silver tableware, acquired by Donald's family in its affluent past and handed down routinely. Donald, with his warmth for antiques, had enjoyed using it, but his pleasure in owning it seemed to have vanished with the goods. Instead of being indignant over its loss, he sounded impersonal, and by the time we had finished the sideboard, decidedly bored.

Faced by the ranks of empty shelves where once had stood a fine collection of early nineteenth-century porcelain, he baulked entirely.

'What does it matter?' he said drearily, turning away. 'I simply can't be bothered . . .'

'How about the paintings, then?'

He looked vaguely round the bare walls. The site of each missing frame showed unmistakably in lighter oblong patches of palest olive. In this room they had mostly been works of modern British painters: a Hockney, a Bratby, two Lowrys, and a Spear for openers, all painted on what one might call the artists' less exuberant days. Donald didn't like paintings which he said 'jumped off the wall and made a fuss'.

'You probably remember them better than I do,' he said. 'You do it.'

'I'd miss some.'

'Is there anything to drink?'

'Only the cooking brandy,' I said.

'We could have some of the wine.'

'What wine?'

'In the cellar.' His eyes suddenly opened wide. 'Good God, I'd forgotten about the cellar.'

'I didn't even know you had one.'

He nodded. 'Reason I bought the house. Perfect humidity and temperature for long-term storage. There's a small fortune down there in claret and port.'

There wasn't, of course. There were three floor-to-ceiling rows of empty racks, and a single cardboard box on a plain wooden table.

Donald merely shrugged. 'Oh well . . . that's that.'

I opened the top of the cardboard box and saw the elegant corked shapes of the tops of wine bottles.

'They've left these, anyway,' I said. 'In their rush.'

'Probably on purpose,' Don smiled twistedly. 'That's Australian wine. We brought it back with us.'

'Better than nothing,' I said disparagingly, pulling out a bottle and reading the label.

'Better than most, you know. A lot of Australian wine is superb.'

I carried the whole case up to the kitchen and dumped it on the table. The stairs from the cellar led up into the utility room among the washing machines and other domesticities, and I had always had an unclear impression that its door was just another cupboard. I looked at it thoughtfully, an unremarkable white painted panel merging inconspicuously into the general scenery.

'Do you think the burglars *knew* the wine was there?' I asked.

'God knows.'

'I would never have found it.'

'You're not a burglar, though.'

He searched for a corkscrew, opened one of the bottles, and poured the deep red liquid into two kitchen tumblers. I tasted it and it was indeed a marvellous wine, even to my untrained palate. *Wynn's Coonawarra Cabernet Sauvignon.* You could wrap the name round the tongue as lovingly as the product. Donald drank his share absent-mindedly as if it were water, the glass clattering once or twice against his teeth. There was still an uncertainty about many of his movements, as if he could not quite remember how to do things, and I knew it was because with half his mind he thought all the time of Regina, and the thoughts were literally paralysing.

The old Donald had been a man of confidence, capably running a middle-sized inherited business and adding his share to the passed-on goodies. He had a blunt uncompromising face lightened by amber eyes which smiled easily, and he had considered his money well spent on shapely haircuts.

The new Donald was a tentative man shattered with shock, a man trying to behave decently but unsure where his feet were when he walked upstairs.

We spent the evening in the kitchen, talking desultorily, eating a scratch meal, and tidying all the stores back on to the shelves. Donald made a good show of being busy but put half the tins back upside down.

The front door bell rang three times during the evening but never in the code pre-arranged with the police. The telephone, with its receiver lying loose beside it, rang not at all. Donald had turned down several offers of refuge with local friends and visibly shook at the prospect of talking to anyone but Frost and me.

'Why don't they go away?' he said despairingly, after the third attempt on the front door.

'They will, once they've seen you,' I said. And sucked you dry, and spat out the husk, I thought.

He shook his head tiredly. 'I simply can't.'

It felt like living through a siege.

We went eventually again upstairs to bed, although it seemed likely that Donald would sleep no more than the night before, which had been hardly at all. The police surgeon had left knock-out pills, which Donald wouldn't take. I pressed him again on that second evening, with equal non-results.

'No, Charles. I'd feel I'd deserted her. D . . . ducked out. Thought only of myself, and not of . . . of how awful it was for her . . . dying like that . . . with n . . . no one near who l . . . loved her.'

He was trying to offer her in some way the comfort of his own pain. I shook my head at him, but tried no more with the pills.

'Do you mind,' he said diffidently, 'if I sleep alone tonight?'

'Of course not.'

'We could make up a bed for you in one of the other rooms.'

'Sure.'

He pulled open the linen-cupboard door on the upstairs landing and gestured indecisively at the contents. 'Could you manage?'

'Of course,' I said.

He turned away and seemed struck by one particular adjacent patch of empty wall.

'They took the Munnings,' he said.

'What Munnings?'

'We bought it in Australia. I hung it just there . . . only a week ago. I wanted you to see it. It was one of the reasons I asked you to come.'

'I'm sorry,' I said. Inadequate words.

'Everything,' he said helplessly. 'Everything's gone.'

Two

FROST ARRIVED tirelessly again on Sunday morning with his quiet watchful eyes and non-committal manner. I opened the front door to his signal, and he followed me through to the kitchen, where Donald and I seemed to have taken up permanent residence. I gestured him to a stool, and he sat on it, straightening his spine to avoid future stiffness.

'Two pieces of information you might care to have, sir,' he said to Donald, his voice at its most formal. 'Despite our intensive investigation of this house during yesterday and the previous evening, we have found no fingerprints for which we cannot account.'

'Would you expect to?' I asked.

He flicked me a glance. 'No, sir. Professional housebreakers always wear gloves.'

Donald waited with a grey patient face, as if he would find whatever Frost said unimportant. Nothing, I judged, was of much importance to Donald any more.

'Second,' said Frost, 'our investigations in the district reveal that a removal van was parked outside your front door early on Friday afternoon.'

Donald looked at him blankly.

'Dark-coloured, and dusty, sir.'

'Oh,' Donald said, meaninglessly.

Frost sighed. 'What do you know of a bronze statuette of a horse, sir? A horse rearing up on its hind legs?'

'It's in the hall,' Donald said automatically; and then, frowning slightly, 'I mean, it used to be. It's gone.'

'How do you know about it?' I asked Frost curiously, and guessed the answer before I'd finished the question. 'Oh no . . .' I stopped, and swallowed. 'I mean, perhaps you found it . . . fallen off the van . . .?'

'No, sir.' His face was calm. 'We found it in the sitting-room, near Mrs Stuart.'

Donald understood as clearly as I had done. He stood up abruptly and went to the window, and stared out for a while at the empty garden.

'It is heavy,' he said at last. 'The base of it.'

'Yes, sir.'

'It must have been . . . quick.'

'Yes, sir,' Frost said again, sounding more objective than comforting.

'P . . . poor Regina.' The words were quiet, the desolation immense. When he came back to the table, his hands were trembling. He sat down heavily and stared into space.

Frost started another careful speech about the sitting-room being kept locked by the police for a few days yet and please would neither of us try to go in there.

Neither of us would.

Apart from that, they had finished their enquiries at the house, and Mr Stuart was at liberty to have the other rooms cleaned, if he wished, where the fingerprint dust lay greyish-white on every polished surface.

Mr Stuart gave no sign of having heard.

Had Mr Stuart completed the list of things stolen?

I passed it over. It still consisted only of the dining-room silver and what I could remember of the paintings. Frost raised his eyebrows and pursed his lips.

'We'll need more than this, sir.'

'We'll try again today,' I promised. 'There's a lot of wine missing, as well.'

'Wine?'

I showed him the empty cellar and he came up looking thoughtful.

'It must have taken hours to move that lot,' I said.

'Very likely, sir,' he said primly.

Whatever he was thinking, he wasn't telling. He suggested instead that Donald should prepare a short statement to read to the hungry reporters still waiting outside, so that they could go away and print it.

'No,' Don said.

'Just a short statement,' Frost said reasonably. 'We can prepare it here and now, if you like.'

He wrote it himself, more or less, and I guessed it was as much for his own sake as Donald's that he wanted the Press to depart, as it was he who had to push through them every time. He repeated the statement aloud when he had finished. It sounded like a police account, full of jargon, but because of that so distant from Donald's own raw grief that my cousin agreed in the end to read it out.

'But no photographs,' he said anxiously, and Frost said he would see to it.

They crowded into the hall, a collection of dry-eyed fact-finders, all near the top of their digging profession and inured from sensitivity by a hundred similar intrusions into tragedy. Sure, they were sorry for the guy whose wife had been bashed, but news was news and bad news sold papers, and if they didn't produce the goods they'd lose their jobs to others more tenacious. The Press Council had stopped the brutal bullying of the past, but the leeway still allowed could be a great deal too much for the afflicted.

Donald stood on the stairs, with Frost and myself at the foot, and read without expression, as if the words applied to someone else.

'. . . I returned to the house at approximately five PM and observed that during my absence a considerable number of valuable objects had been removed . . . I telephoned immediately for assistance . . . My wife, who was normally absent from the house on Fridays, returned unexpectedly . . . and, it is presumed, disturbed the intruders.'

He stopped. The reporters dutifully wrote down the stilted words and looked disillusioned. One of them, clearly elected by pre-arrangement, started asking questions for them all, in a gentle, coaxing, sympathetic tone of voice.

'Could you tell us which of these closed doors is the one to the room where your wife . . .'

Donald's eyes slid briefly despite himself towards the sitting-room. All the heads turned, the eyes studied the uninformative white painted panels, the pencils wrote.

'And could you tell us what exactly was stolen?'

'Silver. Paintings.'

'Who were the paintings by?'

Donald shook his head and began to look even paler.

'Could you tell us how much they were worth?'

After a pause Don said, 'I don't know.'

'Were they insured?'

'Yes.'

'How many bedrooms are there in your house?'

'What?'

'How many bedrooms?'

Donald looked bewildered. 'I suppose . . . five.'

'Do you think you could tell us anything about your wife? About her character, and about her job? And could you let us have a photograph?'

Donald couldn't. He shook his head and said, 'I'm sorry,' and turned and walked steadily away upstairs.

'That's all,' Frost said with finality.

'It's not much,' they grumbled.

'What do you want? Blood?' Frost said, opening the front door and encouraging them out. 'Put yourselves in his position.'

'Yeah,' they said cynically; but they went.

'Did you see their eyes?' I said. 'Sucking it all in?'

Frost smiled faintly. 'They'll write long stories from that little lot.'

The interview, however, produced to a great extent the desired results. Most of the cars departed, and the rest, I supposed, would follow as soon as fresher news broke.

'Why did they ask about the bedrooms?' I said.

'To estimate the value of the house.'

'Good grief.'

'They'll all get it different.' Frost was near to amusement. 'They always do.' He looked up the stairs in the direction Donald had taken, and, almost casually, said, 'Is your cousin in financial difficulties?'

I knew his catch-them-off-guard technique by now.

'I wouldn't think so,' I said unhurriedly. 'You'd better ask him.'

'I will, sir.' He switched his gaze sharply to my face and studied my lack of expression. 'What do you know?'

I said calmly, 'Only that the police have suspicious minds.'

He disregarded that. 'Is Mr Stuart worried about his business?'

'He's never said so.'

'A great many middle-sized private companies are going bankrupt these days.'

'So I believe.'

'Because of cash flow problems,' he added.

'I can't help you. You'll have to look at his company's books.'

'We will, sir.'

'And even if the firm turns out to be bust, it doesn't follow that Donald would fake a robbery.'

'It's been done before,' Frost said dryly.

'If he needed money he could simply have sold the stuff,' I pointed out.

'Maybe he had. Some of it. Most of it, maybe.'

I took a slow breath and said nothing.

'That wine, sir. As you said yourself, it would have taken a long time to move.'

'The firm is a limited company,' I said. 'If it went bankrupt, Donald's own house and private money would be unaffected.'

'You know a good deal about it, don't you?'

I said neutrally, 'I live in the world.'

'I thought artists were supposed to be unworldly.'

'Some are.'

He peered at me with narrowed eyes as if he were trying to work out a possible way in which I too might have conspired to arrange the theft.

I said mildly, 'My cousin Donald is an honourable man.'

'That's an out-of-date word.'

'There's quite a lot of it about.'

He looked wholly disbelieving. He saw far too much in the way of corruption, day in, day out, all his working life.

Donald came hesitantly down the stairs and Frost took him off immediately to another private session in the kitchen. I thought that if Frost's questions were to be as barbed as those he'd asked me, poor Don was in for a rough time. While they talked I wandered aimlessly round the house, looking into storage spaces, opening cupboards, seeing the inside details of my cousin's life.

Either he or Regina had been a hoarder of empty boxes. I came across dozens of them, all shapes and sizes, shoved into odd corners of shelves or drawers: brown cardboard, bright gift-wrap, beribboned chocolate boxes, all too potentially useful or too pretty to be thrown away. The burglars had opened a lot but had thrown more unopened on the floor. They must, I thought, have had a most frustrating time.

They had largely ignored the big sunroom, which held few antiques and no paintings, and I ended up there sitting on a bamboo armchair among sprawling potted plants looking out into the windy garden. Dead leaves blew in scattered showers from the drying trees and a few late roses clung hardily to thorny stems.

I hated autumn. The time of melancholy, the time of death. My spirits fell each year with the soggy leaves and revived only with crisp winter frost. Psychiatric statistics proved that the highest suicide rate occurred in the spring, the time for rebirth and growth and stretching in the sun. I could never understand it. If ever I jumped over a cliff, it would be in the depressing months of decay.

The sunroom was grey and cold. No sun, that Sunday.

I went upstairs, fetched my suitcase, and brought it down. Over years of wandering journeys I had reversed the painter's traditional luggage: my suitcase now contained the tools of my trade, and my satchel, clothes. The large toughened suitcase, its interior adapted and fitted by me, was in fact a sort of portable studio, containing besides paints and brushes a light collapsible metal easel, unbreakable containers of linseed oil and turpentine, and a rack which would hold four wet paintings safely apart. There were also a dust sheet, a large box of tissues and generous amounts of white spirit, all designed for preventing mess and keeping things clean. The organization of the suitcase had saved and made the price of many a sandwich.

I untelescoped the easel and set out my palette, and on a middling-sized canvas laid out the beginnings of a melancholy landscape, a mixture of Donald's garden as I saw it, against a sweep of bare fields and gloomy woods. Not my usual sort of picture, and not, to be honest, the sort to make headline news a century hence; but it gave me at least something to do. I worked steadily, growing ever colder, until the chillier Frost chose to depart; and he went without seeing me again, the front door closing decisively on his purposeful footsteps.

Donald, in the warm kitchen, looked torn to rags. When I went in he was sitting with his arms folded on the table and his head on his arms, a picture of absolute despair. When he heard me he sat up slowly and wearily, and showed a face suddenly aged and deeply lined.

'Do you know what he thinks?' he said.

'More or less.'

He stared at me sombrely. 'I couldn't convince him. He kept on and on. Kept asking the same questions, over and over. Why doesn't he believe me?'

'A lot of people lie to the police. I think they grow to expect it.'

'He wants me to meet him in my office tomorrow. He says he'll be bringing colleagues. He says they'll want to see the books.'

I nodded. 'Better be grateful he didn't drag you down there today.'

'I suppose so.'

I said awkwardly, 'Don, I'm sorry. I told him the wine was missing. It made him suspicious . . . It was a good deal my fault that he was so bloody to you.'

He shook his head tiredly. 'I would have told him myself. I wouldn't have thought of not telling him.'

'But . . . I even pointed out that it must have taken a fair time to move so many bottles.'

'Mm. Well, he would have worked that out for himself.'

'How long, in fact, do you think it would have taken?'

'Depends how many people were doing it,' he said, rubbing his hand over his face and squeezing his tired eyes. 'They would have to have had proper wine boxes in any case. That means they had to know in advance that the wine was there, and didn't just chance on it. And that means . . . Frost says . . . that I sold it myself some time ago and am now saying it is stolen so I can claim fraudulent insurance, or, if it was stolen last Friday, that I told the thieves they'd need proper boxes, which means that I set up the whole frightful mess myself.'

We thought it over in depressed silence. Eventually, I said, 'Who *did* know you had the wine there? And who knew the house was always empty on Fridays? And was the prime target the wine, the antiques, or the paintings?'

'God, Charles, you sound like Frost.'

'Sorry.'

'Every business nowadays,' he said defensively, 'is going through a cash crisis. Look at the nationalized industries, losing money by the million. Look at the wage rises and the taxes and the inflation . . . How can any small business make the profit it used to? Of *course* we have a cash flow problem. Whoever hasn't?'

'How bad is yours?' I said.

'Not critical. Bad enough. But not within sight of liquidation. It's illegal for a limited company to carry on trading if it can't cover its costs.'

'But it could . . . if you could raise more capital to prop it up?'

He surveyed me with the ghost of a smile. 'It surprises me still that you chose to paint for a living.'

'It gives me a good excuse to go racing whenever I like.'

'Lazy sod.' He sounded for a second like the old Donald, but the lightness passed. 'The absolutely last thing I would do would be to use my own personal assets to prop up a dying business. If my firm was that rocky, I'd wind it up. It would be mad not to.'

I sucked my teeth. 'I suppose Frost asked if the stolen things were insured for more than their worth?'

'Yes, he did. Several times.'

'Not likely you'd tell him, even if they were.'

'They weren't, though.'

'No.'

'Under-insured, if anything.' He sighed. 'God knows if they'll pay up for the Munnings. I'd only arranged the insurance by telephone. I hadn't actually sent the premium.'

'It should be all right, if you can give them proof of purchase, and so on.'

He shook his head listlessly. 'All the papers to do with it were in the desk in the hall. The receipt from the gallery where I bought it, the letter of provenance, and the customs and excise receipt. All gone.'

'Frost won't like that.'

'He doesn't.'

'Well . . . I hope you pointed out that you would hardly be buying expensive pictures and going on world trips if you were down to your last farthing.'

'He said it might be *because* of buying expensive pictures and going on world trips that I might be down to my last farthing.'

Frost had built a brick wall of suspicion for Donald to batter his head against. My cousin needed hauling away before he was punch drunk.

'Have some spaghetti,' I said.

'What?'

'It's about all I can cook.'

'Oh . . . ' He focused unclearly on the kitchen clock. It was half past four and long past feeding time according to my stomach.

'If you like,' he said.

The police sent a car the following morning to fetch him to his ordeal in the office. He went lifelessly, having more or less made it clear over coffee that he wouldn't defend himself.

'Don, you must,' I said. 'The only way to deal with the situation is to be firm and reasonable, and decisive, and accurate. In fact, just your own self.'

He smiled faintly. 'You'd better go instead of me. I haven't the energy. And what does it matter?' His smile broke suddenly and the ravaging misery showed deeply like black water under cracked ice. 'Without Regina . . . there's no point in making money.'

'We're not talking about making money, we're talking about suspicion. If you don't defend yourself, they'll assume you can't.'

'I'm too tired. I can't be bothered. They can think what they like.'

'Don,' I said seriously, 'they'll think what you let them.'

'I don't really care,' he said dully: and that was the trouble. He really didn't.

He was gone all day. I spent it painting.

Not the sad landscape. The sunroom seemed even greyer and colder that morning, and I had no mind any more to sink into melancholy. I left the half-finished canvas on the table there and removed myself and trappings to the source of warmth. Maybe the light wasn't so good in the kitchen, but it was the only room in the house with the pulse of life.

I painted Regina standing beside her cooker, with a wooden spoon in one hand and a bottle of wine in the other. I painted the way she held her head back to smile, and I painted the smile, shiny-eyed and guileless and unmistakably happy. I painted the kitchen behind her as I literally saw it in front of my eyes, and I painted Regina herself from the clearest of inner visions. So easily did I see her that I looked up once or twice from her face on the canvas to say something to her, and was disconcerted to find only empty space. An extraordinary feeling of the real and unreal disturbingly tangled.

I seldom ever worked for more than four hours at a stretch

because for one thing the actual muscular control required was tiring, and for another the concentration always made me cold and hungry; so I knocked off at around lunch-time and dug out a tin of corned beef to eat with pickles on toast, and after that went for a walk, dodging the front-gate watchers by taking to the apple trees and wriggling through the hedge.

I tramped aimlessly for a while round the scattered shapeless village, thinking about the picture and working off the burst of physical energy I often felt after the constraint of painting. More burnt umber in the folds of the kitchen curtains, I thought; and a purplish shadow on the saucepan. Regina's cream shirt needed yellow ochre under the collar, and probably a touch of green. The cooking stove needed a lot more attention, and I had broken my general rule of working the picture as a whole, background and subject pace by pace.

This time, Regina's face stood out clearly, finished except for a gloss on the lips and a line of light along inside the lower eyelids, which one couldn't do until the under paint was dry. I had been afraid of seeing her less clearly if I took too long, but because of it the picture was now out of balance and I'd have to be very careful to get the kitchen into the same key, so that the whole thing looked harmonious and natural and as if it couldn't have been any other way.

The wind was rawly cold, the sky a hurrying jumbled mass of darkening clouds. I huddled my hands inside my anorak pockets and slid back through the hedge with the first drops of rain.

The afternoon session was much shorter because of the light, and I frustratingly could not catch the right mix of colours for the tops of the kitchen fitments. Even after years of experience, what looked right on the palette looked wrong on the painting. I got it wrong three times and decided to stop.

I was cleaning the brushes when Donald came back. I heard the scrunch of the car, the slam of the doors, and, to my surprise, the ring of the front door bell. Donald had taken his keys.

I went through and opened the door. A uniformed policeman stood there, holding Don's arm. Behind, a row of watching faces gazed on hungrily. My cousin, who had looked pale
before, now seemed bloodlessly white. The eyes were as lifeless
as death.

'Don!' I said, and no doubt looked as appalled as I felt.

He didn't speak. The policeman leaned forward, said, 'There
we are, sir,' and transferred the support of my cousin from himself to me: and it seemed to me that the action was symbolic as
much as practical, because he turned immediately on his heel
and methodically drove off in his waiting car.

I helped Donald inside and shut the door. I had never seen
anyone in such a frightening state of disintegration.

'I asked,' he said, 'about the funeral.'

His face was stony, and his voice came out in gasps.

'They said . . .' He stopped, dragged in air, tried again. 'They
said . . . no funeral.'

'Donald . . .'

'They said . . . she couldn't be buried until they had finished
their enquiries. They said . . . it might be months. They said . . .
they will keep her . . . refrigerated . . .'

The distress was fearful.

'They said . . .' He swayed slightly. 'They said . . . the body
of a murdered person belongs to the State.'

I couldn't hold him. He collapsed at my feet in a deep and
total faint.

Three

FOR TWO days Donald lay in bed, and I grew to understand what was meant by prostration.

Whether he liked it or not, this time he was heavily sedated, his doctor calling morning and evening with pills and injections. No matter that I was a hopeless nurse and a worse cook, I was appointed, for lack of anyone else, to look after him.

'I want Charles,' Donald in fact told the doctor. 'He doesn't *fuss.*'

I sat with him a good deal when he was awake, seeing him struggle dazedly to face and come to terms with the horrors in his mind. He lost weight visibly, the rounded muscles of his face slackening and the contours changing to the drawn shape of illness. The grey shadows round his eyes darkened to a permanent charcoal, and all normal strength seemed to have vanished from arms and legs.

I fed us both from tins and frozen packets, reading the instructions and doing what they said. Donald thanked me punctiliously and ate what he could, but I doubt if he tasted a thing.

In between times, while he slept, I made progress with both the paintings. The sad landscape was no longer sad but merely Octoberish, with three horses standing around in a field, one of them eating grass. Pictures of this sort, easy to live with and passably expert, were my bread and butter. They sold quite well, and I normally churned one off the production line every ten days or so, knowing that they were all technique and no soul.

The portrait of Regina, though, was the best work I'd done for months. She laughed out of the canvas, alive and glowing, and to me at least seemed vividly herself. Pictures often changed as one worked on them, and day by day the emphasis in my mind had shifted, so that the kitchen background was growing darker and less distinct and Regina herself more luminous. One could still see she was cooking, but it was the girl who was important, not the act. In the end I had painted the kitchen, which was still there, as an impression, and the girl, who was not, as the reality.

I hid that picture in my suitcase whenever I wasn't working on it. I didn't want Donald to come face to face with it unawares.

Early Wednesday evening he came shakily down to the kitchen in his dressing-gown, trying to smile and pick up the pieces. He sat at the table, drinking the Scotch I had that day imported, and watching while I cleaned my brushes and tidied the palette.

'You're always so neat,' he said.

'Paint's expensive.'

He waved a limp hand at the horse picture which stood drying on the easel. 'How much does it cost, to paint that?'

'In raw materials, about ten quid. In heat, light, rates, rent, food, Scotch and general wear and tear on the nervous system, about the amount I'd earn in a week if I chucked it in and went back to selling houses.'

'Quite a lot, then,' he said seriously.

I grinned. 'I don't regret it.'

'No. I see that.'

I finished the brushes by washing them in soap and water under the tap, pinching them into shape, and standing them upright in a jar to dry. Good brushes were at least as costly as paint.

'After the digging into the company accounts,' Donald said abruptly, 'they took me along to the police station and tried to prove that I had actually killed her myself.'

'I don't believe it!'

'They'd worked out that I could have got home at lunch-time and done it. They said there was time.'

I picked up the Scotch from the table and poured a decent-sized shot into a tumbler. Added ice.

'They must be crazy,' I said.

'There was another man, besides Frost. A superintendent. I think his name was Wall. A thin man, with fierce eyes. He never seemed to blink. Just stared and said over and over again that I'd killed her because she'd come back and found me supervising the burglary.'

'For God's sake!' I said disgustedly. 'And anyway, she didn't leave the flower shop until half past two.'

'The girl in the flower shop now says she doesn't know to the minute when Regina left. Only that it was soon after lunch. And I didn't get back from the pub until nearly three. I went to lunch late. I was hung up with a client all morning . . .' He stopped, gripping his tumbler as if it were a support to hold on to. 'I can't tell you . . . how awful it was.'

The mild understatement seemed somehow to make things worse.

'They said,' he nodded, 'that eighty per cent of murdered married women are killed by their husbands.'

That statement had Frost stamped all over it.

'They let me come home, in the end, but I don't think . . .' His voice shook. He swallowed, visibly trying to keep tight control on his hard-won calm. 'I don't think they've finished.'

It was five days since he'd walked in and found Regina dead. When I thought of the mental hammerings he'd taken on top, the punishing assault on his emotional reserves, where common humanity would have suggested kindness and consoling help, it seemed marvellous that he had remained as sane as he had.

'Have they got anywhere with catching the thieves?' I said.

He smiled wanly. 'I don't even know if they're trying.'

'They must be.'

'I suppose so. They haven't said.' He drank some whisky slowly. 'It's ironic, you know. I've always had a regard for the police. I didn't know they could be . . . the way they are.'

A quandary, I thought. Either they leaned on a suspect in the hope of breaking him down, or they asked a few polite questions and got nowhere: and under the only effective system the innocent suffered more than the guilty.

'I see no end to it,' Donald said. 'No end at all.'

By midday Friday the police had called twice more at the house, but for my cousin the escalation of agony seemed to have slowed. He was still exhausted, apathetic, and as grey as smoke, but it was as if he were saturated with suffering and could absorb little more. Whatever Frost and his companion said to him, it rolled off without destroying him further.

'You're supposed to be painting someone's horse, aren't you?' he said suddenly, as we shaped up to lunch.

'I told them I'd come later.'

He shook his head. 'I remember you saying, when I asked you to stay, that it would fit in fine before your next commission.' He thought a bit. 'Tuesday. You should have gone to Yorkshire on Tuesday.'

'I telephoned and explained.'

'All the same, you'd better go.'

He said he would be all right alone, now, and thanks for everything. He insisted I look up the times of trains, order a taxi, and alert the people at the other end. I could see in the end that the time had indeed come for him to be by himself, so I packed up my things to depart.

'I suppose,' he said diffidently, as we waited for the taxi to fetch me, 'that you never paint portraits? People, that is, not horses.'

'Sometimes,' I said.

'I just wondered . . . Could you, one day . . . I mean, I've got quite a good photograph of Regina . . .'

I looked searchingly at his face. As far as I could see, it could do no harm. I unclipped the suitcase and took out the picture with its back towards him.

'It's still wet,' I warned. 'And not framed, and I can't varnish it for at least six months. But you can have it, if you like.'

'Let me see.'

I turned the canvas round. He stared and stared, but said nothing at all. The taxi drove up to the front door.

'See you,' I said, propping Regina against a wall.

He nodded and punched my arm, opened the door for me, and sketched a farewell wave. Speechlessly, because his eyes were full of tears.

I spent nearly a week in Yorkshire doing my best to immortalize a patient old steeplechaser, and then went home to my noisy flat near Heathrow airport, taking the picture with me to finish.

Saturday I downed tools and went to the races, fed up with too much nose-to-the-grindstone.

Jump racing at Plumpton, and the familiar swelling of excitement at the liquid movement of racehorses. Paintings could never do justice to them: never. The moment caught on canvas was always second best.

I would love to have ridden in races, but hadn't had enough practice or skill; nor, I dare say, nerve. Like Donald, my childhood background was of middle sized private enterprise, with my father an auctioneer in business on his own account in Sussex. I had spent countless hours in my growing years watching the horses train on the Downs round Findon, and had drawn and painted them from about the age of six. Riding itself had been mostly a matter of begging the wherewithal for an hour's joy from indulgent aunts, never of a pony of my own. Art school later had been fine, but at twenty-two, alone in the world with both parents newly dead, I'd had to face the need to eat. It had been a short meant-to-be-temporary step to the estate agent's across the street, but I'd liked it well enough to stay.

Half the horse painters in England seemed to have turned up at Plumpton, which was not surprising, as the latest Grand National winner was due to make his first appearance of the new season. It was a commercial fact that a picture called, for instance, *Nijinsky on Newmarket Heath* stood a much better chance of being sold than one labelled *A Horse on Newmarket Heath*, and *The Grand National Winner at the Start* won hands down over *A Runner at Plumpton Before the Off*. The economic facts of life had brought many a would-be Rembrandt down to market research.

'Todd!' said a voice in my ear. 'You owe me fifteen smackers.'

'I bloody don't,' I said.

'You said Seesaw was a certainty for Ascot.'

'Never take sweets from a stranger.'

Billy Pyle laughed extravagantly and patted me heavily on the shoulder. Billy Pyle was one of those people you met on race-courses who greeted you as a bosom pal, plied you with drinks and bonhomie, and bored you to death. On and off I'd met Billy Pyle at the races for umpteen years, and had never yet worked out how to duck him without positive rudeness. Ordinary evasions rolled off his thick skin like mercury off glass, and I found it less wearing on the whole to get the drink over quickly than dodge him all afternoon.

I waited for him to say 'how about a beverage', as he always did.

'How about a beverage?' he said.

'Er . . . sure,' I agreed, resignedly.

'Your father would never forgive me if I neglected you.' He always said that, too. They had been business acquaintances, I knew, but I suspected the reported friendship was posthumous.

'Come along, laddie.'

I knew the irritating routine by heart. He would meet his Auntie Sal in the bar, as if by accident, and in my turn I would buy them both a drink. A double brandy and ginger for Auntie Sal.

'Why, there's Auntie Sal,' Billy said, pushing through the door. Surprise, surprise.

Auntie Sal was a compulsive racegoer in her seventies with a perpetual cigarette dangling from the corner of her mouth and one finger permanently inserted in her form book, keeping her place.

'Know anything for the two-thirty?' she demanded.

'Hello,' I said.

'What? Oh, I see. Hello. How are you? Know anything for the two-thirty?'

''Fraid not.'

'Huh.'

She peered into the form book. 'Treetops is well in at the weights, but can you trust his leg?' She looked up suddenly and with her free hand prodded her nephew, who was trying to attract service from the bar. 'Billy, get a drink for Mrs Matthews.'

'Mrs Who?'

'Matthews. What do you want, Maisie?'

She turned to a large middle-aged woman who had been standing in the shadows behind her.

'Oh . . . gin and tonic, thanks.'

'Got that, Billy? Double brandy and ginger for me, gin and tonic for Mrs Matthews.'

Maisie Matthews' clothes were noticeably new and expensive, and from lacquered hair via crocodile handbag to gold-trimmed shoes she shouted money without saying a word. The hand which accepted the drink carried the weight of a huge opal set in diamonds. The expression on her expertly painted face showed no joy at all.

'How do you do?' I said politely.

'Eh?' said Auntie Sal. 'Oh, yes, Maisie, this is Charles Todd. What do you think of Treetops?'

'Moderate,' I said.

Auntie Sal peered worriedly into the form book and Billy handed round the drinks.

'Cheers,' Maisie Matthews said, looking cheerless.

'Down the hatch,' said Billy, raising his glass.

'Maisie's had a bit of bad luck,' Auntie Sal said.

Billy grinned. 'Backed a loser, then, Mrs Matthews?'

'Her house burned down.'

As a light conversation stopper, it was a daisy.

'Oh . . . I say . . .' said Billy uncomfortably. 'Hard luck.'

'Lost everything, didn't you, Maisie?'

'All but what I stand up in,' she agreed gloomily.

'Have another gin,' I suggested.

'Thanks, dear.'

When I returned with the refills she was in full descriptive flood.

'. . . I wasn't there, of course, I was staying with my sister Betty up in Birmingham, and there was this policeman on the doorstep telling me what a job they'd had finding me. But by that time it was all over, of course. When I got back to Worthing there was just a heap of cinders with the chimney-breast sticking up in the middle. Well, I had a real job finding out what happened, but anyway they finally said it was a flash fire, whatever that is, but they didn't know what started it, because there'd been no one in the house for two days.'

567

She accepted the gin, gave me a brief unseeing smile, and returned to her story.

'Well, I was spitting mad, I'll tell you, over losing everything like that, and I said why hadn't they used sea water, what with the sea being only the other side of the tamarisk and down the shingle, because of course they said they hadn't been able to save a thing because they hadn't enough water, and this fireman, the one I was complaining to, he said they couldn't use sea water because for one thing it corroded everything and for another the pumps sucked up seaweed and shells and things, and in any case the tide was out.'

I smothered an unseemly desire to laugh. She sensed it, however.

'Well, dear, it may seem funny to you, of course, but then you haven't lost all of your treasures that you'd been collecting since heaven knows when.'

'I'm really sorry, Mrs Matthews. I don't think it's funny. It was just . . .'

'Yes, well, dear. I suppose you can see the funny side of it, all that water and not a drop to put a fire out with, but I was that mad, I can tell you.'

'I think I'll have a bit on Treetops,' Auntie Sal said thoughtfully.

Maisie Matthews looked at her uncertainly and Billy Pyle, who had heard enough of disaster, broke gratefully into geniality, clapped me again on the shoulder, and said yes, it was time to see the next contest.

Duty done, I thought with a sigh, and took myself off to watch the race from the top of the stands, out of sight and earshot.

Treetops broke down and finished last, limping. Too bad for its owner, trainer, and Auntie Sal. I wandered down to the parade ring to see the Grand National winner walk round before his race, but without any thought of drawing him. I reckoned he was just about played out as a subject, and there would shortly be a glut.

The afternoon went quickly, as usual. I won a little, lost a little, and filled my eyes with something better than money. On the stands for the last race, I found myself approached by Maisie Matthews. No mistaking the bright red coat, the air of gloss, and the big, kind-looking, worldly face. She drew to a halt on the step below me, looking up. Entirely self-confident, though registering doubt.

'Aren't you,' she said, 'the young man I had a drink with, with Sal and Billy?'

'Yes, that's right.'

'I wasn't sure,' she said, the doubt disappearing. 'You look older out here.'

'Different light,' I said, agreeing. She too looked older, by about ten years. Fifty-something, I thought. Bar-light always flattered.

'They said you were an artist.' Their mild disapproval coloured the way she spoke.

'Mm,' I said, watching the runners canter past on the way to the post.

'Not very well paid, is it, dear?'

I grinned at her, liking her directness. 'It depends who you are. Picasso didn't grumble.'

'How much would you charge to paint a picture for me?'

'What sort of picture?'

'Well, dear, you may say it sounds morbid and I dare say it is, but I was just thinking this morning when I went over there, and really it makes me that mad every time I see it, I was think-ing actually that it makes a crazy picture, that burnt ruin with the chimney sticking up, and the burnt hedge behind and all that sea, and I was thinking of getting the local photographer who does all the weddings and things to come along and take a colour picture, because when it's all cleared away and rebuilt, no one will believe how awful it was, and I want to hang it in the new house, just to show them.'

'But . . .'

'So how much would you charge? Because I dare say you can see I am not short of the next quid but if it would be hundreds I might as well get the photographer of course.'

'Of course,' I agreed gravely. 'How about if I came to see the house, or what's left of it, and gave you an estimate?'

She saw nothing odd in that. 'All right, dear. That sounds very businesslike. Of course, it will have to be soon, though, because once the insurance people have been I am having the rubble cleared up.'

'How soon?'

'Well, dear, as you're halfway there, could you come today?'

We discussed it. She said she would drive me in her Jaguar as I hadn't a car, and I could go home by train just as easily from Worthing as from Plumpton.

So I agreed.

One takes the most momentous steps unawares.

The ruin was definitely paintagenic, if there is such a word. On the way there, more or less non-stop, she had talked about her late husband, Archie, who had looked after her very well, dear.

'Well, that's to say, I looked after him too, dear, because of course I was a nurse. Private, of course. I nursed his first wife all through her illness, cancer it was, dear, of course, and then I stayed on for a bit to look after him, and, well, he asked me to stay on for life, dear, and I did. Of course he was much older, he's been gone more than ten years now. He looked after me very well, Archie did.'

She glanced fondly at the huge opal. Many a man would have liked to have been remembered as kindly.

'Since he went, and left me so well off, dear, it seemed a shame not to get some fun out of it, so I carried on with what we were doing when we were together those few years, which was going round to auction sales in big houses, dear, because you pick up such nice things there, quite cheap sometimes, and of course it's ever so much more interesting when the things have belonged to someone well known or famous.' She changed gear with a jerk and aggressively passed an inoffensive little van. 'And now all those things are burnt to cinders, of course, and all the memories of Archie and the places we went together, and I'll tell you, dear, it makes me mad.'

'It's really horrid for you.'

'Yes, dear, it is.'

I reflected that it was the second time in a fortnight that I'd been cast in the role of comforter, and I felt as inadequate for her as I had for Donald.

She stamped on the brakes outside the remains of her house and rocked us to a standstill. From the opulence of the minor mansions on either side, her property had been far from a slum; but all that was left was an extensive sprawling black heap, with jagged pieces of outside wall defining its former shape, and the thick brick chimney, as she'd said, pointing sturdily skywards from the centre. Ironic, I thought fleetingly, that the fireplace alone had survived the flames.

'There you are, dear,' Maisie said. 'What do you think?'

'A very hot fire.'

She raised her pencilled eyebrows. 'But yes, dear, all fires are hot, aren't they? And of course there was a lot of wood. So many of these old seaside houses were built with a lot of wood.'

Even before we climbed out of her big pale blue car, I could smell the ash.

'How long ago . . . ?' I asked.

'Last weekend, dear. Sunday.'

While we surveyed the mess for a moment in silence a man walked slowly into view from behind the chimney. He was looking down, concentrating, taking a step at a time and then bending to poke into the rubble.

Maisie, for all her scarlet-coated bulk, was nimble on her feet.

'Hey,' she called, hopping out of the car and advancing purposefully. 'What do you think you're doing?'

The man straightened up, looking startled. About forty, I judged, with a raincoat, a crisp-looking trilby and a down-turning moustache.

He raised his hat politely. 'Insurance, madam.'

'I thought you were coming on Monday.'

'I happened to be in the district. No time like the present, don't you think?'

'Well, I suppose not,' Maisie said. 'And I hope there isn't going to be any shilly-shallying over you paying up, though of course nothing is going to get my treasures back and I'd rather have them than any amount of money, as I've got plenty of that in any case.'

The man was unused to Maisie's brand of chat.

'Er . . .' he said. 'Oh yes. I see.'

'Have you found out what started it?' Maisie demanded.

'No, madam.'

'Found anything at all?'

'No, madam.'

'Well, how soon can I get all this cleared away?'

'Any time you like, madam.'

He stepped carefully towards us, picking his way round clumps of blackened debris. He had steady greyish eyes, a strong chin, and an overall air of intelligence.

'What's your name?' Maisie asked.

'Greene, madam.' He paused slightly, and added 'With an "e".'

'Well, Mr Greene with an "e",' Maisie said good-humouredly, 'I'll be glad to have all that in writing.'

He inclined his head. 'As soon as I report back.'

Maisie said, 'Good,' and Greene, lifting his hat again, wished her good afternoon and walked along to a white Ford parked a short way along the road.

'That's all right, then,' Maisie said with satisfaction, watching him go. 'Now, how much for that picture?'

'Two hundred plus two nights' expenses in a local hotel.'

'That's a bit steep, dear. *One* hundred, and two nights, and I've got to like the results, or I don't pay.'

'No foal, no fee?'

The generous red mouth smiled widely. 'That's it, dear.'

We settled on one-fifty if she liked the picture, and fifty if she didn't, and I was to start on Monday unless it was raining.

Four

MONDAY CAME up with a bright breezy day and an echo of summer's warmth. I went to Worthing by train and to the house by taxi, and to the interest of the neighbours set up my easel at about the place where the front gates would have been, had they not been unhinged and transplanted by the firemen. The gates themselves lay flat on the lawn, one of them still pathetically bearing a neat painted nameboard.

Treasure Holme.

Poor Archie. Poor Maisie.

I worked over the whole canvas with an unobtrusive coffee-coloured underpainting of raw umber much thinned with turpentine and linseed oil, and while it was still wet drew in, with a paintbrushful of a darker shade of the same colour, the shape of the ruined house against the horizontals of hedges, shingle, sea and sky. It was easy with a tissue to wipe out mistakes of composition at that stage, and try again: to get the proportions right, and the perspective, and the balance of the main masses.

That done and drying, I strolled right round the whole garden, looking at the house from different angles, and staring out over the blackened stumps of the tamarisk hedge which had marked the end of the grass and the beginning of the shingle. The sea sparkled in the morning sunshine, with the small hurrying cumulus clouds scattering patches of dark slate-grey shadow. All the waves had white frills: distant, because the tide again had receded to the far side of a deserted stretch of wet-looking, wave-rippled sand.

The sea wind chilled my ears. I turned to get back to my task and saw two men in overcoats emerge from a large station wagon and show definite signs of interest in what was left of *Treasure Holme*.

I walked back towards them, reaching them where they stood by the easel appraising my handiwork.

One, heavy and fiftyish. One lean, in the twenties. Both with firm self-confident faces and an air of purpose.

The elder raised his eyes as I approached.

'Do you have permission to be here?' he asked. An enquiry; no belligerence in sight.

'The owner wants her house painted,' I said obligingly.

'I see.' His lips twitched a fraction.

'And you?' I enquired.

He raised his eyebrows slightly. 'Insurance,' he said, as if surprised that anyone should ask.

'Same company as Mr Greene?' I asked.

'Mr Who?'

'Greene. With an "e".'

'I don't know who you mean,' he said. 'We are here by arrangement with Mrs Matthews to inspect the damage to her house, which is insured with us.' He looked with some depression at the extent of the so-called damage, glancing about as if expecting Maisie to materialize phoenix-like from the ashes.

'No Greene?' I repeated.

'Neither with nor without an "e".'

I warmed to him. Half an ounce of a sense of humour, as far as I was concerned, achieved results where thumb-screws wouldn't.

'Well . . . Mrs Matthews is no longer expecting you, because the aforesaid Mr Greene, who said he was in insurance, told her she could roll in the demolition squad as soon as she liked.'

His attention sharpened like a tightened violin string.

'Are you serious?'

'I was here, with her. I saw him and heard him, and that's what he said.'

'Did he show you a card?'

'No, he didn't.' I paused. 'And . . . er . . . nor have you.'

He reached into an inner pocket and did so, with the speed of a conjuror. Producing cards from pockets was a reflex action, no doubt.

'Isn't it illegal to insure the same property with two companies?' I asked idly, reading the card.

FOUNDATION LIFE AND SURETY
D. J. Lagland   Area Manager

'Fraud.' He nodded.

'Unless of course Mr Greene with an "e" had nothing to do with insurance.'

'Much more likely.'

I put the card in my trouser pocket, Arran sweaters not having been designed noticeably for business transactions. He looked at me thoughtfully, his eyes observant but judgement suspended. He was the same sort of man my father had been, middle-aged, middle-of-the-road, expert at his chosen job but unlikely to set the world on fire.

Or *Treasure Holme*, for that matter.

'Gary,' he said to his younger side-kick, 'go and find a telephone and ring the Beach Hotel. Tell Mrs Matthews we're here.'

'Will do,' Gary said. He was that sort of man.

While he was away on the errand, D. J. Lagland turned his attention to the ruin, and I, as he seemed not to object, tagged along at his side.

'What do you look for?' I asked.

He shot me a sideways look. 'Evidence of arson. Evidence of the presence of the goods reported destroyed.'

'I didn't expect you to be so frank.'

'I indulge myself, occasionally.'

I grinned. 'Mrs Matthews seems pretty genuine.'

'I've never met the lady.'

Treat in store, I thought. 'Don't the firemen,' I said, 'look for signs of arson?'

'Yes, and also the police, and we ask them for guidance.'

'And what did they say?'

'None of your business, I shouldn't think.'

'Even for a wooden house,' I said, 'it is pretty thoroughly burnt.'

'Expert, are you?' he said with irony.

'I've built a lot of Guy Fawkes bonfires, in my time.'

He turned his head.

'They burn a lot better,' I said, 'if you soak them in paraffin. Especially round the edges.'

'I've been looking at fires since before you were born,' he said. 'Why don't you go over there and paint?'

'What I've done is still wet.'

'Then if you stay with me, shut up.'

I stayed with him, silent, and without offence. He was making what appeared to be a preliminary reconnaissance, lifting small solid pieces of debris, inspecting them closely, and carefully returning them to their former positions. None of the things he chose in that way were identifiable to me from a distance of six feet, and as far as I could see none of them gave him much of a thrill.

'Permission to speak?' I said.

'Well?'

'Mr Greene was doing much what you are, though in the area behind the chimney-breast.'

He straightened from replacing yet another black lump. 'Did he take anything?' he said.

'Not while we were watching, which was a very short time. No telling how long he'd been there.'

'No.' He considered. 'Wouldn't you think he was a casual sightseer, poking around out of curiosity?'

'He hadn't the air.'

D. J. frowned. 'Then what did he want?'

A rhetorical question. Gary rolled back, and soon after him, Maisie. In her Jaguar. In her scarlet coat. In a temper.

'What do you mean,' she said, advancing upon D. J. with eyes flashing fortissimo, 'the question of arson isn't yet settled? Don't tell me you're trying to wriggle out of paying my cheque, now. Your man said on Saturday that everything was all right and I could start clearing away and rebuilding, and anyway even if it had been arson you would still have to pay up because the insurance covered arson of course.'

D. J. opened and shut his mouth several times and finally found his voice.

'Didn't our Mr Robinson tell you that the man you saw here on Saturday wasn't from us?'

Our Mr Robinson, in the shape of Gary, nodded vigorously.

'He . . . Mr Greene . . . distinctly said he *was*,' Maisie insisted.

'Well . . . what did he look like?'

'Smarmy,' said Maisie without hesitation. 'Not as young as Charles . . .' she gestured towards me, 'or as old as you.' She thought, then shrugged. 'He looked like an insurance man, that's all.'

D. J. swallowed the implied insult manfully.

'About five feet ten,' I said. 'Suntanned skin with a sallow tinge, grey eyes with deep upper eyelids, widish nose, mouth straight under heavy drooping dark moustache, straight brown hair brushed back and retreating from the two top corners of his forehead, ordinary eyebrows, greeny-brown trilby of smooth felt, shirt, tie, fawn unbuttoned raincoat, gold signet ring on little finger of right hand, suntanned hands.'

I could see him in memory as clearly as if he still stood there in the ashes before me, taking off his hat and calling Maisie 'madam'.

'Good God,' D. J. said.

'An artist's eye, dear,' said Maisie admiringly. 'Well I never.'

D. J. said he was certain they had no one like that in their poking-into-claims department, and Gary agreed.

'Well,' said Maisie, with a resurgence of crossness, 'I suppose that still means you are looking for arson, though why you think that anyone in his right senses would want to burn down my lovely home and all my treasures is something I'll never understand.'

Surely Maisie, worldly Maisie, could not be so naïve. I caught a deep glimmer of intelligence in the glance she gave me, and knew that she certainly wasn't. D. J. however, who didn't know, made frustrated little motions with his hands and voted against explaining. I smothered a few more laughs, and Maisie noticed.

'Do you want your picture,' I asked, 'to be sunny like today, or cloudy and sad?'

She looked up at the bright sky.

'A bit more dramatic, dear,' she said.

D. J. and Gary inch-by-inched over the ruin all afternoon, and I tried to infuse it with a little Gothic romance. At five o'clock, on the dot, we all knocked off.

'Union hours?' said D. J. sarcastically, watching me pack my suitcase.

'The light gets too yellow in the evenings.'

'Will you be here tomorrow?'

I nodded. 'And you?'

'Perhaps.'

I went by foot and bus along to the Beach Hotel, cleaned my brushes, thought a bit, and at seven met Maisie downstairs in the bar, as arranged.

'Well, dear,' she said, as her first gin and tonic gravitated comfortably. 'Did they find anything?'

'Nothing at all, as far as I could see.'

'Well, that's good, dear.'

I tackled my pint of draught. Put the glass down carefully.

'Not altogether, Maisie.'

'Why not?'

'What exactly were your treasures, which were burned?'

'I dare say you wouldn't think so much of them of course, but we had ever such fun buying them, and so have I since Archie's gone, and well, dear, things like an antique spear collection that used to belong to old Lord Stequers whose niece I nursed once, and a whole wall of beautiful butterflies, which professors and such came to look at, and a wrought-iron gate from Lady Tythe's old home, which divided the hall from the sitting-room, and six warming pans from a castle in Ireland, and two tall vases with eagles on the lids signed by Angelica Kaufman, which once belonged to a cousin of Mata Hari, they really did, dear, and a copper firescreen with silver bosses which was a devil to polish, and a marble table from Greece, and a silver tea urn which was once used by Queen Victoria, and really, dear, that's just the beginning, if I tell you them all I'll go on all night.'

'Did the Foundation insurance company have a full list?'

'Yes, they did, dear, and why do you want to know?'

'Because,' I said regretfully, 'I don't think many of those things were inside the house when it burned down.'

'*What?*' Maisie, as far as I could tell, was genuinely astounded. 'But they must have been.'

'D. J. as good as told me that they were looking for traces of them, and I don't think they found any.'

'D. J.?'

'Mr Lagland. The elder one.'

Alternate disbelief and anger kept Maisie going through two more double gins. Disbelief, eventually, won.

'You got it wrong, dear,' she said finally.

'I hope so.'

'Inexperience of youth, of course.'

'Maybe.'

'Because of course everything was in its place, dear, when I went off last Friday week to stay with Betty, and I only went to Betty's with not having seen her for so long while I'd been away, which is ironic when you think of it, but of course you can't stay at home for ever on the off chance your house is going to catch fire and you can save it, can you dear, or you'd never go any-where and I would have missed my trip to Australia.'

She paused for breath. Coincidence, I thought.

'All I can say, dear, is that it's a miracle I took most of my jewellery with me to Betty's, because I don't always, except that Archie always said it was safer and of course he was always so sensible and thoughtful and sweet.'

'Australia?' I said.

'Well, yes, dear, wasn't that nice? I went out there for a visit to Archie's sister who's lived there since heaven knows when and was feeling lonely since she'd been widowed, poor dear, and I went out for a bit of fun, dear, because of course I'd never really met her, only exchanged postcards of course, and I was out there for six weeks with her. She wanted me to stay, and of course we got on together like a house on fire . . . oh dear, I didn't mean that exactly . . . well, anyway, I said I wanted to come back to my little house by the sea and think it over, and of course I took my jewellery with me on that trip too, dear.'

I said idly, 'I don't suppose you bought a Munnings while you were there.'

I didn't know why I'd said it, apart from thinking of Donald in Australia. I was totally unprepared for her reaction.

Astounded she had been before: this time, poleaxed. Before, she had been incredulous and angry. This time, incredulous and frightened.

She knocked over her gin, slid off her bar stool, and covered her open mouth with four trembling red-nailed fingers.

'You didn't!' I said disbelievingly.

'How do you know?'

'I don't . . .'

'Are you from Customs and Excise?'

'Of course not.'

'Oh dear. Oh dear . . .' She was shaking, almost as shattered as Donald.

I took her arm and led her over to an armchair beside a small bar table.

'Sit down,' I said coaxingly, 'and tell me.'

It took ten minutes and a refill double gin.

'Well, dear, I'm not an art expert, as you can probably guess, but there was this picture by Sir Alfred Munnings, signed and everything, dear, and it was such a bargain really, and I thought how tickled Archie would have been to have a real Munnings on the wall, what with us both liking the races, of course, and, well, Archie's sister egged me on a bit, and I felt quite . . . I suppose you might call it *high*, dear, so I bought it.'

She stopped.

'Go on,' I said.

'Well, dear, I suppose you've guessed from what I said just now.'

'You brought it into this country without declaring it?'

She sighed. 'Yes, dear, I did. Of course it was silly of me but I never gave customs duty a thought when I bought the paint-ing, not until just before I came home, a week later, that was, and Archie's sister asked if I was going to declare it, and well, dear, I really *resent* having to pay duty on things, don't you? So anyway I thought I'd better find out just how much the duty would be, and I found it wasn't duty at all in the ordinary way, dear, there isn't duty on secondhand pictures being brought in from Australia, but would you believe it, they said I would have to pay Value Added Tax, sort of tax on buying things, you know, dear, and I would have to pay eight per cent on whatever I had bought the picture for. Well, I ask you! I was that mad, dear, I can tell you. So Archie's sister said why didn't I leave the painting with her, because then if I went back to Australia I would have paid the tax for nothing, but I wasn't sure I'd go back and anyway I did want to see Sir Alfred Munnings on the wall where Archie would have loved it, so; well, dear, it was all done up nicely in boards and brown paper so I just camouflaged it a bit with my best nightie and popped it in my suitcase, and pushed it through the "Nothing to Declare" lane at Heathrow when I got back, and nobody stopped me.'

'How much would you have had to pay?' I said.

'Well, dear, to be precise, just over seven hundred pounds. And I know that's not a fortune, dear, but it made me so mad to have to pay tax here because I'd bought something nice in Australia.'

I did some mental arithmetic. 'So the painting cost about nine thousand?'

'That's right, dear. Nine thousand.' She looked anxious. 'I wasn't done, was I? I've asked one or two people since I got back and they say lots of Munningses cost fifteen or more.'

'So they do,' I said absently. And some could be got for fifteen hundred, and others, I dared say, for less.

'Well, anyway, dear, it was only when I began to think about insurance that I wondered if I would be found out, if say, the insurance people wanted a *receipt* or anything, which they probably would, of course, so I didn't do anything about it, because of course if I *did* go back to Australia I could just take the picture with me and no harm done.'

'Awkward,' I agreed.

'So now it's burnt, and I dare say you'll think it serves me right, because the nine thousand's gone up in smoke and I won't see a penny of it back.'

She finished the gin and I bought her another.

'I know it's not my business, Maisie, but how did you happen to have nine thousand handy in Australia? Aren't there rules about exporting that much cash?'

She giggled. 'You don't know much about the world, do you, dear? But anyway, this time it was all hunky-dory. I just toddled along with Archie's sister to a jeweller's and sold him a brooch I had, a nasty sort of *toad*, dear, with a socking big diamond in the middle of its forehead, something to do with Shakespeare, I think, though I never got it clear, anyway I never wore it, it was so ugly, but of course I'd taken it with me because of it being worth so much, and I sold it for nine thousand five, though in Australian dollars of course, so there was no problem, was there?'

Maisie took it for granted I would be eating with her, so we drifted in to dinner. Her appetite seemed healthy, but her spirits were damp.

'You won't *tell* anyone, will you, dear, about the picture?'

'Of course not, Maisie.'

'I could get into such trouble, dear.'

'I know.'

'A fine, of course,' she said. 'And I suppose that might be the least of it. People can be so beastly about a perfectly innocent little bit of smuggling.'

'No one will find out, if you keep quiet.' A thought struck me. 'Unless, that is, you've told anyone already that you'd bought it?'

'No, dear, I didn't, because of thinking I'd better pretend I'd had it for years, and of course I hadn't even hung it on the wall yet because one of the rings was loose in the frame and I thought it might fall down and be damaged, and I couldn't decide who to ask to fix it.' She paused for a mouthful of prawn cocktail. 'I expect you'll think me silly, dear, but I suppose I was feeling a bit scared of being found out, not guilty exactly because I really don't see why we *should* pay that irritating tax but anyway I didn't not only not hang it up, I hid it.'

'You hid it? Still wrapped up?'

'Well, yes, dear, more or less wrapped up. Of course I'd opened it when I got home, and that's when I found the ring coming loose with the cord through it, so I wrapped it up again until I'd decided what to do.'

I was fascinated. 'Where did you hide it?'

She laughed. 'Nowhere very much, dear. I mean, I was only keeping it out of sight to stop people asking about it, of course, so I slipped it behind one of the radiators in the lounge, and don't look so horrified dear, the central heating was turned off.'

I painted at the house all the next day, but neither D. J. nor anyone else turned up.

In between stints at the easel I poked around a good deal on my own account, searching for Maisie's treasures. I found a good many recognizable remains, durables like bed-frames, kitchen machines and radiators, all of them twisted and buckled not merely by heat but by the weight of the whole edifice from roof downwards having collapsed inwards. Occasional remains of heavy rafters lay blackly in the thick ash, but apart from these, everything combustible had totally, as one might say, combusted.

Of all the things Maisie had described, and of all the dozens she hadn't, I found only the wrought-iron gate from Lady Tythe's old home, which had divided the hall from the sitting-room. Lady Tythe would never have recognized it.

No copper warming pans, which after all had been designed to withstand red-hot coals. No metal firescreen. No marble table. No antique spears.

Naturally, no Munnings.

When I took my paint-stained fingers back to the Beach at five o'clock I found Maisie waiting for me in the hall. Not the kindly, basically cheerful Maisie I had come to know, but a belligerent woman in a full-blown state of rage.

'I've been waiting for you,' she said, fixing me with a furious eye.

I couldn't think how I could have offended her.

'What's the matter?' I said.

'The bar's shut,' she said. 'So come upstairs to my room. Bring all your stuff with you.' She gestured to the suitcase. 'I'm so *mad* I think I'll absolutely *burst.*'

She did indeed, in the lift, look in danger of it. Her cheeks were bright red with hard outlines of colour against the pale surrounding skin. Her blonde-rinsed hair, normally lacquered into sophistication, stuck out in wispy spikes, and for the first time since I'd met her her mouth was not glistening with lipstick.

She threw open the door of her room and stalked in. I followed, closing it after me.

'You'll never believe it,' she said forcefully, turning to face me and letting go with all guns blazing. 'I've had the police here half the day, and those insurance men here the other half, and *do you know what they're saying?'*

'Oh, Maisie.' I sighed inwardly. It had been inevitable.

'What do you think I am, I asked them,' she said. 'I was so *mad.* There they were, having the nerve to suggest I'd sold all my treasures and over-insured my house, and was trying to take the insurance people for a ride. I told them, I told them over and over, that everything was in its place when I went to Betty's and if it was over-insured it was to allow for inflation and anyway the brokers had advised me to put up the amount pretty high, and I'm glad I took their advice, but that Mr Lagland says they won't be paying out until they have investigated further and he was proper sniffy about it, and no sympathy at all for me having lost everything. They were absolutely *beastly*, and I *hate* them all.'

She paused to regather momentum, vibrating visibly with the strength of her feelings. 'They made me feel so *dirty*, and maybe I *was* screaming at them a bit, I was so mad, but they'd no call to be so *rude*, and making out I was some sort of criminal, and just what *right* have they to tell me to pull myself together when it is because of *them* and their bullying that I am yelling at them at the top of my voice?'

It must, I reflected, have been quite an encounter. I wondered in what state the police and D. J. had retired from the field.

'They say it was definitely arson and I said why did they think so now when they hadn't thought so at first, and it turns out that it was because that Lagland couldn't find any of my treasures in the ashes or any trace of them at all, and they said even if I hadn't sold the things first I had arranged for them to be stolen and the house burnt to cinders while I was away at Betty's, and they kept on and on asking me who I'd paid to do it, and I got more and more furious and if I'd had anything handy I would have *hit* them, I really would.'

'What you need is a stiff gin,' I said.

'I told them they ought to be out looking for whoever had done it instead of hounding helpless women like me, and the more I thought of someone walking into *my* house and stealing *my* treasures and then callously setting fire to everything the madder I got, and somehow that made me even *madder* with those stupid men who couldn't see any further than their stupid noses.'

It struck me after a good deal more of similar diatribe that genuine though Maisie's anger undoubtedly was, she was stoking herself up again every time her temper looked in danger of relapsing to normal. For some reason, she seemed to need to be in the position of the righteous wronged.

I wondered why; and in a breath-catching gap in the flow of hot lava, I said, 'I don't suppose you told them about the Munnings.'

The red spots on her cheeks burned suddenly brighter.

'I'm not *crazy*,' she said bitingly. 'If they found out about that, there would have been a fat chance of convincing them I'm telling the truth about the rest.'

'I've heard,' I said tentatively, 'that nothing infuriates a crook more than being had up for the one job he didn't do.'

It looked for a moment as if I'd just elected myself as the new target for hatred, but suddenly as she glared at me in rage her sense of humour reared its battered head and nudged her in the ribs. The stiffness round her mouth relaxed, her eyes softened and glimmered, and after a second or two, she ruefully smiled.

'I dare say you're right, dear, when I come to think of it.' The smile slowly grew into a giggle. 'How about that gin?'

Little eruptions continued all evening through drinks and dinner, but the red-centred volcano had subsided to manageable heat.

'You didn't seem surprised, dear, when I told you what the police thought I'd done.' She looked sideways at me over her coffee cup, eyes sharp and enquiring.

'No.' I paused. 'You see, something very much the same has just happened to my cousin. Too much the same, in too many ways. I think, if you will come, and he agrees, that I'd like to take you to meet him.'

'But why, dear?'

I told her why. The anger she felt for herself burned up again fiercely for Donald.

'How *dreadful*. How *selfish* you must think *me*, after all that that poor man has suffered.'

'I don't think you're selfish at all. In fact, Maisie, I think you're a proper trouper.'

She looked pleased and almost kittenish, and I had a vivid impression of what she had been like with Archie.

'There's one thing, though, dear,' she said awkwardly. 'After today, and all that's been said, I don't think I want that picture you're doing. I don't any more want to remember the house as it is now, only like it used to be. So if I give you just the fifty pounds, do you mind?'

Five

WE WENT to Shropshire in Maisie's Jaguar, sharing the driving. Donald on the telephone had sounded unenthusiastic at my suggested return, but also too lethargic to raise objections. When he opened his front door to us, I was shocked.

It was two weeks since I'd left him to go to Yorkshire. In that time he had shed at least fourteen pounds and aged ten years. His skin was tinged with bluish shadows, the bones in his face showed starkly, and even his hair seemed speckled with grey.

The ghost of the old Donald put an obvious effort into receiving us with good manners.

'Come in,' he said. 'I'm in the dining-room now. I expect you'd like a drink.'

'That would be very nice, dear,' Maisie said.

He looked at her with dull eyes, seeing, as I saw, a large good-natured lady with glossy hair and expensive clothes, her smart appearance walking a tightrope between vulgarity and elegance and just making it to the safer side.

He waved to me to pour the drinks, as if it would be too much for him, and invited Maisie to sit down. The dining-room had been roughly refurnished, containing now a large rug, all the sunroom armchairs, and a couple of small tables from the bedrooms. We sat in a fairly close group round one of the tables, because I had come to ask questions, and I wanted to write down the answers. My cousin watched the production of notebook and ballpoint with no show of interest.

'Don,' I said, 'I want you to listen to a story.'

'All right.'

Maisie, for once, kept it short. When she came to the bit about buying a Munnings in Australia, Donald's head lifted a couple of inches and he looked from her to me with the first stirring of attention. When she stopped, there was a small silence.

'So,' I said finally, 'you both went to Australia, you both bought a Munnings, and soon after your return you both had your houses burgled.'

'Extraordinary coincidence,' Donald said: but he meant simply that, nothing more. 'Did you come all this way just to tell me that?'

'I wanted to see how you were.'

'Oh. I'm all right. Kind of you, Charles, but I'm all right.'

Even Maisie, who hadn't known him before, could see that he wasn't.

'Where did you buy your picture, Don? Where exactly, I mean.'

'I suppose . . . Melbourne. In the Hilton Hotel. Opposite the cricket ground.'

I looked doubtful. Although hotels quite often sold pictures by local artists, they seldom sold Munnings.

'Fellow met us there,' Don added. 'Brought it up to our room. From the gallery where we saw it first.'

'Which gallery?'

He made a slight attempt to remember. 'Might have been something like Fine Arts.'

'Would you have it on a cheque stub, or anything?'

He shook his head. 'The wine firm I was dealing with paid for it for me, and I sent a cheque to their British office when I got back.'

'Which wine firm?'

'Monga Vineyards Proprietary Limited of Adelaide and Melbourne.'

I wrote it all down.

'And what was the picture like? I mean, could you describe it?'

Donald looked tired. 'One of those "Going down to the start" things. Typical Munnings.'

'So was mine,' said Maisie, surprised. 'A nice long row of jockeys in their colours against a darker sort of sky.'

'Mine had only three horses,' Donald said.

'The biggest, I suppose you might say the *nearest* jockey in my picture had a purple shirt and green cap,' Maisie said, 'and I expect you'll think I was silly but that was one of the reasons I bought it, because when Archie and I were thinking what fun it would be to buy a horse and go to the races as owners, we decided we'd like purple with a green cap for our colours, if no one else already had that, of course.'

'Don?' I said.

'Mm? Oh . . . three bay horses cantering . . . in profile . . . one in front, two slightly overlapping behind. Bright colours on the jockeys. I don't remember exactly. White racetrack rails and a lot of sunny sky.'

'What size?'

He frowned slightly. 'Not very big. About twenty-four inches by eighteen, inside the frame.'

'And yours, Maisie?'

'A bit smaller, dear, I should think.'

'Look,' Donald said. 'What are you getting at?'

'Trying to make sure that there are no more coincidences.'

He stared, but without any particular feeling.

'On the way up here,' I said, 'Maisie told me everything' (but *everything*) 'of the way she came to buy her picture. So could you possibly tell us how you came to buy yours? Did you, for example, deliberately go looking for a Munnings?'

Donald passed a weary hand over his face, obviously not wanting the bother of answering.

'Please, Don,' I said.

'Oh . . .' A long sigh. 'No. I wasn't especially wanting to buy anything at all. We just went into the Melbourne Art Gallery for a stroll round. We came to the Munnings they have there . . . and while we were looking at it we just drifted into conversation with a woman near us, as one does in art galleries. She said there was another Munnings, not far away, for sale in a small commercial gallery, and it was worth seeing even if one didn't intend to buy it. We had time to spare, so we went.'

Maisie's mouth had fallen open. 'But dear,' she said, recovering, 'that was *just* the same as us, my sister-in-law and me, though it was Sydney Art Gallery, not Melbourne. They have this marvellous picture there, *The Coming Storm*, and we were admiring it when this man sort of drifted up to us and joined in . . .'

Donald suddenly looked a great deal more exhausted, like a sick person overdone by healthy visitors.

'Look . . . Charles . . . you aren't going to the police with all this? Because I . . . I don't think . . . I could stand . . . a whole new lot . . . of questions.'

'No, I'm not,' I said.

'Then what . . . does it matter?'

Maisie finished her gin and tonic and smiled a little too brightly.

'Which way to the girls' room, dear?' she asked, and disappeared to the cloakroom.

Donald said faintly, 'I can't concentrate . . . I'm sorry, Charles, but I can't seem to do anything . . . while they still have Regina . . . unburied . . . just *stored* . . .'

Time, far from dulling the agony, seemed to have preserved it, as if the keeping of Regina in a refrigerated drawer had stopped dead the natural progression of mourning. I had been told that the bodies of murdered people could be held in that way for six months or more in unsolved cases. I doubted whether Donald would last that long.

He stood suddenly and walked away out of the door to the hall. I followed. He crossed the hall, opened the door of the sitting-room, and went in.

Hesitantly, I went after him.

The sitting-room still contained only the chintz-covered sofas and chairs, now ranged over-tidily round the walls. The floor where Regina had lain was clean and polished. The air was cold.

Donald stood in front of the empty fireplace looking at my picture of Regina, which was propped on the mantelpiece.

'I stay in here with her, most of the time,' he said. 'It's the only place I can bear to be.'

He walked to one of the armchairs and sat down, directly facing the portrait.

'You wouldn't mind seeing yourselves out, would you Charles?' he said. 'I'm really awfully tired.'

'Take care of yourself.' Useless advice. One could see he wouldn't.

'I'm all right,' he said. 'Quite all right. Don't you worry.'

I looked back from the door. He was sitting immobile, looking at Regina. I didn't know whether it would have been better or worse if I hadn't painted her.

Maisie was quiet for the whole of the first hour of the return journey, a record in itself.

From Donald's house we had driven first to one of the neighbours who had originally offered refuge, because he clearly needed help more now than ever.

Mrs Neighbour had listened with sympathy, but had shaken her head.

'Yes, I know he should have company and get away from the house, but he won't. I've tried several times. Called. So have lots of people round here. He just tells us he's all right. He won't let anyone help him.'

Maisie drove soberly, mile after mile. Eventually she said, 'We shouldn't have bothered him. Not so soon after . . .'

Three weeks, I thought. Only three weeks. To Donald it must have seemed like three months, stretched out in slow motion. You could live a lifetime in three weeks' pain.

'You're very fond of him, dear, aren't you?' Maisie said.

Fond? I wouldn't have used that word, I thought: but perhaps after all it was accurate.

'He's eight years older than me, but we've always got on well together.' I looked back, remembering. 'We were both only children. His mother and mine were sisters. They used to visit each other, with me and Donald in tow. He was always pretty patient about having a young kid under his feet.'

'He looks very ill, dear.'

'Yes.'

She drove another ten miles in silence. Then she said, 'Are you sure it wouldn't be better to tell the police? About the paintings, I mean? Because you do think they had something to do with the burglaries, don't you, dear, and the police might find out things more easily than you.'

I agreed. 'I'm sure they would, Maisie. But how can I tell them? You heard what Donald said, that he couldn't stand a new lot of questions. Seeing him today, do you think he could? And as for you, it wouldn't just be confessing to a bit of smuggling and paying a fine, but of having a conviction against your name for always, and having the customs search your baggage every time you travelled, and all sorts of other complications and humiliations. Once you get on any blacklist nowadays it is just about impossible to get off.'

'I didn't know you cared, dear.' She tried a giggle, but it didn't sound right.

We stopped after a while to exchange places. I liked driving her car, particularly as for the last three years, since I'd given up a steady income, I'd owned no wheels myself. The power purred elegantly under the pale blue bonnet and ate up the southward miles.

'I'm going to Australia,' I said.

'Can you afford the fare, dear?' Maisie said. 'And hotels, and things?'

'I've a friend out there. Another painter. I'll stay with him.'

She looked at me doubtfully. 'You can't get there by hitch-hiking, though.'

I smiled. 'I'll manage.'

'Yes, well, dear, I dare say you can, but all the same, and I don't want any silly arguments, I've got a great deal of this world's goods thanks to Archie, and you haven't, and as it's partly because of me having gone in for smuggling that you're going yourself at all, I am insisting that you let me buy your ticket.'

'No, Maisie.'

'Yes, dear. Now be a good boy, dear, and do as I say.'

You could see, I thought, why she'd been a good nurse. Swallow the medicine, dear, there's a good boy. I didn't like accepting her offer but the truth was that I would have had to borrow anyway.

'Shall I paint your picture, Maisie, when I get back?'

'That will do very nicely, dear.'

I pulled up outside the house near Heathrow whose attic was my home, and from where Maisie had picked me up that morning.

'How do you stand all this noise, dear?' she said, wincing as a huge jet climbed steeply overhead.

'I concentrate on the cheap rent.'

She smiled, opening the crocodile handbag and producing

596

her chequebook. She wrote out and gave me the slip of paper which was far more than enough for my journey.

'If you're fussed, dear,' she said across my protests, 'you can give me back what you don't spend.' She gazed at me earnestly with grey-blue eyes. 'You will be careful dear, won't you?'

'Yes, Maisie.'

'Because of course, dear, you might turn out to be a nuisance to some really *nasty* people.'

I landed at Mascot airport at noon five days later, wheeling in over Sydney and seeing the harbour bridge and the opera house down below, looking like postcards.

Jik met me on the other side of Customs with a huge grin and a waving bottle of champagne.

'Todd the sod,' he said. 'Who'd have thought it?' His voice soared easily over the din. 'Come to paint Australia red!'

He slapped me on the back with an enthusiastic horny hand, not knowing his own strength. Jik Cassavetes, long-time friend, my opposite in almost everything.

Bearded, which I was not. Exuberant, noisy, extravagant, unpredictable; qualities I envied. Blue eyes and sun-blond hair. Muscles which left mine gasping. An outrageous way with girls. An abrasive tongue; and a wholehearted contempt for the things I painted.

We had met at art school, drawn together by mutual truancy on racetrains. Jik compulsively went racing, but strictly to gamble, never to admire the contestants, and certainly not to paint them. Horse painters, to him, were the lower orders. No *serious* artist, he frequently said, would be seen dead painting horses.

Jik's paintings, mostly abstract, were the dark reverse of the bright mind: fruits of depression, full of despair at the hatred and pollution destroying the fair world.

Living with Jik was like a toboggan run, downhill,

597

dangerous, and exhilarating. We'd spent the last two years at art school sharing a studio flat and kicking each other out for passing girls. They would have chucked him out of school except for his prodigious talent, because he'd missed weeks in the summer for his other love, which was sailing.

I'd been out with him, deep sea, several times in the years afterwards. I reckoned he'd taken us on several occasions a bit nearer death than was strictly necessary, but it had been a nice change from the office. He was a great sailor, efficient, neat, quick and strong, with an instinctive feeling for wind and waves. I had been sorry when one day he had said he was setting off single-handed round the world. We'd had a paralytic farewell party on his last night ashore; and the next day, when he'd gone, I'd given the estate agent my notice.

He had brought a car to fetch me: his car, it turned out. A British M.G. Sports, dark blue. Both sides of him right there, extrovert and introvert, the flamboyant statement in a sombre colour.

'Are there many of these here?' I asked, surprised, loading suitcase and satchel into the back. 'It's a long way from the birth pangs.'

He grinned. 'A few. They're not popular now because petrol passes through them like salts.' The engine roared to life, agreeing with him, and he switched on the windscreen wiper against a starting shower. 'Welcome to sunny Australia. It rains all the time here. Puts Manchester in the sun.'

'But you like it?'

'Love it, mate. Sydney's like rugger, all guts and go and a bit of grace in the line-out.'

'And how's business?'

'There are thousands of painters in Australia. It's a flourishing cottage industry.' He glanced at me sideways. 'A hell of a lot of competition.'

'I haven't come to seek fame and fortune.'

'But I scent a purpose,' he said.

'How would you feel about harnessing your brawn?'

'To your brain? As in the old days?'

'Those were pastimes.'

His eyebrows rose. 'What are the risks?'

'Arson and murder, to date.'

'Jesus.'

The blue car swept gracefully into the centre of the city. Sky-scrapers grew like beanstalks.

'I live right out on the other side,' Jik said. 'God, that sounds banal. Suburban. What has become of me?'

'Contentment oozing from every pore,' I said smiling.

'Yes. So. O.K., for the first time in my life I've been actually happy. I dare say you'll soon put that right.'

The car nosed on to the expressway, pointing towards the bridge.

'If you look over your right shoulder,' Jik said, 'You'll see the triumph of imagination over economics. Like the Concorde. Long live madness, it's the only thing that gets us anywhere.'

I looked. It was the opera house, glimpsed, grey with rain.

'Dead in the day,' Jik said. 'It's a night bird. Fantastic.'

The great arch of the bridge rose above us, intricate as steel lace. 'This is the only flat bit of road in Sydney,' Jik said. We climbed again on the other side.

To our left, half seen at first behind other familiar-looking high-rise blocks, but then revealed in its full glory, stood a huge shiny red-orange building, all its sides set with regular rows of large curve-cornered square windows of bronze-coloured glass.

Jik grinned. 'The shape of the twenty-first century. Imagination and courage. I love this country.'

'Where's your natural pessimism?'

'When the sun sets, those windows glow like gold.' We left the gleaming monster behind. 'It's the water-board offices,' Jik said sardonically. 'The guy at the top moors his boat near mine.'

The road went up and down out of the city through close-packed rows of one-storey houses, whose roofs, from the air, had looked like a great red-squared carpet.

'There's one snag,' Jik said. 'Three weeks ago, I got married.'

The snag was living with him aboard his boat, which was moored among a colony of others near a headland he called the Spit: and you could see why, temporarily at least, the glooms of the world could take care of themselves.

She was not plain, but not beautiful. Oval-shaped face, mid-brown hair, so-so figure and a practical line in clothes. None of the style or instant vital butterfly quality of Regina. I found myself the critically inspected target of bright brown eyes which looked out with impact-making intelligence.

'Sarah,' Jik said. 'Todd. Todd, Sarah.'

We said hi and did I have a good flight and yes I did. I gathered she would have preferred me to stay at home.

Jik's thirty-foot ketch, which had set out from England as a cross between a studio and a chandler's warehouse, now sported curtains, cushions, and a flowering plant. When Jik opened the champagne he poured it into shining tulip glasses, not plastic mugs.

'By God,' he said. 'It's good to see you.'

Sarah toasted my advent politely, not sure that she agreed. I apologized for gatecrashing the honeymoon.

'Nuts to that,' Jik said, obviously meaning it. 'Too much domestic bliss is bad for the soul.'

'It depends,' said Sarah neutrally, 'on whether you need love or loneliness to get you going.'

For Jik, before, it had always been loneliness. I wondered what he had painted recently: but there was no sign, in the now comfortable cabin, of so much as a brush.

'I walk on air,' Jik said. 'I could bound up Everest and do a handspring on the summit.'

'As far as the galley will do,' Sarah said, 'if you remembered to buy the crayfish.'

Jik, in our shared days, had been the cook; and times, it seemed, had not changed. It was he, not Sarah, who with speed and efficiency chopped open the crayfish, covered them with cheese and mustard, and set them under the grill. He who washed the crisp lettuce and assembled crusty bread and butter. We ate the feast round the cabin table with rain pattering on portholes and roof and the sea water slapping against the sides in the freshening wind. Over coffee, at Jik's insistence, I told them why I had come to Australia.

They heard me out in concentrated silence. Then Jik, whose politics had not changed much since student pink, muttered darkly about 'pigs', and Sarah looked nakedly apprehensive.

'Don't worry,' I told her. 'I'm not asking for Jik's help, now that I know he's married.'

'You have it. You have it,' he said explosively.

I shook my head. 'No.'

Sarah said, 'What precisely do you plan to do first?'

'Find out where the two Munningses came from.'

'And after?'

'If I knew what I was looking for I wouldn't need to look.'

'That doesn't follow,' she said absently.

'Melbourne,' Jik said suddenly. 'You said one of the pictures came from Melbourne. Well, that settles it. Of course we'll help. We'll go there at once. It couldn't be better. Do you know what next Tuesday is?'

'No,' I said. 'What is it?'

'The day of the Melbourne Cup!'

His voice was triumphant. Sarah stared at me darkly across the table.

'I wish you hadn't come,' she said.

Six

I SLEPT that night in the converted boathouse which consti-
tuted Jik's postal address. Apart from a bed alcove, new-looking
bathroom, and rudimentary kitchen, he was using the whole
space as studio.

A huge old easel stood in the centre, with a table to each side
holding neat arrays of paints, brushes, knives, pots of linseed and
turpentine and cleaning fluid: all the usual paraphernalia.

No work in progress. Everything shut and tidy. Like its coun-
terpart in England, the large rush mat in front of the easel was
black with oily dirt, owing to Jik's habit of rubbing his roughly
rinsed brushes on it between colours. The tubes of paint were
characteristically squeezed flat in the middles, impatience for-
bidding an orderly progress from the bottom. The palette was a
small oblong, not needed any larger because he used most
colours straight from the tube and got his effects by overpaint-
ing. A huge box of rags stood under one table, ready to wipe
clean everything used to apply paint to picture, not just brushes
and knives, but fingers, palms, nails, wrists, anything which took
his fancy. I smiled to myself. Jik's studio was as identifiable as his
pictures.

Along one wall a two-tiered rack held rows of canvases,
which I pulled out one by one. Dark, strong, dramatic colours,
leaping to the eye. Still the troubled vision, the perception of
doom. Decay and crucifixions, obscurely horrific landscapes,

flowers wilting, fish dying, everything to be guessed, nothing explicit.

Jik hated to sell his paintings and seldom did, which I thought was just as well, as they made uncomfortable room-mates, enough to cause depression in a skylark. They had a vigour, though, that couldn't be denied. Everyone who saw his assembled work remembered it, and had their thoughts modified, and perhaps even their basic attitudes changed. He was a major artist in a way I would never be, and he would have looked upon easy popular acclaim as personal failure.

In the morning I walked down to the boat and found Sarah there alone.

'Jik's gone for milk and newspapers,' she said. 'I'll get you some breakfast.'

'I came to say goodbye.'

She looked at me levelly. 'The damage is done.'

'Not if I go.'

'Back to England?'

I shook my head.

'I thought not.' A dim smile appeared briefly in her eyes. 'Jik told me last night that you were the only person he knew who had a head cool enough to calculate a ship's position for a may-day call by dead reckoning at night after tossing around violently for four hours in a force ten gale with a hole in the hull and the pumps packed up, and get it right.'

I grinned. 'But he patched the hull and mended the pump, and we cancelled the mayday when it got light.'

'You were both stupid.'

'Better to stay safely at home?' I said.

She turned away. '*Men*,' she said. 'Never happy unless they're risking their necks.'

She was right, to some extent. A little healthy danger wasn't a bad feeling, especially in retrospect. It was only the nerve-breakers which gave you the shakes and put you off repetition.

'Some women, too,' I said.

'Not me.'

'I won't take Jik with me.'

Her back was still turned. 'You'll get him killed,' she said.

Nothing looked less dangerous than the small suburban gallery from which Maisie had bought her picture. It was shut for good. The bare premises could be seen nakedly through the shopfront window, and a succinct and unnecessary card hanging inside the glass door said 'Closed'.

The little shops on each side shrugged their shoulders.

'They were only open for a month or so. Never seemed to do much business. No surprise they folded.'

Did they, I asked, know which estate agent was handling the letting? No, they didn't.

'End of enquiry,' Jik said.

I shook my head. 'Let's try the local agents.'

We split up and spent a fruitless hour. None of the firms on any of the 'For Sale' boards in the district admitted to having the gallery on its books.

We met again outside the uninformative door.

'Where now?'

'Art Gallery?'

'In the Domain,' Jik said, which turned out to be a chunk of park in the city centre. The Art Gallery had a suitable facade of six pillars outside and the Munnings, when we ran it to earth, inside.

No one else was looking at it. No one approached to fall into chat and advise us we could buy another one cheap in a little gallery in an outer suburb.

We stood there for a while with me admiring the absolute mastery which set the two grey ponies in the shaft of pre-storm light at the head of the darker herd, and Jik grudgingly admitted that at least the man knew how to handle paint.

Absolutely nothing else happened. We drove back to the boat in the M.G., and lunch was an anti-climax.

'What now?' Jik said.

'A spot of work with the telephone, if I could borrow the one in the boathouse.'

It took nearly all afternoon, but alphabetically systematic calls to every estate agent as far as Holloway & Son in the classified directory produced the goods in the end. The premises in question, said Holloway & Son, had been let to North Sydney Fine Arts on a short lease.

How short?

Three months, dating from September first.

No, Holloway & Son did not know the premises were now empty. They could not re-let them until December first, because North Sydney Fine Arts had paid all the rent in advance; and they did not feel able to part with the name of any individual concerned. I blarneyed a bit, giving a delicate impression of being in the trade myself, with a client for the empty shop. Holloway & Son mentioned a Mr John Grey, with a post-office box number for an address. I thanked them. Mr Grey, they said, warming up a little, had said he wanted the gallery for a short private exhibition, and they were not really surprised he had already gone.

How could I recognize Mr Grey if I met him? They really couldn't say: all the negotiations had been done by telephone and post. I could write to him myself, if my client wanted the gallery before December first.

Ta ever so, I thought.

All the same, it couldn't do much harm. I unearthed a suitable sheet of paper, and in twee and twirly lettering in black ink told Mr Grey I had been given his name and box number by Holloway & Son, and asked him if he would sell me the last two weeks of his lease so that I could mount an exhibition of a friend's *utterly meaningful* watercolours. Name his own price, I said, within reason. Yours sincerely, I said; Peregrine Smith.

I walked down to the boat to ask if Jik or Sarah would mind me putting their own box number as a return address.

'He won't answer,' Sarah said, reading the letter. 'If he's a crook. I wouldn't.'

'The first principle of fishing,' Jik said, 'is to dangle a bait.'

'This wouldn't attract a starving piranha.'

I posted it anyway, with Sarah's grudging consent. None of us expected it to bring forth any result.

Jik's own session on the telephone proved more rewarding. Melbourne, it seemed, was crammed to the rooftops for the richest race meeting of the year, but he had been offered last-minute cancellations. Very lucky indeed, he insisted, looking amused.

'Where?' I asked suspiciously.

'In the Hilton,' he said.

I couldn't afford it, but we went anyway. Jik in his student days had lived on cautious hand-outs from a family trust, and it appeared that the source of bread was still flowing. The boat, the boathouse, the M.G. and the wife were none of them supported by paint.

We flew south to Melbourne the following morning, looking down on the Snowy Mountains en route and thinking our own chilly thoughts. Sarah's disapproval from the seat behind froze the back of my head, but she had refused to stay in Sydney. Jik's natural bent and enthusiasm for dicey adventure looked like being curbed by love, and his reaction to danger might not henceforth be uncomplicatedly practical. That was, if I could find any dangers for him to react to. The Sydney trail was dead and cold, and maybe Melbourne too would yield an unlooked-at public Munnings and a gone-away private gallery. And if it did, what then? For Donald the outlook would be bleaker than the strange puckered ranges sliding away underneath.

If I could take home enough to show beyond doubt that the plundering of his house had its roots in the sale of a painting in Australia, it should get the police off his neck, the life back to his spirit, and Regina into a decent grave.

If.

And I would have to be quick, or it would be too late to matter. Donald, staring hour after hour at a portrait in an empty house . . . Donald, on the brink.

Melbourne was cold and wet and blowing a gale. We checked gratefully into the warm plushy bosom of the Hilton, souls cosseted from the door onwards by rich reds and purples and blues, velvety fabrics, copper and gilt and glass. The staff smiled. The lifts worked. There was polite shock when I carried my own suitcase. A long way from the bare boards of home.

I unpacked, which is to say, hung up my one suit, slightly crumpled from the squashy satchel, and then went to work again on the telephone.

The Melbourne office of the Monga Vineyards Proprietary Limited cheerfully told me that the person who dealt with Mr Donald Stuart from England was the Managing Director, Mr Hudson Taylor, and he could be found at present in his office at the vineyard itself, which was north of Adelaide. Would I like the number?

Thanks very much.

'No sweat,' they said, which I gathered was Australian shorthand for 'It's no trouble, and you're welcome.'

I pulled out the map of Australia I'd acquired on the flight from England. Melbourne, capital of the state of Victoria, lay right down in the south-east corner. Adelaide, capital of South Australia, lay about four hundred and fifty miles north-west. Correction, seven hundred and thirty kilometres: the Australians had already gone metric, to the confusion of my mental arithmetic.

Hudson Taylor was not in his vineyard office. An equally cheerful voice there told me he'd left for Melbourne to go to the races. He had a runner in the Cup. Reverence, the voice implied, was due.

Could I reach him anywhere, then?

Sure, if it was important. He would be staying with friends. Number supplied. Ring at nine o'clock.

Sighing a little I went two floors down and found Jik and Sarah bouncing around their room with gleeful satisfaction.

'We've got tickets for the races tomorrow and Tuesday,' he said, 'And a car pass, and a car. And the West Indies play Victoria at cricket on Sunday opposite the hotel and we've tickets for that too.'

'Miracles courtesy of the Hilton,' Sarah said, looking much happier at this programme. 'The whole package was on offer with the cancelled rooms.'

'So what do you want us to do this afternoon?' finished Jik expansively.

'Could you bear the Arts Centre?'

It appeared they could. Even Sarah came without forecasting universal doom, my lack of success so far having cheered her. We went in a taxi to keep her curled hair dry.

The Victoria Arts Centre was huge, modern, inventive and endowed with the largest stained-glass roof in the world. Jik took deep breaths as if drawing the living spirit of the place into his lungs and declaimed at the top of his voice that Australia was the greatest, the greatest, the only adventurous country left in the corrupt, stagnating, militant, greedy, freedom-hating mean-minded, strait-jacketed, rotting, polluted world. Passers-by stared in amazement and Sarah showed no surprise at all.

We ran the Munnings to earth, eventually, deep in the labyrinth of galleries. It glowed in the remarkable light which suffused the whole building; the *Departure of the Hop Pickers*, with its great wide sky and the dignified gypsies with their ponies, caravans and children.

A young man was sitting at an easel slightly to one side, painstakingly working on a copy. On a table beside him stood large pots of linseed oil and turps, and a jar with brushes in cleaning fluid. A comprehensive box of paints lay open to hand. Two or three people stood about, watching him and pretending not to, in the manner of gallery-goers the world over.

Jik and I went round behind him to take a look. The young man glanced at Jik's face, but saw nothing there except raised eyebrows and blandness. We watched him squeeze flake white and cadmium yellow from tubes on to his palette and mix them together into a nice pale colour with a hogshair brush.

On the easel stood his study, barely started. The outlines were there, as precise as tracings, and a small amount of blue had been laid on the sky.

Jik and I watched in interest while he applied the pale yellow to the shirt of the nearest figure.

'Hey,' Jik said loudly, suddenly slapping him on the shoulder and shattering the reverent gallery hush into kaleidoscopic fragments, 'You're a fraud. If you're an artist I'm a gas-fitter's mate.'

Hardly polite, but not a hanging matter. The faces of the scattered onlookers registered embarrassment, not affront.

On the young man, though, the effect was galvanic. He leapt to his feet, overturning the easel and staring at Jik with wild eyes: and Jik, with huge enjoyment, put in the clincher.

'What you're doing is *criminal*,' he said.

The young man reacted to that with ruthless reptilian speed, snatching up the pots of linseed and turps and flinging the liquids at Jik's eyes.

I grabbed his left arm. He scooped up the paint-laden palette in his right and swung round fiercely, aiming at my face. I ducked instinctively. The palette missed me and struck Jik, who had his hands to his eyes and was yelling very loudly.

Sarah rushed towards him, knocking into me hard in her anxiety and loosening my grip on the young man. He tore his arm free, ran precipitously for the exit, dodged round behind two open-mouthed middle-aged spectators who were on their way in, and pushed them violently into my chasing path. By the time I'd disentangled myself, he had vanished from sight. I ran through several halls and passages, but couldn't find him. He knew his way, and I did not: and it took me long enough, when I finally gave up the hunt, to work out the route back to Jik.

A fair-sized crowd had surrounded him, and Sarah was in a roaring fury based on fear, which she unleashed on me as soon as she saw me return.

'Do something,' she screamed. 'Do something, he's going blind . . . He's going *blind* . . . I knew we should never have listened to you . . .'

I caught her wrists as she advanced in near hysteria to do at least some damage to my face in payment for Jik's. Her strength was no joke.

'Sarah,' I said fiercely. 'Jik is *not* going blind.'

'He is. He is,' she insisted, kicking my shins.

'Do you *want* him to?' I shouted.

She gasped sharply in outrage. What I'd said was at least as good as a slap in the face. Sense reasserted itself suddenly like a drench of cold water, and the manic power receded back to normal angry girl proportions.

'Linseed oil will do no harm at all,' I said positively. 'The turps is painful, but that's all. It absolutely will not affect his eyesight.'

She glared at me, pulled her wrists out of my grasp, and turned back to Jik, who was rocking around in agony and cupping his fingers over his eyes with rigid knuckles. Also, being Jik, he was exercising his tongue.

'The slimy little bugger . . . wait till I catch him . . . Jesus Christ Almighty I can't bloody see . . . Sarah . . . where's that bloody Todd . . . I'll strangle him . . . get an ambulance . . . my eyes are burning out . . . bloody buggering hell . . .'

I spoke loudly in his ear. 'Your eyes are O.K.'

'They're my bloody eyes and if I say they're not O.K. they're bloody not.'

'You know damn well you're not going blind, so stop hamming it up.'

'They're not your eyes, you sod.'

'And you're frightening Sarah,' I said.

That message got through. He took his hands away and stopped rolling about.

At the sight of his face a murmur of pleasant horror rippled through the riveted audience. Blobs of bright paint from the young man's palette had streaked one side of his jaw yellow and blue: and his eyes were red with inflammation and pouring with tears, and looked very sore indeed.

'Jesus, Sarah,' he said blinking painfully. 'Sorry, love. The bastard's right. Turps never blinded anybody.'

'Not permanently,' I said, because to do him justice he obviously couldn't see anything but tears at the moment.

Sarah's animosity was unabated. 'Get him an ambulance, then.'

I shook my head. 'All he needs is water and time.'

'You're a stupid heartless *pig*. He obviously needs a doctor, and hospital care.'

Jik, having abandoned histrionics, produced a handkerchief and gently mopped his streaming eyes.

'He's right, love. Lots of water, as the man said. Washes the sting away. Lead me to the nearest gents.'

With Sarah unconvinced but holding one arm, and a sympathetic male spectator the other, he was solicitously helped away like an amateur production of *Samson*. The chorus in the

611

shape of the audience bent reproachful looks on me, and cheerfully awaited the next act.

I looked at the overturned mess of paints and easel which the
young man had left. The onlookers looked at them too.

'I suppose,' I said slowly, 'that no one here was talking to the
young artist before any of this happened?'

'We were,' said one woman, surprised at the question.

'So were we,' said another.

'What about?'

'Munnings,' said one, and 'Munnings,' said the other, both
looking immediately at the painting on the wall.

'Not about his own work?' I said, bending down to pick it
up. A slash of yellow lay wildly across the careful outlines, result
of Jik's slap on the back.

Both of the ladies, and also their accompanying husbands,
shook their heads and said they had talked with him about the
pleasure of hanging a Munnings on their own walls, back home.

I smiled slowly.

'I suppose,' I said, 'that he didn't happen to know where you
could get one?'

'Well, yeah,' they said. 'As a matter of fact, he sure did.'

'Where?'

'Well, look here, young fellow . . .' The elder of the husbands, a seventyish American with the unmistakable stamp of
wealth, began shushing the others to silence with a practised
damping movement of his right hand. Don't give information
away, it said, you may lose by it. '. . . You're asking a lot of
questions.'

'I'll explain,' I said. 'Would you like some coffee?'

They all looked at their watches and said doubtfully they possibly would.

'There's a coffee shop just down the hall,' I said. 'I saw it
when I was trying to catch that young man . . . to make him tell
why he flung turps in my friend's eyes.'

Curiosity sharpened in their faces. They were hooked.

The rest of the spectators drifted away, and I, asking the others to wait a moment, started moving the jumbled painting stuff off the centre of the floor to a tidier wallside heap.

None of it was marked with its owner's name. All regulation kit, obtainable from art shops. Artists' quality, not students' cheaper equivalents. None of it new, but not old, either. The picture itself was on a standard-sized piece of commercially pre-pared hardboard, not on stretched canvas. I stacked everything together, added the empty jars which had held linseed and turps, and wiped my hands on a piece of rag.

'Right,' I said. 'Shall we go?'

They were all Americans, all rich, retired, and fond of racing. Mr and Mrs Howard K. Petrovitch of Ridgeville, New Jersey, and Mr and Mrs Wyatt L. Minchless from Carter, Illinois.

Wyatt Minchless, the one who had shushed the others, called the meeting to order over four richly creamed iced coffees and one plain black. The black was for himself. Heart condition, he murmured, patting the relevant area of suiting. A white-haired man, black-framed specs, pale indoor complexion, pompous manner.

'Now, young fellow, let's hear it from the top.'

'Um,' I said. Where exactly was the top? 'The artist boy attacked my friend Jik because Jik called him a criminal.'

'Yuh,' Mrs Petrovitch nodded, 'I heard him. Just as we were leaving the gallery. Now why would he do that?'

'It isn't criminal to copy good painting,' Mrs Minchless said knowledgeably. 'In the Louvre in Paris, France, you can't get near the *Mona Lisa* for those irritating students.'

She had blue-rinsed puffed-up hair, uncreasable navy and green clothes, and enough diamonds to attract a top-rank thief. Deep lines of automatic disapproval ran downwards from the corner of her mouth. Thin body. Thick mind.

'It depends what you are copying *for*,' I said. 'If you're going to try to pass your copy off as an original, then that definitely is a fraud.'

Mrs Petrovitch began to say, 'Do you think the young man was *forging* . . .' but was interrupted by Wyatt Minchless, who smothered her question both by the damping hand and his louder voice.

'Are you saying that this young artist boy was painting a Munnings he later intended to sell as the real thing?'

'Er . . .' I said.

Wyatt Minchless swept on. 'Are you saying that the Munnings picture he told us we might be able to buy is itself a forgery?'

The others looked both horrified at the possibility and admiring of Wyatt L. for his perspicacity.

'I don't know,' I said. 'I just thought I'd like to see it.'

'You don't want to buy a Munnings yourself? You are not acting as an agent for anyone else?' Wyatt's questions sounded severe and inquisitorial.

'Absolutely not,' I said.

'Well, then.' Wyatt looked round the other three, collected silent assents. 'He told Ruthie and me there was a good Munnings racing picture at a very reasonable price in a little gallery not far away . . .' He fished with forefinger and thumb into his outer breast pocket. 'Yes, here we are. Yarra River Fine Arts. Third turning off Swanston Street, about twenty yards along.'

Mr and Mrs Petrovitch looked resigned. 'He told us exactly the same.'

'He seemed such a nice young man,' Mrs Petrovitch added sadly. 'So interested in our trip. Asked us what we'd be betting on in the Cup.'

'He asked where we would be going after Melbourne,' Mr Petrovitch nodded. 'We told him Adelaide and Alice Springs,

and he said Alice Springs was a Mecca for artists and to be sure
to visit the Yarra River gallery there. The same firm, he said.
Always had good pictures.'

Mr Petrovitch would have misunderstood if I had leaned
across and hugged him. I concentrated on my fancy coffee and
kept my excitement to myself.

'We're going on to Sydney,' pronounced Wyatt L. 'He didn't
offer any suggestions for Sydney.'

The tall glasses were nearly empty. Wyatt looked at his watch
and swallowed the last of his plain black.

'You didn't tell us,' Mrs Petrovitch said, looking puzzled,
'why your friend called the young man a criminal. I mean . . . I
can see why the young man attacked your friend and ran away if
he *was* a criminal, but why did your friend *think* he was?'

'Just what I was about to ask,' said Wyatt, nodding away
heavily. Pompous liar, I thought.

'My friend Jik,' I said, 'is an artist himself. He didn't think
much of the young man's effort. He called it criminal. He might
just as well have said lousy.'

'Is that all?' said Mrs Petrovitch, looking disappointed.

'Well . . . the young man was painting with paints which
won't really mix. Jik's a perfectionist. He can't stand seeing
paint misused.'

'What do you mean, won't mix?'

'Paints are chemicals,' I said apologetically. 'Most of them
don't have any effect on each other, but you have to be careful.'

'What happens if you aren't?' demanded Ruthie Minchless.

'Um . . . nothing explodes,' I said, smiling. 'It's just that . . .
well, if you mix flake white, which is lead, with cadmium yellow,
which contains sulphur, like the young man was doing, you get
a nice pale colour to start with but the two minerals react against
each other and in time darken and alter the picture.'

'And your friend called this criminal?' Wyatt said in disbelief.
'It couldn't possibly make that much difference.'

'Er . . .' I said. 'Well, Van Gogh used a light bright new yellow made of chrome when he painted a picture of sunflowers. Cadmium yellow hadn't been developed then. But chrome yellow has shown that over a couple of hundred years it decomposes and in the end turns greenish black, and the sunflowers are already an odd colour, and I don't think anyone has found a way of stopping it.'

'But the young man wasn't painting for posterity,' said Ruthie with irritation. 'Unless he's another Van Gogh, surely it doesn't matter.'

I didn't think they'd want to hear that Jik hoped for recognition in the twenty-third century. The permanence of colours had always been an obsession with him, and he'd dragged me along once to a course on their chemistry.

The Americans got up to go.

'All very interesting,' Wyatt said with a dismissive smile. 'I guess I'll keep my money in regular stocks.'

Seven

JIK HAD gone from the gents, gone from the whole Arts Centre. I found him back with Sarah in their hotel room, being attended by the Hilton's attractive resident nurse. The door to the corridor stood open, ready for her to leave.

'Try not to rub them, Mr Cassavetes,' she was saying. 'If you have any trouble, call the reception desk, and I'll come back.'

She gave me a professional half-smile in the open doorway and walked briskly away, leaving me to go in.

'How are the eyes?' I said, advancing tentatively.

'Ruddy awful.' They were bright pink, but dry. Getting better.

Sarah said with tight lips, 'This has all gone far enough. I know that this time Jik will be all right again in a day or two, but we are not taking any more risks.'

Jik said nothing and didn't look at me.

It wasn't exactly unexpected. I said, 'O.K . . . Well, have a nice weekend, and thanks anyway.'

'Todd . . .' Jik said.

Sarah leapt in fast. 'No, Jik. It's not our responsibility. Todd can think what he likes, but his cousin's troubles are nothing to do with us. We are not getting involved any further. I've been against all this silly poking around all along, and this is where it stops.'

'Todd will go on with it,' Jik said.

'Then he's a fool.' She was angry, scornful, biting.

'Sure,' I said. 'Anyone who tries to right a wrong these days is a fool. Much better not to meddle, not to get involved, not to think it's your responsibility. I really ought to be painting away safely in my attic at Heathrow, minding my own business and letting Donald rot. Much more sensible, I agree. The trouble is that I simply can't do it. I see the hell he's in. How can I just turn my back? Not when there's a chance of getting him out. True enough, I may not manage it, but what I can't face is not having tried.'

I came to a halt.

A blank pause.

'Well,' I said, raising a smile. 'Here endeth the lesson according to the world's foremost nit. Have fun at the races. I might go too, you never know.'

I sketched a farewell and eased myself out. Neither of them said a word. I shut the door quietly and took the lift up to my own room.

A pity about Sarah, I thought. She would have Jik in cotton-wool and slippers if he didn't look out; and he'd never paint those magnificent brooding pictures any more, because they sprang from a torment he would no longer be allowed. Security, to him, would be a sort of abdication; a sort of death.

I looked at my watch and decided the Yarra River Fine Arts set-up might still have its doors open. Worth trying.

I wondered, as I walked along Wellington Parade and up Swanston Street, whether the young turps-flinger would be there, and if he was, whether he would know me. I'd seen only glimpses of his face, as I'd mostly been standing behind him. All one could swear to was light-brown hair, acne on the chin, a round jaw-line and a full-lipped mouth. Under twenty. Perhaps not more than seventeen. Dressed in blue jeans, white tee-shirt, and tennis shoes. About five-foot-eight, a hundred and thirty pounds. Quick on his feet, and liable to panic. And no artist.

The gallery was open, brightly lit, with a horse painting on a gilt display easel in the centre of the window. Not a Munnings. A portrait picture of an Australian horse and jockey, every detail sharp-edged, emphatic, and, to my taste, overpainted. Beside it a notice, gold embossed on black, announced a special display of distinguished equine art; and beside that, less well-produced but with larger letters, stood a display card saying 'Welcome to the Melbourne Cup'.

The gallery looked typical of hundreds of others round the world; narrow frontage, with premises stretching back a good way from the street. Two or three people were wandering about inside, looking at the merchandise on the well-lit neutral grey walls.

I had gone there intending to go in. To go in was still what I intended, but I hesitated outside in the street feeling as if I were at the top of a ski jump. Stupid, I thought. Nothing ventured, nothing gained, and all that. If you don't look, you won't see.

I took a ruefully deep breath and stepped over the welcoming threshold.

Greeny-grey carpet within, and an antique desk strategically placed near the door, with a youngish woman handing out small catalogues and large smiles.

'Feel free to look around,' she said. 'More pictures downstairs.'

She handed me a catalogue, a folded glazed white card with several typed sheets clipped into it. I flipped them over. One hundred and sixty-three items, numbered consecutively, with titles, artists' names, and asking price. A painting already sold, it said, would have a red spot on the frame.

I thanked her. 'Just passing by,' I said.

She nodded and smiled professionally, eyes sliding in a rapid summing-up over my denim clothes and general air of not belonging to the jet set. She herself wore the latest trendy fashion with careless ease and radiated tycoon-catching sincerity.

Australian, assured, too big a personality to be simply a receptionist.

'You're welcome anyway,' she said.

I walked slowly down the long room, checking the pictures against their notes. Most were by Australian artists, and I could see what Jik had meant about the hot competition. The field was just as crowded as at home, if not more so, and the standard in some respects better. As usual when faced with other people's flourishing talents I began to have doubts of my own.

At the far end of the ground-floor display there was a staircase leading downwards, adorned with a large arrow and a notice repeating 'More Pictures Downstairs'.

I went down. Same carpet, same lighting, but no scatter of customers looking from pictures to catalogues and back again.

Below stairs, the gallery was not one straight room but a series of small rooms off a long corridor, apparently the result of not being able to knock down all the dividing and load-bearing walls. A room to the rear of the stairs was an office, furnished with another distinguished desk, two or three comfortable chairs for prospective clients, and a civilized row of teak-faced filing cabinets. Heavily framed pictures adorned the walls, and an equally substantial man was writing in a ledger at the desk.

He raised his head, conscious of my presence outside his door.

'Can I help you?' he said.

'Just looking.'

He gave me an uninterested nod and went back to his work. He, like the whole place, had an air of permanence and respectability quite unlike the fly-by-night suburban affair in Sydney. This reputable business, I thought, could not be what I was looking for. I had got the whole thing wrong. I would have to wait until I could get Hudson Taylor to look up Donald's cheque and point me in a new direction.

Sighing, I continued down the line of rooms, thinking I

might as well finish taking stock of the opposition. A few of the frames were adorned with red spots, but the prices on everything good were a mile from a bargain and a deterrent to all but the rich.

In the end room, which was larger than the others, I came across the Munningses. Three of them. All with horses: one racing scene, one hunting, one of gypsies.

They were not in the catalogue.

They hung without ballyhoo in a row of similar subjects, and to my eyes stuck out like thoroughbreds among hacks.

Prickles began up my spine. It wasn't just the workmanship, but one of the pictures itself. Horses going down to the start. A long line of jockeys, bright against a dark sky. The silks of the nearest rider, purple with a green cap.

Maisie's chatty voice reverberated in my inner ear, describing what I saw. '. . . I expect you'll think I was silly but that was one of the reasons I bought it . . . because Archie and I decided we'd like purple with a green cap for our colours, if no one already had that . . .'

Munnings had always used a good deal of purple and green in shadows and distances. All the same . . . This picture, size, subject, and colouring, was exactly like Maisie's, which had been hidden behind a radiator, and, presumably, burned.

The picture in front of me looked authentic. The right sort of patina for the time since Munnings' death, the right excellence of draughtsmanship, the right indefinable something which separated the great from the good. I put out a gentle finger to feel the surface of canvas and paint. Nothing there that shouldn't be.

An English voice from behind me said, 'Can I help you?'

'Isn't that a Munnings?' I said casually, turning round.

He was standing in the doorway, looking in, his expression full of the guarded helpfulness of one whose best piece of stock is being appraised by someone apparently too poor to buy it.

I knew him instantly. Brown receding hair combed back, grey eyes, down-drooping moustache, suntanned skin: all last on view thirteen days ago beside the sea in Sussex, England, prodding around in a smoky ruin.

Mr Greene. With an 'e'.

It took him only a fraction longer. Puzzlement as he glanced from me to the picture and back, then the shocking realization of where he'd seen me. He took a sharp step backwards and raised his hand to the wall outside.

I was on my way to the door, but I wasn't quick enough. A steel mesh gate slid down very fast in the doorway and clicked into some sort of bolt in the floor. Mr Greene stood on the outside, disbelief still stamped on every feature and his mouth hanging open. I revised all my easy theories about danger being good for the soul and felt as frightened as I'd ever been in my life.

'What's the matter?' called a deeper voice from up the corridor.

Mr Greene's tongue was stuck. The man from the office appeared at his shoulder and looked at me through the imprisoning steel.

'A thief?' he asked with irritation.

Mr Greene shook his head. A third person arrived outside, his young face bright with curiosity, and his acne showing like measles.

'Hey,' he said in loud Australian surprise. 'He was the one at the Arts Centre. The one who chased me. I swear he didn't follow me. I swear it.'

'Shut up,' said the man from the office briefly. He stared at me steadily. I stared back.

I was standing in the centre of a brightly lit room of about fifteen feet square. No windows. No way out except through the guarded door. Nowhere to hide, no weapons to hand. A long way down the ski jump and no promise of a soft landing.

'I say,' I said plaintively. 'Just what is all this about?' I walked up to the steel gate and tapped on it. 'Open this up, I want to get out.'

'What are you doing here?' the office man said. He was bigger than Greene and obviously more senior in the gallery. Heavy dark spectacle frames over unfriendly eyes, and a blue bow tie with polka dots under a double chin. Small mouth with a full lower lip. Thinning hair.

'Looking,' I said, trying to sound bewildered. 'Just looking at pictures.' An innocent at large, I thought, and a bit dim.

'He chased me in the Arts Centre,' the boy repeated.

'You threw some stuff in that man's eyes,' I said indignantly. 'You might have blinded him.'

'Friend of yours, was he?' the office man said.

'No,' I said. 'I was just there, that was all. Same as I'm here. Just looking at pictures. Nothing wrong in that, is there? I go to lots of galleries, all the time.'

Mr Greene got his voice back. 'I saw him in England,' he said to the office man. His eyes returned to the Munnings, then he put his hand on the office man's arm and pulled him up the corridor out of my sight.

'Open the door,' I said to the boy, who still gazed in.

'I don't know how,' he said. 'And I don't reckon I'd be popular, somehow.'

The two other men returned. All three gazed in. I began to feel sympathy for creatures in cages.

'Who *are* you?' said the office man.

'Nobody. I mean, I'm just here for the racing, of course, and the cricket.'

'Name?'

'Charles Neil.' Charles Neil Todd.

'What were you doing in England?'

'I live there!' I said. 'Look,' I went on, as if trying to be reasonable under great provocation. 'I saw this man here,' I nodded to Greene, 'at the home of a woman I know slightly in Sussex. She was giving me a lift home from the races, see, as I'd missed my train to Worthing and was thumbing along the road from the Members' car park. Well, she stopped and picked me up, and then said she wanted to make a detour to see her house which had lately been burnt, and when we got there, this man was there. He said his name was Greene and that he was from an insurance company, and that's all I know about him. So what's going on?'

'It is a coincidence that you should meet here again, so soon.'

'It certainly is,' I agreed fervently. 'But that's no bloody reason to lock me up.'

I read indecision on all their faces. I hoped the sweat wasn't running visibly down my own.

I shrugged exasperatedly. 'Fetch the police or something, then,' I said. 'If you think I've done anything wrong.'

The man from the office put his hand to the switch on the outside wall and carefully fiddled with it, and the steel gate slid up out of sight, a good deal more slowly than it had come down.

'Sorry,' he said perfunctorily. 'But we have to be careful, with so many valuable paintings on the premises.'

'Well, I see that,' I said, stepping forward and resisting a strong impulse to make a dash for it. 'But all the same . . .' I managed an aggrieved tone. 'Still, no harm done, I suppose.' Magnanimous, as well.

They all walked behind me along the corridor and up the stairs and through the upper gallery, doing my nerves no slightest good. All the other visitors seemed to have left. The receptionist was locking the front door.

My throat was dry beyond swallowing.

'I thought everyone had gone,' she said in surprise.

'Slight delay,' I said, with a feeble laugh.

She gave me the professional smile and reversed the locks. Opened the door. Held it, waiting for me.

Six steps.

Out in the fresh air.

God almighty, it smelled good. I half turned. All four stood in the gallery watching me go. I shrugged and nodded and trudged away into the drizzle, feeling as weak as a fieldmouse dropped by a hawk.

I caught a passing tram and travelled a good way into unknown regions of the huge city, conscious only of an urgent desire to put a lot of distance between myself and that basement prison.

They would have second thoughts. They were bound to. They would wish they had found out more about me before letting me go. They couldn't be certain it wasn't a coincidence that I'd turned up at their gallery, because far more amazing coincidences did exist, like Lincoln at the time of his assassination having a secretary called Kennedy and Kennedy having a secretary called Lincoln; but the more they thought about it the less they would believe it.

If they wanted to find me, where would they look? Not at the Hilton, I thought in amusement. At the races: I had told them I would be there. On the whole I wished I hadn't.

At the end of the tramline I got off and found myself opposite a small interesting-looking restaurant with B.Y.O. in large letters on the door. Hunger as usual rearing its healthy head, I went in and ordered a steak, and asked for a look at the wine list.

The waitress looked surprised. 'It's B.Y.O.,' she said.

'What's B.Y.O.?'

Her eyebrows went still higher. 'You are a stranger? Bring Your Own. We don't sell drinks here, only food.'

'Oh.'

'If you want something to drink, there's a drive-in bottle

shop a hundred yards down the road that'll still be open. I could hold the steak until you get back.'

I shook my head and settled for a teetotal dinner, grinning all through coffee at a notice on the wall saying 'We have an arrangement with our bank. They don't fry steaks and we don't cash cheques.'

When I set off back to the city centre on the tram, I passed the bottle shop, which at first sight looked so like a garage that if I hadn't known I would have thought the line of cars was queuing for petrol. I could see why Jik liked the Australian imagination: both sense and fun.

The rain had stopped. I left the tram and walked the last couple of miles through the bright streets and dark parks, asking the way. Thinking of Donald and Maisie and Greene with an 'e', and of paintings and burglaries and violent minds.

The overall plan had all along seemed fairly simple: to sell pictures in Australia and steal them back in England, together with everything else lying handy. As I had come across two instances within three weeks, I had been sure there had to be more, because it was surely impossible that I could have stumbled on the *only* two, even given the double link of racing and painting. Since I'd met the Petrovitches and the Minchlesses, it seemed I'd been wrong to think of all the robberies taking place in England. Why not in America? Why not anywhere that was worth the risk?

Why not a mobile force of thieves shuttling containerfuls of antiques from continent to continent, selling briskly to a ravenous market? As Inspector Frost had said, few antiques were ever recovered. The demand was insatiable and the supply, by definition, limited.

Suppose I were a villain, I thought, and I didn't want to waste weeks in foreign countries finding out exactly which houses were worth robbing. I could just stay quietly at home in Melbourne selling paintings to rich visitors who could afford an impulse-buy of ten thousand pounds or so. I could chat away with them about their picture collections back home, and I could shift the conversation easily to their silver and china and objets d'art.

I wouldn't want the sort of customers who had Rembrandts or Fabergés or anything well known and unsaleable like that. Just the middling wealthy with Georgian silver and lesser Gauguins and Chippendale chairs.

When they bought my paintings, they would give me their addresses. Nice and easy. Just like that.

I would be a supermarket type of villain, with a large turnover of small goods. I would reckon that if I kept the victims reasonably well scattered, the fact that they had been to Australia within the past year or so would mean nothing to each regional police force. I would reckon that among the thousands of burglary claims they had to settle, Australian visits would bear no significance to insurance companies.

I would not, though, reckon on a crossed wire like Charles Neil Todd.

If I were a villain, I thought, with a well-established business and a good reputation, I wouldn't put myself at risk by selling fakes. Forged oil paintings were almost always detectable under a microscope, even if one discounted that the majority of experienced dealers could tell them at a glance. A painter left his signature all over a painting, not just in the corner, because the way he held his brush was as individual as handwriting. Brush strokes could be matched as conclusively as grooves on bullets.

If I were a villain I'd wait in my spider's web with a real Munnings, or maybe a real Picasso drawing, or a genuine work by a recently dead good artist whose output had been voluminous, and along would come the rich little flies, carefully steered my way by talkative accomplices who stood around in the states' capitals' art galleries for the purpose. Both Donald and Maisie had been hooked that way.

Supposing when I'd sold a picture to a man from England and robbed him, and got my picture back again, I then sold it to someone from America. And then robbed him, and got it back, and so on and round.

Suppose I sold a picture to Maisie in Sydney, and got it back, and started to sell it again in Melbourne . . . My supposing stopped right there, because it didn't fit.

If Maisie had left her picture in full view it would have been stolen like her other things. Maybe it even had been, and was right now glowing in the Yarra River Fine Arts, but if so, why had the house been burnt, and why had Mr Greene turned up to search the ruins?

It only made sense if Maisie's picture had been a copy, and if the thieves hadn't been able to find it. Rather than leave it around, they'd burned the house. But I'd just decided that I wouldn't risk fakes. Except that . . . would Maisie know an expert copy if she saw one? No, she wouldn't.

I sighed. To fool even Maisie you'd have to find an accomplished artist willing to copy instead of pressing on with his own work, and they weren't that thick on the ground. All the same, she'd bought her picture in the short-lived Sydney gallery, not in Melbourne, so maybe in other places besides Melbourne they would take a risk with fakes.

The huge bulk of the hotel rose ahead of me across the last stretch of park. The night air blew cool on my head. I had a vivid feeling of being disconnected, a stranger in a vast continent, a speck under the stars. The noise and warmth of the Hilton brought the expanding universe down to imaginable size.

Upstairs, I telephoned Hudson Taylor at the number his secretary had given me. Nine o'clock on the dot. He sounded mellow and full of good dinner, his voice strong, courteous and vibrantly Australian.

'Donald Stuart's cousin? Is it true about little Regina being killed?'

'I'm afraid so.'

'It's a real tragedy. A real nice lass, that Regina.'

'Yes.'

'Lookee here, then, what can I do for you? Is it tickets for the races?'

'Er, no,' I said. 'It was just that since the receipt and provenance letter of the Munnings had been stolen along with the picture, Donald would like to get in touch with the people who had sold it to him, for insurance purposes, but he had forgotten their name. And as I was coming to Melbourne for the Cup . . .'

'That's easy enough,' Hudson Taylor said pleasantly. 'I remember the place well. I went with Donald to see the picture there, and the guy in charge brought it along to the Hilton afterwards, when we arranged the finance. Now let's see . . .' There was a pause for thought. 'I can't remember the name of the place just now. Or the manager. It was some months ago, do you see? But I've got him on record here in the Melbourne office, and I'm calling in there anyway in the morning, so I'll look them up. You'll be at the races tomorrow?'

'Yes,' I said.

'How about meeting for a drink, then? You can tell me about poor Donald and Regina, and I'll have the information he wants.'

I said that would be fine, and he gave me detailed instructions as to where I would find him, and when. 'There will be a huge crowd,' he said. 'But if you stand on that exact spot I shouldn't miss you.'

The spot he had described sounded public and exposed. I hoped that it would only be he who found me on it.

'I'll be there,' I said.

Eight

JIK CALLED through on the telephone at eight next morning.

'Come down to the coffee shop and have breakfast.'

'O.K.'

I went down in the lift and along the foyer to the hotel's informal restaurant. He was sitting at a table alone, wearing dark glasses and making inroads into a mountain of scrambled egg.

'They bring you coffee,' he said, 'but you have to fetch everything else from that buffet.' He nodded towards a large well-laden table in the centre of the breezy blue and sharp green decor. 'How's things?'

'Not what they used to be.'

He made a face. 'Bastard.'

'How are the eyes?'

He whipped off the glasses with a theatrical flourish and leaned forward to give me a good look. Pink, they were, and still inflamed, but on the definite mend.

'Has Sarah relented?' I asked.

'She's feeling sick.'

'Oh?'

'God knows,' he said. 'I hope not. I don't want a kid yet. She isn't overdue or anything.'

'She's a nice girl,' I said.

He slid me a glance. 'She says she's got nothing against you personally.'

'But,' I said.

630

He nodded. 'The mother hen syndrome.'

'Wouldn't have cast you as a chick.'

He put down his knife and fork. 'Nor would I, by God. I told her to cheer up and get this little enterprise over as soon as possible and face the fact she hadn't married a marshmallow.'

'And she said?'

He gave a twisted grin. 'From my performance in bed last night, that she had.'

I wondered idly about the success or otherwise of their sex life. From the testimony of one or two past girls who had let their hair down to me while waiting hours in the flat for Jik's unpredictable return, he was a moody lover, quick to arousal and easily put off. 'It only takes a dog barking, and he's gone.' Not much, I dared say, had changed.

'Anyway,' he said. 'There's this car we've got. Damned silly if you didn't come with us to the races.'

'Would Sarah . . .', I asked carefully, '. . . scowl?'

'She says not.'

I accepted this offer and inwardly sighed. It looked as if he wouldn't take the smallest step henceforth without the nod from Sarah. When the wildest ones got married, was it always like that? Wedded bliss putting nets over the eagles.

'Where did you get to, last night?' he said.

'Aladdin's cave,' I said. 'Treasures galore and damned lucky to escape the boiling oil.'

I told him about the gallery, the Munnings, and my brief moment of captivity. I told him what I thought of the burglaries. It pleased him. His eyes gleamed with humour and the familiar excitement rose.

'How are we going to prove it?' he said.

He heard the 'we' as soon as he said it. He laughed ruefully, the fizz dying away. 'Well, how?'

'Don't know yet.'

'I'd like to help,' he said apologetically.

I thought of a dozen sarcastic replies and stifled the lot. It was I who was the one out of step, not them. The voice of the past had no right to break up the future.

'You'll do what pleases Sarah,' I said with finality, and as an order, not a prodding satire.

'Don't sound so bloody bossy.'

We finished breakfast amicably trying to build a suitable new relationship on the ruins of the old, and both knowing well what we were about.

When I met them later in the hall at setting-off time it was clear that Sarah too had made a reassessment and put her mind to work on her emotions. She greeted me with an attempted smile and an outstretched hand. I shook the hand lightly and also gave her a token kiss on the cheek. She took it as it was meant.

Truce made, terms agreed, pact signed. Jik the mediator stood around looking smug.

'Take a look at him,' he said, flapping a hand in my direction. 'The complete stockbroker. Suit, tie, leather shoes. If he isn't careful they'll have him in the Royal Academy.'

Sarah looked bewildered. 'I thought that was an honour.'

'It depends,' said Jik, sneering happily. 'Passable artists with polished social graces get elected in their thirties. Masters with average social graces, in their forties; masters with no social graces, in their fifties. Geniuses who don't give a damn about being elected are ignored as long as possible.'

'Putting Todd in the first category and yourself in the last?' Sarah said.

'Of course.'

'Stands to reason,' I said. 'You never hear about young masters. Masters are always old.'

'For God's sake,' Sarah said. 'Let's go to the races.'

We went slowly, on account of a continuous stream of traffic going the same way. The car park at Flemington racecourse, when we arrived, looked like a giant picnic ground, with hundreds of full-scale lunch parties going on between the cars. Tables, chairs, cloths, china, silver, glass. Sun umbrellas optimistically raised in defiance of the rain-clouds threatening above. A lot of gaiety and booze and a giant overall statement that 'This Was The Life.'

To my mild astonishment Jik and Sarah had come prepared. They whipped out table, chairs, drinks and food from the rented car's boot and said it was easy when you knew how, you just ordered the whole works.

'I have an uncle,' Sarah said, 'who holds the title of Fastest Bar in the West. It takes him roughly ten seconds from putting the brakes on to pouring the first drink.'

She was really trying, I thought. Not just putting up with an arrangement for Jik's sake, but actually trying to make it work. If it was an effort, it didn't show. She was wearing an interesting olive-green linen coat, with a broad-brimmed hat of the same colour, which she held on to from time to time against little gusts of wind. Overall, a new Sarah, prettier, more relaxed, less afraid.

'Champagne?' Jik offered, popping the cork. 'Steak and oyster pie?'

'How will I go back to cocoa and chips?'

'Fatter.'

We demolished the goodies, repacked the boot, and with a sense of taking part in some vast semi-religious ritual, squeezed along with the crowd through the gate to the holy of holies.

'It'll be much worse than this on Tuesday,' observed Sarah, who had been to these junkets several times in the past. 'Melbourne Cup day is a public holiday. The city has three million inhabitants and half of them will try to get here.' She was shouting above the crowd noises and holding grimly on to her hat against the careless buffeting all around.

'If they've got any sense they'll stay at home and watch it on the box,' I said breathlessly, receiving a hefty kidney punch from the elbow of a man fighting his way into a can of beer.

'It won't be on the television in Melbourne, only on the radio.'

'Good grief. Why ever not?'

'Because they want everyone to come. It's televised all over the rest of Australia, but not on its own doorstep.'

'Same with the golf and the cricket,' Jik said with a touch of gloom. 'And you can't even have a decent bet on those.'

We went through the bottleneck and, by virtue of the inherited badges, through a second gate and round into the calmer waters of the green oblong of Members' lawn. Much like on many a Derby Day at home, I thought. Same triumph of will over weather. Bright faces under grey skies. Warm coats over the pretty silks, umbrellas at the ready for the occasional top hat. When I painted pictures of racegoers in the rain, which I sometimes did, most people laughed. I never minded. I reckoned it meant they understood that the inner warmth of a pleasure couldn't be externally damped; that they too might play a trumpet in a thunderstorm.

Come to think of it, I thought, why didn't I paint a racegoer playing a trumpet in a thunderstorm? It might be symbolic enough even for Jik.

My friends were deep in a cross-talking assessment of the form of the first race. Sarah, it appeared, had a betting pedigree as long as her husband's, and didn't agree with him.

'I know it was soft going at Randwick last week. But it's pretty soft here too after all this rain, and he likes it on top.'

'He was only beaten by Boyblue at Randwick, and Boyblue was out of sight in the Caulfield Cup.'

'Please your silly self,' Sarah said loftily. 'But it's still too soft for Grapevine.'

'Want to bet?' Jik asked me.

'Don't know the horses.'

'As if that mattered.'

'Right.' I consulted the racecard. 'Two dollars on Generator.'

They both looked up, and they both said 'Why?'

'If in doubt, back number eleven. I once went nearly through the card on number eleven.'

They made clucking and pooh-poohing noises and told me I could make a gift of my two dollars to the bookies or the T.A.B.

'The what?'

'Totalizator Agency Board.'

The bookmakers, it seemed, were strictly on-course only, with no big firms as in England. All off-course betting shops were run by the T.A.B., which returned a good share of the lolly to racing. Racing was rich, rock-solid, and flourishing. Bully for Australia, Jik said.

We took our choice and paid our money, and Generator won at twenty-fives.

'Beginner's luck,' Sarah said.

Jik laughed. 'He's no beginner. He got kicked out of play-school for running a book.'

They tore up their tickets, set their minds to race two, and made expeditions to place their bets. I settled for four dollars on number one.

'Why?'

'Double my stake on half of eleven.'

'Oh God,' said Sarah. 'You're something else.'

One of the more aggressive clouds started scattering rain, and the less hardy began to make for shelter.

'Come on,' I said. 'Let's go and sit up there in the dry.'

'You two go,' Sarah said. 'I can't.'

'Why not?'

'Because those seats are only for men.'

I laughed. I thought she was joking, but it appeared it was no joke. Very unfunny, in fact. About two-thirds of the best seats in the Members' stands were reserved for males.

'What about their wives and girlfriends?' I said incredulously.
'They can go up on the roof.'

Sarah, being Australian, saw nothing very odd in it. To me,
and surely to Jik, it was ludicrous.

He said with a carefully straight face, 'On a lot of the bigger
courses the men who run Australian racing give themselves
leather armchairs behind glass to watch from, and thick-
carpeted restaurants and bars to eat and drink like kings in, and
let their women eat in the cafeterias and sit on hard plastic chairs
on the open stands among the rest of the crowd. They consider
this behaviour quite normal. All anthropological groups consider their most bizarre tribal customs quite normal.'

'I thought you were in love with all things Australian.'

Jik sighed heavily. 'Nowhere's perfect.'

'I'm getting wet,' Sarah said.

We escalated to the roof which had a proportion of two
women to one man and was windy and damp, with bench
seating.

'Don't worry about it,' Sarah said, amused at my aghastness
on behalf of womankind. 'I'm used to it.'

'I thought this country made a big thing about equality for
all.'

'For all except half the population,' Jik said.

We could see the whole race superbly from our eyrie. Sarah
and Jik screamed encouragement to their fancies but number
one finished in front by two lengths, at eight to one.

'It's disgusting,' Sarah said, tearing up more tickets. 'What
number do you fancy for the third?'

'I won't be with you for the third. I've got an appointment
to have a drink with someone who knows Donald.'

She took it in, and the lightness went out of her manner.
'More . . . investigating?'

'I have to.'

'Yes.' She swallowed and made a visible effort. 'Well . . . Good luck.'

'You're a great girl.'

She looked surprised that I should think so and suspicious that I was intending sarcasm, and also partly pleased. I returned earthwards with her multiple expression amusing my mind.

The Members' lawn was bounded on one long side by the stands and on the opposite side by the path taken by the horses on their way from the saddling boxes to the parade ring. One short side of the lawn lay alongside part of the parade ring itself: and it was at the corner of lawn where the horses' path reached the parade ring that I was to meet Hudson Taylor.

The rain had almost stopped, which was good news for my suit. I reached the appointed spot and stood there waiting, admiring the brilliant scarlet of the long bedful of flowers which lined the railing between horse-walk and lawn. Cadmium red mixtures with highlights of orange and white and maybe a streak or two of expensive vermilion . . .

'Charles Todd?'

'Yes . . . Mr Taylor?'

'Hudson. Glad to know you.' He shook hands, his grip dry and firm. Late forties, medium height, comfortable build, with affable, slightly sad eyes sloping downwards at the outer corners. He was one of the minority of men in morning suits, and he wore it as comfortably as a sweater.

'Let's find somewhere dry,' he said. 'Come this way.'

He led me steadily up the bank of steps, in through an entrance door, down a wide interior corridor running the whole length of the stands, past a uniformed guard and a notice saying 'Committee Only', and into a large square comfortable room fitted out as a small-scale bar. The journey had been one long polite push through expensively dressed cohorts, but the bar was comparatively quiet and empty. A group of four, two men, two women, stood chatting with half-filled glasses held close to their chests, and two women in furs were complaining loudly of the cold.

'They love to bring out the sables,' Hudson Taylor chuckled, fetching two glasses of Scotch and gesturing to me to sit by a small table. 'Spoils their fun, the years it's hot for this meeting.'

'Is it usually hot?'

'Melbourne's weather can change twenty degrees in an hour.' He sounded proud of it. 'Now then, this business of yours.' He delved into an inner breast pocket and surfaced with a folded paper. 'Here you are, typed out for Donald. The gallery was called Yarra River Fine Arts.'

I would have been astounded if it hadn't been.

'And the man we dealt with was someone called Ivor Wexford.'

'What did he look like?' I asked.

'I don't remember very clearly. It was back in April, do you see?'

I thought briefly and pulled a small slim sketch-book out of my pocket.

'If I draw him, might you know him?'

He looked amused. 'You never know.'

I drew quickly in soft pencil a reasonable likeness of Greene, but without the moustache.

'Was it him?'

Hudson Taylor looked doubtful. I drew in the moustache. He shook his head decisively. 'No, that wasn't him.'

'How about this?'

I flipped over the page and started again. Hudson Taylor looked pensive as I did my best with the man from the basement office.

'Maybe,' he said.

I made the lower lip fuller, added heavy-framed spectacles, and a bow tie with spots.

'That's him,' said Hudson in surprise. 'I remember the bow

tie, anyway. You don't see many of those these days. How did you know? You must have met him.'

'I walked round a couple of galleries yesterday afternoon.'

'That's quite a gift you have there,' he said with interest, watching me put the notebook away.

'Practice, that's all.' Years of seeing people's faces as matters of shapes and proportions and planes, and remembering which way the lines slanted. I could already have drawn Hudson's eyes from memory. It was a knack I'd had from childhood.

'Sketching is your hobby?' Hudson asked.

'And my work. I mostly paint horses.'

'Really?' He glanced at the equine portraits decorating the wall. 'Like these?'

I nodded, and we talked a little about painting for a living.

'Maybe I can give you a commission, if my horse runs well in the Cup.' He smiled, the outer edges of his eyes crinkling finely. 'If he's down the field, I'll feel more like shooting him.'

He stood up and gestured me still to follow. 'Time for the next race. Care to watch it with me?'

We emerged into daylight in the prime part of the stands, overlooking the big square enclosure which served both for parading the runners before the race and unsaddling the winners after. I was amused to see that the front rows of seats were all for men: two couples walking in front of us split like amoebas, the husbands going down left, the women up right.

'Down here,' Hudson said, pointing.

'May we only go up there if accompanied by a lady?' I asked.

He glanced at me sideways, and smiled. 'You find our ways odd? We'll go up, by all means.'

He led the way and settled comfortably among the predominantly female company, greeting several people and introducing me companionably as his friend Charles from England. Instant first names, instant acceptance, Australian style.

'Regina hated all this division of the sexes, poor lass,' he said.

'But it has interesting historical roots.' He chuckled. 'Australia was governed nearly all last century with the help of the British Army. The officers and gentlemen left their wives back in England, but such is nature, they all set up liaisons here with women of low repute. They didn't want their fellow officers to see the vulgarity of their choice, so they invented a rule that the officers' enclosures were for men only, which effectively silenced their popsies' pleas to be taken.'

I laughed. 'Very neat.'

'It's easier to establish a tradition,' Hudson said, 'than to get rid of it.'

'You're establishing a great tradition for fine wines, Donald says.'

The sad-looking eyes twinkled with civilized pleasure. 'He was most enthusiastic. He travelled round all the big vineyards, of course, besides visiting us.'

The horses for the third race cantered away to the start, led by a fractious chestnut colt with too much white about his head.

'Ugly brute,' Hudson said. 'But he'll win.'

'Are you backing it?'

He smiled. 'I've a little bit on.'

The race started and the field sprinted, and Hudson's knuckles whitened so much from his grip as he gazed intently through his binoculars that I wondered just how big the little bit was. The chestnut colt was beaten into fourth place. Hudson put his raceglasses down slowly and watched the unsatisfactory finish with a blank expression.

'Oh well,' he said, his sad eyes looking even sadder. 'Always another day.' He shrugged resignedly, cheered up, shook my hand, told me to remember him to Donald, and asked if I could find my own way out.

'Thank you for your help,' I said.

He smiled. 'Any time. Any time.'

With only a couple of wrong turnings I reached ground level, listening on the way to fascinating snippets of Australian conversation.

'. . . They say he's an embarrassment as a Committee man. He only opens his mouth to change feet . . .'

'. . . a beastly stomach wog, so he couldn't come . . .'

'. . . told him to stop whingeing like a bloody Pommie, and get on with it . . .'

'. . . won twenty dollars? Good on yer, Joanie . . .'

And everywhere the diphthong vowels which gave the word 'No' about five separate sounds, defying my attempts to copy it. I'd been told on the flight over, by an Australian, that all Australians spoke with one single accent. It was about as true as saying all Americans spoke alike, or all British. English was infinitely elastic; and alive, well and living in Melbourne.

Jik and Sarah, when I rejoined them, were arguing about their fancies for the Victoria Derby, next race on the card.

'Ivory Ball is out of his class and has as much chance as a blind man in a blizzard.'

Sarah ignored this. 'He won at Moonee Valley last week and two of the tipsters picked him.'

'Those tipsters must have been drunk.'

'Hello Todd,' Sarah said. 'Pick a number, for God's sake.'

'Ten.'

'Why ten?'

'Eleven minus one.'

'Jesus,' Jik said. 'You used to have more sense.'

Sarah looked it up. 'Royal Road. Compared with Royal Road, Ivory Ball's a certainty.'

We bought our tickets and went up to the roof, and none of our bets came up. Sarah disgustedly yelled at Ivory Ball who had at least managed fifth, but Royal Road fell entirely by the wayside. The winner was number twelve.

'You should have *added* eleven and one,' Sarah said. 'You make such silly mistakes.'

'What are you staring at?' Jik said.

I was looking attentively down at the crowd which had watched the race from ground level on the Members' lawn.

'Lend me your raceglasses . . .'

Jik handed them over. I raised them, took a long look, and slowly put them down.

'What is it?' Sarah said anxiously. 'What's the matter?'

'That,' I said, 'has not only torn it, but ripped the bloody works apart.'

'What has?'

'Do you see those two men . . . about twenty yards along from the parade ring railing . . . one of them in a grey morning suit?'

'What about them?' Jik said.

'The man in the morning suit is Hudson Taylor, the man I just had a drink with. He's the Managing Director of a wine-making firm, and he saw a lot of my cousin Donald when he was over here. And the other man is called Ivor Wexford, and he's the Manager of the Yarra River Fine Arts Gallery.'

'So what?' Sarah said.

'So I can just about imagine the conversation that's going on down there,' I said. 'Something like, "Excuse me, sir, but didn't I sell a picture to you recently?" "Not to me, Mr Wexford, but to my friend Donald Stuart." "And who was that young man I saw you talking to just now?" "That was Donald Stuart's cousin, Mr Wexford." "And what do you know about him?" "That he's a painter by trade and drew a picture of you, Mr Wexford, and asked me for your name."'

I stopped. 'Go on,' Jik said.

I watched Wexford and Hudson Taylor stop talking, nod casually to each other, and walk their separate ways.

'Ivor Wexford now knows he made a horrible mistake in letting me out of his gallery last night.'

Sarah looked searchingly at my face. 'You really do think that's very serious.'

'Yes I really do.' I loosened a few tightened muscles and tried a smile. 'At the least, he'll be on his guard.'

'And at the most,' Jik said, 'he'll come looking for you.'

'Er . . .' I said thoughtfully. 'What do either of you feel about a spot of instant travel?'

'Where to?'

'Alice Springs?' I said.

Nine

JIK COMPLAINED all the way to the airport on various counts. One, that he would be missing the cricket. Two, that I hadn't let him go back to the Hilton for his paints. Three, that his Derby clothes would be too hot in Alice. Four, that he wasn't missing the Melbourne Cup for any little ponce with a bow tie.

None of the colourful gripes touched on the fact that he was paying for all our fares with his credit card, as I had left my traveller's cheques in the hotel.

It had been Sarah's idea not to go back there.

'If we're going to vanish, let's get on with it,' she said. 'It's running back into fires for handbags that gets people burnt.'

'You don't have to come,' I said tentatively.

'We've been through all that. What do you think the rest of my life would be like if I stopped Jik helping you, and you came to grief?'

'You'd never forgive me.'

She smiled ruefully. 'You're dead right.'

As far as I could tell we had left the racecourse unobserved, and certainly not one car had followed us to the airport. Neither Greene with an 'e' nor the boy non-artist appeared underfoot to trip us up, and we travelled uneventfully on a half-full aircraft on the first leg to Adelaide, and an even emptier one from there to Alice Springs.

The country beneath us from Adelaide northwards turned

gradually from fresh green to grey-green, and finally to a fierce brick red.

'Gaba,' said Jik, pointing downwards.

'What?'

'G.A.B.A.,' he said. 'Gaba. Stands for Great Australian Bugger All.'

I laughed. The land did indeed look baked, deserted, and older than time, but there were track-like roads here and there, and incredibly isolated homesteads. I watched in fascination until it grew dark, the purple shadows rushing in like a tide as we swept north into the central wastelands.

The night air at Alice was hot, as if someone had forgotten to switch off the oven. The luck which had presented us with an available flight as soon as we reached Melbourne airport seemed still to be functioning: a taciturn taxi driver took us straight to a new-looking motel which proved to have room for us.

'The season is over,' he grunted, when we congratulated and thanked him. 'It will soon be too hot for tourists.'

Our rooms were air-conditioned, however. Jik and Sarah's was down on the ground floor, their door opening directly on to a shady covered walk which bordered a small garden with a pool. Mine, in an adjacent wing across the car park, was two tall floors up, reached by an outside tree-shaded staircase and a long open gallery. The whole place looked greenly peaceful in the scattered spotlights which shone unobtrusively from palms and gums.

The motel restaurant had closed for the night at eight o'clock, so we walked along the main street to another. The road surface itself was tarmacked, but some of the side roads were not, nor were the footpaths uniformly paved. Often enough we were walking on bare fine grit, and we could see from the dust haze in the headlights of passing cars that the grit was bright red.

'Bull dust,' Sarah said. 'I've never seen it before. My aunt swore it got inside her locked trunk once when she and my uncle drove out to Ayers Rock.'

'What's Ayers Rock?' I said.

'Ignorant Pommie,' Sarah said. 'It's a chunk of sandstone two miles long and a third of a mile high left behind by some careless glacier in the ice age.'

'Miles out in the desert,' Jik added. 'A place of ancient magic regularly desecrated by the plastic society.'

'Have you been there?' I asked dryly.

He grinned. 'Nope.'

'What difference does that make?' Sarah asked.

'He means,' Jik said, 'our pompous friend here means that one shouldn't make judgements from afar.'

'You haven't actually got to be swallowed up by a shark before you believe it's got sharp teeth,' Sarah said. 'You can believe what other people see.'

'It depends from where they're looking.'

'Facts are not judgements, and judgements are not facts,' Jik said. 'A bit of Todd's Law from way back.'

Sarah gave me a glance. 'Have you got iced water in that head?'

'Emotion is a rotten base for politics. He used to say that too,' Jik said. 'Envy is the root of all evil. What have I left out?'

'The most damaging lies are told by those who believe they're true.'

'There you are,' Jik said. 'Such a pity you can't paint.'

'Thanks very much.'

We reached the restaurant and ate a meal of such excellence that one wondered at the organization it took to bring every item of food and clothing and everyday life to an expanding town of thirteen and a half thousand inhabitants surrounded by hundreds of miles of desert in every direction.

'It was started here, a hundred years ago, as a relay station for sending cables across Australia,' Sarah said. 'And now they're bouncing messages off the stars.'

Jik said, 'Bet the messages aren't worth the technology. Think of "See you Friday, Ethel", chattering round the eternal spheres.'

With instructions from the restaurant we walked back a different way and sought out the Yarra River Fine Arts gallery, Alice Springs variety.

It was located in a paved shopping arcade closed to traffic, one of several small but prosperous-looking boutiques. There were no lights on in the gallery, nor in the other shops. From what we could see in the single dim street light, the merchandise in the gallery window consisted of two bright orange landscapes of desert scenes.

'Crude,' said Jik, whose own colours were not noted for pastel subtlety.

'The whole place,' he said, 'will be full of local copies of Albert Namatjira. Tourists buy them by the ton.'

We strolled back to the motel more companionably than at any time since my arrival. Maybe the desert distances all around us invoked their own peace. At any rate when I kissed Sarah's cheek to say goodnight it was no longer as a sort of pact, as in the morning, but with affection.

At breakfast she said, 'You'll never guess. The main street here is Todd Street. So is the river. Todd River.'

'Such is fame,' I said modestly.

'And there are eleven art galleries.'

'She's been reading the Alice Springs Tourist Promotion Association Inc.'s handout,' Jik explained.

'There's also a Chinese takeaway.'

Jik made a face. 'Just imagine all this lot dumped down in the middle of the Sahara.'

The daytime heat, in fact, was fierce. The radio was cheerfully forecasting a noon temperature of thirty-nine, which was a hundred and two in the old Fahrenheit shade. The single step from a cool room to the sun-roasting balcony was a sensuous pleasure, but the walk to the Yarra River gallery, though less than half a mile, was surprisingly exhausting.

'I suppose one would get used to it, if one lived here,' Jik said. 'Thank God Sarah's got her hat.'

We dodged in and out of the shadows of overhanging trees and the local inhabitants marched around bareheaded as if the branding-iron in the sky was pointing another way. The Yarra River gallery was quiet and air-conditioned and provided chairs near the entrance for flaked-out visitors.

As Jik had prophesied, all visible space was knee-deep in the hard clear watercolour paintings typical of the disciples of Namatjira. They were fine if you liked that sort of thing, which on the whole I didn't. I preferred the occasional fuzzy outline, indistinct edge, shadows encroaching, suggestion, impression, and ambiguity. Namatjira, given his due as the first and greatest of the Aboriginal artists, had had a vision as sharp as a diamond. I vaguely remembered reading somewhere that he'd produced more than two thousand paintings himself, and certainly his influence on the town where he'd been born had been extraordinary. Eleven art galleries. Mecca for artists. Tourists buying pictures by the ton. He had died, a plaque on the wall said, in Alice Springs hospital on August 8th 1959.

We had been wandering around for a good five minutes before anyone came. Then the plastic strip curtain over a recessed doorway parted, and the gallery keeper came gently through.

'See anything you fancy?' he said.

His voice managed to convey an utter boredom with tourists and a feeling that we should pay up quickly and go away. He was small, languid, long-haired and pale, and had large dark eyes with drooping tired-looking lids. About the same age as Jik and myself, though a lot less robust.

'Do you have any other pictures?' I asked.

He glanced at our clothes. Jik and I wore the trousers and shirts in which we'd gone to the races: no ties and no jackets, but more promising to picture-sellers than denims. Without discernible enthusiasm he held back half the strip curtain, inviting us to go through.

'In here,' he said.

The inner room was bright from skylights, and its walls were almost entirely covered with dozens of pictures which hung closely together. Our eyes opened wide. At first sight we were surrounded by an incredible feast of Dutch interiors, French impressionists and Gainsborough portraits. At second blink one could see that although they were original oil paintings, they were basically second rate. The sort sold as 'school of' because the artists hadn't bothered to sign them.

'All European, in this room,' the gallery keeper said. He still sounded bored. He wasn't Australian, I thought. Nor British. Maybe American. Difficult to tell.

'Do you have any pictures of horses?' I asked.

He gave me a long steady peaceful gaze. 'Yes we do, but this month we are displaying works by native Australians and lesser Europeans.' His voice had the faintest of lisps. 'If you wish to see horse paintings, they are in racks through there.' He pointed to a second plastic strip curtain directly opposite the first. 'Are you looking for anything in particular?'

I murmured the names of some of the Australians whose work I had seen in Melbourne. There was a slight brightening of the lack-lustre eyes.

'Yes, we do have a few by those artists.'

He led us through the second curtain into the third, and from our point of view, most interesting room. Half of it, as promised, was occupied by well-filled double tiers of racks. The other half was the office and packing and framing department.

Directly ahead a glass door led out to a dusty parched-looking garden, but most of the lighting in here too came from the roof.

Beside the glass door stood an easel bearing a small canvas with its back towards us. Various unmistakable signs showed work currently in progress and recently interrupted.

'Your own effort?' asked Jik inquisitively, walking over for a look.

The pale gallery keeper made a fluttering movement with his hand as if he would have stopped Jik if he could, and something in Jik's expression attracted me to his side like a magnet.

A chestnut horse, three-quarters view, its elegant head raised as if listening. In the background, the noble lines of a mansion. The rest, a harmonious composition of trees and meadow. The painting, as far as I could judge, was more or less finished.

'That's great,' I said with enthusiasm. 'Is that for sale? I'd like to buy that.'

After the briefest hesitation he said, 'Sorry. That's commissioned.'

'What a pity! Couldn't you sell me that one, and paint another?'

He gave me a small regretful smile. 'I'm afraid not.'

'Do tell me your name,' I said earnestly.

He was unwillingly flattered. 'Harley Renbo.'

'Is there anything else of yours here?'

He gestured towards the racks. 'One or two. The horse paintings are all in the bottom row, against the wall.'

We all three of us pulled out the paintings one by one, making amateur-type comments.

'That's nice,' said Sarah, holding a small picture of a fat grey pony with two old-fashioned country boys. 'Do you like that?' She showed it to Jik and me.

We looked at it.

'Very nice,' I said kindly.

Jik turned away as if uninterested. Harley Renbo stood motionless.

'Oh well,' Sarah said, shrugging. 'I just thought it looked nice.' She put it back in the rack and pulled out the next. 'How about this mare and foal? I think it's pretty.'

Jik could hardly bear it. 'Sentimental tosh,' he said.

Sarah looked downcast. 'It may not be Art, but I like it.'

We found one with a flourishing signature; Harley Renbo. Large canvas, varnished, unframed.

'Ah,' I said appreciatively. 'Yours.'

Harley Renbo inclined his head. Jik, Sarah and I gazed at his acknowledged work.

Derivative Stubbs-type. Elongated horses set in a Capability Brown landscape. Composition fair, anatomy poor, execution good, originality nil.

'Great,' I said. 'Where did you paint it?'

'Oh . . . here.'

'From memory?' Sarah said admiringly. 'How clever.'

Harley Renbo, at our urging, brought out two more examples of his work. Neither was better than the first, but one was a great deal smaller.

'How much is this?' I asked.

Jik glanced at me sharply, but kept quiet.

Harley Renbo mentioned a sum which had me shaking my head at once.

'Awfully sorry,' I said. 'I like your work, but . . .'

The haggling continued politely for quite a long time, but we came to the usual conclusion, higher than the buyer wanted, lower than the painter hoped. Jik resignedly lent his credit card and we bore our trophy away.

'Jesus Christ,' Jik exploded when we were safely out of earshot. 'You could paint better than that when you were in your cradle. Why the hell did you want to buy that rubbish?'

'Because,' I said contentedly, 'Harley Renbo is the copier.'

'But this,' Jik pointed to the parcel under my arm, 'is his own abysmal original work.'

'Like fingerprints?' Sarah said. 'You can check other things he paints against this?'

'Got brains, my wife,' Jik said. 'But that picture he wouldn't sell was nothing like any Munnings I've ever seen.'

'You never look at horse paintings if you can help it.'

'I've seen more of your pathetic daubs than I care to.'

'How about Raoul Millais?' I said.

'Jesus.'

We walked along the scorching street almost without feeling it.

'I don't know about you two,' Sarah said, 'but I'm going to buy a bikini and spend the rest of the day in the pool.'

We all bought swimming things, changed into them, splashed around for ages, and laid ourselves out on towels to dry. It was peaceful and quiet in the shady little garden. We were the only people there.

'That picture of a pony and two boys, that you thought was nice,' I said to Sarah.

'Well, it was,' she repeated defensively. 'I liked it.'

'It was a Munnings.'

She sat up abruptly on her towel.

'Why ever didn't you say so?'

'I was waiting for our friend Renbo to tell us, but he didn't.'

'A real one?' Sarah asked. 'Or a copy?'

'Real,' Jik said, with his eyes shut against the sun dappling through palm leaves.

I nodded lazily. 'I thought so, too,' I said. 'An old painting. Munnings had that grey pony for years when he was young, and painted it dozens of times. It's the same one you saw in Sydney in *The Coming Storm*.'

'You two do know a lot,' Sarah said, sighing and lying down again.

'Engineers know all about nuts and bolts,' Jik said. 'Do we get lunch in this place?'

I looked at my watch. Nearly two o'clock. 'I'll go and ask,' I said.

I put shirt and trousers on over my sun-dried trunks and ambled from the outdoor heat into the refrigerated air of the lobby. No lunch, said the reception desk. We could buy lunch nearby at a takeaway and eat in the garden. Drink? Same thing. Buy your own at a bottle shop. There was an ice-making machine and plastic glasses just outside the door to the pool.

'Thanks,' I said.

'You're welcome.'

I looked at the ice-making machine on the way out. Beside it swung a neat notice. 'We don't swim in your toilet. Please don't pee in our pool.' I laughed across to Jik and Sarah and told them the food situation.

'I'll go and get it,' I said. 'What do you want?'

Anything, they said.

'And drink?'

'Cinzano,' Sarah said, and Jik nodded. 'Dry White.'

'O.K.'

I picked up my room key from the grass and set off to collect some cash for shopping. Walked along to the tree-shaded outside staircase, went up two storeys, and turned on to the blazing hot balcony.

There was a man walking along it towards me, about my own height, build and age; and I heard someone else coming up the stairs at my back.

Thought nothing of it. Motel guests like me. What else?

I was totally unprepared for both the attack itself, and for its ferocity.

Ten

THEY SIMPLY walked up to me, one from in front, one from behind.

They reached me together. They sprang into action like cats. They snatched the dangling room key out of my hand.

The struggle, if you could call it that, lasted less than five seconds. Between them, with Jik's type of strength, they simply picked me up by my legs and armpits and threw me over the balcony.

It probably takes a very short time to fall two storeys. I found it long enough for thinking that my body, which was still whole, was going to be smashed. That disaster, not yet reached, was inevitable. Very odd, and very nasty.

What I actually hit first was one of the young trees growing round the staircase. Its boughs bent and broke and I crashed on through them to the hard driveway beneath.

The monstrous impact was like being wiped out. Like fusing electrical circuits. A flash into chaos. I lay in a semi-conscious daze, not knowing if I were alive or dead.

I felt warm. Simply a feeling, not a thought.

I wasn't aware of anything else at all. I couldn't move any muscle. Couldn't remember I had muscles to move. I felt like pulp.

It was ten minutes, Jik told me later, before he came looking for me: and he came only because he wanted to ask me to buy a lemon to go with the Cinzano, if I had not gone already.

'Jesus Christ Almighty,' Jik's voice, low and horrified, near my ear.

I heard him clearly. The words made sense.

I'm alive, I thought. I think, therefore I exist.

Eventually, I opened my eyes. The light was brilliant. Blinding. There was no one where Jik's voice had been. Perhaps I'd imagined it. No I hadn't. The world began coming back fast, very sharp and clear.

I knew also that I hadn't imagined the fall. I knew, with increasing insistence, that I hadn't broken my neck and hadn't broken my back. Sensation, which had been crushed out, came flooding back with vigour from every insulted tissue. It wasn't so much a matter of which bits of me hurt, as of finding out which didn't. I remembered hitting the tree. Remembered the ripping of its branches. I felt both torn to shreds and pulverized. Frightfully jolly.

After a while I heard Jik's voice returning. 'He's alive,' he said, 'and that's about all.'

'It's impossible for anyone to fall off our balcony. It's more than waist-high.' The voice of the reception desk, sharp with anger and anxiety. A bad business for motels, people falling off their balconies.

'Don't . . . panic,' I said. It sounded a bit croaky.

'Todd!' Sarah appeared, kneeling on the ground and looking pale.

'If you give me time . . .' I said, '. . . I'll fetch . . . the Cinzano.' How much time? A million years should be enough.

'You sod,' Jik said, standing at my feet and staring down. 'You gave us a shocking fright.' He was holding a broken-off branch of tree.

'Sorry.'

'Get up, then.'

'Yeah . . . in a minute.'

'Shall I cancel the ambulance?' said the reception desk hope-fully.

'No,' I said. 'I think I'm bleeding.'

Alice Springs hospital, even on a Sunday, was as efficient as one would expect from a Flying Doctor base. They investigated and X-rayed and stitched, and presented me with a list.

One broken shoulder blade. (Left.)
Two broken ribs. (Left side, no lung puncture.)
Large contusion, left side of head. (No skull fracture.)
Four jagged tears in skin of trunk, thigh, and left leg. (Stitched.)
Several other small cuts.
Grazes and contusions on practically all of left side of body.

'Thanks,' I said, sighing.

'Thank the tree. You'd've been in a right mess if you'd missed it.'

They suggested I stop there for the rest of the day and also all night. Better, they said, a little too meaningfully.

'O.K.' I said resignedly. 'Are my friends still here?'

They were. In the waiting-room. Arguing over my near-dead body about the favourite for the Melbourne Cup.

'Newshound *stays* . . .'

'Stays in the same place . . .'

'Jesus,' Jik said, as I shuffled stiffly in. 'He's on his feet.'

'Yeah.' I perched gingerly on the arm of a chair, feeling a bit like a mummy, wrapped in bandages from neck to waist with my left arm totally immersed, as it were, and anchored firmly inside.

'Don't damn well laugh,' I said.

'No one but a raving lunatic would fall off that balcony,' Jik said.

'Mm,' I agreed. 'I was pushed.'

Their mouths opened like landed fish. I told them exactly what had happened.

'Who were they?' Jik said.

'I don't know. Never seen them before. They didn't introduce themselves.'

Sarah said, definitely, 'You must tell the police.'

'Yes,' I said. 'But . . . I don't know your procedures here, or what the police are like. I wondered . . . if you would explain to the hospital, and start things rolling in an orderly and unsensational manner.'

'Sure,' she said, 'if anything about being pushed off a balcony could be considered orderly and unsensational.'

'They took my room key first,' I said. 'Would you see if they've pinched my wallet?'

They stared at me in awakening unwelcome awareness.

I nodded. 'Or that picture,' I said.

Two policemen came, listened, took notes, and departed. Very non-committal. Nothing like that had happened in The Alice before. The locals wouldn't have done it. The town had a constant stream of visitors so, by the law of averages, some would be muggers. I gathered that there would have been much more fuss if I'd been dead. Their downbeat attitude suited me fine.

By the time Jik and Sarah came back I'd been given a bed, climbed into it, and felt absolutely rotten. Shivering. Cold deep inside. Gripped by the system's aggrieved reaction to injury, or in other words, shock.

'They did take the painting,' Jik said. 'And your wallet as well.'

'And the gallery's shut,' Sarah said. 'The girl in the boutique opposite said she saw Harley close early today, but she didn't see him actually leave. He goes out the back way, because he parks his car out there.'

'The police've been to the motel,' Jik said. 'We told them

about the picture being missing, but I don't think they'll do much more about it unless you tell them the whole story.'

'I'll think about it,' I said.

'So what do we do now?' Sarah asked.

'Well . . . there's no point in staying here any more. Tomorrow we'll go back to Melbourne.'

'Thank God,' she said, smiling widely. 'I thought you were going to want us to miss the Cup.'

In spite of a battery of pills and various ministering angels I spent a viciously uncomfortable and wide-awake night. Unable to lie flat. Feverishly hot on the pendulum from shock. Throbbing in fifteen places. Every little movement screechingly sticky, like an engine without oil. No wonder the hospital had told me it would be better to stay.

I counted my blessings until daybreak. It could have been so very much worse.

What was most alarming was not the murderous nature of the attackers, but the speed with which they'd found us. I'd known ever since I'd seen Regina's head that the directing mind was ruthlessly violent. The acts of the team always reflected the nature of the boss. A less savage attitude would have left Regina gagged and bound, not brutally dead.

I had to conclude that it was chiefly this pervading callousness which had led to my being thrown over the balcony. As a positive means of murder, it was too chancy. It was quite possible to survive a fall from such a height, even without a cushioning tree. The two men had not as far as I could remember bothered to see whether I was alive or dead, and they had not, while I lay half-unconscious and immobile, come along to finish the job.

So it had either been simply a shattering way of getting rid of me while they robbed my room, or they'd had the deliberate intention of injuring me so badly that I would have to stop poking my nose into their affairs.

Or both.

And how had they found us?

I puzzled over it for some time but could arrive at no definite answer. It seemed most likely that Wexford or Greene had telephoned from Melbourne and told Harley Renbo to be on his guard in case I turned up. Even the panic which would have followed the realization that I'd seen the Munnings and the fresh Millais copy, and actually carried away a specimen of Renbo's work, could not have transported two toughs from Melbourne to Alice Springs in the time available.

There had only been about four hours between purchase and attack, and some of that would have had to be spent on finding out which motel we were in, and which rooms, and waiting for me to go upstairs from the pool.

Perhaps we had after all been followed all the way from Flemington racecourse, or traced from the aeroplane passenger lists. But if that were the case, surely Renbo would have been warned we were on our way, and would never have let us see what we had.

I gave it up. I didn't even know if I would recognize my attackers again if I saw them. Certainly not the one who had been behind me, because I hadn't had a single straight look at him.

They could, though, reasonably believe they had done a good job of putting me out of action: and indeed, if I had any sense, they had.

If they wanted time, what for?

To tighten up their security, and cover their tracks, so that any investigation I might persuade the police to make into a paintings–robbery link would come up against the most respectable of brick walls.

Even if they knew I'd survived, they would not expect any

action from me in the immediate future: therefore the immediate future was the best time to act.

Right.

Easy enough to convince my brain. From the neck down, a different story.

Jik and Sarah didn't turn up until eleven, and I was still in bed. Sitting up, but not exactly perky.

'God,' Sarah said, 'You look much worse than yesterday.'

'So kind.'

'You're never going to make it to Melbourne.' She sounded despondent. 'So goodbye Cup.'

'Nothing to stop you going,' I said.

She stood beside the bed. 'Do you expect us just to leave you here . . . like this . . . and go and enjoy ourselves?'

'Why not?'

'Don't be so bloody stupid.'

Jik sprawled in a visitor's chair. 'It isn't our responsibility if he gets himself thrown from heights,' he said.

Sarah whirled on him. 'How *can* you say such a thing?'

'We don't want to be involved,' Jik said.

I grinned. Sarah heard the sardonic echo of what she'd said so passionately herself only three days ago. She flung out her arms in exasperated realization.

'You absolutely bloody beast,' she said.

Jik smiled like a cream-fed cat. 'We went round to the gallery,' he said. 'It's still shut. We also found our way round into the back garden, and looked in through the glass door, and you can guess what we saw.'

'Nothing.'

'Dead right. No easel with imitation Millais. Everything dodgy carefully hidden out of sight. Everything else, respectable and normal.'

I shifted a bit to relieve one lot of aches, and set up protests from another. 'Even if you'd got in, I doubt if you'd've found anything dodgy. I'll bet everything the least bit incriminating disappeared yesterday afternoon.'

Jik nodded. 'Sure to.'

Sarah said, 'We asked the girl in the reception desk at the motel if anyone had been asking for us.'

'And they had?'

She nodded. 'A man telephoned. She thought it was soon after ten o'clock. He asked if a Mr Charles Todd was staying there with two friends, and when she said yes, he asked for your room number. He said he had something to deliver to you.'

'Christ.' Some delivery. Express. Downwards.

'She told him the room number but said if he left the package at the desk, she would see you got it.'

'He must have laughed.'

'He wouldn't have that much sense of humour,' Jik said.

'Soon after ten?' I said, considering.

'While we were out,' Sarah said, nodding. 'It must have been fairly soon after we'd left the gallery . . . and while we were buying the swimming things.'

'Why didn't the girl tell us someone had been enquiring for us?'

'She went off for a coffee break, and didn't see us when we came back. And after that, she forgot. She hadn't anyway thought it of any importance.'

'There aren't all that many motels in Alice,' Jik said. 'It wouldn't have taken long to find us, once they knew we were in the town. I suppose the Melbourne lot telephoned Renbo, and that set the bomb ticking.'

'They must have been apoplectic when they heard you'd bought that picture.'

'I wish I'd hidden it,' I said. The words reminded me briefly of Maisie, who had hidden her picture, and had her house burnt.

Sarah sighed. 'Well . . . what are we going to do?'

'Last chance to go home,' I said.

'Are you going?' she demanded.

I listened briefly to the fierce plea from my battered shell, and I thought too of Donald in his cold house. I didn't actually answer her at all.

She listened to my silence. 'Quite,' she said. 'So what do we do next?'

'Well . . .' I said. 'First of all, tell the girl on the reception desk at the motel that I'm in a pretty poor state and likely to be in hospital for at least a week.'

'No exaggeration,' Jik murmured.

'Tell her it's O.K. to pass on that news, if anyone enquires. Tell her you're leaving for Melbourne, pay all our bills, confirm your bookings on the afternoon flight, and cancel mine, and make a normal exit to the airport bus.'

'But what about you?' Sarah said. 'When will you be fit to go?'

'With you,' I said. 'If between you you can think of some unobtrusive way of getting a bandaged mummy on to an aeroplane without anyone noticing.'

'Jesus,' Jik said. He looked delighted. 'I'll do that.'

'Telephone the airport and book a seat for me under a different name.'

'Right.'

'Buy me a shirt and some trousers. Mine are in the dustbin.'

'It shall be done.'

'And reckon all the time that you may be watched.'

'Put on sad faces, do you mean?' Sarah said.

I grinned. 'I'd be honoured.'

'And after we get to Melbourne, what then?' Jik said.

I chewed my lip. 'I think we'll have to go back to the Hilton. All our clothes are there, not to mention my passport and money. We don't know if Wexford and Greene ever knew we were staying there, so it may well be a hundred per cent safe.

And anyway, where else in Melbourne are we likely to get beds on the night before the Melbourne Cup?'

'If you get thrown out of the Hilton's windows, you won't be alive to tell the tale,' he said cheerfully.

'They don't open far enough,' I said. 'It's impossible.'

'How reassuring.'

'And tomorrow,' Sarah said. 'What about tomorrow?'

Hesitantly, with a pause or two, I outlined what I had in mind for Cup day. When I had finished, they were both silent.

'So now,' I said. 'Do you want to go home?'

Sarah stood up. 'We'll talk it over,' she said soberly. 'We'll come back and let you know.'

Jik stood also, but I knew from the jut of his beard which way he'd vote. It had been he who'd chosen the bad-weather routes we'd taken into the Atlantic and the North Sea. At heart he was more reckless than I.

They came back at two o'clock lugging a large fruit-shop carrier with a bottle of Scotch and a pineapple sticking out of the top.

'Provisions for hospitalized friend,' said Jik, whisking them out and putting them on the end of the bed. 'How do you feel?'

'With every nerve ending.'

'You don't say. Well, Sarah says we go ahead.'

I looked searchingly at her face. Her dark eyes stared steadily back, giving assent without joy. There was no antagonism, but no excitement. She was committed, but from determination, not conviction.

'O.K.,' I said.

'Item,' said Jik, busy with the carrier, 'one pair of medium grey trousers. One light blue cotton shirt.'

'Great.'

'You won't be wearing those, though, until you get to Melbourne. For leaving Alice Springs, we bought something else.'

I saw the amusement in both their faces. I said with misgiving, 'What else?'

With rising glee they laid out what they had bought for my unobtrusive exit from Alice Springs.

Which was how I came to stroll around the little airport, in the time-gap between signing in and boarding, with the full attention of everyone in the place. Wearing faded jeans cut off and busily frayed at mid-calf. No socks. Flip-flop rope-soled sandals. A brilliant orange, red and magenta poncho-type garment which hung loosely over both arms like a cape from shoulders to crutch. A sloppy white T-shirt underneath. A large pair of sunglasses. Artificial suntan on every bit of skin. And to top it all, a large straw sunhat with a two-inch raffia fringe round the brim, the sort of hat in favour out in the bush for keeping flies away. Flies were the torment of Australia. The brushing-away-of-flies movement of the right hand was known as the great Australian salute.

On this hat there was a tourist-type hat-band, bright and distinctly legible. It said 'I Climbed Ayers Rock'.

Accompanying all this jazz I carried the Trans-Australian airline bag Sarah had bought on the way up. Inside it, the garments of sanity and discretion.

'No one,' Jik had said with satisfaction, laying out my wardrobe, 'will guess you're a walking stretcher case, if you're wearing these.'

'More like a nutcase.'

'Not far out,' Sarah said dryly.

They were both at the airport, sitting down and looking glum, when I arrived. They gave me a flickering glance and gazed thereafter at the floor, both of them, they told me later, fighting off terrible fits of giggles at seeing all that finery on the march.

I walked composedly down to the postcard stand and waited there on my feet, for truth to tell it was more comfortable than sitting. Most of the postcards seemed to be endless views of the huge crouching orange monolith out in the desert: Ayers Rock at dawn, at sunset, and every five minutes in between.

Alternatively with inspecting the merchandise I took stock of the room. About fifty prospective passengers, highly assorted. Some airline ground staff, calm and unhurried. A couple of Aborigines with shadowed eyes and patient black faces, waiting for the airport bus back to dreamtime. Air-conditioning doing fine, but everyone inside still moving with the slow walk of life out in the sun.

No one remotely threatening.

The flight was called. The assorted passengers, including Jik and Sarah, stood up, picked up their hand luggage and straggled out to the tarmac.

It was then, and then only, that I saw him.

The man who had come towards me on the balcony to throw me over.

I was almost sure at once, and then certain. He had been sitting among the waiting passengers, reading a newspaper which he was now folding up. He stood still, watching Jik and Sarah present their boarding passes at the door and go through to the tarmac. His eyes followed them right across to the aircraft. When they'd filed up the steps and vanished, he peeled off and made a bee-line in my direction.

My heart lurched painfully. I absolutely could not run.

He looked just the same. Exactly the same. Young, strong, purposeful, as well co-ordinated as a cat. Coming towards me.

As Jik would have said, *Jesus*.

He didn't even give me a glance. Three yards before he reached me he came to a stop beside a wall telephone, and fished in his pocket for coins.

My feet didn't want to move. I was still sure he would see me, look at me carefully, recognize me . . . and do something

I would regret. I could feel the sweat prickling under the bandages.

'Last call for flight to Adelaide and Melbourne.'

I would have to, I thought. Have to walk past him to get to the door.

I unstuck my feet. Walked. Waiting for every awful step to hear his voice shouting after me. Or even worse, his heavy hand.

I got to the door, presented the boarding pass, made it out on to the tarmac.

Couldn't resist glancing back. I could see him through the glass, earnestly telephoning, and not even looking my way.

The walk to the aircraft was all the same quite far enough. God help us all, I thought, if the slightest fright is going to leave me so weak.

Eleven

I HAD a window seat near the rear of the aircraft, and spent the first part of the journey in the same sort of fascination as on the way up, watching the empty red miles of the ancient land roll away underneath. A desert with water underneath it in most places; with huge lakes and many rock pools. A desert which could carry dormant seed for years in its burning dust, and bloom like a garden when it rained. A place of pulverizing heat, harsh and unforgiving, and in scattered places, beautiful.

Gaba, I thought. I found it awesome, but it didn't move me in terms of paint.

After a while I took off the exaggerated hat, laid it on the empty seat beside me, and tried to find a comfortable way to sit, my main frustration being that if I leaned back in the ordinary way my broken shoulder blade didn't care for it. You wouldn't think, I thought, that one *could* break a shoulder blade. Mine, it appeared, had suffered from the full thud of my five-eleven frame hitting terra extremely firma.

Oh well . . . I shut my eyes for a bit and wished I didn't still feel so shaky.

My exit from hospital had been the gift of one of the doctors, who had said he couldn't stop me if I chose to go, but another day's rest would be better.

'I'd miss the Cup,' I said, protesting.

'You're crazy.'

'Yeah . . . Would it be possible for you to arrange that the hospital said I was "satisfactory", and "progressing" if anyone telephones to ask, and not on any account to say that I'd left?'

'Whatever for?'

'I'd just like those muggers who put me here to think I'm still flat out. For several days, if you don't mind. Until I'm long gone.'

'But they won't try again.'

'You never know.'

He shrugged. 'You mean you're nervous?'

'You could say so.'

'All right. For a couple of days, anyway. I don't see any harm in it, if it will set your mind at rest.'

'It would indeed,' I said gratefully.

'Whatever are these?' He gestured to Jik's shopping, still lying on the bed.

'My friend's idea of suitable travelling gear.'

'You're having me on?'

'He's an artist,' I said, as if that explained any excesses.

He returned an hour later with a paper for me to sign before I left, Jik's credit card having again come up trumps, and at the sight of me, nearly choked. I had struggled slowly into the clothes and was trying on the hat.

'Are you going to the airport dressed like that?' he said incredulously.

'I sure am.'

'How?'

'Taxi, I suppose.'

'You'd better let me drive you,' he said, sighing. 'Then if you feel too rotten I can bring you back.'

He drove carefully, his lips twitching. 'Anyone who has the courage to go around like that shouldn't worry about a couple of thugs.' He dropped me solicitously at the airport door, and departed laughing.

Sarah's voice interrupted the memory.

'Todd?'

I opened my eyes. She had walked towards the back of the aeroplane and was standing in the aisle beside my seat.

'Are you all right?'

'Mm.'

She gave me a worried look and went on into the toilet compartment. By the time she came out, I'd assembled a few more wits, and stopped her with the flap of the hand. 'Sarah . . . You were followed to the airport. I think you'll very likely be followed from Melbourne. Tell Jik . . . tell Jik to take a taxi, spot the tail, lose him, and take a taxi back to the airport to collect the hired car. O.K.?'

'Is this . . . this tail . . . on the aeroplane?' She looked alarmed at the thought.

'No. He telephoned . . . from Alice.'

'All right.'

She went away up front to her seat. The aeroplane landed at Adelaide, people got off, people got on, and we took off again for the hour's flight to Melbourne. Halfway there, Jik himself came back to make use of the facilities.

He too paused briefly beside me on the way back.

'Here are the car keys,' he said. 'Sit in it, and wait for us. You can't go into the Hilton like that, and you're not fit enough to change on your own.'

'Of course I am.'

'Don't argue. I'll lose any tail, and come back. You wait.'

He went without looking back. I picked up the keys and put them in my jeans pocket, and thought grateful thoughts to pass the time.

I dawdled a long way behind Jik and Sarah at disembarkation. My gear attracted more scandalized attention in this solemn financial city, but I didn't care in the least. Nothing like fatigue and anxiety for killing off embarrassment.

Jik and Sarah, with only hand baggage, walked without ado

past the suitcase-unloading areas and straight out towards the waiting queue of taxis. The whole airport was bustling with Cup eve arrivals, but only one person, that I could see, was bustling exclusively after my fast-departing friends.

I smiled briefly. Young and eel-like, he slithered through the throng, pushing a young woman with a baby out of the way to grab the next taxi behind Jik's. They'd sent him, I supposed, because he knew Jik by sight. He'd flung turps in his eyes at the Arts Centre.

Not too bad, I thought. The boy wasn't over-intelligent, and Jik should have little trouble in losing him. I wandered around for a bit looking gormless, but as there was no one else who seemed the remotest threat, I eventually eased out to the car park.

The night was chilly after Alice Springs. I unlocked the car, climbed into the back, took off the successful hat, and settled to wait for Jik's return.

They were gone nearly two hours, during which time I grew stiffer and ever more uncomfortable and started swearing.

'Sorry,' Sarah said breathlessly, pulling open the car door and tumbling into the front seat.

'We had the devil's own job losing the little bugger,' Jik said, getting in beside me in the back. 'Are you all right?'

'Cold, hungry, and cross.'

'That's all right, then,' he said cheerfully. 'He stuck like a bloody little leech. That boy from the Arts Centre.'

'Yes, I saw him.'

'We hopped into the Victoria Royal, meaning to go straight out again by the side door and grab another cab, and there he was following us in through the front. So we peeled off for a drink in the bar and he hovered around in the lobby looking at the bookstall.'

'We thought it would be better not to let him know we'd spotted him, if we could,' Sarah said. 'So we did a re-think, went outside, called another taxi, and set off to the Naughty Ninety, which is about the only noisy big dine, dance and cabaret place in Melbourne.'

'It was absolutely packed,' Jik said. 'It cost me ten dollars to get a table. Marvellous for us, though. All dark corners and psychedelic coloured lights. We ordered and paid for some drinks, and read the menu, and then got up and danced.'

'He was still there, when we saw him last, standing in the queue for tables just inside the entrance door. We got out through an emergency exit down a passage past some cloak-rooms. We'd dumped our bags there when we arrived, and simply collected them again on the way out.'

'I don't think he'll know we ducked him on purpose,' Jik said. 'It's a proper scrum there tonight.'

'Great.'

With Jik's help I exchanged Tourist, Alice Style, for Racing Man, Melbourne Cup. He drove us all back to the Hilton, parked in its car park, and we walked into the front hall as if we'd never been away.

No one took any notice of us. The place was alive with pre-race excitement. People in evening dress flooding downstairs from the ballroom to stand in loud-talking groups before dispersing home. People returning from eating out, and calling for one more nightcap. Everyone discussing the chances of the next day's race.

Jik collected our room keys from the long desk.

'No messages,' he said. 'And they don't seem to have missed us.'

'Fair enough.'

'Todd,' Sarah said. 'Jik and I are going to have some food sent up. You'll come as well?'

I nodded. We went up in the lift and along to their rooms, and ate a subdued supper out of collective tiredness.

'Night,' I said eventually, getting up to go. 'And thanks for everything.'

'Thank us tomorrow,' Sarah said.

The night passed. Well, it passed.

In the morning I did a spot of one-handed shaving and some highly selective washing, and Jik came up, as he'd insisted, to help with my tie. I opened the door to him in underpants and dressing-gown and endured his comments when I took the latter off.

'Jesus God Almighty, is there any bit of you neither blue nor patched?'

'I could have landed face first.'

He stared at the thought. '*Jesus.*'

'Help me rearrange these bandages,' I said.

'I'm not touching that lot.'

'Oh come on, Jik. Unwrap the swaddling bands. I'm itching like hell underneath and I've forgotten what my left hand looks like.'

With a variety of blasphemous oaths he undid the expert handiwork of the Alice hospital. The outer bandages proved to be large strong pieces of linen, fastened with clips, and placed so as to support my left elbow and hold my whole arm statically in one position, with my hand across my chest and pointing up towards my right shoulder. Under the top layer there was a system of crêpe bandages tying my arm in that position. Also a sort of tight cummerbund of adhesive strapping, presumably to deal with the broken ribs. Also, just below my shoulder blade, a large padded wound dressing, which, Jik kindly told me after a delicate inspection from one corner, covered a mucky-looking bit of darning.

'You damn near tore a whole flap of skin off. There are four lots of stitching. Looks like Clapham Junction.'

'Fasten it up again.'

'I have, mate, don't you worry.'

There were three similar dressings, two on my left thigh and one, a bit smaller, just below the knee: all fastened both with adhesive strips and tapes with clips. We left them all untouched.

'What the eye doesn't see doesn't scare the patient,' Jik said. 'What else do you want done?'

'Untie my arm.'

'You'll fall apart.'

'Risk it.'

He laughed and undid another series of clips and knots. I tentatively straightened my elbow. Nothing much happened except that the hovering ache and soreness stopped hovering and came down to earth.

'That's not so good,' Jik observed.

'It's my muscles as much as anything. Protesting about being stuck in one position all that time.'

'What now, then?'

From the bits and pieces we designed a new and simpler sling which gave my elbow good support but was less of a strait-jacket. I could get my hand out easily, and also my whole arm, if I wanted. When we'd finished, we had a small heap of bandages and clips left over.

'That's fine,' I said.

We all met downstairs in the hall at ten-thirty.

Around us a buzzing atmosphere of anticipation pervaded the chattering throng of would-be winners, who were filling the morning with celebratory drinks. The hotel, I saw, had raised a veritable fountain of champagne at the entrance to the bar-lounge end of the lobby, and Jik, his eyes lighting up, decided it was too good to be missed.

'Free booze,' he said reverently, picking up a glass and holding it under the prodigal bubbly which flowed in delicate gold streams from a pressure-fed height. 'Not bad, either,' he added, tasting. He raised his glass. 'Here's to Art. God rest his soul.'

'Life's short. Art's long,' I said.

'I don't like that,' Sarah said, looking at me uneasily.

'It was Alfred Munnings's favourite saying. And don't worry, love, he lived to be eighty plus.'

'Let's hope you do.'

I drank to it. She was wearing a cream dress with gold buttons; neat, tailored, a touch severe. An impression of the military for a day in the front line.

'Don't forget,' I said. 'If you think you see Wexford or Greene, make sure they see you.'

'Give me another look at their faces,' she said.

I pulled the small sketch book out of my pocket and handed it to her again, though she'd studied it on and off all the previous evening through supper.

'As long as they look like this, maybe I'll know them,' she said, sighing. 'Can I take it?' She put the sketch book in her handbag.

Jik laughed. 'Give Todd his due, he can catch a likeness. No imagination, of course. He can only paint what he sees.' His voice as usual was full of disparagement.

Sarah said, 'Don't you mind the awful things Jik says of your work, Todd?'

I grinned. 'I know exactly what he thinks of it.'

'If it makes you feel any better,' Jik said to his wife, 'he was the star pupil of our year. The art school lacked judgement, of course.'

'You're both crazy.'

I glanced at the clock. We all finished the champagne and put down the glasses.

'Back a winner for me,' I said to Sarah, kissing her cheek.

'Your luck might run out.'

I grinned. 'Back number eleven.'

Her eyes were dark with apprehension. Jik's beard was at the bad-weather angle for possible storms ahead.

'Off you go,' I said cheerfully. 'See you later.'

I watched them through the door and wished strongly that we were all three going for a simple day out to the Melbourne Cup. The effort ahead was something I would have been pleased to avoid. I wondered if others ever quaked before the task they'd set themselves, and wished they'd never thought of it. The beginning, I supposed, was the worst. Once you were in, you were committed. But before, when there was still time to turn back, to rethink, to cancel, the temptation to retreat was demoralizing.

Why climb Everest if at its foot you could lie in the sun?

Sighing, I went to the cashier's end of the reception desk and changed a good many traveller's cheques into cash. Maisie's generosity had been far-sighted. There would be little enough left by the time I got home.

Four hours to wait. I spent them upstairs in my room calming my nerves by drawing the view from the window. Black clouds still hung around the sky like cobwebs, especially in the direction of Flemington race-course. I hoped it would stay dry for the Cup.

Half an hour before it was due to be run I left the Hilton on foot, walking unhurriedly along towards Swanston Street and the main area of shops. They were all shut, of course. Melbourne Cup Day was a national public holiday. Everything stopped for the Cup.

I had taken my left arm out of its sling and threaded it gingerly through the sleeves of my shirt and jacket. A man with his jacket hunched over one shoulder was too memorable for sense. I found that by hooking my thumb into the waistband of my trousers I got quite good support.

Swanston Street was far from its usual bustling self. People still strode along with the breakneck speed which seemed to

675

characterize all Melbourne pedestrians, but they strode in tens, not thousands. Trams ran up and down the central tracks with more vacant seats than passengers. Cars sped along with the drivers, eyes down, fiddling dangerously with radio dials. Fifteen minutes to the race which annually stopped Australia in its tracks.

Jik arrived exactly on time, driving up Swanston Street in the hired grey car and turning smoothly around the corner where I stood waiting. He stopped outside the Yarra River Fine Arts gallery, got out, opened the boot, and put on a brown coat-overall, of the sort worn by storemen.

I walked quietly along towards him. He brought out a small radio, switched it on, and stood it on top of the car. The commentator's voice emerged tinnily, giving details of the runners currently walking round the parade ring at Flemington races.

'Hello,' he said unemotionally, when I reached him. 'All set?' I nodded, and walked to the door of the gallery. Pushed it. It was solidly shut. Jik dived again into the boot, which held further fruits of his second shopping expedition in Alice Springs.

'Gloves,' he said, handing me some, and putting some on himself. They were of white cotton, with ribbed wristbands, and looked a lot too new and clean. I wiped the backs of mine along the wings of Jik's car, and he gave me a glance and did the same with his.

'Handles and impact adhesive.'

He gave me the two handles to hold. They were simple chromium-plated handles, with flattened pieces at each end, pierced by screw holes for fixing. Sturdy handles, big enough for gripping with the whole hand. I held one steady, bottom side up, while Jik covered the screw-plate areas at each end with adhesive. We couldn't screw these handles where we wanted them. They had to be stuck.

'Now the other. Can you hold it in your left hand?'

I nodded. Jik attended to it. One or two people passed, paying no attention. We were not supposed to park there, but no one told us to move.

We walked across the pavement to the gallery. Its frontage was not one unbroken line across its whole width, but was recessed at the right-hand end to form a doorway. Between the front-facing display window and the front-facing glass door, there was a joining window at right angles to the street.

To this sheet of glass we stuck the handles, or rather, Jik did, at just above waist height. He tested them after a minute, and he couldn't pull them off. We returned to the car.

One or two more people passed, turning their heads to listen to the radio on the car roof, smiling in brotherhood at the universal national interest. The street was noticeably emptying as the crucial time drew near.

'. . . *Vinery carries the colours of Mr Hudson Taylor of Adelaide and must be in with a good outside chance. Fourth in the Caulfield Cup and before that, second at Randwick against Brain-Teaser, who went on to beat Afternoon Tea . . .*'

'Stop listening to the damn race!' Jik said sharply.

'Sorry.'

'Ready?'

'Yes.'

We walked back to the entrance to the gallery, Jik carrying the sort of glass-cutter used by, among others, picture framers. Without casting a glance around for possible onlookers, he applied the diamond cutting edge to the matter in hand, using considerable strength as he pushed the professional tool round the outside of the pane. I stood behind him to block any passing curious glances.

'Hold the right-hand handle,' he said, as he started on the last of the four sides, the left-hand vertical.

I stepped past him and slotted my hand through the grip. None of the few people left in the street paid the slightest attention.

'When it goes,' Jik said, 'for God's sake don't drop it.'

'No.'

'Put your knee against the glass. Gently, for God's sake.'

I did what he said. He finished the fourth long cut.

'Press smoothly.'

I did that. Jik's knee, too, was firmly against the glass. With his left hand he gripped the chromium handle, and with the palm of his right he began jolting the top perimeter of the heavy pane.

Jik had cut a lot of glass in his time, even if not in exactly these circumstances. The big flat sheet cracked away evenly all round under our pressure and parted with hardly a splinter. The weight fell suddenly on to the handle I held in my right hand, and Jik steadied the now free sheet of glass with hands and knees and blasphemy.

'Jesus, don't let go.'

'No.'

The heavy vibrations set up in the glass by the breaking process subsided, and Jik took over the right-hand handle from me. Without any seeming inconvenience he pivoted the sheet of glass so that it opened like a door. He stepped through the hole, lifted the glass up wholesale by the two handles, carried it several feet, and propped it against the wall to the right of the more conventional way in.

He came out, and we went over to the car. From there, barely ten feet away, one could not see that the gallery was not still securely shut. There were by now in any case very few to look.

'. . . *Most jockeys have now mounted and the horses will soon be going out on to the course . . .*'

I picked up the radio. Jik exchanged the glass-cutter for a metal saw, a hammer and a chisel, and shut the boot, and we walked through the unorthodox entrance as if it was all in the day's work. Often only the furtive manner gave away the crook.

If you behaved as if you had every right, it took longer for any-one to suspect.

It would really have been best had we next been able to open the real door, but a quick inspection proved it impossible. There were two useful locks, and no keys.

'The stairs are at the back,' I said.

'Lead on.'

We walked the length of the plushy green carpet and down the beckoning stairs. There was a bank of electric switches at the top: we pressed those lighting the basement and left the upstairs lot off.

Heart-thumping time, I thought. It would take only a policeman to walk along and start fussing about a car parked in the wrong place to set Cassavetes and Todd on the road to jail.

'. . . *horses are now going out on to the course. Foursquare in front, sweating up and fighting jockey Ted Nester for control . . .*'

We reached the front of the stairs. I turned back towards the office, but Jik took off fast down the corridor.

'Come back,' I said urgently. 'If that steel gate shuts down . . .'

'Relax,' Jik said. 'You told me.' He stopped before reaching the threshold of the furthest room. Stood still, and looked. Came back rapidly.

'O.K. The Munningses are all there. Three of them. Also something else which will stun you. Go and look while I get this door open.'

'. . . *cantering down to the start, and the excitement is mount-ing here now . . .*'

With a feeling of urgency I trekked down the passage, stopped safely short of any electric gadgets which might trigger the gate and set off alarms, and looked into the Munnings room. The three paintings still hung there, as they had before. But along the row from them was something which, as Jik had said, stunned me. Chestnut horse with head raised, listening.

Stately home in the background. The Raoul Millais picture we'd seen in Alice.

I went back to Jik who with hammer and chisel had bypassed the lock on the office door.

'Which is it?' he said. 'Original or copy?'

'Can't tell from that distance. Looks like real.'

He nodded. We went into the office and started work.

'. . . *Derriby and Special Bet coming down to the start now, and all the runners circling while the girths are checked . . .*'

I put the radio on Wexford's desk, where it sat like an hourglass, ticking away the minutes as the sands ran out.

Jik turned his practical attention to the desk drawers, but they were all unlocked. One of the waist-high line of filing cabinets, however, proved to be secure. Jik's strength and knowhow soon ensured that it didn't remain that way.

In his wake I looked through the drawers. Nothing much in them except catalogues and stationery.

In the broken-open filing cabinet, a gold mine.

Not that I realized it at first. The contents looked merely like ordinary files with ordinary headings.

'. . . *moved very freely coming down to the start and is prime fit to run for that hundred-and-ten-thousand-dollar prize . . .*'

There were a good many framed pictures in the office, some on the walls but even more standing in a row on the floor. Jik began looking through them at high speed, almost like flicking through a rack of record albums.

'. . . *handlers are beginning to load the runners into the starting stalls, and I see Vinery playing up . . .*'

Half of the files in the upper of the two drawers seemed to deal in varying ways with insurance. Letters, policies, revaluations and security. I didn't really know what I was looking for, which made it all a bit difficult.

'Jesus Almighty,' Jik said.

'What is it?'

'Look at this.'

'*. . . more than a hundred thousand people here today to see the twenty-three runners fight it out over the three thousand two hundred metres . . .*'

Jik had reached the end of the row and was looking at the foremost of three unframed canvases tied loosely together with string. I peered over his shoulder. The picture had Munnings written all over it. It had Alfred Munnings written large and clear in the right-hand bottom corner. It was a picture of four horses with jockeys cantering on a racecourse: and the paint wasn't dry.

'What are the others?' I said.

Jik ripped off the string. The two other pictures were exactly the same.

'God Almighty,' Jik said in awe.

'*. . . Vinery carries only fifty-one kilograms and has a good barrier position so it's not impossible . . .*'

'Keep looking,' I said, and went back to the files.

Names. Dates. Places. I shook my head impatiently. We needed more than those Munnings copies and I couldn't find a thing.

'Jesus!' Jik said.

He was looking inside the sort of large flat two-foot by three-foot folder which was used in galleries to store prints.

'*. . . only Derriby now to enter the stalls . . .*'

The print-folder had stood between the end of the desk and the nearby wall. Jik seemed transfixed.

Overseas Customers. My eyes flicked over the heading and then went back. Overseas Customers. I opened the file. Lists of people, sorted into countries. Pages of them. Names and addresses.

England.

A long list. Not alphabetical. Too many to read through in the shortage of time.

A good many of the names had been crossed out.

'. . . *They're running! This is the moment you've all been waiting for, and Special Bet is out in front . . .*'

'Look at this,' Jik said.

Donald Stuart. Donald Stuart, crossed out. Shropshire, England. Crossed out.

I practically stopped breathing.

'. . . *as they pass the stands for the first time it's Special Bet, Foursquare, Newshound, Derriby, Wonderbug, Vinery . . .*'

'Look at this,' Jik said again, insistently.

'Bring it,' I said. 'We've got less than three minutes before the race ends and Melbourne comes back to life.'

'But—'

'Bring it,' I said. 'And also those three copies.'

'. . . *Special Bet still making it, from Newshound close second, then Wonderbug . . .*'

I shoved the filing-drawer shut.

'Put this file in the print-folder and let's get out.'

I picked up the radio and Jik's tools, as he himself had enough trouble managing all three of the untied paintings and the large print-folder.

'. . . *down the back stretch by the Maribyrnong River it's still Special Bet with Vinery second now . . .*'

We went up the stairs. Switched off the lights. Eased round into a view of the car.

It stood there, quiet and unattended, just as we'd left it. No policeman. Everyone elsewhere, listening to the race.

Jik was calling on the Deity under his breath.

'. . . *rounding the turn towards home Special Bet is dropping back now and it's Derriby with Newshound . . .*'

We walked steadily down the gallery.

The commentator's voice rose in excitement against a background of shouting crowds.

'. . . *Vinery in third with Wonderbug, and here comes Ring-wood very fast on the stands side . . .*'

Nothing stirred out on the street. I went first through our hole in the glass and stood once more, with a great feeling of relief, on the outside of the beehive. Jik carried out the plundered honey and stacked it in the boot. He took the tools from my hands and stored them also.

'Right?'

I nodded with a dry mouth. We climbed normally into the car. The commentator was yelling to be heard.

'. . . *Coming to the line it's Ringwood by a length from Wonderbug, with Newshound third, then Derriby, then Vinery . . .*'

The cheers echoed inside the car as Jik started the engine and drove away.

'. . . *Might be a record time. Just listen to the cheers. The result again. The result of the Melbourne Cup. In the frame . . . first Ringwood, owned by Mr Robert Khami . . . second Wonderbug . . .*'

'Phew,' Jik said, his beard jaunty and a smile stretching to show an expanse of gum. 'That wasn't a bad effort. We might hire ourselves out some time for stealing politicians' papers.' He chuckled fiercely.

'It's an overcrowded field,' I said, smiling broadly myself.

We were both feeling the euphoria which follows the safe deliverance from danger. 'Take it easy,' I said. 'We've a long way to go.'

He drove to the Hilton, parked, and carried the folder and pictures up to my room. He moved with his sailing speed, economically and fast, losing as little time as possible before returning to Sarah on the racecourse and acting as if he'd never been away.

'We'll be back here as soon as we can,' he promised, sketching a farewell.

Two seconds after he'd shut my door there was a knock on it.

I opened it. Jik stood there.

'I'd better know,' he said, 'what won the Cup?'

Twelve

WHEN HE'D gone I looked closely at the spoils.

The more I saw, the more certain it became that we had hit the absolute jackpot. I began to wish most insistently that we hadn't wasted time in establishing that Jik and Sarah were at the races. It made me nervous, waiting for them in the Hilton with so much dynamite in my hands. Every instinct urged immediate departure.

The list of Overseas Customers would to any other eyes have seemed the most harmless of documents. Wexford would not have needed to keep it in better security than a locked filing-cabinet, for the chances of anyone seeing its significance in ordinary circumstances were millions to one against.

Donald Stuart, Wrenstone House, Shropshire.

Crossed out.

Each page had three columns, a narrow one at each side with a broad one in the centre. The narrow left-hand column was for dates and the centre for names and addresses. In the narrow right-hand column, against each name, was a short line of apparently random letters and numbers. Those against Donald's entry, for instance, were MM3109T: and these figures had not been crossed out with his name. Maybe a sort of stock list, I thought, identifying the picture he'd bought.

I searched rapidly down all the other crossed-out names in the England sector. Maisie Matthews' name was not among them.

Damn, I thought. Why wasn't it?

I turned all the papers over rapidly. As far as I could see all the overseas customers came from basically English-speaking countries, and the proportion of crossed-out names was about one in three. If every crossing-out represented a robbery, there had been literally hundreds since the scheme began.

At the back of the file I found there was a second and separate section, again divided into pages for each country. The lists in this section were much shorter.

England.

Halfway down. My eyes positively leapt at it.

Mrs M. Matthews, Treasure Holme, Worthing, Sussex.

Crossed out.

I almost trembled. The date in the left-hand column looked like the date on which Maisie had bought her picture. The uncrossed-out numbers in the right-hand column were SMC29R.

I put down the file and sat for five minutes staring unseeingly at the wall, thinking.

My first and last conclusions were that I had a great deal to do before Jik and Sarah came back from the races, and that instincts were not always right.

The large print-folder, which had so excited Jik, lay on my bed. I opened it flat and inspected the contents.

I dare say I looked completely loony standing there with my mouth open. The folder contained a number of simplified line drawings like the one the boy-artist had been colouring in the Arts Centre. Full-sized outline drawings, on flat white canvas, as neat and accurate as tracings.

There were seven of them, all basically of horses. As they were only black and white line drawings I couldn't be sure, but I guessed that three were Munnings, two Raoul Millais, and the other two . . . I stared at the old-fashioned shapes of the horses . . . They couldn't be Stubbs, he was too well documented . . .

How about Herring? Herring, I thought, nodding. The last two had a look of Herring.

Attached to one of these two canvases by an ordinary paper clip was a small handwritten memo on a piece of scrap paper.

'Don't forget to send the original. Also find out what palette he used, if different from usual.'

I looked again at the three identical finished paintings which we had also brought away. These canvases, tacked on to wooden stretchers, looked very much as if they might have started out themselves as the same sort of outlines. The canvas used was of the same weave and finish.

The technical standard of the work couldn't be faulted. The paintings did look very much like Munnings' own, and would do much more so after they had dried and been varnished. Different-coloured paints dried at different speeds, and also the drying time of paints depended very much on the amount of oil or turps used to thin them, but at a rough guess all three pictures had been completed between three and six days earlier. The paint was at the same stage on all of them. They must, I thought, have all been painted at once, in a row, like a production line. Red hat, red hat, red hat . . . It would have saved time and paint.

The brushwork throughout was painstaking and controlled. Nothing slapdash. No time skimped. The quality of care was the same as in the Millais copy at Alice.

I was looking, I knew, at the true worth of Harley Renbo.

All three paintings were perfectly legal. It was never illegal to copy: only to attempt to sell the copy as real.

I thought it all over for a bit longer, and then set rapidly to work.

The Hilton, when I went downstairs an hour later, were most amiable and helpful.

Certainly, they could do what I asked. Certainly, I could use the photocopying machine, come this way. Certainly, I could pay my bill now, and leave later.

I thanked them for their many excellent services.

'Our pleasure,' they said: and, incredibly, they meant it.

Upstairs again, waiting for Jik and Sarah, I packed all my things. That done, I took off my jacket and shirt and did my best at rigging the spare bandages and clips back into something like the Alice shape, with my hand inside across my chest. No use pretending that it wasn't a good deal more comfortable that way than the dragging soreness of letting it all swing free. I buttoned my shirt over the top and calculated that if the traffic was bad Jik might still be struggling out of the racecourse.

A little anxiously, and still feeling faintly unwell, I settled to wait.

I waited precisely five minutes. Then the telephone by the bed rang, and I picked up the receiver.

Jik's voice, sounding hard and dictatorial.

'Charles, will you please come down to our room at once.'

'Well . . .' I said hesitantly. 'Is it important?'

'Bloody chromic oxide!' he said explosively. 'Can't you do anything without arguing?'

Christ, I thought.

I took a breath. 'Give me ten minutes,' I said. 'I need ten minutes. I'm . . . er . . . I've just had a shower. I'm in my underpants.'

'Thank you, Charles,' he said. The telephone clicked as he disconnected.

A lot of Jik's great oaths galloped across my mind, wasting precious time. If ever we needed divine help, it was now.

Stifling a gut-twisting lurch of plain fear I picked up the telephone and made a series of internal calls.

'Please could you send a porter up right away to room seventeen-eighteen to collect Mr Cassavetes' bags?'

'Housekeeper . . ? Please will you send someone along urgently to seventeen-eighteen to clean the room as Mr Cassavetes has been sick . . .'

'Please will you send the nurse along to seventeen-eighteen at once as Mr Cassavetes has a severe pain . . .'

'Please will you send four bottles of your best champagne and ten glasses up to seventeen-eighteen immediately . . .'

'Please bring coffee for three to seventeen-eighteen at once . . .'

'Electrician? All the electrics have fused in room seventeen-eighteen, please come at once.'

'. . . the water is overflowing in the bathroom, please send the plumber urgently.'

Who else was there? I ran my eye down the list of possible services. One wouldn't be able to summon chiropodists, masseuses, secretaries, barbers or clothes-pressers in a hurry . . . but television, why not?

'. . . Please would you see to the television in room seventeen-eighteen. There is smoke coming from the back and it smells like burning . . .'

That should do it, I thought. I made one final call for myself, asking for a porter to collect my bags. Right on, they said. Ten-dollar tip I said if the bags could be down in the hall within five minutes. No sweat, an Australian voice assured me happily. Coming right that second.

I left my door ajar for the porter and rode down two storeys in the lift to floor seventeen. The corridor outside Jik and Sarah's room was still a broad empty expanse of no one doing anything in a hurry.

The ten minutes had gone.

I fretted.

The first to arrive was the waiter with the champagne, and he came not with a tray but a trolley, complete with ice buckets and spotless white cloths. It couldn't possibly have been better.

As he slowed to a stop outside Jik's door, two other figures turned into the corridor, hurrying, and behind them, distantly, came a cleaner slowly pushing another trolley of linen and buckets and brooms.

I said to the waiter, 'Thank you so much for coming so quickly.' I gave him a ten-dollar note, which surprised him. 'Please go and serve the champagne straight away.'

He grinned, and knocked on Jik's door.

After a pause, Jik opened it. He looked tense and strained.

'Your champagne, sir,' said the waiter.

'But I didn't . . .' Jik began. He caught sight of me suddenly, where I stood a little back from his door. I made waving-in motions with my hand, and a faint grin appeared to lighten the anxiety.

Jik retreated into the room followed by trolley and waiter.

At a rush, after that, came the electrician, the plumber and the television man. I gave them each ten dollars and thanked them for coming so promptly. 'I had a winner,' I said. They took the money with more grins and Jik opened the door to their knock.

'Electrics . . . plumbing . . . television . . .' His eyebrows rose. He looked across to me in rising comprehension. He flung wide his door and invited them in with all his heart.

'Give them some champagne,' I said.

'God Almighty.'

After that, in quick succession, came the porter, the man with the coffee, and the nurse. I gave them all ten dollars from my mythical winnings and invited them to join the party. Finally came the cleaner, pushing her top-heavy-looking load. She took the ten dollars, congratulated me on my good fortune, and entered the crowded and noisy fray.

It was up to Jik, I thought. I couldn't do any more.

He and Sarah suddenly popped out like the corks from the

gold-topped bottles, and stood undecided in the corridor. I gripped Sarah's wrist and tugged her towards me.

'Push the cleaning trolley through the door, and turn it over,' I said to Jik.

He wasted no time deliberating. The brooms crashed to the carpet inside the room, and Jik pulled the door shut after him.

Sarah and I were already running on ourselves to the lifts. She looked extremely pale and wild-eyed, and I knew that whatever had happened in their room had been almost too much for her.

Jik sprinted along after us. There were six lifts from the seventeenth floor, and one never had to wait more than a few seconds for one to arrive. The seconds this time seemed like hours but were actually very few indeed. The welcoming doors slid open, and we leapt inside and pushed the 'doors closed' button like maniacs.

The doors closed.

The lift descended, smooth and fast.

'Where's the car?' I said.

'Car park.'

'Get it and come round to the side door.'

'Right.'

'Sarah . . .'

She stared at me in fright.

'My satchel will be in the hall. Will you carry it for me?'

She looked vaguely at my one-armed state, my jacket swinging loosely over my left shoulder.

'Sarah!'

'Yes . . . all right.'

We erupted into the hall, which had filled with people returning from the Cup. Talkative groups mixed and mingled, and it was impossible to see easily from one side to the other. All to the good, I thought.

My suitcase and satchel stood waiting near the front entrance, guarded by a young man in porter's uniform.

I parted with the ten dollars. 'Thank you very much,' I said.

'No sweat,' he said cheerfully. 'Can I get you a taxi?'

I shook my head. I picked up the suitcase and Sarah the satchel and we headed out of the door.

Turned right. Hurried. Turned right again, round to the side where I'd told Jik we'd meet him.

'He's not here,' Sarah said with rising panic.

'He'll come,' I said encouragingly. 'We'll just go on walking to meet him.'

We walked. I kept looking back nervously for signs of pursuit, but there were none. Jik came round the corner on two wheels and tore millimetres off the tyres stopping beside us. Sarah scrambled into the front and I and my suitcase filled the back. Jik made a hair-raising U-turn and took us away from the Hilton at an illegal speed.

'Wowee,' he said, laughing with released tension. 'Whatever gave you that idea?'

'The Marx Brothers.'

He nodded. 'Pure crazy comedy.'

'Where are we going?' Sarah said.

'Have you noticed,' Jik said, 'how my wife always brings us back to basics?'

The city of Melbourne covered a great deal of land.

We drove randomly north and east through seemingly endless suburban developments of houses, shops, garages and light industry, all looking prosperous, haphazard, and, to my eyes, American.

'Where are we?' Jik said.

'Somewhere called Box Hill,' I said, reading it on shop fronts.

'As good as anywhere.'

We drove a few miles further and stopped at a modern middle-rank motel which had bright-coloured strings of triangular flags fluttering across the forecourt. A far cry from the Hilton, though the rooms we presently took were cleaner than nature intended.

There were plain divans, a square of thin carpet nailed at the edges, and a table lamp screwed to an immovable table. The looking glass was stuck flat to the wall and the swivelling armchair was bolted to the floor. Apart from that, the curtains were bright and the hot tap ran hot in the shower.

'They don't mean you to pinch much,' Jik said. 'Let's paint them a mural.'

'No!' Sarah said, horror-struck.

'There's a great Australian saying,' Jik said. 'If it moves, shoot it, and if it grows, chop it down.'

'What's that got to do with it?' Sarah said.

'Nothing. I just thought Todd might like to hear it.'

'Give me strength.'

We were trying to, in our inconsequential way.

Jik sat in the armchair in my room, swivelling. Sarah sat on one of the divans, I on the other. My suitcase and satchel stood side by side on the floor.

'You do realize we skipped out of the Hilton without paying,' Sarah said.

'No we didn't,' Jik said. 'According to our clothes, we are still resident. I'll ring them up later.'

'But Todd . . .'

'I did pay,' I said. 'Before you got back.'

She looked slightly happier.

'How did Greene find you?' I said.

'God knows,' Jik said gloomily.

Sarah was astonished. 'How did you know about Greene? How did you know there was anyone in our room besides Jik and me? How did you know we were in such awful trouble?'

693

'Jik told me.'

'But he couldn't! He couldn't risk warning you. He just had to tell you to come. He really did . . .' Her voice quivered. The tears weren't far from the surface. 'They made him . . .'

'Jik told me,' I said matter-of-factly. 'First, he called me Charles, which he never does, so I knew something was wrong. Second, he was rude to me, and I know you think he is most of the time, but he isn't, not like that. And third, he told me the name of the man who I was to guess was in your room putting pressure on you both to get me to come down and walk into a nasty little hole. He told me it was chromic oxide, which is the pigment in green paint.'

'Green paint!' The tearful moment passed. 'You really are both extraordinary,' she said.

'Long practice,' Jik said cheerfully.

'Tell me what happened,' I said.

'We left before the last race, to avoid the traffic, and we just came back normally to the Hilton. I parked the car, and we went up to our room. We'd only been there about a minute when there was this knock on the door, and when I opened it they just pushed in . . .'

'They?'

'Three of them. One was Greene. We both knew him straightaway, from your drawing. Another was the boy from the Arts Centre. The third was all biceps and beetle brows, with his brains in his fists.'

He absent-mindedly rubbed an area south of his heart.

'He punched you?' I said.

'It was all so quick . . .' he said apologetically. 'They just crammed in . . . and biff bang . . . The next thing I knew they'd got hold of Sarah and were twisting her arm and saying that she wouldn't just get turps in her eyes if I didn't get you to come at once.'

'Did they have a gun?' I asked.

'No . . . a cigarette lighter. Look, I'm sorry, mate. I guess it sounds pretty feeble, but Beetle-brows had her in a pretty rough grasp and the boy had this ruddy great cigarette lighter with a flame like a blowtorch just a couple of inches from her cheek . . . and I was a bit groggy . . . and Greene said they'd burn her if I didn't get you . . . and I couldn't fight them all at once.'

'Stop apologizing,' I said.

'Yeah . . . well, so I rang you. I told Greene you'd be ten minutes because you were in your underpants, but I think he heard you anyway because he was standing right beside me, very wary and sharp. I didn't know really whether you'd cottoned on, but I hoped to God . . . and you should have seen their faces when the waiter pushed the trolley in. Beetle-brows let go of Sarah and the boy just stood there with his mouth open and the cigarette lighter flaring up like an oil refinery . . .'

'Greene said we didn't want the champagne and to take it away,' Sarah said. 'But Jik and I said yes we did, and Jik asked the waiter to open it at once.'

'Before he got the first cork out the others all began coming . . . and then they were all picking up glasses . . . and the room was filling up . . . and Greene and the boy and Beetle-brows were all on the window side of the room, sort of pinned in by the trolley and all those people . . . and I just grabbed Sarah and we ducked round the edge. The last I saw, Greene and the others were trying to push through, but our guests were pretty thick on the ground by then and keen to get their champagne . . . and I should think the cleaning trolley was just about enough to give us that start to the lift.'

'I wonder how long the party lasted,' I said.

'Until the bubbles ran out.'

'They must all have thought you mad,' Sarah said.

'Anything goes on Cup day,' I said, 'and the staff of the Hilton would be used to eccentric guests.'

'What if Greene had had a gun?' Sarah said.

I smiled at her twistedly. 'He would have had to wave it around in front of a hell of a lot of witnesses.'

'But he might have done.'

'He might . . . but he was a long way from the front door.' I bit my thumbnail. 'Er . . . how did he know I was in the Hilton?'

There was a tangible silence.

'I told him,' Sarah said finally, in a small mixed outburst of shame and defiance. 'Jik didn't tell you it all, just now. At first they said . . . Greene said . . . they'd burn my face if Jik didn't tell them where you were. He didn't want to . . . but he had to . . . so I told them, so that it wouldn't be him . . . I suppose that sounds stupid.'

I thought it sounded extraordinarily moving. Love of an exceptional order, and a depth of understanding.

I smiled at her. 'So they didn't know I was there, to begin with?'

Jik shook his head. 'I don't think they knew you were even in Melbourne. They seemed surprised when Sarah said you were upstairs. I think all they knew was that you weren't still in hospital in Alice Springs.'

'Did they know about our robbery?'

'I'm sure they didn't.'

I grinned. 'They'll be schizophrenic when they find out.'

Jik and I both carefully shied away from what would have happened if I'd gone straight down to their room, though I saw from his eyes that he knew. With Sarah held as a hostage I would have had to leave the Hilton with Greene and taken my chance. The uncomfortably slim chance that they would have let me off again with my life.

'I'm hungry,' I said.

Sarah smiled. 'Whenever are you not?'

We ate in a small Bring Your Own restaurant nearby, with people at tables all around us talking about what they'd backed in the Cup.

'Good heavens,' Sarah exclaimed. 'I'd forgotten about that.'

'About what?'

'Your winnings,' she said. 'On Ringwood.'

'But . . .' I began.

'It was number eleven!'

'I don't believe it.'

She opened her handbag and produced a fat wad of notes. Somehow, in all the mêlée in the Hilton, she had managed to emerge from fiery danger with the cream leather pouch swinging from her arm. The strength of the instinct which kept women attached to their handbags had often astounded me, but never more than that day.

'It was forty to one,' she said. 'I put twenty dollars on for you, so you've got eight hundred dollars, and I think it's disgusting.'

'Share it,' I said, laughing.

She shook her head. 'Not a cent . . . To be honest, I thought it had no chance at all, and I thought I'd teach you not to bet that way by losing you twenty dollars, otherwise I'd only have staked you ten.'

'I owe most of it to Jik, anyway,' I said.

'Keep it,' he said. 'We'll add and subtract later. Do you want me to cut your steak?'

'Please.'

He sliced away neatly at my plate, and pushed it back with the fork placed ready.

'What else happened at the races?' I said, spearing the first succulent piece. 'Who did you see?' The steak tasted as good as it looked, and I realized that in spite of all the sore patches I had at last lost the overall feeling of unsettled shaky sickness. Things were on the mend, it seemed.

'We didn't see Greene,' Jik said. 'Or the boy, or Beetle-brows.'

'I guess they saw you.'

'Do you think so?' Sarah said worriedly.

'I'd guess,' I said, 'that they saw you at the races and simply followed you back to the Hilton.'

'Jesus,' Jik groaned. 'We never spotted them. There was a whole mass of traffic.'

I nodded. 'And all moving very slowly. If Greene was perhaps three cars behind you, you'd never have seen him, but he could have kept you in sight easily.'

'I'm bloody sorry, Todd.'

'Don't be silly. And no harm done.'

'Except for the fact,' Sarah said, 'that I've still got no clothes.'

'You look fine,' I said absently.

'We saw a girl I know in Sydney,' Sarah said. 'We watched the first two races together and talked to her aunt. And Jik and I were talking to a photographer we both knew just after he got back . . . so it would be pretty easy to prove Jik was at the races all afternoon, like you wanted.'

'No sign of Wexford?'

'Not if he looked like your drawing,' Sarah said. 'Though of course he might have been there. It's awfully difficult to recognize a complete stranger just from a drawing, in a huge crowd like that.'

'We talked to a lot of people,' Jik said. 'To everyone Sarah knew even slightly. She used the excuse of introducing me as her newly bagged husband.'

'We even talked to that man you met on Saturday,' Sarah agreed, nodding. 'Or rather, he came over and talked to us.'

'Hudson Taylor?' I asked.

'The one you saw talking to Wexford,' Jik said.

'He asked if you were at the Cup,' Sarah said. 'He said he'd been going to ask you along for another drink. We said we'd tell you he'd asked.'

'His horse ran quite well, didn't it?' I said.

'We saw him earlier than that. We wished him luck and he said he'd need it.'

'He bets a bit,' I said, remembering.

'Who doesn't?'

'Another commission down the drain,' I said. 'He would have had Vinery painted if he'd won.'

'You hire yourself out like a prostitute,' Jik said. 'It's obscene.'

'And anyway,' added Sarah cheerfully, 'you won more on Ringwood than you'd've got for the painting.'

I looked pained, and Jik laughed.

We drank coffee, went back to the motel, and divided to our separate rooms. Five minutes later Jik knocked on my door.

'Come in,' I said, opening it.

He grinned. 'You were expecting me.'

'Thought you might come.'

He sat in the armchair and swivelled. His gaze fell on my suitcase, which lay flat on one of the divans.

'What did you do with all the stuff we took from the gallery?'

I told him.

He stopped swivelling and sat still.

'You don't mess about, do you?' he said eventually.

'A few days from now,' I said, 'I'm going home.'

'And until then?'

'Um . . . until then, I aim to stay one jump ahead of Wexford, Greene, Beetle-brows, the Arts Centre boy, and the toughs who met me on the balcony at Alice.'

'Not to mention our copy artist, Harley Renbo.'

I considered it. 'Him too,' I said.

'Do you think we can?'

'Not we. Not from hereon. This is where you take Sarah home.'

He slowly shook his head. 'I don't reckon it would be any safer than staying with you. We're too easy to find. For one thing, we're in the Sydney phone book. What's to stop Wexford from marching on to the boat with a bigger threat than a cigarette lighter?'

'You could tell him what I've just told you.'

'And waste all your efforts.'

'Retreat is sometimes necessary.'

He shook his head. 'If we stay with you, retreat may never be necessary. It's the better of two risks. And anyway . . .' the old fire gleamed in his eye . . . 'It will be a great game. Cat and mouse. With cats who don't know they are mice chasing a mouse who knows he's a cat.'

More like a bull fight, I thought, with myself waving the cape to invite the charge. Or a conjuror, attracting attention to one hand while he did the trick with the other. On the whole I preferred the notion of the conjuror. There seemed less likelihood of being gored.

Thirteen

I SPENT a good deal of the night studying the list of Overseas Customers, mostly because I still found it difficult to lie comfortably to sleep, and partly because I had nothing else to read.

It became more and more obvious that I hadn't really pinched *enough*. The list I'd taken was fine in its way, but would have been doubly useful with a stock list to match the letters and numbers in the right-hand column.

On the other hand, all stock numbers were a form of code, and if I looked at them long enough, maybe some sort of recognizable pattern might emerge.

By far the majority began with the letter M, particularly in the first and much larger section. In the smaller section, which I had found at the back of the file, the M prefixes were few, and S, A, W and B were much commoner.

Donald's number began with M. Maisie's began with S.

Suppose, I thought, that the M simply stood for Melbourne, and the S for Sydney, the cities where each had bought their pictures.

Then A, W and B were where? Adelaide, Wagga Wagga and Brisbane?

Alice?

In the first section the letters and numbers following the initial M seemed to have no clear pattern. In the second section, though, the third letter was always C, the last letter always R, and the numbers, divided though they were between several countries, progressed more or less consecutively. The highest number of all was 54, which had been sold to a Mr Norman Updike, living in Auckland, New Zealand. The stock number against his name was WHC54R. The date in the left-hand column was only a week old, and Mr Updike had not been crossed out.

All the pictures in the shorter section had been sold within the past three years. The first dates in the long first section were five and a half years old.

I wondered which had come first, five and a half years ago: the gallery or the idea. Had Wexford originally been a full-time crook deliberately setting up an imposing front, or a formerly honest art dealer struck by criminal possibilities? Judging from the respectable air of the gallery and what little I'd seen of Wexford himself, I would have guessed the latter. But the violence lying just below the surface didn't match.

I sighed, put down the lists, and switched off the light. Lay in the dark, thinking of the telephone call I'd made after Jik had gone back to Sarah.

It had been harder to arrange from the motel than it would have been from the Hilton, but the line had been loud and clear.

'You got my cable?' I said.

'I've been waiting for your call for half an hour.'

'Sorry.'

'What do you want?'

'I've sent you a letter,' I said. 'I want to tell you what's in it.'

'But . . .'

'Just listen,' I said. 'And talk after.' I spoke for quite a long time to a response of grunts from the far end.

'Are you sure of all this?'

'Positive about most,' I said. 'Some of it's a guess.'

'Repeat it.'

'Very well.' I did so, at much the same length.

'I have recorded all that.'

'Good.'

'Hm . . . What do you intend doing now?'

'I'm going home soon. Before that, I think I'll keep looking into things that aren't my business.'

'I don't approve of that.'

I grinned at the telephone. 'I don't suppose you do, but if I'd stayed in England we wouldn't have got this far. There's one other thing . . . Can I reach you by telex if I want to get a message to you in a hurry?'

'Telex? Wait a minute.'

I waited.

'Yes, here you are.' A number followed. I wrote it down. 'Address any message to me personally and head it urgent.'

'Right,' I said. 'And could you get answers to three questions for me?' He listened and said he could. 'Thank you very much,' I said. 'And goodnight.'

Sarah and Jik both looked heavy-eyed and languorous in the morning. A successful night, I judged.

We checked out of the motel, packed my suitcase into the boot of the car, and sat in the passenger seats to plan the day.

'Can't we please get our clothes from the Hilton?' Sarah said, sounding depressed.

Jik and I said 'No' together.

'I'll ring them now,' Jik said. 'I'll get them to pack all our things and keep them safe for us, and I'll tell them I'll send a cheque for the bill.' He levered himself out of the car again and went off on the errand.

'Buy what you need out of my winnings,' I said to Sarah.

She shook her head. 'I've got some money. It's not that. It's just . . . I wish all this was over.'

'It will be, soon,' I said neutrally. She sighed heavily. 'What's your idea of a perfect life?' I asked.

'Oh . . .' she seemed surprised. 'I suppose right now I just want to be with Jik on the boat and have fun, like before you came.'

'And for ever?'

She looked at me broodingly. 'You may think, Todd, that I don't know Jik is a complicated character, but you've only got to look at his paintings . . . They make me shudder. They're a side of Jik I don't know because he hasn't painted anything since we met. You may think that this world will be worse off if Jik is happy for a bit, but I'm no fool, I know that in the end whatever it is that drives him to paint like that will come back again . . . I think these first few months together are frantically precious . . . and it isn't just the physical dangers you've dragged us into that I hate, but the feeling that I've lost the rest of that golden time . . . that you remind him of his painting, and that after you've gone he'll go straight back to it . . . weeks and weeks before he might have done.'

'Get him to go sailing,' I said. 'He's always happy at sea.'

'You don't care, do you?'

I looked straight into her clouded brown eyes. 'I care for you both, very much.'

'Then God help the people you hate.'

And God help me, I thought, if I become any fonder of my oldest friend's wife. I looked away from her, out of the window. Affection wouldn't matter. Anything else would be a mess.

Jik came back with a satisfied air. 'That's all fixed. They said there's a letter for you, Todd, delivered by hand a few minutes ago. They asked me for a forwarding address.'

'What did you say?'

'I said you'd call them yourself.'

'Right . . . Well, let's get going.'

'Where to?'

'New Zealand, don't you think?'

'That should be far enough,' Jik said dryly.

He drove us to the airport, which was packed with people going home from the Cup.

'If Wexford and Greene are looking for us,' Sarah said, 'they will surely be watching at the airport.'

If they weren't, I thought, we'd have to lay a trail: but Jik, who knew that, didn't tell her.

'They can't do much in public,' he said comfortingly.

We bought tickets and found we could either fly to Auckland direct at lunch-time, or via Sydney leaving within half an hour.

'Sydney,' said Sarah positively, clearly drawing strength from the chance of putting her feet down on her own safe doorstep.

I shook my head. 'Auckland direct. Let's see if the restaurant's still open for breakfast.'

We squeezed in under the waitresses' pointed consultation of clocks and watches and ordered bacon and eggs lavishly.

'Why are we going to New Zealand?' Sarah said.

'To see a man about a painting and advise him to take out extra insurance.'

'Are you actually making sense?'

'Actually,' I said, 'yes.'

'I don't see why we have to go so far, when Jik said you found enough in the gallery to blow the whole thing wide open.'

'Um . . .' I said. 'Because we don't want to blow it wide open. Because we want to hand it to the police in full working order.'

She studied my face. 'You are very devious.'

'Not on canvas,' Jik said.

After we'd eaten we wandered around the airport shops, buying yet more toothbrushes and so on for Jik and Sarah, and another airline bag. There was no sign of Wexford or Greene or the boy or Beetle-brows or Renbo, or the tough who'd been on watch at Alice Springs. If they'd seen us without us seeing them, we couldn't tell.

'I think I'll ring the Hilton,' I said.

Jik nodded. I put the call through with him and Sarah sitting near, within sound and sight.

'I called about a forwarding address . . .' I told the reception desk. 'I can't really give you one. I'll be in New Zealand. I'm flying to Auckland in an hour or two.'

They asked for instructions about the hand-delivered letter.

'Er . . . Would you mind opening it, and reading it to me?'

Certainly, they said. Their pleasure. The letter was from Hudson Taylor saying he was sorry to have missed me at the races, and that if while I was in Australia I would like to see round a vineyard, he would be pleased to show me his.

Thanks, I said. Our pleasure, sir, they said. If anyone asked for me, I said, would they please mention where I'd gone. They would. Certainly. Their pleasure.

During the next hour Jik called the car-hire firm about settling their account and leaving the car in the airport car park, and I checked my suitcase through with Air New Zealand. Passports were no problem: I had mine with me in any case, but for Jik and Sarah they were unnecessary, as passage between New Zealand and Australia was as unrestricted as between England and Ireland.

Still no sign of Wexford or Greene. We sat in the departure bay thinking private thoughts.

It was again only when our flight was called that I spotted a spotter. The prickles rose again on my skin. I'd been blind, I thought. Dumb and blind.

Not Wexford, nor Greene, nor the boy, nor Renbo, nor any rough set of muscles. A neat day dress, neat hair, unremarkable handbag and shoes. A calm concentrated face. I saw her because she was staring at Sarah. She was standing outside the departure bay, looking in. The woman who had welcomed me into the Yarra River Fine Arts, and given me a catalogue, and let me out again afterwards.

As if she felt my eyes upon her she switched her gaze abruptly to my face. I looked away instantly, blankly, hoping she wouldn't know I'd seen her, or wouldn't know at least that I'd recognized her.

Jik, Sarah and I stood up and drifted with everyone else towards the departure doors. In their glass I could see the woman's reflection: standing still, watching us go. I walked out towards the aircraft and didn't look back.

Mrs Norman Updike stood in her doorway, shook her head, and said that her husband would not be home until six.

She was thin and sharp-featured and talked with tight New Zealand vowels. If we wanted to speak to her husband, we would have to come back.

She looked us over; Jik with his rakish blond beard, Sarah in her slightly crumpled but still military cream dress, I with my arm in its sling under my shirt, and jacket loose over my shoulder. Hardly a trio one would easily forget. She watched us retreat down her front path with a sharply turned-down mouth.

'Dear gentle soul,' murmured Jik.

We drove away in the car we had hired at the airport.

'Where now?' Jik said.

'Shops.' Sarah was adamant. 'I must have some clothes.'

The shops, it appeared, were in Queen Street, and still open for another half-hour. Jik and I sat in the car, waiting and watching the world go by.

'The dolly-birds fly out of their office cages about now,' Jik said happily.

'What of it?'

'I sit and count the ones with no bras.'

'And you a married man.'

'Old habits die hard.'

We had counted eight definites and one doubtful by the time

Sarah returned. She was wearing a light olive skirt with a pink shirt, and reminded me of pistachio ice cream.

'That's better,' she said, tossing two well-filled carriers on to the back seat. 'Off we go, then.'

The therapeutic value of the new clothes lasted all the time we spent in New Zealand and totally amazed me. She seemed to feel safer if she looked fresh and clean, her spirits rising accordingly. Armour-plated cotton, I thought. Drip-dry bullet-proofing. Security is a new pin.

We dawdled back to the hill overlooking the bay where Norman Updike's house stood in a crowded suburban street. The Updike residence was large but squashed by neighbours, and it was not until one was inside that one realized that the jostling was due to the view. As many houses as could be crammed on to the land had been built to share it. The city itself seemed to sprawl endlessly round miles of indented coastline, but all the building plots looked tiny.

Norman Updike proved as expansive as his wife was closed in. He had a round shiny bald head on a round short body, and he called his spouse Chuckles without apparently intending satire.

We said, Jik and I, that we were professional artists who would be intensely interested and grateful if we could briefly admire the noted picture he had just bought.

'Did the gallery send you?' he asked, beaming at the implied compliments to his taste and wealth.

'Sort of,' we said, and Jik added: 'My friend here is well known in England for his painting of horses, and is represented in many top galleries, and has been hung often at the Royal Academy . . .'

I thought he was laying it on a bit too thick, but Norman Updike was impressed and pulled wide his door.

'Come in then. Come in. The picture's in the lounge. This way, lass, this way.'

He showed us into a large over-stuffed room with dark ankle-deep carpet, big dark cupboards, and the glorious view of sunlit water.

Chuckles, sitting solidly in front of a television busy with a moronic British comic show, gave us a sour look and no greeting.

'Over here,' Norman Updike beamed, threading his portly way round a battery of fat armchairs. 'What do you think of that, eh?' He waved his hand with proprietorial pride at the canvas on his wall.

A smallish painting, fourteen inches by eighteen. A black horse, with an elongated neck curving against a blue and white sky; a chopped-off tail; the grass in the foreground yellow; and the whole covered with an old-looking varnish.

'Herring,' I murmured reverently.

Norman Updike's beam broadened. 'I see you know your stuff. Worth a bit, that is.'

'A good deal,' I agreed.

'I reckon I got a bargain. The gallery said I'd always make a profit if I wanted to sell.'

'May I look at the brushwork?' I asked politely.

'Go right ahead.'

I looked closely. It was very good. It did look like Herring, dead since 1865. It also, indefinably, looked like the meticulous Renbo. One would need a microscope and chemical analysis to make sure.

I stepped back and glanced round the rest of the room. There was nothing of obvious value, and the few other pictures were all prints.

'Beautiful,' I said admiringly, turning back to the Herring. 'Unmistakable style. A real master.'

Updike beamed.

'You'd better beware of burglars,' I said.

He laughed. 'Chuckles, dear, do you hear what this young man says? He says we'd better beware of burglars!'

Chuckles' eyes gave me two seconds' sour attention and returned to the screen.

Updike patted Sarah on the shoulder. 'Tell your friend not to worry about burglars.'

'Why not?' I said.

'We've got alarms all over this house,' he beamed. 'Don't you worry, a burglar wouldn't get far.'

Jik and Sarah, as I had done, looked round the room and saw nothing much worth stealing. Nothing, certainly, worth alarms all over the house. Updike watched them looking and his beam grew wider.

'Shall I show these young people our little treasures, Chuckles?' he said.

Chuckles didn't even reply. The television cackled with tinned laughter.

'We'd be most interested,' I said.

He smiled with the fat anticipatory smirk of one about to show what will certainly be admired. Two or three steps took him to one of the big dark cupboards which seemed built into the walls, and he pulled open the double doors with a flourish.

Inside, there were about six deep shelves, each bearing several complicated pieces of carved jade. Pale pink, creamy-white and pale green, smooth, polished, intricate, expensive; each piece standing upon its own heavy-looking black base-support. Jik, Sarah and I made appreciative noises and Norman Updike smiled even wider.

'Hong Kong, of course,' he said. 'I worked there for years, you know. Quite a nice little collection, eh?' He walked along to the next dark cupboard and pulled open a duplicate set of doors. Inside, more shelves, more carvings, as before.

'I'm afraid I don't know much about jade,' I said, apologetically. 'Can't appreciate your collection to the full.'

He told us a good deal more about the ornate goodies than we actually wanted to know. There were four cupboards full in the lounge and overflows in bedroom and hall.

'You used to be able to pick them up very cheap in Hong Kong,' he said. 'I worked there more than twenty years, you know.'

Jik and I exchanged glances. I nodded slightly.

Jik immediately shook Norman Updike by the hand, put his arm round Sarah, and said we must be leaving. Updike looked enquiringly at Chuckles, who was still glued to the telly and still abdicating from the role of hostess. When she refused to look our way he shrugged good-humouredly and came with us to his front door. Jik and Sarah walked out as soon as he opened it, and left me alone with him in the hall.

'Mr Updike,' I said. 'At the gallery . . . which man was it who sold you the Herring?'

'Mr Grey,' he said promptly.

Mr Grey . . . Mr Grey . . .

I frowned.

'Such a pleasant man,' nodded Updike, beaming. 'I told him I knew very little about pictures, but he assured me I would get as much pleasure from my little Herring as from all my jade.'

'You did tell him about your jade, then?'

'Naturally I did. I mean . . . if you don't know anything about one thing, well . . . you try and show you do know about something else. Don't you? Only human, isn't it?'

'Only human,' I agreed, smiling. 'What was the name of Mr Grey's gallery?'

'Eh?' He looked puzzled. 'I thought you said he sent you, to see my picture.'

'I go to so many galleries, I've foolishly forgotten which one it was.'

'Ruapehu Fine Arts,' he said. 'I was down there last week.'

'Down . . .?'

'In Wellington.' His smile was slipping. 'Look here, what is all this?' Suspicion flitted across his rounded face. 'Why did you come here? I don't think Mr Grey sent you at all.'

'No,' I said. 'But Mr Updike, we mean you no harm. We really are painters, my friend and I. But . . . now we've seen your jade collection . . . we do think we must warn you. We've heard of several people who've bought paintings and had their houses burgled soon after. You say you've got burglar alarms fitted, so if I were you I'd make sure they are working properly.'

'But . . . good gracious . . .'

'There's a bunch of thieves about,' I said. 'Who follow up the sales of paintings and burgle the houses of those who buy. I suppose they reckon that if anyone can afford, say, a Herring, they have other things worth stealing.'

He looked at me with awakening shrewdness. 'You mean, young man, that I told Mr Grey about my jade . . .'

'Let's just say,' I said, 'that it would be sensible to take more precautions than usual.'

'But . . . for how long?'

I shook my head. 'I don't know, Mr Updike. Maybe for ever.'

His round jolly face looked troubled.

'Why did you bother to come and tell me all this?' he said.

'I'd do a great deal more to break up this bunch.'

He asked 'Why?' again, so I told him. 'My cousin bought a painting. My cousin's house was burgled. My cousin's wife disturbed the burglars, and they killed her.'

Norman Updike took a long slow look at my face. I couldn't have stopped him seeing the abiding anger, even if I'd tried. He shivered convulsively.

'I'm glad you're not after *me*,' he said.

I managed a smile. 'Mr Updike . . . please take care. And one day, perhaps, the police may come to see your picture, and ask where you bought it . . . anyway, they will if I have anything to do with it.'

The round smile returned with understanding and conviction. 'I'll expect them,' he said.

Fourteen

JIK DROVE us from Auckland to Wellington; eight hours in the car.

We stopped overnight in a motel in the town of Hamilton, south of Auckland, and went on in the morning. No one followed us, molested us or spied on us. As far as I could be, I was sure no one had picked us up in the northern city, and no one knew we had called at the Updikes.

Wexford must know, all the same, that I had the Overseas Customers list, and he knew there were several New Zealand addresses on it. He couldn't guess which one I'd pick to visit, but he could and would guess that any I picked with the prefix W would steer me straight to the gallery in Wellington.

So in the gallery in Wellington, he'd be ready . . .

'You're looking awfully grim, Todd,' Sarah said.

'Sorry.'

'What were you thinking?'

'How soon we could stop for lunch.'

She laughed. 'We've only just had breakfast.'

We passed the turning to Rotorua and the land of hot springs. Anyone for a boiling mud pack? Jik asked. There was a power station further on run by steam jets from underground, Sarah said, and horrid black craters stinking of sulphur, and the earth's crust was so thin in places that it vibrated and sounded hollow. She had been taken round a place called Waiotapu when

she was a child, she said, and had had terrible nightmares afterwards, and she didn't want to go back.

'Pooh,' Jik said dismissively. 'They only have earthquakes
every other Friday.'

'Somebody told me they have so many earthquakes in Wellington that all the new office blocks are built in cradles,' Sarah said.

'Rock-a-bye sky-scraper . . .' sang Jik, in fine voice.

The sun shone bravely, and the countryside was green with
leaves I didn't know. There were fierce bright patches and deep
mysterious shadows; gorges and rocks and heaven-stretching
tree trunks; feathery waving grasses, shoulder-high. An alien
land, wild and beautiful.

'Get that chiaroscuro,' Jik said, as we sped into one particularly spectacular curving valley.

'What's chiaroscuro?' Sarah said.

'Light and shade,' Jik said. 'Contrast and balance. Technical
term. All the world's a chiaroscuro, and all the men and women
merely blobs of light and shade.'

'Every life's a chiaroscuro,' I said.

'And every soul.'

'The enemy,' I said, 'is grey.'

'And you get grey,' Jik nodded, 'by muddling together red,
white and blue.'

'Grey lives, grey deaths, all levelled out into equal grey nothing.'

'No one,' Sarah sighed, 'would ever call you two grey?'

'Grey!' I said suddenly. 'Of bloody course.'

'What are you on about?' Jik said.

'Grey was the name of the man who hired the suburban art
gallery in Sydney, and Grey is the name of the man who sold
Updike his quote Herring unquote.'

'Oh dear.' Sarah's sigh took the lift out of the spirits and the
dazzle from the day.

'Sorry,' I said.

*

There were so many of them, I thought. Wexford and Greene. The boy. The woman. Harley Renbo. Two toughs at Alice Springs, one of whom I knew by sight, and one (the one who'd been behind me) whom I didn't. The one I didn't know might, or might not, be Beetle-brows. If he wasn't, Beetle-brows was extra.

And now Grey. And another one, somewhere.

Nine at least. Maybe ten. How could I possibly tangle all that lot up without getting crunched? Or worse, getting Sarah crunched, or Jik. Every time I moved, the serpent grew another head.

I wondered who did the actual robberies. Did they send their own two (or three) toughs overseas, or did they contract out to local labour, so to speak?

If they sent their own toughs, was it one of them who had killed Regina?

Had I already met Regina's killer? Had he thrown me over the balcony at Alice?

I pondered uselessly, and added one more twist . . .

Was he waiting ahead in Wellington?

We reached the capital in the afternoon and booked into the Townhouse Hotel because of its splendid view over the harbour. With such marvellous coastal scenery, I thought, it would have been a disgrace if the cities of New Zealand had been ugly. I still thought there were no big towns more captivating than flat old marshy London, but that was another story. Wellington, new and cared for, had life and character to spare.

I looked up the Ruapehu Fine Arts in the telephone directory and asked the hotel's reception desk how to get there. They had never heard of the gallery, but the road it was in, that must be up past the old town, they thought: past Thorndon.

They sold me a local area road map, which they said would help, and told me that Mount Ruapehu was a (with luck) extinct volcano, with a warm lake in its crater. If we'd come from Auckland, we must have passed nearby.

I thanked them and carried the map to Jik and Sarah upstairs in their room.

'We could find the gallery,' Jik said. 'But what would we do when we got there?'

'Make faces at them through the window?'

'You'd be crazy enough for that, too,' Sarah said.

'Let's just go and look,' I said. 'They won't see us in the car, if we simply drive past.'

'And after all,' Jik said incautiously, 'we do want them to know we're here.'

'Why?' asked Sarah in amazement.

'Oh Jesus,' Jik said.

'Why?' she demanded, the anxiety crowding back.

'Ask Todd, it's his idea.'

'You're a sod,' I said.

'Why, Todd?'

'Because,' I said, 'I want them to spend all their energies looking for us over here and not clearing away every vestige of evidence in Melbourne. We do want the police to deal with them finally, don't we, because we can't exactly arrest them ourselves? Well . . . when the police start moving, it would be hopeless if there was no one left for them to find.'

She nodded. 'That's what you meant by leaving it all in working order. But . . . you didn't say anything about deliberately enticing them to follow us.'

'Todd's got that list, and the pictures we took,' Jik said, 'and they'll want them back. Todd wants them to concentrate exclusively on getting them back, because if they think they can get them back and shut us up . . .'

'Jik,' I interrupted. 'You do go on a bit.'

Sarah looked from me to him and back again. A sort of hopeless calm took over from the anxiety.

'If they think they can get everything back and shut us up,' she said, 'they will be actively searching for us in order to kill us. And you intend to give them every encouragement. Is that right?'

'No,' I said. 'Or rather, yes.'

'They'd be looking for us anyway,' Jik pointed out.

'And we are going to say "Coo-ee, we're over here"?'

'Um,' I said. 'I think they may know already.'

'God give me strength,' she said. 'All right. I see what you're doing, and I see why you didn't tell me. And I think you're a louse. But I'll grant you you've been a damn sight more successful than I thought you'd be, and here we all still are, safe and moderately sound, so all right, we'll let them know we're definitely here. On the strict understanding that we then keep our heads down until you've fixed the police in Melbourne.'

I kissed her cheek. 'Done,' I said.

'So how do we do it?'

I grinned at her. 'We address ourselves to the telephone.'

In the end Sarah herself made the call, on the basis that her Australian voice would be less remarkable than Jik's Englishness, or mine.

'Is that the Ruapehu Fine Arts gallery? It is? I wonder if you can help me . . .' she said. 'I would like to speak to whoever is in charge. Yes, I know, but it is important. Yes, I'll wait.' She rolled her eyes and put her hand over the mouthpiece. 'She sounded like a secretary. New Zealand, anyway.'

'You're doing great,' I said.

'Oh . . . Hello? Yes. Could you tell me your name, please?' Her eyes suddenly opened wide. '*Wexford*. Oh, er . . . Mr Wexford, I've just had a visit from three extraordinary people who wanted to see a painting I bought from you some time ago. Quite extraordinary people. They said you'd sent them. I didn't believe them. I wouldn't let them in. But I thought perhaps I'd better check with you. Did you send them to see my painting?'

There was some agitated squawking from the receiver.

'Describe them? A young man with fair hair and a beard, and another young man with an injured arm, and a bedraggled-looking girl. I sent them away. I didn't like the look of them.'

She grimaced over the phone and listened to some more squawks.

'No of course I didn't give them any information. I told you I didn't like the look of them. Where do I live? Why, right here in Wellington. Well, thank you so much Mr Wexford, I am so pleased I called you.'

She put the receiver down while it was still squawking.

'He was asking me for my name,' she said.

'What a girl,' Jik said. 'What an actress, my wife.'

Wexford. Wexford himself.

It had *worked*.

I raised a small internal cheer.

'So now that they know we're here,' I said, 'would you like to go off somewhere else?'

'Oh no,' Sarah said instinctively. She looked out of the window across the busy harbour. 'It's lovely here, and we've been travelling all day already.'

I didn't argue. I thought it might take more than a single telephone call to keep the enemy interested in Wellington, and it had only been for Sarah's sake that I would have been prepared to move on.

'They won't find us just by checking the hotels by telephone,' Jik pointed out. 'Even if it occurred to them to try the Townhouse, they'd be asking for Cassavetes and Todd, not Andrews and Peel.'

'Are we Andrews and Peel?' Sarah asked.

'We're Andrews. Todd's Peel.'

'So nice to know,' she said.

Mr and Mrs Andrews and Mr Peel took dinner in the hotel restaurant without mishap, Mr Peel having discarded his sling for the evening on the grounds that it was in general a bit too easy to notice. Mr Andrews had declined, on the same consideration, to remove his beard.

We went in time to our separate rooms, and so to bed. I spent a jolly hour unsticking the Alice bandages from my leg and admiring the hemstitching. The tree had made tears that were far from the orderly cuts of operations, and as I inspected the long curving railway lines on a ridged backing of crimson, black and yellow skin, I reckoned that those doctors had done an expert job. It was four days since the fall, during which time I hadn't exactly led an inactive life, but none of their handiwork had come adrift. I realized I had progressed almost without noticing it from feeling terrible all the time to scarcely feeling anything worth mentioning. It was astonishing, I thought, how quickly the human body repaired itself, given the chance.

I covered the mementoes with fresh adhesive plaster bought that morning in Hamilton for the purpose, and even found a way of lying in bed that drew no strike action from mending bones. Things, I thought complacently as I drifted to sleep, were altogether looking up.

I suppose one could say that I underestimated on too many counts. I underestimated the desperation with which Wexford had come to New Zealand. Underestimated the rage and the thoroughness with which he searched for us.

Underestimated the effect of our amateur robbery on professional thieves. Underestimated our success. Underestimated the fear and the fury we had unleashed.

My picture of Wexford tearing his remaining hair in almost comic frustration was all wrong. He was pursuing us with a determination bordering on obsession, grimly, ruthlessly, and fast.

In the morning I woke late to a day of warm windy spring sunshine and made coffee from the fixings provided by the hotel in each room; and Jik rang through on the telephone.

'Sarah says she must wash her hair today. Apparently it's sticking together.'

'It looks all right to me.'

His grin came down the wire. 'Marriage opens vast new feminine horizons. Anyway, she's waiting down in the hall for me to drive her to the shops to buy some shampoo, but I thought I'd better let you know we were going.'

I said uneasily, 'You will be careful . . .'

'Oh sure,' he said. 'We won't go anywhere near the gallery. We won't go far. Only as far as the nearest shampoo shop. I'll call you as soon as we get back.'

He disconnected cheerfully, and five minutes later the bell rang again. I lifted the receiver.

It was the girl from the reception desk. 'Your friends say would you join them downstairs in the car.'

'O.K.,' I said.

I went jacketless down in the lift, left my room key at the desk, and walked out through the front door to the sun-baked and windy car park. I looked around for Jik and Sarah; but they were not, as it happened, the friends who were waiting.

It might have been fractionally better if I hadn't had my left arm slung up inside my shirt. As it was they simply clutched my clothes, lifted me off balance and off my feet, and ignominiously bundled me into the back of their car.

Wexford was sitting inside it; a one-man reception committee. The eyes behind the heavy spectacles were as hostile as forty below, and there was no indecision this time in his manner. This time he as good as had me again behind his steel mesh door, and this time he was intent on not making mistakes.

He still wore a bow tie. The jaunty polka dots went oddly with the unfunny matter in hand.

The muscles propelling me towards him turned out to belong to Greene with an 'e', and to a thug I'd never met but who answered the general description of Beetle-brows.

721

My spirits descended faster than the Hilton lifts. I ended up sitting between Beetle-brows and Wexford, with Greene climbing in front into the driving seat.

'How did you find me?' I said.

Greene, with a wolfish smile, took a Polaroid photograph from his pocket and held it for me to see. It was a picture of the three of us, Jik, Sarah and me, standing by the shops in Melbourne airport. The woman from the gallery, I guessed, had not been wasting the time she spent watching us depart.

'We went round asking the hotels,' Greene said. 'It was easy.'

There didn't seem to be much else to say, so I didn't say anything. A slight shortage of breath might have had something to do with it.

None of the others, either, seemed over-talkative. Greene started the car and drove out into the city. Wexford stared at me with a mixture of anger and satisfaction: and Beetle-brows began twisting my free right arm behind my back in a grip which left no room for debate. He wouldn't let me remain upright. My head went practically down to my knees. It was all most undignified and excruciating.

Wexford said finally, 'We want our list back.'

There was nothing gentlemanly in his voice. He wasn't making light conversation. His heavy vindictive rage had no trouble at all in communicating itself to me without possibility of misunderstanding.

Oh Christ, I thought miserably; I'd been such a bloody fool, just walking into it like that.

'Do you hear? We want our list back, and everything else you took.'

I didn't answer. Too busy suffering.

From external sounds I guessed we were travelling through busy workaday Friday-morning city streets, but as my head was below window level, I couldn't actually see.

After some time the car turned sharply left and ground uphill for what seemed like miles. The engine sighed from overwork at the top, and the road began to descend.

Almost nothing was said on the journey. My thoughts about what very likely lay at the end of it were so unwelcome that I did my best not to allow them houseroom. I could give Wexford his list back, but what then? What then, indeed.

After a long descent the car halted briefly and then turned to the right. We had exchanged city sounds for those of the sea. There were also no more Doppler effects from cars passing us from the opposite direction. I came to the sad conclusion that we had turned off the highway and were on our way along an infrequently used side road.

The car stopped eventually with a jerk.

Beetle-brows removed his hands. I sat up stiffly, wrenched and unenthusiastic.

They could hardly have picked a lonelier place. The road ran along beside the sea so closely that it was more or less part of the shore, and the shore was a jungle of sharply pointed rough black rocks, with frothy white waves slapping among them, a far cry from the gentle beaches of home.

On the right rose jagged cliffs, steeply towering. Ahead, the road ended blindly in some workings which looked like a sort of quarry. Slabs had been cut from the cliffs, and there were dusty clearings, and huge heaps of small jagged rocks, and graded stones and sifted chips. All raw and harsh and blackly volcanic.

No people. No machinery. No sign of occupation.

'Where's the list?' Wexford said.

Greene twisted round in the driving seat and looked seriously at my face.

'You'll tell us,' he said. 'With or without a beating. And we won't hit you with our fists, but with pieces of rock.'

Beetle-brows said aggrievedly, 'What's wrong with fists?' But what was wrong with Greene's fists was the same as with mine: I would never have been able to hit anyone hard enough to get the desired results. The local rocks, by the look of them, were something else.

'What if I tell you?' I said.

They hadn't expected anything so easy. I could see the surprise on their faces, and it was flattering, in a way. There was also a furtiveness in their expressions which boded no good at all. Regina, I thought. Regina, with her head bashed in.

I looked at the cliffs, the quarry, the sea. No easy exit. And behind us, the road. If I ran that way, they would drive after me, and mow me down. If I could run. And even that was problematical.

I swallowed and looked dejected, which wasn't awfully difficult.

'I'll tell you . . .' I said. 'Out of the car.'

There was a small silence while they considered it; but as they weren't anyway going to have room for much crashing around with rocks in that crowded interior, they weren't entirely against it.

Greene leaned over towards the glove compartment on the passenger side, opened it, and drew out a pistol. I knew just about enough about firearms to distinguish a revolver from an automatic, and this was a revolver, a gun whose main advantage, I had read, was that it never jammed.

Greene handled it with a great deal more respect than familiarity. He showed it to me silently, and returned it to the glove compartment, leaving the hinged flap door open so that we all had a clear view of his ultimate threat.

'Get out, then,' Wexford said.

We all got out, and I made sure that I ended up on the side of the sea. The wind was much stronger on this exposed coast, and chilling in the bright sunshine. It lifted the thin carefully combed hair away from Wexford's crown, and left him straggly bald, and intensified the stupid look of Beetle-brows. Greene's eyes stayed as watchful and sharp as the harsh terrain around us.

'All right then,' Wexford said roughly, shouting a little to bring his voice above the din of sea and sky. 'Where's the list?'

I whirled away from them and did my best to sprint for the sea.

I thrust my right hand inside my shirt and tugged at the sling-forming bandages.

Wexford, Greene and Beetle-brows shouted furiously and almost trampled on my heels.

I pulled the lists of Overseas Customers out of the sling, whirled again with them in my hand, and flung them with a bowling action as far out to sea as I could manage.

The pages fluttered apart in mid-air, but the offshore winds caught most of them beautifully and blew them like great leaves out to sea.

I didn't stop at the water's edge. I went straight on into the cold inhospitable battlefield of shark-teeth rocks and green water and white foaming waves. Slipping, falling, getting up, staggering on, finding that the current was much stronger than I'd expected, and the rocks more abrasive, and the footing more treacherous. Finding I'd fled from one deadly danger to embrace another.

For one second, I looked back.

Wexford had followed me a step or two into the sea, but only, it seemed, to reach one of the pages which had fallen shorter than the others. He was standing there with the frothy water swirling round his trouser legs, peering at the sodden paper.

Greene was beside the car, leaning in; by the front passenger seat.

Beetle-brows had his mouth open.

I reapplied myself to the problem of survival.

The shore shelved, as most shores do. Every forward step led into a stronger current, which sucked and pulled and shoved me around like a piece of flotsam. Hip-deep between waves, I found it difficult to stay on my feet, and every time I didn't I was in dire trouble, because of the black needle-sharp rocks waiting in ranks above and below the surface to scratch and tear.

The rocks were not the kind I was used to: not the hard familiar lumpy rocks of Britain, polished by the sea. These were the raw stuff of volcanoes, as scratchy as pumice. One's groping hand didn't slide over them: one's skin stuck to them, and tore off. Clothes fared no better. Before I'd gone thirty yards I was running with blood from a dozen superficial grazes: and no blood vessels bleed more convincingly than the small surface capillaries.

My left arm was still tangled inside the sling, which had housed the Overseas Customers since Cup Day as an insurance against having my room robbed, as at Alice. Soaking wet, the bandages now clung like leeches, and my shirt also. Muscles weakened by a fracture and inactivity couldn't deal with them. I rolled around a lot from not having two hands free.

My foot stepped awkwardly on the side of a submerged rock and I felt it scrape my shin: lost my balance, fell forward, tried to save myself with my hand, failed, crashed chest first against a small jagged peak dead ahead, and jerked my head sharply sideways to avoid connecting with my nose.

The rock beside my cheek splintered suddenly as if exploding. Slivers of it prickled in my face. For a flicker of time I couldn't understand it: and then I struggled round and looked back to the shore with a flood of foreboding.

Greene was standing there, aiming the pistol, shooting to kill.

Fifteen

THIRTY TO thirty-five yards is a long way for a pistol; but Greene seemed so close.

I could see his drooping moustache and the lanky hair blowing in the wind. I could see his eyes and the concentration in his body. He was standing with his legs straddled and his arms out straight ahead, aiming the pistol with both hands.

I couldn't hear the shots above the crash of the waves on the rocks. I couldn't see him squeeze the trigger. But I did see the upward jerk of the arms at the recoil, and I reckoned it would be just plain silly to give him a stationary target.

I was, in all honesty, pretty frightened. I must have looked as close to him as he to me. He must have been quite certain he would hit me, even though his tenderness with the pistol in the car had made me think he was not an expert.

I turned and stumbled a yard or two onwards, though the going became even rougher, and the relentless fight against current and waves and rocks was draining me to dish-rags.

There would have to be an end to it.

Have to be.

I stumbled and fell on a jagged edge and gashed the inside of my forearm, and out poured more good red life. Christ, I thought, I must be scarlet all over, leaking from a hundred tiny nicks.

It gave me at least an idea.

I was waist-deep in dangerous green water, with most of the

shore-line rocks now submerged beneath the surface. Close to one side a row of bigger rock-teeth ran out from the shore like a nightmarish breakwater, and I'd shied away from it, because of the even fiercer waves crashing against it. But it represented the only cover in sight. Three stumbling efforts took me nearer; and the current helped.

I looked back at Greene. He was reloading the gun. Wexford was practically dancing up and down beside him, urging him on; and Beetle-brows, from his disinclination to chase me, probably couldn't swim.

Greene slapped shut the gun and raised it again in my direction.

I took a frightful chance.

I held my fast-bleeding forearm close across my chest: and I stood up, swaying in the current, visible to him from the waist up.

I watched him aim, with both arms straight. It would take a marksman, I believed, to hit me with that pistol from that distance, in that wind. A marksman whose arms didn't jerk upwards when he fired.

The gun was pointing straight at me.

I saw the jerk as he squeezed the trigger.

For an absolutely petrifying second I was convinced he had shot accurately; but I didn't feel or see or even hear the passing of the flying death.

I flung my own right arm wide and high, and paused there facing him for a frozen second, letting him see that most of the front of my shirt was scarlet with blood.

Then I twisted artistically and fell flat, face downwards, into the water; and hoped to God he would think he had killed me.

The sea wasn't much better than bullets. Nothing less than extreme fear of the alternative would have kept me down in it, tumbling and crashing against the submerged razor edges like a piece of cheese in a grater.

The waves themselves swept me towards the taller breakwater teeth, and with a fair amount of desperation I tried to get a grip on them, to avoid being alternately sucked off and flung back, and losing a lot more skin.

There was also the problem of not struggling too visibly. If Wexford or Greene saw me threshing about, all my histrionics would have been in vain.

As much by luck as trying I found the sea shoving me into a wedge-shaped crevice between the rocks, from where I was unable to see the shore. I clutched for a hand-hold, and then with bent knees found a good foothold, and clung there precariously while the sea tried to drag me out again. Every time the wave rolled in it tended to float my foot out of the niche it was lodged in, and every time it receded it tried to suck me with it, with a syphonic action. I clung, and see-sawed in the chest-high water, and clung, and see-sawed, and grew progressively more exhausted.

I could hear nothing except the waves on the rocks. I wondered forlornly how long Wexford and Greene would stay there, staring out to sea for signs of life. I didn't dare to look, in case they spotted my moving head.

The water was cold, and the grazes gradually stopped bleeding, including the useful gash on my forearm. Absolutely nothing, I thought, like having a young strong healthy body. Absolutely nothing like having a young strong healthy body on dry land with a paint-brush in one hand and a beer in the other, with the nice friendly airliners thundering overhead and no money to pay the gas.

Fatigue, in the end, made me look. It was either that or cling like a limpet until I literally fell off nervelessly, too weak to struggle back to life.

To look, I had to leave go. I tried to find other holds, but they weren't as good. The first out-going wave took me with it in no uncertain terms; and its incoming fellow threw me back.

In the tumbling interval I caught a glimpse of the shore.

The road, the cliffs, the quarry, as before. Also the car. Also people.

Bloody damn, I thought.

My hand scrambled for its former hold. My fingers were cramped, bleeding again, and cold. Oh Christ, I thought. How much longer.

It was a measure of my tiredness that it took the space of three in and out waves for me to realize that it wasn't Wexford's car, and it wasn't Wexford standing on the road.

If it wasn't Wexford, it didn't matter who it was.

I let go again of the hand-hold and tried to ride the wave as far out of the crevice as possible, and to swim away from the return force flinging me back. All the other rocks were still there under the surface. A few yards was a heck of a long way.

I stood up gingerly, feeling for my footing more carefully than on the outward flight, and took a longer look at the road.

A grey-white car. A couple beside it, standing close, the man with his arms round the girl.

A nice quiet spot for it, I thought sardonically. I hoped they would drive me somewhere dry.

They moved apart and stared out to sea.

I stared back.

For an instant it seemed impossible. Then they started waving their arms furiously and ran towards the water; and it was Sarah and Jik.

Throwing off his jacket, Jik ploughed into the waves with enthusiasm, and came to a smart halt as the realities of the situation scraped his legs. All the same, he came on after a pause towards me, taking care.

I made my slow way back. Even without haste driving like a fury, any passage through those wave-swept rocks was ruin to the epidermis. By the time we met we were both streaked with red.

We looked at each other's blood. Jik said 'Jesus' and I said 'Christ', and it occurred to me that maybe the Almighty would think we had been calling for His help a bit too often.

Jik put his arm round my waist and I held on to his shoulders, and together we stumbled slowly to land. We fell now and then. Got up gasping. Reclutched, and went on.

He let go when we reached the road. I sat down on the edge of it with my feet pointing out to sea, and positively drooped.

'Todd,' Sarah said anxiously. She came nearer. '*Todd.*' Her voice was incredulous. 'Are you *laughing*?'

'Sure.' I looked up at her, grinning. 'Why ever not?'

Jik's shirt was torn, and mine was in tatters. We took them off and used them to mop up the grazes which were still persistently oozing. From the expression on Sarah's face, we must have looked crazy.

'What a damn silly place to bathe,' Jik said.

'Free back-scratchers,' I said.

He glanced round behind me. 'Your Alice Springs dressing has come off.'

'How're the stitches?'

'Intact.'

'Bully for them.'

'You'll both get pneumonia, sitting there,' Sarah said.

I took off the remnants of the sling. All in all, I thought, it had served me pretty well. The adhesive rib-supporting cummerbund was still more or less in place, but had mostly come unstuck through too much immersion. I pulled that off also. That only left the plasters on my leg, and they too, I found, had floated off in the mêlée. The trousers I'd worn over them had windows everywhere.

'Quite a dust-up,' Jik observed, pouring water out of his shoes and shivering.

'We need a telephone,' I said, doing the same.

'Give me strength,' Sarah said. 'What you need is hot baths, warm clothes, and half a dozen psychiatrists.'

'How did you get here?' I asked.

'How come you aren't dead?' Jik said.

'You first.'

'I came out of the shop where I'd bought the shampoo,' Sarah said, 'and I saw Greene drive past. I nearly died on the spot. I just stood still, hoping he wouldn't look my way, and he didn't . . . The car turned to the left just past where I was . . . and I could see there were two other people in the back . . . and I went back to our car and told Jik.'

'We thought it damn lucky he hadn't spotted her,' Jik said, dabbing at persistent scarlet trickles. 'We went back to the hotel, and you weren't there, so we asked the girl at the desk if you'd left a message, and she said you'd gone off in a car with some friends . . . With a man with a droopy moustache.'

'Friends!' Sarah said.

'Anyway,' Jik continued, 'choking down our rage, sorrow, indignation and what not, we thought we'd better look for your body.'

'Jik!' Sarah protested.

He grinned. 'And who was crying?'

'Shut up.'

'Sarah hadn't seen any sign of you in Greene's car but we thought you might be imitating a sack of potatoes in the boot or something, so we got out the road map, applied our feet to the accelerator, and set off in pursuit. Turned left where Greene had gone, and found ourselves climbing a ruddy mountain.'

I surveyed our extensive grazes and scratches. 'I think we'd better get some disinfectant,' I said.

'We could bath in it.'

'Good idea.'

I could hear his teeth chattering even above the din of my own.

'Let's get out of this wind,' I said. 'And bleed in the car.'

We crawled stiffly into the seats. Sarah said it was lucky the upholstery was plastic. Jik automatically took his place behind the wheel.

'We drove for miles,' he said. 'Growing, I may say, a little frantic. Over the top of the mountain and down this side. At the bottom of the hill the road swings round to the left and we could see from the map that it follows the coastline round a whole lot of bays and eventually ends up right back in Wellington.'

He started the car, turned it, and rolled gently ahead. Naked to the waist, wet from there down, and still with beads of blood forming and overflowing, he looked an unorthodox chauffeur. The beard, above, was undaunted.

'We went that way,' Sarah said. 'There was nothing but miles of craggy rocks and sea.'

'I'll paint those rocks,' Jik said.

Sarah glanced at his face, and then at me. She'd heard the fervour in that statement of intent. The golden time was almost over.

'After a bit we turned back,' Jik said. 'There was this bit of road saying "No through road", so we came down it. No you, of course. We stopped here on this spot and Sarah got out of the car and started bawling her eyes out.'

'You weren't exactly cheering yourself,' she said.

'Huh,' he smiled. 'Anyway, I kicked a few stones about, wondering what to do next, and there were those cartridges.'

'Those what?'

'On the edge of the road. All close together. Maybe dropped out of one of those spider-ejection revolvers, or something like that.'

'When we saw them,' Sarah said, 'we thought . . .'

'It could have been anyone popping off at seabirds,' I said. 'And I think we might go back and pick them up.'

'Are you serious?' Jik said.

'Yeah.'

We stopped, turned again, and retraced our tyre treads.

'No one shoots seabirds with a revolver,' he said. 'But bloody awful painters of slow horses, that's different.'

The quarry came in sight again. Jik drew up and stopped, and Sarah, hopping out quickly, told us to stay where we were, she would fetch the bullet cases.

'They really did shoot at you?' Jik said.

'Greene. He missed.'

'Inefficient.' He shifted in his seat, wincing. 'They must have gone back over the hill while we were looking for you round the bays.' He glanced at Sarah as she searched along the side of the road. 'Did they take the list?'

'I threw it in the sea.' I smiled lopsidedly. 'It seemed too tame just to hand it over . . . and it made a handy diversion. They salvaged enough to see that they'd got what they wanted.'

'It must all have been a bugger.'

'Hilarious.'

Sarah found the cases, picked them up, and came running back. 'Here they are . . . I'll put them in my handbag.' She slid into the passenger seat. 'What now?'

'Telephone,' I said.

'Like that?' She looked me over. 'Have you any idea . . .' She stopped. 'Well,' she said. 'I'll buy you each a shirt at the first shop we come to.' She swallowed. 'And don't say what if it's a grocery.'

'What if it's a grocery?' Jik said.

We set off again, and at the intersection turned left to go back over the hill, because it was about a quarter of the distance.

Near the top there was a large village with the sort of store which sold everything from hammers to hairpins. Also groceries. Also, upon enquiry, shirts. Sarah made a face at Jik and vanished inside.

I pulled on the resulting navy tee-shirt and made wobbly tracks for the telephone, clutching Sarah's purse.

'Operator . . . which hotels have a telex?'

She told me three. One was the Townhouse. I thanked her and rang off.

I called the Townhouse. Remembered, with an effort, that my name was Peel.

'But, Mr Peel . . .' said the girl, sounding bewildered. 'Your friend . . . the one with the moustache, not the one with the beard . . . He paid your account not half an hour ago and collected all your things . . . Yes, I suppose it is irregular, but he brought your note, asking us to let him have your room key . . . I'm sorry but I didn't know you hadn't written it . . . Yes, he took all your things, the room's being cleaned at this minute . . .'

'Look,' I said, 'can you send a telex for me? Put it on my friend Mr . . . er . . . Andrews' bill.'

She said she would. I dictated the message. She repeated it, and said she would send it at once.

'I'll call again soon for the reply,' I said.

Sarah had bought jeans for us, and dry socks. Jik drove out of the village to a more modest spot, and we put them on: hardly the world's best fit, but they hid the damage.

'Where now?' he said. 'Intensive Care Unit?'

'Back to the telephone.'

'Jesus God Almighty.'

He drove back and I called the Townhouse. The girl said she'd received an answer, and read it out. 'Telephone at once, reverse charges,' she said, 'and there's a number . . .' She read it out, twice. I repeated it. 'That's right.'

I thanked her.

'No sweat,' she said. 'Sorry about your things.'

I called the international exchange and gave them the number. It had a priority rating, they said. The call would be through in ten minutes. They would ring back.

The telephone was on the wall of a booth inside the general store. There was nothing to sit on. I wished to God there was.

The ten minutes dragged slowly by. Nine and a half, to be exact.

The bell rang, and I picked up the receiver.

'Your call to England . . .'

The modern miracle. Half-way round the world, and I was talking to Inspector Frost as if he were in the next room. Eleven-thirty in the morning at Wellington: eleven-thirty at night in Shropshire.

'Your letter arrived today, sir,' he said. 'And action has already been started.'

'Stop calling me sir. I'm used to Todd.'

'All right. Well, we telexed Melbourne to alert them and we've started checking on all the people on the England list. The results are already incredible. All the crossed-out names we've checked so far have been the victims of break-ins. We're alerting the police in all the other countries concerned. The only thing is, we see the list you sent us is a photocopy. Do you have the original?'

'No . . . Most of it got destroyed. Does it matter?'

'Not really. Can you tell us how it came into your possession?'

'Er . . . I think we'd better say it just did.'

A dry laugh travelled twelve thousand miles.

'All right. Now what's so urgent that you're keeping me from my bed?'

'Are you at home?' I said contritely.

'On duty, as it happens. Fire away.'

'Two things . . . One is, I can save you time with the stock list numbers. But first . . .' I told him about Wexford and Greene being in Wellington, and about them stealing my things. 'They've got my passport and traveller's cheques, and also my suitcase which contains painting equipment.'

'I saw it at your cousin's,' he said.

'That's right. I think they may also have a page or two of the list . . .'

'Say that again.'

I said it again. 'Most of it got thrown into the sea, but I know Wexford regained at least one page. Well . . . I thought . . . they'd be going back to Melbourne, probably today, any minute really, and when they land there, there's a good chance they'll have at least some of those things with them . . .'

'I can fix a Customs search,' he said. 'But why should they risk stealing . . ?'

'They don't know I know,' I said. 'I think they think I'm dead.'

'Good God. Why?'

'They took a pot-shot at me. Would bullet cases be of any use? Fortunately I didn't collect a bullet, but I've got six shells.'

'They may be . . .' He sounded faint. 'What about the stock list?'

'In the shorter list . . . Got it?'

'Yes, in front of me.'

'Right. The first letter is for the city the painting was sold in; M for Melbourne, S for Sydney, W for Wellington. The second letter identifies the painter; M for Munnings, H for Herring, and I think R for Raoul Millais. The letter C stands for copy. All the paintings on that list are copies. All the ones on the longer list are originals. Got that?'

'Yes. Go on.'

'The numbers are just numbers. They'd sold 54 copies when I . . . er . . . when the list reached me. The last letter R stands for

Renbo. That's Harley Renbo, who was working at Alice Springs. If you remember, I told you about him last time.'

'I remember,' he said.

'Wexford and Greene have spent the last couple of days chasing around in New Zealand, so with a bit of luck they will not have destroyed anything dodgy in the Melbourne gallery. If the Melbourne police can arrange a search, there might be a harvest.'

'It's their belief that the disappearance of the list from the gallery will have already led to the immediate destruction of anything else incriminating.'

'They may be wrong. Wexford and Greene don't know I photocopied the list and sent it to you. They think the list is floating safely out to sea, and me with it.'

'I'll pass your message to Melbourne.'

'There's also another gallery here in Wellington, and an imitation Herring they sold to a man in Auckland . . .'

'For heaven's sake . . .'

I gave him the Ruapehu address, and mentioned Norman Updike.

'There's also a recurring B on the long stock list, so there's probably another gallery. In Brisbane, maybe. There may also be another one in Sydney. I shouldn't think the suburban place I told you about had proved central enough, so they shut it.'

'Stop,' he said.

'Sorry,' I said. 'But the organization is like a mushroom . . . it burrows along underground and pops up everywhere.'

'I only said stop so I could change the tape on the recorder. You can carry right on now.'

'Oh.' I half laughed. 'Well . . . did you get any answers from Donald to my questions?'

'Yes, we did.'

'Carefully?'

'Rest assured,' he said dryly. 'We carried out your wishes to the letter. Mr Stuart's answers were "Yes, of course" to the first question, and "No, why ever should I" to the second, and "Yes" to the third.'

'Was he absolutely certain?'

'Absolutely.' He cleared his throat. 'He seems distant and withdrawn. Uninterested. But quite definite.'

'How is he?' I asked.

'He spends all his time looking at a picture of his wife. Every time we call at his house, we can see him through the front window, just sitting there.'

'He is still . . . sane?'

'I'm no judge.'

'You can at least let him know that he's no longer suspected of engineering the robbery and killing Regina.'

'That's a decision for my superiors,' he said.

'Well, kick them into it,' I said. 'Do the police positively yearn for bad publicity?'

'You were quick enough to ask our help,' he said tartly.

To do your job, I thought. I didn't say it aloud. The silence spoke for itself.

'Well . . .' his voice carried a mild apology. 'Our co-operation, then.' He paused. 'Where are you now? When I've telexed Melbourne, I may need to talk to you again.'

'I'm in a phone booth in a country store in a village on the hills above Wellington.'

'Where are you going next?'

'I'm staying right here. Wexford and Greene are still around in the city and I don't want to risk the outside chance of their seeing me.'

'Give me the number, then.'

I read it off the telephone.

'I want to come home as soon as possible,' I said. 'Can you do anything about my passport?'

'You'll have to find a consul.'

Oh ta, I though tiredly. I hung up the receiver and wobbled back to the car.

'Tell you what,' I said, dragging into the back seat, 'I could do with a double hamburger and a bottle of brandy.'

We sat in the car for two hours.

The store didn't sell liquor or hot food. Sarah bought a packet of biscuits. We ate them.

'We can't stay here all day,' she said explosively, after a lengthy glum silence.

I couldn't be sure that Wexford wasn't out searching for her and Jik with murderous intent, and I didn't think she'd be happy to know it.

'We're perfectly safe here,' I said.

'Just quietly dying of blood-poisoning,' Jik agreed.

'I left my pills in the Hilton,' Sarah said.

Jik stared. 'What's that got to do with it?'

'Nothing. I just thought you might like to know.'

'*The* pill?' I asked.

'Yes.'

'Jesus,' Jik said.

A delivery van struggled up the hill and stopped outside the shop. A man in an overall opened the back, took out a large bakery tray, and carried it in.

'Food,' I said hopefully.

Sarah went in to investigate. Jik took the opportunity to unstick his T-shirt from his healing grazes, but I didn't bother.

'You'll be glued to those clothes, if you don't,' Jik said, grimacing over his task.

'I'll soak them off.'

'All those cuts and things didn't feel so bad when we were in the sea.'

'No.'

'Catches up with you a bit, doesn't it?'

'Mm.'

He glanced at me. 'Why don't you just scream or something?'

'Can't be bothered. Why don't you?'

He grinned. 'I'll scream in paint.'

Sarah came back with fresh doughnuts and cans of Coke. We made inroads, and I at least felt healthier.

After another half-hour, the storekeeper appeared in the doorway, shouting and beckoning.

'A call for you . . .'

I went stiffly to the telephone. It was Frost, clear as a bell.

'Wexford, Greene and Snell have booked a flight to Melbourne. They will be met at Melbourne airport . . .'

'Who's Snell?' I said.

'How do I know? He was travelling with the other two.'

Beetle-brows, I thought.

'Now listen,' Frost said. 'The telex has been red-hot between here and Melbourne, and the police there want your co-operation, just to clinch things . . .' He went on talking for a long time. At the end he said, 'Will you do that?'

I'm tired, I thought. I'm battered, and I hurt. I've done just about enough.

'All right.'

Might as well finish it, I supposed.

'The Melbourne police want to know for sure that the three Munnings copies you . . . er . . . acquired from the gallery are still where you told me.'

'Yes, they are.'

'Right. Well . . . good luck.'

Sixteen

WE FLEW Air New Zealand back to Melbourne, tended by angels in sea green. Sarah looked fresh, Jik definitely shop-worn, and I apparently like a mixture (Jik said) of yellow ochre, Payne's grey, and white, which I didn't think was possible.

Our passage had been oiled by telexes from above. When we arrived at the airport after collecting Sarah's belongings in their carrier bags from the Townhouse, we found ourselves whisked into a private room, plied with strong drink, and subsequently taken by car straight out across the tarmac to the aeroplane.

A thousand miles across the Tasman Sea and an afternoon tea later we were driven straight from the aircraft's steps to another small airport room, which contained no strong drink but only a large hard Australian plain-clothes policeman.

'Porter,' he said, introducing himself and squeezing our bones in a blacksmith's grip. 'Which of you is Charles Todd?'

'I am.'

'Right on, Mr Todd.' He looked at me without favour. 'Are you ill, or something?' He had a strong rough voice and a strong rough manner, natural aids to putting the fear of God into chummy and bringing on breakdowns in the nervous. To me, I gradually gathered, he was grudgingly offering the status of temporary inferior colleague.

'No,' I said, sighing slightly. Time and airline schedules waited for no man. If I'd spent time on first aid we'd have missed the only possible flight.

'His clothes are sticking to him,' Jik observed, giving the familiar phrase the usual meaning of being hot. It was cool in Melbourne. Porter looked at him uncertainly.

I grinned. 'Did you manage what you planned?' I asked him. He decided Jik was nuts and switched his gaze back to me.

'We decided not to go ahead until you had arrived,' he said, shrugging. 'There's a car waiting outside.' He wheeled out of the door without holding it for Sarah and marched briskly off.

The car had a chauffeur. Porter sat in front, talking on a radio, saying in stiltedly guarded sentences that the party had arrived and the proposals should be implemented.

'Where are we going?' Sarah said.

'To reunite you with your clothes,' I said.

Her face lit up. 'Are we really?'

'And what for?' Jik asked.

'To bring the mouse to the cheese.' And the bull to the sword, I thought: and the moment of truth to the conjuror.

'We got your things back, Todd,' Porter said with satisfaction. 'Wexford, Greene and Snell were turned over on entry, and they copped them with the lot. The locks on your suitcase were scratched and dented but they hadn't burst open. Everything inside should be O.K. You can collect everything in the morning.'

'That's great,' I said. 'Did they still have any of the lists of customers?'

'Yeah. Damp but readable. Names of guys in Canada.'

'Good.'

'We're turning over that Yarra gallery right this minute, and Wexford is there helping. We've let him overhear what we wanted him to, and as soon as I give the go-ahead we'll let him take action.'

'Do you think he will?' I said.

'Look, mister, wouldn't you?'

I thought I might be wary of gifts from the Greeks, but then

I wasn't Wexford, and I didn't have a jail sentence breathing down my neck.

We pulled up at the side door of the Hilton. Porter raised himself agilely to the pavement and stood like a solid pillar, watching with half-concealed impatience while Jik, Sarah, and I eased ourselves slowly out. We all went across the familiar red-and-blue opulence of the great entrance hall, and from there through a gate in the reception desk, and into the hotel manager's office at the rear.

A tall dark-suited member of the hotel staff there offered us chairs, coffee, and sandwiches. Porter looked at his watch and offered us an indeterminate wait.

It was six o'clock. After ten minutes a man in shirt and neck-tie brought a two-way personal radio for Porter, who slipped the ear-plug into place and began listening to disembodied voices.

The office was a working room, lit by neon strips and furnished functionally, with a wall-papering of charts and duty rosters. There were no outside windows: nothing to show the fade of day to night.

We sat, and drank coffee, and waited. Porter ate three of the sandwiches simultaneously. Time passed.

Seven o'clock.

Sarah was looking pale in the artificial light, and tired also. So was Jik, his beard on his chest. I sat and thought about life and death and polka dots.

At seven-eleven Porter clutched his ear and concentrated intently on the ceiling. When he relaxed, he passed to us the galvanic message.

'Wexford did just what we reckoned he would, and the engine's turning over.'

'What engine?' Sarah said.

Porter stared at her blankly. 'What we planned,' he said painstakingly, 'is happening.'

'Oh.'

Porter listened again to his private ear and spoke directly to me. 'He's taken the bait.'

'He's a fool,' I said.

Porter came as near to a smile as he could. 'All crooks are fools, one way or another.'

Seven-thirty came and went. I raised my eyebrows at Porter. He shook his head.

'We can't say too much on the radio,' he said. 'Because you get all sorts of ears listening in.'

Just like England, I thought. The Press could turn up at a crime before the police; and the mouse might hear of the trap.

We waited. The time dragged. Jik yawned and Sarah's eyes were dark with fatigue. Outside, in the lobby, the busy rich life of the hotel chattered on unruffled, with guests' spirits rising towards the next day's race meeting, the last of the carnival.

The Derby on Saturday, the Cup on Tuesday, the Oaks (which we'd missed) on Thursday, and the International on Saturday. No serious racegoers went home before the end of things, if they could help it.

Porter clutched his ear again, and stiffened.

'He's here,' he said.

My heart, for some unaccountable reason, began beating overtime. We were in no danger that I could see, yet there it was, thumping away like a steam organ.

Porter disconnected himself from the radio, put it on the Manager's desk, and went out into the foyer.

'What do we do?' Sarah said.

'Nothing much except listen.'

We all three went over to the door and held it six inches open. We listened to people asking for their room keys, asking for letters and messages, asking for Mr and Mrs So-and-So, and which way to Toorak, and how did you get to Fanny's.

Then suddenly, the familiar voice, sending electric fizzes to my fingertips. Confident: not expecting trouble. 'I've come to collect a package left here last Tuesday by a Mr Charles Todd. He says he checked it into the baggage-room. I have a letter here from him, authorizing you to release it to me.'

There was a crackle of paper as the letter was handed over. Sarah's eyes were round and startled.

'Did you write it?' she whispered.

I shook my head. 'No.'

The desk clerk outside said, 'Thank you, sir. If you'll just wait a moment I'll fetch the package.'

There was a long pause. My heart made a lot of noise, but nothing much else happened.

The desk clerk came back. 'Here you are, sir. Paintings, sir.'

'That's right.'

There were vague sounds of the bundle of paintings and the print-folder being carried along outside the door.

'I'll bring them round for you,' said the clerk, suddenly closer to us. 'Here we are, sir.' He went past the office, through the door in the desk, and round to the front. 'Can you manage them, sir?'

'Yes. Yes. Thank you.' There was a haste in his voice, now that he'd got his hands on the goods. 'Thank you. Goodbye.'

Sarah had begun to say 'Is that all?' in disappointment when Porter's loud voice chopped into the Hilton velvet like a hatchet.

'I guess we'll take care of those paintings, if you don't mind,' he said. 'Porter, Melbourne City Police.'

I opened the door a little, and looked out. Porter stood four-square in the lobby, large and rough, holding out a demanding hand.

At his elbows, two plain-clothes policemen. At the front door, two more, in uniform. There would be others, I supposed, at the other exits. They weren't taking any chances.

'Why . . . er . . . Inspector . . . I'm only on an errand . . . er . . . for my young friend, Charles Todd.'

'And these paintings?'

'I've no idea what they are. He asked me to fetch them for him.'

I walked quietly out of the office, through the gate and round to the front. I leaned a little wearily against the reception desk. He was only six feet away, in front of me to my right. I could have stretched forward and touched him. I hoped Porter would think it near enough, as requested.

A certain amount of unease had pervaded the Hilton guests. They stood around in an uneven semicircle, eyeing the proceedings sideways.

'Mr Charles Todd asked you to fetch them?' Porter said loudly.

'Yes, that's right.'

Porter's gaze switched abruptly to my face.

'Did you ask him?'

'No,' I said.

The explosive effect was all that the Melbourne police could have asked, and a good deal more than I expected. There was no polite quiet identification followed by a polite quiet arrest. I should have remembered all my own theories about the basic brutality of the directing mind.

I found myself staring straight into the eyes of the bull. He realized that he'd been tricked. Had convicted himself out of his own mouth and by his own presence on such an errand. The fury rose in him like a geyser and his hands reached out to grab my neck.

'*You're dead,*' he yelled. '*You're fucking dead.*'

His plunging weight took me off balance and down on to one knee, smothering under his choking grip and two hundred pounds of city suiting; trying to beat him off with my fists and not succeeding. His anger poured over me like lava. Heaven knows what he intended, but Porter's men pulled him off before he did bloody murder on the plushy carpet. As I got creakily to my feet, I heard the handcuffs click.

He was standing there, close to me, quivering in the restraining hands, breathing heavily, dishevelled and bitter-eyed. Civilized exterior all stripped away by one instant of ungovernable rage. The violent core plain to see.

'Hello, Hudson,' I said.

'Sorry,' Porter said perfunctorily. 'Didn't reckon he'd turn wild.'

'Revert,' I said.

'Uh?'

'He always was wild,' I said, 'underneath.'

'You'd know,' he said. 'I never saw the guy before.' He nodded to Jik and Sarah and finally to me, and hurried away after his departing prisoner.

We looked at each other a little blankly. The hotel guests stared at us curiously and began to drift away. We sat down weakly on the nearest blue velvet seat, Sarah in the middle.

Jik took her hand and squeezed it. She put her fingers over mine.

It had taken nine days.

It had been a long haul.

'Don't know about you,' Jik said. 'But I could do with a beer.'

'Todd,' said Sarah, 'start talking.'

We were upstairs in a bedroom (mine) with both of them in a relaxed mood, and me in Jik's dressing-gown, and he and I in a cloud of Dettol.

I yawned. 'About Hudson?'

'Who else? And don't go to sleep before you've told us.'

'Well . . . I was looking for him, or someone like him, before I ever met him.'

748

'But why?'

'Because of the wine,' I said. 'Because of the wine which was stolen from Donald's cellar. Whoever stole it not only knew it was there, down some stairs behind an inconspicuous cupboard-like door . . . and I'd stayed several times in the house and never knew the cellar existed . . . but according to Donald they would have had to come prepared with proper cases to pack it in. Wine is usually packed twelve bottles in a case . . . and Donald had two thousand or more bottles stolen. In bulk alone it would have taken a lot of shifting. A lot of time, too, and time for housebreakers is risky. But also it was special wine. A small fortune, Donald said. The sort of wine that's bought and sold as an asset and ends up at a week's wage a bottle, if it's ever drunk at all. Anyway, it was the sort of wine that needed expert handling and marketing if it was to be worth the difficulty of stealing it in the first place . . . and as Donald's business is wine, and the reason for his journey to Australia was wine, I started looking right away for someone who knew Donald, knew he'd bought a Munnings, and knew about good wine and how to sell it. And there, straightaway, was Hudson Taylor, who matched like a glove. But it seemed too easy . . . because he didn't *look* right.'

'Smooth and friendly,' said Sarah, nodding.

'And rich,' Jik added.

'Probably a moneyholic,' I said, pulling open the bed and looking longingly at the cool white sheets.

'A what?'

'Moneyholic. A word I've just made up to describe someone with an uncontrollable addiction to money.'

'The world's full of them,' Jik said, laughing.

I shook my head. 'The world is full of drinkers, but alcoholics are obsessive. Moneyholics are obsessive. They never have enough. They *cannot* have enough. However much they have, they want more. And I'm not talking about the average hard-up man, but about real screwballs. Money, money, money. Like a drug. Moneyholics will do anything to get it . . . Kidnap, murder, cook the computer, rob banks, sell their grandmothers . . . You name it.'

I sat on the bed with my feet up, feeling less than fit. Sore from too many bruises, on fire from too many cuts. Jik too, I guessed. They had been wicked rocks.

'Moneyholism,' Jik said, like a lecturer to a dimmish class, 'is a widespread disease easily understood by everyone who has ever felt a twinge of greed, which is everyone.'

'Go on about Hudson,' Sarah said.

'Hudson had the organizing ability . . . I didn't know when I came that the organization was so huge, but I did know it was *organized*, if you see what I mean. It was an overseas operation. It took some doing. Know-how.'

Jik tugged the ring off a can of beer and passed it to me, wincing as he stretched.

'But he convinced me I was wrong about him,' I said, drinking through the triangular hole. 'Because he was so careful. He pretended he had to look up the name of the gallery where Donald bought his picture. He didn't think of me as a threat, of course, but just as Donald's cousin. Not until he talked to Wexford down on the lawn.'

'I remember,' Sarah said. 'When you said it had ripped the whole works apart.'

'Mm . . . I thought it was only that he had told Wexford I was Donald's cousin, but of course Wexford also told *him* that I'd met Greene in Maisie's ruins in Sussex and then turned up in the gallery looking at the original of Maisie's burnt painting.'

'Jesus Almighty,' Jik said. 'No wonder we beat it to Alice Springs.'

'Yes, but by then I didn't think it could be Hudson I was looking for. I was looking for someone brutal, who passed on his violence through his employees. Hudson didn't look or act brutal.' I paused. 'The only slightest crack was when his gamble went down the drain at the races. He gripped his binoculars so hard that his knuckles showed white. But you can't think a man is a big-time thug just because he gets upset over losing a bet.'

Jik grinned. 'I'd qualify.'

'In spades, redoubled,' Sarah said.

'I was thinking about it in the Alice Springs hospital . . . There hadn't been time for the musclemen to get to Alice from Melbourne between us buying Renbo's picture and me diving off the balcony, but there had been time for them to come from *Adelaide*, and Hudson's base was at Adelaide . . . but it was much too flimsy.'

'They might have been in Alice to start with,' Jik said reasonably.

'They might, but what for?' I yawned. 'Then on the night of the Cup you said Hudson had made a point of asking you about me . . . and I wondered how he knew you.'

'Do you know,' Sarah said, 'I did wonder too at the time, but it didn't seem important. I mean, *we'd* seen *him* from the top of the stands, so it didn't seem impossible that somewhere he'd seen you with us.'

'The boy knew you,' I said. 'And he was at the races, because he followed you, with Greene, to the Hilton. The boy must have pointed you out to Greene.'

'And Greene to Wexford, and Wexford to Hudson?' Jik asked.

'Quite likely.'

'And by then,' he said, 'they all knew they wanted to silence you pretty badly, and they'd had a chance and muffed it . . . I'd love to have heard what happened when they found we'd robbed the gallery.' He chuckled, tipping up his beer can to catch the last few drops.

'On the morning after,' I said, 'a letter from Hudson was delivered by hand to the Hilton. How did he know we were there?'

They stared. 'Greene must have told him,' Jik said. 'We certainly didn't. We didn't tell anybody. We were careful about it.'

'So was I,' I said. 'That letter offered to show me round a vineyard. Well . . . if I hadn't been so doubtful of him, I might have gone. He was a friend of Donald's . . . and a vineyard would be interesting. From his point of view, anyway, it was worth a try.'

'Jesus!'

'On the night of the Cup, when we were in that motel near Box Hill, I telephoned the police in England and spoke to the man in charge of Donald's case, Inspector Frost. I asked him to ask Donald some questions . . . and this morning outside Wellington I got the answers.'

'This morning seems several light years away,' Sarah said.

'Mm . . .'

'What questions and what answers?' Jik said.

'The questions were, did Donald tell Hudson all about the wine in his cellar, and did Donald tell *Wexford* about the wine in the cellar, and was it Hudson who had suggested to Donald that he and Regina should go and look at the Munnings in the Arts Centre? And the answers were "Yes, of course", and "No, why ever should I?", and "Yes".'

They thought about it in silence. Jik fiddled with the dispenser in the room's in-built refrigerator and liberated another can of Foster's.

'So what then?' Sarah said.

'So the Melbourne police said it was too insubstantial, but if they could tie Hudson in definitely with the gallery they might believe it. So they dangled in front of Hudson the pictures and stuff we stole from the gallery, and along he came to collect them.'

'How? How did they dangle them?'

'They let Wexford accidentally overhear snippets from a fake report from several hotels about odd deposits in their baggage

752

rooms, including the paintings at the Hilton. Then after we got here they gave him an opportunity to use the telephone when he thought no one was listening, and he rang Hudson at the house he's been staying in here for the races, and told him. So Hudson wrote himself a letter to the Hilton from me, and zoomed along to remove the incriminating evidence.'

'He must have been crazy.'

'Stupid. But he thought I was dead . . . and he'd no idea anyone suspected him. He should have had the sense to know that Wexford's call to him would be bugged by the police . . . but Frost told me that Wexford would think he was using a public phone booth.'

'Sneaky,' Sarah said.

I yawned. 'It takes a sneak to catch a sneak.'

'You'd never have thought Hudson would blaze up like that,' she said. 'He looked so . . . so dangerous.' She shivered. 'You wouldn't think people could hide such really frightening violence under a friendly public face.'

'The nice Irish bloke next door,' Jik said, standing up, 'can leave a bomb to blow the legs off children.'

He pulled Sarah to her feet. 'What do you think I paint?' he said. 'Vases of flowers?' He looked down at me. 'Horses?'

We parted the next morning at Melbourne airport, where we seemed to have spent a good deal of our lives.

'It seems strange, saying goodbye,' Sarah said.

'I'll be coming back,' I said.

They nodded.

'Well . . .' We looked at watches.

It was like all partings. There wasn't much to say. I saw in their eyes, as they must have seen in mine, that the past ten days would quickly become a nostalgic memory. Something we did in our crazy youth. Distant.

'Would you do it all again?' Jik said.

I thought inconsequentially of surviving wartime pilots looking back from forty years on. Had their achievements been worth the blood and sweat and risk of death: did they regret?

I smiled. Forty years on didn't matter. What the future made of the past was its own tragedy. What we ourselves did on the day was all that counted.

'I guess I would.'

I leaned forward and kissed Sarah, my oldest friend's wife.

'Hey,' he said. 'Find one of your own.'

Seventeen

MAISIE SAW me before I saw her, and came sweeping down like a great scarlet bird, wings outstretched.

Monday lunch-time at Wolverhampton races, misty and cold.

'Hello, dear, I'm so glad you've come. Did you have a good trip back, because of course it's such a long way, isn't it, with all that wretched jet lag?' She patted my arm and peered acutely at my face. 'You don't really look awfully well, dear, if you don't mind me saying so, and you don't seem to have collected any suntan, though I suppose as you haven't been away two weeks it isn't surprising, but those are nasty gashes on your hand, dear, aren't they, and you were walking very *carefully* just now.'

She stopped to watch a row of jockeys canter past on their way to the start. Bright shirts against the thin grey mist. A subject for Munnings.

'Have you backed anything, dear? And are you sure you're warm enough in that anorak? I never think jeans are good for people in the winter, they're only cotton, dear, don't forget, and how did you get on in Australia? I mean, dear, did you find out anything useful?'

'It's an awfully long story . . .'

'Best told in the bar, then, don't you think, dear?'

She bought us immense brandies with ginger ale and settled herself at a small table, her kind eyes alert and waiting.

I told her about Hudson's organization, about the Melbourne gallery, and about the list of robbable customers.

'Was I on it?'

I nodded. 'Yes, you were.'

'And you gave it to the police?' she said anxiously.

I grinned. 'Don't look so worried, Maisie. Your name was crossed out already. I just crossed it out more thoroughly. By the time I'd finished, no one could ever disentangle it, particularly on a photocopy.'

She smiled broadly. 'No one could call you a fool, dear.'

I wasn't so sure about that. 'I'm afraid, though,' I said, 'that you've lost your nine thousand quid.'

'Oh yes, dear,' she said cheerfully. 'Serves me right, doesn't it, for trying to cheat the Customs, though frankly, dear, in the same circumstances I'd probably do it again, because that tax makes me so mad, dear. But I'm ever so glad, dear, that they won't come knocking on my door this time, or rather my sister Betty's, because of course I'm staying with her again up here at the moment, as of course the Beach told you, until my house is ready.'

I blinked. 'What house?'

'Well, dear, I decided not to rebuild the house at Worthing because it wouldn't be the same without the things Archie and I bought together, so I'm selling that plot of seaside land for a fortune, dear, and I've chosen a nice place just down the road from Sandown Park racecourse.'

'You're not going to live in Australia?'

'Oh no, dear, that would be too far away. From Archie, you see, dear.'

I saw. I liked Maisie very much.

'I'm afraid I spent all your money,' I said.

She smiled at me with her well-kept head on one side and absent-mindedly stroked her crocodile handbag.

'Never mind, dear. You can paint me *two* pictures. One of me, and one of my new house.'

*

I left after the third race, took the train along the main line to Shrewsbury, and from there travelled by bus to Inspector Frost's official doorstep.

He was in an office, chin-deep in papers. Also present, the unblinking Superintendent Wall, who had so unnerved Donald, and whom I'd not previously met. Both men shook hands in a cool and businesslike manner, Wall's eyes traversing the anorak, jeans and desert boots, and remaining unimpressed. They offered me a chair, moulded plastic and armless.

Frost said, faintly smiling, 'You sure kicked open an ant-hill.'

Wall frowned, disliking such frivolity. 'It appears you stumbled on an organization of some size.'

The gaze of both men swept the mountain of paper.

'What about Donald?' I asked.

Frost kept his eyes down. His mouth twitched.

Wall said, 'We have informed Mr Stuart that we are satisfied the break-in at his house and the death of Mrs Stuart were the work of outside agencies, beyond his knowledge or control.'

Cold comfort words. 'Did he understand what he was hearing?'

The Wall eyebrows rose. 'I went to see him myself, this morning. He appeared to understand perfectly.'

'And what about Regina?'

'The body of Mrs Stuart,' Wall said correctively.

'Donald wants her buried,' I said.

Frost looked up with an almost human look of compassion. 'The difficulty is,' he said, 'that in a murder case, one has to pre-serve the victim's body in case the defence wishes to call for its own post-mortem. In this case, we have not been able to accuse anyone of her murder, let alone get as far as them arranging a defence.' He cleared his throat. 'We'll release Mrs Stuart's body for burial as soon as official requirements have been met.'

I looked at my fingers, interlacing them.

Frost said, 'Your cousin already owes you a lot. You can't be expected to do more.'

I smiled twistedly and stood up. 'I'll go and see him,' I said.

Wall shook hands again, and Frost came with me through the hall and out into the street. The lights shone bright in the early winter evening.

'Unofficially,' he said, walking slowly with me along the pavement, 'I'll tell you that the Melbourne police found a list of names in the gallery which it turns out are of known house-breakers. Divided into countries, like the Overseas Customers. There were four names for England. I suppose I shouldn't guess and I certainly ought not to be saying this to you, but there's a good chance Mrs Stuart's killer may be one of them.'

'Really?'

'Yes. But don't quote me.' He looked worried.

'I won't,' I said. 'So the robberies were local labour?'

'It seems to have been their normal method.'

Greene, I thought. With an 'e'. Greene could have recruited them. And checked afterwards, in burnt houses, on work done.

I stopped walking. We were standing outside the flower shop where Regina had worked. Frost looked at the big bronze chrysanthemums in the brightly lit window, and then enquiringly at my face.

I put my hand in my pocket and pulled out the six revolver shell cases. Gave them to Frost.

'These came from the gun which the man called Greene fired at me,' I said. 'He dropped them when he was reloading. I told you about them on the telephone.'

He nodded.

'I don't imagine they're of much practical use,' I said. 'But they might persuade you that Greene is capable of murder.'

'Well . . . what of it?'

'It's only a feeling . . .'

'Get on with it.'

'Greene,' I said, 'was in England at about the time Regina died.'

He stared.

'Maybe Regina knew him,' I said. 'She had been in the gallery in Australia. Maybe she saw him helping to rob her house . . . supervising, perhaps . . . and maybe that's why she was killed, because it wouldn't have been enough just to tie her up and gag her . . . she could identify him for certain if she was alive.'

He looked as if he was trying to draw breath.

'That's all . . . guessing,' he said.

'I know for certain that Greene was in England two weeks after Regina's death. I know for certain he was up to his neck in selling paintings and stealing them back. I know for certain that he would kill someone who could get him convicted. The rest . . . well . . . it's over to you.'

'My God,' Frost said. 'My God.'

I started off again, towards the bus-stop. He came with me, looking glazed.

'What everyone wants to know,' he said, 'is what put you on to the organization in the first place.'

I smiled. 'A hot tip from an informer.'

'What informer?'

A smuggler in a scarlet coat, glossy hair-do and crocodile handbag. 'You can't grass on informers,' I said.

He sighed, shook his head, stopped walking, and pulled a piece of torn-off telex paper out of his jacket.

'Did you meet an Australian policeman called Porter?'

'I sure did.'

'He sent you a message.' He handed me the paper. I read the neatly typed words.

'*Tell that Pommie painter Thanks.*'

'Will you send a message back?'

He nodded. 'What is it?'

'No sweat,' I said.

*

I stood in the dark outside my cousin's house, looking in.

He sat in his lighted drawing-room, facing Regina, unframed on the mantelshelf. I sighed, and rang the bell.

Donald came slowly. Opened the door.

'Charles!' He was mildly surprised. 'I thought you were in Australia.'

'Got back yesterday.'

'Come in.'

We went into the kitchen, where at least it was warm, and sat one each side of the table. He looked gaunt and fifty, a shell of a man, retreating from life.

'How's business?' I said.

'Business?'

'The wine trade.'

'I haven't been to the office.'

'If you didn't have a critical cash flow problem before,' I said, 'you'll have one soon.'

'I don't really care.'

'You've got stuck,' I said. 'Like a needle in a record. Playing the same little bit of track over and over again.'

He looked blank.

'The police know you didn't fix the robbery,' I said.

He nodded slowly. 'That man Wall . . . came and told me so. This morning.'

'Well, then.'

'It doesn't seem to make much difference.'

'Because of Regina?'

He didn't answer.

'You've got to stop it, Donald,' I said. 'She's dead. She's been dead five weeks and three days. Do you want to see her?'

He looked absolutely horrified. 'No! Of course not.'

'Then stop thinking about her body.'

'Charles!' He stood up violently, knocking over his chair.

760

He was somewhere between outrage and anger, and clearly shocked.

'She's in a cold drawer,' I said, 'and you want her in a box in the cold ground. So where's the difference?'

'Get out,' he said loudly. 'I don't want to hear you.'

'The bit of Regina you're obsessed about,' I said, not moving, 'is just a collection of minerals. That . . . that *shape* lying in storage isn't Regina. The real girl is in your head. In your memory. The only life you can give her is to remember her. That's her immortality, in your head. You're killing her all over again with your refusal to go on living.'

He turned on his heel and walked out. I heard him go across the hall, and guessed he was making for the sitting-room.

After a minute I followed him. The white-panelled door was shut.

I opened the door. Went in.

He was sitting in his chair, in the usual place.

'Go away,' he said.

What did it profit a man, I thought, if he got flung over balconies and shot at and mangled by rocks, and couldn't save his cousin's soul.

'I'm taking that picture with me to London,' I said.

He was alarmed. He stood up. 'You're *not*.'

'I am.'

'You can't. You gave it to me.'

'It needs a frame,' I said. 'Or it will warp.'

'You can't take it.'

'You can come as well.'

'I can't leave here,' he said.

'Why not?'

'Don't be stupid,' he said explosively. 'You know why not. Because of . . .' His voice died away.

I said, 'Regina will be with you wherever you are. Whenever you think of her, she'll be there.'

Nothing.

'She isn't in this room. She's in your head. You can go out of here and take her with you.'

Nothing.

'She was a great girl. It must be bloody without her. But she deserves the best you can do.'

Nothing.

I went over to the fireplace and picked up the picture. Regina's face smiled out, vitally alive. I hadn't done her left nostril too well, I thought.

Donald didn't try to stop me.

I put my hand on his arm.

'Let's get your car out,' I said, 'and drive down to my flat. Right this minute.'

A little silence.

'Come on,' I said.

He began, with difficulty, to cry.

I took a long breath and waited. 'O.K.,' I said. 'How are you off for petrol?'

'We can get some more . . .' he said, sniffing, '. . . on the motorway.'